EMPIRE

EMPIRE

ELYSIUM'S MULTIVERSE | BOOK 4

Ranyhin1

Published in 2025 by Podium Publishing
www.podiumentertainment.com

Podium

EMPIRE

CHAPTER 1

Riven sat in an underground room on a blood-covered rocking chair, smoking a cigar, red eyes glinting in the darkness. He'd cast his armor to the side for just a moment after not having felt the air on his bare skin in so long—and he looked almost ridiculous in just a pair of undergarments.

He didn't care. Wearing those Chalgathi artifacts had made him really appreciate the finer things in life—like being able to take clothes off.

This place was mostly devoid of light save for lanterns hung along the walls that cast dim shadows over the blood and corpses of the cultists he'd killed there, but that didn't bother someone like him in the least. And in the hallway nearby, the tortured screams of the man who had kidnapped and abused Fay rang loud and clear—music to his ears.

Riven had only checked on her once, watching as she'd cut off his fingers one by one before making the cultist down a health potion—shattered glass and all. Giving her this opportunity was the least Riven could do after what she'd been through, and he felt like even this wasn't enough.

But what else was there?

In front of him, a swirling dark ball of mana collected energy, drawing in the shadows and blood bit by bit from around the room in an almost phantasmal portrait. It was here that his Chalgathi artifacts were now doing . . . something. He wasn't entirely sure what just yet, and he hadn't even seen the other two pieces he'd picked up before his own Gluttony-tinted artifacts had begun to change them.

"This is the first time I've seen you without your artifacts on," Luke stated absentmindedly, staring at him from where he too smoked a cigar they'd looted off the dead. The old elf thrall had calmed down a lot since Riven's massacre at Daskus, the city of canyons, and was now back to his usual self.

Whether or not this was because of the thrall contract Riven could not tell, but he was glad for it.

Riven grinned over at the man, and then at Azmoth—who was rifling through the pile of loot they'd collected on a nearby bench near the cultists' ritual circle.

Riven was going to take a look at the loot himself eventually, but he needed to calm his nerves after all that'd happened. "How do you like the cigar, friend?"

Luke glanced over at him again, coughed, then grinned. Pulling a hand through his silver hair and tapping the ashes of his cigar on the chair arm, he gave Riven a nod. "It's pretty good. Though I must admit, I'm used to smoking out of a pipe. Not this commoner stuff."

"Cigars are sophisticated."

"As sophisticated as a blind hag's wrinkled old ass."

The sound in the hallway ended with a high-pitched squeal; a notification appeared concerning the death of another Chalgathi participant, and then it was followed by a long bout of silence. The door creaked open to reveal Fay. The blue-skinned succubus let out long exhales of breath, one after the other—and then she trotted over with exhaustion evident. Slapping the severed head of the man who'd abducted her on the floor next to Riven's rocking chair, she wordlessly sat on his lap and curled up in a ball with her arms around Riven's neck.

"I feel a little bit better now," Fay whispered. Tears had dried on her skin, but she wasn't shaking anymore and the hours of sleep before her torture session had done a lot of good to calm her nerves. She was still missing her severed wings, but those could be regrown after spending some time in the nether realms. "I left your weapon back in the hall. It's still lodged in his ass."

Riven's eyebrows raised, and he took another puff of cigar before putting it out and tossing the thing aside. As he hugged Fay firmly, the two continued to rock back and forth on the curved arches of the chair. "Glad to hear it."

Fay snorted a mellow laugh but closed her eyes—just enjoying the comforting touch. "Thanks again for saving me."

"You say that like you think I wouldn't have come."

She glanced up at him, black eyes staring into red for a time, before nestling back in and closing them once more. She let out a deep, content sigh. "Many warlocks wouldn't. Some would, and I'm just glad you're one of the good ones. You're the best."

"I know."

He got a jab and an amused chuckle for the snark, but grinned all the same, and after sitting in silence to calm his nerves a little while longer, he pulled up the notifications he'd recently received. It was a lot to take in.

[Quest Completed: Find Your Succubus Princess—You have found and saved Fay and have re-bound her as a minion. A map and notes concerning the location of a Dao treasure relating to Sin has been deposited in your bag of holding. The Puzzle-Box Cube Labyrinth from Daskus has also been placed in your storage space as a bonus prize due to your high performance on this quest—and your first attempt at the Cube Labyrinth has been reset.]

[You have grown from level 83 to level 112 after massacring an entire city's inhabitants. XP intake has been drastically reduced for all enemies below level 75 after reaching level 100. From here on out, anyone who is not at least three-fourths your own level will have significantly fewer XP gains for killing them—exponentially scaling the lower their levels go.]

[System Notice: You have ascended tiers and have climbed out of the Paragon rank. Elysium has assessed your level of power, and <u>you are now an Apex ranker on this world's power ladder.</u> You are currently listed at <u>spot number five</u> on the power ladder. <u>This shift of power on the world stage is noted by Elysium, and video footage of your climb to the peak has been uploaded to the world forums along the main page for anyone to view.</u> With this increase in rank, the system will provide better opportunities for you in the future as Panu's integration continues. Congratulations! The ranking categories are as follows: Apex rank (top 10), Paragon rank (top 1,000), S rank (top 0.0001%), A rank (top 1%), B rank (top 15%), C rank (top 30%), D rank (top 50%), E rank (bottom 50%).]

[You have reached the level 100 marker. Congratulations! You're now able to upgrade your class. Please select from the following options: Warlock Summoner or Warlock Devastator. Please click this notification for more information or visit your status page.]

[You have acquired a Sin Class as a secondary class slot, which may only be filled by Sin-based classes. You have acquired a second and unique class: Harbinger of Gluttony. Your Core of Original Sin— Gluttony has been created successfully. Bonuses: ??? Please click this notification or select your soul's sin core for more information.]

[You, Riven Thane, have acquired seven of five set pieces for Chalgathi's inheritance. Redistribution has commenced: Extra pieces have been redistributed to other newly appointed Chalgathi's chosen who do not have pieces. You now have five of five set pieces, are the third person to acquire all five set pieces for Chalgathi's inheritance, and the first noncultist to do so. Only two full sets remain to be claimed. Please wait for further world quest updates until after your Chalgathi armor set has completely oriented itself to your chosen aspect: Gluttony. Your ability to ping Chalgathi artifacts has been permanently removed.]

[Riven Thane's Status Page:
• Level 112

- **Pillar Orientations:** Unholy Foundation, Blood Specialty: Profane Cyclone (Tier 1 of the Path of Red and Black), Infernal, Shadow (subserviently linked to Blood Specialty pillar), Sin Core (Gluttony)
- **Core of Original Sin—Gluttony:** Allows access to Sin (Gluttony). Allows access to a secondary Sin Class. (Sin Class—Harbinger of Gluttony, currently under construction) Bonuses: ???
- **Traits:** <u>Race: Pure-blooded Vampire</u> (Extreme Darkness Regeneration) (Sunlight Decay) (Extreme weakness to silver weapons, Sun pillar, and Light pillar attacks), <u>Primary Class: Warlock Adept, Sin Class: Harbinger of Gluttony,</u> Adrenaline Junkie (Blood) (+15% to Agility), <u>Accomplishment Title:</u> Bloodthirsty 1 (+5% increased blood mana from corpses, +1% dmg for blood magic)
- **Abilities:** Blessing of the Crow (Unholy), Wretched Snare (Unholy), Silvertongue (Unholy), Bloody Razors (Blood), Crimson Ice (Blood), Blood Lance (Blood) (Tier 2), Blood Nova (Blood) (Tier 3), Hell's Armor (Infernal), Blaze of Profane Glory (Infernal) (Tier 3), Riftwalk (Shadow), Gluttonous Sacrifice (Sin)
- **Stats:** 149 Strength, 366 Sturdiness, 888 Intelligence, 466 Agility, 10 Luck, -584 Charisma, 256 Vampiric Perception, 267 Willpower, 9 Faith
- **Free Stat Points:** 203
- **Minions:** Athela, Level 60 Arshakai [0 Willpower Requirement, currently INACTIVE with lingering soul shard]. Azmoth, Level 73 Hellscape Brutalisk (Infernal Crusader Initiate) [58 Willpower Requirement]. Fay, Level 39 Succubus [29 Willpower Requirement]. Luke Blissfallen, Level 15 High Elf Thrall (Stormrazor Battle Priest) (Warning: 72% soul decay detected) [10 Willpower Requirement]
- **Equipped Items:** Jackal (894 dmg, 305% mana regen, 8% stamina regen, Shadow and Blood dmg +36% with 10% decreased ability cost, Black Lightning, Gluttony's Riptide, Jackal's Lunge), Undergarments, Witch's Ring of Grand Casting (+26 Intelligence), Negrada's Modified Bag of Holding]

His weapon Jackal appeared from the hallway, having taken canine form. Trotting over to sit beside Riven's chair, the eerie, shadowy dog lay down next to him and accepted some ear scratches while Riven reviewed the system logs.

Two hundred and three points to spend, eh? And his passive XP sharing concerning the minion contracts had given both Azmoth and Luke some extra levels. That was nice, but it was far from everything. He also had to select a new class upgrade, had to check out the second class he'd received from Gluttony, had to deposit the puzzle box back in Brightsville and eventually needed to finish it, had to sift through the cultist loot, had to wait for his Chalgathi artifacts to finish modifying so he could continue on with the world quest, had to check out the map concerning the Dao treasure relating to Sin, and needed to see just what the system had posted on the world forums concerning his actions. Hopefully Elysium hadn't painted him in too bad of a light, but anyone who'd seen what he'd done would no doubt think him a monster. It was going to be a rough ride from here on out concerning social interactions, because everyone he met would likely be afraid of an apocalyptic, city-destroying rampage should he visit. And that was only if they didn't outright run or try to kill him on the spot—should they ever think they had a chance.

His eyes lingered on Athela's notification. She was considered a lingering soul shard and would need to be brought back somehow . . . He didn't know how just yet, but he'd figure it out. That was a certainty, and a priority. He needed his sassy spider back ASAP.

"Jesus this is a lot of stuff." Riven rubbed at his temple with one free hand while his other rubbed Fay's back. "All right, I'll just start at the top. Here goes nothing . . ."

Trying to get things done fast, he started with his status page. He slammed fifty points into Strength, twenty-five points into Willpower, twenty-five points into Sturdiness, and 103 points into Intelligence.

On to the next topic: classes.

He pulled up his new class, the one supplied by Gluttony.

- **Harbinger of Gluttony (Sin Class Title)—the Harbinger of Gluttony is the most basic sin class specific to the Original Sin of Gluttony and creates a secondary self-regulating soul clone to fight alongside you. Successfully landing any offensive attack with your soul clone will cause soul damage to your opponent, decreasing all mana, stamina, divinity, and health regeneration until the enemy soul has healed. +2 Sturdiness, +9 free points per level.**

Riven blinked. Soul clone? Self-regulating?

What did that even mean?

He looked around, patted himself down, and internally willed whatever soul clone was there to come on out. Nothing happened. He looked at his inner soul aperture next, and although he did see that his core was fully formed with a runic sigil concerning his Gluttonous Sacrifice miracle, he didn't find any change about a soul clone.

Odd.

Well, he was probably going to find out eventually, so until it showed itself, he'd just move on. He was more than happy with the vast increase in free points to use.

Closing it out and examining the next set of information after clicking his primary class options, he grinned in satisfaction at the list. This was where things got spicy . . . as either option was a good one.

[Level 100 Class Upgrade Options:

- <u>Warlock Summoner</u>: The Warlock Summoner is a direct upgrade from the class Warlock Adept, and even further emphasizes demonic minions. Your stat points all get a minor increase per level-up, and you gain an additional four demonic minion slots that can be unlocked at combat levels 110, 120, 135, and 150. <u>Class Trait</u>: All demonic minions acquire a 5% bonus to all stats. Bonus structure for Staves, Cloth Armor, Willpower, and Intelligence included.
- <u>Warlock Devastator</u>: The Warlock Devastator is a direct upgrade from the class Warlock Adept, but branches more into close combat than a pure mage role. Gain an additional one demonic minion slot. Significant increase compared to last class concerning Strength and Sturdiness stats per level. <u>Class trait</u>: All physical strikes are naturally imbued with bonus Unholy damage equal to 1% of your current total mana pool, not costing any actual mana, with the most passive damage being done at full mana capacity. Bonus structure for Heavy Armor, Two-Handed Weapons, Intelligence, and any Body Enhancement spells.]

CHAPTER 2

Warlock Summoner versus Warlock Devastator.

An interestingly beneficial pathway regardless of which choice he took. On one hand, with the Summoner option, he could have four additional minions, with all his minions adding 5 percent to all stats. On the other hand, with the Devastator option, he was still able to acquire at least one more minion while focusing primarily on himself—having his passive physical damage increased by 1 percent of his mana pool at any given time depending on how full it was. It didn't cost him mana to use, either—the effect was passive Unholy damage.

And 1 percent of his mana pool was nothing to scoff at. In fact, that was a very, very large number when compared to most people. It was more than enough to annihilate a normal person multiple times over, and just by looking at the class he got a very distinct notion—likely from the system itself—that he could deactivate this passive trait at will.

Which was good, seeing that he didn't want to accidentally blow someone up if he gave them a teasing shove or inadvertently stepped on their foot.

This was even more the case because Devastator was the one he was going to pick now that he was focusing on shoring up his close-combat abilities—which had been an inherent weakness up until recently. Yeah, four new minions would be great, but he was quickly beginning to realize that even though they were extensions of himself, he as a person was the real power player here. Though Athela and Azmoth were both far stronger than most enemies they came across, and Fay was a great utility demon to have on his side, he was confident in his ability to beat any of them in a fight one-on-one if the heavens descended and decided to see who was stronger. Though this had not been the case in the early levels of his development—back then his minions had been way stronger than he and had saved his life countless times.

Even with his given weakness to rogue-like characters, Athela—who was far more dangerous than most rogues or assassins they'd come across—would still have a very hard time beating him if they ever went all out in a sparring match. His regeneration and massive amount of magical firepower alongside his insanely strong aura were just too far above her for the demoness to compete.

That didn't mean they were useless—they were far from useless—but in the end they truly were extensions of himself and his own power, according to the system. He had to weigh just how beneficial four more would be when compared to the passive trait this Devastator class gave, and the passive was, in his opinion, better. At least for now, but that didn't mean his demons couldn't catch up to him in both level and Dao insights. In fact, he very much meant to invest in their own growth when things calmed down, because he needed—and wanted—a squad that was equal or at least close to equal to his own strength. Still thinking of the early days during the integration—they'd literally carried him through hell as a weak and clueless novice warlock; they'd been with him through thick and thin, and now it was his turn to carry them to even greater heights.

[You have selected Warlock Devastator as your new primary class. Congratulations! You have gained one additional demonic minion slot: 2,863,496 demons have already applied to be your new minion prior to this notification.

Warlock Adept's +2 Willpower, +3 Intelligence, +2 free stat points, -5 Base Charisma, -1 Charisma per level has been changed. Warlock Devastator now applies +3 Strength, +2 Sturdiness, +2 Willpower, +4 Intelligence, +2 free stat points, -5 Base Charisma, -1 Charisma per level.

Devastator trait has been acquired.

Devastator trait: When this trait is toggled on, physical strikes apply additional passive Unholy damage equal to 1% of your current total mana pool. This trait does not require any actual mana to use, with the most passive damage being done at full mana capacity.

Warlock Devastator class gives additional bonuses as follows: 12% defense for all Heavy Armor, 9% damage for Two-Handed Weapons, +3% bonus applied to Intelligence stat, and 25% increased effectiveness to all body-enhancement spells of any category cast by yourself.]

Wow. That was . . . a LOT of applications.

How the hell was he supposed to go through them all? Why was he suddenly such a popular choice? What had happened between now and the last time so that literally millions of demons had taken notice of him?

It was definitely a good problem to have, though. He only wished Athela was here to vet them like last time . . . Ugh. And if any of them even thought they could replace Athela, which was a likely upcoming scenario, they could get fucked. He immediately became angry upon thinking it, then realized just how ludicrous it was to act that way and began to internally laugh at himself. He really did like that crazy spider bitch.

Fay, who'd been watching his screens with him, smiled slightly after seeing the number of demonic applications. Letting out a still shaky but content sigh, she rubbed her cheek affectionately against his chest. "I got in before all those other idiots realized how great you were."

Looking down and blushing slightly at just how sincere she was being, he suddenly became very aware of how this may look when Luke winked at him and head-bobbed to the demoness in his lap. Riven quickly and subtly shook his head, though—this wasn't the time or the place to even think about that kind of thing after what Fay had just been through. "Thank you, Fay. It means a lot hearing that from you."

Still rocking in the chair and comfortingly rubbing the traumatized succubus's back, he abruptly felt a surge of Unholy-flavored power coalesce around his core. Internally watching his soul aperture, he saw a new wave of disjointed runes beginning to float about the soul space—not really having any pillar or piece of the core acting as a true attachment. Rather, they acted to soak up mana leaking from the surrounding pillars—making his energy use far more efficient and empowering what he believed to be his new passive Devastator trait.

Very interesting.

Readying himself to put intent into the action, as well as toning down his flow of passive power down to only a fraction—to avoid blowing up the room—he snapped his fingers while focusing on the air as his target.

A large spark of black, green, and a hint of red cracked over his hand just with the mere snap, and he'd not used a single mana point to do it.

Now he could only wonder just how much 1 percent would truly look like, and a wide smile crossed his lips. "Fay, I'm going to get up and see what Azmoth has looted from their wares. Is that okay?"

She aggressively shook her head and tightened her hold around him. "No."

He sputtered a laugh, grinning down at her as she pursed her lips defiantly up at him. "Oh, come on!"

"You can't leave."

"I'll only be a few feet away!"

"No."

He was about to roll his eyes and get up anyway, but quickly realized that she was being serious. When he shifted, she began to tremble again—and it was very apparent to him that she was still only barely holding on by the way her breathing picked up. She was still very traumatized after being kidnapped, and it'd likely be that way for quite a while.

He let his body slump back down. His eyes softened and he nodded down at her, feeling her body stop its trembling seconds later as her breathing slowed down to normal levels.

"I'll stay right here," Riven said with a comforting smile, and he motioned at Azmoth with a head bob. "Hey, man, mind bringing that table over—"

He didn't get to finish the sentence as Azmoth screamed out in victory while jumping up and down—startling everyone in the room with just how excited the huge demon had become over the course of the last two seconds.

"AZMOTH FIND IT!" The huge armored demon yelled, whirling around and stomping over to where Riven and Fay sat while cupping something small within two of his hands. "AZMOTH FIND IT!"

Reminding himself that although Azmoth was sometimes more mature than his age should indicate, this demon was still a newborn. Chuckling at the brutalisk while Fay scowled menacingly up at the armored titan, Riven glanced down at Azmoth's clawed hands. "What is it you have there, buddy?"

Azmoth breathed a cloud of hot air through his razor teeth. flames simmering from his mouth in excitement along the obsidian plates of his eyeless face. "Azmoth's stone."

The demon opened up his hands and, to Riven's shock and surprise, revealed a small red bauble. It was slightly different than how Riven remembered it from the depths of Negrada's hellscape, but it was definitely the same thing. It just lacked the inherent energy and power that'd once been contained inside, and there was a crack along one edge of the glass-like, red orb.

"Is this . . ." Riven picked up the bauble presented to him, turning it around in his hand with a curiously raised eyebrow. "Wow. It is. Azmoth, have you kept this bauble the entire time?"

[Dark Arts Miracle Stone (Unique) (Broken): The prayers to Jograz Metz were heard, the blood price had been paid, and he answered with this gift. This stone once housed the demon Azmoth, an infant Hellscape Brutalisk, before the stone was used and Azmoth's departure left the stone inadequate for proper functioning. Now it appears to only be a memento, but it does still hold faint traces of Jograz Metz's aura.]

Azmoth took the stone back when it was offered to him, and the large demon reverently put it in his mouth before swallowing it whole. As he sadly shook his head, Azmoth's shoulders sagged and he gave the impression of a kicked puppy dog as he let out a long, high-pitched groan very uncharacteristic of the behemoth. "I not have stone. I gave to Athela as present. Cultists take stone from Athela when kill her."

He looked up, staring at Riven wordlessly until he managed to get out a slowly phrased question. "Will Athela come back? I miss Athela."

Riven nearly died of cuteness overload, and he reached out to pat the large demon's lower left hand. He'd not realized that Azmoth had given Athela this memento as a present, nor had he realized that she'd kept it on her person so long. It must have some significant meaning for them to have shared it like that. "Yeah. She'll be back. I promise I'll find a way. I have that soul shard, don't I?"

Azmoth hesitantly nodded. "Yes. When, though?"

"I don't know, bud. I'll have to figure that out, too, but it's a priority. That I promise."

Riven wiped the blood off his lips, licking his fingers and tossing the cultist's arm to the side.

The items these cultists had acquired outside the realm of Chalgathi artifacts were rather niche, most of them oriented toward ritualistic magic that Riven had only touched on in passing. There were some rings that Riven could use, though, and some other stuff that was actually oriented toward utilizing miracles—though only a few of them were outside the realm of Unholy. Though they were scarce, he handed these items over to Luke for whenever his soul repaired to properly function.

"Horned Helm of Soothsaying, Godsent Charm Box, and the Bristled Pinewood Cloak. These are for you." Riven shoved the items across the table to Luke, who donned them one by one—a leather helm with deer antlers stuck to the front, a small wicker box with some kind of plant akin to pinecones inside, and a cloak with interwoven pine needles stitched into the fabric. Each was a miracle-boosting item, each oriented toward the Fae foundational pillar and the Forest subpillar. "How's your recovery coming along, by the way?"

Luke tightened the cloak around his waist with a cloth belt, then made sure the charm box was appropriately fastened to it. Adjusting the horned helmet one more time, the silver-haired old elf smiled widely. "I can feel the soul slowly starting to repair itself. I even went down 1 percent in terms of soul damage. It's slow going, but changing into a thrall was the best decision I could have ever made. It's actually healing me!!!"

Riven nodded, appreciating just how happy and excited the old man was. "Good to hear. I noticed it, too, but I figured I wouldn't say anything yet. Do you think you'll be able to use those items when your abilities are back in business?"

Luke nodded, suddenly going serious. "Yes, though I specialized more in Storm than Forest. I still have a few Forest miracles, however, as long as the pillar etchings weren't utterly destroyed."

"Good."

Riven went back to sorting the materials on the table. There were odds and ends, including string, animal bones, human hair, a scalp, oddly colored salts, shriveled herbs, and a number of different-colored chalk pieces rolled up in parchment.

"I don't know what any of this shit is."

Riven deposited them into his inventory nonetheless, not wanting to waste them as they'd obviously been useful to these cultists—so they probably had SOME value. The dead cultists and the eldritch demon had also carried some caster equipment for mages, specifically warlocks, but it was a little bit below what he wanted to equip himself with in terms of value. It'd still be good to bring back to his budding empire, though, as he was sure some novice warlocks would be able to use the wands, gloves, and two amulets he'd found.

But there were five items he did find interesting. Two were basic enchanted gold rings, each of them boosting his Intelligence by a small amount, that he slipped onto his fingers next to the Witch's Ring of Grand Casting. Then there was a basic brown Whip of Debaucherous Taming, which was . . . unique. There was also the white blade with black runes, a demon-slayer blade that'd been used to kill Athela—he promptly stored that for experimentation purposes. And lastly there was Fay's outfit, which had been so kindly stored away upon her kidnapping—they'd no doubt kept it for the enchantment value, and he'd promptly given it back to her after tearing them new assholes.

[Gold Band of Minor Intelligence: +7 Intelligence]
[Gold Band of Minor Intelligence: +9 Intelligence]
[Whip of Debaucherous Taming: 15 average damage on strike, induces pain and pleasure when struck, with an enchantment effect that causes any humanoid target to be more prone to following your commands.]
[Chelfine (Demon-Slaying Blade): 102 average damage on strike, with the chance to apply Holy burns. Utilizing this weapon against a demon can cause the demon's soul to degrade at a rapid pace, permanently killing them regardless of contract.]

The whip would be a good present for Allie, considering she had her own man-harem going on. If not, well, he'd figure out someone who could use it. Would be a waste to simply toss it.

Placing the whip and the blade in his bag of holding, and adjusting the rings on his fingers, he glanced over his shoulder to where Fay was passed out on the bed, wearing her purple witch's hat, skirt, and crop top, chest rising and falling. The feathered boots he'd gotten her that helped with her flying were set beside her on the floor, and if Riven had to guess, she'd be out of it for quite some time, even though she'd slept earlier that day.

"We've got some drugs here." Luke held up a bag of herbs and tossed it over to Riven. "We used to smoke that stuff as kids in the highlands near my village back home. It's called reeter weed—makes you feel happy and hungry."

"Sounds familiar to something from my own planet." Riven grinned, stuffing the bag of herbs into a side pocket and nodding in appreciation. "We're going to get so high after this . . ."

"Definitely deserve it."

"Agreed. This waking nightmare I've been living in is going to run me ragged. Anything back beyond that hallway?"

"No. Just a small, closeted room that didn't have anything of value in it."

A faint whisper echoed throughout the chamber, drawing Riven's attention to the swirling, black-and-red mass. Slowly, ever so slowly, the ball of swirling energy began to dissipate—and in place of his items was a more unified version of the artifacts he'd come to know . . . but they shifted eerily, as if they hadn't taken completely solid form yet.

[The Apocalypse Beasts, Chalgathi, Personal Quest Update: Five of five set pieces for Chalgathi's inheritance have been acquired. Checkpoint reached. Current Chalgathi artifacts have had their stat pages completely revealed due to acquiring all five pieces. Chalgathi Cultist Breastplate, Chalgathi Cultist Amulet, Chalgathi Cultist Pauldrons, Chalgathi Cultist Claws, and Chalgathi Cultist Mask are ready to completely merge into one set item after acquiring necessary aspect from soul. As this is a system world quest, this prize is meant to be a boon to the wielder and not a detriment—thus this query is being issued: Do you wish to keep the connection between Gluttony's Sin Core with this item set? Doing so will allow the armor to evolve and grow with you, but will give you compulsions from time to time that can become overwhelming if your Willpower isn't regularly increased to combat the effect.]

Riven blinked. "I increase my Willpower all the time anyways, and I have Gluttony already knocking at my door through the core. Why would I care? Gimme that evolving armor set!"

He slapped the button real, real hard.

[Connection to Sin Core has been maintained. Analyzing and configuring now.]
[Chalgathi Cultist Amulet (The Great Maw), Chalgathi Cultist Pauldrons (Twin Cannibals), Chalgathi Cultist Mask (Fallen Apostle), Chalgathi Cultist Claws (Bloodfallen Rippers), and Chalgathi Cultist Breastplate (Hunger's Despair) have all converged into one item after completing this item set.]
[Chalgathi Cultist Armor Set: Messenger has been completed.]

[Messenger (Mythic Heavy Armor Set, Sin Artifact, Gluttony Aspect) (Evolving Symbiote) (World Quest Item: Panu) (Unique Soul-Bound Sentient): This Mythic-tier armor set was created on the world of Panu during its integration cycle by the pure-blooded vampire Riven Thane. Having far surpassed the realm of normalcy, this armor set has been afflicted with the Original Sin of Gluttony. As a messenger of sin and a holder of a sin shard, Gluttony has blessed this armor to even further heights so that the wielder may one day become the tidebringer of wanton destruction Gluttony seeks. All shall perish before the great maw; all hail the abyssal depths.
> Devour: This amulet can use shadowy tendrils to attack and pull in prey for devouring. If bitten, a potent paralytic poison is applied to your enemy. Devouring enemies allows this item set to grow slowly.
> Identifier's Clause: Wearing this item increases your ability to identify information concerning items or living creatures, being the equivalent of a low-tier identifier class. Your own basic information will be much harder to identify.
> Blood in the Eyes: These pauldrons passively absorb blood mana from your surroundings up to a maximum of double your normal mana pool. These pauldrons act as a reservoir for your passive vampiric regeneration, this suit's Launch ability, and act as a mana font to pull from as you would environmental resources. Once the pauldron's eyes dim, your extra resource pool has run out.
> Ripping Claws: Punching someone with the spikes of your gauntlets will cause massive hemorrhaging damage over time.

> Launch: The back of your suit can open up, creating a blast of sin energy that damages enemies and acts as a propulsion method to blast you in a given direction at speeds dependent on how much energy you drain from the stored reservoir of your pauldrons.
> +20% to all base stats
> +300 Strength, +600 Sturdiness, +300 Agility
> +1,858 defense to all plated areas of armor
> +965 defense to all bloodsilk areas between plates
> Natural sunlight does not affect you while wearing this suit
> Liquid breathing is bestowed upon you while wearing this suit
> All senses enhanced by 40% while wearing this suit
> Allows passage free from harm in any underverse controlled by Gluttony
> Immediately identifies and locks on to nearby sins or commandments
> This armor set will occasionally urge you to undertake feeding frenzies. Wear at your own risk. A high Willpower is needed to combat the urges.]

Mythic. That was one Riven hadn't heard of before. He'd heard of elite tier and legendary tier, though he'd had very little information about them before now. He knew Allie had legendary-tier soul-woven armor after she'd sacrificed a group of people in the tutorial, but Mythic? Not even Negrada's merchants had talked to him about this.

So . . . he assumed this was a pretty good armor set?

And by the looks of the rest of the status page, he couldn't be more right. He had a little bit fewer than 400 Sturdiness right now, and this item set not only gave him a 20 percent boost to those base stats—supplying him with somewhere around 75 more Sturdiness points—but it also gave a flat 600 Sturdiness stat points off the bat. Same could be said about his Strength, which was only 199 right now—yet this suit gave him an additional 20 percent to those numbers and then another 300 flat Strength points? He had 466 points of Agility already, but he was ALMOST doubling it with the 20 percent boost and then another 300 flat Agility points after that.

"Is this even fair?"

Chalgathi and/or Gluttony must really want him alive . . . or perhaps this was just how all the Chalgathi item sets were. If that were the case, then each of the five people who made it to this next part of the world quest would be overpowered as all hell—just with different flavors of aspects dependent on their own souls and how those souls bonded to their artifact pieces.

Though Riven had a very hard time believing other people in this quest line had an aspect as powerful or as dangerous as Gluttony.

Riven stopped his gawking to look up when the shimmering around the item set began to clear. Slowly the colors began to fade, and in place of the swirling energies was a completed, single item that combined all five of the artifacts he'd acquired. The pieces were so interlinked, however, that he doubted he'd be able to detach them from one another if he tried.

And it looked a lot more intimidating now that it was all finished, with many similarities to his original pieces but also some major differences.

The second difference was the helmet. And it *was* a helmet. No longer a porcelain mask, but a very smooth, ivory-colored metal that shimmered in the firelight. It had slits for his eyes and was molded in the form of two jaws coming together to interlink vertically down the middle like two halves had been smashed together to create the intricate helmet. The seven crimson peacock feathers had changed—morphing into shorter, neon-red feathers that almost looked like blades coming down the spine of the helmet and along the back of the neck.

Where the helmet stopped, a red bloodsilk layer connected it to the rest of the armor. Coming down the neck and attaching to the top of the full-body chest armor and pauldrons, it could also be seen in patches of crimson between different layers of plating where the ivory metal extended along the armor and farther into gauntlets.

The gauntlets were absolutely wicked, with slightly elongated points at the knuckles that crackled with red and black energies. The pauldrons were almost exactly the same as they had been—horned vampiric skulls with brilliant, glowing red eyes. The full-body chest armor had the same vertical maw of black teeth down the center, and it had what looked like four flat patches of black metal embedded in the ivory along the back. These black slabs each sparked with a similar energy to the gauntlets, but instead of sparks, they exuded wisps of red and black that drifted into mist, similar to what happened when Riven charged a Blood Lance.

No doubt those black slabs were the equivalent of thrusters used for his suit's new ability, Launch. The techies working on mechs in Chicago would be so jealous of this baddie. Perhaps they could even study it? That'd be neat.

The armor's metal cut off at the waist, but it fully encompassed the upper half of his body. Two additional large flaps of bloodsilk hung down from the armor's back to cover the posterior and sides of his thighs down to his knees before ending entirely. Perhaps the flaps were to keep his thrusters from burning his legs? That'd make sense. He walked around it, admiring the item set as he gave a low whistle. He'd have to find boots and leg armor to complete the outfit, but that was certainly doable.

Curiously enough, Jackal—his weapon now in canine form—was looking intensely at the armor set with a cocked head and intense expression. When the armor set Messenger turned its helmet to stare back at the shadowy dog on the floor, Riven nearly keeled over in surprise.

The stare-down between Gluttony-blessed weapon and Gluttony-blessed armor continued for another ten seconds until Jackal gave a nod of approval and settled back down. The armor suit then slowly turned in the air, where it hovered, stopping only when it faced Riven. Wordlessly, the great maw split apart, as did the bloodsilk along the neck and then the two sides of the helmet where the metal looked like two jaws coming together.

The arms peeled open next, and the gauntlets turned outward.

The suit was inviting him in.

"I'm not going to be trapped inside you if I wear you again, am I?" Riven asked hesitantly, wanting to put the suit of armor on but also not willing to trap himself again if that was a prerequisite.

A low hiss from the armor echoed through the room, but the armor eventually turned its ivory helmet back and forth in a no gesture.

Riven nodded in approval. "Very good, then."

Stepping forward and turning around, he let himself walk backward into the armored suit. The breastplate snapped shut with the teeth interlocking on his chest, then the bloodsilk along his neck zipped up. The helmet came after, letting his glowing red eyes look out through the slit in the metal, and his arms and gauntlets were after that. Lastly, a bloodsilk layer began stretching down along his legs, over his undergarments, and all the way down to cover his feet. Immediately he felt a rush of power flood his body, and Riven gasped at the immense weight of all this newfound energy he felt bounding through his muscles.

He felt like a fucking god.

He was . . . the GOAT.

"You really need to put on your metal boots and leggings," Luke commented while stroking his chin, only to have Azmoth agree with a nod. "Amazing up top, but it also looks like you . . . what was the phrase Athela used earlier? 'Skipped leg day at the gym one too many times,' I believe?"

Azmoth snickered, and Riven gave Luke a frowning glare.

"Fine. I'll go put on the leggings, but now the colors won't match. Damn, I've gotta find some ivory-colored spray paint so I can color-code this outfit."

"Color-code?" Luke repeated, the corners of his mouth lifting up with ill-hidden amusement. "Never thought I'd hear the day a vampire started talking about color-coding their outfits."

"Well, how many vampires have you known? I bet they ALL like to color-code. I'll tell you this—" Riven held up one ivory-encased finger. "The vampires at the Blood Moon Requiem's trading post are all very fashionable."

Luke snorted and rolled his eyes. "Perhaps you're right. Now, what's the plan? Do we head back to Brightsville after this? We still have the option to teleport to your guild hall, right?"

"That or we can use Jackal. My weapon has the ability to create portals, too, and one of them is registered to Riven's Eye—the world-spanning wormhole." Riven gestured down at the shadowy dog, who silently stared up at them from beside the severed cultist head. "I'm a man of culture, my dear friend Luke. I have not one but two methods of getting us back home. Problem is it'll still take a bit to channel the effects. But twenty-four hours from now, we'll be right as rain."

"And the demonic contract you can acquire?"

"That'll wait for now . . . I'd preferably want Athela to be here when I do it, but we'll see. I'll talk to Allie first and decide when we get back home."

"And the Dao treasure map? Weren't you going to check on the world forums?"

"Oh, for fuck's sake, Grandpa, just let me have some time, okay?!"

CHAPTER 3

[World Quest 2, The Apocalypse Beasts: Ah, this is one of my personal favorites. I present to you the apocalypse beasts! Your world has been cursed with three tyrannical creatures of astronomical power that are currently being incubated and grown into their adult forms. Each of these absolute monstrosities is able to turn the world on its head, demolishing countries in its path and tearing the very fabric of reality apart. Know that if these creatures are allowed to awaken, you will likely not live much longer than the five years' limit. Each of these monsters have cultist worshippers from their own planets, given knowledge of these creatures before the integration even began. They will try to awaken the monsters' adult forms to destroy your world entirely, leading to astronomical amounts of power as a reward for the cultists in their success when they leave the smoldering wreckage of Panu. Your goal is to stop and kill their cult worshippers and find out where these creatures are being incubated so that you will have a world to live on when the five years of time runs out.

Current Threat Level: Extremely High. Catastrophe upon failure of completion when five years has passed: Nekra, the Skeletal Devourer, will be unleashed onto Panu. Chalgathi, the Plague Dragon, will be unleashed onto Panu. Chubin, the Glass Kraken, will be unleashed onto Panu. Advanced Details Have Been Unlocked: Upon completing this quest and finding the incubation chambers of any given apocalypse beast, you may either kill it before it is born for an item of immense power or claim its eggs for yourself. Killing them will bless you with a unique tier-50 spirit item, while claiming their eggs for yourself will link them to you as a minion. Claiming them as a minion will not produce them in their adult form, but rather they will begin as an infant version of themselves and must be cultivated to higher grades of power over time before coming into their true potential. You have already been in contact with Chalgathi's starter quests, thus you will soon receive an update on his particular quest line now that the World Quests have been distributed.]

[Chalgathi, The Apocalypse Beasts World Quest, Panu, has updated: Congratulations on being the third person to collect all five Chalgathi artifacts. Now that all artifacts have coalesced into one item set, you are to be given eventual access to the subevent: the Altars of Despair and Hope.

The Altars of Despair and Hope are exclusive areas designated by the Elysium administrator, where only the chosen of the apocalypse beasts who've acquired the five needed artifacts, as well as abducted involuntary participants from across the multiverse, may enter. This applies to all apocalypse beasts, not only Chalgathi. Here at the Altars of Despair and Hope you will be divided into two groups: cultists and noncultists. As previously described, the outcomes of this world quest differ greatly depending on which of the chosen acquires the prizes for these quests. Thus, cultists will be pitted against noncultists when reaching these altars. Noncultists across all three apocalypse beast categories will arrive at the Altar of Hope, and cultists across all three apocalypse beast categories will arrive at the Altar of Despair. You will be highly incentivized to work together with your given team upon arrival, and severe punishments will be handed down to those who intentionally harm any others within your own category while involving yourself in this subevent of the quest line; more details will arrive upon event initiation.

The Altars of Despair and Hope will first open with an event initiation in four months, one week, three days, and five hours from now. Upon opening the altars, the next phase of World Quest 2, The Apocalypse Beasts, will begin. You can expect to enter an alternate pocket realm at that time along with other various people, places, artifacts, and events drawn in from around the multiverse, and can expect to be gone for approximately one year. Participants who do not collect all the necessary apocalypse beast artifacts upon event initiation will still be able to join the Altars of Despair and Hope subevent upon completion of the item sets.]

It looked like he had some time before the next set of events concerning the world quest. That was if he didn't get assassinated in the meantime by other participants, who could no doubt track his location with the Ping Chalgathi Artifacts ability.

Then again, perhaps his growing and sinister reputation would cause the others to fuck right off. That Japanese man had certainly tucked tail and run when Riven had appeared last time, leaving his compatriots to be slaughtered.

His red eyes gazed over the information for the third time since it'd appeared. Silently closing the notification, Riven continued to meditate in a hovering position with steepled hands—cross-legged in the air. He wore his new upper-body plate armor, Messenger, and had put on his dark steel leggings and boots. Meanwhile, his weapon Jackal continued to channel the portal ability as it created an orb of multicolored light above the blade in the center of the room. It was almost time, but he had another five minutes until they were able to teleport back to Riven's Eye Wormhole near Brightsville.

Using this time to his advantage while his minions got ready, he pulled out the map that'd been deposited in his spatial bag concerning the Sin-related Dao treasure.

Unlike most treasure maps, this one was actually a three-dimensional hologram. It emerged from a small metal cylinder, the top of the cylinder creating a very intricate diagram of a part of Panu from a zoomed-out view.

The hologram displayed a tropical island with a volcano at its center. It had a very distinct boot-shaped protrusion that formed a cove on one side, with trees and other features on the island so tiny that they were smaller than a pinhead but still somewhat discernible. The map spanned many meters across in any direction from the cylinder, and he was even able to get up and walk through it—identifying a glowing dot underneath the volcano through a large sprawling set of ancient ruins underneath the island. There, where a ruined city lay long forgotten by the looks of how decimated the architecture was, were flowing rivers of magma that eventually led to an odd-looking temple.

It was here, at this temple, that the icon continued to flash.

It had no description otherwise, no details, only the outline of the island, the ruins, and the path down the magma rivers leading to the temple where the Dao treasure of Sin was located. The very large problem he now had, though, was that he had zero clue where this island was. It could be literally anywhere, and he had no doubt that the combination of three merging planets would only make it all the harder to find.

"At least it's a start."

He looked up from the slit in his helmet, neon-red feathers along the spine of his helmet flashing slightly when the portal ahead of him finally materialized. His weapon Jackal returned to his hand when he stretched his arm out—and looking through the ovoid gate, he could see that it was likely afternoon or early evening on the other side. The location was directly outside Riven's Eye Wormhole, and he could see not only thousands of people traveling between the Elysium altar, downtown Brightsville, the slave farms, and Chicago on the wormhole's other side, but he could also see patrolling helicopters and fighter jets in the sky through a very thin layer of mist that'd become prevalent in his Unholy-tainted lands. The silver grasses, black-wood trees with similarly silver or neon-teal leaves, and the red vines were very distinct.

He stepped through shortly afterward without a word, metal boots flattening the grass underneath him with the wormhole's brilliant white-blue lights churning to his left.

"FREEZE!" a military man in uniform called out, turning around with others under his command to raise a gun Riven's way. "STOP RIGHT THERE!"

The man's squad was a rather odd thing to look at. It included two cyborgs—a man and a woman with orange and yellow lines of power lighting up their arms, guns, and eyes. There were a couple of soldiers as well, a two-story humanoid mech that sported plasma cannons on its back, looking like it'd been pulled out of a manga, and two skeletal Unholy mages with staves and a whole slew of goblins that looked rather different from the ones Riven was used to.

Riven couldn't quite place it, and he stared at the little green men for quite some time while ignoring the startled soldier and his squad. The goblins were slightly bigger, but that wasn't it . . . they looked more self-aware. Intelligent, even, by the way they weren't picking their noses and dawdling about, or how they interacted with each other or the passing travelers.

Or by the way one of those goblins was the first to recognize him before any of the others did.

The goblin at the forefront of the mixed squad, a small green creature about three and a half feet tall, wearing body armor native to Earth, was warily clutching at his own daggers. The weapons had obviously been enhanced by Chicago's engineers due to the way the tips of their blades were plasma-based, but the little man's buggy eyes went wide when he saw Azmoth and Fay step out of the portal beside Riven.

"YOU FUDGING IDIOT! THAT IS OUR KING!" The goblin promptly slammed a booted foot into the soldier's shin, causing his commanding officer to fall with a cry of surprise before others of their unit abruptly took in the goblin's words. "HOW DARE YOU RAISE A WEAPON TOWARD HIM!"

The red eyes, Riven's weapon, and the minions were recognizable from video footage. The armor was, too, but only to a certain extent. The maw across the front was obviously the same, as were the pauldrons and the bloodsilk connecting various plate-armor pieces, but everything else was different. The helmet and plate armor surrounding his torso were vastly improved, as were the ivory gauntlets he wore, and the flaps of bloodsilk out behind Riven's waist were also far different from his original look. He didn't wear a cloak, either, but rather remained in full plate armor, as the ridge of feathers along the top of his helmet wouldn't allow it.

The goblin quickly bowed with an apologetic and wary smile, and soon the entire squad followed suit. Even the mech took a knee, its pilot saluting Riven from the cockpit in the central body, and travelers who'd been vanishing into the wormhole or coming back out completely stopped their foot traffic to look at him as Riven's own portal closed from behind. Rat-kin traders from Deepnest, humans from Dawn and the Necropolis, the undead created from Allie's bone garden, green-skinned orcs and goblins alike—they all quickly came to a hushed silence when he appeared.

Many of them fell to their knees in silent respect—prostrating themselves. Others spoke in hushed whispers and avoided being seen by hiding behind trading carts, cargo trucks, or nearby buildings on the perimeter of the wormhole. It was very apparent that Riven inspired respect here, but he also inspired a sense of fear.

The soldier on the ground, a man who no doubt came from the military units of Chicago, Milwaukee, and Rockford, shakily put his head to the ground. "I'm sorry, my king, I did not realize it was you and I . . ."

His voice trailed off into a hushed whisper, and it was obvious by the way he shook that he was terrified.

Riven frowned. "Has it really been long enough that you forgot what I did for your city? I'm not some crazed lunatic out to kill everyone, despite how the world forums paint me. You don't have to be afraid—you did nothing wrong."

The soldier gave a relieved shudder but remained prostrated like the crowds of silent people behind him. Out of everyone present, it was only the high elf slaves who remained standing in the immediate area. They glared daggers at him, silently seething with hate while shackled and collared—forced into manual labor against their will. There were hundreds—no, thousands of them now, just in the immediate area across the farmlands on either side of the main road leading to the trading hub at the Elysium altar. It was very apparent that the number of high elf slaves had grown, no doubt from Allie's war efforts against the towns and one major elf city she'd conquered in his absence.

He'd read the updates in the local forums about it.

But even the high elves fell to their knees when his eyes turned their way, shuddering with fear as his aura softly pulsed out over the crowds on a subconscious level. He hadn't even realized he'd been doing it until then, but he didn't bother retracting the aura, either. Nor did he feel compassion for the enslaved elves anymore. He had too much to worry about; too many lives were at stake across the world for him to give a damn about the many tens of thousands of inherently racist people who'd started wars and fights they couldn't finish.

Perhaps if they'd not been so intent on elvish supremacy, perhaps if he'd not been betrayed in Greenstalk, perhaps if these high elves hadn't kept human slaves of their own—he may have more sympathy. But now they were merely cattle. Property of the empire, fuel to be used for the country's growth.

He paused as this thought passed him by. How different his outlook was now . . . Why was that?

Numerous reasons, really. An additive effect over time after his poorly based assumptions about the world had been whittled down little by little. His morals from the old world were almost entirely dead now, though in his opinion he and Allie could have been a lot harsher with the captives they'd taken. And he still had ideas concerning programs to reintegrate any of the high elves who complied and became productive members of society; it'd just take a bit to implement them. Those who stuck to their guns of being racist, violent bigots could stay slaves for all he cared.

Turning on his heel and walking through the crowds, Riven began to make his way to his manor. Fay had been wanting to see her brother, Tupper, and he was curious how Genua's training was coming along. He'd given Tupper express commands to turn her noncompliant, bad attitude around in Riven's absence, and he was still salty about how she and her family had made him feel so at home before trying to murder him.

No, she was the only one remaining of the people he'd come to trust before that betrayal. She would bear the humiliation for her dead family as an atonement for their transgressions. Though Riven couldn't help but wonder how Len was doing and how far the little girl had come along in her reeducation.

He pulled out his communication orb, modified with Machine-pillar tech before he'd left to extend to a longer range. The black bauble with mechanical ribbing on its outer shell pulsed in his hand when he infused mana into it—and he felt the connection settle ten seconds later when Allie picked up on the other line.

Riven smiled. "Hello, little sister."

"RIVEN!" Allie's excited voice came over the line. "YOU'RE BACK!"

He chuckled, passing another group of rat-kin traders carrying sacks, who all gave him a deep bow of respect. "It's good to hear your voice. We have a lot to talk about. Where are you?"

There was a pause, then the sound of shuffling papers on the other side.

"Getting ready for an exam!" Allie's voice called through the orb. "I'm attending that academy we talked about before you left. I've even made a friend! You should meet him; he's really nice."

"He?"

"Yeah, he. Why is that important?"

"Just curious. How's your man-harem doing?" Riven looked down to his bag where the enchanted whip he'd found lay in wait, and he shook his head with another chuckle. "I have a present for you."

"They're fine, but I haven't really seen any of them since coming here. Hey, do you think you'd be able to meet up for coffee in Dawn's capital sometime? Bring a disguise. I don't want you scaring everyone here shitless after the stunts you pulled in that canyon city."

Riven raised his eyebrows, giving Fay the thumbs-up to fly ahead in order to meet her brother. He watched the succubus take off over the crop fields infested with chained elves using plant-based magics alongside their guards. "A disguise, you say? Very well. When do you want to meet? I was going to drop in and take a nap at the manor, though. I'm exhausted, and I could really use a comfortable bed for once."

CHAPTER 4

Things had certainly changed at the guild hall manor in Riven's absence, and it left Riven wondering why Allie hadn't told him about it.

Kathrine Vonsilla Crushada the Ninth, eldest daughter to the duke and duchess of House of Crushada, 107th in line for the vampiric throne, was somehow standing in front of Riven's multistory home in a pristine black dress adorned with bright-red flowers. Her brown hair was swept to one side, shining elegantly in the light of numerous lanterns that now illuminated the outer walls of the manor. Soldiers encircled the large metal fences around the front courtyard and a large pond fringed with beautiful Death-attuned flowers, and along the back of the garden, even more of the soldiers guarded his compound. Two banners hung from the upper balconies, one of them displaying the Blood Moon Requiem's sigil of a red crescent moon on a black backdrop. The other was just blue with a black question mark.

Beside Kathrine stood Tupper, wearing a butler's outfit and engaged in deep conversation with his sister, Fay—and there were a number of very pretty high elf slaves present, too. They were almost all female, far more scantily clad than Riven remembered the previous maids' outfits to be. They essentially wore enchanted iron collars signifying their rank and were lined up with hands in front facing ahead. They had been outfitted in black skirt-bikinis and thin slip-on shoes—and they all wore expressions of nervousness as Riven slowly approached. In fact, the only males Riven saw were the ones Allie had taken into her man-harem—which made Riven wonder where the other men who'd been in line to become butlers had gone.

He stopped ahead of Kathrine, leveling his red gaze to meet her own where she stood ahead of the others. "I didn't realize you could leave the confines of your trading commune. Tell me, what brings you to my home?"

Kathrine's visage of confidence briefly faltered at his cold tone, but the young woman remained in good posture as she addressed him with chin held high. "You're a busy man, Riven Wraithtide."

"Riven Thane," Riven corrected with a slow blink of his eyes.

Kathrine hesitated, then nodded. "Very well. Riven Thane it is. Our elder High Queen Nephridi has informed me that my efforts to make contact with you and form relations have been less than adequate, and she told me I needed to redouble my efforts. Because I am unable to contact you outside the commune's borders under most circumstances, I asked your sister, Allie, if it would be all right for me to assign myself as an attendant."

There was an awkward silence following her words.

"And Allie said yes?" Riven asked, pulling up the status page of his guild hall, which was connected to his own status page as guild hall owner.

> **[Guild Hall: Stone Manor (Unnamed)**
> - **Assigned Guild: Unassigned. Owned by Riven Thane. Administrative privileges also set to Allie Thane.**
> - **Homeward Teleportation: Very long channel time. Only hired attendants or guild members can utilize this teleportation function. Currently, there is no guild assigned to this guild hall, and there are no attendants, so the teleportation function is limited to Riven Thane.**
> - **Fifteen attendant spots available, six hundred Elysium coins per month per active attendant are taxed by the system administrator. You may either mentally link this guild hall to the nearest friendly Elysium altar that you have access to in order to hire attendants from the general store, or you may hire attendants from associated factions at that altar. Attendants Currently Enlisted (2/15): Tupper (Incubus Butler), Kathrine Vonsilla Crushada (Pure-blooded Vampire Diplomat)**
> - **Three-mile exploration radius for attendants before forced retrieval back to guild hall**
> - **Core Sturdiness: Moderate**
> - **Defensive wards: None**
> - **Change Guild Hall Location: one year of channeling needed.]**

Allie had guild hall privileges, as he'd set it to be that way, but he was surprised he'd not been notified. He glanced back up to see Kathrine fidgeting nervously, and his eyes narrowed. "Answer me honestly. Why?"

"Excuse me?" Kathrine replied, brows furrowed.

"Why go out of your way now? What's changed? Why leave the relative safety of all your guards, servants, and immediate access back home through your commune portal in order to be here?"

"I . . . I'm not sure what you mean. I've been trying to get a hold of you—"

"And I've actively been ignoring your efforts, yes, I know," Riven stated flatly, stepping forward again and causing Kathrine to cringe. "What makes it so important to you that you'd leave the comfort of your lavish commune to be here—a mere pauper's hut compared to what you have at the altar?"

Kathrine frowned, her hands tightening around one another as she huffed. "You underestimate your importance as a prince in the empire."

Riven wasn't buying it. "You're one hundred and seventh in line for the throne. I'm what—thirtieth? Thirty-fifth? I can't even remember. I'm not an immediate heir and we haven't even been to the Blood Moon Requiem."

"You are the son of the queen's favorite granddaughter, and you are a holder of the gift."

"Malignant prophecy?"

Kathrine nodded. "As previously stated, not many of the empire's royalty have that ability. It is a key asset, one that is valued above all others. The fact that you and your sister both have it is a tremendous boon, one that cannot be lost to us."

There was a pause.

"I see." Riven gave his distant cousin a wary up-and-down look. She seemed very nervous. "Kathrine . . . what happens if you fail to establish good relations with me?"

At this, Kathrine blanched. She stuttered at first, then calmed herself and cleared her throat. "I will be executed. Along with my entire family. None of us possess the gift . . . and although we are technically royalty, we're only barely so."

Riven's eyebrows raised. Sighing and shaking his head, he mentally willed his helmet to dislodge from his face so he could rub at his temple to relieve his building headache. The helmet peeled back and hung off the back of his neck, revealing his face—to the abrupt inhale of many of the slaves nearby.

Stopping mid-temple rub, he glanced up at the wide-eyed slaves who were gawking and staring. Frowning, he looked down at his outfit, then back up. One of the slave girls was even covering her mouth subconsciously.

"Am I really that scary?" Riven asked with an exhausted, deflated hunch of his shoulders. His eyes fell to Kathrine, and even she wore a similar expression—which was unusual, as she'd met him before. "What is it?"

"You look . . . rather good. Better than I remember," Kathrine eventually said hesitantly, stepping in closer to get a better look. "Do not take this the wrong way, but . . . perhaps you should look in a mirror."

He snorted, then turned to Azmoth and Luke. "Do I look any different? What are they talking about?"

Luke and Azmoth both simultaneously shrugged.

"Whatever. Anyways, I'm off to take a nap. Kathrine, you're more than welcome to stay and we can talk about ways to build relations later. I won't let you or your family be executed, and you can tell the queen that I'm interested in maintaining a positive connection with the empire, but I'm rather busy. I just haven't had time to deal with diplomacy when I have a series of world-ending events I need to deal with, especially since I'm now in the top ten."

Kathrine's features brightened immediately with relief, then confusion. "Top ten?"

"I'm ranked fifth on the world power boards. I have a responsibility now more than ever."

Her eyebrows shot up in surprise, then delight. "The queen will be pleased to hear it. We don't have access to the ranking boards of integrating worlds as outsiders—but it is a great honor. If you don't mind, I do have some important matters to talk to you about before you go to sleep . . . The incubus and I actually have a dinner prepared for your arrival. Would it be all right if we—"

"It can't wait?" Riven asked impatiently, glaring down at his distant relative with exasperation. "I don't think you realize how awful this last trip was for me. I really just want to pass out."

Kathrine hesitated, then shook her head. "Hours matter. It involves your off-world estates, ones that you and Allie technically own as heads of the Wraithtide household. Large amounts of wealth and numerous lives will be affected by your decision or lack thereof. Allie . . . has been less than cooperative dealing with this matter, as she's busy at her academy. Beyond that, you're the elder brother and the inheritance technically belongs to you."

Riven groaned. "Lives are going to be affected? Numerous? What does that even mean?"

"The Wraithtide household is in a state of disrepair, and other nobles are seeking to absorb your assets by bribing lesser members of your house. You need to sign a decree so I can take it to the commune and transport it from there back to the empire through a messenger, establishing yourself as a present entity and denying access to those who would seek to buy and sell your rightful property in your absence."

"You're saying other members of my distant family are trying to pawn off my inheritance?"

"Correct."

Riven scratched his chin. "Doesn't really bother me that much. What exactly is it that I technically own?"

"Your inheritance is that of a single high-grade planet, a trading hub in the Vartesh sector named Luteski. Because your parents have been gone so long, the house of Wraithtide has fallen to lesser nobility, and they see your return as a threat to their own wealth. They wish to sell what they can now before you return, and then they will relocate."

Riven's eyes widened. "I own a planet?"

"You do, and you lord over all its inhabitants—dictating what laws are established there as long as they do not conflict with the high queen's own. The inhabitants of the planet number over fifty million vampires and six billion slaves, and your net worth is . . . rather high. For lesser members of your family to pawn it off is not technically illegal, but the high queen wanted me to inform you that you should take matters into your own hands now if you wish to keep the inheritance."

Riven's jaw dropped slightly. "I see. That does sound slightly important . . . All right. Let's talk about this inside."

Kathrine bowed, smile widening more than he'd ever seen before. "As I said, Tupper and I prepared you a meal. But since you are tired, perhaps we can discuss this in your room and bring the food to you as you rest?"

Riven pondered this, grinned, and nodded. "I do believe that sounds rather nice. Dinner in bed. I'll see you up there."

The inside of the manor that'd once been unfurnished was now lavishly decorated. Sculptures of different animals lined the hallways, beautiful paintings adorned the large receiving room, and chandeliers glowed faintly with orange-yellow light. While waiting for the meal to be brought up to his room, he was shown around by the incubus concerning all the amendments they'd bought. The furniture was especially lavish, and it looked like he'd just entered a Victorian-era mansion out of an HBO TV series.

"My lord," Tupper said as they approached the spiral staircase leading to the third level. He turned, black eyes narrowed slightly underneath tiny black horns very similar to his sister's own. He glanced back over his shoulder to where Fay and Kathrine had briefly stopped to talk to Luke about the decorations, and then turned his attention back to Riven with a bow. "I wish to express my utmost gratitude for what you did for my sister . . . When I heard she might not last, I . . . I nearly decided to end my life. Without Fay, I have nothing left. She is the only family that cares about me, and that you went out of your way to get her back and save her life means more to me than anything else ever could. Thank you for caring, and I hope the man who took her died painfully."

The incubus stood up, gave Riven a quivering smile that he quickly calmed after a deep inhale, and tilted his head in a firm nod—extending his hand to shake. "I know it means little to someone like you, but you've earned a life debt from me."

Riven smiled, glancing over to where his succubus was laughing alongside Kathrine. Then he took Tupper's hand and firmly shook it with a nod of his own. "Of course. Fay is important to me, as are all the demons I've bonded with."

Tupper stared, tightened his wings closer to his body, then cleared his throat to break his building emotions. "Indeed."

"By the way—" Riven gestured over to where one of a dozen different scantily clad slaves stood at attention, a silver-haired young woman carrying a tray of refreshments shooting him wary glances from time to time while putting on a very obvious display of swaying her hips whenever she walked by.

He followed the elf as she walked by, then glanced back over to Tupper, who stood at attention beside him. "I do appreciate the obvious eye candy you've invested in concerning . . . the slave girls. God, that sounds bad . . . but why did you do it? You do realize I have no interest in using them like that. Right?"

Tupper immediately smirked and leaned over as if talking about a conspiracy. "No doubt my sister would be quite jealous if you did, but Allie insisted on it."

"Allie?"

"Yes. She said, word for word, 'Riven hasn't been laid in over a year now. Fill up the mansion with a bunch of pretty girls and see what happens.' She was quite insistent."

Riven sputtered a laugh, chuckling to himself and rolling his eyes. "That sounds exactly like what Allie would do. She should know better, though. I'm not going to force myself on someone like she does."

Tupper opened his mouth to reply, shut it, thought for a moment, then held up a finger. "If I may, Your Majesty. I don't believe any of them would need to be *forced* into doing something like that."

"You don't say."

"Indeed." The incubus gestured over to where another of the collared young elf women clad in a black skirt-bikini was blatantly staring at both of them before being caught in the act, and she colored with a deep blush while going back to cleaning the mantel above a fireplace before shuffling out of the room. "They might be slaves, but that doesn't mean they don't find you suitable. Did you not see the way they all looked at you when you took off your helmet?"

"I'd thought they were just scared of me like everyone else."

Tupper paused. "Yes, that is likely part of it. No doubt your negative Charisma and position of power do intimidate them—to a drastic degree. However, just like my own kind, incubi—you vampires, especially purebloods, have a very enticing figure. Not only that, but they likely see you as a meal ticket out of their current situations."

"That doesn't inspire me to act."

The incubus shrugged and noted a signal from Kathrine—the other pure-blooded royal. "Take it as you will. I am merely following orders. Anyways, the food preparations are likely ready now. I know vampires have special interests in blood, so I had Kathrine help me prepare what she deemed an acceptable course for a royal like yourself. Please, follow me, Your Majesty—Kathrine is very ada-mant on discussing this subject of your inheritance before the vultures swoop in."

Following his incubus butler up the stairs, Riven eventually reached the third floor and came to the door of his own room. Three of the slave servants bowed low and then stood at attention right outside, awaiting orders.

Azmoth and Luke had stayed downstairs, with Luke being shown to his own room by one of the girls and Azmoth having gone to the nearby chapel adjacent to the manor on the guild hall property.

Tupper came to the door, opened it, and bowed again with a sweeping gesture of his hand to let Riven in. "After you, Your Majesty."

"Call me Riven," he replied, stepping inside and coming to a quick halt only a few feet in the room.

His quarters had definitely changed. Someone—Allie, no doubt—had pinned up a bunch of posters concerning different anime and manga he'd been into presystem integration, which he found hilarious. It was a stark contrast to the red-gold sheets and draped bedding on what had to be an emperor-size, fluffy bed. Two couches, an ornate wooden table, a long mirror, and two dress-ers were inside along with the adjacent bathroom. There was even a TV that actually worked—which was very surprising to him. It was playing a news story concerning some kind of bandit activity along the outskirts of Milwaukee, where a human reporter was interviewing a group of skeletal skresh body hunters assigned to track the bandits down.

But what really caught his attention was the food.

"Do you like it?" Kathrine asked as she came inside, standing next to Riven, who was stunned into silence. She grinned rather proudly, then looked back over to the spread. "We usually dine like this in the Blood Moon Requiem, though ours are a little bit more exotic than even this. I was told you don't like eating humanoid meat if you can help it, and that you like to treat your slaves well, so we didn't butcher any of the slaves and included only pork and venison. I hope it is to your liking—I did the artwork myself."

He didn't know how to reply to that. In front of them and at the center of the room between two couches, on top of the table, was Genua—and Riven wasn't sure whether to be turned on, impressed, or utterly sickened.

The elf was certainly alive, but she'd been stripped naked and tied up while kneeling on a large platter made of solid gold—surrounded by brilliant red flowers. A bright-green apple had been stuffed into her mouth, so that she very much resembled how medieval kings would display a butchered hog for their feasts. Her long blonde hair was tied in a knot to tightly attach at her bound wrists, which were positioned at her curvy lower back, cranking her neck backward at an awkward angle as her nostrils flared while staring ahead and exposing her chest.

Some kind of sauce, no doubt infused with blood by the smell of it, was slathered all over the naked woman's entire body below the neck. There were also patches of artwork made from hardened chocolate decorating her skin in a very thin layer, creating various depictions of mythical creatures, warriors, and cities in incredibly intricate detail. A tower of stacked fruit surrounded by flowers had been placed in a bowl on her back that she attempted to keep as flat as possible—stabilized on either side by the hair tightly tied to her wrists. Four hot wax candles had melted onto her skin on either side of the fruit bowl—they still burned and flickered with yellow light.

On either side of the kneeling slave were other displays of food. Three large bottles of blood-infused wine, a cabbage salad display cut into the shape of flowers, numerous slabs of meat, cubes of different cheese, and loaves of steaming fresh bread were all there as well. Plates and utensils, enough for two, were placed on one side of the table.

"She volunteered," Tupper quickly stated when Riven shot him a cold look. The incubus raised both hands. "Genua did volunteer for this. She's been taking her training very well and wanted to show you that she's submissive, subservient to your will—and she's ready for you to feed on her as live cattle right here on the table, instead of the more stale options otherwise presented if you wish it. I know you vampires like your blood fresh. Her previous attitude problems have completely vanished over the time you've been gone, enough so that we've even started to keep her here in your room—as she is your personal attendant and a source of blood for your feeding, after all."

Tupper gestured over to the other side of the bed where a large cage had been placed, collar and chain included.

Riven blinked, noted how Fay had abruptly stiffened on his left, and merely sagged his shoulders. ". . . Fine."

He was surprised at his own lack of caring. Once upon a time, a sight like this would have infuriated him. Once upon a time he'd also never have considered laying waste to an entire city to meet his own ends, either. Once upon a time he'd been more trusting and compassionate, and he'd have been infuriated at the mere idea of slaves even if they had been criminals of war.

Now, however, he just didn't care. He was physically and mentally exhausted. He was constantly on the move, trying to figure out what to do next, was involved in world-ending events—many of which hadn't even presented themselves yet— and he'd been hunted for what he was. He'd been betrayed by Jalel and the elves, he and his sister had nearly been assassinated by other nobility of the Blood Moon Requiem, they'd had a holy war waged against them by the man called Prophet, he had some kind of strange entity called Chalgathi always fucking with his life . . . Riven simply couldn't find it in his heart to give a shit anymore.

Sighing with true exhaustion, he only shrugged and proceeded to the bed, where he set his spear-staff down on the thick covers. Then he allowed his armor to peel off and laid it next to the weapon before glancing down at his bare chest. He'd become rather athletic, so he admired his own abdomen for quite a while and then noiselessly approached the table.

Kathrine went around to the other side and sat down, only to raise her eyebrows when Riven pulled his own chair out and gestured for Fay to come sit.

The succubus paused wordlessly, blushed, and smiled before taking his invitation and sitting down in the chair he'd presented her. Pushing the chair in as Fay sat down, Riven went out to the balcony to another set of chairs and brought one in. Glancing at the TV, which was still talking about the current events in Milwaukee, he smiled faintly and pulled his seat up to the table at the end between Fay and Kathrine—reaching over for a bottle of blood wine and popping the cork before chugging.

He belched, grinned at Fay when she rolled her eyes, and set the bottle down. "All right, Kathrine. Let's talk about this inheritance of mine."

A smile spread widely across her pale face, displaying her fangs underneath her bright-red eyes. "Yes, of course. I'd also like to discuss the tutoring proposition as well, and potential training. We want you to succeed even more than you know, Riven Thane. If it is within my power to help you do so, then all the better. Now, as for the inheritance . . ."

CHAPTER 5

"So your inheritance, the planet Luteski, is a very prominent trading hub that manages transported goods throughout the Blood Moon Requiem and a number of our allies. This is in large part for three different reasons. The first is that the planet has a natural Shadow alteration built into its atmosphere; I'm not sure on the exact details, but it allows the inhabitants to easily create or redirect wormholes." Kathrine gave Riven a knowing look. "This means that it's both easy to defend and easy to invite people into—a double positive. It also allows those with high Shadow affinities to cultivate there more easily, which is a very good thing for many of us vampires, who often have high Shadow affinities. Not only that, but it's located on the outskirts of the empire but in a rather safe quadrant. Not only do our own forces defend the planet, but so do many of our allies, who are heavily invested in trading with us due to the easy access and expedient travel time it allows them. It is a gold mine, frankly."

"Why not just use Elysium altars and trading communes?" Riven asked curiously.

Kathrine smiled and pulled out a pipe, lighting it up with a conjuration of Infernal flames, and started to smoke. She puffed out a cloud, then crossed her legs in contemplation. "The short answer to that question is twofold. First and foremost is taxes. The system taxes on trade are incredibly high when you use communes, and you can avoid taxes to the system altogether by just traveling there yourself through ships or portals."

"Spaceships?"

"We call them by a variety of names, but essentially yes. They travel through space."

"Neat. What's the second reason?"

"The second reason is that communes have limitations on how much you can buy or sell per year. It won't matter to you on this planet because it's in the early stages of integration, but when planets start to develop and trade starts to pump out, there's a far larger scale of goods being exchanged—and these are limited by the system. So when you hit that limit, the altar goes stale until the next year."

Riven leaned back in his chair and took another swig of the blood wine, accidentally spilling some of it down his bare chest. Choking slightly and wiping his mouth with one arm, he set the bottle back down and picked up a slab of meat—sharing a plate with Fay with a warm smile when she pushed it halfway between them to start eating. "I see. That's good to know—I wasn't aware there was a limit on the altars, but I suppose it makes sense. So the name of the planet is Luteski, it has fifty million vampires and six billion slaves, it's a profitable trading hub, it has a Shadow affinity, and my punk relatives are trying to sell it off. What else can you tell me about it? Who are they trying to sell it to?"

Kathrine cocked her head and picked a peeled fruit off the bowl atop Genua's back. Rubbing it in the blood sauce covering the bound elf, Kathrine bit into the fruit and chewed slowly. "As I said, they're trying to sell it to other nobles who are looking to capitalize before your eventual return to the fold. It's not just one but many different major households that are looking to buy different establishments or parts of the planet. The transactions can be stopped, but you must act now."

The royal held out a hand and activated a ring on one finger, lighting up a black gemstone with white light before a scroll appeared over her hand. When she unfurled the scroll, a very fancy document adorned with different wax seals and exquisite ink handwriting appeared—and as she unfurled the item it also portrayed a series of changing pictures.

The images shifted one by one every couple of seconds. First it was a dark planet orbiting a white dwarf star, with swirling clouds of black and green in the atmosphere that only allowed brief glimpses of the continents below. Next came images of various cities under dark clouds that glowed with orange and yellow lights, each with sprawling metropolises and towering skyscrapers that had fleets of alien airships docked or sailing overhead. Some of the airships looked very similar to normal ships from Earth, but those were few and far between. There were armored capsules, enormous creations made out of living flesh or plants, tiny sleek silicone jets, and innumerable other types of ships that were often grouped together by design depending on where they hailed from. After the fleets of ships and cities, the images of his planet showed vast networks of mines, inhabited by humanoids with pale eyes, purple skin, white hair, and two smooth antennae that looked rather soft, fleshy, and malleable as opposed to those of insects. One of these depictions showed a deep crevice splitting the earth, with dim lights illuminating a vast complex stretching miles down where hundreds of thousands of these humanoids worked to acquire minerals under their vampire overseers.

"Those creatures are called Sarak, and they were the natives on this planet before it was conquered by our empire almost two millennia ago." Kathrine noted when he took particular interest in the last photo, but then she slapped the paper on the table and pushed it his way. Leaning forward, she dismissed the images by tapping on one of the wax seals along the top of the parchment. "You need to read and sign this today. Doing so will establish that you are the acting head of the household unless your parents return, and that you retract the right for any of the lower-tiered members of your house who are trying to pawn it off. I have also added some amendments stating that funds that've been going to the lower nobility will be rerouted into your own personal coffers from here on out, as they've been stealing outlandish amounts of money from your parents already. The problem is your parents are assumed dead and you weren't known to have existed, so what they did was treading a fine line between legal and illegal means of acquiring their wealth. If you wanted to, you could have their case heard in the upper courts, as is your right—but you cannot outright kill them, either. Not without punishment, because they are still carriers for Malignant Prophecy, even if they don't have the gift themselves. It would likely be up to the queen if you wanted to pursue vengeance for theft."

Riven snorted, then shook his head. "No, I don't want to kill them. For all they knew, I wasn't even around and my parents were dead. Just reroute the funds to my own coffers, wherever they are off-world—and if they try to sell my stuff again or cheat me in some way, then notify me. I'm counting on you entirely for this, Kathrine, because I don't know anything about it."

Kathrine nodded, then began to amend the document with a quill that magically rearranged some of the wording on the parchment below. "Very well. I will notify the courts. Before signing, there's also the topic of laws."

Kathrine pointed to another section of the parchment down below, clicked one of the highlighted subjects in black ink, and an entirely new display appeared on the parchment like it would a system screen—only it was now medieval-flavored. "These are all the current laws on Luteski. You have the right as head of your household and owner of this planet to modify them as long as they do not contradict the queen's laws. Change what you want, if you want to, and I'll let you know if there's a contradiction. It may take a while, so let's get at it."

"Protection for children, one day of rest each week, no child labor, no more forced gladiator battles between slaves, torture without reason is prohibited, butchering is prohibited in favor of regular blood drains that don't outright kill the slaves . . ." Kathrine looked up from his list with a frown. "You even have a small compensation built into our taxes for slaves who donate more blood than others do over the course of a year. These are rather hard boundaries to set, and you're going to upset a lot of the vampires under your banner if you do this."

"Do any of them contradict the queen's laws?"

Kathrine hesitated, then shook her head. "No . . . but this is going to have a major impact on the society there. I haven't heard of any planet in our empire with such protective laws concerning our slaves. You do realize that we regularly kill and eat these creatures like you would cows or pigs. Right? The Sarak are cattle. We literally breed and keep some of them in pens to fatten up so we can eat them later."

"Are they intelligent?" Riven asked curiously while wiping another slab of meat across Genua's naked body, soaking up more of the sauce and chocolate before ripping into it rather ravenously. His voice was beginning to slow, and he could feel the intoxication setting in. "This shit is really good, by the way."

On the sidelines Fay was drinking herself more and more into a silent stupor, and while she was at it she was practicing how to withdraw her regrown wings into her back to look more human—and the succubus seemed rather happy at having achieved it.

But Kathrine was frowning deeply at Riven, and she gave a low hum of disapproval. "The Sarak are rather stupid."

"How do they compare to humans?"

"They're about equal in terms of intelligence. Equally stupid."

Riven snorted a laugh, a little more amused than he'd normally be concerning the situation. "Tough shit, then. These are the laws I want. These Sarak are innocent and have been for dozens of generations, so just be happy I'm not some kind of wannabe savior. At the very least I can give these people lives worth living instead of the garbage that you've presented me with. They'll still be forced to work the mines there, and I'm not even restricting the use of personal slaves, but I want their quality of life to get better."

"I think you'd have an outright riot on your hands if you changed those particular things."

"I realize that. That's why I'm not doing it." Riven gave her a flat look, cup of wine touching his lips. "I know how the vampires there will likely view me after I come in out of the blue as some unknown and start uprooting their way of life. But think of just how unfair it would be, being born into a race of intelligent people who are enslaved across your planet, only to be used in the mines while you're healthy and later when you get older, you're eaten alive."

Kathrine cringed and sighed deeply, then slumped her shoulders in defeat. She hiccuped and took an entire bottle to drain the last of it with a belch unbecoming of vampire royalty. "I . . . will let the planetary guard know of your changes to their laws. At the very least, it'll be interesting . . . I've never heard of anything like this before. Are there any other changes you'd like to make? Any announcements you want coupled with these laws?"

Riven paused, then nodded. "You said the planetary guard are the ones who'll be enforcing these, right?"

"Yes."

"And they are loyal to my house?"

"To your house second, but first to the queen."

"Do you think they'll accept these terms if I'm not personally there to oversee it?"

Kathrine hesitated before answering. "I'm not sure. Probably half-heartedly."

"What if I bribed them?"

She raised her eyebrows. "How would you do that?"

"By setting aside 50 percent of the profits through trade and mining over the course of the next five years and giving those profits to the planetary guard instead of them going to my own coffers or any of the other nobles. Let them know it's an investment to make sure these laws are followed."

Kathrine smirked, then bobbed her head side to side—almost falling over as Riven and Fay laughed. Quickly correcting her posture and flushing a bright red, she straightened up and tried to get control of her body once again. "It is possible that they'd be more willing that way . . . but you need to include that amendment in the document."

She scribbled new text down and rearranged it again, infusing a magical residue into the ink through the quill. After she pushed it back over to Riven, he read it over and signed yet again.

"There's my royal decree." Riven smirked with a dismissive wave of his hand. "Let me know how it goes."

"I certainly will," Kathrine noted with another nod, leaning back and putting the parchment away before taking another long inhale from her pipe. Blowing the smoke out toward the ceiling in a cloud of purple-gray, she passed the pipe over to Fay, who'd been listening quietly. "Do you mind going over a planned schedule for tutoring and martial training next?"

Riven yawned while the alcohol continued to overcome him, covering his mouth with one arm before standing up and coming over to where Genua's neck was cranked back at an awkward angle due to the way her hair was tied to her wrists. Leaning down and extending his fangs, he abruptly sank his teeth into the middle-aged woman—causing her to squeal loudly through the apple in her mouth as her eyes went wide and her nostrils flared even wider.

The elf quivered under his grip, tears welling up under her eyelids, but otherwise she remained still as she let her owner drink her lifeblood. Kathrine and Fay were silent as well while Riven sucked, and eventually he pulled back with a satisfied sigh, wiping the blood off his face as Fay passed the pipe back to Kathrine.

The small puncture wounds only lasted for a little while before slowly sealing up. Vampiric venom naturally healed the wounds over time if there wasn't any trauma, allowing a vampire to repeatedly feed on victims.

"You're right, live food is better." Riven chuckled mercilessly and roughly tousled Genua's hair before flopping back down into his seat. "Especially when I have no qualms about feeding on this particular person. It is . . . invigorating, and freeing."

"How so?" Kathrine asked, puzzled, as she threw both of her long, pale legs up on the table while leaning back in her chair with the smoking pipe in one hand. Her neat dress already had spots where food and drink had accidentally spilled, but she was too drunk to care.

"I grew up a human. Feeding on people does not come naturally to me, and I felt a sense of guilt whenever I thought about it before." Riven gestured to the hog-tied elf. "But her, I feel no remorse. Anyways, enough about that. As I've already said, I don't have a lot of time to spare, but I suppose I could carve some out once in a while before I leave for the Chalgathi quest line in four months. Got anybody who's a master with the spear?"

"We certainly do," Kathrine replied, and she giggled with a slightly buzzed smirk while pulling out a small bag of green powder. Placing it on the table, she took a very small spoon from within the bag and snorted the powdery substance for good measure—clutching her head with one hand while her smile spread. Winking at Riven slyly, she nudged him with a foot under the table. "Want to try some? It's good stuff, the highest quality."

The vampire passed the powder over to Fay first, who looked curiously at the bag and small spoon, hesitating. Hiccuping and peering down harder, she eventually shrugged and without question snorted a small spoonful of the powder just like Kathrine had.

"Good, right?" Kathrine mused, a silly smile across her lips as the succubus began to giggle. "I wish I could do this back home without my parents intervening."

"Is this illegal back on your home world?" Riven asked curiously, poking at the powder and watching when Kathrine took a very large spoonful and whispered into Genua's ear. The elf's eyebrows raised on the questioning words Riven couldn't hear, but then she nodded hesitantly. The princess smiled in approval and then roughly shoved the powder up Genua's nostrils—violently smushing it against the sputtering elf's face until she was satisfied.

Kathrine then glanced back his way, her eyes narrowing wickedly. "No . . . but my parents still wouldn't be happy knowing that I have it. Hey . . . did you know that we're not technically real cousins? Funny fact."

Riven frowned, noting that Fay was beginning to salivate and Genua's eyes were beginning to glaze over. "What do you mean we're not cousins? That's not what you told me earlier."

Kathrine rolled her eyes with exaggeration—then she began to count on her fingers. "I mean, we're as much cousins as you are to any other vampire. We're all related to the blood god, but aside from that . . . I suppose our great-great-great-great-great-great-great-great-great-great-great-great-great-grandparents were siblings. Hold on . . . Yeah, that many generations."

"How many?"

"Fifteen generations ago we share common ancestors."

Riven pursed his lips. "Interesting. Why are you telling me now, though?"

"Because I'm tutoring you!" Kathrine laughed, nearly tipping out of her chair again before Riven caught her fall. Pulling herself up his arm, she reached for the bag again and snorted another small spoonful, eyes rolling back while she giggled profusely. "I have lots to tutor you in! We're going to be great friends, you and me. Now try this!"

"I don't know what it is."

She shoved the bag his way, then scowled when he gave her a skeptical look. "If it was poison, the three of us would already be dead! It's just a drug specifically meant for vampires! It's like . . . what did Allie say about it . . . like catnip for vampires, I believe!"

"Allie's tried it, too?" Riven, who was still quite buzzed, glanced over to where Fay was giving him a side-eye. She had a deep flush now and was still salivating and taking deep breaths. Genua was in a similar position, drool literally dripping from the apple in her mouth while her head bobbed up and down in an attempt to keep it upright. "It looks like it works on other people aside from vampires, too."

"Pussy." Kathrine cackled, jabbing him under the table again with her foot. "Just do it! You have armed guards outside and there's no way that you're in any danger . . . Come on!"

She grabbed his wrist, sliding her hand up his arm to where his bicep was. "Your sister said you needed some relaxation time, so just go ahead and relax! We'll be here with you!"

Riven was about to ask about what it was again, but thought it over once more. Up until recently he'd been so uptight about everything. It was almost his motto—it'd gotten so bad because he always felt like he was the one responsible for the lives of others. His choices affected hundreds of thousands of other people on a daily basis, and if you included the world quests—they'd affect far, far more than that. Billions, even. Stack the new planet he apparently owned on top of that and it emphasized the problem even more.

Well, Fay and the other two women hadn't died yet. They seemed more jovial than usual, even, and when Fay pushed the bag over in his direction with a flushed grin, he couldn't stop himself.

"Fuck it. But if I die, I'm coming back to haunt you, Kathrine." He chuckled at the laughter of the other vampire, then took the small spoon and snorted some of the green powder.

The effect was immediate. The movement around him became more sluggish, and he had a spike of dopamine slam into his brain with the weight of a freight train. Everything became better instantaneously, and . . .

And Kathrine's soft hand felt really good on his arm.

Looking up, he saw her shoulder dip as one half of Kathrine's dress began to slide off—exposing pale, bare skin underneath. Fay growled in irritation immediately after that, then stood up with arms straight out at her side.

The succubus twitched her tail back and forth with hesitation, but the drugged state she was in won over—and irritation was quickly replaced again by a giggling fit. Slowly removing her skirt and letting it drop to the floor, exposing athletic thighs, she stepped over Riven's legs to straddle him—locking her arms around his neck while her usually sky-blue skin flushed violently. "You're pretty cute, Riven . . . did I ever tell you that? Or was it just in my head?"

The succubus nuzzled her nose against his own, then slowly planted a warm kiss on one cheek to hold it there.

"It was an aphrodisiac. A really good one!" Kathrine drawled sloppily, starting to get up only to trip and fall over her own feet when she tugged the other side of her dress down to expose her perky white breasts. She landed on both Riven and Fay and knocked them to the floor in a pile of bodies.

She grinned slyly, lying on the other two and pressing her body against theirs and letting the silence drag on for a while amid their staring—hands starting to grope and legs intertwining as the seconds ticked by.

When Kathrine dragged her hand over to Fay's, and then brought it down to Riven's nether regions, the vampire and succubus simultaneously looked up at a rather stunned but obviously excited man underneath them. It only made Kathrine's breathing pick up when she noticed. "Oops! Sorry . . . Didn't mean to. I promise!"

Riven woke up the next morning to the sounds of chirping birds. Apparently they were still flourishing here, even in the Unholy-oriented lands surrounding his altar. He blinked with a loud yawn to clear his head.

God, did he have a headache.

But the events of last night were still mostly there . . . they were just a little fuzzy.

All four of them were absolutely naked, and thankfully it wasn't cold enough to matter that they didn't have any covers on. Kathrine was on her side facing him, drooling into a pillow, completely fried and almost dead to the world by the way she was snoring. Fay was on top of him, her very round blue breasts pushing into his chest with her body weight while she slept with a content smile—her two long legs encircling one of his own in a vise grip. On his left, the elf slave Genua still had her large ass propped up where she'd passed out—facedown in a pillow and wrists still bound, but he could at least remember that she'd liked and even volunteered for it. She'd even said yes when asked if she wanted to partake of the drug.

Riven . . . didn't know what to think about what'd happened. Nor did he really put much effort into figuring it out after a mental grin when he thought about what Jose would have said after seeing him like this. Fuck, he missed that guy.

It was a nice one-night stand, and it'd definitely blown off steam. He doubted it'd happen again, but he had no regrets, and it'd be a memory he probably kept until the end of time. It was a damn good one.

Getting up and letting the passed-out succubus take his spot, he yawned and winced at the bright rays of sunlight coming through the balcony. Sighing and picking Genua up, he dragged the still-sleeping older woman into the box cage set out for her. He collared the elf, locked the barred door after putting a pillow inside, and went over to tuck the other two women into bed.

Coming over to a desk and pulling out some paper, he borrowed Kathrine's quill and wrote out a letter to let them know where he was going. Yawning one more time and exiting the balcony, he looked for one of the patrolling helicopters that often circled this area.

It was time to pay his sister a visit in Dawn.

CHAPTER 6

Riven's stomach churned, and a seed of doubt had been planted. It was both unexpected, and unwanted, and he'd forced the helicopter to turn back around only half an hour into their trip after telling Allie that he'd be later than expected.

"Fuck, I'm such an idiot!" He slammed an open palm into his forehead and gritted his teeth, scouring the aisles of the Brightsville herbalist's market in search of a perfect set of flowers. "Goddamn it, the first time I do this and it's on fucking drugs. She was just held hostage by some other guy and I'm too much of an idiot to even think about staying?! FUCK me!"

Azmoth patted his shoulder comfortingly, trying to calm him down while people nearby gave him gawking stares or wary glances. "It okay, Riven. You'll be fine, she like you."

"Yeah, well, I probably made her feel like shit after just up and leaving like that; I was just in too much of a hungover haze to even think straight and now . . ." He threw up his hands and spun around on his large armored summon, shaking his head in wonder at his own stupidity. "Man, I'm not even sure if she would have done what she did if she wasn't high on drugs herself. She might not even like me like that . . ."

Doubt overshadowed him. He glanced over at the bouquet of blue flowers positioned on a nearby stall, nervously fidgeting with his hands and looking like a schoolboy who'd made a huge mistake. "It might have just been the intoxication."

Azmoth let out a loud snort at that remark. "Doubtful."

"What if I fuck this up, Azmoth?"

"You won't."

"I might. And I might look really fucking stupid when I walk in there with flowers only for her to laugh at me."

"Riven." Azmoth took ahold of both shoulders this time, then rapidly shook him back and forth like a rag doll. "Stop. This. Now. Get flowers; go ask her. Just because succubus does not mean she want only sex. Does not mean only drugs. Need ask, and assume the best."

Dim daylight trickled through gray clouds overhead, a common phenomenon due to his transformation zone of Unholy attunement. Glancing down at his fidgeting hands, Riven took in a deep breath and let it out to calm himself. "I've done far harder things than this. Get ahold of yourself, man, grow a pair of balls."

Turning around and stalking over to the cashier who wore a frightened, pale look, he picked up three differently colored bouquets: one blue, one white, and one purple. "How much for all of these?"

"M-my king . . ." the cashier stuttered with a bow, her portly frame nearly tipping over in the act. "No need to buy—"

He didn't have time to waste. Slamming a sack full of gold and platinum coins onto the counter, he leaned over with a fierce look in his eye. "Tell me where the best spot is for a first date. I'm talking an EPIC first date. Can you do that?"

The startled woman's eyes went even wider, and she quickly nodded. "Y-yes, there's a nice little restaurant on the river back near Baker's Bend . . . Do you happen to know where that is?"

Fay was curled up in her own room, alone. She did not want to talk to her brother at all after what had happened. Kathrine had walked back to the altar as right as rain with a skip in her step to leave Fay—unknowingly—to think rather depressed thoughts.

It wasn't that the sex had been bad. It had been beyond great, and it was fun to involve Kathrine and Genua, too. But Riven had just gotten up and left the next morning without saying a word, like it was no big deal . . . and to Fay, it was a very big deal. She'd spent less than six months with Riven, but during that time she quickly came to care for him on a much deeper level than she would've ever expected before the contract was signed. He was kind, had a good heart, and treated her like a person with real feelings. This was a first for her, and she'd never had this kind of connection with her previous summoner, who only saw her as a sex toy.

Maybe that's what she was to Riven, too.

Tears welled up under her eyes. She vividly remembered the feeling she'd had upon realizing Riven had come to save her in that underground lair where she'd been taken by Chalgathi cultists. Her heart slammed in her chest so hard that she thought was going to pop out and burst. He didn't need to come get her; he could have easily left her for another succubus or demon, but he came—and he comforted her. He cared.

Yeah, he . . . he cared.

Or maybe she was just being stupid.

Sniffling and drawing up the covers over her face, she let out a sound akin to a dying cat amid a stifled sob. "I'm so fucking stupid! Fucking, fucking, FUCKING stupid!"

She sobbed again and punched the pillow with an angry, balled-up fist, and then slapped herself three times as punishment for believing something that obviously was a falsehood. If Riven wanted to use her like that, it was his right. He was her summoner and she was a succubus. Emotions didn't apply. So she just had to swallow that fact and accept—

A loud knock at the door interrupted her thoughts, and she sniffled again with red-rimmed eyes to glare over her shoulder under small black horns. Her voice quivered angrily as she spoke, but despite her attempt to hide the hurt she felt, it was still obvious she was very distraught. "I s-said get lost, Tupper! I'm trying to sleep, okay?!"

To her mounting rage, the door creaked open. With fires of anger lit under her soul, she ripped herself off the bed and stormed over to the doorway to fling it open the rest of the way. Then she began to screech. "TUPPER! I said—"

Fay came to an abrupt halt midsentence, the snarl leaving her lips while tears clung to her face. In the doorway, Riven stood holding three bouquets of very pretty flowers to his chest. He looked at her with shame, face turning a shade darker as he held his breath, and his crimson eyes aimed at the floor.

"Um . . . Fay . . . I need to talk to you. Can I come in?"

She remained speechless, still not fully dressed. "Aren't . . . aren't you supposed to be seeing your sister?"

Her words came out as a whisper, and she searched his face for a time before her eyes landed on the flowers again.

Shamefaced, Riven avoided her stare for a moment. "I was supposed to, yes . . . but I think this is more important. What happened last night . . . I wanted to talk to you about it. But if I'm being stupid and you don't feel the same way—"

"Feel what way?" Fay cut in, her voice cracking with pent-up emotions as one hand clutched at her stomach.

Hesitantly he looked back up. "I . . . Well, these are for you." He pushed the flowers over to her and stepped back.

Unsure of how to react, she took them in both arms while continuing to stare out at him—tears beginning to dry on her light-blue skin.

"For me?" she said in a whisper, lips pursing as her face scrunched up in an attempt not to cry again.

Riven nodded, clenching and unclenching his hands as he stood in the hallway. Taking in a deep breath, he cleared his throat. "Um, can I be blunt?"

Fay slowly nodded, lips quivering.

He let out another breath. "I'm not sure if what happened last night was anything important to you, but I wasn't thinking straight when I left this morning. I was still hungover and the drugs were still somewhat in my system, and I was tired so my mind was hazy anyways. But on the chopper ride over, I began to realize that I really care about you. And . . . I mean, if you don't feel that way, too, I can back off and pretend like this never happened, but . . ."

He met her eyes again, losing his momentum when she didn't react. She hadn't reacted at all.

She only stared. He paled beyond what was normal even for him, and his shoulders sagged. "Sorry. This was a really, really stupid idea."

Giving Fay a half-hearted smile, he nodded once and stepped back. Clearing his throat one more time, he turned to go.

And she let him go.

Fay watched him wordlessly while he slowly meandered down the hall to the spiral staircase. She watched without action as he muttered again about how stupid he was under his breath and he slammed a palm into his face to drag it down his cheek before exiting into the stairway.

Riven was utterly defeated. His heart hurt, and the rejection had been so brutal that he couldn't even believe it.

Jesus. He'd really fucked this one up. Sighing and leaning against the outer wall of his manor, he lightly banged a fist against the wall and shook his head in silence. He'd even made her cry because he'd overstepped so badly. To think that she'd had such a terrible reaction—she'd fucking cried—because he'd wanted to ask her on a date was just devastating, and he put his back against the wall and slid down to sit with a thud.

Farther into the garden, he saw Jose's tombstone. Giving it a thumbs-up and a half-hearted laugh, he caught the lump in his throat and covered his face with one hand. "Goddamn it, Jose. I've always been terrible with girls. I wish you were here, man. I wish you were here to give me that dumbass advice you always used to give, and even though it never worked, it always was such a fucking self-esteem boost!"

He let out a true laugh this time, still feeling the pit in his stomach like a thousand pounds of weight settling in to curl in a massive ball of anxiety. "Damn. She might not even want to be contracted to me after this. Fuck, man, I didn't realize just how much I liked her . . . and Athela is going to kill me when she gets back and realizes her friend doesn't want to be with us anymore because I'm a creep. Goddamn it."

Birds continued to chirp overhead, just like they had earlier that morning. No doubt some sparrows had built a nest in the tree above, and as he was hiding his face in shame, he felt bird shit land on his boot.

Looking down at the white liquid dung, he felt it an appropriate punishment for his stupidity. Fay was way too pretty to be with someone like him, anyway. Wherever he went people lusted after her, so why the fuck would someone like that want to be with someone like him?

A light breeze rustled his hair, and a moment later he felt the light touch of soft fingers on his hand alongside a nearby heartbeat. "Riven?"

Startled slightly, he looked up—coming face-to-face with Fay.

"Oh! Hey . . ." Riven awkwardly, nervously grinned back up at her before avoiding her gaze. "I—I'm sorry for bothering you like that. It was completely out of line. I shouldn't have . . . I mean . . . I was going to ask you on a date after I gave you the flowers and . . . I . . ."

"Stop." Fay held up one finger to his lips, shushing him when he began to protest, and she slid down the wall to sit next to him with a quivering, uncertain smile. Her wings retracted into her body, and her thin black tail flipped nervously from side to side. "Just . . . be quiet for a moment. Okay?"

Riven promptly shut up, and his gaze faltered again.

The two of them sat there, looking out over the garden in the shade of the trees and the manor under a slight breeze. He could still feel deep regret and shame flooding his mind, could still feel the bitter bite of her shocked expression—and the utter lack of response on her part after he'd very stupidly confessed he'd had a crush. All those times she'd played around with him, they'd just been teasing. It'd all just been fun and games with the little comments she'd made here or there. She was a succubus, he should have expected as much, and now he'd made things very awkward between the two of them. She only wanted the sex, and nothing more.

"Riven, what do you see when you look at me?"

Riven's eyes narrowed, and he turned his gaze fully on the woman beside him, who stared back at him with big black doe eyes. "What do I see when I look at you?" He repeated the question again in a half whisper, uncertain of what she was getting at, but she stayed silent. "I see one of my good friends, and I see a girl way out of my league."

He gave an apologetic smile, this one being genuine. "Fay . . . I truly am sorry about earlier. I didn't ever mean to make things awkward. I had a stupid thought enter my head when we had sex last night and I just jumped the gun, but I promise it won't happen again. Please don't leave because of this . . . Athela would kill me if you did."

Fay wordlessly continued to stare, mouth opening slightly—only to close again as she took in air and pushed her long white hair over one ear. Arms wrapped around her knees, she slowly turned to look at the ground in front of her feet, and tears began to trickle down her face again before she squinted her eyes shut hard.

The ball of anxiety quickly returned to Riven's throat and gut. "Hey . . . I can go if you want me to. I can give you space, I just really—"

Fay's hand whipped around and slapped him full across the face, leaving a hard red handprint across his pale white skin. She was fuming, tears continuing to stream down while her hands shook at her sides. Getting up into a kneeling position, she glared daggers at him like he was something she had nothing but hate for—and her breathing became loud and ragged within seconds.

Shock, despair, and humiliation. Those were the three emotions that quickly crossed his mind, and all he could do was slowly nod without any words. Holding one hand to his bruised cheek, he began to climb to his feet—only for one of Fay's slender hands to yank him back down by his shirt.

He let her pull him back, hitting the ground with his knees to stare in confusion back at her. No words were spoken while she fumed, continuing to shake and cry, only for her to gently reach up and touch his bruised face with a quivering hand.

"Sorry," she muttered under her breath with a croak, using a voice that sounded like it'd been crying too hard and too much for her to speak properly. "I just needed to get that out."

Then she cupped his cheeks in both hands, drew herself into his embrace, and locked lips with him while softly pushing him into a sitting position.

The warm touch of her skin on his as she kissed him was like a tidal wave of mixed emotions. First there was shock again, then confusion, and then finally a deep-set warmth and happiness that spread up through his abdomen and into his chest. His arms wrapped around her scantily clad body, pulling her in more closely as she pushed herself toward him to straddle him.

Gasping for breath seconds later, she pulled back a few inches to stare into his eyes—searching for something in his returned gaze. "You were really going to take me on a date?"

Snapping himself out of his dumbstruck state, he blinked a couple times and nodded. "Yeah . . . I was. Fay, please don't do this if you're just trying to appease me. Okay?"

He tilted his head and gave her the most sincere but also hesitant look he'd ever given anybody. "You don't have to do this just because I'm your contracted warlock. That's . . . not what I'd want."

WHAM

She hit him full across the face again, leaving a bruised handprint on the other side of his face to match the first.

"You're a fucking idiot!" Fay said, voice quivering as she reached down to his shirt and yanked. The fabric ripped, then it ripped again, and then it finally tore. When she pushed Riven violently to the ground, Fay's tail whipped back and forth as she aggressively pressed her lips against his again—this time sticking her tongue into his mouth while her hands traveled across his toned chest and abdomen.

When her own clothes started to come off and the moaning started, that's when the four onlookers from around the corner of the manor all started to snicker.

Well, at least they gave their own versions of a snicker. Jackal's ears just flapped up and down in its shadowy dog form, Azmoth gave the childish tee-hee-hee laugh he used to do in earlier days back during his travels in Negrada, and Luke just slowly clapped with a grin.

Jackal quickly followed, and Azmoth came next. But Azmoth had to come back and yank the old elf thrall away before the sounds became even more passionate only ten seconds later.

Riven yet again lay naked with Fay on his chest, only this time he was outside and underneath the shade of the garden's largest tree. When he ran his fingers in and out of Fay's silky white hair, she hummed in contentment while her own fingers traced his left bicep.

"So . . . are you still wanting to go?" Riven asked after a long time of relaxation, turning his head to kiss her as she snuggled up into his arms. "On the date, I mean?"

"Of course I do, silly! Just let me know when you've got it planned." Fay grinned widely back at him, then furrowed her brows before jolting upright. "Wait, do you mean today?!"

He let out a loud laugh, nodding and sweeping the hair out of her face while tracing her cheek with one hand. "That's what I meant, yes."

"WELL, OF COURSE I WANT TO GO! WHAT ARE WE STILL DOING HERE?!"

Shooting to her feet, Fay almost fell over as she attempted to put on her panties and bra again. Cursing to herself under her breath, she swatted at him with her tail and glared at him over her shoulder while he continued to laugh. "You OWE ME for making me cry! So where are we going?!"

Sighing with a smile, he let her pull him up and took her into a hug again while she jumped up repeatedly on her tiptoes like a little kid at a candy shop. "I've reserved a place . . . It's waiting for us now. Perks of being a king, or a prince, I guess. I don't want to ruin the surprise until we get there, and I'm kind of bad at this dating thing . . . but I think you'll like it. If this works out . . . do I get to call you my girlfriend?"

Riven wiggled his eyebrows enticingly her way, and she snorted a laugh before pinching him and shoving him back. "First you have to get on something presentable, then you can try to woo me again afterward. Go on! I expect only the fanciest outfits! And you BETTER NOT wear that ghastly armor of yours; it's scary. Even for me."

She lifted herself up on her tiptoes one more time, kissed him for the millionth time in the past hour, and winked. "HURRY UP! We've gotta go, and I'm super excited!!!"

CHAPTER 7

Allie stood in her usual soul-woven bone armor, staring with red eyes out of a skull mask with her thrumming wand twirling around in her hand at blurring speed. She'd gotten the hang of flipping it around absentmindedly between her fingers and could now do it with one hand and not even bother looking.

It was just a neat party trick, nothing more.

Vin and Nin, the skresh necromancers, stood beside the ghoul Mara in an underground cave a dozen miles outside Dawn's capital, the city of Mandon. The large cavern was easily big enough to house an entire legion, but that wasn't the purpose of this place. Instead, it was merely a laboratory—one that was hidden from the view of the normal populace, and a safe house for her to retreat to in case Dawn was less than trustworthy in days to come. It had dozens of tunnels through the underdark, found by some of her allies from Deepnest at her request, and accessed the outer rim of Tereen's lands as well. Most importantly, one of these tunnels was incredibly large and had been dug all the way out to the surface to a hidden pit in a nearby forest.

The size of that particular tunnel was going to be very important for what she had planned.

Concerning Dawn, she could honestly say that the relations with this human kingdom were going quite well. Trade had drastically increased, and the two kingdoms were more or less dependent on one another for certain valuable resources each had. The Thane Necropolis provided Dawn with numerous alchemy ingredients that could only be found in the Unholy-affiliated landscapes surrounding Brightsville, such as Death-attuned herbs or feral ghoul body parts. Chicago also had a large amount of mana-infused salts along its coastline that were very good for improving enchantments on weapons. Then there was the direct access to Deepnest, which provided both the Thane Necropolis and Dawn with valuable minerals in exchange for weapons and mercenaries for their stalemated war against the dwarves.

On the other hand, Dawn was providing her forces with two things the Thane Necropolis very much wanted outside of the normal goods merchants often carried in their caravans. The first was something the system called Sky Ink, a treasure in its own right that allowed her mechanical units from Chicago to operate at a much higher level. Any mechanical units like cyborgs, machines, or even weapons would have their basic functions increased by a very large margin—though she didn't know where the king was getting this strange blue fluid, either. Whatever the source was, Dawn had hidden it. The second thing they were trading were roc eggs—with each one coming at a very steep price in Elysium coins.

But it'd be worth it one day when she was able to have her own roc riders flying overhead. The large golden birds were just as fast as many of the helicopters, and they were able to grow levels, too, and some of them were inherently born with Storm martial arts that produced lightning attacks.

And that was all aside from all the elf and dwarf slaves to man their farms and bodies Allie had acquired from the wars. Both the war with the Tereen elves, and the war with the dwarves in the underdark had resulted in massive numbers of casualties that further fueled her undead acquisition. The number of undead that she'd created from the bone garden had skyrocketed, and the population of their necropolis was now numbering in the hundreds of thousands of undead due to the violence. It only served to make the necropolis that much stronger—and the bone garden that much more valuable.

Not that her bone garden was a normal one. It also produced avenues of access to off-world undead who weren't affiliated with any of the other major multiverse factions, ones that were below a certain level threshold, due to early quests in their war against Prophet. It had been upgraded three times now, and losing it would mean a drastic decrease in undead output if she had to build a replacement. A new one simply wouldn't do as well, as these upgrades were all unique to the system. There was the upgrade to allow off-world undead to come over, which she'd gotten for being the most notable native undead faction on the planet Panu that allowed for far less resource consumption per undead produced, and an upgrade she'd acquired for finishing a quest to sacrifice a city's populace to the Death subpillar. This last upgrade had been achieved using one of the elf cities, and though she didn't like losing all those slaves, the upgrade she'd gotten was more than worth it, allowing for spontaneous upgrades to random undead who were within a zone of influence ranging fifty miles out around Brightsville.

She snapped out of her thoughts when Gurth'Rok and Dr. Brass entered through the tunnels, leading another five of Gurth'Rok's orc warriors along with seven more unfamiliar orcs. The unfamiliar warriors all wore blue-painted feathers in their braided hair, and their tusks were slightly smaller than the orcs of the Yellow Skull Tribe, who'd been incorporated into the necropolis.

Passing the huge pile of rotting bodies, skeletons, and the alchemy lab set up that bubbled and hissed in large vats and cauldrons to their right, the seven new recruits warily sidestepped a pair of heavily armored cyborgs who carried enchanted plasma blades on their backs and automatic rifles in their hands.

"All clear." The voice of a scout came from the entrance through the walkie-talkie at Allie's side.

Allie gestured for the seven orcs to step forward, passing some of the larger vats of bubbling green liquid casting eerie light along the walls. Stopping alongside Mara, she pushed her wand and her hands into the dark pockets of her cloak.

"Kneel before our queen," Gurth'Rok said, his red eyes glinting in the dim light of the cavern and his wooden cobra staff slamming into the stone floor.

The seven newcomers did as he told them, getting on their knees to prostrate themselves. They did not speak until spoken to.

"Your tribe is called . . . what was it . . ." Allie said, kneeling to examine some of the blue feathers adorning their braids by picking one up in a gauntleted hand. "The Blue Hawk Tribe? Is that right? You may rise."

She let the feather and the man's braid go, standing as they did. She peered up at the taller orc chieftain in front of her and hummed curiously to herself while circling him with light steps.

"Queen Allie Thane of the Thane Necropolis—" The orc chieftain, a very muscular man with a strong jaw who carried an axe at his side, bowed low. "I am humbled that you would spare time to meet with me personally. Your reputation precedes you."

Allie giggled slightly, coming back around to stop in front of him with another twirl of her wand. "And what reputation is that?"

The orc chieftain didn't skip a beat, giving her a menacing smile. "Your brutality, bloodlust, and ruthlessness. They are all qualities we desire in a leader— especially when they're directed toward high elves."

The other greenskins chuckled ruthlessly, and the orc chieftain gestured to two of his men. Together they dragged the body of a blonde elf man forward, still covered in blood and wearing what had once been pristine clothing that was now shredded. The pointed ears were still intact, but his eyes had been gouged out and the expression rested in a silent scream, a deep wound torn across his chest. "I present to you the prince of the Tereen. My clan and I ambushed his honor guard when crossing the twin rivers to the northwest."

Allie took the body in her free hand, noting the tattoo of the royal family on the man's neck. Turning to Mara, she gestured to the marking while prodding it with her wand. "Have our sources confirmed the prince's death?"

Mara nodded. "They have. That is the genuine article."

In response, Allie pulled out a sack of coins from her spatial bag and slapped it into the outstretched palms of the orc chieftain representing the Blue Hawk Tribe. Then she stored the body of the prince for later use. "Very good. Here's your bounty. Run along now."

"Eh . . . My queen," Gurth'Rok interrupted, bowing low and hesitating with a glance the other orc chieftain's way. "What about the other matter?"

"Other matter?" Allie asked, puzzled. She blinked twice, then snapped her fingers in realization. "Oh, yes. They can join the necropolis if they want to, but it's your responsibility to make sure their tribe acclimates just like yours did. You'll be speaking for them, Gurth'Rok. I don't want any more incidents like the last one where your soldiers were caught torturing a slave. I'd hate to hang more of them from the tower as another display of what happens to those who damage the property of the crown."

Gurth'Rok grimaced slightly but nodded—and the other orcs present remained absolutely silent while he spoke. "Of course, Your Majesty. I will make sure they understand the consequences of damaging any of your slaves again, and I will let them know what the norms of our country are. Do I have permission to take funds and build another residential area?"

"Where?"

"Likely renovated buildings from Brightsville itself."

"Then yes, you do."

"And the other stipend? I promised the chieftain of the Blue Hawk Tribe that he'd be paid for integrating his people, as is your policy. They bring another two thousand orcs ready to serve you, most of them civilians, as their numbers were culled by the Tereen."

"Oh, yes. Sorry, my mind has been elsewhere lately ever since I enrolled in the academy." Allie pulled out yet another bag of coins, this one much bigger than the first—which she tossed onto the ground for the greenskin leaders to pick up.

"Thank you, my queen!" Gurth'Rok replied happily while the other greenskins of both tribes grinned widely. They were just happy to have more of their own kin now, as both of their tribes had been almost decimated during the early integration. The Blue Hawks were the fourth orc tribe to join, and their numbers were growing fast. "You will not regret this! Our people are steadfast in our loyalty and your kindness will not go unreciprocated! Now if you do not mind, I need to attend a hunt. My people are tracking locust wraiths spawned in the outer reaches of our lands, and they breed rapidly with other feral undead to produce small swarms if not put down."

Allie nodded, then waved them away rather impatiently with a shooing motion. The orcs packed up and left, laughing to one another and speaking excitedly about what to expect when moving into the suburbs of Brightsville, which were being rebuilt and renovated as more people arrived from the surrounding wildlands or other less protected areas.

Then, when they'd finally left, Allie motioned to the two elite cyborgs nearby. One was female, the other male, and both wore very stern looks of hardened military veterans with various metal pieces incorporated into their bodies. "Follow the Blue Hawk leadership after Gurth'Rok lets them depart. If they seem to be gallivanting off with the money given to them and don't take a route toward the necropolis, assassinate them and bring the money back. I don't want a repeat of the Bloodhound Tribe's treachery."

Both cyborgs nodded silently, then activated stealth fields and disappeared entirely. The only reason Allie knew they were there was due to their heartbeats that continued to disappear down the cavern and then out a tunnel exit the way the orcs had departed.

"Back to the drawing board!" Allie turned heel toward the center of the cavern, and as she did, her friends Vin and Nin activated the sigils that'd been placed there. "Is it ready?"

The sigils on the stone floor glowed a faint neon teal, shimmering with black wisps as death mana poured into the magical construct and slabs of stone began to rise at intervals akin to an evil Stonehenge.

The loud bubbling of the chemical vats nearby came up an octave when lines of power connecting them and the sigils began to intertwine, and Vin nodded expectantly while rubbing his skeletal hands together. "Yes, Allie, we're good to go! Do you have the corpse?"

Allie nodded, walking over to the circle. She lifted a hand and withdrew a small bauble. One that Riven had gifted to her after defeating and containing the dungeon boss he'd saved Hakim's team from across the planet.

Then, when she smashed it between her fingers almost effortlessly, the corpse appeared before her.

The drake was enormous, far larger than she'd thought it would be—and it almost instantly took up half the cavern. It was only just big enough to fit on the runic sigils and in between the pillars of stone, and she nodded approvingly at the scaled blue behemoth while noting the wounds still kept fresh by the time freeze in her spatial sack.

"Riven killed this thing, huh?" Allie muttered, rubbing at her neck and giddily skipping backward to the edge of the runic circles while clapping her hands together. Then, with a hand stretched to the right, Mara placed a soul stone they'd crafted together just for this particular occasion from a combination of soul shards.

With a recent breakthrough Allie could now say that, though she couldn't completely resurrect people yet without damage to the original soul, she could mix and match different pieces of souls and imbue these newly created true souls into bodies. It was a grand step in the direction of complete revival and was supposedly not often done even in the outer reaches of the multiverse.

"I don't know of anyone who can completely revive a soul from true death without immense cost to themselves," Kathrine had told Allie months ago when she'd asked.

Well, fuck that. Not just anyone had a 100 percent affinity to the Death subpillar, either. Other people might not be able to do it, but Allie was hell-bent on figuring out a way.

Mara nudged Allie with a wide smile. "Good luck! I'm excited. To your first captain undead!"

Captain undead minion slots were those reserved by Allie's swarm necromancer class. She had two of these slots. The captains, which she hadn't successfully created until now, were supposed to be intelligent and could control the other undead she commanded, giving her swarm a command stat buff whenever they were nearby. However, she'd failed every time when trying to create a captain-type undead, as it required the soul to remain completely intact; while simultaneously she needed to have complete control over the souls she used to animate them.

But that problem was now gone. Mostly, anyway.

"Here goes nothing." Allie cracked her neck, then concentrated on the unique soul she and Mara had infused into the soul stone clasped between her fingers. The stone lit up, becoming a bright neon teal that flared and pulsed over and over again with each infusion she channeled into it. Cracks started appearing on the stone one after the other, little pieces of crystal chipping off it and falling to the ground until eventually—suddenly—it burst.

Blinding teal light roared to life as the uniquely crafted soul—a true chimera masterpiece created from their most deadly enemies—was let loose and directed into the body of the drake. Power flowed and pulsed, charging forward and slamming into the huge, blue-scaled monster.

The corpse shivered and trembled.

The ground shook with the infusion of necromantic power.

The runes along the stone pillars and cavern floor lit up and pulsed from teal to white.

Scales began to fall off the massive dead beast, leaving behind exposed flesh that crackled and tore at the air with smoldering necromancy. Diseased flesh rotted away and was replaced with thick cords of black miasma. Membranes along the wings decayed and fell away, only to be replaced with a similar black power that stretched between exposed bones—integrating little trickles of neon-teal light like blood vessels would do.

The drake then opened its eyes to reveal a dull gray-white color, and the undead creature slowly rose to its feet.

[You have created a new minion with additional boost enchantments to the soul aperture. New minion's soul has been fed numerous other souls to strengthen its core. Affinity with body is still intact due to 43% of current soul being utilized from previously deceased drake. Your minion's affinity to the Death pillar has increased after being imbued with your blood. New Captain Minion has been applied to your status page and can control all other minions you possess as long as those orders do not contradict your own:

Undead Drake, Level 60, Unnamed

Ability Synopsis is shown below; see individual status page for this minion for more details:

- **Deathfire Blast—Breathe death-attuned flames at your enemies**
- **Winds of Rot—Cast a billowing torrent of black winds that rot away your enemies, or use it to boost your own speed**
- **Wraithflight—Increases flight movement drastically by turning your body into a wraith's form. Can move in between the lands of the dead and the living at will, at high mana cost. Affects any adjacent items or riders**
- **Pulsating Roar—This martial art sends a shock wave of kinetic energy at your enemies and potentially silences them for a short time**

- **Unholy Slash—Imbue your claws with Unholy energy, empower-ing your slash attack for additional speed and physical damage]**

"Bravo," Mara muttered under her breath while clapping slowly, watching the titanic monster stand to its full height—though it had a hard time stretching its wings out without touching the cavern ceiling. "Bravo, bravo, bravo . . ."

"Oh yeah, baby!" Allie humphed triumphantly while the other undead around the room cheered or gawked and let the drake's enormous skeletal head drive itself forward to get a better look at her.

A deep rumbling sound came from the monstrous, zombified, skeletal drake—and it breathed a brief bout of flames out its nostrils while side-eyeing her when it turned its head. The eye itself was larger than she was, but it centered on her position with intent.

When it spoke, the noise was like a demonic hiss that echoed through the caves and tunnels beyond. "You are . . . Master."

"Allie Thane, and yes. I am the one who created you."

The drake picked its head up to look at her from another angle, then let off another rumbling sound. "Allie Thane . . . is a good name. My memories are . . . jumbled. My understanding of this world is . . . limited. Please advise me on what my purpose is and what I was created to do."

"Your purpose is to serve me," Allie replied, staring up at the large creature with a devilish gleam in her eye. "And your first order of business is to educate yourself."

Allie gestured over to Vin and Nin, the two skeletal humanoids. "They will be your tutors here in the cavern while I'm gone. Learn about what our situation is, about the world outside, and I will be back to claim you in due time. As for the rest of you . . ."

She turned on her heel to stare at the others who'd gathered here in the cavern, witnesses to her new mount's birth. "Prepare yourselves for an assault. You'll all be coming with me in upcoming days. Riven will be, too, but he's currently on a long-needed date and I have my own plans at the academy. So it'll wait. The assault will take place in two days."

"Assault?" Mara asked curiously, shoving her hands into her pockets with another side-eye at the large draconic creature looming over them. "This is the first time I'm hearing about it. Who are we attacking? Are you and Riven going to break the frontline stalemate with the Tereen?"

Allie shook her head. "No, we're going to let our own forces continue that fight. They need the levels; the system rewards those who kill, and champions will rise from this war. No need for me or Riven to get involved, because we'd simply end a good opportunity. No, we are going to be attacking the dungeon that is supporting the Tereen, Dungeon Alibast. I hear it has lots and lots of treasures."

CHAPTER 8

The barely present drizzle splashed on the cement pathway leading them along the river's edge. A metal railing separated them from a small drop-off into the water below, and numerous restaurants that'd reopened along the riverwalk were now in full bloom with people sitting underneath umbrellas, eating or drinking. Flowers even lined the roadside, and there was a guard patrol in case any monsters managed to make it this far into the city.

It was a rarity now that the city was under complete control, but the city was big and a lot of the population had been culled upon integration—so there were still a few spots here or there that just simply hadn't been swept yet.

That being said, Brightsville had been pretty safe since the Thane siblings had taken over. There were even human kids running around and playing on a nearby playground with their parents . . . and this in turn made Riven think of the little elf girl Len.

Fay's hand tightened around his own, and she pulled him closer while they walked—catching a lot of attention from other couples taking a stroll or people dining nearby along the riverwalk. "Are you okay? We've been having such a good time! Why so down?!"

Taking a large bite out of the chocolate ice cream cone and tugging on Riven's hand to get his attention, she leaned over and kissed him with a wide smile. "And the restaurant was really nice. Thanks for the date, Riven. This has been a great experience. I hope to repeat it again. Also—the suit really fits you well!"

Yeah. Now was not the time to think about the elves. He'd just need to introduce those programs and get it rolling so it was out of his hands.

Turning to face the beauty beside him, he let go of her hand while they walked and slung his arm around her shoulders to bring her in—passing by another couple who shot them wary smiles. Then, coming up to a bench, Riven motioned for her to sit after wiping the bench off the best he could. Holding an umbrella out so they wouldn't get wet, he joined her shortly after and sat down to take in the view. "Thanks, Fay. I've got to admit, I haven't worn a suit like this in many years now." He grinned, gesturing to the red tie and black suit jacket he had on while crossing his legs. "Many years."

"But why?! You look so good in it!"

Riven snorted and out of nowhere ripped the ice cream cone out of her hand—causing her to gasp as he snarfed the last of it down.

"Hey!" Fay jabbed him in the rib while he began to cackle through mouthfuls of food, her jaw hanging down in fake disbelief before she too began to laugh. "You jerk! You owe me another!"

"Fay, you've already had three! You're going to get fat. I'm just saving you from that fate by eating all your calories for you."

"Am not! Have you ever seen a fat succubus?!"

"No, but I don't usually meet many succubi, so you can't hold me to that standard!"

"Well, I'll have you know that I won't get fat no matter what I eat! My metabolism is god-level, Riven! GOD-LEVEL!" She gave him a rather rude gesture with one middle finger and then licked some chocolate remnants off his face before shoving him off the bench and into the rain. Snatching the umbrella as he laughed, she humphed and crossed her legs while glaring down at him. "Oh, get up! You're going to make me look bad if you just sit there. All these people are going to think I'm committing treason or something by attacking you."

He covered his face to subdue a belch, then stood up and brushed off his suit while enjoying the slight drizzle. "Maybe I should call the guards over and have you arrested. Ooh . . . They could handcuff you and stuff you in my room so I could deal with you later."

"I actually kind of like that idea." She winked, then patted the bench and took on a more serious expression. "Hey, Riven . . . can we talk?"

Riven's eyebrows lifted, then he nodded and came to sit next to her. "Yes?"

Fay fidgeted for a bit, then huffed and turned her entire body to face him with one knee tucked under her body. "I've been thinking about . . . us. And about what happened—HEY! Stop that sad expression RIGHT NOW! That's not what I mean!"

She pursed her lips and scowled until his frown departed, and she reached out to grip his hand tightly while leaning forward. "Don't even think I'm trying to let you down easy. That's not it at all, and what we talked about earlier is true. But there is a topic surrounding this that we need to discuss, and it's an important one. It's Athela."

"Athela?" Riven repeated, unsure of what to think. "What does Athela have to do with . . ."

His words trailed off as she stared at him, and he eventually shook his head. "I don't think she likes me like that."

"Riven, don't be an idiot." Fay cocked her head to the side and her lips thinned into a straight line. "You love her. I saw the video footage where you said you did."

"Oh. Is that what this is about?" Riven shrugged helplessly. "Well, I do love her. She's my very best friend. I'd die for her without a thought if it came down to a choice. Is this a jealousy thing because I'm close with her?"

Fay leaned back, closing her eyes, and gathered herself. "Yes, Riven, I know. And I don't expect that to change. What I'm saying is that she's got her sights set on you."

"Doubtful."

"I'm being serious."

"Has she ever even once told you so?"

Fay hesitated, then shook her head. "No . . . but I can tell."

Riven smirked, then leaned back to put his arms behind him over the backrest of the bench. Looking out over the river, he stayed motionless for a time while pondering what to say next. "I don't think you're right. She probably has some actual spider lover in the nether realms."

"And what if I am right?" Fay asked bluntly. "If Athela came to you tomorrow, if she told you that she wanted you to be with her instead of me . . . What would you do? Would you pick me—or her?"

Riven's eyebrows furrowed, and he stared at Fay for a long moment. "Fay . . . Athela and I aren't like that—"

She held up a hand to silence him, pushing her fingers up against his lips. Huffing again, it was her turn to shake her head, causing her long white hair to flow back and forth. "You asked me earlier if you could be blunt with me. Now let me be blunt with you. I like you a lot, Riven. I'm falling in love with who you are. But let's be realistic, I'm a succubus and you're a summoner—"

"That has nothing to do with anything," Riven said angrily, pushing her hand away and glaring at her. "How can you even say that?"

"I'm not saying that we can't have a relationship of some kind," Fay clarified, keeping eye contact. "But I am saying that putting a label on it so early would be bad. I know you joked about calling me your girlfriend, and honestly my heart just wanted to jump right out of my chest and hug you for it! But it'd be idiotic to do that. To make it exclusive would put a target on my back, and if I'm right about Athela, she'd never forgive me for stealing you when we find a way to bring her back."

Riven's scowl deepened, but he didn't get mad or raise his voice despite being irked by her words. He hesitated, then shook his head again as his eyes fell. "Was bringing you here a mistake?"

"NO!" Fay exclaimed, gripping his arm hard and tugging on him to get his attention. "Stop it! Fucking stop it, okay?! That's not what I'm saying . . . Goddamn it. Please just listen and stop interrupting, okay?"

Riven looked up, still frowning, but remained silent and waited for her to finish.

She huffed once more, straightened her shoulders, and held her head high. "Here's me being blunt. You are a prince of an intergalactic multidimensional empire run by some of the most powerful vampires in existence. You are a prince of an S-grade faction, and I'm not talking about S-grade like how you were S-grade here or how Allie is S-grade now. Those are planetary grades. I'm talking about S-grade by multiverse standards. Riven, I'd be assassinated within a year if you let it be known that I was your official girlfriend—let alone wife. And it'd be a permanent assassination, likely from some other woman who wanted to get your attention who comes from a rich and powerful family much further up the food chain than my own. A prince of the Blood Moon Requiem is a very steep prize to attain, and you're going to have a lot of women trying to draw your attention."

Riven opened his mouth to protest, but she shut him up again with another finger to his lips.

"Nope, not finished," she stated with a sad smile. "Let me give an example. You already have Kathrine here, who is DEFINITELY trying to gain your favor, and by the way, she skipped off this morning so full of energy after having lain with you; last night in her mind is no doubt a political success."

"Kathrine wouldn't have you assassinated, Fay."

"Oh, she wouldn't?!" Fay drew her hands back and placed them on her hips, letting go of the umbrella, only for Riven to catch it and hold it upright. "Let me ask you this, Riven: Why wouldn't she? Until last night she'd utterly failed at establishing a connection with you, she's a very minor princess of a branch family WITHOUT the gift of Malignant Prophecy. If she doesn't succeed here by their high queen's standards, she and her entire family will be executed. Killed. Murdered for lack of results. I have zero doubt in my mind that if she thinks I'm in her way, she'll not even think twice about getting rid of me. You may not THINK it's her when I'm dead, but that wouldn't change the reality of it. She is going to be doing everything in her power to get you hitched, engaged, whatever you want to call it—or at the very least she's going to want to become your concubine."

Riven snorted a laugh and rolled his eyes. "I think she has higher sights set than becoming someone's concubine. As you said, she's princess of—"

"A MINOR princess! She isn't anyone of importance on the grand scale of things! At least not when compared to you! You just don't see it now because you're stuck on this little rock of a planet; you haven't seen the scale and gravity of the empire your family rules over!" Fay stated loudly, holding her hands out to either side to emphasize her words. "Look, Riven, I'm not going to sit here and argue with you about this. All I'm saying is that putting an official label on it would be bad for multiple reasons. I absolutely adore you and I want to be with you, but making me the sole recipient of your affections would mean a very bad time for me."

Riven blinked. "Fay, are you telling me that I should also be sleeping with other women?"

"That's precisely what I'm saying."

"You wouldn't be jealous of that?"

"Did I seem jealous when you were making love with Kathrine and Genua last night?"

Riven raised an eyebrow, and Fay started to blush profusely before folding her arms and glaring at him.

"Okay, I might have been a little bit jealous from time to time last night, I admit it. But still—I'm not stupid enough to officially label myself and then get myself killed. All I want from you is your affection, your genuine affection, and . . ." Her voice trailed off, becoming faint while her blush grew stronger and her eyes darted to the ground.

"And what?" Riven asked, somewhat amused.

"And for you to love me. Eventually, I mean. I know you probably don't love me NOW, not yet, anyway . . ." Fay gave him a sheepish smile and clasped her hands in front of her chest. "But I want to get there one day! Beyond anything else, I just want true emotion involved. Emotion between us, a real connection—and for you not to view me as just a thing to use. I want to be loved, and I want to love in turn. Eventually."

He snorted and reached out to pull her into a hug. Rubbing her back and feeling her sigh in contentment, he leaned back again and brushed the hair out of her face while continuing to maintain eye contact. "Fay . . . I'm not really sure about all that."

"What do you mean?"

"I mean that, although I'm certainly not entirely opposed to the idea of being with multiple women—what straight guy wouldn't like that . . . I just don't know if it's what I really want in the end." He gave her a shrug, then put his hands on his knees and sighed. "It'd be great for the bachelor's life, and god knows my sex life has been lacking. Last night was amazing. But when it comes to truly dating someone, and starting a genuinely caring relationship with someone, I've always wanted to be with a person who knows me intimately. I've always had a vision of growing old with that person and having kids, and not needing to worry about being cheated on or lusting after other women. I want a soul mate, not just someone I get to fuck. So, to reiterate: although I did have a great time yesterday and wouldn't mind repeating it here or there, I am looking for someone who I can give my all to as a lifelong partner."

"But what if you could have that with more than one person?"

"I'm not sure I could. Maybe, but it feels dirty to think about it."

"What if it did work, though, theoretically? That you could feel that way about multiple people at once?"

Riven pondered this for a while and scratched his chin, waving to another passing family farther on the path. "Theoretically it would be fine, except that I wouldn't want those people becoming jealous of each other, either. Realistically, I don't feel like it'd be an easy thing to find, because one person or multiple people are always going to feel like they're being neglected. I've had friends who were in committed open relationships before, and they almost always fell through because one person would always get jealous. Or, even worse, one person would fall out of love and find someone else."

Fay hesitated. "I see. I'm not entirely disagreeing with you, either. Just . . . keep an open mind for now. I want you, and I want to be with you, just . . . let's keep it out of the public eye for now until you, I, and Athela have a chance to talk about it together. Bare minimum. Then after that, we can discuss things like Kathrine, the tens of thousands of other succubi currently asking to be your familiar right now, and intergalactic politics that will involve themselves in the form of hungry brides wanting a bite out of an S-tier–faction prince."

Riven shot her another wary look. "I like you a lot, Fay, but I'm not entirely sure I want the same thing you do. I'll do as you say and keep an open mind for now . . . and I'll talk with Athela even knowing she doesn't feel that way about me. But is this about something else? Like, are you into girls? Is that it?"

Fay rolled her eyes dramatically. "Somewhat, but that literally has nothing to do with what we're talking about. Riven, do you trust me?"

"Yes."

"Then trust that everything I've said is the absolute truth." She squeezed his hands and pulled him into another kiss, getting an exclamation of "EWWWW" from a little boy who'd been walking by—only to have his parents quickly usher him away while others on the sidelines chuckled.

Fay pulled back, gave Riven another peck on the forehead, and softly pinched his cheek. "I'm falling for you, hard. I have been for a while. Trust me, this is not me pushing you away. I want you more than you know, it's just that . . . things are more complicated because of who you are. Now, are you ready to take me on that big wheel in the sky over there or not?"

Riven grinned, then gestured for her to stand. "It's called a Ferris wheel, and yes. I'm ready. Let's grab another two ice cream cones, though."

She held up three fingers with gusto. "THREE ICE CREAM CONES!"

He laughed. "Three it is, then. Now come on, there's a lot more to show you about human Earth culture."

CHAPTER 9

YEAR 1 SCHEDULE:
Beginners' Magic Theory—Instructors, Kremsin Bots and Ori Orumi
- **Mornings**

Beginners' Battle Abilities 1: Applications of Magic, Miracles, and Martial Arts—Instructors, Jaimest Vorvus and Thoi Jorsem
- **Afternoons**

Beginners' Battle Abilities 2: Combined Warfare Tactics—Instructor, Mince Quarteple
- **Afternoons**

Combined Combat Class—Instructors, Nester Rose, Jokzofrie Belfast, and Jupis Astirith
- **Evenings**

Beginners' Healing and First Aid—Instructors, Nuthak Ororin and Jan Wetzle
- **Evenings**

Lahn Lucio put his parchment away in the bright lighting of the academy hall, stuffing the schedule into his bag with his right hand as he struggled to maintain balance with his left despite it being shriveled and weak. His matted brown hair was damp from the rain, and the family maid assigned to him had been pulled off her duty to attend to his brother instead—per his brother's request. No doubt to cause Lahn even more trouble getting to class on time, as his two siblings were always trying to find ways to make his life harder. For what reason, Lahn didn't know. Perhaps they were embarrassed he was here, perhaps they were just malicious, but regardless of the why, the results were always the same.

At the very least they were years ahead of him, so his classes were devoid of their harassments. Mostly.

He'd gone to his Beginners' Magic Theory and Battle Abilities courses earlier that morning, and had been disappointed to see that Allie'd skipped out again. She usually skipped Beginners' Battle Abilities 1 after the incident with instructor Thoi Jorsem, but the other courses she often attended. Occasionally she'd miss due to family matters, as did many of the other nobles who were inheriting their parents' estates, but she was certainly an outlier for how often it happened.

And seeing as she was one of only a few people who gave him the time of day and didn't shun him outright, Lahn had grown very fond of his new friend—always disappointed when he ended up sitting in class alone.

So he took in a deep breath, already late to Combined Combat class—as if HE would ever see combat—and rattled the door.

The metal knob squeaked and turned, and it took a good bit of effort to push the door open and wheel the rolling chair he used into the crack before it shut. Inside he could already see that the class had started—with numerous people getting into groups and firing off basic projectiles of different sources toward a target at the back of the gymnasium.

"Late again, Mr. Lucio?" a motherly voice called out from the right, and he managed to push himself through the door entirely when the teacher strode over and helped open the heavy wooden obstacle.

Instructor Nester Rose was the kindest of the three Combined Combat instructors. She was middle-aged, redheaded, and a very committed teacher—even for someone like him. "Come now, Mr. Lucio, we can't have you always being late just because your siblings steal your help. You need to leave earlier. Overcome, adapt, and struggle against the odds—I have faith you will one day see success."

These were some of the kindest words he'd ever heard from his teachers, and she always told him thus any time he came late. She knew what he was going through, and he gave a smile of appreciation for the encouragement. "Thanks, Instructor Rose, I appreciate it."

The middle-aged woman wiped down her finely made, richly colored blue robes and nodded with a thin-lipped smile. "Very good. Now, find a group to join and get started. We're practicing projectile magics today. I know you have at least one."

Lahn sighed and nodded with a grimace. "Yes, Instructor Rose. I do."

"Very good. Now move along; you've already missed a third of the class."

When Lahn nodded and wheeled himself farther into the room, the instructor left to go attend to other trainees in the gym. Half of the class was on his right, half was on his left, and they were all facing away from him as they practiced their various spells and miracles. There were even a few martial arts being practiced, but most of these included projectiles like arrows that were infused with power rather than an outright energy projectile that the other types of energy produced.

Though there were always exceptions to every rule.

He scanned the room, looking for a very particular person, until his eyes landed on her. His face brightened and he quickly began to wheel himself toward the back left corner where Allie was currently leaning against a wall, looking bored as would-be suitors of various noble houses tried to talk to her and gain her attention. They looked like flies drawn to a corpse the way they swarmed her, and the reason it'd taken Lahn so long to find her was because of just how packed it was over on this side.

That and he was in a sitting position and it was hard to get a good view.

"This spot is taken," a snobby female voice sourly called out when he neared one of the groups to pass them by, an orange-haired young woman in bright yellow judgingly glaring at him as he gave a sheepish smile and continued on.

It wasn't like he was wanting to ask that group anyway. He knew Precilla was a jerk and wouldn't have taken him unless he groveled.

He was struggling and breathing hard now after the exertion of wheeling himself across campus with only one arm, occasionally needing to correct his direction by reaching over to the other side and taking the left wheel with his right hand. It truly was a struggle.

Huffing and puffing, he came across another young man who only glared down at him, refusing to move, so Lucio had to wheel around him and then tried to make a straight line in Allie's direction.

"Allie!" Lahn called out excitedly, getting a few glares or mocking laughter from some of the men surrounding her position. He ignored them. "Hey, Allie!"

The room was loud, and she didn't hear him despite his two attempts. She continued to watch, bored, as some of the other young men tried to impress her with displays of their own fireballs, tiny ice lances, Holy smites, or sparks of electricity. Instead, one of the men who was already looking disgruntled by being shoved to the back of the crowd around her took notice.

It was none other than Gleetus Nefrand.

God, how Lahn hated this guy. But Gleetus's own frown of annoyance quickly turned to wicked malice when noticing Lahn, and Gleetus quickly adjusted his pristine Victorian-style jacket—complete with buttons and a frill—before walking in Lahn's direction. Gleetus took a comb and touched up his already perfectly gelled brown hair, eyes narrowing like a snake ready to strike, before he stopped directly in front of Lahn with a sneer.

"What are you doing here?" Gleetus asked in a low hiss, his hands clasped behind his back and his chest puffed out arrogantly. One finely made boot tapped on the gymnasium floor, as if impatiently waiting for an answer even though he'd only just asked. "Lady Wraithtide is busy. You'll have to come back later after more suitable men speak with her first. If you are trying to woo her, don't bother. No one would want to court a cripple like you, Lucio."

"I wasn't trying to woo anyone! She's just my friend!" Lahn retorted in a half snarl, barely containing his anger. He tried to wheel around Gleetus, only for the bigger man to step in front of him again. "Get out of my way, Gleetus! Allie and I always partner up!"

"Hardly," Gleetus said down the bridge of his nose in a nasally sigh. Then he inspected his nails, one by one, enjoying every second of being in a position of power over Lahn. "You barely know her. Do not act like she is your friend. I realize you're desperate for any kind of social interaction—even your maids don't want to be near you. I feel sorry for your siblings, having the family name marred by one such as you. Your lies about being on good terms with Lady Wraithtide only further insult that name. Begone, before I report your misgivings to your elder brother again. I'm sure he'd not want to hear you're dragging their reputation through the mud once more."

"I'm not desperate," Lahn growled through gritted teeth, glaring up hatefully at his longtime nemesis. "And I'm not trying to court her. I know she wouldn't want to be with someone like me. I am merely her friend. That's all. Just because you're at the back of the line and can't get a good spot with all these other guys jockeying for position doesn't mean you need to take it out on me."

Lahn had obviously hit the nail right on the head by the way Gleetus froze and began to redden in the face.

When he stepped forward menacingly and hissed low so that only Lahn could hear him, his eyes were barely slits—and his hands trembled. "Watch your insolent mouth, Lucio, or I will break that other leg of yours so you know your place."

"LAHN!" Allie's voice called out excitedly, and Gleetus abruptly straightened and turned around with a wide, bright smile to intercept.

"Lady Wraithtide!" Gleetus said sweetly while stepping in front of her as she pushed her way through the crowd. "I'd been hoping—"

She merely walked around Gleetus, completely ignoring him like he wasn't even there, and knelt in front of Lahn's wheelchair with a brilliantly white smile. The way she walked, the formfitting leathers she wore that were far different than most ladies of the court, the way her hips moved, the way her perfect features shone like the sun and her now-blue eyes twinkled were enough to captivate any man's heart—and Lahn felt himself flush a bright red when she got down on her knees to put a hand on his own. She was utterly stunning, an angel having taken human form—there were no other words for it.

"My favorite person! I've been waiting all day for you!" she said with a laugh, brushing her silky brown hair to the side and tilting her head. "Have you been practicing with those tips I gave you?! The way you form your intent when casting?"

Lahn was very aware of all the hostility oozing out from the dozen or so other young men, and he gulped while avoiding their gazes—but kept his eyes locked onto hers. "Uh, yeah! I've been practicing . . . can't say I'm all that great at it. But I'll get there! And there is NO way you've been waiting all day. You've been skipping again."

A sly grin etched itself across her features, and she shrugged—standing up and getting behind his wheelchair to push him forward through the group of nobles to the front. "Well, I can't say you're wrong. I'm a slacker."

A fake laugh from one of the other men, and Lahn was almost shellshocked to see it was Braden Rooze. Braden was probably the most popular man in their year. He was incredibly handsome, muscular, had a father who was a frontline war hero who'd even achieved the prestigious A-class category on the world power boards, and his family was filthy rich due to owning many of the laboratories in Dawn used to create potions for the war effort. That being said, Braden had never been mean or vile toward Lahn—so Lahn didn't necessarily think poorly of the man, either.

"I wouldn't say that you're a slacker, Lady Wraithtide," Braden cut in with a swish of his blonde hair, stuffing his hands into his pockets. "From my perspective, you're just more advanced than the rest of us and don't need to attend those classes. And hello, Lahn. How are you today?"

A small pit of jealousy built inside Lahn's gut, but he quickly pushed that back down. He knew there wasn't anything between himself and Allie anyway, and Braden would make a great suitor for someone like her. So instead, he put on a warm smile and reciprocated the friendly gesture with a wave. "Hello, Braden. I'm doing well, though I'm obviously a bit wet from the rain."

Braden chuckled warmly with a nod of understanding. "Yes, that tends to happen when you have . . . a lack of help. Lady Wraithtide has been telling me a lot about how she's teaching you tips and tricks. It must be nice to have such a beautiful tutor. I tried to get her to teach me, too, but she said she doesn't have time and we merely settled on lunch."

Lahn caught Allie's brief smile, one directed toward Braden, and his heart sank even though he knew it shouldn't. "Oh! You had lunch together?"

"We did." Allie nodded in confirmation, putting a hand on Lahn's shoulder and directing him to the marked line where people would stand to cast spells. "Braden is slightly less insufferable when compared to many of the other people here. It was a nice chat."

Braden's victorious smile cut like a knife, not only to Lahn, but to many of the other nobles present, too. Four of them left wordlessly right there and then, with two more following shortly thereafter—silently admitting defeat.

Allie seemed not to notice, and she focused on coaching Lahn instead. "All right, so show me what you've got. Remember, the intent part is far more important than anything else, and the imagery of what you need should be incorporated simultaneously when you channel the power through your Holy pillar. Got it?"

Swallowing the lump in his throat, Lahn nodded and began to cast. Raising his good arm, he closed his eyes and focused inward on his soul apparatus. He could see the faint sparks of white energy channeling up the pillar, could see them etch themselves into the foundation, and slowly he opened his eyes again to see a small sphere of brilliant light forming in front of his outstretched hand.

"GREAT!" Allie exclaimed excitedly, jumping up and down just once and pointing toward the target carved into enchanted stone at the end of the gymnasium. "Now fire!"

Lahn concentrated, imagining the arc the Holy bolt would need to take, and the orb began to move forward.

Only it veered left.

When it slammed into another projectile farther down the gymnasium, he saw his small Holy projectile get crushed by a flurry of ice and snow—torn apart instantaneously by another more proficient caster who began to shriek in outrage.

"GET AHOLD OF YOUR MAGIC, LUCIO!" A shrill, high-pitched scream from Precilla echoed through the room—getting a bout of laughter from multiple groups who'd seen the two magics collide. Her face was flushed red in irritation, and her yellow dress swayed when she pointed his way. "I had PERFECT MARKS until your stupid sphere made contact! Now look! The marker is going to record my attempt as a miss!"

Lahn visibly recoiled. "Sorry . . ."

"Fuck off, bitch," Allie called out with a dismissive wave of her hand. "It's not like that pissant attempt at an ice flurry would have killed anyone anyways."

This resulted in even more laughter, and Precilla's red face almost matched the color of her orange hair as she stomped one foot into the ground. "I have had PERFECT marks thus far, Lady Wraithtide! Unlike you, who fails to even attend the most basic schedule of classes! It is apparent that only one of us is taking our training seriously, and we'll see just who is superior by the end of the year for it!"

"Whatever," Allie called back with a bored yawn. "Just shut the fuck up and stop screeching. Your annoying voice is nearly making my ears bleed."

Even more laughter erupted from different parts of the audience, and Precilla's anger was visibly rising. Strutting across the room right over to where Allie stood looking back at her with an impassive expression, Precilla stopped directly in front of her and pointed a finger in Allie's face.

"If you're so confident, you low-class country bumpkin, I challenge you to a restricted duel."

Excited muttering quickly replaced the laughter, and even the instructors were now looking over to see what the commotion was about.

Allie glanced over to Instructor Nester Rose, and then to Instructor Jupis Astirith. "Is that allowed here? Or do we need to take it out to the colosseum?"

Instructor Rose waltzed over, her thin-lipped smile quirking in amusement as she gazed down at Lahn as if telling him she knew he was the cause of this dispute. Perhaps she did know and had seen it from the beginning. "We can do it here, though we'll have to take up one side of the gymnasium to do it. It appears everyone is rather interested to see the end result anyways. Is that all right with all of you?"

Everyone's attention was now drawn to the dramatic scene, Precilla heaving angrily with every breath she took, and Instructor Rose got a unanimous affirmative answer from the audience.

"Very well. Everyone spread out. The other instructors and I will set up a mana field."

"Allie!" Lahn hissed under his breath as muttering began to pick up around the room and Precilla stomped off to be with her friends. "She's really good! Probably just as good as you are. You don't need to do this! You could lose!"

Allie's amused giggle made her eyes sparkle, and she covered her mouth with a warm expression directed his way. "We'll see about that."

Gleetus sneered at them from the sidelines after watching the friendly interaction, then muttered something under his breath to a friend, who only nodded with distaste in Lahn's direction.

It didn't take long for the instructors to set up a rectangular mana barrier, encompassing a field about half the size of the gymnasium with everyone present watching. They'd had very minor practice bouts with pseudo-sparring sessions in the colosseum before, but Allie had never faced Precilla before, and they were arguably two of the most competent people in the room, alongside a few others.

Instructor Rose began the usual speech. "As usual, these restricted duels come with protective gear. Neither of you can or should remove the bracelets we dispense to you, unless you want to accidentally die. They are meant to save your life in case of an attack too potent, and will heal any wounds you receive afterward—within reason. Any wounds that the bracelets do not heal can be dealt with by us or by the medical bay staff should they be severe. Outside of mortally wounding your opponent, you can do whatever you want in order to win—but you must stop if the instructors pause the fight. Failing to stop when instructed by our staff will result in immediate expulsion. Any equipment damaged during a fight is not our problem, and it is your responsibility to get it repaired if needed. Do I make myself clear?"

Allie nodded calmly with her arms crossed. Meanwhile, Precilla continued to snarl and drew out a very decorated wand with gold trimmings and diamond studs.

"Very well. Are there any further questions or words you'd like to have before the fight begins?"

"Yes, I do." Precilla raised her hand to garner the attention of the class. She smiled wickedly Allie's way, then raised her nose up as if in disgust. "I'd like to make a bet."

Allie's eyebrow quirked up in amusement. "What kind of bet?"

Precilla paused, dramatically looking Allie up and down and then gesturing with an upturned lip at Allie's outfit. "I would like to have a wager of wealth on this fight . . . though I'm not sure how much you can afford to bet."

Laughter yet again echoed from around the room at Precilla's jab at Allie's outfit.

Precilla paused, waiting for the laughter to sink in. "I know your family is from a poor and poorly known country estate. Based on how you dress, I am concerned you may not be able to match me, but if you can, I'd like to bet my wand."

Precilla held the sparkling, gold- and diamond-encrusted wand out for the admiration of everyone else. "It is worth at least a hundred platinum, if not two hundred. Do you have anything to match? Anything at all?"

The noble lady in training cocked her prominent hip out to one side and rested her free hand on it, waiting expectantly with a confident smirk.

Allie hesitated for a moment, tapped her pointer finger on her chin, then shrugged. "I might."

Allie first made a display of rummaging around in her spatial sack. Spatial sacks were very rare and of high value in of themselves, and no one had known up until now that it even was a spatial sack. They'd thought it merely a bag she carried around. But when Allie pulled out a book that was far larger than the sack itself, two realizations hit the class simultaneously.

The first realization was that the bag was indeed a spatial sack and worth more than the wand itself. The second realization was that this book was of even far greater value, and although not many of them had identification classes or items to help them, the basic description of this book along with the way its aura pulsed through the room made things very obvious.

[The Prophets' Call (Holy Grimoire, Legendary Holy Relic): ???]

Brilliant white and gold inscriptions were written on the back, front, and spine of the hard silver cover. It was rather large, and magic literally danced around the object like a thin cloud of radiance. The book's presence was palpable, spreading warmth through the room like a cozy campfire on a cold winter's day, and many of the people there felt not only rejuvenated but energized just by looking at it.

"I believe this should suffice as reasonable compensation should I lose the bet," Allie said plainly, handing the book to Instructor Rose, who just gawked at the item. "Though I highly doubt I'll lose. I do believe that wand will look rather nice strapped at my hip."

Precilla's eyes were large, round with greed, and her fingers twitched while almost reaching out across the room as if to take the book now. "What is an Unholy-based caster doing with such an item? That book is obviously not meant for you."

Allie grinned, remembering how she'd stripped it from Prophet's corpse. "Let's just say it was a gift. Now, are you going to stop gawking? Or do I need to wait?"

Turning back to glare at Allie despite the murmurings of admiration concerning the relic, Precilla nodded with a fire in her eyes. "Instructor Rose, please let us know when to proceed. I have a lowly country bumpkin to squash and a bet to win."

Instructor Rose, who'd been turning the book over in admiration, quickly cleared her throat and stepped back from the wall of mana that encompassed the two combatants. "Very well. Are you both ready to begin?"

Both women nodded. Allie remained silent, arms folded, while examining the protective bracelet meant for dueling, and Precilla took a casting stance with wand pointed in Allie's direction.

"Then BEGIN!"

Instructor Rose made a chopping motion with her hand, and Precilla immediately went on the offensive.

A blast of ice and snow similar to the one Lahn's tiny projectile had interrupted crossed the space between Precilla and Allie over the course of two seconds. Lahn took in a quick inhale of breath when he thought it was going to collide with Allie's face, only to let out a sigh of relief and shock when the ice magic shattered and dispersed.

Precilla blinked rapidly, not understanding what had happened, and she swung her arm around in the air dramatically for another casting. Ice yet again billowed out and shot Allie's way, only this time the rebuttal was more obvious.

Death mana, radiating out in waves of neon-teal and black energy, briefly pulsed from Allie's figure when she casually began to walk forward. The energy rebuffed the ice immediately, whipping forward and crushing the glacial magic in an instant.

"Is that an aura?" Braden Rooze asked one of his acquaintances in a shocked whisper. "How does someone at this level already have an aura?!"

Becoming enraged, Precilla conjured a different spell. This time, a spike of ice three fingers in diameter jutted out from the ground right behind Allie and ripped toward her left calf muscle.

Yet the same thing happened, and the ice shattered the moment it made contact with the aura surrounding Allie's figure.

"What kind of treachery is this?!" Precilla shrieked, trying yet again as Allie continued to approach casually.

The ice shattered for the fourth time, leaving Precilla in shock and building dismay. But things changed even more dramatically when Allie took out her own wand.

It was a thin instrument, longer than most other wands and created from black wood and ivory bone—with a very sharp end to it and jagged edges on one side akin to small vertebrae. She'd drawn the weapon from her spatial sack, and the moment it appeared, an overwhelming aura of dread overtook the entire room, similar to what the book had done. This aura was far more malicious, though, and it literally staggered not only Precilla but many of the watching nobles, too, with one of them even keeling over right there and then. It was as if their very souls had been humbled in the wand's presence.

The weapon hissed, and then it let out an ear-piercing shriek when Allie lifted it to point in Precilla's direction.

Lahn's jaw dropped as a billowing cloud of black and teal flames roared to life around Allie's wand-holding hand, then her arm. Her silky brown hair whipped backward with the explosion of power, and an uncharacteristic, malicious grin spread across her face as she laser-focused on Precilla in front of her.

The four walls of the containment field shuddered and cracked, and with another piercing scream from the wand in Allie's hand, dozens of flaming strings tore forward to attack the other caster.

Precilla screamed in horror and anguish as she was penetrated all across her body. Needlelike threads of death mana ripped open her skin along her abdomen, neck, face, arms, legs, and feet in a simultaneous flash of darkness. Precilla crumpled, seizing on the ground with dozens of burn marks as the attack immediately ceased. Her yellow dress was utterly destroyed.

The classroom remained silent aside from the calm footsteps of Allie's boots. She came to stand over the seizing girl with a look of utter disgust, bent down, and ripped the diamond-studded wand out of Precilla's hand.

"Oh my! How pathetic!" Allie said with a giggle, a hand daintily covering her mouth, her malicious intent having gone as quickly as it had come. She attached the diamond-studded wand to her hip, nodded in approval as she spun around, and then walked over to the barrier wall between her and Instructor Rose. Allie tapped the mana barrier with a finger just once, and the magical construct the instructors had created shattered into a million pieces, drifting away into the air. Taking the Holy relic out of Instructor Rose's hands, she turned heel and sauntered over to where Lahn was gawking. "I think I'm over this class today. How about we go get some food? I'm hungry!"

Braden Rooze was quick on the uptake, nudging past another admirer and putting his handsome self at Lahn's side. "I would be glad to accompany you for another meal in his stead if you don't mind, Lady Wraithtide! Your display was quite remarkable, and I do believe I'd like to continue the conversation from earlier!"

Braden put a hand forward and touched Allie's lower back, a little thing but something with tremendous weight behind the gesture. Lahn didn't fail to notice it, and his eyes faltered, but he was surprised when Allie took a step away from Braden with raised eyebrows.

"My dear sir," Allie said with a soft smile, tsking at him and removing his hand. "Don't get so frisky. I'm not spoken for yet, but that doesn't mean you're the man to do the job."

She turned back to Lahn, smiled, and then knelt. "You ready to go? I have some stuff I want to talk to you about, and we can practice together in a more private setting in the colosseum later!"

Lahn gulped and nodded, watching as some of Precilla's friends helped her back up and carried her out of the room toward the medical bay. "Yes, I'd love to go! But don't you want to stay and keep practicing?"

The question was absurd after what he'd just witnessed. He and everyone else there knew it, but he couldn't help but ask. He felt obligated to do so out of respect for Instructor Rose despite Allie's utter display of dominance. It was obvious that she didn't need to be here, and she was likely only here—if Lahn had to guess—for political connections.

But if that was the case, then why had she chosen him? He was a nobody. Maybe she wanted to connect with his family?

"I'm fine, and I'd much rather have a scone," Allie mused with another light-hearted laugh, coming around to Lahn's back and beginning to push him forward out of the room. "I actually only came today so that I could meet up with you and then leave. I'm very much wanting to try those new cream cheese dumplings, too . . . or the candied apples. This place has all sorts of tasty treats, and I haven't experienced even half of them yet!"

CHAPTER 10

The food courts at the academy were truly something to behold. There was one in the east and one in the west. Allie had chosen to take them to the eastern plaza.

"There's someone I'd like you to meet!" Allie exclaimed excitedly while rolling Lahn down the cobblestone pathways lined in marble that'd been swept free of snow. "I'm stoked!"

Lahn looked back over his shoulder and gave an interested smirk. "I'm not too sure anyone would be all that excited to meet me, but I'll do my best to give a good impression for whoever it is."

Allie only rolled her eyes.

Coming up to one of the restaurants, where two butlers and a maid in very fancy uniforms greeted them, Allie stopped when they gave her a bow. The entrance was created from elegant crystal, the floors were made of polished wood lined with gold, and it had to be the gaudiest place Lahn had ever seen.

"My lady, my lord. We've been expecting you." The foremost butler gave another low bow, then gestured them inside.

Lahn looked over his shoulder again. "They were expecting us? What exactly is this place?"

"You don't get out much, do you?" Allie asked with a chuckle, following the man inside, where numerous flowering plants were in full bloom and illusionary butterflies soared through the air. There was even an artificial sun overhead, burning with a dull warmth in the main lobby, which had a glittering pool underneath filled with multicolored fish—and it was surrounded by numerous tables on the bottom and top floors of the two-story establishment.

Lahn gawked, looking around and seeing numerous high-profile people he'd seen his father talk to in the past at house parties—though Lahn had never once been introduced to them himself. Still, he got recognizing glances from time to time due to his unique look, and even one wave from a high-ranking general who oversaw the recruitment of new officers into their military from this very academy.

"What is this place?" Lahn repeated as they circled around, following the butler into a secluded hallway that led to a double door twice the size of a normal man on either side. Two soldiers in heavy plate armor bearing the king's sun sigil on their breastplates stood at attention on either side of the hallway, but they shifted at Allie's approach to open the doors and let her in.

Inside, in a private room, sweet aromas lingered in the air, an artificial sky overhead was bright blue and dotted with clouds, more illusionary butterflies permeated the air here as well—and there were at least a dozen different servants all wearing butler and maid uniforms standing along the walls. Three personal chefs were cooking food in front of another group of feasting onlookers that included two men and a woman.

The first man was familiar to Lahn. He had red hair, a short, neatly trimmed beard, and a wide, happy expression, and he was laughing alongside the other man while downing a swig of very expensive alcohol from a golden bottle. The redheaded man was burly, roughly mannered, yet wore exquisite clothing with the king's sigil on the front of his shirt as well.

The second man was very pale, extremely good-looking, and wore a basic black combat robe, and Lahn could immediately guess at who he was. He had to be a relative of Allie's, possibly even a brother, because he had the same striking blue eyes and the same strange amulet around his neck that she did.

The last person at the table was also extremely pretty—even giving Allie a run for her money in the looks department. She was blonde, fit, wearing a striking silver dress, and had proportional curves and a nearly perfect face. Lahn couldn't see a single blemish on her, and she had both hands wrapped around the second man's hand.

"Lady Allie Wraithtide!" the first man called out with a wide grin, beckoning her to come join them at the square table and motioning at a servant.

Immediately one of the servants pulled out a chair, but they hesitated when they saw Lahn.

"I'll be sitting next to him," Allie stated simply with a gentle nod, and she pushed the chair over a tad in order to make room for Lahn. Putting Lahn's wheelchair in place and pulling the chair back behind her, she slumped down and immediately started picking at some of the exquisite fruit displays that'd been thoroughly decorated with chocolate. "Hello, Your Majesty. How are you this afternoon?"

"I'm quite well!" the bearded man said with a hearty laugh, slapping the pale relative of Allie's on the shoulder as they smiled at one another. "Especially since getting to know this fine young man. Your brother is quite the guy!"

Lahn's heart immediately dropped into his gut as he realized just who the first man was. This was the king, King Arthur Brix, the man who'd sat on the throne of Dawn for well over two centuries now. He didn't look a day past forty, and Lahn had a very faint memory of meeting him once as a child at a palace party.

Lahn stuttered when the king's eyes rested on him, and he attempted to wheel himself out for kneeling and bowing as was proper—but he was immediately stopped by Allie as she firmly caught his wrist.

"You're fine. This is a private meeting, so there is no need for formality. Right, Your Majesty?" Allie stated with a look of intent to Lahn, glancing over at the king.

"She's right," King Brix said with a grin, then gestured to Lahn's chair. "I remember you. You're that Lucio boy, the second son. Is that correct? Your father is a close friend of mine."

Lahn's eyes went wide, and he immediately caught a lump in his throat. Clearing his head, he took in a deep breath and nodded mechanically just once. "Yes, Your Majesty. I am sorry for my improper attire. I was not aware that I'd be meeting you today!"

He shot a glare at Allie, who just smirked back and teasingly poked his ribs.

King Brix watched the interaction with interest, though he feigned ignorance when Lahn's gaze returned to him and downed more of the alcohol. Passing another entire bottle of the gold liquid over to the second man and the woman, who were still holding hands, he gestured to them next. "Have you both met Mr. Lucio yet? Or is this your first time?"

"Travis Wraithtide," the second man said, extending a hand to introduce himself with a warm smile of his own. He shook Lahn's hand, then pulled it back to look at the woman as she held his other one.

She only looked back, blinking rapidly and then furrowing her brow in confusion.

"You can let go of my hand now. I promise it'll be here when you're done introducing yourself," Travis stated, amusement creeping onto his lips as she immediately flushed a bright red.

"Sorry!" the woman said as she extended her hand out rather aggressively to shake Lahn's own a second later. "My name is Fay Wraithtide! Er—not Wraithtide, just Fay!"

The admission of her last name caused her to blush an even deeper red. Her eyes went wide, and she squeaked something inaudible under her breath as Allie and Travis both laughed loudly.

"This is my brother," Allie said, pointing to Travis. "He's kind of a knucklehead, but I love him. This is his new . . . friend? Girlfriend?"

Allie raised an eyebrow in question, and Fay covered her face with both hands while groaning.

"I've been giving her shit about that all day," Travis said, pouring himself fine wine out of the bottle and into a crystal glass. "Apparently she'd rather just be my ho."

"That is NOT what I said!" Fay reprimanded him, slapping his thigh and getting an "OW!" from Travis. "I SAID that I just need time to think about how I can avoid ASSASSINATION from competitors if I'm dating you!"

"That is definitely not what she said," Travis mused, swirling the wine in his glass and sipping at it while staring back at Fay—who only glowered back at him in an unsaid threat. "Honestly, I don't think she knows what she wants."

"Travis! Stop it, that isn't true!"

"I do believe it is."

Allie and the king exchanged looks.

"Is this how it's been since he got here?" Allie asked King Brix rather curiously, giving Lahn a comforting nudge when she realized he'd gone nearly as pale as she was.

The king smirked, nodded, and made room for a freshly cooked plate of food—venison slathered in hot butter, steaming vegetables decorating a half sphere of mashed potato, and finely cut fruits surrounding a cylindrical tower of ice cream. "Yes, that's how it's been since they got here. Riv—*Ahem*. I mean, Travis has been telling me all about how he and Fay went on their very first date, only for her to not want to really date him. It's been quite a . . . what was it you called it? A soap opera?"

"That is not how it is!" Fay exclaimed, clamping onto Travis's hand so hard that her knuckles turned white. Tears were welling up under her eyes and her lips were pouting. It looked very much to Lahn like she was going to cry. "It was just a misunderstanding and I'm worried! Stop teasing me; this isn't funny!"

Allie side-eyed the blonde woman, shrugged, then pointed to the king's plate as she got one of her own set in front of her. "These are quite interesting first courses."

"Travis told me you were more informal and that dessert always comes first with the meal. Is that not true?" King Brix asked curiously, only to get a smirking laugh from Travis a moment later.

Allie sputtered her own laugh and shook her head, sighing dramatically and leaning over to put an elbow on Lahn's shoulder. "My brother has always eaten dessert at the exact same time as the normal meals. It's weird."

"You can't dip your sausage-egg muffins in ice cream if you don't have the ice cream with the muffins!" Travis chided Allie from across the table, getting a scoff of disgust from one of the chefs and laughter from another. Travis then pointed to the chef who'd scoffed. "And you stop giving me attitude, Jerrard! I've had enough of your shit for one night! I eat as I please!"

This time the entire room, with the exception of the man who'd been singled out, erupted into laughter, including the king and all the servants. The rather thin chef who'd been called out muttered something under his breath after that. "No self-respecting person would dip sausages, eggs, or muffins in ice cream. It is a disgrace."

Travis belched in the king's presence, to Lahn's horror, and he got up while gesturing to a back hallway. "I'm going to hit the restroom. I'll be back in a bit."

"Take your time!" King Brix said with a chuckle, watching Travis go until he disappeared—then turning around to face Allie. "I do believe I very much like him. Reminds me of one of my sons. Certainly not what I expected."

Lahn's brain was still trying to catch up to the present. Just who were these people? Who was Allie truly affiliated with, in order to get a seat here so informally with the king of Dawn? Was their family somehow related? Were their parents childhood friends of the king? Why was he, Lahn, an absolute nobody, invited to this luncheon? His mother might congratulate him for finding a way here, but his father and his siblings would have had heart attacks thinking about how many different ways Lahn would bring disgrace to the family name at such an important social event.

All eyes at the table turned to Fay when she let out another low groan, putting her elbows on the table like no proper lady would do, and swept her hair back to stare at the food that'd just been placed in front of her. "I screwed up that date so badly."

There was a pause.

Then Allie took the bait. "Why? What happened?"

Looking over her shoulder to make sure Travis wasn't back yet, Fay smacked herself upside the forehead in a form of self-punishment.

"I don't think that's healthy," Lahn said, worried. "Are you okay?"

"I'm anything but okay!" Fay muttered. Then, raising her eyes to Allie, she let out a long sigh. "Allie, I know we don't know each other very well, but I need your help. The date was just . . . perfect, until I screwed it up."

"Yes, but you haven't said what you did . . ." Allie muttered with furrowed brows and steepled fingers. "He doesn't seem upset . . . What did you do?"

Fay glared up at Allie from underneath the hands supporting her forehead. "The very short version is that I told him I didn't want to be his girlfriend publicly, because I'm afraid someone like Kathrine would eventually assassinate me to get me out of the way. When I tried to tell him why, I could tell he got upset even if he didn't say it . . . and then I brought up . . . the other girl he's close with."

"Why would you be assassinated just for dating someone?" Lahn asked hesitantly, getting looks from the others but no outright answer.

Fay turned to Allie again. "I talked about how the other woman . . . she's coming back, and that she'd be angry if I went ahead and took Travis for myself."

"But do you want Travis for yourself?" Allie asked curiously, putting her chin on her hands with a confused stare.

"Of course I do!" Fay hissed in irritation, throwing up hands to either side as the king chuckled and continued to drink and pick at his venison. "That's the problem! He's a very important person, and if I'm seen as an obstacle, I'm as good as dead! Not necessarily by that other particular person, but by ANYONE in the future who sees him as an opportunity! So I told him he should also court other girls; that way I wouldn't be a target!"

Allie's eyes rose in shock, and she frowned a little more deeply than she had been. "You don't think Travis could protect you?"

Fay huffed, looking rather conflicted as her eyes darted back and forth, and then she hung her head. "I don't know. I'd hope so, but the kind of people he's going to be mixed up with are far beyond what you two can manage right now. It'd be safer for everyone if I remained a background character. But I don't want to be a background character!"

Lahn's brow furrowed. If they knew the king to talk with him so informally, couldn't they just ask him to help with potential assassins somehow? Surely that would be the case.

Allie churned over the information bit by bit, putting the pieces of the puzzle together while twirling a fork in her right hand. "What I'm getting out of it is you're upset that you want Travis for yourself but believe you can't realistically or safely have it that way. Yet, you're the one pushing the agenda of remaining a background character, and not being his actual girlfriend—or the woman he is 'courting'—from an official point of view. Because you're afraid of being killed, and because you're afraid of hurting that other particular woman's feelings when she returns from . . . her extended vacation."

"Exactly!"

"I'm still confused," Allie said bluntly. "Is Travis truly upset about this, too, then?"

Fay growled under her breath, fingers clenching the wooden table in a viselike grip. "The problem is that I don't actually WANT him to see other girls because I WANT him for myself! But I'm scared. And when I told him as much, he took it to mean that I am not interested in dating him but rather am just wanting him for other reasons."

"Like?"

"I don't know! But I could immediately tell that he was put off by the idea! At first I'd thought letting him see other women while also dating me would be something any normal man would want!"

The king raised a toast to that. "Hear, hear."

Fay ignored the king despite a snickering laugh from Allie. "But instead, Riv—um, Travis gave me a speech about how he's wanting to find a soul mate! And that it might not be me, because we want different things! But I DO want only him and I want him to only want me, and I think that he doesn't want me anymore because he doesn't think I want him the same way! I WAS JUST SCARED AND THOUGHT HE'D WANT TO BE WITH OTHER GIRLS WHILE DATING ME, TOO!"

The very end of her admission went up an entire octave as she covered her mouth with both hands and let out a squeal of despair, tears starting to stream down her cheeks while the king tried to hide his amusement across the table.

Meanwhile, Allie just stared flatly back at the succubus with a puzzled expression—as the king outright laughed.

"THIS ISN'T FUNNY!" Fay screamed before hiding her face in her hands again and letting out a sob. "I'm genuinely upset!"

"Fay, you're overthinking things." Giving Fay a pitying look, Allie noticed "Travis" was standing in the hallway now, listening to their conversation while leaning against the wall with a soft expression directed at Fay's back.

Clearing her throat, Allie then touched Fay's arm and urged her to look up. "Hey. Perhaps instead of spilling this to us, you should just talk to him about it again to clear the air."

"Ah, to be young," King Brix stated before munching on some chocolate-covered fruit. "But yes, I do believe the topic of conversation has arrived."

"Travis" had taken Fay to the back, where they could have a private conversation after her emotional breakdown, leaving Allie, King Brix, and a very nervous Lahn to eat on their own.

Lahn's hand trembled slightly, still very nervous that he would do something stupid in front of their kingdom's legendary leader, but Allie was speaking to King Brix almost as an equal. As if they were even friends to some extent, though Lahn knew that couldn't be the case. No, there was something more to this odd scenario that he just hadn't grasped yet.

But his thoughts were snapped out of his trancelike state when he heard his name brought up.

"So Lahn is the one you're bringing to the royal ball?" King Brix asked, intrigued, as he leaned back in his chair to reevaluate the crippled young man across the slew of food and drink. "Very . . . very interesting. I'm sure that his father will be proud to know he's attending such a grand event after all, especially with such an esteemed guest."

Lahn's face twitched with confusion. "Did you say royal ball?"

He turned to look at Allie, who was smiling fondly back at him, her chin resting on two hands.

"That's what he said," Allie replied with a wink. "As long as you're up for it. I hear that the rest of your family is already invited, so you'll know at least a few of the people there."

CHAPTER 11

King Brix stood on the balcony of the academy's finest restaurant, watching the four younger people depart through snow-swept streets while loudly talking about some kind of prank Riven had once pulled on Allie when she was young. He stroked his short red beard with mild amounts of curiosity and chuckled as he thought about the recent luncheon. "Certainly not what I expected of the rank-five vampire on our world roster. Wouldn't you agree, Kassius?"

Kassius, the king's spymaster, unhinged himself from a nearby shadow and took human form, warping from obscurity into the light of day. He wore a black outfit, a veiled mask, and his face was completely hidden as he clasped his gloved hands behind his back. "Yes, Your Majesty. I can honestly even say that, as long as he's wearing that amulet you provided him, he's very likable. It really is a shame that he has such a high negative Charisma—one day he'll need something much stronger than your gift to hide among the human masses in order not to scare them half to death just by walking by."

"Isn't that the truth!" King Brix bellowed a laugh and slapped Kassius on the back. "He was downright scary when we first met him!"

"Do you think it is wise to let him travel our city alone, though?" Kassius muttered absentmindedly, following the group of four until they passed out of sight around a bend in the road—heading toward the barracks. "I may like his character when it was set to neutral, but he did murder an entire city in order to bring one of his demons back. Half a million souls or more, by current estimates, were wiped out in the blink of an eye. We don't want that to happen here should he become enraged for some reason."

King Brix raised one eyebrow and side-eyed the slender man. Folding his arms over the sun crest on his tunic, King Brix gave a loud humph. "And what would be the alternative? Following him would let him know that we don't trust him, should he find out. No, I do believe it is better to make friends and to not give him or his sister reasons to distrust us. Without their help, we very well could have fallen to the Tereen and their blasted spirit saints by now. Who knows, maybe I'll even be able to pawn off one of my daughters or granddaughters to him as a bride. And if not . . . perhaps that Lucio boy will surprise us concerning Allie. I would find it hard to believe from an outside perspective, but there's always hope."

"You hope to make ties by blood?"

"Oh yes. Whether or not that can be done is to be seen, but I have very high hopes. Not many civilizations will survive this integration, Kassius, but some will rise from the ashes at the end. I intend ours to be one of them, and those two vampire siblings would be a great set of allies to have on our side in the long run—not just for this war with the elves."

Of Mandon's ten city levels, each spanning over a hundred miles of stacked earth, the top seven were aboveground and three existed underground. They were labeled by the populace as Lower Three through Lower One and Upper One through Upper Seven. The lower the floor, the poorer the citizens usually were—so here on the highest level it was a given that most of the most expensive items Dawn's capital city had to offer could be found.

"'Drak's Magical Emporium, the place where all your wondering wizardful whims come true,'" Travis read with a doubtful expression cast over his shoulder while standing in front of the large three-story building. "We'll see about that."

Fay tugged him inside the large, bustling, upper-floor shop with a loud giggle, passing many gawking well-dressed customers who stared at any one of the three abnormally attractive people with what appeared to be mixed emotions. "Come on! You said you'd start a magical tinkering with me! You need to teach me all about totems and runes and how to make them. Even Allie said she'd help with the soul imbuement!"

"Oh, don't do that, you know I'm only barely experienced!" Travis chuckled and motioned to Lahn. "Don't let her make you think I'm any kind of pro. I'm barely a beginner."

Grinning and leaning forward to kiss Fay in the doorway, he let the beautiful blonde woman in her silver dress pull him through and followed her toward a series of displays that had various gadgets lined up for sale.

Pushing Lahn inside, Allie followed them, the wheels of Lahn's wheelchair bumping over the doorframe's bottom ledge. "Doing okay, Lahn? You look down!"

From where he sat in front of her, Lahn's mind was indeed in darker places than normal. He couldn't pinpoint exactly what it was . . . but should he need to say it out loud, it was probably a mixture of a couple things.

Here he was, having one of the best days of his life up until his sudden epiphany. He'd had Allie stand up for him in class—beating Precilla handily in a restricted duel. He'd gone out on what was almost—at least in his mind—a luncheon date with one of the most, if not the absolute most, beautiful girl in the entire academy, and she'd picked him over none other than the class stud, Braden Rooze. Lahn had then been taken to one of the most expensive restaurants on academy grounds, which was abnormal for him because his father and siblings didn't want to be seen with him in public—yet he'd gotten to meet the king and talk to him on a very personal level. Then Allie had asked him to come along on a double date.

She'd literally called it that.

"Come on, Lahn!" Allie had said with the most beautiful smile, teasing him with a jab at his rib cage again while looking down at his crippled form. "My brother and his new *girlfriend* are going shopping. Let's make it a double date! You should come with me as I tag along! It'll be fun! Who needs class anyways, right?!"

He'd been so shocked and so excited to hear her say those words that he'd nearly fallen out of his wheelchair. But now, after thinking things over, he was sure this was just Allie being nice or trying to get into touch with the rest of his family. There was little to no chance that she, realistically, was interested in someone like him. So Lahn dwelled and stewed internally, wondering if it was his father's connections or his brother's inheritance that she was after. He wondered just when this daydream was going to end, how it was going to end, and how harshly the disappointment of losing his only friend would affect him when this window into a happier life collapsed around him.

Leaving Lahn alone once more.

"I'm fine!" Lahn said with a fake smile, but it was the best he could muster given his current state of mind, and he cleared his throat while redirecting attention from himself to a couple of stone engravings on slates to their left, each square in shape and about two by two feet in size. "Those are some good models to use for runecrafting if your brother is interested. They're beginner's guides, and there's even an Unholy type! Maybe we should grab it for him?! Hopefully it's not too expensive . . ."

For a moment, Allie came around to his side to scrutinize him suspiciously, but she eventually nodded and pushed him forward to where the stone tablets were located. Pushing some of the square stone slabs aside and grabbing the one that Lahn had pointed out, Allie placed it in his lap and let her fingers trail over his withered left hand with a light touch that made him quiver. "Nice find, Lahn. He'll definitely like it. Now, as we continue to browse . . . tell me about this little animal sanctuary you're working on."

Lahn blanched, then looked up in shocked surprise while clutching the stone slab in his good hand. "How do you know about the animal sanctuary?! No one knows about that!"

Allie's mischievous grin quirked at the side of her mouth. "I have my ways."

"Are you spying on me?!"

". . . perhaps." Allie chuckled low and wickedly, rubbing her hands together theatrically while Lahn caught his breath.

How had Allie known about his animal sanctuary?

The very first day they'd met, when Lahn had seen her at the pond in the gardens beyond the academy, he had actually been traveling between his sanctuary and the school's inner grounds. He went once a day with his maid, or even sometimes by himself, bringing a bag of food for the animals he picked up on the lower levels.

Going from pale to a bright pink, Lahn felt his ears grow hot as deep embarrassment set in. "Do I really have to talk about it? I know it's peasant, feminine work and I don't like the idea of being made fun of by you, too."

Allie's expression went from teasing to shocked. "Peasant work? Feminine? Lahn, creating a secret animal sanctuary is one of the cutest, most adorable things I've ever heard of! Are you kidding me?! Who on earth bad-mouthed you for it like that?!"

Lahn's brows furrowed, and he gave Allie a curious once-over. "Who on earth? That's an odd expression. But it was my brother, Parius Lucio, and my father, Lord Nikola Lucio, who told me so. I had another animal sanctuary back home, because animals . . . they're kind. They're innocent. Especially dogs, and they made me happy to work with."

Lahn's face fell into a soft, contemplative smile, finally feeling himself lose the hard edge he'd had concerning doubtful thoughts on Allie's intentions. "I, um, go down to the poorer floors of Mandon. The capital's lower levels are very thick with stray dogs, so I pick up the ones I can and bring them back to take care of them. I got permission from Zefima, the archmage of the academy, to keep them far out in the gardens in a gated area I made. It was very nice of her . . . and it makes me happy. Before you came along, I had no friends, and the dogs were the only company I had."

There was a pause as Allie digested this information. The voice of her brother cut in from behind Lahn as Travis walked around to stand at her side.

"I personally like dogs more than most humans," Travis said with a nod of approval. "I totally get it. Would you like help taking care of them?"

Allie's eyes brightened, and she gave Travis a warm smile—continuing to stare at his feet.

But then Lahn's head snapped up, as if struck, and he stared back at both Travis and Allie with curious surprise. "You want to help me? You want to help take care of stray animals?"

Allie nodded enthusiastically, clasping her hands together in front of her and leaning into Travis with a nudge. "Absolutely! That sounds so fun!"

"But you're not afraid to be made fun of for doing peasant work?"

"Since when is taking care of sick and homeless animals peasant work?"

Lahn's face grew doubtful. "It's always been peasant work. Nobles don't do that kind of thing."

"You do," Allie protested with a humph, folding her arms in front of her.

Lahn's face fell, and he let out a deep chuckle, shaking his head. "I am not what you would call normal, and I'm only barely nobility. I'm sure that if it weren't for my loving mother, my father would have cast me out into an orphanage. I am nothing like the rest."

Another customer, a plump man sporting a large mustache, a cane, and a top hat that looked like he'd been dragged out of a Victorian steampunk magazine, snorted loudly at them while tapping his cane on the floor. His voice was high-pitched and nasally, and he had two servant girls far younger than he was carrying books, manuscripts, and various odds or ends that were obviously quite heavy. "You four! You four right there! Move yourselves so that I may pass through! You are taking up the entire aisle!"

Slowly, Travis and Allie looked over to glare at the man. The aisle was only halfway filled, with more than enough room for him to get through, and the two vampires wordlessly shared a look before Travis stepped around to confront the man.

"No, it was easily big enough for you to go around," Travis stated, stepping up to widen his stance, towering over the man with the cane, who took a step back at his approach. "You see where I am now? This is me taking up the entire aisle. Go the fuck around."

Lahn's eyebrows raised in surprise. He was very much nonconfrontational—he hated confrontations—and yet Allie had confronted Precilla earlier that day and Travis was confronting this man he didn't even know in the store like they were made of toughened steel. Both of these siblings truly had guts, because Lahn would have just cowed and moved without a word.

The man with the mustache sputtered something unintelligible, then picked up his cane and menacingly jabbed it into Travis's gut. "I daresay! You should know when to respect your—"

Travis whipped his hand forward with a blur so fast that Lahn couldn't even follow the motion, ripping the cane out of the man's grasp and snapping it in half before tossing it to the ground before the man with the top hat could blink.

A few eyes from around the store settled on the scene, silently watching the standoff, until the man with the top hat grew redder in the face and lost his nerve. Shaking, with balled-up fists, he stormed out of the establishment and into the street—losing himself with his servants among the high-class crowds in this section of the market.

After that the mood quickly went back to normal, and the shopkeeper at the front desk let out an audible sigh of relief.

"Travis . . ." Lahn asked hesitantly when Allie's brother came back from kicking the pieces of cane out the door. "You've seen combat. Haven't you?"

"What makes you say that?" Travis asked curiously, stuffing his hands into the pockets of his black combat robe. Then he looked down at his outfit and chuckled.

"Are you a warrior?" Lahn pressed, even more curious now. "Do you serve in the army?"

". . . you could say that." Travis waved up at Fay, who was rummaging through bookshelves on the second level near a balcony railing, and she blew him a kiss while scurrying around trying to collect things that they could use for practicing runecraft. "God, she's so pretty."

"GAG!" Allie gasped, poking a finger into her throat and making a vomiting noise, to the laughter of both Travis and Lahn. "Ooh, god, you're gonna make me puke!"

From the stairway leading up to the second level, a familiar voice called out to Lahn—one he hadn't heard in quite a while now but one that he instantly recognized. "Lahn?! Is that you?!"

As he turned his wheelchair with his good arm, his heart sank and he felt like he wanted to crawl under a rock. There at the bottom of the stairs stood not one but two people he knew. One of them he knew very well, and the other he'd only met in passing once, when his mother had tried to set him up with a potential lady of the court to wed.

The voice that'd called out to him was none other than Marsia Bortrost, daughter of Lord Armando and Lady Niltini Bortrost—friends of his mother. Marsia had been brought over via carriage to specifically meet him at the bidding of both their parents, only for her to—in private and not so nicely—tell him that she was by no means interested in even pretending to court him.

Marsia, a woman of nineteen years of age, was in her prime years to get married to another of the court. She wasn't spectacular to look at for most people, but she certainly wasn't ugly, with brown hair and large dimples just like her parents. She wore a bright-green dress. And she stood with a shocked expression right beside Lahn's older sister, Linela Lucio.

His sister was quite pretty, from what Gleetus often said about her when rubbing salt into the wounds he inflicted any time that asshole interacted with Lahn. And honestly Lahn couldn't disagree. Linela was blonde, unlike Lahn's own chestnut hair, and she was tall with a thin but very symmetrical frame. She was wearing a similar green dress to match Marsia, and they had three manservants in suits following a few paces behind to carry their luggage.

Linela remained quiet, with her dainty hands clasped in front of her lower waist just like Marsia, but she wore an equally surprised expression to that of Marsia while quietly evaluating both Lahn and the company he held.

"Lahn, is that you?!" Marsia eventually said again, stepping forward with perfect posture—her brunette hair pulled up in a bun while her high heels clicked against the polished floor. "I didn't realize you'd hired new help!"

Allie and Travis shared a glance, then they both burst into laughter—clearly amused at the obvious probe for information concerning who they were.

"They are not hired help . . ." Lahn said in an exasperated tone, letting out a deep sigh and already dreading this interaction. "This is Lady Allie Wraithtide and her brother, Lord Travis Wraithtide. They're nobility as well, and Allie attends the academy, too. She's in my classes—that's how we met."

"Who's that?" Allie asked, casually resting a hand on one hip and giving Marsia an unconcerned glare upon seeing Lahn's cringing reaction to the women's presence. "Friend of yours?"

"Family friend," Lahn muttered, then he gestured with his good hand to Linela. "That's my sister, Linela."

Linela curtsied, then took the opportunity to join the others while giving Travis a once-over. "I didn't realize Lahn kept such good company. Usually he is found mingling with the lower class. Are you attending the academy, too? I daresay I would have noticed someone like you. Your features are quite striking."

Lahn inwardly cringed again at the flirtatious jab oriented toward Travis, as well as the fluttering eyelashes his sister gave Allie's brother. "He doesn't attend—"

"I wasn't speaking to you, Lahn." Linela quickly cut him off with a scornful glare, then returned a flirtatious smile on Travis again. "Let Lord Wraithtide speak for himself."

Travis's eyelids dropped slightly, unamused by the interaction. "As Lahn was about to say, I do not attend the academy."

"Then what is it you do? Are you running a family estate of some sort? What exactly does your family oversee since the integration began? I assume you're one of the newly risen nobles, after the political landscape was oh so rearranged given the merging of worlds?" Linela took another step forward, a little close for comfort, to get a better look at him. "You smell wonderful, by the way."

Lahn could almost hear Allie's cringe to match his own, but it got even worse when Marsia did the same.

"He does smell good!" Marsia exclaimed happily, almost pushing herself past Lahn's wheelchair in order to get in close. "We saw your interaction with that snob from earlier. You were quite fast! Are you a soldier?! Have you fought in the war?"

"My father, the esteemed Lord Nikola Lucio, is on the front lines," Lahn's sister Linela exclaimed with a proudly puffed chest, head held high. "He's an A-ranker. Perhaps you have heard of him?"

CHAPTER 12

"I . . . have heard of your father," Riven replied slowly. He hadn't heard GOOD things about Linela's father, but he was also Lahn's father—and he didn't want to overstep by saying something rude. "A-ranker, huh . . . That's . . . impressive."

Linela beamed with pride and smoothed the front of her green dress to try and emphasize her curves. "Indeed it is. He's even a personal friend of the king, believe it or not. Not meaning to brag, of course, but I have even had the opportunity to personally deliver the king a letter—and he acknowledged my family's house name in passing. So we ARE known to him!"

Linela let out a proud humph and her chin raised even higher.

"You . . . delivered a letter . . . to the king?" Riven replied, a little dumbfounded and not sure if this was supposed to be impressive. "That's very . . ."

"Honorable, I know." Linela smiled brightly and flipped her blonde hair out to the side. "My little brother, Lahn, probably wouldn't know this because he is unable to attend such events, but my father was even given tokens to attend the upcoming royal ball next month. If you'd like, I could extend you an invitation . . ."

She let the words trail off, waiting for the expected reaction of shock and awe to set in. Instead, she got something else entirely. And not from Riven, or "Travis," but rather from Allie.

"Why isn't Lahn able to attend?" Allie asked, confused and more than a little irritated.

Linela frowned, barely cast Lahn a glance in his wheelchair, and raised an eyebrow. "Isn't it obvious? He's a cripple—and a cursed one at that. How is he supposed to dance and mingle in the crowd when half his body is afflicted with some kind of obscure, damnable rot? I do truly feel bad for him, but we aren't allowed to bring our own servants into the royal palace and none of us real family members can spare the time to babysit him."

Lahn's face fell, but he remained silent.

Allie was torn. Torn because she wanted to violently kill the dumb bitch for being so mean, and because she wasn't sure if killing his sister would upset Lahn. She also wasn't sure if telling Linela about her own invitation to Lahn as a date to the ball would be met with further problems for him, so she merely scowled and kept silent.

"I know you must feel bad. I used to as well," Linela said with a fake pout and a tut. "But Lahn here has a different path in life. If I could change it, I would. But I can't, so why bring shame to the family name by dragging him out in public? It would only lead to embarrassment for him anyways. Better he become a librarian or something like that instead of dealing with the politics of the noble houses or war efforts against the Tereen. Since you're at the academy yourself, I can assume you're also interested in either political or military aspirations, so be honest with yourself. Do you ever see Lahn fighting on the front lines against the elves when he can't even walk properly?"

Both Wraithtide siblings remained silent, and Linela took this as the go-ahead for her to continue—and that they agreed. "The only reason he's here is because Mother has a soft spot for him. We all know it, and we all know it's a massive waste of time. Father was furious about the entire ordeal, and it took weeks of Mother arguing with him in order to even let him leave the house, much less attend the academy. I'm sure she spent many a night on her knees in order to woo Father so he'd do as she asked."

She let out a dramatic sigh and rolled her eyes at that last statement, to which Lahn got visibly angry. Shaking in his chair and face flushed red, he pointed his one good hand up at his older sister with a wavery voice.

"Don't you dare talk about Mother like that!" Lahn hissed. "She's your mother, too!"

Linela hummed with amusement, hands clasped in front of her while other high-class people in the shop continued to move around them while browsing. "Truly, she is. Though I do believe you're misinterpreting my intentions when concerning Mother. That woman is a true master of manipulation and seduction when it comes to Father, one I aspire to be like."

Linela gave Travis a wink and let her eyes linger on his. "So what do you think? Would you like to attend the royal ball with me or not? Do not dawdle—it would be a great opportunity for connections, and I will only extend the invitation once."

Marsia Bortrost, the young woman who'd shunned Lahn all those months ago at the Lucio compound, did not like being put on the back burner. Even if it was by her friend and peer Linela. "Linela—I do believe you have already offered your accompanying spot to Lord Bortrude's son, did you not? Perhaps Lord Wraithtide should go with me instead, as I have not given my extra token away yet."

Linela shot Marsia a look that could kill, and her fingers tightened around one another with venom clear in her words. "Lord Bortrude the Second will have his offer retracted if Lord Wraithtide so wishes, as it was mere charity that allowed my initial exchange in the first place."

"Is that so?" Marsia asked plainly, ignoring Linela's frown and pushing farther into Travis's personal space to pull out an invitation. "Well, it just so happens that I have my extra invitational spot with me. Do you have yours?"

Linela froze, and centered a building stormy glare on her peer while her eyes darkened. "I happen to have left it at home."

Travis remained unconcerned, his hands stuffed in his pockets. "I already have an invitation."

Both women turned immediately, shocked into forgetting their brief squabble.

"You have an invitation to the king's ball already?" Linela pressed with a frown. "I've never even heard of your house before. How would a small house such as yours gain such a boon?"

In response, Riven pulled out a letter with the king's seal. Opening it and letting them read it for themselves for only a few seconds, he ripped it out of Linela's grip when she reached for it and stuffed the letter back into his pocket. "My sister and I will both be attending."

"How . . ." Marsia began, but she was cut off by Linela, who beamed at the opportunity to deny Marsia a win.

"Then perhaps we can both plan to meet there!" Linela stated with a wide smile, pushing past Marsia and getting up right next to Travis, who now had his back pressed to a shelf with arms folded. "I'd love to show you around! As a newcomer to the political ambitions of the kingdom, I'd be a lot of help navigating the social ladder—"

The sound of books and supplies crashing into the floor interrupted their chatter.

"TRAVIS?! Is that you?!" Fay's singsong voice called out from behind the manservants near the stairwell, and everyone turned their heads to watch as the succubus in disguise made her appearance.

She looked just like she had at the king's luncheon earlier that day: wearing the guise of a young blonde woman with extremely pretty features and wearing a formfitting silver dress that put both of the other girls attempting to woo Travis to shame. In truth, Fay looked almost exactly like she normally did, only that her skin color had gone from sky blue to a mild tan, her demonic features were missing, and her hair wasn't a bright silky white in her current state.

Coming over from where she'd dropped an entire armload of supplies she'd intended to use with "Travis" to learn runecrafting and totem making together, she completely ignored both of the other young women and even pushed between them. Wrapping her slender arms around Travis's neck, she planted a long, passionate, drawn-out kiss on his lips, to the shocked inhales of Linela and Marsia.

Allie only snickered in delight at their reactions.

"I've been looking all . . . over . . . for . . . you . . ." Fay said, booping him on the nose flirtatiously at every pause she made during her sentence. Again kissing him briefly with another peck, she turned to look at the two stunned ladies of the court with raised eyebrows—giving each of them a once-over and solidifying her spot next to Travis by wrapping her left arm around his waist. "Travis, have you been trying to pick up the local whores again? I've told you, no more prostitutes! EVEN IF THEY'RE PUSHY! You have me now and that should be enough."

Marsia gasped in horror and outrage, eyes wide at the sheer audacity this newcomer had in calling them both prostitutes—and Linela's eyes narrowed with a tightening grip along the lower seams of her dress.

"Did you just insinuate—" Linela began, but Fay cut her off with a loud giggle.

"Oh my, I'm sorry if I offended you two. I didn't mean it! You were both just pressing yourselves up against my man in the aisle and I assumed you were trying to sell yourselves." Fay rolled her eyes playfully, reached around to grope his ass—making Travis yelp in surprise while grinning dangerously back at Linela while maintaining eye contact. "Unfortunately this fine specimen is taken by someone better—**me**. Go along and find yourselves another man. For someone like you two—I'd suggest a pimp of some sort."

Marsia let out another exaggerated and shocked gasp of disgust. "HOW DARE YOU!"

"How dare you!!!" Fay repeated in a high-pitched and whiny voice while poofing out her cheeks, and she poked her fingers into the sides of her face, creating impromptu dimples that were far exaggerated from what Marsia had—but the point was taken. It was a mockery. Absolute mockery.

"MY WORD!" Marsia huffed, now red in the face and stamping down a heeled foot with trembling hands clasped in front of her in an attempt to maintain as much of a ladylike appearance as possible. "HOW IMMATURE!"

Linela looked from Travis to Fay, from Fay to Travis, and kept her frown to a thin-lipped look of discontent. "Is this one yours, Lord Wraithtide?"

Travis looked down at Fay, who suddenly became sheepish under his gaze—something that Linela definitely caught. Then he smiled warmly. "Yes. I am courting her."

"I see," Linela replied flatly, glaring back at Fay—who'd just become public enemy number one. "Well, then. I am Lady Linela Lucio, daughter of Lord Nikola Lucio—high inquisitor of His Majesty. Who might you be?"

"Why should I share my name with you?" Fay replied, gaining her composure now that she'd turned her attention away from Travis—but also feeling bolstered and glowing with a new warmth as his hand came to settle on her waist. "I have no desire to do so."

"Yes, well, seeing that I've never noticed you at any of the public events, I'm rather tempted to say that you're not nobility at all. You're a commoner, aren't you?" Linela let the question hang in the air, and when she didn't get a reply, she grinned wolfishly. "Yes. As I thought. Lord Wraithtide has decided to take a pretty commoner over her betters, diluting the gene pool for superficial looks rather than good genetics with high affinities for the pillars or good heritage in wealth. A tragedy, but that's how men work, I suppose."

Fay's nostrils immediately flared, and she took an aggressive step forward—coming into Linela's personal space and meeting the other woman eye to eye. Travis couldn't exactly pinpoint what had set Fay off, but something in that line of sentencing had flipped a switch. Something Linela had said not only made Fay mad, but truly triggered her to a degree that Fay looked like she was going to strike the girl down.

How curious.

"And what if I am not nobility?" Fay asked curiously, green eyes narrowed with a venomous smile—fingers twitching and almost ready to cast a spell. "When I become Lord Wraithtide's bride one day, I will be then. Won't I? Does that hurt your pride, knowing you are being bested by a mere commoner? My name is Fay. I don't need a house name and Daddy's money in order to secure a man, unlike you flat-chested little whores that continue to run ragged attempting to take other women's belongings."

Linela held up one dainty hand, laughing dramatically into the back of it with her head thrown back. "Quite the fangs on you! Well, then, commoner trash. How about you put your bluster to the test. A bet, perhaps? One that is enforced by Elysium itself—we could even get a magistrate to recite the rites."

"And what did you have in mind?" Fay asked with a fake smile that twitched at the edges. "I do love tests, especially if it involves putting you in your place."

Linela snapped her fingers, summoning one of her manservants over while not looking away from her newly found archnemesis—and held out a hand for her manservant to deliver a small, pristine card.

Checkmate.

She took the small white card, laced with platinum trimmings, and extended it to Fay with a smug smirk. "This is a pass that allows you into the High Tide Women's Tea Club. I wouldn't expect you to know anything about it, seeing as you're lowly commoner trash, but it's a well-known establishment here on the top level of the capital. Inside, seven days hence, we will have a competition between the two of us. It will involve things that proper ladies of the court and wives of the nobility must know how to do in order to satisfy their men. Seeing that you are oh so desperate to be one of us, I'm sure you won't shirk your duty to show us all just how superior you really are . . . right? If you have any questions about what I mean, which I'm sure you will, perhaps you can ask my crippled brother about it. He should at the very least be able to tell you that much, even if he is otherwise useless."

Allie scowled on the sidelines and was about to come up and smack a bitch—but Lahn reached out to grip her wrist with a pleading glance.

Fay glanced down at the card, stiffly clasping it between her hands while glaring at the other blonde woman. "And what is it that you intend to bet, harlot? What exactly could you entice me with so that I would attend such a senseless kind of competition? What do I have to gain?"

"What is it you want?" Linela said with a wicked sneer—and by this point the clerk at the counter was spellbound, fascinated by the verbal catfight taking place in front of him. "I'm sure that I could come up with something to appease someone as poor and lackluster as you."

Fay raised her eyebrows, thought about it for a moment, then grinned in satisfaction as her eyelids narrowed. "You obviously have the upper hand in this bet, so why not make the winnings all that more dangerous? If I win this pathetic little competition of yours, you have to work cleaning cow shit out of the stables for a week. It would be a fitting place for you."

Silence followed.

Linela paled slightly but regained her sneering composure when Fay began to snicker. She straightened, and to everyone's surprise, she agreed. "Fine. I accept, on one condition."

Fay's grin grew wider. "Which is?"

"If I win, I get to take your man to the royal ball."

Fay's smile immediately dropped, and Allie butted in a moment later. "You can't pawn my brother off like that."

"Can't I?" Linela asked curiously, sizing Allie up before checking Travis out again with a grin. "I'm sure I'd do a much better job making him happy than this commoner could. Perhaps I'd even be able to steal him afterward, just as this Fay has accused me of trying to do. I think I'd like that very much."

Fay hesitated, and her face grew dark with anger. "I can't do that. We've already made plans."

"Oh? Intimidated? Getting cold feet now after all that false bluster? How pathetic!" Linela laughed, then turned to wave at her manservants in the back. "Well, if you change your mind, do let me know. I'll be there in seven days' time, waiting for you at noon—just in case!"

"We can make another bet," Fay stated promptly, only getting a side-eyed and demeaning look of one who thought themselves superior.

"No, my dear. We can't. You're obviously not quality material, not confident enough in yourself to win against someone like me—as it should be. You are not worthy of someone like him, and it is a sad thing to see indeed. Sad that nobility like him would fall for trash like you."

They glared at each other, both seething under their falsely polite smiles, before Lahn's sister turned heel. With a humph and a straightening of her shoulders, Linela walked out of the store with Marsia and all their servants carrying luggage—only looking back to blow Travis a kiss and seductively wink his way.

CHAPTER 13

Lahn's little animal sanctuary was positioned in the gardens on the outskirts of Dawn's Imperial Academy, located between hills and secluded from the surrounding area. Enclosed by a tiny wooden fence only big enough to keep the rescued dogs inside, it was adjacent to a pond with a couple heating stones positioned in tiny wooden doggy homes to keep the animals warm during winter months.

There were about two dozen dogs there, half of them puppies, and as he pushed open the latched wooden fence, they came barreling over to him with yips, yaps, and happy tail wags as he laughed and laughed and laughed.

"Jesus, that's so cute!" Allie whispered to the others with a warm smile, latching the fence behind her as they all stepped inside to be assaulted by the licking, panting dogs themselves soon thereafter.

Riven reached down and picked up a tiny brown mutt that looked like a cross between a basset hound and a wiener dog. It was only a few months old at most, and the excited licks, barks, and pawing at his arm was more than enough for him to appreciate what Lahn had done.

"You little rascal! I didn't give you that; come back here!" Riven said with another laugh as he chased the tiny puppy around the enclosure after it snagged one of the many treats they'd brought in paper bags.

Fay watched him go, clutching at her waist where Riven had held her for the entire trip to the sanctuary in order to hold her close. Smoothing out her silver dress and laying the paper bags down, she began to pull out bones, chew sticks, and various dried meats, distributing them to the ferocious pack of yipping puppies, strays, and even a few hobbling older dogs that were more than friendly. Many of them nuzzled up against her, and she even had one of the older dogs yawn and lie down on her lap to go to sleep.

"This has GOT TO BE the CUTEST FUCKING THING I'VE EVER SEEN!" Allie exclaimed while being bombarded by the animals.

Lahn, meanwhile, was introducing the individual animals by name to Allie, or at least the names he wanted to give them. Only a few of them actually responded to their given names, but it was adorable nonetheless.

Though he paused to consider Fay after a while of playing with the dogs when seeing that she looked rather down. "Fay? Are you doing all right?"

Fay, who was now staring at her own reflection and kneeling along the side of the pond, jolted out of a thoughtful stupor. "Oh! Yes, I'm fine. This has been quite fun! Why do you ask?"

Lahn glanced over to where the Wraithtide siblings were having a very serious discussion about puppy adoptions and playing fetch with some of the toys Lahn had brought. "I feel bad about the interaction you had concerning my sister. I'm sorry you had to deal with her like that. Don't feel bad—there's nothing wrong with being a commoner, and you're far prettier than she is anyway. She's just jealous."

Fay's eyebrows rose in surprise, then she grinned. "Thanks! And it's okay, nothing that you did warrants an apology. I came off a little aggressive, too, when I saw her hitting on Travis, and I think she only responded so poorly because of my initial prompting. I was rude, too."

"Yeah, but it was nice to see someone finally say those things to her. The evil bitch." Lahn wheeled himself up to the pond, tossing some bread into the water and smiling as beautifully colored fish came up to the surface to nibble at the bread before diving back down again. "It must be nice, having a sister that actually cares about you. I'm jealous of Travis by a lot."

"It's obvious Allie cares about you, too, you know. Which brings me to my question—just what DID you do to get her attention?" Fay asked, giving him a curious smirk.

Lahn blushed furiously, shaking his head from side to side as snowflakes began to fall slowly and land on his skin. "I think you have the wrong idea! We're just friends. There's no way she'd be interested in me like that."

"I do believe you're wrong," Fay stated with a simple shrug. "But believe what you will."

There was a very long silence after that as Lahn considered her words. He glanced up from his hand to look over the pond toward Allie, then looked back to Fay, brows furrowed. "Why do you think she's interested in me like that? It seems almost impossible."

Fay held her hands out to either side. "I'd thought it would be impossible for her to settle down at all. She has a lot of suitors. A LOT of suitors. And she's . . ."

Fay held her tongue, wanting to say that she'd acquired thralls to use as sex slaves one after another until recently. Fay wanted to tell him that Allie had abruptly stopped visiting her man-harem after she'd started talking to them about Lahn. Fay wanted to also tell him that although she didn't know Allie very well, she'd come to view Allie as a bloodthirsty, ruthless killing machine and a cutthroat queen who was very much transformed into a blushing schoolgirl in Lahn's presence—but Fay couldn't say any of that. Nor could she voice her more personal thoughts—such as she didn't know why Allie would take a liking to Lahn, either, but then again, the more time Fay spent with Lahn, the more likable he became. Perhaps Lahn's personality really had won Allie over.

"She's . . . what?" Lahn pressed, frowning at Fay's hesitation.

Fay sighed, then began giggling when a beagle started nuzzling its nose under her arm to begin licking her hand. As she petted the dog, her shoulders lost their tension. "She just seems different. I think you're good for her. It may not be romantic, but it also may be that way, I don't know. At the very least, I do believe it's possible, so keep your chin up. I can tell you're very hard on yourself because of your disabilities, but you shouldn't be. After all, it's not your fault you have an Azagnitide Rotworm living inside you."

Lahn's face blanked. "What?"

Fay's smile widened mischievously. "I said, it's not your fault you have an Azagnitide Rotworm living inside you."

Lahn blinked. "I'm not sure I know what you're talking about."

Fay pointed to his left arm, then his left leg, where the flesh had withered and shriveled into black and green, almost mummified limbs. "It's eating you away, you know. You'll likely die within three years, and I'm surprised you've lasted this long. You're getting sick more often, aren't you?"

Lahn's face scrunched up in confusion, and his mouth opened and closed repeatedly while he tried to find the words to reply. "Yes, I have been getting sick more frequently. How did you know that? I never even told any of you that I had bouts of sickness. Do you know what my condition is? Have you seen it before?"

His voice picked up an octave, hope shining in his eyes. "No one has ever found out the source of my sickness! Do you have a clue about how to treat it?! And what is an Azagnitide Rotworm?"

Fay nodded slowly and sagely, standing up to brush dog hair from her form-fitting silver dress. "Oh yes, I am very aware of your predicament. You see, I'm a curse specialist. I only have a few spells under my belt, but I was schooled in many different theories and I know a lot of the lore. One of my lore lessons, taught to me by my mother, talked about your condition in detail."

Fay reached out, touching his withered hand. "Essentially, your life force is being slowly drained over time to fuel a void beast. It first takes parts of your body, then at the end of your life it takes your soul and eats that, too. Azagnitide Rotworms are very common parasites in the void, but elsewhere . . . Not as much. They use high-grade curses of flesh melding to blend in with your body—disguising themselves from healing magics to avoid purging. I'm not sure how you ever came into contact with one, but it is possible to cure your condition entirely. Allie actually asked me to come along today in order to evaluate your condition after hearing that you thought it was a curse, and I'm glad to say that I think I'll be able to get the resources together for a sufficient ritual. It may take a while, but it's certainly worth a shot."

Lahn's breathing picked up dramatically, and he nearly jumped out of his chair due to the excitement, which then caused him to fall over. Fay had to catch him as he sputtered a reply, but she calmed him down—getting curious glances from the Wraithtide siblings as they started to walk around the pond to Lahn's location.

"You can CURE me?!" he asked, heart slamming inside his chest—which was very evident to the two vampires nearby. "You're not just saying that?!"

"Whoa, now!" Fay stated with a stern glare. "I am NOT making any promises. I am merely saying it's possible and that I'll try. First I have to get the right ritual set up, and that'll require some digging through old texts from my mother's library. I'll have to pay her a visit. Then I'll have to collect the right ingredients and we'll have to have a healer on standby—because, by the hells, if it works, the purging of that worm is going to be a very painful process."

Allie wheeled Lahn back to his dormitory, right outside the first-floor entrance where other fledgling lords and ladies of Dawn's high society bustled in and out. Many stopped to stare at the three immensely attractive people talking to Lahn, but not a single one paid him any attention at all.

In fact, they treated him like he was some sort of plague-ridden ghost—even going out of their way to avoid him most of the time.

"Those puppies you saved are adorable, and I'm glad we got to meet them today," Allie said, getting on one knee and clasping his good hand in her own. "And try not to think so much about what Fay said! I know you're excited, but we aren't sure if it can be done yet."

Lahn, meanwhile, was staring back at her the same way he stared at his mother all those years growing up. He suppressed a sob, clenched her hand harder, and tried to swallow the ball in his throat. His voice was shaky, and it was all he could do not to cry and embarrass himself in front of everyone there. "No one has ever done anything like this for me before. No one but my mom."

He promptly shook his head to cut her off when she began to protest. "No, I mean it. I've only known you a relatively short time, and you're already one of the best things that has happened to me since I was very little. I couldn't ask for a better friend. Thank you for at least trying, Allie, and even if it doesn't work, the mere fact that you tried says and means more to me than you can ever imagine. Thank you."

Lahn then coughed loudly into his withered hand, getting disgusted looks from one of the other noble brats walking by. Sheepishly putting his bad hand back in his lap, Lahn shifted his eyes toward Allie and the others again. "Sorry. Anyways, thank you all. Fay, I appreciate your efforts no matter how it goes. I'll be waiting eagerly to try, but I need to be off. I have to study for tomorrow's test . . . Are you going to be there to take the test tomorrow, Allie?"

Allie smiled, pressed her hands against his, and stood to shake her head. "No. Family business calls. My brother and I have some things to do."

Lahn immediately looked disappointed. "Things?"

"It involves the war effort," Allie stated, then winked. "Classified."

"Against Tereen?" Lahn said, open-mouthed. "Wait, are you really caught up in the war already? That would explain why you're so strong! Are you already an officer? What are you doing here?!"

Travis and Allie both chuckled.

"She did say 'classified,'" Fay stated with a wink. "Do you need one of us to help you to your room?"

"NO! No, that'd be embarrassing," Lahn replied with a reluctant exhale. "Fine! Keep your secrets! I'll figure them out later anyway!"

With a teasing grin, Lahn turned his wheelchair around and headed into the dormitory. Waving at Allie and his two new friends, he turned left and started wheeling himself toward his room. It was only a couple doors down from the main entrance, intentionally placed there for easy access, and he ignored the stares he got from other academy students while fumbling with his keys. Finding the correct one and inserting it into the lock, he looked down the hall the way he'd come as if to see whether Allie had followed.

And of course she hadn't.

He gave a wistful sigh, turned the key, and entered the room.

His maid wasn't there. She'd probably been called off on an errand for his brother again, as she did technically serve the entire Lucio household and not just Lahn. Locking the door behind him and laboriously pushing himself past the main dining area and into the bedroom, Lahn took out the royal ball invitation Allie had given him. When he peeled open the parchment imbued with the king's sigil and read the golden texts, his excited smile was accompanied by a light laugh of disbelief.

"What's that?" his sister's familiar voice called out from the dark interior of the kitchen, and Lahn whirled around as fast as he could in his chair to give the three figures a startled look.

There, sitting or leaning against the countertops in the kitchen, were his brother, his sister, and none other than his archnemesis Gleetus Nefrand. Gleetus wore a look of malicious glee, cracking his knuckles and glaring down at him while Linela hopped off the counter to coldly jut her nose upward in Lahn's direction.

Meanwhile, his older brother, Parius Lucio, stalked forward with slow steps, his boots thunking against the carpeted floor. Parius was one of the most handsome men around and always had flocks of girls trying to catch his eye. He was blonde, a lot like Lahn's sister, Linela, and wore his hair in a ponytail. Much like Gleetus, Parius also wore a Victorian-style buttoned coat with frills coming up off the collar. His blue eyes glared down at Lahn between the other two figures, obviously the alpha in this situation, and he snatched the invitation to the royal ball out of Lahn's hands with a sneer.

Then, as his eyes traced the lettering amid the dead silence of the room, his eyebrows lifted. Parius flicked the page twice with his pointer finger and turned his attention back to his crippled younger brother. "Who did you steal this from, little brother?"

Lahn paled. "I didn't steal it from anyone! It was given to me!"

"By who?" Parius questioned again.

Lahn's fists curled. "Lady Allie Wraithtide!"

Gleetus, who'd remained silent up until now, sputtered in exaggerated disbelief. "No, no, no. Parius, your little brother has been stalking that poor girl ever since she arrived here. Allie Wraithtide is a new, beautiful, rather rich young lady of the court and is quite popular in our classes. No doubt during one of his attempts to stalk her, he snatched this invitation from her bag when she wasn't looking."

"I can attest to that," Linela said with a snobbish flip her hair. "I saw him stalking the poor girl and her brother at the magic shop in town just earlier today. It was rather pathetic, if I may add. She wanted nothing to do with him, but he continued to follow her like a kicked dog."

Gleetus snickered.

"That isn't true!" Lahn said desperately, his eyes pleading with his older brother as he extended a hand for the parchment. "That is an invitation for me! She personally gave it to me so I could attend with her!"

"AS HER DATE?! HERS?!" Gleetus roared with laughter, and even Linela seemed genuinely amused this time. "THAT'S OUTRAGEOUS! Now I'm CERTAIN he stole it from her! Parius, if you saw this woman for even a moment, you'd understand just how absurd it would be for someone like her to ask him to the ball."

"Agreed!" Linela spat, with her arms crossed. "If I didn't know better—"

Parius snapped his fingers, still glaring down at Lahn, and the other two people in the room quickly shut up. Folding the invitation into his coat pocket, he patted it twice and clasped his hands behind his back. He let out a weary sigh, shook his head, and slowly began to exit the room. Coming to the door leading out, he stopped and briefly glanced back. "I'll be heading out to return the invitation you stole, Lahn. Your very existence is already shame enough to the family, as your performance at this school has been. I will try to correct this by returning the invitation to her and making amends before even more shame is brought onto the Lucio name, and in the meantime I urge you to reconsider just what it is you're trying to accomplish here. Gleetus, you may proceed."

Turning the knob to leave the room, Parius quickly exited and locked the door behind him with a click.

Lahn just stared at the door shut behind his older brother, a combination of embarrassment, fury, and despair sinking in as tears welled up under his eyes.

"Oh, are you going to cry now?!" Gleetus laughed alongside Linela, who began to laugh behind a hand covering her mouth. Cracking his knuckles and walking over to where a fire poker was set next to the cold fireplace at the end of the room, he picked up the metal object and gave it a few swings. "Well, don't get too hasty now. Do you remember what I said to you in class? About how I'd break your legs if you kept that attitude of yours up so that you'd remember your place?"

Gleetus turned around, smiling menacingly at the crippled young man in the wheelchair. "Well, now you're about to find out that I'm not all just bluster after all!"

Gleetus dashed forward, and Lahn yelled out in surprise and fear as Gleetus swung the fire poker as hard as he could—slamming the metal object into Lahn's good leg.

There was a snap of bone, a shrill scream, and Linela began to laugh.

"WHAT ARE YOU DOING?!" Lahn yelled, falling out of his chair as he tried to escape and bleeding from a gash along the leg that didn't want to hold his weight anymore. "HELP! SOMEONE HELP ME!"

CRACK

The metal object slammed into the back of Lahn's thigh, tearing out a small strip of flesh as Gleetus started to angrily and repeatedly hit Lahn's good leg as hard as he could. Over and over, Gleetus struck the downed man while Linela watched from the sidelines, and over and over, Lahn let out horrified whimpers and screams for help.

CHAPTER 14

The creature was exactly as the hologram had depicted her—a large red-and-black spider that was pretty for an arachnid, which was odd, considering how he'd always thought most spiders looked disgusting. Athela's blood-tipped legs tapped rapidly in excitement as she looked around, and as her two red eyes settled on him, she lifted the two front legs and spread her fangs while getting up on her hind legs. "Hi there, Master! How's your day going?"

Riven was taken aback. The spider could talk? The voice was high-pitched, feminine, and was the equivalent to a soft summer's breeze or wind chimes. It was nice, pleasant to hear, and he couldn't help but chuckle. Not only was the spider very pretty for an animal, but even her voice was pleasant and friendly?

He gave the dog-size arachnid a mixed expression of confusion and amusement before getting up and walking over to her. Extending a hand and shaking one of her rather cold, sharpened front legs, he smiled down as she clicked her mandibles together. "You're rather cute. How'd I get so lucky with my minion choice?"

He could have sworn that the spider flushed pink for a moment before she shook his hand vigorously with dramatic affect.

"Now, now, human, I can't have you hitting on me right after summoning me. We're different species and it wouldn't work out."

Riven blinked, and the memory faded.

Chopper blades whirred overhead, creating a symphony of beating metal against the wind as two dozen Apache attack helicopters and a couple transports zoomed over the forested landscape beneath. The birds of prey had come to roost in the dying light of sunset. Their destination had been set to Dungeon Alibast.

A burning village, a battalion of marching undead, and ruined battlegrounds were swept away by their passage. The front lines were fast approaching, and once they even encountered an elvish strike squadron on horseback running down men from Dawn's armed forces—only for the Apaches to annihilate the elves in a storm of gunfire imbued with power from the Machine pillar. The Apaches had been modified by system engineers, classers that could upgrade mechanical units various ways—the equivalent of mages for the Machine pillar. Thus, the magically imbued arrows and lightning strikes that did manage to connect with the helicopters only burned out and fizzled away when the plasma shields activated—lighting up the mechanical runes along the sides of the machines' heavy armor.

The attack finished just as fast as it began—ending in an abrupt bloodbath, and the men of Dawn below cheered their thanks while the Apaches rapidly passed them by.

"I'm surprised they haven't surrendered yet," Riven said through a microphone incorporated into his Messenger helmet by one of Chicago's engineers. His red eyes shifted over to Allie, who merely shrugged and laughed back at him through the coms.

"Most of their elite troops have been wiped out, but they're far from done putting up a fight," Mara yelled over the whirring of the helicopter blades through her own mic, gripping the side of the transport helicopter with white knuckles. "It's only guesswork as to why they haven't given up yet, but some think they're too proud—and others think their king has gone mad. Either way, it means more bodies for us from both sides of the conflict—and they have a lot of soldiers left."

"But if this goes right, they might even surrender today," Allie chimed in through the mic. "Regardless, we still win. When the war is over, we'll split the land between Dawn and the Necropolis, with a third of their empire going to Dawn and two-thirds going to us. I've already laid claim to the capital. It's a prize I won't give up—the city is supposed to be full of natural treasures and has an enormous population we can use to our own ends."

"It is very generous of you to even give them a third, my queen," Gurth'Rok, the vampiric orc chieftain, cut in with a harsh cough. "We did most of the work in this war. If it was up to me, I'd have given Dawn nothing. It was prize enough to save them from eventual disaster and enslavement."

Allie's chuckle rang clear. "True enough, but it is nice to have a real ally for once. Think of it as an investment. We can't just go kill and conquer everyone we see, and extending an olive branch now may prove useful in the future."

The transport choppers landed two miles from the dungeon on a secluded plateau at the end of the mountain range, dropping off their loads and quickly making a break back toward the necropolis with their Apache escort.

Riven watched them go but eventually turned around when they were out of sight beyond the mountains in the northeast. He then abruptly found himself being watched—by everyone.

They expected him to lead.

Fay leaned over and nudged him with a chuckle, tipping her witch's hat and spreading her wings to encompass his body, armor and all. Azmoth just stood beside him with all four arms folded and his massive molten war hammer head-down on the ground. Allie and Gurth'Rok came to stand beside him in solidarity, both turning around with Allie's hands clasped behind her back and Gurth'Rok putting weight on his cobra staff.

"So you are our best and brightest," Riven said aloud, evaluating them one by one. "I only very briefly introduced myself earlier, but I'm sure you all know me. Now it's my turn to know all of you. You were all recommended by Allie, Gurth'Rok, or General Bruner—so I expect great things. Tell me about yourselves and what you can do; we'll start down the line. Brief descriptions only."

The group consisted of a mix and match of different races, classes, and abilities. Each of them were in the low to high A-tier brackets—being between levels 49 and 56—and introductions didn't take long. Including Riven and his two demons, there were thirty-six of them total.

There were three cyborg sharpshooters with modified, silenced sniper rifles and plasma swords for close combat—but they were primarily for long-range fighting. Each of them had had various pieces of their previously human bodies replaced with technological equivalents, brought about by their pillar orientations and classes, and they each wore formfitting, self-repairing black nanotech armor.

Two hackers and one combat engineer followed—with the energy hackers being able to not only track energy signatures but to indicate what type of incoming attack would target their group if they identified it fast enough. Sometimes they were even able to misdirect enemy energy signatures and use them to their own ends—meaning they could turn enemy spells and martial arts around on their casters—hence the Hacking aspect of their class. The combat engineer was confined between plates of metal in a medium-size mech a little bit bigger than Azmoth, with various utility gadgets attached to different appendages that included repair kits, healing rays, a large mining laser, 3-D mapping technology and tracking beacons, utility arms for rapid construction, and a couple of self-defense measures that mostly included short-range burst fire from a machine gun on one arm. What was most unique about the mech, though, was that it was integrated into the man's Machine pillar and subpillars—becoming an extension of himself. It wasn't something he could just give up or give away, which wasn't always apparently the case—but doing this made his mech all that much more powerful because he could level it up.

Twelve warriors in enchanted heavy plate armor made up the front line— seven muscular orc death knights, three ghoul death knights, and two hulking flesh golem Unholy berserkers with exposed musculature and metal plates or spikes protruding from their red-and-white bodies.

Two skeletal skresh assassins, a single ghoul assassin, two human rogues, and a lone goblin thief were all present on the subterfuge department—they'd been outfitted with varieties of equipment that gave stealth bonuses. Each of them had an assortment of plasma daggers—which were quickly becoming a staple of the Necropolis forces—enchanted crossbows, silenced pistols, handheld energy bombs supplied by Chicago's engineers, and a variety of Shadow-subpillar abilities that attributed to stealth.

Then, last, were the mages—not including Riven, Gurth'Rok, and Allie.

There were obviously Mara, Nin, and Vin—all of them necromancers and dark arts practitioners. But there were a couple Infernal-based bombardment mages in their ranks, too—three humans and a defense-oriented orc shaman who was able to cast healing spells and air-based defensive domes, having forgone the transition into the Unholy foundational pillar at Riven's altar in favor of keeping the Fae foundational pillar. Healers were a rarity, it turned out, thus the shaman was highly valued—as was Gurth'Rok and the utility-based combat engineer with his mech's healing rays.

Unlike the shaman, though, Gurth'Rok HAD taken the plunge into the Unholy pillar. He'd had to after his vampiric heritage clashed with his Fae pillar, and it'd meant he'd had to relearn a bunch of new spells. However, the transition hadn't been a complete reset—because many of his old spells had been mutated or warped into Unholy versions of their Fae counterparts. This ended up giving Gurth'Rok a lot of Blood-related spells that were actually healing oriented, and Riven knew he probably would need to learn at least one of them from the orc. The problem was that his Blood subpillar was filling up in terms of runic space, and they'd even started transitioning to etching themselves into his soul core rather than the pillar itself. He had room for potentially one to three more Blood-based abilities in his pillar—depending on runic size—and a few more in his core from any orientation. Not all spells took up the same amount of space. When the Blood subpillar filled up, Riven wouldn't be able to create the sigils needed for lock-and-key access to new spells unless they were of different pillar orientation—as the other pillars he had could place their own oriented spells on their part of the soul aperture, but they wouldn't allow spells oriented to other pillars to be drawn onto them, unlike his core, which was a free-for-all. He currently had Bloody Razors, Crimson Ice, Blood Lance, and Blood Nova—with the Crimson Ice and Blood Nova taking up enormous portions of his Blood subpillar just by themselves. Not immediately, but soon if he wanted to learn new Blood spells after his core filled up, he'd need to start sacrificing other abilities to learn them.

So he had to choose wisely on which new abilities he wanted for the future.

"Let me be clear," Riven said, slamming the butt of his spear-staff into the ground with the black blade pointing upward. "I am here to help ensure your safety, but I want this experience to go to all of you. I will intervene if I feel it is absolutely necessary in order to save your lives, but I cannot promise you won't die. I'll do my best, but the coming world quests will need more than just me to see them through. We have liches, snow giants, invaders from out of this world, and more that we don't even know about coming to fuck our day up."

He let his words sink in, watching his soldiers unwaveringly stare back at him. Riven nodded in approval. "We are entering this dungeon for the same reason we are allowing this senseless war with Tereen to continue: it is because we are in the business of raising this world's elites to combat the bigger threats of the future. Conflict breeds heroes in this new multiverse, and though I'm sure not all of you will make it that far, I'm willing to bet that some of you will. This venture into the dungeon is going to be on all of your shoulders. From this expedition and later expeditions: Allie and I will select future guildmates to accompany us regularly to participate in only god knows what when the guild system finally comes. I am told by our allies in the Blood Moon Requiem that guilds have a large part to play in upcoming events across the multiverse, even beyond this planet, so do your best to impress us. Think of this almost as a tryout. You'll be evaluated the entire way through—but all of you already knew that when you signed up, didn't you?"

He got nods and grunts of acknowledgment from the party in front of him.

"Dungeon Alibast, as many of you know, has been supplying Tereen with many of its dungeon creatures to fight alongside the elves in the war. It should have a couple thousand creatures inside right now, despite sending most of its forces to help aid the enemy." Riven continued, red bloodsilk flaps of his lower back armor rustling in the breeze. "I do not intend to destroy the dungeon outright. This dungeon will be temporarily put down in favor of looting its wares, and if all goes well, we'll be able to do so a few times before it either relocates entirely or becomes a training dungeon for us. We'll see how things go. Now, aside from myself, you'll all be participating—including my sister, Allie, my minions who need the levels as well, and Gurth'Rok. There may come a time where we split up into teams, but only for short intervals. No need to senselessly waste such good talent on a training expedition—so most of the expedition is going to be together where I can intervene if need be. Any questions?"

"No, sir!" one of the cyborg sharpshooters called out, and many of the others shook their heads in silence.

"Good. I expect great things from all of you. Now let's move out."

The dungeon's entrance was an enormous cave, built into the side of the last mountain in the chain, where a couple dozen large plantlike humanoids were playing cards with high elf sentries. The system called the plantlike creatures lesser dryads, and they were the dominant creature Dungeon Alibast produced. Aside from that, there'd been a number of other plant-type monsters that ranged from carnivorous walking trees and flowers to living, rolling masses of vines that sucked the blood and bile right out of your body. There'd also been a few reports on greater dryads, too, though they were patchy and contradictory at the best of times.

"Stealth team A is in position. Targets have been eliminated on the eastern slope."

"Stealth team B in position."

"Overwatch team is in position."

"Bombardment team is on standby and ready to nuke 'em."

Riven clicked his tongue, watching from the hillside where he held a dead elf archer by the neck—one of many that would be raised from the dead to act as temporary cannon fodder by the necromancers. He mentally activated his coms. "Begin."

Immediately three of the sentries standing around the table watching the card game were decapitated in single-strike blasts of targeted gunfire. The shock from the dryads as well as the elves was only short-lived, but it was enough time for the sniper rifles to take out another four of their number.

"WE'RE UNDER ATTACK!" a young elf with blonde hair yelled while drawing a white long sword from a scabbard.

He was quickly cut down by a skeletal hand wielding a dagger as one of the skresh assassins ruptured from a nearby shadow.

The defenders died within seconds, and Riven nodded in appreciation at the skill these soldiers showed while coming down from his hiding place at a vantage point.

Stopping near the man who'd called out to try and raise the alarm, Riven frowned. He wondered just what kind of lies he'd been told, what kind of pay he'd been enticed with, what morals he held that allowed him to stay here and fight this war. Perhaps the young elf wasn't all that different from himself, or at least he might not have been before becoming a corpse.

"They started this war," Allie reminded him upon seeing his gaze linger on the dead young man, barely older than a boy. "They were committing atrocities, purging entire villages and towns—enslaving people from Dawn without cause and treating those slaves a lot more brutally than you allow us to do with the elvish prisoners of war. Remember that."

Riven didn't look back; instead he turned toward the cave entrance, peering into the darkness. "Yes. I know."

George Kalsky's yellow bionic eye zoomed down the iron sight of his silenced sniper rifle on thought. Positioned on a ledge that overlooked the roaring battle below, he took a moment to soak in the field.

As a Navy SEAL, he'd had his fair share of warfare. But this was a lot more intense than what he'd been used to back on his missions in the Middle East and southern Asia. The line of heavily armored, fully plated death knights were beating back a horde of carnivorous vines akin to snakes, as well as a multitude of their plantlike dryad masters that looked like people carved from wood, stems, and flowers. Heavy metal tower shields were held out in front of the knights as each of them wielded swords that let off soul flame of neon-teal and black energies. The death magic ripped through the plants, and various body enhancements were obviously in full glow as they carved through the dungeon's defenses like a meat grinder, but their main job was to tank for the real damage doers in the back.

Black holes overhead soaked in both light and life as the necromancers continued to suck in enemies and raise the dead—sending the undead creations back toward the still-living dryads in a never-ending wave. Blasts of fire akin to mortars and bombs tore holes in the hundreds of racing enemies charging their position—decimating the underground caverns that'd once been littered with flowering plants. Stealth-based classers darted in and out of the shadows on the sidelines, killing stragglers or enemies that'd been separated from the main groups, while also looking out for occasional enemy stealth types.

Feeling the pulse of his Armaments subpillar flare in his soul, George set his sights on one of the back-line druid casters and began channeling the Tier-2 martial art True Shot—one of the most basic but useful abilities of his class.

The silenced sniper rifle, a magnificent, sleek black gun half the size he was, shimmered with pale light and let an infused projectile rocket out of the chamber. Tearing through the air, the bullet infused with True Shot passed by an erected energy shield and made contact with the first physical item behind it—the shaman's heart.

[You have landed a critical hit. Max Damage x9.]

The dryad's chest blew out the back, showering his allies in gory plant matter to the enraged screams of the other defenders.

Grinning wolfishly, George turned his closely shaved head to the next target and readjusted his aim. This time it was a mutant treeant, a large, hulking humanoid created out of thick bark, branches, and enormous limbs. It was gigantic, from racing straight for the front line and shrugging off flaming bolts of fire and darkness fired by the back-line casters, but it wasn't about to get there alive.

He channeled another True Shot and fired. The bullet howled through the air, slamming into the tough defenses of the treeant's hide and completely ignoring the outer layer of energy shielding the creature—but the thick bark was more than just for show. The bullet, as fast as it was, only lodged in half an inch and caused the treeant to stagger.

"Shit."

Getting to one knee and making sure that there wasn't an enemy coming up from behind, he exposed himself to activate another ability, Plasma Cannon.

It was the very first skill he'd acquired from the Armaments subpillar, and it temporarily shifted his arm into a weapon. When he held out his right hand in a straight line, his entire arm began to change. Metal pieces quickly shifted, churned, rotated, and clicked into place as his fingers were reincorporated into his body and a long, hollow steel barrel glowing with orange light replaced it. Neon lights etched through lines of power across his entire extremity, and a whirring noise began to rumble within the limb as small fanlike blades began to rotate inside.

THRUM

The orange energies congregated, forming an orb inside the small cannon attached to his arm—and he took a more careful aim as he felt the plasma begin to charge. A percentage counter began ticking up, letting him know what kind of energy output he'd unleash.

178 V.

204 V.

267 V.

305 V.

He didn't know what the V stood for, but it definitely correlated to the power output of his cannon—and when his arm started to shake and overheat around 509 V, he let the cannon rip.

The ball of orange energy roared forward and rocked the dungeon's room, nearly blowing him backward with an aftershock as the ball of plasma collided head-on with the incoming tree giant.

The monster roared as half its body shattered into splinters of wood. It fell over, crushing many dryads underneath it—and George's arm began to simmer with heat as it cooled down.

"Fuck yeah!" he muttered to himself with a smile, narrowly dodging a wooden spike that was launched in retaliation from the enemy back lines.

And that's when he heard the crunch of wood on stone behind him.

Eyes narrowing, he whirled, barely seeing the incoming root before he dodged left.

The root passed him by and skewered the stone he'd been lying on, then whipped back around and retracted into a green woman with vines for hair and a pink flower for her left eye that covered half her face. She wore a long dress made of interwoven leaves, and her legs trailed with roots that supported her weight and helped her move as if her feet were hovering a few inches above ground.

She hummed with amusement and held up a hand as George raised a pistol, deflecting numerous bullets as the semiautomatic weapon chipped away at the bark shield she conjured. "Quite the little rascal, aren't you?"

Her voice was like honey, too human for George's liking, and he quickly drew from his belt a plasma knife that flared to life with neon light. Yellow rectangular runes of the Machine pillar began to light up his arms and legs as body-empowerment abilities activated, and he set himself into a combat-ready stance for close combat.

[Greater Dryad, Wood Priestess, Level 70 Elite]

The notification glowed in golden flames, signifying the elite status that he'd heard rumors about but hadn't actually seen until now. And she was level 70 to his level 55.

This did not look good.

But he steadied himself anyway, ready to match her attack as she simply smiled and blinked back at him through the roar of battle.

Then another figure appeared from the hallway from whence the expedition had come. And then another, and another, and then even more. They poured in, silently evaluating the battle from the ledge George had decided to use as a vantage point—and his body grew cold when he saw the last of the figures emerge from around the bend. She was only a little girl and looked a lot like the dryads—she had vines and leaves for hair and half of her right arm was covered in bark, but her small body was otherwise created from green stalks and dozens of small flowers.

[Greater Dryad, Wood Priest, Level 61 Elite]
[Greater Dryad, Flower Priestess, Level 72 Elite]
[Greater Dryad, Earth Shaman, Level 69 Elite]
[Reincarnation of Gaia, Planet Earth–Based Demigoddess, Level 103, Legendary]

The little girl looked up to George, studied him through narrowed hazel eyes, and frowned. "George . . . Why are you attacking me?"

Caught off guard by the monster knowing his name, George abruptly took a step back. "Huh? Do I know you?"

"I know all the people who were born on my world . . . or at least I used to." The little girl put on a sad smile. Then she walked over, unperturbed by the violence below, and stood to watch the massacre of her people. "George . . . Can you bring Allie and Riven to me so I may speak with them?"

She turned around, a bastion of innocence. "I do believe there has been a misunderstanding."

CHAPTER 15

Riven stared at the young girl sitting a few feet away from him, red eyes narrowed through the visor slit and vertical jaws along his ivory plate armor hissing from time to time. Jackal had taken its dog form, a shadowy canine that glared over at Gaia's reincarnation wordlessly as its body shimmered with black wisps of shadow. "So let me get this straight. You're saying that you've been quarantined here, unable to control any of the monsters you create—"

"I do not like to refer to them as monsters," Gaia replied sweetly, a smile adorning her lips while new flowers began to bloom from her outstretched palm. "They are my children, just like you."

Riven blinked. "Right . . . You are unable to control your children outside this dungeon because the elves have . . . What, mind-controlled them somehow by using nature-attuned magics?"

"That is correct. My children are very susceptible outside my dungeon realm, and I cannot leave this dungeon myself until I have matured," Gaia stated with a nod, letting the flower grow into a fully formed crystallized multicolored rose, shimmering with light, and plucking it to set the flower on the floor between them. "This is for you as a sign of good faith. I know you better than you think you know yourself, Riven Thane. Being born on my world before the integration, I knew you even better back then, and there are both many secrets that I can share as well as many boons that I can give you, should you help me."

The fighting had stopped entirely now. Gaia's treeants, plant creatures, and dryads had all retreated to a safe distance on the opposite end of the cavern from Riven's own forces. Gaia claimed that no harm had been done because she could resurrect any of these creations with their souls intact as long as they didn't leave Dungeon Alibast, whose avatar was actually one of the greater dryads watching over the goddess reincarnate. The elves, apparently, had been regularly taking the dryads from the dungeon to use as cannon fodder in the war—abducting them to warp their minds with some kind of ritualistic magic Riven was unfamiliar with. Due to the high affinities of the Fae pillar that these elves had, and the dryads' high affinities to it as well, the dryads were very susceptible to this kind of mental attack and were even identified as minions to the elvish masters by Elysium's status pages. This made Gaia very angry, because once they died outside this dungeon, there was no way to bring them back to life. They were gone for good, and thus the elves of Tereen had essentially kidnapped and murdered many of her newly created children.

Riven hesitated, then picked the glittering rose off the floor, which had been covered in soft layers of moss over the last few minutes just by being in Gaia's presence. He personally didn't feel any different, but many of the still-human soldiers he'd brought along and the orc shaman who'd remained unaffiliated to the Unholy pillar claimed that they'd felt rejuvenated just by seeing her.

It was . . . interesting, to say the least.

"Do you know what happened to my parents?" Riven asked slowly while Allie caught her breath on the sideline, waiting expectantly for Gaia's answer. "Since you are apparently the Mother Nature of Earth on our old world reincarnated, perhaps you could let me know?"

Gaia slowly shook her head. "Unfortunately I am unable to tell you exactly what happened because they were not born on my body, but elsewhere. I did not have a connection to their spirits as I did yours, or Allie's, or the others' prior to integration. However, I did have eyes and ears. The plants and animals spoke to me even then, and I do know snippets of the things that passed before they left my body together."

"Together?" Riven repeated, eyebrows raised. "My father left years before my mother disappeared, and I was half convinced they'd died. You're saying they not only left alive, but they left with each other?"

"That is correct," Gaia said with visible empathy etched into her features. "I am sorry. I know how thoroughly it broke the two of you at that time. I would have been more involved in situations like yours if the gods of Olympus hadn't banished me and worked with other pantheons to steal the magic of our planet. All I could do was watch as my children, like you two, suffered unjustly."

That response raised a lot more questions. "The gods of Olympus are real?"

"As are many of the other pantheons you humans considered mythology," Gaia said. "They were all banished to their own versions of reality when the magic left, after they failed to harness the world's power properly. It is why Earth was devoid of magic and why magic was a myth to you when the other two worlds Earth merged with during the integration already had some knowledge of the subject. I believe that now many of them will be making an appearance just like me, likely secluded to different dungeons or instance events the administrator has created until . . . until we are deemed ready to emerge into the combined world of Panu."

"Back to our parents—" Allie cut in, irritated that the subject had gotten off track. She stepped forward, only to be met with flares of power from the greater dryads and Dungeon Alibast's dryad avatar—each having auras that matched Allie's own.

She stepped back, grunting in irritation and glaring down at the little flowering-plant girl. "Why did they leave? Why couldn't you see them and why don't you know where they went or what happened, if plants and animals in their area told you?! That doesn't make sense!"

Gaia looked up to Allie, sighing softly and shaking her head, causing the vines that were her hair to shift. "I don't know why your father left you all those years ago, but he remained on my body until he left with your mother much later. When he left you, he entered a complex of some kind that shielded my gaze—it was underground, with Unholy auras permeating the structure. I only ever saw him when he came out to feed on my other children. Eventually, when your mother was being chased by . . . some kind of otherworldly creature not native to Earth, she killed the beast and made preparations for the two of you. She wiped clean any traces connecting her to her two children and headed for the same complex your father had stayed at all those years. It was then attacked by similar shadowy creatures, and I felt a rip in space as a portal activated. Soon after that, the presence of your parents disappeared and the complex blew up to stop the monsters from pursuing. That is all I can tell you."

"What did the creatures look like?" Allie pressed, concern evident while she bit her bottom lip.

"I cannot say," Gaia stated again with a helpless frown. "My state at the time was weakened, and I could not make out their true bodies. All I know is that they were Shadow-oriented creatures of some kind, and they were dangerous. They killed many of the other people in your father's facility before the underground complex exploded, and they were dragging the bodies out by the many dozens to use their parts in sacrificial rituals of some kind before everything was purged with Infernal flames. I apologize for not knowing more."

Allie paused, taking in the information, but let out a shaky breath and slumped. "Thank you anyway. It's more information than we've ever gotten before."

Riven took Allie's hand and squeezed reassuringly, then turned his attention back to the flower. It looked crystalline in nature, was multicolored and shimmered in the light. He couldn't get a read on it even with his suit's low-tier identification ability, so he held it up and asked, "What does this do, exactly?"

Gaia turned her gaze from Allie to Riven, and then to the brilliant crystal flower she'd plucked from her palm. "That is a piece of my soul."

Riven stared. "Why would you give me a piece of your soul? What use do I have for this?"

"Do you not have someone you love waiting to be revived?" Gaia asked, a small grin creeping onto her face. "Think of this as an up-front payment. Do not worry—my soul will regenerate over time as long as the core piece is intact—and Athela's core is what attached itself to your own soul aperture. What do I want in return? Free my children from this quarantine the elves have placed on my home, destroy the runic glyphs that siphon my power to keep my growth stagnant, destroy the seals that keep us inside, stop Tereen's king from mind-controlling my children by taking his head—and you will have a lot more than this. That I promise you. And you will have made an ally of me as well. I cannot leave the dungeon myself yet, even if you do destroy the glyphs, but I will be able to do so eventually.

When that time comes, you will need me for the invaders that seek to take this new planet for themselves."

Riven barely heard her after the first sentence. "This can help Athela come back?"

Gaia nodded. "It can. It will also impart a gift to her in the form of my own power, should she choose to take it. The art of soul mending is a thin line between utter failure and creating a new being—but this rose already has the commands programmed into it that would allow Athela's soul to regrow properly while keeping Athela herself."

The little girl held up a finger before Riven could speak. "I also suggest that you are very careful about letting in too much aspect, concerning the sin of Gluttony you have acquired. Athela's soul was created out of nothing by the power of your sin shard, from what I can gather by looking at it. Is that correct?"

"That is correct."

"Then Athela will be very in tune with Gluttony's power when she revives. Be very careful that Gluttony does not consume her outright in an attempt to claim my gift, and that the core of her soul remains intact. If done right, she will likely take both the power of Gluttony and my own gifts to combine them into something unique—but it will be up to you to hold back the greed and hunger Gluttony represents when that shard realizes the gift I have given you isn't for yourself but rather for your minion. Eat the flower now, and within one week's time, your minion will be back in your company. Lastly, I would heavily advise against trying this again with her or with anyone else. Soul mending can go very wrong, as I have mentioned, and you could very well destroy the essence of who she is if it isn't done right. An example of this would be even now, should you fail to keep out Gluttony's shard from devouring my preset sigils of power, you could very well lose Athela entirely."

". . . is there not a safer way?" Riven asked hesitantly, glancing down at the flower.

Gaia gracefully held out one hand to either side. "Probably, but not a way I know of."

While Riven, Allie, and the others were destroying the sigils and various magical constructs left in place by the elves surrounding Dungeon Alibast, Fay decided to enter the nether realms. She'd been dreading going back home to see her family after what'd happened with Tupper, but she wouldn't simply stand by and watch her relatives torture her brother for what they considered improper behavior. It was just ludicrous.

Personal nether realms were available to all demons, just like angelic races; it was an inherent part of what they were. Fay could retreat to her own personal nether realm and create a small space where she was able to relax, protected from harm or fear, untouchable to the greater universe beyond. But when nether realms were shared entities between groups of demons like clans . . . that's when things got a little tricky. They became more physical and real in nature, and it was also a lot less safe.

Stepping out of her portal, she touched down onto a large stone temple adorned with flowers and large marble statues depicting different incubi and succubi in various lewd poses. Her feathered boots hit the floor, and her black wings flapped twice before settling into a folded position behind her. Various demons were talking, eating, drinking, or outright mating with one another right there on the temple grounds—which was pretty typical for her breed of demons. Unlike the variously colored succubi and the incubus she'd seen at Dungeon Negrada's trading commune, her clan were all like her—with short black horns, black eyes, a black tail, silky white hair, and characteristic sky-blue skin.

"Welcome back home to the Sojavi clan's nest, dear sister!" a familiar light-hearted voice called out as Nitidi, Fay's favorite older sister, came skipping through the crowd of various bodies from a temple doorway.

Fay's smile widened. "Nitidi! One of only two people I want to see today!"

Her older sister laughed, and quickly they embraced in a strong hug. Nitidi was pretty tall for a succubus and her horns curled slightly more than Fay's did. Her thighs were slightly thicker, too, but otherwise the two sisters looked very similar.

"I see you've brought back some fashion statements!" Nitidi teased, letting go of Fay and flicking the witch's hat before motioning to the feathered knee-high boots and the torn purple skirt outfit. "You really need to get that skirt and top replaced. You can have some of mine—I've been collecting clothes just for you while you've been gone . . . It's the least I could do to make you feel better after what happened."

Fay's body suddenly went rigid, but she played it off with a cough and another friendly smile. No doubt Nitidi was talking about how Fay had been kidnapped, tortured, and used by the cultists. Fay had seriously thought she was going to die, permanently, after seeing Athela get cut down and the sheer pleasure that blonde man had taken from seeing Fay in pain.

She looked down at her outfit, which, even though it did have some minor self-repair enchantments, hadn't mended itself properly after being torn apart a couple times. "Um . . . Thanks, Nitidi. It is appreciated."

An awkward silence ensued, and then Nitidi perked up with a nudge to Fay's side. "But hey! That new man you've got . . . I'm jealous! What a hottie, right?! And the title of GIRLFRIEND?! Now THAT is something you've got to tell me about! How did you manage that?! Most guys just want to use us for fun, but emotional investment?! Mother is most pleased."

Fay's deep blush said it all, causing Nitidi to chuckle viciously.

"Is Mother truly happy with me?" Fay managed to mutter under her breath as they began walking toward the temple's entrance. "I was afraid she and the other elders would be angry after I helped Tupper escape."

Nitidi scoffed, brushing the comment aside with a flip of her hair. "Not at all. They're happy to be rid of him. I think it was best for all parties involved."

Fay let out a deep, long sigh of relief. "Good. I was afraid of what they'd say."

"It's not like they should care anyways. Just let Tupper do what he wants to do and let it be—no need to pressure him to follow the family line of work."

"Yes, I agree."

Stopping at a small windowless room on the left, Nitidi quickly picked up a couple stacks of clothes and deposited them into a sack, then handed it to Fay with a wink. "I included some edible lingerie so you and Riven can have some fun."

Fay slapped a hand over her face, and her blush deepened. "Nitidi! Stop, you're embarrassing me!!!"

"Fay, you're a succubus. Get used to the idea!" Nitidi laughed, poking Fay in the stomach and letting her younger sister carry the bag as they continued down the hall toward their mother's library.

Finally getting to the large door and opening it, Fay stepped inside and beheld the massive number of books her clan had collected.

The room was huge. Utterly massive. It contained textbooks, novels, documentaries, maps, lore, scrolls, and other ancient texts from numerous worlds across the multiverse. Most of them had been taken from previous warlock masters their clan had bound themselves to at one point or another, while others had been traded for, stolen, or bought while on the job. Fay's mother, Saemi, was a book fanatic and, as one of the clan elders, had ordered the library be added to whenever they got the chance.

"Fay!!! You've finally arrived!" Saemi exclaimed upon seeing her youngest daughter, getting up and pushing off one of her bare-chested incubus suitors, rudely gesturing for him to get lost as he scurried out of the room. Saemi smiled widely down at Fay and took her head in both hands, turning Fay's face back and forth before kissing her on the cheek. "I've been wondering when you'd come back to talk to me! I got so worried . . . but I'm glad to see your summoner cared enough to save you."

Saemi raised one eyebrow, her finger tracing down Fay's chest to her poorly repaired top. "We need to do something about this. This just simply will not do. Nitidi, did you get Fay some new clothes with seduction enchantments as discussed?"

"They're in the bag. They all have Depravity-associated boons, too. I made sure of it," Nitidi replied with a smile, plopping down onto one of the many cushioned chairs in the library and crossing her legs to swing her foot back and forth while watching her mother and sister interact.

Saemi nodded approvingly and took a step back to further evaluate her youngest child. Saemi was somewhere between Fay and Nitidi in height, wore the equivalent of a belly dancer's outfit, white against her sky-blue skin, and didn't have any shoes on. It was obvious where Fay got her looks. "I simply can't believe how well you've done! You've struck gold, daughter! Securing a prince of the Blood Moon Requiem as a master—you'll be his servant and have the opportunity to grow for millennia, if not far longer! Vampires do not age, after all!"

"I think he wants her to be more than just a servant . . ." Nitidi cut in with a low chuckle, causing Fay's eyes to hit the floor and avoid her mother's gaze.

But Saemi's smile only widened. "Yes . . . I saw that. Very interesting. As I said, you've done splendidly. Be sure that even if you don't feel the same way about him, do not let him know. This is a once-in-a-lifetime opportunity even for us demons who live eternal lives should we not get murdered."

Fay's fingers clenched. "But I do feel the same way about him."

There was a brief pause, and then Saemi laughed and pulled her daughter into a hug. "Of course you do! You're so adorable. I'm sorry! I didn't mean that to sound bad. I almost forgot that he's only your second summoner—and hopefully the last! Who knows, right? By the hells, this is SUCH an upgrade from your last warlock!"

Her mother winked down at her before letting Fay go again. "Perhaps your brother will take some lessons on obedience from you while under your care . . . I can only hope. Anyways, is there a particular reason you're returning today? Or was it just to catch up?"

Fay's eyes brightened, and she turned to look up at the soaring stacks of books along many hundreds of extremely tall bookshelves. "I was hoping to find information regarding Azagnitide Rotworms. Riven's sister has a friend who is afflicted with one, and I was wanting to find a ritual to get rid of it."

Saemi's eyes narrowed, and she bit her lower lip while tapping a finger along one cheek. Turning her head up to inspect a particular bookshelf farther down the way, she gestured for Fay to follow. "Perhaps I know where to look. Come now, follow me and we can discuss things further. You, too, Nitidi—this conversation involves you as well."

Launching herself up off the floor, their mother began soaring into the massive pathways between bookshelves, taking a sharp right with her two daughters quickly flying behind her.

Saemi's grace was unnatural. Some people in the clan often compared her to the angels and how they used their feathers to better adjust with wind currents, but that's what you got after many tens of thousands of years to practice flying and to acquire new traits.

Zipping in between the bookshelves a couple dozen yards off the ground, Saemi eventually came to a stop near a large, elevated wooden platform. Adjusting a lever and moving the platform to the right a little ways, Saemi stopped the contraption and reached out to pick out two separate leather-bound books.

"I believe these two volumes are exactly what you're looking for," Fay's mother stated, extending them to Fay with both hands. However, she withdrew them a moment later, a clever smile painting her lips. "But there is something you must do for me first."

Fay, who'd been reaching for the books to put in the bag Nitidi had gifted her, frowned. "What trickery are you up to this time, Mother? I hope you're not scheming again and trying to prank me like the last time. You know I get embarrassed easily."

Nitidi and Saemi both loudly laughed at her innocent accusation.

"I don't know what you mean by that, Fay! I'm only looking out for the clan's welfare and growth!" Saemi replied with another low chuckle. "Those slugworms were harmless—it's not MY fault you reacted the way you did. Anyways! I was hoping we could have a quick chat about Nitidi here."

Fay lifted her gaze, just as confused as Nitidi by the look they exchanged. "What about her?"

"Well, she finally escaped that foul man who was using her in sacrificial blood orgies," Saemi stated with a prompt huff. "Took forever to use that contractual loophole, but we managed to get her out."

"Oh!" Fay said with an excited bounce on the balls of her feet, still holding the sack of clothes. "Congratulations, Nitidi!"

"Yeah, it's way better now," Nitidi admitted with pursed lips. "But what does my old master have to do with Fay?"

"Well, it's obvious, isn't it?" Saemi said simply. "You need a new one, and Riven has an open slot. Does he not? Last I checked there were over three million demons angling for that single spot, and we need it to go to our clan. Not another."

A pause followed.

"You want Nitidi to bind to Riven, too?" Fay said skeptically. "Why? Not that I'd mind, but I thought you wanted our influence spread out across different sectors for information accumulation. Our clan is an information broker, after all."

"Riven is not a normal summoner; the benefits of binding two daughters to him outweigh the benefits of binding you to separate warlocks," Saemi said simply. "If I were a low enough level to meet the requirements, I'd bind to him myself. But unfortunately I can't, as I'm well above level 4,000 now. System regulations won't permit it—and it's not often any summoner at all manages to make it that far anymore. Unfortunate, truly. Now, if I wish to gain access to the mortal realms, I have to beat my way through the hells to do it, and we all know how that usually goes for succubi. Those damnable devils are truly barbaric."

Fay grimaced and wrinkled her nose, but hesitated when her mother gave her an expectant look.

"Are you . . . jealous?" Saemi asked, amusement creeping into her voice while she rolled her eyes. "Come on now. I know you had fun with that vampire princess and elf slave woman, didn't you? It wouldn't be much different than that."

Fay huffed with irritation. "That was a little bit different than this. And no, I'm not opposed to the idea of Nitidi coming if Riven wants to do so, but I won't speak for him, and I'll need both of you to respect any boundaries I set. Riven is mine. He belongs to me. I . . . I'm very much attached to him, and I don't want any other woman taking his heart from me."

"AHHH!!!!" Nitidi gasped with hands on either side of her cheek. "That's so cute! You really DO like him!"

Saemi once again rolled her eyes, then extended the books once more. "Well, at least ask him; you know how hard it is to find a decent summoner. It doesn't have to be sexual—I'll leave that decision up to you since you've already made a claim on your prince charming, but do let us know. Go on and rid that other poor soul of the Azagnitide Rotworm. I do hear they're rather foul, and I believe the rituals you need will be in these texts."

CHAPTER 16

Lahn's body . . . hurt. It was painfully obvious to Lady Shovi Lucio, his mother, whenever she looked at him, and her fury had never known such heights. Not until the day he'd withdrawn from the academy a physically and mentally broken man.

"YOU NEED TO DO MORE!" Shovi screamed at his father, the esteemed Lord Nikola Lucio, right outside Lahn's room. Furiously throwing a vase at the wall and causing it to shatter into hundreds of tiny porcelain pieces, Lahn's mom heaved with a red face, shoulders raising and hands quivering violently with ill-contained rage. "GET OFF YOUR ASS AND FIND OUT WHO DID THIS!"

Slamming the door as hard as she could in front of her shocked husband and not bothering to even look back at her other children, who'd done nothing but make jabs about Lahn's situation since he'd withdrawn from the academy, Shovi sank into a chair next to his bedside and tried to contain a sob.

Her glistening, watery eyes slowly lifted to meet his own as he struggled to breathe. "Don't worry, Lahn. I won't stop until whoever hurt you is found."

Lahn didn't reply. He couldn't. Or he could, but he didn't want to. He claimed not to know who the culprits were. He'd expressionlessly watched his sister sneer at him from the hallway when he'd been wheeled back into the room with his good leg and good arm both broken in multiple spots—something her mother had noticed and homed in on with a suspicious glare, but she had no foundation for any accusation thus far.

How had she ever raised such uncaring, pompous brats? Of her three children, only Lahn had ever shown any compassion or interest for anything other than their own well-being. In large part she blamed the man she married, but she also knew she was partially to blame for not failing to correct such behavior. Now, as they'd reached young adulthood, she feared it was far too late.

She turned her eyes back to her broken, kind, loving son on the bed. His jaw was shattered; his ribs were broken. His arms were so mangled after the brutal beating that she didn't even know if he'd have *any* good limb after all was said and done—and the good healers were all on the front lines helping keep people alive. The ones left here in the capital were either absolutely swamped with more serious cases than his or simply inadequate. He was still in a massive amount of pain any time he attempted to budge, and it caused her to sob uncontrollably at random times.

Rearranging the pillows and making sure Lahn was as comfortable as he could be, Shovi stepped back to the window and opened it for some sunshine. It was still winter and sunshine wasn't all that abundant, but it was better than nothing. She took out a brush and nervously smoothed her brunette hair like she usually did whenever she was upset, staring out across their courtyard, only to notice a new carriage had parked itself right outside.

Curiously frowning down at it, she heard a knock at the door and wondered who it could be.

"Lahn . . . I believe we have company," Shovi said in a shaky, hoarse voice from all the screaming and crying she'd done lately. Clearing her throat and flattening down her green dress, she clasped her hands and put on as kind a smile as she could while trying to catch the gaze of her broken son.

He only barely acknowledged her with a brief glance, then turned his lost gaze back to the window, not moving for fear of causing himself more pain.

Not knowing what else to say, she excused herself and started for the main hall. Stepping gracefully to the first platform overlooking the entrance hall, where a painting of Shovi and her husband hung above the first flight of stairs, she furrowed her brows even more when she saw the new guests.

There were three of them, none of whom she recognized. One was an extremely attractive, extremely pale man with startling blue eyes and an athletic build, dressed in a very basic yet stylish vest, shirt, and pants. Beside him on either side were two startlingly beautiful young women, one tan and blonde with green eyes and wearing a formfitting silver dress, and the other brunette, pale, and blue-eyed just like the man—probably a sibling. This last woman wore a very bright red dress that hugged her body to reveal toned musculature along her hips and abdomen. Her shoulders were bare. She also wore long red gloves that left her fingers bare and had a strange amulet strung around her neck similar to one the man beside her wore—likely a family sigil if Shovi had to guess.

They were talking to her husband, and there were two maids on standby along the right wall.

"You're here for Lahn?" Nikola asked curiously, his deep voice echoing throughout the room as Shovi made her way down. "What were your names again?"

Lord Nikola Lucio, high inquisitor of the king's court, was a very thickly built man and more resembled his eldest son, Parius, than anyone else. Nikola was blonde, hazel-eyed, with a neatly trimmed beard and a short, stylized haircut. Whenever he was out of his armor and not on the front lines, he could be seen in attire that most of the nobles wore—frilled, Victorian-style jackets over long-sleeved white shirts with militaryesque pants and boots.

"Lady Allie Wraithtide is my name," the stunning woman in the red dress said politely, though the way neither she nor the others smiled or even attempted to address Lord Lucio properly in his home made it obvious she was not in a friendly mood. "I've said that twice now. Where is Lahn?"

"Are you friends of Lahn?" Shovi asked, hurrying down the hall and becoming excited at the prospect of Lahn having made friends. He'd always struggled with that, and although this wasn't likely the case, Shovi could hope. Lahn could use all the positive energy he could muster . . .

Allie's eyes settled on Shovi, and her piercing gaze was oddly unsettling.

Coming to stand beside her husband, who was frowning at the three people in their entryway, Shovi put a hand on Lord Lucio's wrist to squeeze meaningfully. "What business do you have with my son?"

Lady Allie Wraithtide paused, her gaze almost calculating while she coldly evaluated both parents before clasping her hands behind her back. "He is my class partner. I was on a family business trip and heard he was beaten half to death . . . Lahn and I have become close. I was hoping to speak with him."

Lord Nikola Lucio's eyes widened in surprise, giving the young woman a once-over—and Shovi's breath caught in her throat.

"You . . . are close with my youngest son?" Lord Lucio responded skeptically. "And you are an academy student? I have not heard of House Wraithtide before."

"Father? Who is that?" a young male voice called from the kitchen area on the first floor, and soon Parius came into the light from beyond the next corner. Strutting over with a rather cocky attitude often found in the scions of noble houses, he nearly tripped when he laid eyes on both Allie and Fay. Then his gaze landed on Travis, and it was as if he was a peacock that'd gotten its tail feathers in a tussle.

Immediately assuming an air of better-than-thou-ness, Parius walked directly up to square off with Riven, evaluating the man of equal height with a piercing gaze as Riven casually stared back.

"I do not believe we've met," Parius said, extending a hand to Riven for him to shake. "Parius Lucio, heir to this house."

Riven glanced down at the extended hand, back up to Lahn's brother, and, without smiling, shook it wordlessly. "Travis Wraithtide."

"You're being rude, Parius," Shovi sighed. "You cannot just barge into the middle of a conversation like that."

"Agreed. Mind your manners, boy," Lord Nikola Lucio said with a crisp tone, getting a wince from his son.

Parius abruptly nodded but spared both Fay and Allie sidelong glances. "I apologize. I was just so taken with the looks of these young women that I forgot myself."

He gave his most charming smile, which neither woman returned—throwing him off as he sheepishly stepped back in line.

Lord Nikola Lucio let out a long sigh and placed his hands on his hips. "Excuse the rudeness of my eldest. As for my other son, Lahn, he is not well. It is true that he was severely beaten, but he has not identified the perpetrators and the matter is being investigated. It is best if you leave him be."

"Nonsense," Shovi said with a growl, stepping forward and reaching out to Allie with an approving nod. "My boy would love to have visitors. You must tell me about how the two of you met. He hasn't brought many friends over to our house before! This is good news!"

Meanwhile, Parius blinked in confusion. "That's because Lahn doesn't have any friends, Mother . . . Wait, what are your names?"

Allie gave an exasperated sigh, gritting her teeth and closing her eyes. "Lady. Allie. Wraithtide."

"OH!!!" Parius exclaimed, his fist smacking into his other open palm. "I have heard of you from my sister, Linela! You're the girl Lahn was stalking at school!"

Nikola immediately stiffened at the news, flushing with anger and embarrassment while giving a sideways glare up the stairs to Lahn's room. Shovi's heart sank.

"Stalking . . . ?" Shovi repeated with an awkward laugh. "Surely not . . . Lahn wouldn't do that."

"He would," Parius shot back, irritation showing in his flick of the wrist to motion in the same direction his father had glared only a moment ago. "You know how desperate he is for attention, Mother. You of all people should know. You need to stop babying him. Lahn even went as far as to steal an invitation to the royal ball from this young woman! Is that not true, Lady Wraithtide?"

Parius stared back at Allie eagerly, pleased that he'd made the connection, and let his eyes wander across her body rather thoroughly in ill-hidden lust. "I'm sure that's the real reason you've come, is it not? Lahn admitted to stealing it and handed it over to me. I actually have it stored in my room—I was going to find and give it to you to make amends. Would you like it back?"

Allie blinked, the clockworks ticking rapidly in her mind as the other two people with her silently glared Parius's way. Then her demeanor abruptly changed, and Allie shifted from being outwardly cold to being very polite and charming. She put on a fake but convincing smile, fluttered her eyelashes, and stepped in close with an extended hand. "I would certainly like it back."

Parius nodded, blushing at her close proximity and clearing his throat. "I will retrieve it, then! I should say that, although I've never met you before, I'm excited to think about you attending the ball! I'll be there as well. Perhaps giving back the ticket that my little brother stole will earn me a dance?"

Allie didn't reply, only keeping her hand extended expectantly—and Parius cleared his throat and quickly walked away and up the stairs toward his own room on the opposite side of the house from Lahn's.

Shovi was utterly crestfallen. While her husband continued blushing with shame over what Lahn had done, she was pale and felt like all the hope she'd had about potential friends coming to visit her crippled boy was out the window. "We . . . um, we apologize for our son's behavior."

"Which one?" Allie asked Shovi with a raised eyebrow.

Lord Lucio barked a scoffing laugh, shoving his hands into his pockets and muttering to himself while glaring at Allie, then up the stairs toward Lahn's room again, before huffing and turning back to Allie once more. "Of course we speak of our youngest boy. I'm mortified to think that he'd stalk you, much less steal something so valuable from you. I was confused at first at your appearance, but it appears Parius and Linela know who you are and intervened in time to reacquire your invitation. I am glad for it. Invitations to social events like that are in high demand, and I can understand why you came personally to fetch it. You have my most sincere apologies. I am sure that, should time permit it, I will take time away from the king to speak to your parents and also offer my apologies."

Allie stared back at Lahn's father, the fake smile still plastered there for many seconds. "Lord Lucio, I am afraid you're mistaken."

Lahn's father shuffled slightly, then raised an eyebrow. "Oh? How is that?"

Allie's eyes narrowed in turn. "That invitation was given to your son so he could attend the ball as my date. Lahn never stole that invitation, which begs the question as to why your daughter, Linela, accused him of stealing it—and why Parius has it now. I'm quite curious."

Dead silence filled the entrance hall.

"You're taking Lahn? Lahn, my youngest son? To the royal ball?" Lord Nikola Lucio sputtered, disbelief plain. He gestured up and down at Allie. "You?"

"That's all you got out of what I just said?" Allie asked, her words now coming out venomous as her anger began to rise. Her teeth clenched again, and for a brief moment her eyes flashed a brilliant red as the amulet around her neck abruptly cracked. But it came so fast that neither of Lahn's parents were sure that it'd actually happened. Rather, their attention was drawn down to the amulet, where a tiny piece of the oddly shaped sigil had chipped and fallen to the floor.

Shovi didn't know what to think. On one hand, she was internally reeling that this stunning young woman would go out of her way to ask Lahn to the ball. A mysterious young lady of the court, an academy student, and one as gorgeous as her? Shovi couldn't ask for more concerning her youngest boy, but what exactly was Lady Allie Wraithtide implying here? Surely she didn't think that Lahn's siblings had had anything to do with his beating. Linela and Parius weren't bastions of innocence and had grown up into poor excuses for adults, being spoiled all their lives and being taught by their father that they were better than everyone else, but to claim that they were involved in Lahn's injuries? That was preposterous. There was certainly another reason why Parius had the invitation, and Shovi could think of many possibilities off the top of her head even now. Perhaps Parius had acquired the invitation after the beating, finding it in Lahn's room and assuming he'd stolen it. Perhaps Lahn had given it up out of shame when the incident had occurred. Perhaps Lahn knew he couldn't go to the ball and had spun a lie to his brother and sister so they'd take the invitation and put it to good use. There were many, many ways Parius could have acquired that invitation.

Parius's footsteps came thudding back. The young nobleman proudly extended the invitation to Allie, who snatched it without a word.

"Well? A promise to a dance?" Parius asked eagerly, folding his arms, sucking in his stomach, and puffing out his chest to make himself look bigger. "I'd love to take you as a date, if you don't already have someone attending the ball with you!"

Allie's eyelids dropped. "I'll have to decline. I'm attending with your brother."

There was a pause. Then Parius nearly choked, and his eyes narrowed in confusion. "Huh? Surely this is a jest . . . Wait, are you being serious? Is this out of pity for what happened to him? He won't be able to attend the ball the way he is anyways! He's a cripple, and he's been so badly beaten—"

"Then I will sit with him in his room as he recovers and simply forgo the ball," Allie replied flatly. Turning away from the shocked father and son duo, Allie smiled Shovi's way. "Please take me to Lahn. I have a lot to talk to him about. I hope it doesn't feel like an intrusion."

Shovi nearly choked as well, but her reason was far different than her flabbergasted eldest son. "Not at all! Oh my, Lahn will be so excited to see you! Come! Come, he's up the stairs to the left."

CHAPTER 17

The portal between worlds opened, and legions spilled forth.

Hundreds of thousands of armored soldiers marched in columns through fiery gates, singing songs of war to the beat of thousands of drums. The sky was filled with the fleet of the Empire of Dying Suns, bearing a flag emblazoned with an angled sword piercing a ball of flames on a golden backdrop.

The time for the invasion of Panu had finally arrived.

"Captain Vros Kinal." The general addressed him as they stood alongside the king on a flagship in the sky, watching their armies venture into unknown lands to conquer whatever lay in wait. The old man's tone caught the captain off guard, and the general stroked his chin while inspecting the muscular younger man before abruptly saluting. "Good luck. May you bring glory to the Empire of Dying Suns, may you find victory upon the boundless path of eternal war, and may you bring this new world of Panu under control. A lot is riding on this expedition, Captain. I hope you realize that."

Captain Vros Kinal saluted back, armored gauntlet slamming into his pristine breastplate as the robed, elderly king stepped forward to place a hand on his pauldron.

"Captain," the king said with a smile. "You are the best we can afford to send. You will encounter four other invading forces, aside from the locals, as well as whatever other planetary quests the system decides to throw down as a gauntlet for the inhabitants to bypass. You will need to crush them all. Do so by the end of five years and the planet is ours, but if it comes down to it, you merely need to hold on and root yourself into position, keeping the beacon intact so reinforcements can arrive. Survival trumps supremacy, but supremacy will bring great honor. Do you understand what I am telling you?"

The captain nodded, piercing eyes shining out of the barbute helm he wore. "Yes, my king!"

The old man smiled, letting go of the other man's pauldron. "Good. Now go—the other factions who have acquired invasion tokens will no doubt be looking for a place to plant their own beacons, too. Find out where they are, dispose of them early, and smash the locals into submission. For the glory of the empire."

"For the glory of the empire!" the surrounding officers repeated in unison.

[World Quest 3 Update, Invaders From Beyond: Other factions of the multiverse have been watching your small planet greedily, wanting its resources for themselves. Be it mass slavery, genocide, forced societal integration, or being farmed as literal food, your planet's people are in danger. Invasion tokens have been distributed, and the invasion portals have finally been opened.

Invading forces have until the end of the five integration years to either conquer Panu entirely or alternatively survive that long in order to acquire reinforcements from the homeland. Any invading force left at the end of five years will have free access through system portals until a victor is decided. To rid this planet of an invading force, you must destroy their beacon, which will be highlighted by a marker in the sky above its location with the symbol of their empire. Maximum level for entry invaders has been set to level 80, with growth still enabled after arrival.
Invading Forces:
The Empire of Dying Suns
Pagaroth
The Kingdom of Shatterstone
The Black Sky Azag Hive Cluster
Rippenvire
Prepare yourselves, natives of Panu. The enemy is coming.]

Allie dismissed the notification almost as quickly as it'd come. She had other, more important things to worry about. It was a far different reaction than Lahn's brother and father, who immediately exited the manor to head for the palace.

Even Lady Shovi Lucio was troubled, and she hesitated at Lahn's door on the second floor of their household to read the world quest update twice over before glancing Allie's way. "Do you need to get back to your family?"

Allie didn't even blink. "No. I'd like to see Lahn."

Nodding in appreciation, Shovi opened the door—letting Allie, Riven, and Fay inside.

Allie had hardened herself to extreme degrees since the integration had begun, so she didn't flinch when she saw the broken body on the bed. Lahn was bruised, swollen, with his two good limbs wrapped in soft casts and some kind of ointment having been spread along his jaw and rib cage. The extent of the damage was obvious, and there were even a couple of isolated areas where the fire poker that'd been used to beat him half to death had left imprints of its shape.

There were even a few open, oozing wounds—though most of those had already been closed by the mediocre healers that'd been available here in the capital.

Riven, Fay, and Shovi watched from the door in silence as Allie came around the bed to sit on the side where the window let light in. She glanced down at him as he stared absently through the glass, then looked out alongside him. Wordlessly they sat together until she reached out her hand and clasped his own shriveled one.

Tears began to accumulate under his eyes, and his lips began to quiver at the contact. He managed to get out a hoarse whisper after that, and rapidly started blinking to try to control his emotions. "Thank you for coming. But . . . why?"

She turned to look at him, kindly squeezing his hand in her own. "Why what?"

He choked back a cough, still only whispering through his teeth in order to keep his broken jaw from hurting. "Why did you come?"

"You're my friend. Of course I would come."

"Why, though?"

"Why are you my friend?"

"Yes."

Allie paused, considering his question. "Because you're genuinely kind. You are internally strong. You deserve to have friends—don't think otherwise."

Lahn scoffed, then winced as his jaw moved in a way that caused the fractures to grind against one another. "I am not any of those things."

"Why do you think that?"

"Because being kind and internally strong are the defaults I am forced to abide by. Being weak makes me act that way; I don't have a choice. These are not admirable qualities. If I were to have power, if I were to be physically capable, and then I were to act the way I do with kindness—then it would be admirable. But being weak and therefore not having a choice in how I act should not grant me the same kind of admiration that a truly powerful man would get, because I don't have that choice."

Allie shook her head. "That's not true. Not true at all. Those stray dogs you keep in your little animal sanctuary are proof of that. Even how you are now, you still have power over those helpless animals. Do you not?"

Lahn looked like he was going to protest, but he instead decided to remain silent.

"And can you honestly tell yourself that you'd be a different person should you be granted power today?" Allie asked curiously, his shriveled hand still clutched in her own.

Lahn let out a sputum-filled cough, then managed a barely visible shrug. "I don't know. I'd probably be the same, but that's something I'll never know. Not after this. The injuries are too far gone; even the best healers we have—should they come back from the front lines—won't be able to completely heal me when the bones reset the way they are now. Even if you do manage to get rid of that worm, whatever Fay called it, and cure me . . . I'll still be a broken man."

Shovi immediately furrowed her brows, contemplating whether to ask about this worm and the cure he was talking about—but she didn't want to ruin the moment and chose to stay silent. She was just happy someone had cared enough to come and happy that her son was finally willing to talk with someone. Watching the child that she loved not have any support at all aside from her had broken her heart—so this was an incredibly welcome surprise and it made Shovi's heart swell to watch.

"I agree with you about one thing—you'd probably still be the same," Allie said, pushing his hair out of his eyes to get a better look at his bruised face. Her expression turned sad. "I haven't known you for long, but I can honestly say that I'm pulled to you. I haven't met anyone like you before, and I don't think it's just because you're weak."

To this, Lahn began to laugh. It was a sardonic laugh. Despite his injuries, he just couldn't help it, and with every laugh came a wince. "Drawn to me. I don't understand. Truly, I don't. Don't get me wrong, Allie, I've loved being around you . . . but you could have such better friends. Friends that don't hold you back and friends who don't need to be pushed around in a chair just to follow you into a café. Friends that have higher social status than me. Friends that have brighter futures than a cripple who will hold no true position of power in the ruling classes despite my noble birth. I have nothing to offer you, and I don't know why you're wasting your time. You have everything, Allie—you're incredibly kind, stunningly beautiful, and talented. You have a far brighter future than I do. Being friends with me will only push away potential suitors that would no doubt make your family proud, as they'd probably get the wrong idea about your intentions and find spending time with me inappropriate—even if it is innocent and just as friends."

Allie threw up her hands in mock despair. "Oh, god! Not that! Whatever will I do should the suitors decide to go away?!"

Riven failed to hide his grin.

Then Allie gave Lahn an exasperated but still kind stare. "Come on, Lahn. Catch a hint."

Leaning down and brushing her long brown hair behind one ear, Allie slowly pressed her lips against his—earning a sharp and excited gasp from his mother.

Letting the kiss linger, Allie eventually pulled back and poked a very confused and very bright-red Lahn in the chest—getting a wince from him when she forgot that he had broken ribs. "Oh, sorry! I forgot you're injured."

She winked. "And you look like an apple right now, you're so damn red. You almost match the color of my eyes or my dress."

The silence was palpable, and it took a while for the young crippled man to gain his bearings again as Allie laughed and the other two women held hands over their mouths with grins underneath.

"Your eyes are bright blue! They're not red!" Lahn said snarkily through clenched teeth, trying and failing to hide his growing, giddy smile as his heart hammered loudly in his chest to the ears of the vampires in the room. "But yes, I can see why you'd . . . um . . . compare my face to your dress. I kind of daydreamed this would happen . . . but I never thought you'd actually be interested in someone like me. Why me? You have so many other options."

Allie flicked his nose. "Does it matter?"

"It does. I want to understand. You're just so . . . you're everything I'm not. As I said before, you're kind, beautiful, talented, and I just don't see what you see in me. And Mother, please! You're embarrassing me! Stop making those cutesy noises!"

Riven chuckled while Shovi mumbled an excited but hushed apology.

Allie raised an eyebrow, the smile fading. She turned to face him on the bed with one knee bent and tucked under her other thigh. "Lahn . . . I have been called many things since arriving on Panu. Kind is not one of them."

Lahn blinked. "Huh? What are you talking about? You're one of the nicest people I've ever met!"

Shovi was eating this up like an old woman watching midday soap operas with both hands still clasped over her incredibly wide smile. She was so, so excited for her son and she'd been desperate for him to find someone—but not many people had been interested in pitching their daughters to a crippled man. Yet here Allie was—far better than anything Shovi could have hoped for, and it made Shovi just as giddy as Lahn to see it.

Allie straightened on the bed, her back becoming stiff, and she hesitantly glanced over to Riven, who gave her a nod of encouragement. Then her hand wrapped around the amulet around her neck, and her grip tightened. "No. I'm not a good person, Lahn. In fact I'm probably one of the worst people you'll ever know."

Confusion struck him like a freight train. "What are you talking about?"

Allie gave him another sad smile, and she pulled away slightly. "I like you, Lahn. I like you a lot. You inspire me to be a better person, I want you to know that. I admire you, in many ways, and you remind me of my brother back before he was forced to change. Perhaps that's why I like you so much. Anyways . . . I've done some terrible things, and I think you should know before you get too excited about—well, me."

"There isn't a lot that you could tell me that'd change my mind," Lahn replied with a lighthearted laugh. "It's not like you're a mass murderer, Allie. What did you do? Embezzle funds? Bribe some officials? Is your family caught up in the syndicate or something? Because if that's the case, then—yeah, that's bad, but . . . but I'll work through it. I was thinking you and your brother were kind of odd in that way—mysterious even. I doubt whatever you did is unforgivable, though."

Allie's face had become rigid as he spoke. She let out a deep breath. "No . . . No, I'm not part of any kind of syndicate. I didn't realize there was an organization like that here to begin with. I'm afraid it's far worse than that. Lahn, I *have* killed people."

Lahn blinked. "Oh! Like, in the war . . . right? Is that what this is about? I forgot you went on that trip concerning the elves . . ."

His voice trailed off as she shook her head.

"I mean . . . yes, I've killed a lot of elves, too," Allie said hesitantly.

"A . . . LOT of elves?" Lahn repeated, concern etched into his face. "Too?"

Allie nodded. "Yeah. Funny that you mention it, but I actually am a mass murderer. I think I've killed well over ten thousand people just by myself, and I've ordered many, many more to die, too. Some people I killed out of need or revenge, but I've killed other people because it's fun."

Lahn's confusion and concern matched Shovi's own as his mother stood stiffly in the background. None of this was making any sense to either of them.

"Perhaps you'd better recognize me as Queen Allie Thane of the Thane Necropolis, vampire princess of the Blood Moon Requiem, or by what the elves are calling me—Butcher of Carnis—rather than Allie Wraithtide. Wraithtide is my parents' family name, while Thane is the name Riven and I used growing up." Sighing and firmly tightening her hand one last time on the amulet around her neck, Allie gave it a tug—snapping the latch in the back and putting the item on the bed. Within a matter of seconds, her eyes went from bright blue to crimson, and her vampiric aura along with her vast negative Charisma hit the room like a cannon.

It was as if Shovi and Lahn had both been physically slapped, and the reaction only got more pronounced as Allie's red dress faded away into her spatial sack, only to be replaced by a very famous set of soul-stitched bone armor. Boots, pauldrons, cuirass, gauntlets, underlying bone-linked chain mail, black robe, and finally the skull mask appeared on Allie's body one after the other. When the mask finally came to rest on Allie's face and her crimson eyes gleamed out at him, she took it off and placed it on Lahn's chest.

"Tell me, Lahn," Allie said with a hesitant smile, displaying her small fangs. "What do you think of me now?"

Shovi was as pale as the sheets on Lahn's bed, and slowly her eyes traced across the room to land on Riven. Putting one and two together, she started to shake— and her thoughts were only confirmed a moment later when Allie spoke.

"Riven . . ." Allie said softly, still maintaining eye contact with the broken young man on the bed and softly holding Lahn's withered hand in her own slender fingers. "What do we do to the people who harm our friends?"

Riven's eyes narrowed, and his amulet shattered as a pulse of his aura rocked the entire manor in a sheen of red—causing Shovi to stumble and catch herself against the wall while maids downstairs could be heard screaming. "We brutally kill them."

Allie's eyes slowly lifted to Riven's own as his aura began to fade. "I agree. Would you do me a favor and bring me the lordling Gleetus Nefrand? I do believe he has a very special role to play today after our ritual is complete. You know where to find him."

Riven grinned. "I'm going to enjoy this."

"Really? You've changed, Riven. Perhaps destroying that city was good for your character after all—you no longer balk when circumstance comes calling."

"Perhaps, but I very much approve of your proposed methods concerning this scenario. I'll be back soon." Riven raised a hand, and a shadowy rift flared to life in front of him. Stepping through it, he disappeared and closed the portal behind him.

Fay began to walk around the bed, stopping beside Allie and dismissing her illusion to show what she truly looked like—which kept her facial features the same, while her skin color changed to blue, her eyes turned black, her hair turned white, and her demonic horns and tail were on full display. She kept her wings retracted. "Hey, Lahn! I found some textbooks regarding the ritual we need to get rid of that worm . . . The problem is that it'll be very painful, and normally we'd have to battle it when it gets out. Thankfully I believe Allie should be able to handle it rather easily, and it'll only be a very minor struggle, so there isn't any need to switch locations. Are you ready to begin?"

CHAPTER 18

Scented smoke filled the room and where sunlight filtered through a glass window illuminating various books, chairs, and a central table where the three men sat. Otherwise it was pretty dark, as there was only one window and the room was rather large.

Gleetus belched loudly over the laughter of his two friends while giving them a rude gesture, yet he smiled, too. "Just because you can't do it doesn't mean I can't do it!"

"She is out of your league, my friend!" another of the young men said with a cackle, smacking the ass of a passing maid. The young woman yelped, angrily scowled at the man, and then hurried out of the lake house with more laughter following her.

Gleetus grumbled to himself and held a glass of wine to his lips, sipping it out of frustration and thinking of the new lady of the court he had a crush on. "I just don't understand why Allie wastes her time with that maimed twat! He's useless to everybody and the only person she ever talks to is him!"

"I heard even Braden Rooze was shot down. She must be a real looker," the other of Gleetus's friends said thoughtfully, smoking on a pipe and blowing out rings of smoke. "Either way, at least you taught Lahn to stay away from your girl. Don't worry, she's from a poor country household and I'm sure your father's influence will be enough to pressure her into some kind of courtship."

Adjusting his frilled, buttoned jacket and looking out the window onto the shimmering lake nearby, Gleetus only grunted. "Yes, you're probably right. I've already told my father about it, and he said he'd look into House Wraithtide soon. Perhaps I'll be able to meet with their head of household sometime to apply pressure this week."

"There's no need for that. We're already here."

Gleetus nearly fell out of his chair in surprise, and one of the other lordlings screamed just as an aura of extreme malice slammed into them like a sledgehammer. The third man abruptly vomited all over the table.

Gleetus, who cried out as red frost began to accumulate along the surroundings and even along his skin, shoved the chair back and wheeled around in a panic. But there was no one there. "What the hell?!"

The sound of bone on wood cracked the silence, and Gleetus wheeled around again to see his two companions slump to the floor on either side of a hooded man clad in black, feet up on the table in a relaxed position. He stared at Gleetus with glowing crimson eyes, arms crossed and face otherwise shadowed in the light of the single window.

They just stared at one another, the unknown intruder very calm while Gleetus felt his heart rapidly pounding in his chest. He didn't know who this guy was, but his soul roared at him to run—telling him that this man was dangerous. How had he not heard this person enter? Why was Gleetus's mana not coming to his call? Why was the air so frigidly cold?

There was only one option. Gleetus was the definition of a coward, thus he decided to abandon his friends to their fate. Shakily, Gleetus made his move— bolting for the door only to stagger and fall when Crimson Ice swept up one leg to hold in him place.

Gleetus flopped forward, hitting the ground and breaking his ankle with a shrill scream when the ice halfway up his foot didn't budge and the rest of his body kept going. "HELP! HELP, WE HAVE AN INTRUDER! GUARDS! GUARDS, COME NOW!!!"

"Your guards have been . . . incapacitated," Riven said, not having moved from his spot on the chair between the two crumpled men. "Let me introduce myself . . . I am Allie Wraithtide's brother. My name is Riven Wraithtide, also known as Riven Thane."

Gleetus, who'd been bawling and wailing on the ground while intermittently calling out to the soldiers his family hired as personal security, froze upon hearing Riven's words. His eyes went wide, and his breathing picked up between tearful coughs of pain. "Wait . . . what?"

The shock was apparent, but Riven didn't say it again. Instead, Riven slowly lifted a finger—and abruptly a spike of Crimson Ice shot up from the floor and punctured Gleetus's left thigh.

Again, Gleetus screamed.

"Allie sent me to collect you," Riven stated, only whispering but infusing his voice with mana to amplify the sound over the wails of the bleeding man on the floor. "For what you did to Lahn."

Again, Riven lifted a finger and another spike lanced out from the frost-covered floor to skewer Gleetus in the right shoulder.

"I DON'T KNOW WHAT YOU'RE TALKING ABOUT!" Gleetus yelled between choked sobs. "WHAT IN THE HELLS IS WRONG WITH YOU! WHO ARE YOU REALLY?!"

Another finger lifted, skewering him this time in the left hand.

Gleetus flailed, writhing about and trying to rip his body off the magics while his heart beat like a Cherokee drum in a panic.

"No . . . No, that will not do," Riven said, getting ready to lift another finger. "Admit what you did and tell me why so that I can upload this recording to the

Dawn forums. We were going to get Lahn to do it, but we found out that he'd already tried. Apparently subterfuge is still somewhat protected unless certain circumstances are met—that clause covers your little stunt in the barracks the other day. So I'm going to continue torturing you until you tell me in vivid detail what you did that day—and why."

Another finger lifted, another crimson spike skewered Gleetus's arm.

"I'M INNOCENT!!! I WASN'T THE ONE TO—"

Another spike skewered his pelvis.

Gleetus screamed. "FINE! FINE, IT WAS ME!!! I BEAT THE SHIT OUT OF HIM WITH A FIRE IRON! BUT I WAS ONLY TEACHING THAT LITTLE CRIPPLED BITCH THAT STALKING YOUR SISTER WAS—"

Another spike skewered his good ankle, causing Gleetus to break down into violent sobs. Blood was everywhere, and he'd pissed himself halfway through the exchange. He couldn't even move properly anymore with the number of spikes sticking through his extremities.

"He wasn't stalking my sister at all," Riven said flatly, kicking his legs off the table and leaning forward with a chuckle. "If anything, my sister was stalking him. She had a crush, you see, and it even appears you and those twat siblings of his stole the invitation to the royal ball that she'd given him—after you beat him half to death. I'm convinced, by the looks of him, you actually meant to murder him right then and there. It was only luck his maid came in time to get some help. He would have died if she hadn't—which brings us to now . . . You tried to kill Allie Thane's friend. That was a very big mistake. So tell me the real reason why you did it. Not some made-up hocus-pocus about stalking—because we both know that's a lie."

"M-my family w-will—"

"Your family will do nothing, unless they want to join you in hell after you're dead," Riven said, cutting him off with narrowed eyes. "You pathetic little meatbag."

Riven started channeling energy through his Unholy pillar, and the next words he used were infused with the ability of Silvertongue. His voice reverberated unnaturally, and Gleetus seemed to shrink back when Riven spoke. "Give me the real reason you decided to try and kill Lahn."

[Silvertongue (Unholy): Soak your words with Unholy mana to briefly capture the minds of lesser beings, allowing only those with less Willpower than you to be affected and enabling you to persuade them more easily. This spell scales with both Willpower and negative Charisma, as well as the amount of mana you put into it. This spell may be developed into a better version of itself by acquiring the Depravity subpillar. Extremely high mana cost, low cooldown.]

Gleetus's eyes glazed over, his words slowed as if he was drunk, and his body became relaxed despite the numerous red spikes skewering his limbs. "I did not mean to kill him. I only meant to beat him badly—but I got carried away when he started crying. It was just too easy; he was such an easy mark to pick on. It made me look better in front of the other nobility, and it was fun—especially when his sister urged me to go on. Lahn spoke back to me in class not long ago when your sister was there; he was the reason your sister ignored me. So I took care of him to get the attention of your sister—and even if it was bad attention, I'd have used the threat of potentially ending him next time to manipulate her to sleep with me. My father is a powerful man, and he could have shielded me from a small noble house such as yours. At least I thought so until now—I did not realize who she really was if what you say is true."

Riven let the spell drop, and the far-off look on Gleetus's face vanished—only to be replaced with the pained horror of what was happening when he began to scream again.

Another finger rose, another spike punctured the floored victim, and Riven sneered when Gleetus began to beg.

Fay continued to draw out the ritual circle, once in a while taking time to evaluate the sigils, runes, and diagrams in the books her mother had given her before going back to the chalk she was scribbling with on the bedroom floor. Occasionally she'd take an item from a pouch at her side, such as an odd marble, a rodent's skull, and some of Lahn's hair—circling them with different diagram outlines before continuing with the rest.

She was trying not to smile at the two on the bed. They were fucking adorable, and Lahn's reception of who she was had gone over very well. He'd obviously been surprised but otherwise hadn't changed his opinion of Allie in the slightest.

Allie lay there next to him, still armored up, eyes locked with Lahn's and holding his hand while whispering to him, occasionally laughing at whatever he was saying in reply. The two had fallen into their own little world despite Fay's presence and Lahn's mother—Shovi—who'd taken up residence in a chair in the corner of the room after guaranteeing the maids of the household that everything was all right.

Shovi didn't know what to make of this situation. On one hand Shovi was incredibly happy for her son, not only because he'd found a friend and a potential lover—which were both long shots for him prior to now given the social circles he was introduced to alongside his condition—but these were very dangerous waters he was treading. Not only for himself, but for the family. Shovi had often heard rumors of Queen Allie Thane, Butcher of Carnis, the she-devil who struck fear into the hearts of Dawn's enemies while inspiring awe in the most veteran of the king's men on the battlefield. Up until now Shovi hadn't seen any footage that displayed Allie's or Riven's faces—perhaps there was some obscure video somewhere, but even after going back through the forums, it hadn't been found. How was Shovi supposed to know these two abnormally pale siblings were the Thane siblings?

With a snap of their fingers, either one of them could spell disaster for the kingdom of Dawn. Allie wasn't as powerful as Riven, but she was still a walking disaster, and she was the primary figurehead of their allied kingdom of the undead to the north. While her brother was just a gods damned monster who had literally wiped out an entire city of hundreds of thousands of people, if not more than that, over the course of a few minutes when he'd become enraged.

Yet here Allie was . . . snuggling up to Shovi's crippled son on the bed and giggling at his stupid jokes while occasionally giving him giddy kisses. Meanwhile, Riven's demon—THE Riven Thane's demon—was creating a ritualistic cure for her boy. What would her husband say? What would he do? Would he finally acknowledge Lahn if things changed for the better? Daring to look up and watch Allie crinkle her nose with another high-pitched laugh at Lahn's whispers, Shovi blushed with pride and unbridled glee—but quickly averted her gaze uncertainly when Allie looked her way.

"Do you wish move closer, Lady Shovi?" Allie asked with a bright smile as she propped her head up on one elbow. "Come tell me about what your husband and eldest son are likely up to. I know they left for the palace due to the announcement of foreign invaders, but I know little of the internal politics and military mindsets here in the capital. It was one of the reasons why I even accepted the king's invitation to come—I wish to be acquainted with your people to get a better idea of who you all are."

Shovi's eyebrows lifted in surprise, and she abruptly stood up to curtsy in respect before pulling the chair over to the edge of the bed—being careful not to step on any of Fay's chalk drawings. Sitting down with an elegant flare of her green dress, she spared an excited wink for her blushing son. "Well, I can't tell you too much because I simply don't know. My husband has always been rather tight-lipped about the happenings of the capital. Though I'm sure if you wanted to know more, other ladies of the court could fill you in at our regular gatherings. Other husbands are more liberal in what they say—so they potentially have some insight that I would not."

Allie began to grin—just barely displaying her small fangs—and Lahn rolled his eyes. "I see. Are you inviting me to one of these . . . gatherings, then?"

"Precisely so! It isn't anything important, just teatime and gossip with some good food." Shovi beamed, clapping once with a delighted nod. "Oh, I'm so very excited to get to meet and speak with you! It's truly an honor, Your Majesty!"

"Oh, please! Call me Allie. And certainly, I'd love to come. When's the next one?"

Lahn huffed. "Don't let her wrangle you into those boring tea parties; they're dreadful. I've had to sit through them myself and I nearly want to roll my chair off the deck to end it all whenever my attendance is required!"

"LAHN!" Shovi exclaimed to the laughter of her son and Allie both, putting her hands on her cheeks in mock anger. "How could you say something like that?! All my friends just LOVE being around you!"

"They treat me like a broken puppy dog," Lahn stated with a knowing look. "But yes, at least they're nice to me. Could certainly be worse."

"Indeed it could. And don't you ruin this opportunity for me to show off your new lady friend to my posse! That's just rude!" Shovi paused midsentence and hesitated, then lifted a finger of inquiry. "May I ask . . . Would it be too forward to assume that you and my son are courting?"

"MOTHER!" Lahn exclaimed, only to get more laughter from Allie while she blushed.

"That's only correct if Lahn wants it to be so," Allie replied warmly, having dismissed her gauntlets to wrap her slender fingers around Lahn's own again—not withdrawing in disgust at all like so many others had before her when his withered flesh touched her own. "I was aiming for that, but I don't know if I'm good enough for him."

"Allie, shut up," Lahn stated flatly—getting a wide-eyed glare from his mother.

But Allie's reaction showed Shovi just how close the two had become in such a short time. It'd only been a few months that Lahn had been enrolled in school, and things had been a roller coaster since then—but they'd turned out brilliantly here at the end.

Shovi cleared her throat, and her nerves calmed as she realized that not only did Allie not take offense, but she even enjoyed the banter and the fact that he'd teasingly told her to shut it. Perhaps telling her son to be extremely respectful would be a bad idea, but it'd been the first knee-jerk thought Shovi had when learning Allie's true identity. No, she'd not interfere in any major way and just let it take its road. He obviously was doing something right by the way Allie looked at him. "So how did you and Lahn meet, if you don't mind me asking?"

Allie opened her mouth to reply—but a dark portal appeared and a flash of black propelled both Riven and Gleetus into Lahn's room. Riven was hauling Gleetus by the collar, yet the limp, whimpering man that Riven tossed to the ground with a splat of blood was far from what Allie remembered Gleetus to be.

The young lordling bully was broken, far worse than what Gleetus had done to Lahn. His legs and arms were snapped backward in multiple places at awkward angles, and he looked like a bloody pincushion with dozens of spikes sticking out of him. The blood that did seep out of his body was being rerouted back into his vessels as Riven manipulated it—keeping him alive—and he smiled widely at his sister with a thumbs-up when he appeared.

"I just learned my first healing spell! Er . . . Perhaps *healing* isn't the right word for it. Maintenance-of-life spell, perhaps?" Riven said with a laugh. "It's pretty decent, actually. If people can't go into shock because of blood loss, they don't die. Simple but effective. I've essentially kept this asswipe alive for the past hour by mapping out his blood vessels to replicate them, whereas any normal person would bleed out in minutes."

Pulling up a screen and ignoring the horrified, shocked looks of Shovi and Lahn, Riven showed Allie the new spell. Though he did note that the shock and horror was quickly replaced by rage in Shovi, whereas Lahn, looking down at the man who'd tormented him for years, was overcome with an emotion Riven couldn't quite place.

> **[Voodoo Doll (Blood) (Tier 2): Scan your target to map out their vessels and infuse your mana into their bloodstream. You then gain the ability to replicate their bloodstream regardless of whether they have extensive wounds—enabling you to keep them alive as long as their brain remains intact. You may also use this ability on hostiles to form painful blood clots. Heart attacks caused by this ability do critical strike damage. Dependent on both Intelligence (90%) and Willpower (10%) stats. Medium cooldown. This is a channeling ability and will not work if interrupted by using other spells.]**

Allie's eyes widened and she shifted off the bed, putting her boots on the floor and exclaiming her excitement with a laugh, hands on her head. "Riven! That's so good! Can you show me?"

"I'm showing you right now," Riven stated, confused. "I can cancel it and reshow you if you'd like to see the hand gestures, if that's what you're getting at. I've done it a couple times already when casting portals to jump across this capital city. Um . . . Mandon is the name of this city—right?"

"No! I mean, yes—it is called Mandon, but no! I meant the blood clots!" Allie stood up and walked over to the sniveling man who was coughing blood intermittently on the floor and shaking violently. "Give him a heart attack and watch him squirm a bit before saving him again! You can do that, right?"

Riven thought about it a moment, scratching his chin, then underwent the proper motions for his new Tier-2 spell. He flared his fingers, spreading them apart before pointing his open palm in Gleetus's direction in a grasping motion to test it out.

Immediately Gleetus began to gasp, turning white and spasming on the ground even more violently. Allie began to laugh and clap her hands, violently kicking Gleetus in the rib cage to the sound of snapping bones that sent the lordling slamming into a far wall, still spasming.

Riven shifted his hand slightly, and Gleetus gasped for air—beginning to sob violently. "He's like a little porcupine! Isn't he cute?!"

"Allie . . . can you please stop?"

Both vampires turned curiously back to where Lahn was trying to sit up on the bed. He was giving it quite the effort, and his mother next to him had turned pale.

"Our house is going to be in a lot of trouble if you murder him . . ." Lahn said hesitantly, glancing over to his mother where she looked to be beginning to have a nervous breakdown by the way her mouth and eyebrow twitched while she scraped her nails against her thighs. "Please don't kill him. Gleetus has a very powerful father who—"

"We'll kill his father," Allie said in an upbeat, chipper tone, bending down to pull Gleetus up by the hair and bringing his wide bloodshot eyes to meet her own as he dangled limply under her strength. She gave the lordling a wide fanged smile. "That'll be after we kill Gleetus first, though! When we change you into a vampire, Lahn, your first meal will be this guy!"

Allie roughly shook the man, sending droplets of blood everywhere like a dog would shake off water—but they quickly retracted and sank back into the streams of blood across Gleetus's ruined, torn body, flowing out of his severed vessels in many places due to Riven's magic.

That's when Gleetus began to beg. "P-please, Allie! I didn't know—"

Her other fist slammed into his gut, causing Gleetus to lose the air in his lungs before her hand ripped out part of his lower intestine. She flung the organ to the floor, sneering at the man in her grasp. "You don't get to talk! No, no, no . . . You're just—"

"Allie!" Lahn called out, timid but also fearful. "Allie, you're scaring me! Please stop!"

For the first time since Riven had reconnected Allie after the integration, Riven saw doubt and uncertainty in her eyes. She glanced over to where Lahn's chest was heaving despite broken ribs, and her eyes softened.

"Allie . . ." Lahn said warily, grimacing due to speaking too fast with his broken jaw. His eyes fell to the sobbing face of Gleetus when Allie flung him across the room with another splat, before Lahn took in a deep breath. "Allie, for me . . . please don't kill him."

"But . . ." Allie said, frowning. She took a couple steps toward the bed, past Lahn's mom, who was pale and staring at the entrails that'd been ripped out of the young lordling, and sat beside her crippled friend. "Why? He hurt you, severely. He tried to kill you, Lahn. I'd thought you would want this . . . and you'll need to feed if you become a vampire. When the change occurs, you become crazed because you start out starved! When I turn you—"

"Allie!" Lahn said, exasperated—trying to hold up a hand but grimacing as he did so. "Allie, you're amazing, and I appreciate that you're trying to protect me—but this isn't what I want. I don't want to . . . to feed on him. You never even asked me, Allie—you just assumed. But I don't want to become a vampire."

He gave her a sheepish smile, and Allie's face froze in shock.

"You see!" Gleetus gasped with a horrified, blood-flecked rattle to his voice. He was frantic, despite all his injuries, and he grasped onto Lahn's words despite the shock of what was going on in this situation and all the things he'd learned in the past hour. "He doesn't want me dead! You don't need to do this! Spare me!"

"Shut the fuck up." Riven, who was standing nearby, kicked him, the motion a blur so fast that neither Lahn nor Shovi could follow it. In turn, Gleetus's head was literally snapped off his body—hitting the ceiling and bouncing down onto the floor.

Shovi screamed.

Lahn went pale.

Fay giggled.

Allie sighed. "Riven! He just said that he didn't want us to kill him!"

"Oh, he's not dead." Riven casually gestured to the head where blood was still streaming into the arteries of the decapitated neck. "I haven't stopped channeling yet. This voodoo doll magic is really neat! I figured that'd work, just wanted to see for myself—but his brain cells aren't dying because I'm still supplying them with blood."

Indeed, Gleetus's shocked face with a smashed-in nose and unhinged jaw was blinking rapidly—eyes darting around to let out a silent scream. But he didn't have lungs, and although the blood streams were drawing his head back toward the rest of his body, he wasn't able to utilize anything below the neck because Riven had kicked his head off.

Allie gawked for a moment, shook herself out of her stupor, then turned back to Lahn. Clasping his withered hand, she returned his sheepish smile. "I . . . guess I got ahead of myself. I'd just assumed you'd want to become like me . . . it'd make you a lot stronger, and we'd be able to fit together better because of it."

"I don't need to be a vampire to fit together with you, as long as you'll have me as a human," Lahn replied, having let himself drift back into a thick pillow underneath his head. Sighing, he closed his eyes. "That's just a very, very big decision to make. Maybe I'll change my mind one day, just . . . just don't throw it on me so fast. Is that okay?"

"That's absolutely okay!" Allie said in turn, smiling gently down at the young man she'd fallen for. "I'm so sorry, I was being stupid. And I also kind of wondered how you'd react . . . so we have a backup plan on feeding Gleetus to you. Fay, how's the ritual coming along?"

Fay glared up at Riven, pooching her lips and humphing at where some of Gleetus had smeared the chalk diagrams. "It'd be done if Riven hadn't bounced Gleetus's head onto the drawings. I'll have to redraw it. Another two minutes, tops."

"Good!" Allie replied, rubbing her hands together wickedly to glare daggers at the ruined man on the floor. "Time for plan B!"

"Which is?" Riven asked curiously.

"Well, we're going to take Lahn's worm and shove it up Gleetus's ass, of course! What else is there if Lahn isn't going to eat him?!"

CHAPTER 19

"Slayfather, the advance force has launched their assault on the natives." Peskus bowed at the waist, black tailcoat billowing in the wind as he and his superior officer stood atop a huge half-flesh, half-machine abomination that was burrowing itself into the coastal cliff face. It mutated and convulsed but took care not to dislodge any of the many tens of thousands of people still inside the construct.

It was a living fortress created from a combination of Unholy and Machine foundational pillars, with huge spires, battlements, guns, and steampunk defensive tech mounted at intervals all along the outer wall. Tunnels were being dug, causing the ground to shudder as the drills went to work—but soon the entire cliff would be one big defensive layer that would be almost impenetrable to any army without immense casualties.

The Slayfather glanced back from underneath his black top hat, red eyes narrowed while he supported himself with his intricate cane. Not that he needed to—it was more of a fashion statement than anything else. "Are the harvesters with them?"

"They are," Peskus said, maintaining the bow and blinking through his monocle. "The first order of business, as you instructed, was to acquire a food source. We sent them to a merfolk lair to the north, and after that they are to travel to a coastal city run by humans. Our scouts indicate it's prime real estate with lots of cattle for the picking, and I do know how you like your humans."

The Slayfather grinned, displaying his vampiric fangs. Holding up one steampunk gauntlet that ticked with a compass of some sort in the back side of his hand, he nodded enthusiastically. "Oh, I haven't had one of those in days . . . That sounds rather good right now. Once they're back, bring me the fattest, most plump human you can find—I feel like gorging myself right about now and I am oh so weary of the nargles we've had to settle for due to food shortages back home in Rippenvire."

At Lahn's request, Riven had force-fed Gleetus a couple healing potions and stabilized the man while Allie and Fay performed the ritual. It was a lot of chanting, sitting, praying, and hand gestures that Riven simply found boring.

But it was working.

He casually watched from the sidelines next to a cowering, sniveling Gleetus on the floor. Hands clasped behind his back, Riven stared at Lahn's body as the young man groaned and occasionally whimpered in pain—yet his necrotic, unnatural rot was beginning to fade away. It was being replaced with new skin, and his mother, Shovi, was crying hysterically in the hallway—having removed herself after being overcome with emotion that her son was going to be cured of the ailment that'd plagued him nearly his entire life.

Internally glancing at his soul aperture where the crystal flower he'd recently eaten—a piece of Gaia's soul—was wrapped around Athela's core piece, he saw the piece flare with pulsing light again. It'd done that a few times now, and her soul piece was beginning to grow larger—exponentially so. Whereas it'd only been a speck when he'd first gotten it, the soul piece was now a fourth of the size of his core.

Riven smiled. He was excited to see his friend again.

A draconic roar, and then the sound of large talons crashing into the ground outside caused Riven's head to turn slightly. Casually walking to the window, he saw Allie's undead pet drake. Its black wings were marked with glowing neon-teal veins; bones made up most of its body with black strings of mana and neon-teal miasma shimmering off the huge creature. He'd remembered that fight—before it'd become an undead toy. It'd been a hard thing to kill, but what was it doing here?

"Allie, isn't that your new pet?" Riven asked with a sidelong glance, but his sister shushed him despite the lumbering creature that shook the ground with every step—causing the people downstairs to scream in horrified echoing cries. "Allie, seriously, your pet is here."

Allie huffed loudly in irritation and stood up, ending the chant while Fay continued almost in a trance. Walking over to the window as Shovi looked open-mouthed at the huge skeletal dragon head staring in with one eye, Allie pushed the glass open and angrily grumbled at the monster. "Tyranus, this better be good! You KNOW you're not supposed to come here in broad daylight—even if the king DID tell the fleet to let you through! And you're SUPPOSED to be guarding Dungeon Alibast so the elves stop enslaving dryads!"

Tyranus? So that's what she'd named it.

Riven chuckled at the dumb expression the creature gave her for being chided, but perhaps that was all in his head. Gleetus screamed and wet himself when he saw the huge drake after sparing a glance—and one of the maids ran up the stairs to report the huge monster in a panic only to swoon when she saw the huge head staring into Lahn's room.

When the drake spoke, his words were deep and raspy—but boomed loud enough for everyone in the house to hear them. "I was told to come by Gaia, to bring you a message."

"Well, spit it out, then. What's Gaia's message?" Allie said, tapping her foot impatiently.

The drake paused, cocking his head as if trying to remember what the Fae goddess had imparted to him. "A new enemy approaches."

Allie and Riven both exchanged looks.

"That's surely not all she said," Riven stated flatly. "What else?"

The drake's pale eye shifted to Riven, then back to Allie. "A wave of death unsettles the land, imbalances nature, and culls the living. She says that you are needed on the coast, that an independent city-state is now fighting for their lives against something called Rippenvire—one of the outworld factions. They are here, and soon they will head inland to slaughter our own citizens if you choose not to take the fight to them now. Gaia says they are strong, and many, and that if you cannot defeat them, perhaps seeing what they are capable of is itself a boon to use later, when the time is right."

Allie frowned deeply, rubbing at her chin. "One of the invading forces is already at our southern coast? Isn't there a town there controlled by Dawn?"

"T-there is . . ." Shovi cut in from behind at the doorway, still hesitantly peeking in due to the huge skull-faced drake at the window.

"But the city being attacked is independent?" Riven asked, confused. "Do we know of any city-states along the coast nearby?"

No one said anything until Shovi cleared her throat. "There was a recently confirmed report of such a city farther south . . . but it's over two hundred miles from here. That's what my husband told me. We don't know much about them yet."

Again, Allie and Riven exchanged glances.

"Tyranus . . ." Allie said slowly, turning to the large beast in the window. "Do you know where it is, exactly?"

"I do not," the drake immediately replied.

Frowning, Allie sighed. "All right. Riven? Want to join me on a little scouting expedition?"

Riven nodded. "Certainly. Tweedle, Berry, you're to stay with Fay and make sure her ritual goes according to plan."

Out of the shadows, a skresh assassin alongside a human rogue nodded and knelt.

"Yes, my king," the skeletal skresh assassin said, bone hand clasped against his heart and hooded head bowed. "Nothing will befall her."

"The boy will continue the ritual as planned. We will take care of the worm when it arrives . . ." The human rogue trailed off, setting his eyes on Gleetus, who sat dumbstruck that there'd been two other stealthed people in the room without him even knowing. "And if this one causes problems, I'll just cut off his head."

"I very much like that idea," Riven replied with a chuckle. Walking over to where Fay was glaring up at him, giving him a pouting expression despite continuing to chant and make motions with her hands amid flickering lights in the air, he bent down and gave her a kiss on the cheek. "Keep safe. When I get back, let's go for a nature walk. Or fishing. Or something outdoors. I think it'd be fun."

Fay blushed, nodded, but kept doing what she was doing as he turned to jump out the window. Allie said something to Lahn and Shovi, talking to them for a few minutes before following Riven out.

"Ever ridden on a dragon before?" Allie asked with a giddy smile, clambering up the monster's huge back to where a pair of saddles were stationed between spines. "It's pretty funnnnn!!!"

Riven snorted and followed her up, strapping himself in as his clothes were changed out by warping them between his spatial sack and the stuff he had on his body. Soon, Jackal was in spear-staff form and the heavy armor set Messenger was also encompassing his body with an ivory-painted pair of steel boots and leg armor. "I can't say I've ever ridden one, no. But I'm glad to see you're putting my hard-won victories to work—now show me what this guy can do. Let's go see just who and what Rippenvire actually is."

Athela's eyes opened, and once again she found herself before her new god.

Gluttony, the great maw, hovered over her, a thousand times larger than she and hissing down at her. In an abyssal black hell, Athela was utterly nothing in comparison to this ancient entity that'd existed even at the dawn of time.

"HEY!" Athela snapped, angrily shaking a fist up at the toothy bastard. "SEND ME BACK AND STOP INTERFERING WITH MY RESURRECTION! You fuckin' toothy BABY-BACK BITCH! You KNOW the system won't stand for this rule breach!"

She gave the great maw a sideways glare, and she felt it mentally reach out to her again—but she humphed and turned away. "NOPE! NOT happening! I know what you want and you ain't gonna get it!"

There was an ominous pause, and the maw's hissing stopped.

"You do not have a choice . . ." Gluttony muttered—the ancient voice coming in from all directions in a way that made even Athela's bones shudder. "You do not . . . have a choice . . . I will pay the price for defying Elysium, but you will obey me on this . . . it is a certainty . . ."

Athela, for all her posturing, was terrified. She felt the cold pressure of the original sin weighing down on her mind, breaking her mental defenses like they were nothing. She felt the sensation of icy tendrils wiggling their way into her body and semiformed soul aperture.

She was scared, but she swallowed the pit of fear forming in her throat and squinted hard to fight the presence off—to reclaim herself and to stop it from getting what it wanted.

Athela would not betray Riven. She would not do it, not even to save herself. She'd rather stay dead than have that happen, so despite the mental anguish that abruptly racked her brain as her mind was pulled apart, she held on for what felt like the millionth time. Time, after all, worked differently here—but she kept going no matter what.

Because she knew she'd get to see Riven again one day.

That little twerp had it coming after all the shit he'd put her through.

She would see him again . . .

She would see him . . .

She would see . . .

She would . . .

She would eat him.

Athela's eyes lifted to the maw in the sky, where a crystalline flower was slowly emerging from Gluttony's mouth.

She would devour everything in her path.

WHAM

She smacked herself across the face as hard as she could, shaking herself from her stupor. "NO! NO, NO, NO!"

Athela shook her head back and forth like a wet dog. "Come on, come on, come on, stay sane—stay sane—stay sane! I just have to wait until Riven gets me out of here and I'll be fine. I just have to hold on . . . hold on . . . hold . . . on . . ."

She needed to . . . to feed . . . on Riven's core . . . to take the . . . the . . .

Athela's mind went dark, but then a distant light began to brighten her otherwise fading consciousness. The blooming crystal rose showed itself to her once more, and she felt a warmth spread over her as petals began to sprout along her skin.

Gluttony shrieked in rage with a roar that trembled the heavens.

Her demonic soul shivered with greed.

The rose wrapped itself around her, and she was finally at peace—awaiting the day that she would return home.

[You have acquired the trait Fae-Unholy Hybrid. Gluttony has been punished by Elysium for attempting to circumvent its rules. You have stolen a shard of Gluttony, Original Sin.

Evolutionary changes commencing.]

CHAPTER 20

The huge African guy who'd first dived into the fray was covered in shallow cuts and large bruises, but he stood tall and limped over to where Riven was panting. Holding out a hand of friendship, he bowed his head in appreciation. "Thank you for doing what others would not. You are a good man. What is your name?"

The man's voice had a thick accent, Nigerian, maybe, but Riven couldn't be sure.

Riven gingerly collected the hatchet from the corpse at his feet, casually smiled, and took the man's handshake with a nod of thanks. He had to look up just slightly in order to meet the man's eyes even though Riven himself was over six feet tall. "Riven. My name is Riven . . . what's yours?"

"FEARRRRRR MEEEEEEEE!!!!!"

The dancing spider was hopping up and down on her six hind legs while wiggling her front ones up in the air and gnashing her teeth. Athela was chittering loudly as she did it, bouncing around, moving her butt up and down, and hissing every couple seconds while decorating herself with the innards of the men she'd killed. She was wearing a headdress made of intestines, and all Riven could do was look away and pretend not to know her.

"Hakim," the man said with a small smile, releasing Riven's bloody hand without a second thought. "You were very brave. Is that your pet?"

"Nope. I don't know her."

"Are you sure about that?"

"Uh . . . Yes. I mean, no. Okay, she's mine. Don't call her a pet, though, she doesn't seem to like it."

"Should I call her a demon, then? Identifying her says she's a level 3 Blood Weaver demon."

Riven gave the spider a sideways glance. "You guessed it."

Riven was quite enjoying himself, hands behind his head as he was taken on a joy ride unlike anything he'd experienced before.

Wind whipped Allie's face and her hood flapped violently due to their speed. Tyranus's wings beat slowly but powerfully. Mountains had turned to sprawling forests, forests had turned to plains, and they reached the coastline soon thereafter before making an abrupt change from south to southwest as they followed the beach.

"How are you doing down there?!" Allie screamed through the coms over the roar of wind as the sun began to set on the horizon.

Riven whooped loudly and gave two thumbs-up, being strung along by a long, thick cord of Wretched Snare that he'd used to connect himself to the dragon instead of sitting directly behind her. The snare had held easily, and it was almost as if they'd decided to go inner tubing—where Tyranus was the boat, and the Wretched Snare was the rope pulling the inner tube behind. That and they were high up in the sky soaring through clouds versus being on a lake.

It was slightly more intense than the original version of the beast. Even Jackal was enjoying the ride, sending pulses of excitement through its connection to Riven while it remained latched to Riven's back.

"Ah, man . . . Athela would love this kind of joyride." Riven smiled sadly but dismissed the emotion soon after. She'd be back. Her soul was already forming, but the spunk she always brought to the party was sorely missed. He'd probably cry like a little girl when she finally did get back, and if he did she'd no doubt make fun of him.

The snare he'd attached himself to was firmly secured around his waist. The thick, heavy, Gluttony-infused armor, Chalgathi's five-piece set that'd now turned into the item Messenger, was much more indifferent to the experience than Riven or Jackal. The red feathers down the center of the helmet occasionally swayed back and forth, and the eye sockets in his horned vampiric pauldrons flared whenever a nearby bird passed. Sometimes even the maw along the front of his breastplate rumbled and hissed, but it wasn't anything other than grumbling about wasting time as they hadn't killed anything in quite a while now. Messenger was becoming impatient.

But the coastline was truly a sight to behold, especially from this far up. With the sun setting, brilliant orange, red, and yellow hues lit up the horizon like a painted masterpiece. Allie had to avoid the sight by keeping her hood down, but Riven's armor gave him the ability to watch without being afflicted with the vampiric debuff pertaining to sunlight. So watch he did, as he was dragged along far behind the huge drake and his sister with a relaxed sigh. He even started to doze off after another hour of the same, until he heard a sharp cry from in front.

"RIVEN! LOOK!"

He yawned, blinked, and squinted—looking down the coast and then out to sea. His eyes widened in shock, and Allie's drake, Tyranus, slowed while adjusting their trajectory more inland to ride the outskirts of the catastrophe that no doubt awaited them.

There was indeed a city, but a large portion of it burned with ongoing explosions that could be seen even from here.

Thousands of airships, the details of which were hard to distinguish from this distance, soared through the sky. But it did look like they were firing on the city.

Far more land forces had accumulated, too, having encompassed the city perimeter entirely as they laid siege. Then, farther out to sea, there was more commotion as more of the airships were being engaged by what looked like huge krakens along with various creatures flinging magics up from the depths.

Were those merpeople?

Wasn't this supposed to be a human city?

Drawing himself up along the long rope of his Wretched Snare, Riven clambered back onto the drake and sat behind his sister while they flew closer.

"What's the plan?" Allie asked over her shoulder while Riven stared out toward the ongoing battle. "Just a scouting mission, right? No commitments? We don't know how strong these invaders are supposed to be, but if there are only five of them and they're supposed to conquer the planet . . ."

"They're likely far stronger than the natives, yes," Riven said solemnly. He gestured to a group of hills to the north of the city just on the outskirts of the battle. "Let's land there. We can leave Tyranus and go on foot. We'll be less likely to be noticed that way. Tyranus is huge."

"Eh . . ." Allie trailed off, obviously not liking the idea. "I mean, yeah . . . he is. But I think you should stay with him. Stay as my backup in case I need it—you'll be close by and I can do the scouting myself."

"Why?" Riven asked rather curiously.

Allie chuckled. "Because you're too much of a hero for your own good. If I go in there and see innocent people dying, I'll stick to the plan and not endanger us to help them. You, on the other hand? You'd go guns blazing. Even if you are rank five on this planet's leaderboard, that doesn't mean the invaders won't stack up to you. We need to know how strong they are first, and we need to be smart about it before you get yourself killed. In the end, that's the smarter thing to do even from a saving-people perspective—because if you die, you won't be able to save anyone else later on. And yes, if it looks like we can help the natives without risking our lives, then by all means you can go aggro on their sorry asses. Agreed?"

"No, absolutely not. I'm going in with you—don't be stupid. Now, let's see about where we can park this baddie . . . We have a battlefield to explore."

They landed without issue, touching down in between two large hills that only barely hid Tyranus's large frame when he lay down. The creature was massive, but thankfully he was more than okay with taking a rest break after the long flight.

Allie hopped off, hitting the ground with a thud before she was landed on with an *UMPH* when Riven intentionally plopped down onto her. "You fucking cuck! Get off me!"

Riven cackled and violently ruffled up her hair to the screeches and protests of his little sister before getting up and lending a hand. "I just have to remind you who's big bro from time to time, Miss Queen Bee."

"Goddamned turd nugget . . ." Allie grumbled, taking his arm and pulling herself up to her feet with a humph, then brushing her bone armor off. "All right—so, wanna escort me to the border of the fight?"

Riven paused, then nodded. "Sure. But I'm coming in with you whether you like it or not. I wouldn't be able to live with myself if you got killed in there, and we don't know how strong these guys are."

"No, I'm sure you'll start World War Three up in this bitch if you follow me. I guarantee there are things in there where you wouldn't be able to just stand by, and it's important we do that. Frankly, I'm more ruthless than you are, and it'll be something I can live with, whereas you won't be able to do that." She gave him a playful nudge on the shoulder on one of his large pauldrons.

Riven, however, was adamant. "I will literally fucking drag you back to the necropolis and go in myself if I have to argue my point about coming inside to make sure you're okay. Got it?"

"Bleh. FINE! Just keep your head on your shoulders and don't go killing things just to play hero, okay?!"

With that she turned heel and walked away, through the crevice between the hills and to the right—where the sounds of magics, gunfire, and distant explosions could be heard a few miles away.

Riven glanced down at his boots, then up to Tyranus. The undead, skeletal drake only stared back, probably not even knowing that it'd been Riven who'd been responsible for killing the previous inhabitant of that body. "We're gonna take a walk. Catch ya later, big guy. Stay hidden."

The drake only grunted with a flare of teal flames out of his nostrils, closing his eyes and curling up with a yawn.

Pulling out Jackal in its weapon form, Riven went to follow his sister.

The space they traveled was truly flatlands, rolling fields of grass and wildflowers with only scattered trees all the way to the coastline, where a raging battle was ensuing. Missiles—both magical and mechanical—flew through the air in both directions. Barriers and shields of various sorts behind barricades on either side of the quarantined city would flare and deflect an oncoming barrage—but it was apparent that the aggressors had the upper hand due to the airships raining down hell.

There were only two reasons, by Riven's guess, why this city likely hadn't been bombarded into dust already. One, what was the point of taking a city if you didn't leave SOMETHING intact to lay claim to? Two, the ocean was in an uproar where creatures and what were probably merpeople had begun shooting down the invaders' airships. Rippenvire had thus been engaged on two fronts. The airships themselves were for the most part very big, thick, bulky things made of metal and what he assumed to be flesh—looking almost like upside-down turtle shells with attached cannons sprouting from their bottoms.

"It'll be tough getting inside at this angle. Airships are landing on the coastal edge of the city where Rippenvire looks to be in control." He pointed over the army surrounding the city, past the northern front lines of combat toward what appeared to be large transport versions of the vampiric airships on the southern side. "Looks like they've set up a temporary headquarters that way. That's where we'll probably be able to gather the most valuable information."

"Remember, no unnecessary risks," Allie chided with a growl.

"We're about to walk into a city full of hostiles, potentially from both sides as they won't know whose side we are on," Riven shot back with a raised eyebrow. "You got any stealth spells?"

"No."

"Then we do our best without them. Let's . . ." Riven paused as he caught sight of two small children racing across the plains in their direction. They'd somehow gotten past the battlefield and were crying, screaming, and running for their lives from a group of six-legged dog creatures and their masters in black uniforms just as one child fell. The other, a little boy, tried to pick up the little girl who'd fallen— only to have his head ripped apart by the dog a second later.

Riven's eyes narrowed and his grip clenched. "Motherfuckers."

"Oh, goddamn it, Riven! This is EXACTLY what I was talking about!"

"RUN, CHILDREN! DON'T LOOK BACK!"

Sister Anita's voice echoed in Alipe's ears, and she wept. The old woman had tried to fight the bad, red-eyed men off with a kitchen knife and her cane. But they'd eaten her. Sister Anita had been too weak—and her screams and sobs haunted Alipe's mind while the little girl raced as fast as she could into the foothills outside the city. Their orphanage was somewhat displaced from the rest because the nuns had believed it would be good for the children to experience nature—and the governor had even supplied them with guards to fend off animal attacks.

But animals hadn't been the only things that'd attacked that day. It'd been far worse.

Though there were those mean dogs that'd eaten Alipe's friends. They were still probably chasing her, and the thought scared her so much that she covered her face with Teddy to stop herself from seeing as she sobbed and sobbed and sobbed.

Her flip-flops rapidly snapped against the bottoms of her feet, and her pink shorts tore on a bush when she tripped and fell—screaming to land shoulder-first on the hard dirt beneath.

Her friend Sam quickly caught up and huffed to try and pick her up. "ALIPE, GO! WE CAN'T STAY HERE; THEY'LL EAT US, TOO!"

But Alipe was too scared to move. Instead of getting up, she covered her face and just continued to cry and shake despite him trying to tug her to her feet. It was hopeless—the bad men and evil dogs were almost here.

And a moment later Sam's scream right next to her was abruptly silenced when the snarling of a hound and ripping sounds caused Alipe to hold Teddy even more tightly against her face. She didn't want to see it. She didn't want to see what'd come to eat her. She was so scared, and her short blonde hair was abruptly splashed in warm liquid—from where she didn't know.

She felt hot breath on her cheek and heard the panting of an animal along with the deep chuckle of an approaching man.

"She's burying her head in a toy! That's hilarious!" one of the bad men cackled to another of his comrades. "It's even kind of cute! Too bad they said we have to feed the dogs this way, but they've gotta eat, too. Have at it . . ."

The man's voice trailed off, and a deep chill settled over Alipe's body.

The dog abruptly yelped, and there was another splash of warm fluid—this time covering her legs. The hot breath went away, though, and so did the panting.

But Alipe did not move.

She could not move.

She was just too scared.

Riven glared at the five vampires chasing the children and their . . . . what exactly were these things?

[Tiki Hound, Level 32]

Well, whatever the fuck tiki hounds were, they were ugly little shits. The remaining beast he hadn't already killed was essentially a six-legged dog, with a mouth that opened in three directions a lot like the sandworms in the *Dune* movies did. The maw produced squirming, writhing, tentacle-like appendages that came out of its hissing throat as the creature backed up—obviously sensing the danger Riven posed and not wanting to engage.

"So much for subterfuge." Allie followed Riven with a sigh, casually examining the oncoming vampires behind the hound.

If all the Rippenvire enemies were like this, then Rippenvire was essentially an army of steampunk vampires. Another group following the first that'd come with the hounds were also accompanied by similar dogs, but their various pets had warped versions of machines inserted into their bodies, and Riven had already seen them systematically cutting down the defenders at a distance.

Riven shifted his thoughts back to the present, turning his glowing crimson eyes to the sobbing little girl burying her head in her teddy bear—with her little dead friend next to her. If he wasn't so shocked at the complete brutality of it all, he'd likely have already killed the vampires who'd chased her down along with their strange tiki dogs. He thought he'd been bad, but this?

He knew he was being hypocritical. He was sure he'd killed children when he'd wiped out that city in the canyons, but it'd been detached and it was very quick. This felt very real; it was far more brutal than a purging fire—they were feeding these kids to their animals.

It made him physically sick to think about.

As he was thinking, the five other vampires just stared—awestruck at his and his sister's presence. One of them even knelt before them, and he was soon joined by a second and a third. Each of them wore dark buttoned-up coats and top hats, along with various mechanical gadgets infused with Unholy, Blood, Death, and Shadow powers of various sorts. Riven also felt various types of Machine pillar influence as well. Though he was less attuned to the latter, he could tell it was still unmistakably Machine pillar after spending so much time in Chicago. They also wore different shades of tinted goggles, but their eyes were still unmistakably red. Though their eyes also didn't glow like his, and instead of a bright crimson they were rather dull in color. Perhaps another breed of vampire?

[Lesser Vampire, Restrainer, Level 62]
[Lesser Vampire, Restrainer, Level 75]
[Lesser Vampire, Animal Tamer, Level 41]

"My apologies . . . I didn't realize the nobility had sent one of their scions to the field . . ." one of the restrainers stated hesitantly, taking a step back to reach for a pirate-style pistol and eyeing the black spear-staff that pulsed with writhing streams of blood along its surface. "I do not mean offense. If you wish to take that one as your own meal, or as a meal for your companion, then do so—but this is a sanctioned war effort. Killing us or our charged hounds needlessly will be punishable, even for a scion such as yourself. The council demands results, and infighting is prohibited. You know this."

Riven's glare was interrupted by a blink.

Oh. So that's what it was. He'd almost forgotten—he was a pureblood, as was Allie. That's why this man likely thought them to be scions of Rippenvire's elite.

He merely shook his head, pools of blood beginning to swirl around him as the ground started to freeze over for dozens of yards in all directions. "Oh no. I do believe you've got this all wrong. I'm not from Rippenvire. I'm a native, and I'm about to tear you guys a new asshole. I don't use lube."

The ground shook with power, causing the others to fall back in confusion, and Black Lightning tore through Jackal as he twirled the staff around to point at the oncoming invaders. "Prepare yourselves."

CHAPTER 21

Jestus was a tall greater vampire, and like so many others of the Rippenvire faction he preferred a top hat and suit jacket with coattails as his primary attire. Gold trimmings laced a vest underneath with a pocket watch, a pocket protector, and two ornate pirate-style pistols holstered under either arm. He wore tall black boots up to his knees and dark baggy trousers, and his red eyes glowed slightly brighter than those of all the lesser vampires he lorded over on this harvesting expedition. One thing the vampires always faced as an initial trial on these world-conquering invasion missions was a lack of food—because unlike other factions that could just bring their food with them, vampires also required mortal blood. That gave Rippenvire two options—either decrease the number of vampiric soldiers they could bring with them to conquer a planet in order to bring cattle, or bring as many vampires as they could and just kill or enslave the local population to feed on. Rippenvire always chose the latter, often settling on a mass execution of anything and anyone around their initial breach point to secure their borders and have a reserve supply of blood without needing to use other more basic but still valuable food supplies other than blood to feed the slaves. After Rippenvire secured a foothold, they'd then start enslaving rather than just mass slaughtering for blood. They simply didn't have the early resources for keeping a large supply of slaves or cattle just yet.

"Those merfolk really didn't like it when we came and harvested that outpost of theirs, did they?" Jestus Bloodrain said with a chuckle, swirling the red wine in his goblet while casually observing the battle over the ocean underneath his flagship. "Truly pesky little things."

His lieutenant nodded, staring over the flagship's steel rails at a kraken that'd been tamed by the natives while its limbs reached skyward to try and pluck at their airships. "We could always pull our fleet over to the city in its entirety to avoid a double-sided battle, Your Excellency."

"Nonsense. More merpeople means more bodies we can harvest from the sea—and they are quite terrible at attempting to kill us. Wouldn't you agree?" Jestus snorted and sipped at his wine as the bowl-like underside of the flesh-metal hybrid airships continued to carpet-bomb the merpeople ruthlessly while they in turn did their best to use various water-based magics to strike out at the vampiric fleet. "In fact, I do believe—"

An ominous feeling of dread spread over Jestus right before an explosion echoed from the battlefield across the besieged city and a pulse wave of power crashed into the enormous flagship. Alarms immediately began ringing and he was nearly thrown over the rail into the sea before a nearby soldier latched onto his ankle. The sky turned an ominous red and black as crimson snow tore into the fleet, and dozens of the domed airships of metal and flesh were tipped over entirely—spilling many of their crew into the waiting hands of the merpeople far below.

"WHAT THE BLOODY HELL IS HAPPENING?!" Jestus roared over a torrent of power that even now continued to push down on him, making him feel small and almost helpless in a way he'd never experienced in real battle before, red eyes wide and holding on to the railing for dear life. The flagship slowly tipped back to right itself as a black cloud blanketed the sky overhead to cover the sun.

Normally that would be a welcome sight, but not this time. The flaming teal eye of some unknown god opened up to reveal itself through hundreds of large spatial tears in the miasmic cloud—glaring down on the besieged city and everything around it to judge the unworthy.

Jestus screamed as his body began to tear apart in dozens of places right before the defensive shields of the ship sprang to life. He abruptly hit the deck, gasping and spitting blood while leaking fluid from numerous wounds as the shields flared in response to some kind of Death-attuned attack.

He didn't even have time to question it as his eyes lifted to see another of the airships with its turtle shell–like bottom, cannons still blasting, rocket toward the large flagship with half its hull missing. He watched in real time when a torrent of red and black lances ripped through the ship moments later, then felt the jarring impact of similar lances crashing into the shields right before the allied airship did so with the sound of snapping ligaments and tearing metal.

CRASH

The allied airship had been caught completely unaware, not having had time to activate its own shields, which left it only a heaping chunk of metal and muscle that crunched and sagged against the Unholy barrier surrounding Jestus and his men.

He watched as soldiers on the other ship who'd somehow miraculously survived until this point were smashed up against those same shields, watched their bodies splatter, and he hastily made his way back into the inner command chamber while other officers scrambled and alarms continued to blare across other ships of the fleet.

"Your Excellency!" one of his underling officers called out, pulling up a 3-D image of the battlefield, which was now in complete chaos when compared to the rather controlled scenario of only twenty seconds ago. "Two enormous mana signatures are on the northern end of the city's edge! OH GODS! THE ENTIRE GROUND FORCE HAS BEEN WIPED OUT—THEY'RE ALL JUST GONE! ALL GONE! AND WE HAVE INCOMING!"

"Incoming?!" Jestus spluttered, his dead heart beating fast in his chest as he stared slack-jawed at the two mana signatures on the hologram. They were both enormous, with even the weaker signatures being leagues above anything he'd seen anyone at his level of 80 perform before. The sensors of the flagship were comparing one of these readings that continued to hover around 1,400, while the other was now even surpassing a power level of 3,000 . . . and it was continuing to RISE. "IMPOSSIBLE! CAPTAIN, SEND WORD FOR REINFORCEMENTS IMMEDIATELY AND ROUTE ALL POWER INTO SHIELDS! GET US ABOVE THOSE DAMNABLE FISH AND WITHDRAW THE FLEET—"

CRASH

The flagship shuddered—sending Jestus sprawling onto the floor as another volley of SOMETHING blasted into its shields. A wave of heat along with Infernal mana bathed the shields that began flickering as one by one airships on the hologram began to melt away and dissolve amid a burning cloud of hellfire.

Orders were sent out over the communication as he picked himself up, and soon the engines started ticking up while cannon fire from the main guns continued to blare.

"FIND OUT WHO OR WHAT THOSE MANA SIGNATURES ARE!" Jestus screamed while officers yelled over encrypted lines calling for backup from the main base. His eyes then shifted to the dots racing toward his fleet. First it was five, then twelve, then twenty—and the number just kept growing. "AND ACTIVATE THOSE GODS DAMNED TOTEMS—WHATEVER IT IS ATTACKING US ISN'T PLAYING AROUND AND WE'RE GOING ALL OUT!"

The combined storm of Death, Blood, and Shadow energies Allie and Riven wove together was astronomically devastating. The entire ground force of Rippenvire on this side of the city had been wiped cleanly off the face of the planet within twenty seconds, all their defensive barriers and talismans having been pointed in the opposite direction of the two Thane siblings. It'd been like taking candy from a baby, and now their combined storm was focused on the fleet on the opposite side of the city.

Allie's Unholy obelisk sang overhead, the teal eye of some foreign behemoth laser-focusing all enemies with a crushing wave of oppression. Crimson Ice spun with crackling arcs of lightning that shattered machine and flesh alike. Airships warped and tore, bodies began falling into the sea, and the entire harvesting strike force of the invaders was upended in a violent display of power. Massive numbers of weaker enemies were quite easy for area-of-effect mages to deal with; they were essentially just XP fruits for the picking—so this kind of battle with the enemy backs turned in closely knit formations was exactly the kind of scenario both she and Riven would excel at.

Riven stood in full Gluttony-attuned plate armor at the central eye of the storm, looking over the field of death atop a mound of corpses, his black weapon flaring with streams of blood magic as he cradled the sobbing young girl in his arms. She still held her teddy bear close, but was beginning to calm down while answering Riven's questions and even asking some of her own as she became more comfortable with the idea that she was safe.

Allie cackled as the level increases raced in, squaring her shoulders and typing furiously into her laptop while hovering cross-legged a few feet in the air—communicating with the approaching squadrons as officers checked in one by one.

"Alpha team on lock."

"Bravo team on lock."

"Charlie team on lock. Now that our two walking tactical nukes have done their deeds, I hear these so-called invaders have a good amount of oil to plunder, and they could use some good old-fashioned freedom! Ain't that right, my lady?!"

"FUCKING RIGHT! I want these motherfuckers liberated with some red, white, and blue!" Allie crowed over chat, having had this conversation with the squadron leaders before on other raids against the elves. Laughter from the fighter pilots echoed across the coms channels, and the modified F-35 fighter jets were soon seen on the horizon in seven V formations. Eighty-one of these things had been produced with shield and radar upgrades and weapon boosts since the integration had begun—and each of them was a terror of the skies. If the people of Earth had been lacking in magic, it'd more than made up for it when finding ways to kill each other using technology. This was only emphasized even more since the system had come into play. "We'll take the storm down a notch right when you arrive—go guns blazing, gentlemen, and do the necropolis proud. No risky moves; we want you all to level up your piloting classes and we can't have you die on us early. Gain your XP, bail or eject if you have to, and give them hell. Good luck, ladies!"

"For the necropolis!" came the simultaneous call over the main coms before each squadron separated into its own respective chat channels. Allie watched them spread out in the sky.

Riven turned around and casually came to a stop near his sister, looking down at her with a crimson glare under his feathered helm as the storm thundered around them. "This little girl's name is Alipe. I'm going to drop her and her teddy off with Tyranus, then we're heading in for the big kahuna."

"Yup. So much for the stealthy approach. We're all in now. Whatever happens, by the way—this is your fault." Allie gave a thumbs-up, still looking at the screen and sending private messages to different squadron leaders. Priority targets had already been selected by drones sent by engineers who were currently piloting them from Brightsville. There were a few heavy-hitting artillery flesh golems on the enemy side that had built-in siege cannons along their arms or chests, and these were for the most part still located within the city after the outer perimeter had been wiped clean. They would be a problem and a danger for her jets, and the drones were currently pinging well over twenty of their locations even now—with some other very fast and agile vampiric rogues that'd already been seen wiping out sky-bound human-made missiles from the defenders of this Earth-originating city on the coast. If these melee fighters were fast enough to take out missiles midflight by slicing at them with daggers while acrobatically flipping around in midair, as ridiculous as it was, they'd likely be dangerous if the jets got too close to the ground.

It was just something to keep in mind with how the system worked now. Though it might seem stupid not to solely use long-range spells or weapons during a fight, she'd already seen numerous instances of classers who were built around Sturdiness both in this battle and battles against the elves—they'd often been able to just blow off explosions, bullets, cannon fire, magical blasts, or other ranged onslaughts entirely if they were at a high enough level. She'd seen her own flesh golems or bone giants charge into a swarm of elvish magic–infused arrows or windstorms without so much as a blink, and she'd seen elvish griffons tank bombs with barely a scratch before tearing off the heads of her ghouls. It was why she was creating a frontline legion of death knights back at the capital; they'd be used as line breakers and shock troops in the future for quarantined siege situations exactly like this one.

Before Riven got back, Allie sent a final declaration for the drones to redistribute across all Machine pillar–related communication lines. "The Thane Necropolis has claimed this city as part of its empire, starting now. Should Rippenvire give an immediate unconditional surrender and lay down its arms, we will spare you. Otherwise, prepare to meet the afterlife. Veni, vidi, vici, motherfuckers—signed, Allie Thane, queen of the Thane Necropolis and princess of the Blood Moon Requiem."

[Jackal (Ascended Legendary Weapon. Type: Vampiric Artifact, Sin Artifact, Sorcerer's Spear-Staff): 894 average damage on strike with each physical strike dealing additional Shadow damage. Each physical strike steals health from the enemy, heals you, and repairs this item. Mana regeneration is increased by 305%. Stamina regeneration increased by 8%. All Shadow and Blood abilities cost 10% less mana while dealing 36% additional damage. This item has an abnormally high endurance and is hard to destroy. Requires vampiric heritage and a piece of Gluttony's Original Sin to wield.

- **Sacrificial Kill: Killing strong opponents has a chance to imbue this weapon with additional attributes, stats, or bonuses.**
- **Gluttony's Riptide: Passively builds up an elongated blade of sin energy that can extend by swinging this weapon in an arc. Recharge rate and damage output depend on control and insight concerning Gluttony.**
- **Black Lightning: This staff can passively build up charges of Black Lightning. Power of Black Lightning depends on the amount of charge emitted.**

- **Jackal's Lunge:** Point this weapon in any direction and activate this innate and unique martial art, charging the blade with blood mana to create the visage of a jackal's maw and blasting forward. When your blade strikes an enemy, the red jackal will close down on them to deal additional blood and sin damage.
- **Portal Master:** This weapon can sync to any stabilized portal you have permission to use from the maker and master. Current locations available for access: Dungeon Negrada, Riven's Eye Wormhole. Takes one week of channeling in the same place to use this ability.
- **Beastform:** This weapon can turn into a shadow jackal. This form is not offensively compatible but is a way for the weapon to experience the world around it outside of combat—matching the will of the blade.]

Space split apart and Riven tore through a portal, exiting out the other side to clear the distance instantaneously before the other vampire even knew what'd hit him. Blood frost bloomed in the air all around, and Black Lightning thundered along Riven's curved blade as his spear-staff blurred ahead with the roar of a thousand storms.

The ground shuddered.

BOOM

The city buildings around the two combatants exploded as the Rippenvire officer's legs snapped under Riven's strike. His weapon barely held, blocking the blow just as another Rippenvire rogue came in from the side to slip a dagger into the underside of Riven's armor where the plate mail was gone and only bloodsilk remained.

Yet the stamina-infused dagger strike didn't pierce even that, sliding off Messenger with sparks flying before Riven's armored elbow crashed into the rogue's face—snapping his jaw ninety degrees to the left in a clean break, teeth flying everywhere.

"I fucking HATE ROGUES!" Riven snarled, blurring left to slice through the stunned man's torso and backflipping over a mana attack similar to his own Blood Lance. Quickly identifying the two vampire mages that'd targeted him, he swung his spear-staff and activated Gluttony's Riptide.

The image of Gluttony's maw roared behind him, paralyzing his targets with fright as dark sin magics flashed forward, instantly ripping apart the two men and the buildings behind them for many blocks.

The docked Rippenvire transports were continually being downed by necropolis F-35 jets, being priority targets that were marked by drone pilots whenever they did manage to get off the ground—and the remaining Rippenvire forces that'd entered the city were now scrambling in a panic. Allie and Riven, along with Azmoth and a legion of undead who'd been summoned not long ago to help guard from any would-be assassins, were quickly tearing through the poorly entrenched vampires after their frontline gains across the city had been bulldozed. The swarming undead were kept in the back surrounding Allie and chasing down any nearby enemies while she focused on cleaning up ships in the sky to support the fighter jet squadrons, and Riven took the very front with Azmoth as a spearhead effort to break any enemy lines that tried to form a defensive hold.

So far, Riven could honestly say that these Rippenvire vampires weren't pushovers.

They were certainly not a match for him and Allie combined, at least not here and now, but if this was just a part of their invading army—which he assumed to be the case—the Thane Necropolis would have a hard time beating them should they muster their true forces. Already he'd met multiple level-80 vampires that'd put up real fights despite their lower levels. True, he was focusing on honing his close-combat abilities and was also utilizing his magics and aura to rip into the fleet above as a distraction—but he was still surprised with the quality of these enemies nevertheless. As usual, the rogues and stealthy types were the ones that gave him the most issue—but there were a few heavily armored knights wielding claymores that he'd also come to respect.

They had regeneration abilities similar to his own, were completely covered in very thick mechanical bodysuits, and were massive—obviously somehow augmented by both Blood and Armaments subpillars. How this was possible he didn't know, but he intended to find out—as five of these Azmoth-size vampiric beings now stood in front of him with claymores drawn. They glared out at him, suits sparking with electricity and Unholy miasma, unblinking in the sunset as the fleets overhead crashed into one another amid a storm of magic. They were some of Rippenvire's elites, and Riven's eyes narrowed as he read their descriptions.

[Greater Vampire, Bloodborg Paladin, Level 85]
[Greater Vampire, Bloodborg Paladin, Level 81]
[Greater Vampire, Bloodborg Paladin, Level 78]
[Greater Vampire, Bloodborg Paladin, Level 80]
[Greater Vampire, Bloodborg Paladin, Level 86]

Azmoth snapped the neck of another enemy, cackled, and stomped over to settle in beside his master while giving a demonic smile to the five large enemies ahead of them. "Azmoth take two. Riven take three. Deal?"

Riven grinned underneath his helm, and his aura of malice exploded forward like a physical entity that caused the five brave warriors ahead of him to stumble. The crowds of fleeing vampires boarding transport ships simultaneously stutter-stepped or fell over completely, and a sign on one of the buildings with Chinese lettering snapped off to crash to the ground.

"Deal."

Azmoth launched himself forward with his Propulsion martial art, sending flames behind him in the dash as he slammed into both of his marks with a heavy four-handed swing of his giant stone maul.

Riven, on the other hand, launched a dozen Storm razor balls at his enemies and riftwalked to teleport along their side, smashing magics into his three marks before activating Jackal's Lunge. His curved blade shimmered with sin energy, and the red maw of a fanged jackal roared ahead of his weapon when he pointed it toward the lined-up targets who'd braced against his initial magic strike.

The jackal's maw snapped and he blasted forward—hitting all three at the same time his red-and-black Storm razor balls collided with the enemy vampires.

The first body tore apart effortlessly, but the second and third heavy front liners turned with amazing speed, almost matching his own. The first claymore he came into contact with blocked and parried his strike using a defensive shielding ability but sent the man stumbling to the left just as his comrade activated his own martial art—claymore glowing red with blood magic that left a red ribbon in its wake and crashed into Riven's pauldron.

Riven was sent rolling, crashing through a concrete wall, only to whirl about to catch an incoming sword strike that clipped his staff. He snarled at the oncoming paladins, striking back in a flurry of blows as his weapon collided with the other two claymores in a blur of metal, sparks, blood magic, and Black Lightning. The building around them was blown apart under the furious assault, and Riven soon found himself locked into a melee combat of epic proportions. Concrete shattered and explosions of power sent debris flying as the three combatants went at it—with Riven beginning to smile underneath his visored helmet.

Should he dismiss the storm overhead to deal with these two?

No. That would leave the squadrons at a disadvantage and cost lives.

And he'd almost forgotten what it was like to struggle. This was kind of fun.

CHAPTER 22

Lahn gasped, lurched, and screamed as Fay's mana tendrils literally ripped the worm out of his skin. The sightless brown creature was long, the width of Fay's arm, wicked-looking with numerous thorns, and had a gaping sucker that pulsed and slurped at the air using its tongue. Lahn's mother, Shovi, gasped in horror-stricken awe, and even the two rogues assigned to escort Fay were a little unnerved by the sight of the disgusting creature. But the succubus reached out a slender blue hand to grasp the thing by its throat as it wriggled, not thinking twice and smiling victoriously as she held it aloft.

"I told you so! There it is!"

The magics of the ritual circle died away, and she quickly pulled out two glass vials of healing potion to pour onto Lahn's numerous wounds where the worm had been taken out of his withered side. They were pretty high-grade, a cherry-red liquid that smelled quite nice as it washed over his skin. She also had Shovi help feed him another one so it'd work from the inside out, and within seconds Lahn's body began to heal.

It was literally right before their very eyes. His shriveled limbs remained skinny due to years of muscle atrophy, but they were covered in new, HEALTHY skin without the shriveled look. He gasped, almost seizing on the bed as his mother and Gleetus just gawked—but when Gleetus made a move to leave, he was sent sprawling back along the floor with a kick to the gut.

"You're not going anywhere," the skresh assassin said in a faint whisper, its skull chattering as a blade twirled in its hand. "My lady Fay? Do you wish us to proceed as planned?"

"Yes . . . Take him to the designated spot for now. Allie wants to do it personally." The succubus nodded, handing the worm over to the human rogue before the two stealth personnel dragged Gleetus out of the room kicking and screaming—while also carrying the odd, squirming creature she'd ripped out of Lahn.

Shovi only stood, dumbfounded, staring with tears in her eyes at the young man in the bed. Reaching out and touching Lahn's completely cured left arm, she pulled down the covers to reveal his leg was the same. The bed was soaked in blood and potion, but neither she nor Lahn cared as he continued to pant in a puddle of his own sweat. "Lahn . . . Lahn, you're healed! YOU'RE HEALED!"

Shovi screamed and barreled into the reclining young man, hugging him and sobbing as Lahn grimaced—but even he had tears in his eyes as he shakily examined his left hand.

"I . . . I don't even know what to say . . ." Lahn muttered shakily, voice quivering. He hugged his mother back, then glanced down at the foot of the bed where Fay was smiling warmly at him. "You know, I've been thinking a lot about the first time I met you and Riven at that dinner. A lot of what you said now makes sense."

Fay blushed with embarrassment and rolled her eyes. "Yes, well . . . I'm a bit obsessed with Riven. I will admit it."

She strode over to the bedside and sat down on the edge, giving Lahn and Shovi their space as she straightened out her silver dress. Night was falling now; it'd been many hours since the ritual had begun, and still Lahn's father and brother hadn't come back. She stared out at the starlit night sky and snorted at the memory of her mental breakdown. "Sorry if I came across as crazy."

Lahn smiled and shook his head. "No. Not crazy. Just stricken, and even if you were crazy, I wouldn't care anyways. Not after what you did for me."

Fay turned her face in the candlelight. Her small obsidian horns glistened, and she tucked her long white hair behind her ears with a smooth motion of her hands. "I appreciate that."

There was a moment of silence as Lahn let his mother continue sobbing into the bed while she lay on top of him, hugging him tight, but then he cleared his throat and looked around—finally realizing that Allie was gone. He'd been so out of it and in so much pain during the hours-long ritual that he'd lost track of time, and his frown deepened at the note of her absence. "Hey, Fay . . . where did Riven and Allie go?"

Fay cocked her head to the side, amused. "You really don't remember?"

He shook his head.

"They're fighting right now," Fay replied absentmindedly, turning her gaze back to the starlit sky. "Spearheading the fight against one of the invading forces on the southern coast of this continent."

"The invaders?!" Lahn asked, bewildered. "They're already here?!"

Fay raised an eyebrow. "Oh yes. They're here, all right, though this particular group I believe bit off a bit more than it could chew having selected this area of the world to start in."

The heavens roared with conflict, and the battle raged to new heights.

Riven and Azmoth both crashed through the deck of the flagship as it began to fall from the sky. Sinewy flesh snapped and metal creaked ominously, fires raged and the injured screamed.

Rolling to his feet, he blurred to unleash a wall of Crimson Ice that blocked an incoming scimitar. The weapon smashed halfway through the wall, lodging itself into the magic before he countered with Bloody Razors that quickly morphed into their Storm-ball variant—tearing through the air and smashing into the lightning-fast blade of the vampire expedition leader.

"I AM JESTUS BLOODRAIN, SON OF THE GRAND DUKE AND A SCION OF RIPPENVIRE—YOU INSOLENT WHELP!" Jestus screamed in rage, wisps of black exploding out of him in a cloud that hid his location right before a torrent of Blood Lances blew holes in his ship.

Jestus's voice echoed out again through the unnatural darkness that even Riven's eyes could not see through. "I WILL TEAR YOUR HEAD FROM YOUR BODY AND FEED IT TO MY DOGS!"

Azmoth cackled and charged four more paladins that rushed them through the black, colliding with one via a shoulder charge and snapping another man's head with a maul strike. Riven's Wretched Snares rapidly incapacitated the remaining two paladins, leaving them as easy prey for the brutalisk to tear apart as Jestus leaped from a position behind Riven's own.

The scimitar whistled forward, and the vampire's red eyes gleamed underneath his top hat as he struck out at Riven's neck.

Riven's own body exploded with crackling lightning and blood wisps as he activated Blessing of the Crow, forming a smoothly flowing cloud of energy that rippled along his armor and shot him left before a supersonic counterstrike with Jackal caused the enemy leader to stagger.

Blades collided, and Jestus found his arm missing a second later in a spray of blood.

The vampire screamed and then cursed even more furiously when Messenger's maw opened up and shot out black tendrils to wrap around one of his legs. "NOOOOO!!!"

Unhesitating, Jestus cut off his leg to evade the snaring, gluttonous armor and kicked off the floor to launch himself up into the air by twenty meters—before free-falling overboard to be lost from sight.

Riven grimaced, tsking in annoyance as he lost track of his enemy in the madness surrounding him. Fires continued to flare up and the flagship was still creaking ominously as it fell from the sky. Not far off, Allie's drake, Tyranus, was breathing neon-teal blasts of flame onto any ships that remained—or she'd downright land on them and let the drake have a buffet as it gorged itself on the screaming vampires. F-35 jets raced through the retreating enemy fleet, slightly fewer than they'd started with when entering the fray but all squadrons still largely intact—and the merfolk were ravenously picking off and killing any of the invaders that fell overboard into the ocean.

Riven's peripheral vision and an uptick in a nearby heartbeat caused him to turn and block an incoming sword strike—catching the blade in his free hand while glaring out at the hyperventilating vampiric female officer.

Yanking her sword out of his hand while he stood watching her apathetically, she screamed and drove the blade forward again—only for him to catch it once more, rip it out of her hand, and behead her in a single swift motion.

The woman's body staggered and fell, and her head spun through the air to bounce along the metal floor.

CLANG

Riven grunted and spun as a bullet slammed into the back of his helmet, bouncing off it completely and giving him a slight headache. Seeing another man in a buttoned coat stationed on a deck above with a large ornate wooden rifle similar to the pirate-style pistols so many of the others carried, Riven's eyes narrowed.

He began to activate Launch, an inherent ability his suit had, and sin energy began gathering along four panels at his back. Black and red churned and writhed in streams of power, building up and then bursting into red flames as the suit torpedoed him through the air fist-first into the man's face.

The blow would have been enough on its own to completely tear the man's head off, but with the Ripping Claws buff attached to his gauntlets, the vampire was quite literally torn apart in a blur and explosion of rage.

Riven exited the falling flagship the same way he'd come—in a blaze of profane glory and red flames while his suit torpedoed him through the air like a jet pack. Air whistled by and he narrowly dodged another falling ship, zipping over Allie as she rode her dragon through the mess of sky-bound debris and giving her a thumbs-up before readjusting his trajectory toward the half-destroyed city. There were still a lot of Rippenvire survivors, including their expedition leader, the self-proclaimed duke's son, and he was intent on finding and killing them all.

[Messenger (Mythic Heavy Armor Set, Gluttony Aspect) (Evolving Symbiote) (World Quest Item: Panu) (Unique Soul-Bound Sentient): This Mythic-tier armor set was created on the world of Panu during its integration cycle by the Pure-blooded vampire Riven Thane. Having far surpassed the realm of normalcy, this armor set has been afflicted with the Original Sin of Gluttony. As a messenger of sin and a holder of a sin shard, Gluttony has blessed this armor to even further heights so that the wielder may one day become the tidebringer of wanton destruction Gluttony seeks. All shall perish before the great maw; all hail the abyssal depths.

> Devour: This amulet can use shadowy tendrils to attack and pull in prey for devouring. If bitten, a potent paralytic poison is applied to your enemy. Devouring enemies allows this item set to grow slowly.

> Identifier's Clause: Wearing this item increases your ability to identify information concerning items or living creatures, being the equivalent of a low-tier identifier class. Your own basic information will be much harder to identify.

> Blood in the Eyes: These pauldrons passively absorb blood mana from your surroundings up to a maximum of double your normal mana pool. These pauldrons act as a reservoir for your passive vampiric regeneration, this suit's Launch ability, and act as a mana font to

pull from as you would environmental resources. Once the pauldron's eyes dim, your extra resource pool has run out.

> Ripping Claws: Punching someone with the spikes of your gauntlets will cause massive hemorrhaging damage over time.

> Launch: The back of your suit can open up, creating a blast of sin energy that damages enemies and acts as a propulsion method to blast you in a given direction at speeds dependent on how much energy you drain from the stored reservoir of your pauldrons.

> +20% to all base stats

> +300 Strength, +600 Sturdiness, +300 Agility

> +1,858 defense to all plated areas of armor

> +965 defense to all bloodsilk areas between plates

> Natural sunlight does not affect you while wearing this suit

> Liquid breathing is bestowed upon you while wearing this suit

> All senses enhanced by 40% while wearing this suit

> Allows passage free from harm in any underverse controlled by Gluttony

> Immediately identifies and locks on to any nearby sins or commandments

> This armor set will occasionally urge you to undertake feeding frenzies. Wear at your own risk. A high Willpower is needed to combat the urges.]

Jestus Bloodrain watched in horror-filled fascination from a rocky outcropping along the coast while his body regenerated. Watched his fleet, the one his father had vouched for him to command, burn to the ground in what was probably one of the most humiliating defeats of any integration invasion mission to date. Rippenvire hadn't ALWAYS conquered the planets they visited, but they'd never been defeated so soundly in any battle that'd been recorded to his knowledge.

Simply put, he was doomed. He was no doubt going to bring his house shame after this major blunder, and although this had just been a relatively small harvesting force of the military might Rippenvire had brought with them, that wouldn't be an excuse he could use.

The huge flagship hit the plains with a brilliant plume of flame, the shearing sound of metal tearing across the landscape in an ear-piercing screech. Jestus had to cover his ears and winced when a shock wave of radiation tore through the ground and into the ocean, no doubt caused by the large generator meant to power the shields of that behemoth.

The same shields those fucking monsters had ripped through like they were nothing.

Specifically, the armored vampire who'd nearly killed him.

Thinking back to the brilliant crimson eyes of his opponent, Jestus shuddered. That was, without a doubt, a pureblood. How one even existed on this planet, and as a self-proclaimed native, was an absolute mystery to him. How the natives here knew of the Blood Moon Requiem to make false claims about their origins was an even bigger mystery . . . and it made him second-guess himself concerning their true origins.

Perhaps the message that Allie bitch had sent out was true. Perhaps she really was a princess of the Blood Moon Requiem and the man with her had been one of her champions . . . but that simply didn't make sense. Invasion tokens were public knowledge and the Blood Moon Requiem hadn't had one of them. Not only that, but that kind of empire would never allow its scions—especially its princess—to engage in a world-conquering activity like this. Their bloodlines were too valuable to risk due to the heritage of Malignant Prophecy, and entire sector-ending wars had been started in order to retrieve their lineage from the hands of other forces in millennia past. There was no way the high queen of the Blood Moon Requiem would allow it.

So who the fuck were those two?

A slight breeze, a ripple in space, and a cold sensation tearing down his spine sent Jestus into an abrupt panic. He whirled around and limped when his still-injured leg hit the rock he was hiding behind, his eyes darting left and right. But at his back had only been the slowly crashing waves of the ocean.

Sending out tendrils of mana, then divinity, and then stamina, he didn't catch any significant signs of life . . . so he began to relax. Turning back around to watch the rest of his humiliating defeat at the hands of these unknowns, he—

CRACK

SNAP

RIP

Jestus fell limply to the ground, a hole in his chest where his heart had been and his skull caved in with large claw marks torn through his bone and brain. And there, standing over him, was a woman with pitch-black skin. Her brilliant red eyes bore down into the dead man lying at her feet, and six bladelike limbs gently brought the man's heart to her opening mouth—utterly silent—before she chomped down onto it. Raven hair billowed in the wind while she chewed absent-mindedly, staring at her victim with distaste.

Looking toward the city, where she felt the tangible presence of her master, Athela wanted to run to him. She wanted to find him, to hug him, to cry in his arms . . . to tell him how she really felt about him. To let him know that she was back, and to revel in the reaction she knew he'd have once he saw her. And her feelings only welled up to greater heights when she replayed the video of the moment he'd confessed. The video that was circulating Panu's cortex like wildfire, one that she would not put aside now that she knew how he felt.

"But you're a good man!" Luke croaked out with desperation, waving to the carnage and destruction Riven had wrought and was continuing to spill down onto the surrounding city. "What's the point of this, Riven? You're killing indiscriminately because you're upset? Because you're angry at the world?"

Riven slowly cocked his head to the side. Then he chuckled. "That isn't true at all. Let me pose a question, Luke. Just how far would you go, just how far would you push yourself, to save the ones you love? This . . . this is my answer to that question."

Not bothering to wait for a reply, Riven looked back up to the writhing ball of hellfire overhead—and his free hand began to move. It created a circle of flames, pushed through the center of that circle with a clenched fist, and then his forearm twisted while he chanted. "Rain fire upon mine enemies, cast doubt upon divine providence, and bathe the land in a blaze of profane glory."

She watched Riven burn that city in the canyon to ashes, sacrificing his morals and all the people there to save a small piece of her soul so that she would one day return. He'd killed them all . . . for her. She smiled with giddy and warm sensations she'd never experienced before now, emotions that boiled up to a precipice inside her evil little heart. Then it clenched, and a livid rage overtook her when her thoughts turned to Fay.

"That bitch," Athela sneered, clawed fingers curling, turning her athletic hips to walk down the coastline along the beach—northward, to where she knew the other contracted demoness was. Since Athela's mutation into an archdemon, she could hide her presence from the others. She was simply that powerful now and had even blinded Riven's own sight to her return after wanting to surprise him. But what she'd found was . . . was this pretender, this succubus cunt who'd stolen Riven while Athela had been dead.

This would not stand. Riven was HERS.

Athela's body began to crack, snap, and shift, rapidly mutating from her stealth variant into her new siege variant. She grew to be thirty times larger, dwarfing even Azmoth and equaling the size of a small house. She retained the upper body of a beautiful woman, though she grew another set of red eyes, for a total of four, and her entire body became a brilliant bright white—a stark contrast to the otherwise pitch-blackness of her original form. Her lower body in turn grew the abdomen and legs of a spider, and crystalline flowers began blooming all along her body and the path she walked. A large crystalline, vertical maw erupted across her lower abdomen and down into her arachnid half—groaning as she hungrily rumbled across the beach. Picking up speed and summoning the power of blizzards and wind to her, she raced north toward her new target in a storm of Fae magic.

Fay had known how Athela felt. Athela had seen their interactions through Riven's memories in her time dead, and Fay hadn't tried very hard to correct Riven's assumptions that Athela wasn't head over heels for him. The succubus very well knew what she'd done, and thus had whatever punishment Athela could devise coming.

Fay had crossed a line.

She had this coming.

CHAPTER 23

Metal creaked and groaned as cogs in the gigantic landstrider continued to churn. They were the only sounds left now in the dark interior of the council's room—only lit by a faint blue hologram of a map on the tabletop. Peskus shifted nervously in his seat, his eyes meeting the Slayfather's only briefly before rapidly dropping to look at the metal table in front of him.

Other officers of Rippenvire did the same, not wanting to be the targets for the wrath or ire of their commander.

Pale hands steepled in front of the man at the head of the table, and he took in a deep breath and let it out very slowly as he closed his red eyes. "That report was from five minutes ago. A fourth of our entire fleet, lost within a little over a day of arriving on this planet. That is not acceptable, and I do not intend to be held responsible for such humiliation when I return home. I assume you all feel the same way, unless you want to be shunned for the remainder of your lives for such a blunder."

Peskus nodded in agreement. "If I may, Your Excellency?"

The Slayfather curiously glanced left, then leaned back in his chair and motioned for Peskus to continue. "Go on."

Peskus cleared his throat. "Those same reports also indicate that we know from whence these vermin come. The battle is only now finishing, and although we may not be able to reach the remnants in time to clean up, we can use this opportunity to strike back."

Murmuring agreements echoed through the dark room over the next dozen seconds.

"I propose we strike now," Peskus continued, growing in confidence from the audible support. His finger landed on the hologram. "This should be their capital, and I doubt they are advanced enough to have any kind of protections against portaling in. There is no doubt in my mind that the ones who attacked our harvesting fleet are the strongest they have. I would have thought it impossible to encounter such strong natives this early in the integration, but I am more than certain they do not have more. We should strike now and hit their home base before they come back, and then when they arrive to see the smoldering ruins of their great city, they will truly know what it means to attack Rippenvire."

"AGREED!" one of the other officers roared out, standing. "KILL THEM ALL!"

One by one the officers stood, shouting their encouragement and urging their leader to take action. "Kill them all."

The Slayfather held his hand up for silence, and when the room became quiet, he too stood up and tipped his top hat in Peskus's direction. "I suppose it wouldn't be a bad start. In the meantime, collect what information you can on the name Allie Thane. Send a message back to the homeland and seek out whether her claims concerning the Blood Moon Requiem are true. As all of you know, I am highly skeptical that a princess of their empire would be here on a frontier integration planet, but it is better to be certain. The fact that a native even knows of their name is somewhat concerning, and although it is likely a bluff, thoroughness in all things is a virtue. If it's true, if by some miracle she really is who she says she is, taking her as a prisoner for breeding purposes so we can acquire the bloodline for ourselves is a new and top priority. Prepare the legions and the fleets."

Peskus saluted. "Yes, Your Excellency. Which ones?"

The Slayfather raised an eyebrow and tapped his cane on the metal floor with a resounding crack. "All of them."

Fay leaned over her cup of tea, cooling it with a soft whispering puff of air, then sipped. The warm amber liquid was gentle on her tongue, with traces of scented herbs mixed into a sweet and soothing taste. "This is quite nice. Thank you, Shovi."

Lahn and his mother both smiled back at her, sipping on their own tea as they sat at a wicker table on the back porch of their estate, overlooking a large garden with a flowing brook full of brilliantly colored fish similar to the ponds in the gardens of the academy. This place had a nice view, as the Lucio estate was positioned on a hill overlooking some of the other well-kept neighborhoods of middle- to upper-class citizens—and little, tiny lights dotted the streets along the roads where merry nightlife was still in abundance.

Shovi yawned and glanced up at the starry night sky where airships of the royal fleet were gathering a few miles out. There were thousands of them, mostly created from wood and styled in a way that would allow them to act as regular ships of the sea should they need to let their engines cool down. Smaller drakes and rocs along with their riders were also swarming the area—landing on large flat hover platforms to join the gathering horde. "I wonder . . . It is not often to see such a large amount of the fleet here at one time."

"News of the invaders is quite a topic on Dawn's forums, especially here in Mandon," Lahn said softly, giving his thin but now healed left arm a once-over again. "They speak of the legions assembling, retreating from the front lines and heading home. I am not sure if they expect an attack or not . . . but it is certainly concerning. To just give up all the ground we fought for overnight . . ."

The quick slapping steps of a hired maid rushing through the house became louder when the back door opened, and a young woman came to bow before Shovi. "My lady! News from your husband—a quarantine is about to be announced and all people are to shelter on the lower floors! The academy and the palace are both being evacuated! Your husband is joining the fleet as we speak, and your other two children are being escorted with the other academy students on campus to floor six!"

Shovi frowned deeply. "Quarantine? Take shelter? We are on the seventh upper level, the very top of the city. Why would we go down? Are we expecting an attack from the sky?"

The maid hesitated. "I am not sure, my lady, it is merely the message your husband sent via letter. He says it is important, and—"

The hired maid's voice was cut off by the blaring sound of alarm bells just as a booming echo radiated out from overhead. High up in the sky and a few miles to the left, a gigantic vortex began swirling about with yellow and red light. War horns sounded next, blasting out from the fleet across the city as the thousands of airships began to take formation and magics flared to life. Shields, barriers, and swarms of individual aerial riders made themselves visible, and the glowing sigil of Dawn's sun illuminated the scattered clouds.

Lahn's jaw dropped and Shovi gasped in horror along with the other staff members nearby. A tray clattered and porcelain plates shattered, and an enormous *BOOM* from the swirling, ominous portal sent shock waves across the landscape. A layer of hot air billowed out to rustle the plants nearby, sending Fay's hair into a frenzy as the succubus stood up—and it nearly knocked Shovi over completely.

There, far above and distant to Dawn's own fleet, was another—an unknown swarm of incoming airships. These ones were far different from the wooden galleon-style ships of Dawn; instead they were made of metal and flesh. Many were domed, with cannons hoisted up on mounted turrets, bottom and top. Others were larger, more boxy, illuminating the ocean of dark figures on the other side of the portal with red lights. And there was one in particular that dwarfed all others . . .

It was an absolute mammoth of a construct and spanned many hundreds of yards in all dimensions. Looking like an enormous spiked ball, there were hundreds of levels where figures illuminated by red lights were outlined on battle stations. Huge turret guns and a few plasma cannons beginning to charge up along the forward side glowed in the darkness, and huge writhing appendages made from metal and muscle stretched out like the arms of an octopus—letting off sparks of yellow lightning that crackled and simmered against the dark backdrop of the huge construct.

The blaring war horns and clamoring alarm bells of Dawn's forces were met in turn with a deep, ominous boom of a single echoing horn from the gigantic spiked ball miles out. The portal expanded, and behind it came many thousands more airships. Quickly these newcomers began to double, triple, and then quadruple Dawn's own numbers as their slow radvance was set and spread out across the sky-line—incoming red lights dotting the horizon.

"By the gods . . ." Shovi whispered with wide eyes, her voice shaky as she staggered to her feet. Then she whirled. "GET THE CARRIAGES READY! GET LAHN'S CHAIR—HE CAN'T WALK YET! WE LEAVE FOR THE SIXTH-LEVEL STAIRWAY IMMEDIATELY! GET EVERYONE, AND ONLY TAKE WHAT YOU NEED! DO IT NOW!"

Fay watched as dozens of bright-crimson torpedoes rocketed out of the enemy ships. Considering their trajectory was not aimed at the royal fleet but rather at the city itself, and considering that these brightly colored torpedoes were only a couple dozen in comparison to the many thousands of airships, it confused her. That wasn't nearly enough to do any real damage to the city's top level, was it?

Her mind quickly changed when she saw what they did.

One, two, and then three more explosions sounded out upon impact at various points along the cityscape, with accompanying flares of red and neon light in the distance. Fay's eyes went wide as she realized that they were even more portals. They were smaller versions of the one bound to the sky, but the problem with these was that they were located directly on the city's seventh floor. One of them had even appeared in a nearby city street down the hill where merry nightlife had been in abundance with music and drinking only minutes before.

And within moments, surging hordes of mechanical abominations, fleshy hounds, and red-eyed steampunk vampires began to pour out in a blitzkrieg. The neighborhood was quickly set aflame, and the screams of the innocent filled the air as they were burned to ash, eaten alive, or butchered to the tune of laughter and mayhem.

The sky was alight with combat as the two fleets clashed, sounding like rumbling thunder over a decimated landscape.

And Shovi's attempt to run with her son, Fay, and hired servants had been put to rest—at least temporarily.

The nearest stairway to the sixth floor was jam-packed with refugees trying to flee the luxurious, uppermost seventh level. Tens of thousands of people trying to cram down one spiral staircase that only fit a few hundred people at one time led to infighting, stampedes, and outright panic while city garrisons tried to keep the citizens safe in a desperate attempt to hold the vampiric hordes back.

This particular stairwell was also next to the central-most city waterfall, the one that spanned all seven upper floors and the lower floors before the water was cleaned, recycled, and reused. Hundreds of people had already been pushed off the edge or had outright jumped in order to avoid the vampires who'd been able to break past the local garrisons where fighting was most fierce—only to find the soft underbelly of untrained, panicking women, children, and elderly that died like flies in a nest of spiders.

"We can't get through!" Shovi coughed out with a desperate squeal of panic, looking out the carriage window where her driver was trying to control the horses amid the absolute madhouse of running people. "Gods damn it!"

Lahn remained quiet, shocked into silence as two of the other maids, a butler, and Fay rested across or next to him in their seats.

Fay was quietly summoning and discharging curse traps, laying them in the path of any oncoming enemy. Flickering runes of green light would ebb and fade away, only to be tripped by anyone she considered an enemy—blowing them to smithereens from a distance in showers of gore or torn metal. Unfortunately she wasn't able to use her curse of rot, because should she try, she'd likely bathe the entire area in a cloud of death and cause all the civilians nearby to rot away before she even got close to the vampires.

And she dared not leave the carriage. The enemies still had quite a ways to go through the crowds before they got here. Not only that, but she needed to stay and protect Lahn for Allie's sake . . . at least that's what she was telling herself. Yet she knew that wasn't the only reason. She was afraid, torn between leaving Lahn and his mother entirely to fly away to safety. She still remembered what'd happened the last time she'd fought someone—she'd been abducted, tortured, and . . . and things had not ended well for her. Not until Riven had come to save her from the fate she otherwise would have endured until death. She'd be so broken, and she shuddered outwardly at the memory before she turned her attention back to the hordes of vampires illuminated by burning buildings. The enemies screamed bloodthirsty cries while they clashed against lines of human mages, firing archers, and armored city guards, trying their best to join what other of their compatriots had found a way around to the terrified, fleeing citizens. What little organization the defenders did have was minimal at best and only available to them because the portals that'd ripped open along Dawn's top floor were spread out and disorganized themselves. It'd become a vast free-for-all, the city had been breached, and every man was for himself as far as the noncombatant citizens were concerned.

Shovi rapidly ducked back inside the carriage when a galloping man on horseback skidded along the side, running people over in an attempt to save himself while clutching the limp, bloodied body of a young boy to his chest. She took in a sucking breath and shakily clasped her hands, rocking back and forth with tears welling up in her eyes. "Fay? Does Riven know what's happening? Are Allie and Riven coming to save us?"

Lahn's mother looked up, hope still present but the fear obviously apparent while she and the other occupants tried not to panic like everyone else outside.

Fay nodded, clutching a communication stone in her hands while staring out the window. It was so, so loud, and the fighting was getting closer. Her Unholy runes kept popping up and exploding, and she'd gained numerous levels since this event had begun, but she was constantly on the verge of running out of mana—even after having downed numerous mana potions. "They know. They're coming, as are reinforcements from the necropolis. Even Deepnest is sending one of their hive swarms to help defend the city, but the fastest of them won't be here for a few hours."

"Who's closest?" Lahn asked, a mixture of relief and worry crossing his face.

Fay hesitated. "Um . . . let me ask . . ."

A shrill scream erupted from overhead and the ground beside the carriage split apart as a twelve-foot-tall gargoyle with leathery wings and red eyes skewered a man right outside, shrieking in delight and tearing out the man's neck. People abruptly began to scatter—only for the gargoyle to trigger a nearby rune and explode in a shower of gore. The horses bucked and charged, bulldozing another couple people with the crunch of bodies underfoot.

Fay sighed uncomfortably as Shovi and the maids screamed, but they quickly calmed themselves when they realized the threat was dealt with and the driver was bringing the horses under control.

"T-thank you, Fay . . ." Shovi muttered under her breath, violently trembling now and reaching out to take Lahn's hand as she cowered against the wooden carriage wall.

Fay looked out the window again, frowning, and then gestured to the sky. "Don't thank me yet. I think we may need to forgo the stairway altogether . . . things aren't safe here."

Immediately overhead more of the gargoyles clashed with rocs, small dragons and their riders—blood magics colliding with Holy and fire spells as the smaller aerial units of both fleets duked it out over the crowds of civilians. Bodies began to fall more and more frequently, and a couple hundred yards away a smoking galleon spiraled down to crash into a pub with an explosion of fire.

Then, the chanting could be heard.

It grew louder, starting as a faint echo and building into a roar as the vampires withdrew to congregate along a city street. The marching footsteps of leather boots, the sounds of rifles and pistols firing, the clash of sword on sword, and the snarling barks of vampiric hounds rose up like a wave.

That's when Fay saw them. Thousands of enemies, led by one of the gigantic vampire paladins wielding a huge claymore, marched in a mob toward the defending lines. Arrows bounced off him, magics splashed against his mechanical armor, but he just kept coming in a steady, monotonous rhythm of heavy footfalls.

But then he abruptly stopped and turned. His eyes went right, and the chanting died down as he gave an obviously perplexed look of surprise. The defenders and what civilians that weren't frantically trying to rush down the spiral staircase or simply couldn't fit followed his gaze—all settling on the same area.

There, coming out between buildings, were shadowy cloaked figures. Fay's heart skipped a beat and she let out a quivering sigh of relief when she saw them, though it was far from over and she wasn't sure if they could win. Still, it was a hope to latch on to, and despite being a contracted demon, Fay was still traumatized by the very real experience of almost true death not long ago.

Did that make her a coward?

Absolutely. But she didn't care.

There, coming out into the open to face the vampiric horde from the side where Mandon's defenders and the advancing vampires were standing off from one another, was a swarm of undead. Zombies, skeletons, and flesh golems—many of which gave off clouds of pestilent green gas or flickered with shadow magics— came to a silent halt. Three necromancers, all cloaked and hooded, held wands at the ready. Two skresh and a beautiful, pale-eyed ghoul woman.

Mara's dead eyes shifted to the carriage where Fay and Lahn were kept, and she nodded once before raising her wand. Teal wisps of light began to gather around her as her body flared, and the other two skresh necromancers followed suit with the same exact spell.

Then the horde of undead charged, the vampires roared to meet them or continued their mad dash into the human ranks, and all hell broke loose.

CHAPTER 24

Carnage erupted behind them, and they'd had to abandon their carriage and walk due to the crowds. They'd even lost all their hired servants, who'd either been pushed aside, left behind, or had simply gone off on their own to try and force their way to the enormous spiral stairway and ramps leading to lower floors. But they'd finally made it, given time by the defenders of this city sacrificing their lives—and the timely intervention of Mara, who even now continued to battle topside in a violent struggle against the vampire hordes.

Fay's guilt was building because of it. She'd even flown over to assist for a time but had been yelled at by the ghoul necromancer, telling her to get back to help Lahn walk and escort his mother down to the next level. So Fay did just that, flying back and landing in the startled crowds before morphing back into the figure of a normal human woman to avoid attention as much as possible.

And it was true. After the servants had been separated from Lahn and his mother, only Shovi was there to help Lahn get down the stairs while simultaneously trying to avoid being trampled. Her son was still weak; though his flesh was not withered any longer on the left side, it still had significant muscle atrophy from years of disuse. So Fay took up the burden of supporting him, urging Shovi to focus on herself amid the jostling of the crowds.

The slope of the spiral staircase and adjacent ramp was not steep, traveling deeper into the landmass holding up the seventh city level, but it was very large with long, drawn-out arcs coming around the spiral to maintain something of a flat but slanted surface so people wouldn't simply roll down if they accidentally fell. It was also wide enough to fit a couple hundred people across at one time, but even so there were still dozens upon dozens of bodies underfoot that'd been trampled to death in the mass panic taking place.

"Are you okay?!" Fay asked, yelling over the thunderous crash of powers up above as the chunk of tectonic plate this level of the city had been built upon shook around them. "Do we need to stop?!"

The echoing screams filtered through the relative darkness, with only lanterns along the stone walls illuminating their surroundings. Shovi had stuttered and almost fallen, but she'd caught herself on a bigger man in front of them before righting herself again with a shake of her head. She was panting, high heels clacking on the stone floor, and Fay wished it was only one of them that she had to babysit—because at least that way she could fly that person down.

But here she was.

And she was relatively sure Allie would not be happy if she let either of these two people die.

"We need to keep moving!" Shovi yelled over the booms and screams, brunette hair plastered across her face with sweat. "We can't stop! We'll be run over!"

Fay merely nodded, considering whether she could fly them down one at a time—but she'd already had to physically beat off people from steamrolling both of them, so Mara was right; she couldn't leave them alone, and if she did she wasn't sure she'd be able to find the other again in this mass of bodies.

Twenty minutes passed before they finally made their way through the landmass and into the sky of upper level six.

The stairway continued to spiral down, with nearly a mile of space between their position and the floor. Far below them, various subsections of the city with parks, industrial buildings, manors, residential neighborhoods, and marketplaces were scattered out as far as Fay could see. This capital city, Mandon, was truly enormous—but even so there were scattered areas of burning buildings on the sixth level. How many people did Dawn have under its thumb? Thousands of people were filing down this staircase alone, with some being accidentally pushed off or falling to their deaths in the mad rush, while other enormous staircases to their left or across the central waterfall on either side also showed similar events. One of them even showed large amounts of fighting halfway down, with vampiric soldiers rushing along the steps after civilians to cut them down by the dozens every second.

Fay grunted when Lahn tripped again, and the communication bauble in her pocket started vibrating furiously. Pulling it out, she held it to her chest with her free hand that wasn't supporting Lahn's left side and pushed mana into it for the contraption to work. "Hello?!"

"YOU NEED TO GET OUT OF THAT STAIRWAY NOW!" Mara's voice screeched through the black bauble. "WE WERE UNABLE TO HOLD THEM BACK! THEY'RE PREPPING A—"

A shrill gasp, an audible scream from Mara, and a *SHUNK* cut through the noise before the connection cut off entirely.

Fay looked down, wide-eyed, shock apparent. Had she just heard Mara die?

Fay's gut formed a knot and she looked up behind her, where crowds continued to roll down the large stone construct, but flashes of eerie light radiated from the tunnel of tectonic plate, and ominous roars echoed out to follow their advance.

And then it came.

A wave of red lava that devoured everything in its path, blindingly hot, roared down the steps like an avalanche down the face of a mountain. Fay's eyes widened as she saw hundreds of people swallowed and engulfed in the molten metal in mere seconds, and the flood of destruction was rapidly descending on her position.

"Fuck."

Grabbing Shovi by the collar as the older woman screamed and yanking Lahn to the nearby edge, she decided on the long shot. She didn't have much of a choice, and, jumping over the waist-high barrier, she dove off the stairway and into the air.

Just in time.

The rolling wave of molten metal washed over everyone that'd been around them in a splash of heavy, searing-hot pain—muffling their screams as soon as it swallowed them up. Despite this, the enormous wave of magma was also pouring off the sides of the stairway, splashing Fay's left wing midflight and causing her to swerve with a pained grimace as Lahn clutched her, pale-faced.

Meanwhile Shovi shrieked in panicked horror, squirming in Fay's grasp as they fell toward the ground a mile down.

"STOP STRUGGLING! I'M GOING TO DROP YOU BY ACCIDENT!" Fay screamed over the roar of wind while they plummeted. "I NEED TO GET A BETTER HOLD!"

Shovi only continued to panic, and levels of the spiral staircase blurred by as their speed picked up.

During this time, despite the panicking woman, Fay closed her eyes to go over the options she had. Her magically infused, bat-like wings were not strong enough to carry both Lahn and Shovi, but it was still possible to blunt the landing or perhaps drift for a very short time before the strength of her wings gave out.

It was really her only option, otherwise . . .

Fay sensed the stamina signature before she actually saw the creature, and she quickly accelerated their fall with a burst of speed to avoid the tearing claws of a gargoyle's empowered slash. Looking up, the succubus saw the following monster as it howled in a rage—joined quickly by three of its kin as more of the beasts swarmed out of the upper levels to descend on the sixth city level below.

She sneered.

Plumes of black clouds tore out of her outstretched hand as she momentarily dropped Shovi, hitting two of the pursuing gargoyles head-on. They shrieked and banked left, their bodies starting to decay while the succubus turned her attention back to Shovi—wrapping her arm around the other woman's waist and altering their trajectory to avoid another dive-bomb swipe from a monster.

Fay dodged expertly, then created a dreamwalker zone around her, burning through her mana to create hallucinations that would hide them from the gargoyles that continued to grow in number while simultaneously sending out illusions of herself.

The gargoyles scattered, following the hallucinations off into different directions while screeching and roaring their hate with thick gray skin flexed and talons open.

Rapidly approaching the bottom of the staircase and aiming for a lake, Fay managed to infuse as much mana as she could into her wings with a monumental effort. Pulling back and feeling the mana channels in her musculature almost pop, she screamed in pain and felt one of her wing membranes tear on the right side before she, Shovi, and Lahn plunged into the deep end of the waters below.

Cold fluid engulfed them, but the angle was right and the pullback was enough that no serious damage was done to anyone. Gasping when she came up for air, she managed to pull Lahn up with her while Shovi wildly dog-paddled to the surface and began to cough violently.

Fay felt her mana flicker and die in that instant, completely running out of juice, and Curse of the Dreamwalker ran dry. She also wouldn't be able to fly, so she retracted her injured wings and began to tug on Lahn—kicking and paddling to the shoreline while shrieks of gargoyles, screams of civilians, and the thunder of pouring lava was heard overhead.

"Come on, Lahn! We have to move!" Fay gasped, coming up beside Shovi while the older woman coughed up lungfuls of water on the shore. Lahn wasn't in good shape, either; he'd used all the strength he had on his right side just to hold on—and he'd been nothing but deadweight since they'd abandoned the carriage. Only having one side of his body to use made him strained at best, and his breathing was ragged.

A thundering roar reverberated from above and the ground beside them quaked when an enormous body hit the sand. Fay staggered, accidentally dropping Lahn to catch herself—only to look up with wide eyes when she saw a gaping maw looking back at her.

There, only a couple feet in front of her, was an enormous, red-eyed gargoyle. It was far, far larger than most of the others that'd been pursuing her, but it was certainly one of them. Saliva dripped from its mouth, and huge talons extended from its hands and feet while rippling gray musculature flexed in anticipation. Wings outstretched, it stood to its full height of twenty feet and snickered down at the three smaller individuals.

"I have come . . ." the gargoyle began with a wicked grin, pointing a clawed hand directly at Fay while other gargoyles began to swoop down, landing behind their bigger cousin with roars of their own ". . . to try my very first piece of succubus meat. I have heard it tastes quite nice . . . I hope you do not disappoint!"

Fay blanched. Even though she likely would be sent to the nether realms should she die, the other two people next to her would not. They'd be permanently dead. She felt her legs begin to shake in fear. Trauma from recent events was still fresh in her mind, and she began to cry silently while her body quaked.

And as the gargoyle's large maw opened up with a snarl, the creature lunged forward in a flash of speed—and another, even larger figure crashed down onto the monster.

Blood splashed everywhere as the huge monster screamed in anguish, its bones cracking and lungs bursting while one enormous, white arachnid limb skewered the gargoyle like a kebab.

The other gargoyles backed up in shock, and Fay had to wipe the monster's viscera from her face before she could see properly. Her eyes traveled up, staring wide-eyed at the creature looking down at her.

Fay felt a mixture of emotions when she recognized the arachnid's face. It was a combination of fear, of shame, regret, sadness, happiness, and relief all jumbled around into one condensed moment. Fear, shame, and regret for having betrayed Athela's trust to pursue her own wants. Sadness knowing that Athela was likely very, very angry at her, judging by the way this arachnid was glaring down—and that they'd been good friends for a few months before Athela's death. Happiness and relief that Athela was resurrected, if not having been very much changed since doing so. Because even if Athela was angry, and even if Athela would potentially find a way to take revenge, Fay truly liked her and was glad to see her back.

But all those emotions quickly gave way to awe after the initial shock of seeing her co-bonded demoness.

Athela now stood as tall as a house, from the waist up a beautiful young woman with four narrow crimson slits for eyes. Her lower body was that of a gigantic spider, with a vertical maw along her front similar to that of Riven's Messenger armor—but this one looked like it was made of crystal or ice. Even now it breathed out swaths of frostbitten air, chilling the area around them and causing ice to accumulate on anything it touched, with similarly crafted flowers blooming spontaneously along Athela's huge body like shimmering, translucent-white roses.

The rest of her body was also a bright white, even her hair, and when she sneered—so too were the rows of sharp fangs that she bared at the succubus in a hot rage.

"Athela . . . !" Fay exclaimed, hesitantly taking a step back, as did the other gargoyles behind her. They were all very aware just how much stronger this new demon was by the way she'd flattened their largest companion like a pancake, and by her billowing aura of absolute malice. "Athela, I didn't realize you were back! Is Riven here, too?!"

Athela continued to stare, and as one of the gargoyles gained enough courage to shriek and lunge with claws outstretched, a dismissive backward wave with one of Athela's arachnid limbs sent a spiraling crash of elemental chain lightning that instantaneously eviscerated all the dozen or so gargoyles that'd been lined up around them.

Their charred husks fell to the ground in pieces, flesh peeled from bones and streaks of smoking earth slathered in gargoyle body parts. It'd been so effortless, and the fact that Athela had just shown off an ability that was without a doubt from the Fae foundational pillar completely shocked the succubus into silence.

Demons should not have access to the Fae foundational pillar or its subpillars at all.

Ignoring the two humans, the house-size demoness approached the smaller succubus to tower over her—and with one feminine hand, Athela reached down and grabbed Fay by the waist.

Bones snapped and Fay screamed as she was brought to eye level with the glaring arachnid, which was no doubt some advanced variation of a drider—but far more powerful than what was normal.

"You . . . little . . . cunt . . ." Athela bit the venomous words off one by one, sharp and distinct from the others. Her grip tightened, and another rib snapped—causing Fay to scream in pain yet again.

Overhead and to the west, one of the spiral staircases blew up—showering the distant cityscape in thousands of tons of rubble amid a wave of fire. Rippenvire airships were beginning to descend through the gigantic hole in the center of the city where the waterfall rushed down, either entering the sixth city layer or passing it by entirely to travel to the lower levels and wreak havoc there, too.

"Please!" Fay gasped for breath, shuddering when one of her fingers snapped under Athela's grip. "You're hurting me!"

"LET HER GO!" Lahn screamed up at the arachnid, not knowing who or what Athela was while Shovi frantically tried to drag her son away.

Athela turned her head, all four red eyes settling on Lahn and his mother with confusion before the faint memories she'd accumulated through her bond to Riven's soul materialized. "Ah . . . you're Allie's new plaything. She does have unique tastes, doesn't she? Well, little one—this has nothing to do with you. This is between Fay and me, demonic sisters of the same warlock master. We have a score to settle . . . do not worry, I will take care of you and make sure you come out safe. But as for Fay . . ."

Athela's four red eyes narrowed, and her grin widened to display the rows of daggerlike teeth while Fay struggled to breathe. "Do you have anything to say for what you've done?"

Her grip loosened around the succubus, and Fay shuddered as air finally found its way into her lungs. Around them, the carnage and chaos around the city only continued to escalate.

Fay grimaced, but her determined look had resolve etched into it. "I . . . I'm sorry."

"Sorry you got caught upon my return, without Riven here to stop me?" Athela mused thoughtfully, one slender finger tapping at her lips. "Or, perhaps, sorry that you betrayed my trust—knowing full well how I felt about him, yet deciding to use my temporary death as an opportunity to take him away from me? Do tell."

Fay huffed, but she couldn't manage to feel angry despite her broken bones and bruises. She understood how Athela must feel, and if anything, there was only guilt in Fay's heart. "I'm sorry that I hurt you, and I'm sorry that I likely lost a friend. I . . . I was weak. When I nearly died that day and Riven came to save me, all that pent-up emotion just came out and it never left . . . It was the first time I'd ever felt that way so deeply. About anyone."

Athela raised an eyebrow. "Do you regret what you did?"

Fay hesitated, then slowly shook her head. "I regret that I hurt you . . . but no. I don't regret my actions. I am falling in love with Riven. I want him, even if it means . . . even if it means that you're angry with me. I care about him, a lot. And I care about you, too, I just . . ."

Fay's voice trailed off, and Athela's glare grew more angry.

With her free hand, Athela lifted a palm—presenting a shimmering block of ice. That ice began to fade away, and her smile returned as the item within the ice began to present itself to the world.

Fay's face blanched, and true fear overcame her when Athela's grip tightened.

There, in Athela's palm as the arachnid gave the succubus an evil smile, was the demon-slaying sword Athela had been killed with.

"I took this from Riven's bag without him noticing . . ." Athela mused, letting the sword hover there over her hand while Fay began to puke in fear as she realized what was about to happen. "You know . . . I have two bodies now. This one, which is more geared toward large-scale battles, and the other . . . a modified version of my original Arshakai body. That version of myself is very adept to stealth and assassination, even more than it was before, so stealing something like this was merely child's play. Who'd have imagined that I of all demons would ascend, becoming an archdemon by passing through the veil of death? By defying one of the original sins itself? To gain the boon of a fallen Fae goddess? It is both laughable and absurd . . . but it happened. So here I stand—a demigod among my lesser demonic peers."

Icy tendrils connected to the sword from Athela's bright-white palm, taking the hilt and turning the blade toward Fay's neck. The weapon drew just the barest hint of blood from Fay's sky-blue skin, and the succubus began to convulse as she thrashed and screamed in a panic while searing pain erupted along her soul aperture.

The amusement was completely gone from Athela's cold stare, and her grip tightened to crunch down again. "You may have thought me weak . . . or a pushover, because I would act silly in Riven's presence. Perhaps you thought I wouldn't actually find a way to strike back at you without Riven protecting you . . . but let me tell you something, you scheming little bitch. I am far more malicious, cunning, and vile than you will ever know. To take something that is precious to me . . . leaves me with only a few options. The most forward of these options, right now, is to simply kill you. To sentence you to an everlasting death, and if Riven is not here . . . even if his skill wasn't on millennia-long cooldown . . . how would he then save you like he saved me, hmmm?"

Fay was hyperventilating, sobbing, and quivering in Athela's grip—but slowly the sword began to pull away, becoming encased again before the block of ice vanished into a mist of frost.

Athela still glowered, but eventually her features softened and she let out a long and defeated sigh. "But that . . . would unfortunately make Riven angry with me. Riven is . . . important to me. So permanently killing you would be a self-defeating thing to do, even if you do deserve it. I just wanted to let you know that, if I wanted to, I could have easily ended you right here and now. Forever. Do those big breasts you use for brains understand that?"

Fay, who was still crying but not nearly as violently, nodded, humbled, with wide, wet eyes. She shuddered involuntarily. "I understand."

"Good. Then you'll also understand that this is a declaration of war. I will have Riven for myself." Athela cocked her head to the side, waiting for Fay's reaction, but the succubus only let her gaze sink solemnly to the ground beneath them. "No words, eh? Very well. Then, lastly, I have one more thing that I need to do."

Fay's eyes hesitantly blinked, then lifted again to the large demon holding her. She sniffled. "What's that?"

Athela grinned jovially. "Well, I'm not going to permanently kill you. Riven will no doubt resurrect you soon, but I'm certainly going to show you how I feel about all this!"

Opening up her mouth to display a gaping maw of sharp teeth, Athela chomped down on the abruptly screaming succubus. With a rip and a tear, Athela tore off Fay's upper body and swallowed Fay's head and chest in a single gulp.

She pulled off Fay's boots to give back to the succubus later, knowing they were one of Riven's gifts to Fay and were important. Tossing Fay's lower half to the side and licking her lips, she turned to Shovi and Lahn, who remained on the ground—gawking up at her. "What are you two looking at?! It's personal business, and don't worry! I'm sure Fay will be back in the next day or two. Now, let's find the two of you a nice place to hide so I can go kill some stuff!"

CHAPTER 25

Gurth'Rok jogged at a fast pace, his green skin sweating from the exertion of getting here with the rest of the legion behind him—but he was far from too tired to fight. The sounds of war drums beat into the night sky where clashing fleets continued to battle it out over the elevated city-level slabs of land stacked on top of one another. The clank of heavily armored death knights or heavy orc berserkers, many hundreds strong, led the way with dark-arts assault mages, necromancers, archers, sharp-shooters, and swarms of mindless undead minions on either side of the column. Farther back and catching up quickly were two regiments of tanks and heavy assault mechs—humanoid in form but very thick, each standing as tall as the bone giants that took up the rear of the undead columns. Behind the tanks came another column of support mages, system engineers, mana hackers, and a large group of cyborg elites that'd been utilized as a strike force against the elves not long ago.

And that was just the beginning. More forces were pouring in from the north, including two more undead legions, another three armored divisions from Chicago's side of the portal, a fleet of well over 150 modified Apache helicopters, more of Dawn's own armies withdrawing from the front lines against Tereen, and swarms of rat-kin from Deepnest. These forces were going to be dispersed over the course of hours, and Mandon held over a million civilians over the area of its ten city levels with the majority of them being completely noncombat related. Already slaughters had been reported, and it was unknown just how many civilians their forces could save even if they won this battle.

Then there was the fleet to the south, with Allie and Riven heading at break-neck speed to this location. Gurth'Rok wanted to do them proud before they arrived, and he bared his vampiric fangs in a grin as he clutched his cobra staff and rushed headlong toward the ground level of Dawn's capital.

Even here, only a few hundred yards away, Gurth'Rok could see them fighting. Dozens of red-eyed vampires armed with pistols, sabers, hand cannons, flame-throwers, mechanical gadgets that produced force fields, and flesh-machine hybrid abominations of various sorts. Some were hounds, while others were large flesh golems with iron spikes and steel skulls, ripping apart any human who got close.

Here on the city's edge, civilians screamed, ran, and scattered—many of them heading toward the oncoming forces of the Necropolis in an attempt to gain sanctuary, attempting to outpace their pursuers while their city burned behind them.

Gurth'Rok gave the first signal with a wave of his cobra staff, illuminating it with blood magic to send off a flare as his heartbeat picked up in excitement. The forces behind him began to spread out, swarms of mindless skeletons and ghouls racing left and right while the death knights—fully kitted in heavy dark-gray plate mail—began to pulse with Unholy power. Their tower shields lifted in unison, and their long swords were unsheathed.

A war horn blew from the edge of the city, where the battalion of enemy vampires was wreaking havoc among the civilians, and the vampires quickly began to gather upon seeing the forces of the necropolis approach from down bloodstained cobblestone roads.

"GET IN LINE AND WAIT FOR MY COMMAND!" one of the vampiric captains, also wearing a top hat, screamed at his men. Top hats seemed to be a status symbol among these black-coated, red-eyed, pale people. "SMIDGES TO THE FRONT AND SIDES!"

Civilians were quickly disregarded as the vampires stopped giving chase, forming lines and raising their pistols, rifles, and hand cannons to take aim—some of them ignoring the commanding officer and firing at the oncoming horde early as more and more of the vampires gathered. They took care not to hit their own units while dozens and then hundreds of barking split-faced hounds, along with Mecha-flesh golems, began taking a frontline stance.

"SHIELD WALL!" Gurth'Rok called out, backing behind the frontmost line of heavily armored foot soldiers while they sprinted ahead. The shields linked together, fused with stamina energies and abilities each of these warriors now possessed after training in the yards together over past months. The tower shields reinforced one another, forming a long line of seemingly impenetrable metal with barriers of death energies roiling in front of the charging row. Metal boots thundered on the ground, and supporting caster mages in the very back flung up additional buffs to aid their passage forward.

The rumbling of the undead swarm turned into a roar, muffling the enemy vampire captain's command as the first volley was unleashed into the necropolis forces just as Gurth'Rok's second signal bloomed in a red burst overhead.

The mad rush of their cannon fodder charged to the right and left of the death knight column, a wave of mindless carnage sprinting headlong into bullets, bombs, and various blood magics.

Bullets and blood and death energies also crashed into the line of death knights and orc berserkers, most of them bouncing harmlessly off the reinforced shield wall and the barriers of death mana immediately ahead of them—but a few of the repeatedly hit front liners went down. One man's helmet exploded right next to Gurth'Rok when a torpedo of some kind was launched over the horde of skeletons and ghouls—crashing into the eye socket of the orc berserker with a squelch of brain matter. A skeletal skresh death knight hissed in rage at his friend's untimely demise, and he roared—pulsing with mana and anger that was quickly joined by the others.

The Rippenvire front line charged, red hounds and golems crashing into the cannon fodder swarm to defend the vampires at their backs—just as the final flare went up from Gurth'Rok's staff.

Dozens of Infernal suns, each the size of a car, bloomed behind them, created by numerous assault mages working together before they ripped forward into the vampiric ranks with explosions of melting, searing heat. The vampires retaliated with barriers and exchanged fire of their own, but well over two hundred of them were left piles of ash or charred corpses while dozens more screamed and writhed, flaming on the ground.

Gurth'Rok roared over the din of battle, pointing down the middle of the fight where the two swarms of cannon fodder had left an opening. "RUSH THEM NOW!"

In conjunction the tower shields flared, and as one, the front line of death knights utilized Shield Charge. Flares of deathly energies roiled when the martial art activated, and they blurred ahead—clearing the distance and smashing into the poorly organized enemy ranks like a steamroller.

BOOM

The vampiric captain screamed as his lower body was torn off when a twenty-foot-tall, steel-plated assault mech tore into him with a nine-foot plasma blade extending out of a metal forearm. The blue sword shimmered and hissed when the vampire's blood hit the searing energy, the pilot cackled in delight through speakers on its side—and then the mech lifted a huge mechanical foot to smash down onto the disbelieving captain who'd been completely caught off guard from the side.

The vampire's skull crunched, and the death knights tore through the Rippenvire golems and hounds like a scythe through wheat, their bloodthirsty rage pulling them forward to where the back-line vampires continued taking potshots. More mechs raced ahead in a pincer attack, thundering with each step or using thrusters from their backs to jump or even fly briefly—landing amid dozens of enemies and tearing them down in a brutal display of carnage.

Tanks barreled through a defensive blockade to the right, speeding farther into the city as dozens of them cleared a path while booming out explosive shots and machine-gun fire—their objective being the closest stairwell to the second floor.

Gurth'Rok's own blood magic continued to heal those around him, making sure the injured front liners were okay before turning his attention to occasional blasts of simmering red orbs that tore into some of the hounds that tried to run. "This . . . this is what we have been waiting for!!! COME ON, BOYS! WE HAVE SOME OUTLANDERS TO KILL!"

The orcs, undead, and human forces alike roared as one and continued to beat back the enemy, routing this particular section of Rippenvire forces and claiming the edge of Mandon's ground level for the necropolis.

Peskus cursed internally, watching in silence as his palms began to sweat—still clutching his large saber and trying to calm his nerves.

Why had the Slayfather chosen HIM to lead the spearheading charge into the city's lower levels? Why couldn't he have just stayed topside on the seventh where they had support of the fleet?

The greater vampire, along with the many dozens of other vampiric heirs and paladins of their order, shuddered in fear as the creature continued to approach.

The massive figure moved through the mists like a reaper of death, no doubt a demon—but unlike any that Peskus had seen or even heard of before. It was some kind of unique variant that somehow accessed Fae and Unholy pillars simultaneously, and his identifiers had told him it was some sort of archdemon—but what would an archdemon be doing here in an integrating world? What kind of summoner had been able to even BOND to an archdemon so early?

Was this some kind of sick joke?

The monster screeched out an ominous giggle, causing Peskus to flinch involuntarily while her huge frame cast shadows from inside clouds of mist and ice. The monster's huge, sleek, pointed legs crunched onto the mountain of corpses underneath her, the elemental frosted mists obscuring most of her body while radiating out of the many crystalline flowers along her skin that occasionally glinted through the foggy backdrop, and four brilliant red eyes locked onto him from a shroud of white and gray.

The head of General Brimblood, a vampire almost on equal terms with Peskus himself, was flung from the mists and bounced once, twice, and three times to roll to a stop in front of his feet.

Peskus blinked twice, going pale even for one of his own race, and red magic flared along the polished wooden pistol he carried. He looked up again, examining her as best he could through the shimmering cloud surrounding her.

"Sir . . ." one of the paladins warily asked in a low whisper, eyes flitting back and forth as eerie figures darted about in the mists surrounding the enormous, shrouded monster staring them down. "I believe a retreat is in order . . . If General Brimblood is dead, that means . . ."

"That means this abomination wiped out all eight strike groups under his command." Peskus finished the sentence for him, looking around at the mutilated bodies of his kin that painted the surrounding road, buildings, and landscape with their entrails. "Fuck. What are the odds . . ."

His voice cut off and he abruptly stiffened—yanking his empowered pistol and activating Red March with a blast of energy, encasing his body with blood magic that shimmered and flickered in the mists that continued to surround their ninety or so elites.

Just in time to dodge a quickly moving lance of ice.

WHIP

BOOM

Dozens of ice pillars tore through the mists to violently impale numerous vampires at once. Crackling thunderbolts tore out from different directions, not just from where the demon was standing, and nearly twenty of the vampires died in an instant from the brutal attack.

Instantly the vampires returned fire with their own weapons, launching Blood subpillar–infused projectiles and various magics, with five of their paladins exploding forward with Mecha-based movement martial arts.

The monster giggled and laughed, letting the attacks hit her one by one without so much as moving—many of the projectiles being rebuffed by the icy mists surrounding her. Others bounced off her silky, graceful skin like pebbles slamming into a concrete wall, and when the five paladins made it to her, the scythe-like arachnid limbs blurred so fast that none of them could react in time.

CRUNCH

SNAP

"AHHHHHHHHH!!!" The cry of the last paladin quickly snuffed out when another arachnid limb skewered his skull.

And then the creature was gone.

Peskus frantically looked around, in absolute shock at having lost so many of their elites in such a short amount of time, not even realizing that the creature had left until it was already completely obscured. Other vampires under his command sent out radiating waves of death mana, hoping to disperse the mists around them, but they were rebuffed effortlessly despite combining spells to stack onto one another.

"GODS DAMN YOU!" Peskus roared, empowering his pistol and firing off explosive rounds that decimated buildings one by one—but every time the blood magic would explode to disperse the mist, the icy fog would merely float right back to where it'd been seconds later—filling in the gap and leaving them blinded again.

Then a man was yanked out of their formation, screaming in horror before he too was cut off with an earsplitting squelch.

A giggle came in from the opposite side where another vampiric officer, a woman with a long ponytail, was yanked by her hair into the mists and gutted ruthlessly, judging from the pained screams.

The vampires panicked, utilizing different methods, magics, gadgets, bombs, defensive wards, enchanted talismans, or martial art abilities to blast everything around them. They didn't know what they were hitting, if they were doing anything at all, and above the building ruckus, the feminine giggle of the archdemon continued to rise like a gleeful child's laugh.

Chittering sounds began whispering through the mists next despite the bombardment, and in the periphery, just outside the range of their attacks, a set of four blue eyes snapped open. Peskus centered his attention on this set of eyes, quickly snapping his pistol up and firing—hearing a squelch and a screech of pain. His heart lurched in excitement when he realized he'd hit something, only to see another set of four blue eyes settle to his left.

He fired again, but this time the eyes disappeared back into the mist and three more sets of four eyes appeared on his right.

The chittering grew in volume, still whispering all around him until the whispers overlapped into a torrent of ill-fitting sounds not meant for this world. The remaining vampires all backed up to cluster around one another, forming a tight defensive circle as more and more of these blue eyes glared out at them from the mists, bodies obscured through the haze of frost.

Then the single set of red eyes appeared, far larger and higher up than the smaller, more numerous sets of blue. The monster appeared before them now, stepping out of the fog to put her entire body on display.

She was truly beautiful but utterly terrifying as the vertical crystalline maw along her front crunched down onto one of Peskus's men—casually eating him while she slowly walked forward. Her upper half was humanoid, her lower half was that of a giant spider, and crystalline flowers that'd been producing the mists cut off the fog—letting some of it disperse to reveal their surroundings at a limited extent.

As the fog very slowly began to move away, the figures behind the blue eyes were revealed next. Dozens, then hundreds, and then thousands of dog-size, crystalline spiders chittered eagerly and hissed in the direction of the vampires. They screeched in anticipation, an ocean of them all around as Peskus's heart dropped in horror.

There were so many.

The enormous archdemon clicked her tongue, letting out an amused hum while keeping her nose arrogantly lifted—intentionally looking down on the smaller vampires from her great height. "I do believe I've stomped babies sturdier than you . . . Do you have any last words, meatlings?"

A man beside Peskus screamed in rage and charged—only to be blasted with a crackle of lightning so powerful that it didn't leave a single remnant of his Mecha suit intact. His body exploded in a shower of flesh and metal, creating a crater in the place he'd been only a second before.

"We can come to terms!" Peskus tried, his voice catching in his throat as the hissing spiders began to advance all around him. "Please! Whatever you're doing here, we can offer you or your master recompense! We can strike a deal!"

It was a far-fetched gamble, and one that did not pay off.

Athela only hummed in amusement. "I'm afraid . . . not."

With a snap of her fingers, the horde of crystalline spiders roared forward like a tidal wave onto the small island of remaining vampiric elites—cutting down their people amid the screams, wails, and futile last efforts to fight back.

Standing over the vampires her children were eating alive, Athela tsked and turned her attention to one of the massive nearby stairways leading up to the next city level. She could sense someone or something very powerful approaching her, something . . . not familiar. A vampire, certainly, she could tell that much by the aura it gave off, but it wasn't Riven or Allie, either.

Smiling to herself and wondering whether this one would finally be a match, one that could push her new body to the limits to see what she could truly do with it, her large arachnid limbs carried her forward.

It was time to meet a true champion of these puny, pathetic creatures. It was time to show them just what a spider princess could truly do.

CHAPTER 26

Lahn watched in silence beside his mother and the other refugees hiding here in a pub's cellar. Funnily enough, he even noted how a small group of other students from the academy were here—no doubt having fled down the stairway long before he did. But overall it was the locals—the pub owner and his family, a farmer and his three sons, a couple of women from the local brothel, and a few merchants with their kids.

They were all terrified to stay here given the battle raging right outside, but options had run out. There was nowhere left to go with almost every level of the city experiencing some kind of fighting, with the exception of the lowermost levels underground—but there was no way Lahn and his mother could make it there. They were on upper floor six, and by foot it'd take one or two hours just to get down a single flight of stairs between levels.

The forums were lit up with activity, with various people in Mandon streaming things that were happening while begging for help or coordinating evacuations or rescues. But it was dire, and people were beginning to lose hope. The king had been critically injured in the battle with some guy called the Slayfather and had to be evacuated by air to a more secure location—at the cost of many lives. The royal fleet had lost half of its total numbers and was on the back foot, hard-pressed to assist anyone else and unable to intercept the large blocky transports that shuttled down invading strike groups to the lower floors along the edges of the city. People were dying by the tens of thousands, being butchered outright or set up in containment areas with shackles and slave collars—no doubt prizes to be brought back to Rippenvire's home base after the battle was won.

But not all was lost.

Reinforcements continued to flood in through the lower levels as frontline fighters who'd been combating the elves retreated home. Legions from the Thane Necropolis were already securing most of the ground city level, but fighting was still fierce even here. News of armies from Deepnest, headed by the rat-kin queen herself, was also circulating, and most important of all—Riven Thane was reportedly heading here now.

Lahn's eyes fell as he thought back to having met the man. He liked Riven, or Travis, as he'd called himself while hiding his identity, but he didn't know what would happen when Riven got here. Past events showed Riven was quite literally an army- and city-killing machine, specializing in massive area-of-effect magic that could potentially be the saving grace of Dawn. But what kind of damage would take place in the city should Riven go all out?

And what if Riven wasn't enough?

Slayfather Tikus, a man with a long silver katana and a top hat in a billowing black suit coat, continued to calmly walk off the stairs onto flat land—his hundreds of undead thralls tearing into enemies ahead of him so that he merely had to continue raising the dead. So far, the only man he'd really had to put any effort into was the king himself, who was now fleeing across the sixth level and almost out of sight.

No matter. It wasn't as if they'd escape. It was merely a feeble attempt at prolonging the inevitable.

His pale lips curled up into a grin to expose his fangs when one of the king's guards desperately tried throwing an empowered, electrified lance of Holy light his way—but Slayfather Tikus smashed the weapon with an effortless flick of the wrist.

Weak.

But he paused as he came across the corpse of a man he knew. Just a lieutenant in the Rippenvire army, but still more real to him than any of the other deaths he'd seen so far. His brows furrowed in irritation; that man had given him a sense of real promise.

Looking back up to the fleeing, severely wounded king and his guards, across bloodied cobblestones and hundreds of bodies, past burning buildings where screams of the dying echoed over the cityscape, the Slayfather locked onto the limping leader of this city.

This city of cattle—cattle that would be butchered to fuel Rippenvire's expansion into this sector of the multiverse.

Tikus narrowed his eyes. Perhaps taking his time finishing this would indeed be . . . unwise of him. After all, he wouldn't be able to call in reinforcements from the homeland for years—so why not put in the effort and save the lives of his men just by helping them out a bit?

He sighed, and with another flick of his wrist, the undead thralls around him exploded into red orbs of blood magic. The combined power of their sacrifices thrummed and then blasted across the two-hundred-yard gap between himself and the king, and with cries of alarm the king's guard set up a shield formation right before the wave of red crashed into them.

The impact was devastating.

Half of the heavily armored guards were ripped apart completely, two more were knocked unconscious with severe wounds, and only five of them maintained their stands in a flood of penetrating power.

The king and the man helping him limp away were both crushed, slamming them through a brick wall and out the other side, where their mangled bodies remained barely breathing and bleeding out on the ground.

A blur of silver and his katana caught an assassin's attack to his left, flaying the semi-invisible man alive with an audible squelch over the roars. Tikus sneered down at the assassin, who was clutching his throat as fluid spilled out, and the Slayfather put a foot on the man's chest to push him onto his back. "I have heard your heartbeat for well over two minutes, imbecile. If you're going to hide your presence against a vampire, and a greater vampire at that, you need to do more than just . . ."

Slayfather Tikus slowed his speech, abruptly noticing that his thralls weren't making noise anymore. In fact, the entire area around him had gone eerily silent . . .

He blinked. His eyes lifted slowly from the dying man in front of him, taking in a scene that very much confused him. All across the two-hundred-yard gap between himself and the remnant of the king's guards who were desperately trying to get to Dawn's leader, were the bodies of his undead minions.

They were dead. All dead, and for good this time. He hadn't even heard them drop, but their bodies were scattered about like someone had just run them through a meat grinder. And there, sitting on top of a central pile of them, was a small spider.

Small was a relative term; rather, it was a little larger than half the size of the vampiric hounds Rippenvire had brought with them. The spider was black and red, with two eyes and twelve legs. It was . . . a demon, if he wasn't mistaken. One called a Blood Weaver that he'd seen in textbooks before, even a favorite of vampiric warlocks if he remembered correctly due to their high affinity for the Blood subpillar, and it wore a ruby-studded black tiara on its head while simultaneously decked in a cape of fresh entrails. It stood proudly, almost humorously staring at him with mandibles splayed open in a spider's version of a wide grin. The creature's heartbeat and power signature were both absolutely and utterly hidden, and if Slayfather Tikus didn't see the creature with his own eyes he wouldn't have believed it was even there.

That was disturbing.

But what really got his attention were the five heads it'd impaled on a stick. That stick was being held much like a staff, too large for the spider's size, but the implication was clear—and Tikus recognized each of these faces immediately.

They were five of his generals.

Five of seven generals. The best men of this conquering expedition aside from himself. Some were even his friends.

All had been beheaded and strung up like a kebab.

That . . . that got his attention. These events during the invasion were on full display for his homeworld to see, for all of Rippenvire to watch as the invasion unfolded.

What shame had they brought to their houses by dying so fast? What shame had they brought to him and his house, considering they'd been under his command when they'd died?

Slayfather Tikus rarely felt anger, but when he did, his enemies knew it. Power slowly began to build with his aura, a field of ominous death energies whirling about him as his teeth gritted in rage. Slowly he pulled out the pistol at his side, the weapon flaring with blood magic as his silver katana began to radiate with black-and-teal death energy. The aura billowed out and roared to life around him, red eyes flaring as he focused his rage and intent on the creature in a display that caused the top layer of ground to explode with debris and rot away.

But the spider remained in its stance atop the bodies of his thralls, mockingly wiggling the kebab staff his way.

"HELLO, PLEBEIAN WHELP!" Athela called out in her Blood Weaver form, bouncing her arachnid rump up and down while prancing back and forth amid the aura of death that encompassed this area. She wiggled the kebab staff of stacked heads his way again, cackling with a chittering laugh. "ARE YOU THE LEADER OF THIS BAND OF MERRY MISFITS?! I'm supposed to save that king, you know—you gotta get past me if you wanna get him! AND I'VE BROUGHT YOUR FRIENDS TO WITNESS YOUR DEMISE—HOW NEAT!!!"

Slayfather Tikus narrowed his red eyes, confused that his aura had no effect on what was supposed to be a lower-tier demon species. But perhaps her level was just that high. Species didn't mean everything. He took a step forward, coattails billowing in the winds of his aura's power. The ground cracked underneath his weight as he walked, and tortured thoughts of what he would do to this little arachnid bastard crossed his mind in a thousand different ways—making his angry snarl turn into a crazed, malicious grin with bared fangs. "I certainly am the leader of this invasion. Congratulations, you've found me. You've found your death. Slayfather Tikus, at your service . . . Now . . . Tell me who you are, or who you serve, so that I may know the names of the people I will so ruthlessly flay before feeding your corpses to my dogs for murdering my men."

Dramatically, Athela whipped her entrail cape out to the side and stood proud on her hind legs while crossing her front ones over her chest—with exception of the two legs holding the kebab staff. "VERY WELL! I shall introduce myself. I am **PRINCESS** Athela! I AM THE MOST RENOWNED BABY STOMPER THERE EVER WAS, TEHHHH GREATEST SMASHER OF SUCCUBI WHELPS, TEEHHHHH BRINGER OF CHAOS! I am . . . ATHELA, FUTURE CONQUEROR OF WORLDS! MWAHAHAHAHAHAHAAA!!!"

She jiggled the kebab staff once more and flung back her head, tiara gleaming in the light of burning buildings around them while cackling to the heavens. "ALL SHALL FEAR TEHH GREAT SPIDER ATHELA, BABY-STOMPER, CONQUEROR EXTRAORDINAIRE!"

Abruptly her face whipped back down, mandibles dripping with dark-green venom as her red eyes matched his own with a glint of frenzied insanity. She pointed two of her sharp, arachnid legs at the advancing vampire with a screech. "Now . . . DIE!"

Time froze, and Slayfather Tikus was almost floored by the notification that appeared next. His mind reeled, and he suddenly began to take this a lot more seriously than he had just moments before. Because for the system to consider this a boss fight, for HIM . . . Well, boss fights outside of dungeons not only gave huge boons if you won them—but they only occurred when you had a very real possibility of losing and usually had the odds stacked against you.

This was not what Tikus had been expecting to see.

WARNING

WARNING

WARNING

WORLD QUEST BOSS FIGHT: ARCHDEMON ATHELA (THREE FORMS), CUTE WITTLE BLOOD WEAVER/ GLUTTONOUS ARSHAKAI/GLUTTONOUS FAE DRIDER, PRINCESS BABY STOMPER AND FUTURE CONQUEROR OF WORLDS, HAS BEEN INITIATED. YOU MUST KILL ALL THREE FORMS TO WIN THIS FIGHT.

[This fight is now being broadcasted to Panu's cortex, front page, and all local channels.]

ELYSIUM HAS SEALED OFF YOUR POINT OF EXIT WITH A DIAMETER OF FIVE MILES UNTIL THE BATTLE IS COMPLETE, THOUGH ENEMY AND ALLY FORCES CAN STILL ENTER THIS ZONE UNTIL ONE OF YOU IS KILLED DUE TO WORLD QUEST AND INVASION PARAMETERS.

[Fifty million Elysium coins, a custom Legendary item, and a Legendary Dao treasure relating to blood will be provided to the victor.]

BEGINNING BATTLE IN
5 . . .
4 . . .
3 . . .
2 . . .
1 . . .

The system had the audacity to name this creature FUTURE conqueror of worlds?! What the—

Time resumed, a white wall of power from the system closed off a five-mile area, and the spider launched herself off the pile of bodies with an explosive force that made Tikus reel.

"YOU SURLY, UGLY LITTLE COW!" Tikus barely had time to raise his pistol and fire with a blur of speed that caused the air to crack with the effort, sending an explosive round right into the spider's trajectory—only for the demon to veer left with flurries of webbing that extended in all directions from various legs.

It pulled her left, up, and then back around while maintaining momentum as she veered into him with a gleeful cackle. "GOTCHA, BITCH!"

CRACK-CLING-CLANG-WHIP-BOOM-SNAP

Athela's sharpened legs blurred, smashing against the vampiric general as he backpedaled while cursing and focusing his aura into his silver katana. Just as quickly, he fired off bullets every time she gave him room, bullets and blade meeting arachnid legs and sprays of red webbing or acidic venom clouds in movements so fast that the cortex viewers watching the exchange could only gawk at the sheer display of power and speed.

The ground tore up beneath them, building with momentum as the crazed spider continued cackling, jiggling the kebab of heads, and exchanging attacks with the Slayfather on equal footing. It absolutely enraged him.

Sending out a shock wave of death energy in all directions to give him some space, Tikus snarled and summoned two shadow lords—elemental void creatures of the beyond—to fight for him. Each was twice his size, looking like a cloaked wraith made of black wisps that tore through the air toward the spider—but Athela merely crackled with green light and sent a shock wave of her own energy back at the creatures.

The wall of green rapidly expanded and burst, colliding with the shadow elementals and causing them to scream as their bodies turned to clouds of pink flower petals. Those same flower petals quickly sharpened, and in a flurry of thousands of tiny little blades, they expanded to all sides before collapsing on the Slayfather's position.

FAE MAGIC FROM A DEMON?!

Tikus cursed in shock and disbelief, activating a martial art called Danger Sense that prioritized incoming attacks based on lethality, giving him an edge to concentrate on and defend what was important. Then he activated another martial art, Soulsaint Swordstorm, which sent a thousand silver cuts empowered with death energy at the wall of petals in front of him. Translucent blades tore through the air and scattered the petals, only to—

WHAM

Tikus reeled backward, holding his nose when the kebab spiraled through the air and crashed into his face. Blinking rapidly and staring dumbfounded at the decapitated heads on a stick that'd smacked him upside the skull, he turned his angry red gaze to glare back at the loudly cackling demon that pointed his way while dancing around in a victory circle. He'd not seen it coming because he'd been too invested—via his Danger Sense—on the truly lethal strikes of the petals, but being smacked upside the head with the decapitated faces of his friends was humiliating.

"I will teach you to mock me!" Tikus said under his breath, spitting blood and wiping it away from his broken nose just before it snapped back into position and healed. **"You will regret making a fool of me!"**

Athela had resorted to making turkey-gobbling noises, hopping up and down on her hind legs, and wiggling her cape of entrails while her tiara bobbed up and down a few dozen yards off. "SOME VAMPIRE YOU ARE! I'D THOUGHT VAMPIRES WERE HOT SHIT AFTER BONDING TO MY MASTER, BUT IT APPEARS I WAS MISTAKEN! YOU'RE JUST A BLOODSUCKING FAIRY WITH A BIG EGO!"

"CURSE YOU BACK TO THE HELLS, FOUL DEMON WENCH!" Tikus blurred forward and unleashed a Trick Shot martial art, causing multiple blood-infused bullets to swerve left and right before veering back to take Athela in the sides as he carved down with the silver blade.

CHING-CHING-CHING-CHING-CHING

Athela's legs met his attacks almost simultaneously, the rapid exchange sounding like a Gatling gun before she sprayed acid all over the Slayfather's face.

Tikus screamed, and then he felt one of her legs rip through his chest.

Immediately he exploded into a cloud of blood, re-forming three dozen meters away and snarling at the wound in his vest that dripped blood. Black-green venom began combating his natural regeneration, and the skin on his face sizzled with the acid that slowly began to fade away under his vampiric healing qualities.

"I do believe I underestimated you in the beginning, little one . . ." Tikus said, slowly taking off his top hat and tossing it aside. Ripping off his ruined coat and then his vest, he exposed his pale and muscular chest to the air while baring his fangs. When he dropped his sword and gun, veins began to pulse and swell all along his arms, abdomen, and upper body until his red eyes bulged out of his sockets. "But I won't make that mistake again. BEHOLD! MY ULTIMATE FORM!"

Athela's cackling came to an abrupt halt as the area around them exploded again in a massive surge of power. The city shook under the immense weight of the vampire's strength. Blood and death energies intermixed as a roaring howl reverberated around their white-walled enclosure many miles wide, and the vampire began to change before her very eyes.

Wings blasted out of his back in a spray of blood. His skin darkened from bright white to a deep gray. Hair sprouted along his back; nostrils enlarged and became vertical slits. His jaw protruded, with large, pointed teeth growing in his mouth—emphasizing his fangs most of all—and his fingers became long, scythe-like talons. His body also became larger, three times the size of the man he'd once been, and bones cracked as his legs reverted to a more T. rex–like figure that rippled with muscle.

He was huge, menacing, and bat-like.

And Athela was caught off guard as the Slayfather broke the sound barrier to engage her once again. In an instant, her small body was ripped asunder, sending her upper and lower halves scattering apart to skip along the ground . . .

Before her next body began to re-form from the pieces.

CHAPTER 27

Despite the abrupt surge in power, despite revealing his ultimate form to combat this demonic arachnid, Tikus felt both inferior and small when the creature began to re-form. His gray wings sagged, his flex claws that'd so recently torn the spider's body in half stiffened, and his eyes widened in shock as he beheld the creature's new body recreating itself before his very eyes.

Bones snapped. Scythe-like legs each bigger than he was snapped out and crashed into the ground. Four narrowed red eyes looked down at him like he was some kind of bug to squash, and an expanse of jagged teeth smiled wide.

What was once a dog-size spider had now rapidly warped from the pieces of its mutilated body and grown to hundreds of times its original size. Black flesh turned to white, crystalline flowers bloomed along the creature's skin, and a drider far larger than any should ever become grinned down at him with teasing malice as Athela licked her lips.

She oozed power. The very air around her became frosty, and occasional sparks of lightning crackled around forming snowflakes as a crystalline maw down her lower midsection opened with a hiss—tendrils of black and blue snaking out in his direction with slow, monotonous intent. She was beautiful, but also a creature that could be torn out of nightmares, and her own aura composed of something primal—something that reached out to him with a hunger at the most basic essence of conscious thought—tore into his very soul with probing feelers.

Tikus took a step back without thinking, whispering under his breath, "What in the hells?!"

A war horn echoed to his left, and both Tikus and the large demon took a moment to look. Marching toward them, were over five hundred vampiric paladins wielding claymores and mechanical armored biosuits—activating various buffs, speed boosts, and martial arts in preparation for battle. They were some of Rippenvire's elites, and the Slayfather's heart grew firm with resolution. He still stood a chance.

Though the demon . . . laughed, and she didn't seem intimidated or worried at all.

Athela lifted up one arm, and the ground shuddered when a pillar of ice tore out of the earth in front of her. Red runes intermixed with deep black, writhing along the pillar that continued to rise out of the ground like a monument to her glory. Ice sculpture carvings, figurines of beautiful women and men, demon and fairy alike, but most of all, hundreds of spiders all climbed atop one another to try and reach the summit while being weighed down by rune-inscribed chains of red-black flame. Half the zone within the five-mile battle bubble began to simultaneously burn and freeze, spiraling around her in a great cycle that interchanged in waves of elemental Fae ice and sin-based flame.

Her hands raised higher, the pillar climbed, the ice sculptures screamed out as one—and the great maw along her midsection roared with a pulse of energy that breathed a storm of destruction. It wove into the cycle, creating a huge tornado of ice and dark fire that roared and shook the earth with voluminous, expanding, ripping force.

Tikus flared his wings, channeling his mana as the paladin elite of his homeworld joined him in solidarity. One by one they saluted him and formed a line, awaiting his orders with red eyes flaring alongside their auras. "MEN OF RIPPENVIRE!"

"YES, SLAYFATHER!" the hundreds-strong soldiers yelled back, claymores simmering with Unholy light—and as one they conjured large tower shields that crashed into the ground with a resounding boom.

A defiance in the face of the immense power of this archdemon. And Tikus? He couldn't be more proud of them.

Towering over the others and drawing a battle formation, the equivalent of dozens of sigils and empowered circles of dark mana, that reinforced a given area for all defenders inside it—the large winged vampire snarled at the oncoming tornado that continued to build. The formation boomed and roared, unleashing a wall of miasma that tore through the sky of the enclosed system-made dome—and Tikus pointed. "YOU WILL FALL, DEMON! THE MEN OF RIPPENVIRE WILL NOT FAIL HERE! AND I WILL MOUNT YOUR GIGANTIC HEAD ON MY WALL!"

"Hmmm…hmm—hmmmhmm—haaahahahaha—AAAHAAHAHAAHAAA!!!!" Athela's laugh grew and her hands wove tapestries of intricate keys, unlocking the mechanisms of her spell until a single gigantic Celtic-style rune ripped the sky overhead. The pillar of ice, flaming chains, and climbing sculptures with red and black sigils made contact with the sky-bound mark—and as soon as it did, the earth thundered.

CRRASSSSSSSHHHHHHH

It was like an atomic bomb had gone off. Rows of buildings froze, burned, and crumbled. Fire tore through the earth, ice froze the very air, and the barrier erected by the vampiric elite crumbled in a flash.

Tikus screamed in fear when he realized what that strange energy really was. Watching pieces of his hand alight as he kept an arm over his eyes, he felt pieces of his very soul apparatus begin to be chewed away.

He hadn't been sure before, but now he was certain. This was SIN energy.

This creature had somehow acquired a piece of original sin . . . and now that he was sure of it, he saw with mounting horror the giant vertical maw along her front for what it really was.

This was a harbinger of Gluttony, and an instant after the area-of-effect attack went off—the giant creature was among them.

WHIP

SNAP

CRACK

BOOM

Blood sprayed everywhere.

Athela's scythe-like legs tore through the vampiric paladins like they were a child's dolls. If he hadn't known better, Tikus never would have guessed these were the strongest soldiers of their level prior to being let into this newly integrated world. This was not how things were supposed to go, this was not how the invasion was supposed to proceed. How could he let himself die within less than a week of arriving on this new planet?

How had this happened?

The demon's hands rapidly summoned magics that crashed into her surroundings as dozens, then hundreds, and then thousands of spiders poured out of her giant maw like an avalanche. It was so fast that the vampires nearby were buried within seconds, and only their screams were heard as the dog-size white-and-blue arachnids—a variant of Blood Weavers—poured over the vampiric invaders like a wave of hunger.

Electrified snowflakes rippled and swirled, latching onto the mechanical armor of the paladins and stunning them while the spiders attacked—and thick, icy mists rapidly bloomed out of the flowers all along Athela's body as she moved three times faster than any of the vampiric host could.

Tikus coughed blood and then screamed as he felt one of the thousands of spiders tear into his leg, but he smashed the ice-made creature with a single blow.

Only to have three more launch themselves his way—taking him down with frenzied screeches and biting fangs that spread frostbite all along his body.

It would have been his final moments, lying there being devoured alive by the archdemon's summoned minions, but then something odd happened.

Time froze yet again, similar to when the world-boss fight had started, and a new notification appeared with screens blipping into existence in front of all participants currently locked in combat inside the dome.

WARNING

WARNING

WARNING

A JUDGMENT DESCENDS.

THREE HARBINGERS OF GLUTTONY HAVE COME TO

JOIN THE BATTLE. THEY SEEK TO CLAIM SHARDS OF SIN

**FOR THE GREAT MAW, READY TO TAKE BACK WHAT IS
RIGHTFULLY OWNED BY THE HUNGERING ONE. ALL WILL
SUFFER, ALL WILL PERISH, ALL WILL BECOME FUEL FOR
THE TIDE OF THE HUNGERING CHOSEN.
DESPAIR.
BEGINNING BATTLE IN**

5 . . .

4 . . .

3 . . .

2 . . .

1 . . .

Tikus felt numb, his chest burst and split, and before his very eyes, tendrils of darkness ripped out of his heart and buried themselves into his limbs. His mind faded into the background as something else, a new sinister entity, overcame his thoughts—overpowering his will and creating nothing but a husk of the man who'd once been Slayfather of the Rippenvire invasion fleet.

And in his place, a monster began to rise.

Athela watched in silence as her own shard of Gluttony screamed at her to eat and devour the three newcomers, the three apostates that would dare defy the maw's will.

Odd that this particular piece of Gluttony viewed other pieces as nothing but food for its own growth—but so was the will of the great maw. Until only one remained, they would eternally be in conflict, trying to devour each other until a singular entity finally remained.

Her spiderlings withdrew, the wave of white and blue spreading rapidly through the mists as her four red eyes narrowed into slits. She took a step back when the three bodies, each of them previously having been ranking vampires of the Rippenvire, exploded in showers of gore. Vertical maws ripped out of their chests and screamed to the heavens, black tendrils emerging from the void and devouring any nearby biomass—fueling the transformation of the three harbingers while their bodies rapidly grew.

The first was a giant burning stag with a skull for a face, sightless and horns radiating even more brilliantly than the rest of its body.

The second grew into a grotesque abomination, fat and full of rolls with various arms, legs, and eyes. It had two main humanoid legs and two arms, while it carried a large morning star with a shadowy spiked ball on a chain.

The third was more human in shape and size when compared to the giant abominations who first appeared, but this one was by far the most powerful. A creature built of shadow, this was without a doubt a dread-wraith. A void creature, partially built of spirit and partially from empty space itself, dressed in black robes with a black hood and black scimitars. In fact it was so black that the only thing giving off any true definition was Gluttony's maw up and down the front of its chest.

Which was a similar trait that the other two shared, though each of these maws had its own unique characteristics. Gluttony's maw on the dread-wraith was created from shadow, Athela's was created from crystalline ice, the abomination's maw breathed out toxic rotting fumes and leaked flesh, while the stag's was made of Infernal flames.

Each monster emitted auras that matched Athela's own, each was a true powerhouse just as she was, and each of them hungrily eyed her as the four seeds of Gluttony roared and screeched at one another in anticipation of the fight to come. It also appeared that because the stag particularly had claimed the Rippenvire Slayfather as a temporary host, Athela couldn't end this event without killing the creature inhabiting him, too.

"Athela . . ." The shadowy wraith spoke her name as a whisper, but the voice was so filled with power that her very body trembled involuntarily. It took a step forward and held out a hand to her, black blades forming in either palm and one of them pointing in her direction. "We have come to claim your soul . . . In the name of the great maw, we have judged you unworthy. Prepare to . . ."

The wraith's head turned left, and within only seconds the entire domed arena Elysium had set up shook and quaked. A feeling of utter rage set upon them all, red frost beginning to coat the ground rapidly from the point where this malicious aura crept from. The sky of the event dome turned red, then bright crimson, and through the wall of shimmering light, Riven walked.

His plated foot touched solid ground with a resounding boom, his own maw across Messenger's ivory breastplate screamed in anticipation, and red eyes flared as he leveled the blade rippling with ribbons of blood at the three monsters aligned against his friend. The weapon roared, the seeds of Gluttony all simultaneously screamed, and the city shattered under his feet when he launched himself forward.

High Queen Nephridi cackled with delight on her balcony as she watched her great-grandson demolish the Rippenvire fleet over the course of mere minutes. And the fact that it was Rippenvire, a vassal of the Blood Moon Requiem's most prominent but still friendly rival, made it even sweeter. And hilarious. Entire squadrons fell in the blink of an eye, torn asunder by powers far beyond anything that should be expected at this level. Clouds of blades, torrents of crimson ribbons, and thunderous clouds of black bolts vaporized absolutely everything that got in his path.

Truly her grandson was something special. In the beginning, Nephridi had had higher hopes for Allie—and although her granddaughter had shown incredible promise, it still paled in comparison to her brother now.

If Riven continued to grow this rapidly, if he continued to gain insights this fast, if his seed of Gluttony was able to absorb the other pieces here, then she had no doubt that he'd be almost unstoppable when thrown against the other forces on this planet. Riven was developing into an army killer, one that did better against larger numbers than against smaller groups of concentrated power. Each death fueled him even more, if only temporarily. She was already betting the other invaders were avidly hoping for his downfall here against the unforeseen judgment, but should he live . . .

Should he live, the only way to kill him with the forces they'd mustered would be to make sure he didn't engage their united armies. They'd have to take him out with fewer numbers of elites, perhaps some supreme treasures if they'd brought any, to make sure his power didn't grow to exponential heights like it had now. The accumulation of death and blood in the area had empowered him to match even the Harbingers of Gluttony in a one-on-one battle, but it was only temporary. It was a boon granted to him by all the carnage he'd created amid the weaker members of the Rippenvire fleet, now reduced to hundreds of thousands of mangled corpses that would no doubt feed his sister's army of undead. All that blood energy mixing in with a man who had a 100 percent Blood affinity was just astronomically terrorizing, and she had to give it to him—he'd been the first to have that particular affinity reach 100 percent ever since herself.

It made her wonder just how alike they'd be in terms of how they handled blood mana, and she was interested to find out should they ever meet.

When she turned her attention to Allie and her own activities concerning that human boy, High Queen Nephridi's smile faded into a frown. She tsked and caught the attention of her manservant who held a tray of tarts to her side while overlooking the capital city. "I do hope she doesn't fall for that whelpling . . . There are so many others who'd literally kill to take her as a bride. Even now, bidding for her hand in marriage has begun—and I'd hate to break it to her the hard way that she now belongs to the Blood Moon Requiem."

Her manservant raised an eyebrow, red eyes shining almost as brightly as hers. Though he was merely a servant, to serve the queen meant he had to be at minimum a pureblooded vampire himself—lest he tarnish her presence with his filth. "Do you not feel the same way about your grandson?"

"What about him?"

"His relationship with . . . that succubus. The people of the empire watching these events unfold on the frontier are eating it up rather nicely, I must say. Many are cheering for her, but then again—many are rooting for Athela, too."

High Queen Nephridi giggled, then laughed loudly while watching the battle unfold between five Harbingers of Gluttony—a rare sight indeed. "No, dear, those are demonic contracts. They are toys, nothing more, so he can play with them however he chooses. Do not worry—we will find Riven a good pure-blooded wife. And I do believe that, according to Kathrine's reports, she's already managed to woo him once. Her family is delighted, and the bidding wars on him are already raging just as fiercely . . . though should she claim his heart before integration ends, I have already told her that she may have the spot regardless of who wins the bidding. We will see how it all unfolds, and five years from now when we bring them to their family's inheritance, I hope to see them both bear us children. They both have the gift, and chances of passing the prophecy on to future generations are exponentially increased by ones who are more than just passive genetic carriers."

CHAPTER 28

Despite the Rippenvire fleet having been for the most part wiped out, many hundreds of dropships had landed troops on different layers of the stacked city and were continuing to wreak havoc. The royal fleet of Dawn was also decimated, and the country's forces were already engaged at numerous points. The vampires continued to slaughter civilians as fast as possible, either out of spite or simply because they didn't know they'd lost yet. But the fact remained that without the surging hordes of allied reinforcements coming up from the lower levels, this city would certainly have been lost. Even now forces from both Brightsville and Deepnest had reclaimed the first three upper levels and two lower levels, with another four contested city pieces to go.

Though honestly when Allie had flown over floor seven, there'd been almost nothing left. The entire top side was a ruined husk of what it'd once been, littered with smoking corpses and broken airships, while the academy was nothing but rubble and flame.

Allie's footsteps echoed through the long hall, the corpses around her twitching and rising in silence as wisps of teal light trickled out of her body to animate the dead. Ahead of her, two more vampiric sets of eyes glared back at her through the dark, leveling pistols her way before firing.

The bullets sizzled and hissed through the air, exploding on contact when Allie's wand shot forward and eradicated them in an instant. Not speeding up or slowing down, she continued her monotonous walk while more bullets continued peppering the walls around her.

"BLOOD TRAITOR!" one of the vampires screamed, drawing out a scimitar and dashing forward when he realized the bullets weren't doing anything.

His companion soon joined him in the frontal assault, and Allie conjured four flaming skulls before letting them loose like cannon fire.

The walls on either side of her shuddered in the darkness, only illuminated by the deathly flames as the skulls screeched forward and exploded on impact. The two vampires died immediately, and she effortlessly stepped over their charred remains while casually continuing toward her goal.

"Insects . . ." she hissed, turning right and approaching a barricaded door where one of the vampiric hounds was digging its way through the old wood into the room. On the other side, screams of civilians and the weeping of children were audible.

The monster didn't even know she was there, too obsessed with the scent of nearby prey, and it too died in a flash of death mana that left it dropping to the floor with a loud yelp.

"Is this it?" Allie asked, turning to Mara, who was in terrible shape and missing an arm along with half her lower torso.

The ghoul necromancer, along with the skeletal brothers Vin and Nin, all nodded. Mara held up a hand, and out of the darkness a shadow elemental in the form of a rat tore itself off a wall to land on her outstretched palm. "He is here."

Ignoring the screams and sobbing on the other side of the door, Allie turned back to the old, thick wood and unleashed thin threads of power. They dug into the hinges, the locks, the perimeter of the wooden outline and in a second tore the door off the wall and flung it aside. Then they continued to fling pieces of debris and junk, stuff that the people on the other side of the door had piled up against it as a barricade, and the screaming grew louder.

She stepped inside, looking around the candlelit room with red eyes through her skull mask as one man threateningly brandished a dagger at her. There were a couple dozen people here, all scattered throughout a cellar.

But another pair of people, a middle-aged husband and wife, quickly recognized her with a gasp when she didn't move to attack anyone. Immediately they got down onto their knees and prostrated themselves, and the woman began to call out to her, "Queen Thane of the Necropolis!"

The mood immediately shifted, but everything else that was said filtered in through one ear and out the other when Allie's shoulders sagged in relief. In one corner of the room, still alive, were Lahn and his mother, Shovi.

They locked eyes, and without another word Allie picked up her pace while taking off her mask. Lahn tried to stand up, but he was still weak—and he stumbled to catch himself against the wall right before Allie flung her arms around him.

"Good on you for not dying," Allie said softly, sighing when she felt his returned embrace as the room went silent. "That would have made me very sad."

Lahn, somewhat speechless with tears welling up under his eyes, nodded just once. "Thanks for coming. But don't you have better things to do, other than rescue me?"

She smiled, then shook her head. "No. This is the most important thing, and if I hadn't come you'd have been dead within a few minutes when the vampires broke down that door. We need to move you and your mother to a more secure location, then Tyranus and I are going to join Riven in his fight against the harbingers."

Her red eyes shifted to where one of the people had a system cortex screen up displaying the fight, and already it was becoming a fight of the ages. She ignored that for now; Riven would be fine until she got there.

"My queen," Mara said from under a black hood, looking over her shoulder to where Nin and Vin had exited toward the sounds of clashing metal and screams farther back. "The vampires are approaching in great numbers. We cannot stay; another of their elite groups is sweeping this part of the city and fighting them would stall you even longer from reaching your brother. We need to leave unless you want to get locked into a drawn-out conflict."

Allie abruptly nodded and let go, seeing Shovi sniffle and give her a wide, shaky smile. "Come on, everyone, you heard Mara. Let's get going."

Malice.

Hate.

Rage.

These were the feelings coursing through him when his eyes locked onto those who would dare try to rip Athela's soul apart to acquire her newly found shard of sin. These motherfuckers didn't know who they were messing with, and there was no way he was about to let these would-be thieves take Athela away from him when she'd just gotten back.

A giant flaming stag.

A fat, fleshy abomination wielding a morning-star flail.

A shadowy, dual scimitar–wielding wraith.

He was going to crush them all into paste.

His foot exited the dome of light, coming to the other side of the five-mile-wide system-made arena. His aura roared for blood, shaking the very ground he stood on as his entire being radiated with fury and his eyes locked onto the three interlopers.

[You have entered an event: World Quest Boss Fight—Tikus, Slayfather of Rippenvire, versus Archdemon Athela, Baby Stomper and Future Conqueror of Worlds.

Warning—This event has been modified. Slayfather Tikus and the forces of Rippenvire have been either devoured or possessed by three Harbingers of Gluttony. This event will not end until either the three harbingers have perished or Athela dies.]

Oh, there would be some perishing, all right.

Wisps of blood condensed around his weapon and a gaping red jackal's maw roared ahead. Black and red wisps lit up along his body, smoldering with power under the upgraded version of Blessing of the Crow. The back of his thick ivory plate armor bloomed with torrential red flames, and a lightning strike five times larger than he was encompassed him in a protective shell as he prepared the move.

Then the city shattered underneath Riven's feet as he launched himself forward faster than the speed of a hypersonic bullet.

- **Black Lightning:** This staff can passively build up charges of Black Lightning. Power of Black Lightning depends on the amount of charge emitted.
- **Jackal's Lunge:** Point this weapon in any direction and activate this innate and unique martial art, charging the blade with blood mana to create the visage of a jackal's maw and blasting forward. When your blade strikes an enemy, the red jackal will close down on them to deal additional blood and sin damage.
- **Launch:** The back of your suit can open up, creating a blast of sin energy that damages enemies and acts as a propulsion method to blast you in a given direction at speeds dependent on how much energy you drain from the stored reservoir of your pauldrons.
- **Blessing of the Crow:** Activate this ability up to once per day for an hour's worth of increased stamina regeneration with a significant boost to Agility.

Riven collided with the flaming stag, his jackal's maw snapping down onto its skull as the blade skewered its brain. But it wasn't enough to kill the creature.

The stag roared, blooming with retaliatory fire and forcibly being torn off the ground by the immense impact. The huge monster was sent careening with Riven's blade impaling it, screeching in pain and rage as a storm of blood magic ripped through its body while it tried to regain a footing against its uncontrolled, thunderous roll.

The fight was on.

Thousands of crystalline spiders screeched and rushed forward, swarming toward the fat flesh abomination with hundreds of hungry mouths as it charged Athela. Her cloud of frost became a blizzard, intermixing with electrified snowflakes that whirled about her as she opened her maw of Gluttony to unleash a cannon blast of fire, ice, and lightning at the wraith.

But the wraith vanished, leaving Athela only a moment to counter the incoming scimitars aimed at her neck as the shadowy figure roared with blazing torrents of void energy—smashing into Athela's outstretched hand that blocked the attack. But her scream of pain as blue blood began pouring out of the deep wound gave Riven pause across the battlefield.

Ripping his weapon out of the stag's skull and turning only briefly, he saw Azmoth's armored, flaming figure crash a huge stone maul into the back of the wraith.

"AZMOTH SAVE TINY ATHELA!!!"

The wraith was floored in a shower of shadowy wisps, flames, and debris, but immediately recovered even under the enormity of that strike with a quick flip and blur of shadowy blades as it created five more illusions of itself. Snarling, it began the assault—exchanging places with its illusionary bodies from time to time and making it hard for the two demons fighting it to pinpoint its exact location. Each strike it made was met with thunderous claps of discharging shadow, and in turn Athela's frosted, scythe-like legs and Azmoth's flaming maul created shock waves of their own.

The multimouthed flesh monster was roaring and smashing aside dozens of spiders at a time, only being weighed down temporarily by the swarm of arachnids and not taking much if any damage from them—but at least it was being held back for now to buy them time. Clouds of noxious green fumes were spraying from the many mouths and its huge, sickly belly jiggled with every thunderous step it took to crush more spiders underfoot, flail spiraling in the air and sending out sprays of earth every time the weapon crashed into the ground with storms of arachnid body parts.

Riven didn't have much more time to look, needing to trust in his two minions to deal with the wraith. He needed to finish off this stag before the abomination laid waste to the arachnid swarm.

"RUK-RUK-RUK-RUK-RUK!" The stag in front of him had regained its legs, letting out an odd bellowing call with its mangled mouth toward the sky and antlers lighting up an even brighter orange-red as the flames pulsed. A circle formed in the sky above them, and Riven's eyes widened when the circle of flames opened a portal—conjuring swarms of flaming, molten chains that spiraled down toward him like snakes.

And they were fast.

The maw along Riven's chest opened and unleashed a torrent of black tendrils to intercept the first few, but he was forced to riftwalk backward to avoid the collision of the molten storm.

The ground thundered upon impact, and the chains began spiraling out to chase him down while the stag charged.

CRASH

Sparks ignited along Riven's blade and left pauldron as he stood his ground and took the hit, flaming antlers smashing into his smaller figure and causing the surprised stag to stumble and trip. Counterattacking with a wide swipe of his weapon and simultaneously conjuring dozens of Bloody Razors that rapidly morphed into ripping storm balls through Profane Cyclone's Path of Red and Black, he split the stag's side open in numerous places and sent it staggering once again.

His weapon radiated amid the screech of the flaming maw across the stag's chest, and right before the swarm of chains connected with him, the visage of Gluttony appeared behind him as he unleashed his attack.

- **Gluttony's Riptide: Passively builds up an elongated blade of sin energy that can extend by swinging this weapon in an arc. Recharge rate and damage output depend on control and insight concerning Gluttony.**

Before the stag hit the ground, a torrential amount of sin energy cut down with the swing of his blade and tore through the line of motion hundreds of yards out. The ground was torn asunder and the stag's internals were sent spraying—

BOOM

Riven was hit head-on with the swarm of molten chains, causing him to reel backward and scream as searing heat began working its way through the slit in his helmet. When he abruptly activated Hell's Armor, the pain went away and he sighed in relief, but his eyes were burned out and he couldn't see until his regeneration kicked in.

Cursing and using his mana to feel out the remaining—

CRASH

The stag's horns slammed him into the ground, and he felt a hoof twice the size he was repeatedly stomp him into the ground with radiating kinetic energy—causing some of his bones to shatter even though his armor didn't give. Messenger was holding firm, but so too was his Hell's Armor, which gave him an additional layer of obsidian plates along with an Infernal shroud of flame and heat resistance.

Somehow the stag had survived the attack after being cleaved in two.

BAM-BAM-BAM

The stomps kept coming, with force that would no doubt crush armored tanks repeatedly barreling into him.

He coughed blood but managed to fight through the pain with his regenerative properties as flaring blood mana rippled up his arm. Forming his hand into a claw, a Blood Lance tore out of his body—passing through the Path of Red and Black to imbue it further with Black Lightning. He infused as much power as he could within those two seconds, and the torpedo blindly crashed into the body of the stag, resulting in an echoing scream.

He kicked off the ground with a burst of blood energy out of his pauldron reservoirs, tearing through the binding chains that shattered under the mental flex and sending himself out of the crater he'd been smashed into. After he landed a ways off and shook his head to clear it of the ringing, his eyesight slowly started to return. Cursing, he ripped away some of the magma that was still glued to his face, his red eyes glared out through the visor, and he blinked rapidly through the flames of Hell's Armor and wisps of Blessing of the Crow, settling his gaze on the creature before him.

This monster was no pushover.

The huge hellish stag was now in one piece again, though some of the wounds from his earlier attacks were still present. How that was possible he didn't know, but the way his body ached and the still-broken bones mending told him one thing—he probably shouldn't try to fight this monster up close. It was physically stronger than he was, and he'd have the advantage if—

The monster rocketed toward him in a blast of flame similar to Azmoth's own gap-clearing martial art, causing Riven to stumble back and throw out another Black Lightning strike the size of his thigh.

But the creature barreled through it heedlessly, coming at him like a comet from the heavens and smashing into him again.

Riven was launched through the air at high speed, his mind going in and out due to the massive strike until he regained consciousness midflight and activated the thrusters on his armor.

Steadying himself in midair and barely avoiding a crash into the domed wall a few hundred feet up, he held out his arms to either side. "You motherfucker . . ."

The air around him swirled and roared, tearing apart the buildings underneath him while a storm of red began collecting about his body like a cyclone. Dark lightning, red ice, and shrieking winds howled as he poured mana into his aura and his Crimson Ice spell. He poured in all the blood energy he'd accumulated after tearing through the Rippenvire fleet—causing the dome encompassing them all to tremble under his power.

He lifted his hand, and like a god condemning a mortal to a life of damnation, he let the magic go. "Let's see what you think about this."

A tidal wave of roaring power soared through the air directly toward the stag from all directions, causing the ground to quake and shudder under the approaching strike.

The stag backpedaled with wide eyes, panicking with a cry of fear, and a halo of fire bloomed over its head as the incoming storm of red and black rushed forward. A blinding flash lit up from the halo, illuminating the entire combat zone in a quick instant—and Riven had to blink away the afterimage of the halo exploding.

The storm of his mana was gone. The halo was gone. The remaining molten chains were gone. The noxious clouds of the titanic flesh abomination were gone. Even Athela's swarm of crystalline spiders was gone.

The stag had dispelled all the active attacks to save itself from the impending collision, but the way the monster sagged made it obvious that it'd expelled almost all of its own energy to do so.

Riven gawked. "You've gotta be fist-fucking me!"

Then, to his amazement and brief confusion, he saw the flesh abomination tear out toward the stag to swing its large spiked flail directly at the creature's head.

The weakened hell stag only had a moment to scream before the huge ball of spikes crushed its skull entirely, obliterating its brain and sending the monster's flaming body into a spasm before it too exploded in a storm of fire.

The flesh abomination roared with all its many mouths in triumph—letting its own visage of Gluttony send out spiraling tendrils that dug into the body and soul of the stag within seconds.

Riven watched, both horrified and fascinated, as the abomination's shard of Gluttony ripped and tugged—pulling out the stag's own and beginning to devour it. The visage of the maw that it yanked out of the stag's soul was similar to what Riven had seen back in Negrada's hellscape when he'd first acquired it out of that jar, a ghostly maw of red and black, but this time it was the one being eaten.

Eaten by another piece of itself.

The maw screamed and roared in rage as the other piece of Gluttony chomped down, splitting it apart and absorbing it like a leech would suck blood out of prey.

And as soon as it was done, the flesh abomination began to shiver. Its aura rose, and the monster screamed in glee before it completely disappeared in a flash of light.

His eyes narrowed. That certainly made things easier on his end, but it left a lot of disturbing questions . . .

He turned his attention to Athela and Azmoth where they were battling the wraith. It was fast, very fast, and its strikes were on par with anything that any of them could throw out to boot. A storm of strikes from the two scimitars whirled around it as the wraith flipped, teleported, dashed, and ducked between the two demons like it was nothing.

Athela's body was covered in deep wounds that flared with black wisps, draining out blood as she tried to pinpoint where the wraith was in between the fading figures of its illusions.

Azmoth, on the other hand, was worse off, missing three of his arms so only one remained. He'd dropped the maul in favor of using his claws now that he couldn't wield the weapon properly, and part of the armor covering his face had been ripped away to reveal a deep, oozing wound on the side of his obsidian skull.

Riven calmed his nerves. Despite having lost most of his mana in that recent, failed attack on the stag, his mana regeneration was quite good. He waited another couple seconds, landing on one of the rooftops that was still somehow standing despite the absolute desolation surrounding him. He slammed his blade into the rooftop beneath, clawed his fingers, and conjured a Blood Lance to take aim.

Back in Chicago, Riven had acquired the Snipe upgrade for his Blood Lance ability as a reward for defeating the Azag Hive Cluster. He'd not had a good time to use it in battle until now, but this would be a perfect opportunity to try it.

The crimson lance shimmered in the light, crackling with Black Lightning courtesy of his path and forming a Wretched Snare along its back for additional propulsion via his slingshot method. Strings of mana were sent out, feeling for the enemy's true position as his eyes closed, and then time slowed when his vision changed from that of his eyes to that of the lance itself.

It was like looking down the sight of a barrel.

His vision zoomed in during that frozen moment, identifying one of twelve figures that could be the wraith. It was still midtransition between illusionary bodies, but Riven was pretty sure this was the right one based on how his mana strings couldn't penetrate this particular body.

Activating the second stage of his Snipe ability, the Blood Lance was empowered. It sharpened, becoming thinner and sleeker than its previous form, and the tip of the lance darkened. The air around it shimmered, condensed, and the Blood Lance pulled back on his Wretched Snare slingshot for an additional boost. Everything else around him still remained frozen—which made him wonder what other people would see when watching this from an external perspective—and then time resumed.

The lance tore through the half mile almost instantaneously, leaving a long, linear tear through space itself as it crashed into the chest of the wraith.

Black goop sprayed out the other side of the creature, causing it to gasp as a hole in its body was left crackling with Riven's power.

His two demons capitalized, moving in unison to charge the wraith during its staggered moment of vulnerability. Athela's shriek of glee echoed through the dome as one of her legs ripped into the body of the wraith, leaving a line of frost in her wake just as another flash of light erupted from behind her.

Riven's heart nearly stopped when he saw that it was the abomination he'd assumed had left. Whether it was using illusion, spatial warping, or some kind of other means to mask its presence, the creature was still here, and its many mouths grinned ominously as the giant morning star flail crashed through all three of the combatants in front of it.

And this time, it imbued the strike with a massive amount of Unholy energy.

Azmoth died on the spot.

The wraith died, too.

And Athela? Her house-size body was crushed into the ground—smashing her brains across the rubble as the abomination began to cackle furiously.

Riven screamed and blasted forward with what little mana he had left—throwing his arm back and heaving Jackal forward to throw it like a spear.

The weapon launched forward, smashing into the huge abomination and tearing a hole through its chest that caused it to howl in anger and turn toward him.

CRACK

The flail spun around so fast Riven didn't have time to adjust his trajectory, and he felt his ribs all snap at the same time with the groan of metal when the weapon impacted his armor.

BOOM

He landed in a cloud of rubble, gasping for air and watching from a limp, supine position while the abomination began consuming the wraith next.

Unearthly screeches tore out of the wraith's soul as it tried to escape, but it could not. The huge fleshy, abnormally fat monster roared in victory once again as its maw of Gluttony ripped and tore at yet another shard, sending the monster's aura spiking even more than the first time.

The ground underneath it tore apart, pieces of earth and rubble rising into the air all around it while it continued to scream a victory cry—hands raised above while Unholy power radiated around it. And soon it turned its attention to Athela, wanting to consume her soul, too, but it paused with a multitude of frowns when it realized she wasn't there.

Then, appearing beside its neck on top of one massive shoulder, the slender form of Athela's Arshakai body blipped into existence.

It was the form Riven was most accustomed to now. Long, slender black legs, black hair, two red eyes, and a very feminine, humanoid figure. Six arachnoid blades ripped out of her back, and an evil smile focused on one of the creature's fleshy, bloodshot eyes. "Looking for me?"

She ripped into the eye and dived into its body, a whirlwind of blades digging a tunnel into the monster's neck before she ripped out the other side in a spray of gore.

The monster howled, clutching at its neck, and tried to swat her away—but she easily landed with a backflip and gracefully flung the monster's fluids off her in a single logic-defying motion.

Riven managed to get to his knees, then, with effort, pushed himself up to stand. Their eyes locked, and Athela's wicked grin faltered into something else—some kind of emotion that he could not pinpoint passing over her.

With a nod, she blurred forward again, far faster than she'd ever been, and crashed into the flesh abomination with whirlwinds of strikes—using her long black tongue, necrotic poisons, claws, blades, and blood thread needles to attack the larger monster mercilessly. All the while, she dodged attack after attack as the abomination spewed clouds of acidic smog, smashed down with its flail, and tried to body slam or stomp her to death.

From what Riven could see, Athela's current body had mostly remained the same, but with two key differences. The first was that it was far faster and more agile than she'd been previously, by a scale of double or triple her previous power. The second change was a little less obvious.

From time to time, Riven caught glimpses of Gluttony's visage on her body, opening up along random places in various sizes to suck away the smog or lash out with necrotic tendrils, before the maw would vanish into her body like it'd never been there.

If he had to guess, it was somehow utilizing her body's shapeshifting abilities to hide itself and appear as needed in different places.

He held out his hand and Jackal soared back into its rightful place. Spinning the weapon around once and having let his vampiric regeneration fully heal him once again, he charged.

CRASH

THUD

BOOM

He struck and slashed at the monster over and over again, drawing its attention away from Athela as best he could to provide a less mobile but sturdier target for the monster to focus on.

And the enraged monster took the bait.

Roaring and giving up on catching Athela for now, the creature tried body slamming Riven underneath a mountain of flesh—crashing into the floor with a resounding boom that shook the earth right after Riven riftwalked away to put distance between them.

He reengaged, smashing Jackal into the creature's exposed shoulder and tearing out a good chunk of flesh before the flail connected with him yet again in a blurring crash.

But bracing himself with Crimson Ice, which glued his legs to the ground, he was able to take the hit head-on. The weapon smashed against Messenger, and even though Riven felt his legs snap—so too did the spiked ball.

The flail shattered amid Riven's scream, and Athela took the moment to go for the monster's brain.

Rapidly digging with the Flurry martial art on repeat, she was able to carve a five-meter hole into the monster before another cloud of acidic gas caused her to retreat. Flipping up over the monster's back, she dived for the back side as it lay prone and activated the martial art Backstab with all six of her sharpened, bladelike legs.

The effect was immense, far more than she'd anticipated. Critical strike notifications bloomed before her eyes and torrents of kinetic energy mixed with Shadow energy rippled along the monster's back, causing it to scream and flail. Internal organs ruptured and she quickly dived off when the abomination rolled—only to be flung sideways by a shock wave of force when the creature simultaneously belched from all its mouths.

"Shit!" Riven cursed when he saw Athela thrown aside, and he began charging up another Snipe when a ripple in the dome above caught his attention.

And with a roar, Tyranus dived through the dome.

The giant skeletal drake dive-bombed the other monster with outstretched claws, deathly flames billowing from its mouth while Allie summoned hundreds of deathly globes that shot forward to bombard the creature below. The drake roared, sending one martial art after the other as it activated Pulsating Roar in waves of kinetic energy to knock the struggling creature back down—flattening it and sending its fat belly jiggling to all sides. Then the Deathfire Blast came next, barreling toward the creature after Allie's bombardment in an immense storm of teal and black flames.

The hundreds of death balls peppered the monster with tiny explosions and the drake's fire blast smashed into the screaming monster, burning it alive before Allie and her drake crashed into the smoldering wreckage of the beast underneath.

Claws and teeth tore into it, and Allie's wand lifted to send out lacerating strikes of death mana ripping all across the beast's surface.

Riven didn't think twice and immediately started firing off more of his Bloody Razors, and Athela dived back in with a scream of glee.

The flesh abomination struggled against the equally large drake atop its body, but it was weakened now. Despite being higher leveled and more powerful than the drake would be in most circumstances, the damage the flesh abomination had taken was too great.

Acid spewed up onto Tyranus's bone claws, but the undead drake ignored it and continued tearing into the monster with reckless abandon while its wings pinned down the abomination's arms. Then, when the large gluttonous maw across the abomination's chest opened up to let loose dozens of tendrils to try and combat the drake, Tyranus reared back and fired a blast of flame directly into the maw.

The abomination bellowed, puffed up, and exploded in a shower of gore that threw smoldering body parts everywhere.

Then, as the victory notifications began to seep in and the dome began to fade away, Tyranus, with Allie on his back, lifted his enormous body up on his hind legs, spread his wings, and roared to the heavens in victory as black and teal death energies burned all around him.

CHAPTER 29

The seeds of Gluttony inside the flesh abomination called to him, but they might as well have been whispers on the wind—the last thing on Riven's mind.

Because standing there next to the large eviscerated corpse . . . was Athela. Staring back at him with a vulnerable, almost sheepish glance before her eyes hit the ground.

It was really her. How had he not known she'd come back?

He'd choked back his emotions upon first seeing her to maintain a clear head, masked them with anger during the fight, but now that things were calmer . . .

Riven began to step forward, slowly at first but with increasing speed. He threw Jackal to the side as it warped into its canine form, and flung his helmet back off his face to hang from the bloodsilk bindings along the back of his neck.

Riftwalking through a portal and coming within ten yards of her, he stopped dead to stare at Athela with wide, wet eyes.

"Um . . . Hey, Riven," Athela said meekly, hands nervously clasped in front of her, eyes searching his face for clues on what he was feeling. "I . . ."

He broke into a run—crashing into Athela with a muffled sob as he gripped her tightly, eyes shut in a futile attempt to block out tears, his entire body shaking with both arms wrapped around her smaller, lithe frame. His voice came out as a whisper. "Back in the city of canyons, I thought I'd lost you forever. Athela, I missed you so, so much . . . I'm . . . I'm glad to have you back."

Athela didn't reply, but she pursed her lips into a tight line, eyes squinting with unbidden tears coming to her as well. Burying her face in his chest and clinging to him with her arms around his torso, she let out a long high-pitched, drawn-out whimper that lasted for a couple seconds before she quietly began to sob.

Allie watched silently from atop her skeletal drake, standing guard over them with a warm half smile across her lips—though she didn't know how Fay was going to feel about the intense and raw emotion during this reunion. Where was Fay, anyway? Allie felt like she needed to leave to give them some space, but with three or more shards of Gluttony within the corpse underneath her draconic mount—as well as the enormous pile of Elysium coins and the glowing Dao treasure that'd appeared as event prizes for Athela's victory—Allie just couldn't bring herself to leave. She knew that given their reunion, it was very unlikely that either of them would realize it if someone came up and started stealing under their very noses. They'd simply be too invested in each other to care, so it was now up to her to make sure these treasures remained guarded until Riven and Athela got their heads on straight.

"Riven . . ." Athela said with a quivering voice, sniffling and keeping her head against his chest as they embraced. "I need to talk to you. I have an admission to make. I also did something bad . . . but I don't regret it. And I need you to know why I did it, which may have something to do with the original admission. You might be mad at me."

Riven shook his head, holding on to her for dear life. "There's nothing you could have done that I wouldn't forgive you for. I'm just happy to have you here with me."

Athela paused, letting the words sink in as the feelings of happy butterflies and wavering dread intermixed. She didn't want this moment to end, but she peeled out of his grasp to stand a foot away, still holding him by the hands. "Promise me?"

Riven raised an eyebrow, then chuckled. "Of course, silly. I promise."

Another pause before Athela gained the courage to go through with what she was about to do, with a deep inhale and slow exhale. "All right. Close your eyes."

Riven wiped away a tear with a happy but confused smile, cocking his head to the side with red eyes staring into her own. "Close my eyes? That's an odd request. Weren't you going to tell me something?"

"Just do it, idiot!" Athela meekly replied in a soft, wavering voice. She crossed her long, slender, pitch-black legs, avoiding his gaze for a moment before giving him a pleading look. "I have to tell you with your eyes closed. Please trust me."

The sound of explosions echoed in the distant city, but neither of them turned to look.

Riven blinked just once, sighed with a gentle smile, and did as she asked. He felt Athela's hands let go of his own, and then felt her arms gracefully glide around his neck before the warm press of her lips met his.

Up on her tiptoes, pulling him in, she held the kiss for a long, long time before letting go. "I love you, Riven."

"THAT WRETCHED BITCH!" Fay flung a vase to shatter across the wall in the Sojavi clan's nether realm, then screamed at one of the lower-class members of their large family to get out before slumping down into a huddling position to sob against a stone wall, head in her hands.

Fay's sister Nitidi sat down next to her with a comforting arm laid across her shoulders.

"There is a saying from his homeworld . . ." Saemi, Fay's mother, stated while sprawled out on a couch with a frown, watching the events on Panu unfold. "'All is fair in love and war,' I believe it was. She played her cards well."

"You're not helping, Mother!" Nitidi scolded the older succubus before turning to hug Fay tighter while the blue-skinned succubi continued to occupy the inner library sanctum. "This is not over, Fay. You'll be back and can set things right. She's just taking advantage of you not being there—"

"Like I did to her?!" Fay spat back, self-loathing and venom in her words while still clutching her face—digging her nails into her skin. "DAMN IT! This could NOT have gone worse!"

Saemi frowned at her youngest daughter, giving Fay a once-over before sighing loudly. "What exactly did you expect for her to do after she came back? Just roll over and let you take him? You have to fight for what you want, Fay. It is the law of the multiverse, and in the arena of lust and love, you of all people have an advantage. You are a succubus—stop acting like such a spoiled child."

Fay looked up to glare at her mother, but Saemi didn't back down. "This isn't about competition, Mother. This is about how Riven sees me for ME, and not as a SEX OBJECT like all of **your** previous masters. You wouldn't understand."

Fay winced when her mother snapped forward to whip Fay across the face with her tail. It left a long red mark on one cheek, and the younger succubus immediately went silent.

"You will not talk of my previous masters, little girl," Saemi stated with gritted teeth, but she settled back down on the cushioned couch a moment later with a calming breath. "There were a couple of them that I liked very much. Just because you are hurting, child, doesn't mean you need to inflict that same emotional pain on others."

The anger toward her mother immediately simmered down, and Fay glanced up to see there was genuine hurt behind Saemi's eyes. Fay had struck a nerve, probably a half truth or even a full truth, and she immediately felt guilty. "I—I'm sorry, I didn't mean to hurt you. As you said, I am just . . . I am not okay."

Fay's quivering voice hiccuped, and she tried to let out another calming breath while warm tears streamed down her cheeks. Looking up at the ceiling and wrapping one of her own arms around her silent sister sitting next to her—returning the embrace—Fay let out a wry chuckle. "I suppose I deserve this."

There was a long pause, and Saemi gave her daughter a sad smile. "Child . . . you have a long, long ways to go on this road if you ever wish to find success. A minor setback like this is nothing in the grand scale of the true game."

Fay sniffled. "And what would the true game be, exactly?"

Saemi smiled but did not answer that question. Instead, she waved her hand to summon the image of the Blood Moon Requiem's capital city. Gesturing to it, she began to speak. "Did you know that both Riven and Allie are being sold by the high queen as breeding stock?"

Fay sniffled yet again, wiped her eyes, then frowned with furrowed eyebrows. "What do you mean?"

"I mean that, just like all the ones who have the active gift of Malignant Prophecy, their marriages are being auctioned off to other pure-blooded royal houses. To be wed to the most prominent supporter and highest bidder." Saemi's gaze remained fixed on Fay.

When her daughter didn't reply, only staring back at her in silence, Saemi continued. "To have a better chance at creating more just like them. Simply put, he is property of their high queen. The Blood Moon Requiem has destroyed entire empires and has committed genocides against trillions of people over even a slim chance of letting that gift of prophecy fall into the wrong hands, and in equal measure it seeks to create more users to solidify their power in the multiverse. If you really wish to pursue this man and don't wish to simply find another, perhaps you should consider whether you're able to recognize that you may never have a choice in the matter of being the only woman with him. Even if that's what he wants, the high queen could and would simply force him into arranged marriages—or worse. Bidding for his hand in an official marriage has already reached absurd heights, going as far as offering up three planets and a trove of supreme Dao treasures to the crown for the chance at acquiring his genes and house name. The same can be said about Allie, but for her it is even more of an unfortunate circumstance. She can only bear one pregnancy at a time, while Riven can have many children at once. This in turn means that the high queen will be less intrusive into your own relationship with the man, while Allie . . . Allie will likely be prohibited from seeing anyone else at all—aside from the person the high queen picks for her. Be happy that Riven is a man, Fay, because if it'd been Allie you'd fallen in love with and if you were an incubus—there'd be no hope for you whatsoever."

[You have an abnormally high number of stat points to spend. Be advised that it is in your best interest to invest them soon.]

Riven watched, mind elsewhere, as his shard of Gluttony violently consumed the three other shards one by one out of the monstrous corpse remnants ahead of him. Athela had told him how Fay had betrayed her trust, how Athela had just been hesitant to ruin their friendship by making a move, and how she'd recently killed Fay—temporarily—in order to get some time alone to tell Riven all about what'd happened. To tell Riven how she felt about him.

Fay had originally made it seem like she wasn't certain of Athela's intentions, yet she'd lied to Riven about that, too. Which bothered and angered him. He was also bothered and angered by Athela's admission about killing and eating Fay, because Fay had already been recently traumatized and was still in a fragile state.

He didn't even know what to think at this point. He was currently dating Fay, but when Athela had admitted how she felt about him on the world stage . . .

He sighed, eyes distant amid the violent ripping and tearing of his own original shard of Gluttony feasting on other shards. Funnily enough, the changes mostly didn't portray themselves on his own body—but rather had a true link through his armor and weapon. The link was inside his soul, sure—he could even see it there as it connected to the other shards and grew in size, but the stats of his armor and his weapon both increased by leaps and bounds for every other shard consumed—rather than his own body being changed like the harbingers' or Athela's.

Well, there was one odd change he noted on his body—but it wasn't anything out of place. Instead of a new arm, a mouth growing out of his chest, or some weird tail extension, he got another tattoo.

It was a sleeve tattoo, covering his entire right shoulder and traveling all the way to his fingertips. There were a couple of stationary sin-affiliated glyphs along with various Unholy-affiliated runes—but most of the pitch-black tattoo was fluid, moving. Patterns crossed, wove about one another, and shifted randomly all along the inner part of his tattoo's borders—and a cold, chilling sensation continued to seep into his bloodstream from the ominous black ink.

[You have absorbed five pieces of Gluttony. Mark of the Sinner is under construction.]

Five?

His vision turned inward. He only saw four, all rotating about his sin core . . . until he noticed the faint connection between Athela's shard in her own soul aperture and his own.

Five it was, then.

And if that's how it was going to work . . . perhaps he should distribute his pieces across all his minions.

Which brought him back to needing to fill his last demonic contract slot, which he still hadn't done. He'd been waiting this entire time for Athela to get back, wanting her opinion above all others' before choosing, but now . . .

Ugh. He loved Athela, and he was attracted to her, but did he love her the same way she loved him? He'd never thought about her romantically before. Not only that, but what about Fay? He was dating Fay, wasn't he? How would she react to all this? Did he even want to date her after she'd kept such sensitive information to herself before making a move—knowing it'd hurt Athela?

"That was . . . somewhat expected," Allie said softly, standing beside him as helicopter squadrons patrolled the skies overhead. She looked back over her shoulder the way Athela had left, giving Riven the time he needed to compute what had just happened.

"Take all the time you need. I'll be waiting. I don't need an answer now, I just . . . I just need to know soon."

That's what Athela had told him before going, and she'd given him another hopeful kiss before disappearing into the desolate city to find vampires to kill. What did that even mean?

Riven shook his head and let himself fall back onto his ass with a thud, not bothering to catch himself when he sprawled out. Closing his eyes and spreading out his arms, he couldn't even be bothered to snort. "I don't know what I'm supposed to do, Allie. What should I do?"

It was Allie's turn to sigh, and she plopped down onto the ground beside him—poking at the shifting tattoo on his right arm with mild curiosity. "Do what feels right. Don't feel obligated to either of them. Don't act out of a sense of right or wrong. Just . . . pick whoever you feel would be best for you. Pick the one you think will love you the most, the one you could love the most, and hope that it doesn't go wrong. And give it your all, because if it fails—you want to make sure that you have no regrets. Other than that, it's up in the air. I'm no good at this relationship stuff. I had a man-harem up until recently, remember? You might be asking the wrong girl."

CHAPTER 30

Captain Vros Kinal, champion of this expedition to Panu, harbinger of the Empire of Dying Suns, was quite amused. "How long has it been now? A few days?"

The other officers in plate armor cackled or snickered while drinking the rum of conquered locals as they sat atop a keep on a large hill—making the scantily clad new slaves dance for them as they talked about recent events.

"You'd be correct!" one of Kinal's subordinates called out. "How pathetic! This is hilarious! Rippenvire is done here! No doubt they'll be off the planet and out of our hair in a few days, having abandoned Panu due to their embarrassing defeat."

"I give it a single day!" another officer yelled over the laughter—chugging a glass of ale.

"Two days!" another one cried, slamming his fists merrily into the polished wood as scenes of the battle circulated over the Panu cortex.

Captain Vros Kinal grinned, sipping at his own drink and adjusting some of the documents in front of him before pushing a stack over to the previous queen of this newly conquered country. He slammed a finger into the top paper and gave the beautiful brunette a knowing look—then head-bobbed over to where he'd hanged her husband from a support beam down the way. "These are the public decrees you're going to make, and you're going to make them today. Don't give me any more attitude or you'll end up like your husband, and we'll move on to your children next. Do we have an understanding?"

The woman's head nodded and she smoothed out her dress, but she'd been crying so hard that she wasn't able to speak. Instead, she just took the papers and pulled them closer to her, beginning to read while trying to maintain a semblance of dignity.

"Good," Kinal said while leaning back in his chair. "Believe me, Your 'Majesty.' This is better for everyone involved—this way we don't have to slaughter your people to make an example of them . . . in due time, I'm sure you'll all come around to see the light."

Fourteen days later . . .

[Riven Thane's Status Page:

- **Level 130**
- **Pillar Orientations:** Unholy Foundation, Blood Specialty: Profane Cyclone (Tier 1 of the Path of Red and Black), Infernal, Shadow (subserviently linked to Blood Specialty pillar), Sin Core (Gluttony)
- **Core of Original Sin—Gluttony, five shards collected:** Allows access to sin pillar (Gluttony). Allows access to a secondary Sin Class. (Sin Class—Harbinger of Gluttony, currently under construction) Mark of the Sinner: Under Construction. Bonuses: ???
- **Traits:** <u>Race: Pure-blooded Vampire</u> (Extreme Darkness Regeneration) (Sunlight Decay) (Extreme weakness to silver weapons, Sun pillar, and Light pillar attacks), <u>Class: Warlock Devastator</u>, Devastator class trait (physical strikes are imbued with Unholy damage equal to 1% of damage being done at full mana capacity). Adrenaline Junkie (Blood) (+15% to Agility), <u>Accomplishment Title:</u> Bloodthirsty 1 (+5% increased blood mana from corpses, +1% dmg for blood magic)
- **Abilities:** Blessing of the Crow (Unholy), Wretched Snare (Unholy), Silvertongue (Unholy), Bloody Razors (Blood), Crimson Ice (Blood), Blood Lance (Blood) (Tier 2), Voodoo Doll (Blood) (Tier 2), Blood Nova (Blood) (Tier 3), Hell's Armor (Infernal), Blaze of Profane Glory (Infernal) (Tier 3), Riftwalk (Shadow), Gluttonous Sacrifice (Sin)
- **Stats:** 217 Strength, 427 Sturdiness, 1,063 Intelligence, 538 Agility, 10 Luck, -638 Charisma, 274 Vampiric Perception, 328 Willpower, 9 Faith
- **Free stat points:** 126
- **Minions:** Athela, Level 127 Archdemon (Unique, three forms, Cute Wittle Blood Weaver/Gluttonous Arshakai/Gluttonous Fae Drider) [190 Willpower Requirement]. Azmoth, Level 95 Hellscape Brutalisk (Infernal Crusader Initiate) [66 Willpower Requirement]. Fay, Level 48 Succubus [29 Willpower Requirement]. Luke Blissfallen, Level 17 High Elf Thrall (Stormrazor Battle Priest) (Warning: 29% soul decay detected) [10 Willpower Requirement]. One open demonic slot is available. Current number of offered contracts: 36,799,092
- **Equipped Items:** Jackal (1,390 dmg, 305% mana regen, 8% stamina regen, Shadow and Blood dmg +36% with 10% decreased ability cost, Black Lightning, Gluttony's Riptide, Jackal's Lunge), Messenger (1,858 def/965 bloodsilk def, Devour, Identifier's Clause, Blood in the Eyes, Ripping Claws, Launch,

+20% all stats, natural sunlight does not afflict debuffs, liquid breathing, senses enhanced 40%, passage through Gluttony's realms, sin and commandment identification), Plate Leggings (257 def), Witch's Ring of Grand Casting (+26 Intelligence), Negrada's Modified Bag of Holding]

His heavy plate armor glinted in the midday sun, his eyes unaffected from the bright light of early spring.

Riven sat on the southernmost mountain's peak, looking out over Dawn's distant capital city—Mandon. Smoke still billowed out even from here, and although the armies of Rippenvire had been thoroughly crushed, remnants of them still remained on the planet. Interrogations had led to the finding of their original base location, but the fortress they'd brought with them had . . . moved itself. Apparently.

"I am surprised you don't want to be there with your sister," Gaia said, the little dryad girl playing with flowers that wove and moved to dance on the ground in front of her. She glanced up at her partner in meditation, looked over the status screen he'd left up for well over an hour now, and sighed. "My child, it is unhealthy for you to seclude yourself like this."

Riven spared the smaller figure of Gaia a brief glance. It'd only been a couple days since she'd been able to exit her dungeon, but he was glad to have her present here. Despite isolating himself from Athela, Fay, and Allie after recent events for introspection and some soul-searching, he couldn't deny that her insight and wisdom were appreciated. "Allie is giving her speech today. For the fallen who died fighting to save the city. The people love her; they're obsessed with her. She is an ever-present figure who symbolizes change and improvement in their lives, with only a few exceptions—namely for the elvish slaves. As for me? I'm merely a figurehead, an unsaid threat. A weapon to be used in the background. People fear me for what I did in the city of canyons, and I can't say I blame them. My presence will not be missed, I have no desire to stay in the spotlight beyond what is necessary, and I needed to clear my head after . . ."

His words faltered, and his gaze slid to the ground—red eyes piercing the dirt through the visored slit in his feathered plate-armor helmet. The bloodsilk around his body rippled, and a comforting, soothing notion from both Messenger and Jackal in his lap oozed through him.

It was nice seeing that his two items were there for him, though he did find it odd that this was the case considering what they were at the core of their beings. Ever since the completion of each item, they'd been nothing but supportive both in battle and with mental fortitude. It was like having two quiet guardian angels keeping watch on either shoulder at all times, and ever since his acquisition of the other shards of Gluttony—that presence of theirs had increased drastically with the increase in their stats.

Speaking of stats . . .

He turned back to his status page. One hundred and twenty-six stat points to assign, and over thirty-six million demonic contracts to sort through. How was he supposed to dig through all of that on his own?

He wished Athela was here to help him decide.

But he still needed to process everything that had happened. When Fay had arrived back on Panu, the two women had screamed and shouted at one another until Fay left crying and even Athela remained a little shaken. Riven didn't know what the hell to do.

If he was being honest with himself, he cared a lot about both of them. But . . .

Fuck. He couldn't bring himself to say it.

Shouldn't he be consoling one or the other, or both of them, in their time of crisis?

Yet here he was, sitting atop a mountain, avoiding the entire situation. It was very apparent to him that should he take one wrong move, he might very well lose one or both of them.

He wished he could go back to the days where they were all just friends.

To him, it'd be worth it. Then he wouldn't have to be so terrified of seeing one of them leave.

- **Stats: 217 Strength, 427 Sturdiness, 1,063 Intelligence, 538 Agility, 10 Luck, -638 Charisma, 274 Vampiric Perception, 328 Willpower, 9 Faith**
- **Free stat points: 126**
- **Minions: Athela, Level 127 Archdemon (Unique, three forms, Cute Wittle Blood Weaver/Gluttonous Arshakai/Gluttonous Fae Drider) [190 Willpower Requirement]. Azmoth, Level 95 Hellscape Brutalisk (Infernal Crusader Initiate) [66 Willpower Requirement]. Fay, Level 48 Succubus [29 Willpower Requirement]. Luke Blissfallen, Level 17 High Elf Thrall (Stormrazor Battle Priest) (Warning: 29% soul decay detected) [10 Willpower Requirement]**

He sighed and did the math again. After Athela's massive evolution, her Willpower requirement had spiked to 190 points. Adding them all up, including Luke—who he hadn't seen in a while after leaving him back in the Brightsville manor, he had 295 of his Willpower stat points utilized in containing his minions. That left thirty-three available points for a new demonic contract.

That wouldn't be enough. Not if he had such a large number of demons to choose from, as he had no doubt the best and brightest of them would be far more of a tax on his Willpower than that.

So he pushed all 126 of his free stat points into Willpower, making it rise to 454 and giving him 159 Willpower points to work with concerning the new contract he was going to make.

"Hiding here will not make your problems go away," Gaia eventually said after she caught Riven staring off into space yet again. "You have yet to focus on your cultivation since experiencing insights during the last battle, you have made little to no progress concerning the two women you have feelings for, Athela has been waiting for you to use her Dao treasure as it requires a bonded partner, and you have yet to enter the cube you took from Daskus, the city of canyons. News from the Blood Moon Requiem's outpost here talks of slave rebellions on your inherited planet in another sector, probably a farce and a political play from enemies you don't even know you have yet—with details from that vampiric princess Kathrine otherwise being withheld until she speaks to you specifically. You need to acquire your new minion. After seeing your display on Mandon, the elvish kingdom of Tereen has surrendered, and they are wanting to become your vassals in exchange for an end to the war and the return of their people—with talks still on hold because you're sitting here in seclusion. The king of Dawn has continually tried to contact you for unknown reasons and you simply ignore him, which could have political ramifications. Allie also wants to teach you about the Death subpillar before the time comes to enter Chalgathi's next trial. If it was anyone else, I would tell them to take the time needed to clear their heads. But you are an important person, Riven, and you cannot afford to sit around and waste time if the goals you have are real. If you don't figure out your problems, you will bring that stress and anxiety with you into events that will affect the lives of billions. Please consider this, just as I asked Athela and Fay to consider it in your stead."

Riven raised an eyebrow, looking over at the dryad demigoddess while perched on their ledge. "You asked them what, exactly? What do you mean by that?"

Gaia gave him a warm smile. "I just gave them some insight as to what this internal strife they caused has done to you. They are waiting for you to speak to them, back at your manor in Brightsville. I think you should go; it has been long enough already, and pushing this confrontation back even further will only make things worse. It is time for the three of you to decide what happens next, for better or for worse, so that you can all move forward in your lives and allow for some much-needed healing."

There was both celebration and mourning in the city of Brightsville as Riven, like a zombie, slowly made his way through the crowds—dreading the confrontation to come. Upon seeing him, people prostrated themselves—calling him a hero aloud while keeping their distance and giving him fearful glances as he passed them by.

He ignored them. Not because he didn't care about their well-being, but because he knew they were more scared of him than anything else. He was a monster now. There was no point in making himself feel good about false praise.

Hundreds of feet above the huge markets now set up around the Elysium altar was the giant cube they'd taken from Daskus, shifting randomly like a Rubik's cube with blue runes etched into each square. People were lined up to try their hand at acquiring power from its trials—risking their lives to do so.

He got some shout-outs from various representatives of both the Blood Moon Requiem and Negrada when passing along the perimeter of the trading communes at the Elysium altar, but these too he blatantly ignored. Instead he continued his trudging death march toward the manor a few miles away on the southern edge of the city, beyond the farms where elf slaves tended the fields.

God, how he hated the fact that they kept slaves.

And if Tereen's proposal was right, if they were able to maintain a vassal state with the elves under their thumb, Riven was sure to get rid of those slaves as long as their people were reeducated to fit the bill. They needed peace, not more hate, and if that meant indoctrinating the elvish children, then so be it.

The rest of the trip seemed like a blur, and Riven eventually came to a stop in front of the manor, where a large group of people already awaited him. And some of the people here were certainly a surprise to see—including the king of Dawn in plate mail with some of his bodyguards, and Genua's wide-eyed daughter Len, who wore a familiar red dress and held her mother's hand tightly.

He didn't know if they'd all been told by Gaia, but that'd probably been what happened upon his descent from the mountains. The pure-blooded vampire heiress Kathrine; a line of uniformed maids—including Genua and her little girl; Fay's incubus brother, Tupper; Dr. Brass; Riven's thrall Luke Blissfallen; Gurth'Rok, the orc chieftain-turned-vampire; Allie; Mara; Vin and Nin, the skresh necromancers; Lahn; Lahn's entire family—including the two sibling brats Riven seriously disliked from the stories he'd heard; General Bruner; the new mayor of Chicago; and his minions were all there.

Azmoth stood with four folded arms in between Athela and Fay, both women staring fixated on his position and having various emotions crossing each of their faces. Nervousness, anxiety, fear, hope, love . . . they were all present.

But why was Allie here? Shouldn't she be giving that speech in Mandon? And the king of Dawn, too?

Riven's shoulders sagged when Gaia walked out of the back line, escorted by two of her greater dryad companions, and stopped at the very front with a calming aura filtering in the air around her. "Thank you for coming, Riven. I took it upon myself to get everyone here to help ease the transition of things needing to be done. Otherwise it may take many more weeks than we have to get situated. Now, first and foremost—you, Fay, and Athela are going to have a discussion about your future together. I am sorry if I am acting like an overbearing parent here, but I believe it is needed."

"The king and queen of Tereen have also surrendered and are being escorted here now by our troops. They should arrive by tonight," Allie chimed in from the side.

Riven couldn't give two shits whether or not the leaders of Tereen were coming, and the body language he had accompanied by the expression he wore even underneath his helmet was an obvious takeaway on exactly how he felt.

Silence reigned.

And it was Azmoth who eventually broke that silence. "I come with you. We all speak inside. Follow me and we fix this."

The large obsidian demon, akin to a hell-spawned paladin of legend, stepped forward, gesturing for the maids to create a path as the doors to the manor swung open. Kathrine looked like she was about to speak, too, but quickly shut up at a glare from Allie.

Athela and Fay both turned to follow Azmoth, but each of them glanced back to make sure Riven was coming, too, before entering the three-story stone manor.

Hesitating only for a few moments, Riven silently walked through the crowds of his friends, servants, and acquaintances until he was at the staircase leading up to his room on the third floor. Then, after he followed Azmoth and his other two demons into his private chambers, the four of them shut the door to have a private conversation about the things that'd happened over the past couple weeks.

CHAPTER 31

Athela sat on the bed, a downcast expression on her face, while she fiddled with the crown Riven had given her as a gift months ago.

Fay remained standing, nervously shifting her weight from foot to foot while occasionally giving him sideways glances.

Azmoth took it upon himself to direct Riven near the bathroom to a stool someone had brought into the room during his long absence. It'd been a while since he'd come home, and Azmoth closed the balcony windows after a few seconds of listening to helicopters passing by overhead.

The resounding silence was long and awkward. Riven would much rather be in a life-or-death situation than something like this, and he inwardly cringed at just what he'd have to do if these two forced his hand.

He didn't want to face the music. Not like this.

"Um . . . Riven?" Athela asked shakily, getting a vengeful glare from the succubus nearby. "I know this is hard . . . but can you talk to us, please? We need to know."

Fay cleared her throat, anxiously stepping side to side as he stared at his feet. She took in a deep breath and folded her arms to hug herself tightly. "I agree. I can't keep going on like this. The last two weeks have been a living nightmare for me. I keep thinking about . . . about you choosing her and . . ."

Fay's words trailed off, eyes settling on the ground.

Riven dismissed Messenger, the armor peeling itself off his body and floating to the side—only leaving a thin linen vest on as he took in a deep breath of his own. He looked up to meet each of their gazes one at a time, a sad smile on his lips. "I really wish you two hadn't done this to me."

"It's HER fault!" Fay began, pointing to Athela with venom in her words. "She should have taken what she wanted, not waited until I started dating you to decide she would act! This is so utterly—"

"You knew I was going to tell him," Athela cut in, voice soft but firm and eyes glued to Riven as the succubus glared her way. "You knew, Fay."

"AND YET YOU DID NOTHING ABOUT IT!" Fay shrieked, tears coming to her eyes as her voice quivered. "And now that he is mine, you've chosen to try and steal him from me! Can you not see how miserable you've made him?! Can you not see how happy we were?! And you came in to ruin it!"

Fay choked back a loud sob, and Athela finally met her eyes. Only this time it was Athela's turn to start crying. Her pitch-black lips quivered, and tears started forming under her red eyes while her fists clenched and her whole body began to shake.

Athela shook her head. "I couldn't live with myself if I didn't tell him how I felt. You waited until I was dead, not telling him—"

"I DID TELL HIM!" Fay screamed, motioning to where Riven sat watching the two of them in silence. "I told him that I thought you may like him and—"

"May?" Athela asked, becoming visibly angry when she aggressively got to her feet—only to be sat back down by Azmoth's hand planted on her shoulder. She glared up at the armored demon, brushed his clawed hand off, and snarled back at the succubus. "I thought you were my **friend**. You had an absolute knowledge that I planned to tell him how I felt—do not act like you didn't know. There was no maybe, no *may* about it. You knew. Yet you betrayed my friendship anyway to get him for yourself when I wasn't around. You stabbed me in the back, Fay."

Riven cleared his throat, getting the attention of all of them while three heads swiveled to meet his face. He took in a deep breath, gave a defeated, half-hearted laugh, and rubbed his fingers along the sides of his temple. "I believe this is partially my fault."

No one said a word, waiting for him to continue.

Riven met their eyes again, a lump forming in his throat while he thought about just what was going to happen when and if he was forced to break the news. "It may be entirely my fault. I . . . I didn't know you felt the way you did, Athela. Fay tried to tell me, and though she didn't outright say she knew—she did hint at it. We can at least give her credit for that."

Fay seemed to calm somewhat at his words, while Athela's face creased in worry.

He continued, "I don't know what was said between the two of you before Daskus, when Athela died and Fay was kidnapped, but Fay did tell me it may be possible you felt that way. I just didn't believe it, because . . . I don't know why. I just didn't realize it was the truth. I'd always looked at you as my best friend, rather than as a potential romantic partner."

Athela's face scrunched up with emotion, and she tried to reply—but all that came out was a choked, muffled sound while her hands clenched tightly around one another, tears streaming down her face again.

Riven paused, gritting his teeth. "Honestly, if it were up to me . . . we'd all go back in time to the way things were. Before all of this happened and the conflict between the two of you started, before either of you admitted your feelings for me. That way I wouldn't have to choose. Let me ask you both . . . What happens if I choose the other?"

The silence was palpable once again, and this time it lasted for a full minute before Fay spoke up.

"I've asked my mother to forcibly cut my contract with an artifact if you choose her over me," Fay stated softly, a sad smile playing across her lips. "It isn't that I want to punish you if you do choose her, it's that I couldn't stay if you did. I'm falling for you, just as Athela has. I intimately understand how she feels about you because I feel the same way. I wouldn't mind if . . . if you even slept with other girls. But not her. She's a threat to my bond with you, because I want to be the one that is most important to you. Physically, we succubi and incubi are very involved and the drive is high—sex is only sex, but emotionally . . . I want that emotional connection. If you choose her over me, it means your heart is with her rather than me. I know you love her, I've heard you say it, but I believe it isn't a romantic love. Is it? I'm hoping not, because I want to be the only romantic love you have."

"You'd really just leave? Just like that?" Riven asked in a whisper.

Fay nodded. "Yes."

Riven's eyes stared up at her for a moment, then he turned to Athela. "And what about you? What happens to you if I choose to continue dating Fay?"

Athela slowly opened her mouth to reply, hesitated, choked back a weak sob, and cleared her throat while blinking rapidly. "I . . . I'm not sure."

She paused, mulling over her tumultuous thoughts. "Riven . . . do you really love me like you said you did back in Daskus? After I was killed, when you slaughtered all those people to bring me back?"

Riven's eyes softened. "Of course I do."

"But it wasn't a romantic love then? As Fay implies?"

He hesitated, then slowly shook his head. "No, it hadn't been."

Athela's lips quivered. "And . . . and do you think there'd be any chance of that changing?"

Riven did not reply.

She took in deep breaths, trying to calm herself while tightly closing her eyes. "Perhaps this was foolish of me after all."

She let the words hang in the air, and her shoulders sagged—hands coming up to hide her face while she rested her elbows on her knees in a hunched position. "Honestly I . . . I don't think I know. I would try to stay if you choose her, I really would, I just . . . My feelings toward you have changed since we first met. I can't help it . . . I just am so infatuated with you. I get butterflies just being around you, and I've worked so, so hard to try and build up the courage to talk to you about it . . ."

Athela bit her lip to stifle another sob, voice quivering, letting out a feminine whimper as blood trickled down her chin from where her teeth dug into flesh. "I just . . . I worked so, so hard . . . to get the courage. And when I finally had it, I was betrayed by someone I thought a friend. It's hard . . . hard to wrap my mind around. That I am losing not only a friend, but the man I love. Losing him to that person I previously thought a friend. It hurts a lot more than I thought it would. It . . . it feels like my heart is going to rip out of my chest. I don't know how to handle this . . ."

"Athela . . ." Riven began, but she held up a hand to stop him, sniffling, as she straightened her posture and blinked away more tears.

"No, I have more to say." She sniffled, wiping her face with the backs of her hands and forcing a smile as wide as she could. "No matter what happens, I want you to choose whoever is best for you. But I hope that it's me. I want to be the one that you marry one day. I know it may seem silly, coming from a demon, but the idea makes me giddy. It also makes me physically sick thinking you'd want to be with someone other than me. Ever since we first bonded, back in Chalgathi's trials, I knew that I'd likely come into a humanoid form. I have many aunts and uncles with humanoid forms; it is just part of the evolutionary process . . . and the day you saved me from being eaten in Negrada was the first day that I really considered it. But over time that feeling grew, and it grew fast. I remember the day we went clothes shopping in Brightsville after we trudged through that sewer, covered in gore and sludge after the fight with the worms . . . I remember how bad we both smelled."

She gave a little laugh. "I remember how you told me that the dress I'd picked out would look good on me, and how you hugged me . . . and how it felt to have your arms around me. I remember being so jealous of that elf, Ethel, and how I thought I'd never measure up to someone as pretty as that. Humans have a thing for elves, after all, and I didn't have blonde hair, I was naturally violent, and my demonic side was perhaps too ugly for you—but I wanted to believe you'd one day see me as a woman rather than as a pet."

Athela turned her eyes on Fay, becoming stiff when the succubus's glare made contact with her own. "And I was so intimidated when we ended up choosing Fay as the third minion, you wouldn't even believe it. Fay is so pretty, unnaturally so, just like all of her race. It's what her kind is good at, wooing mortals, but I told you to choose her anyways because she was the right fit for you. It was better than that overgrown eyeball of a demon who tried to trick you into signing a bad contract, and I don't regret that decision even now. Because Fay and I became friends. Or at least I thought we had. But now . . ."

Athela's words trailed off, and a look of guilt overcame Fay when the succubus winced.

"I guess I'd probably leave, too," Athela eventually said with a mournful expression, downcast gaze hitting the floor. "I'd try to stay, I really would. I want you to be happy. But it might be too painful to watch you continue on this path with her when I want it to be me instead. The dates you had, the dinner you took her to, the way you held hands and the love you made with her . . . I wanted that. I still want that. I want to be the one woman you love forever, and if not . . . then perhaps it is time for me to finally move on. Maybe I'd enter the wars in hell as an independent mercenary and cut all ties, or maybe I'd just stay in the nether realms until I calm down enough to come back. I just don't know, and I don't think I will know until the time comes."

Athela avoided his gaze after that, sullen and downcast on the bed with her hands clasped in front of her.

"Don't abandon me . . ." Fay whispered under her breath, eyes wide as she stepped closer to Riven with a hand hesitantly stretching out. "Please . . . These have been the happiest months of my life. You showed me that I don't have to be a sex object like my sisters, aunts, and mother all were. You treated me like a real person; you are so different from the last summoner I had . . . and I have found true happiness. Don't take that away from me."

Athela couldn't even manage to glare at the succubus again, instead just choking up.

Riven took a shaky breath, then slowly stood up. He took Fay's hand in his own, wrapping his fingers around hers, and gave Athela a sad look as the arachnid demoness returned a teary-eyed glance. "Athela, I really wish you would have told me sooner."

Their eyes locked, Athela's expression pleading as she silently mouthed the words *I love you* as she violently wrung her hands together.

"Please leave the room, Athela."

Athela's eyes went wide, and she broke out into a loud sob before she rushed out—slamming the door behind her with a loud bang.

Sighing and heart clenching, Riven turned to Fay, who looked up at him with an emotional smile, hand still wrapped around his own as she began to press up against him, arms wrapping around his chest with a shaky sigh of relief.

Until he stopped her short.

She gave him a confused glance but was brought down to a sitting position on the bed as he joined her to face her head-on—tears coming to his own eyes while he gathered the courage to do what needed to be done.

Deep breaths.

"Fay . . . the time we spent together was special. It still is special. You are special to me," Riven said softly, feeling her pull away as her expression began to change. He stayed strong, having prepared himself over the past two weeks for this, and outwardly shuddered. "You mean a lot to me. Honestly, this fucking sucks. This entire situation sucks. I wish it'd never happened."

"Don't abandon me . . ." Fay whispered again, beginning to break down with choking sobs as her eyes squinted and she withdrew from him on the bed.

Riven's gaze hit the floor, a lump forming in his throat. "You two are forcing me to choose. It isn't fair, and I don't want to do it. Is there any way that the three of us could work this out? You and I are dating now, but . . . maybe we could make it work with the three of us. You said you're okay with me sleeping with other women—why make me choose between you and her? I've told you that I always wanted the one, a soul mate to grow old with, but this is cruel. What the two of you are doing to me is cruel. I'd rather not lose either of you, and despite what I want, I'd rather try it with both of you first."

Fay stared at him for a time, mixed emotions crossing her features, but she shook her head to reply with a whisper. "No. Neither I nor Athela want that. We both want to be the one your heart is bound to; the physical stuff isn't much of an issue—but not with her. Not with an emotional threat like that. You could end up loving her more than me. I couldn't and wouldn't do it. You don't even want that, either—you said it yourself many times now, and you just said it again; you want a soul mate just like we do. You need to choose."

Riven's expression fell, and he took in a shuddering breath. His shoulders sagged. "All right, then. If that's how it is, then I have to choose Athela. I'm sorry, Fay, I really am."

It was as if he'd slapped her across the face. She remained sitting there, stunned, before letting out a final muffled sob. Shaking violently and stumbling to her feet, she nearly fell over. She then began taking off the feathered boots he'd given her—setting them down clumsily on the floor while streams of water poured down her cheeks and her lips trembled. She then let out a whisper. "Please let Tupper stay. I hope Athela makes you happy . . . Mother, take me home."

In a flash of light, Fay was gone, leaving Riven speechless on the edge of the bed. When he saw the notification appear before his very eyes, he began to sob silently, his shoulders heaving up and down while he clutched his face in his hands to try and keep the tears back.

[Fay's contract has been forcibly broken. A demonic contract slot has opened up. Two of four demonic contract slots are now available.]

CHAPTER 32

Tupper gulped, nervousness overcoming him while he traversed the halls of his clan's compound. He was already getting glares from numerous members of his family, but as long as he found Fay before his father found HIM, then he'd be fine.

Hopefully.

Cringing at the memory of how that last encounter with his father had gone, he mentally brushed it aside with supreme will and headed toward his mother's chambers. Fay wasn't in her room, and he needed to make sure she wasn't making a huge mistake.

Passing by another succubus-incubus couple sitting on a couch and turning left down the pristine hall of this shared nether realm pocket dimension, Tupper came up to the ornate doors that signified the clan mother. Taking in a deep breath and looking around to make sure no one else was there, he knocked.

"Come in, Tupper, we've been waiting for you."

Tupper's face paled. *We?*

Hopefully that wasn't who he thought she meant.

Gathering his courage and entering the room, he let out an audible sigh of relief when he saw his sister Nitidi and Saemi, his mother. His father was nowhere to be seen. But he still noted the look of distaste Saemi gave him before she gestured for him to sit on one of the nearby beds.

He took a seat, the usual suit he wore back on Panu gone in favor of a more free-flowing robe with a large slit down the middle to reveal his chest—a chosen garment many of their kind wore. His black eyes met his mother's, and he shuddered. "Hello, Saemi. I was hoping you'd know where Fay went."

His sister Nitidi frowned, exchanging a look with the older succubus before Saemi leaned forward with hands clasped together. "We know exactly where she went. Why would you want to know?"

Tupper blinked, then firmed his will. "I believe she is making a mistake by leaving. I am . . . just confused. Confused as to why it was said she used an artifact to leave, for one. I know there's no chance any of you would ever use an artifact to cut her contract like that unless she was in mortal peril. Is there an explanation for why she would say that to Riven?"

Saemi raised an eyebrow. "Is that all?"

"No, it isn't, but it is the first of a few questions."

"I believe you just want her there because you'd miss her rather than it being the right choice."

Tupper's mood immediately darkened. "Of course I'd miss her, but—"

Saemi cut off his words with a raised hand, leaning back against a stack of pillows with a snort. She turned to her left, picking up some fruit and beginning to chew softly before swallowing—then glanced back at her son. "I did not use an artifact."

"Then how did she break the contract, and why would she lie?"

This time, it was Nitidi who chimed in. "It's because her contract stated that in order for her to stay, Riven could not harm her. Why she lied about it? We don't know."

Tupper's eyes widened, and a look of shock overcame him. "He was hurting her?"

"Not physically. But emotionally, yes. It was enough for the system to consider it torture—mental anguish can bring even more pain than physical. So it allowed her to break the contract on the spot."

"But that's utterly ridiculous!" Tupper exclaimed, standing up with hands outstretched. "This makes no sense! She's acting out of emotion only and not thinking logically! Riven still cares for her, I know he does. There was still a chance for her to make things work if she'd just stay, instead of forcing him into choosing between her and ATHELA, who Riven has been with since the beginning of the integration! He even said he cared for Athela in a nonromantic way, and for all Fay knows it may be like asking him to choose between his love interest and a family member! Fay has known him for half the time she has, and the Blood Moon Requiem is going to use him as a prized stallion to breed anyways—whether he likes it or not. She does realize this, right? WHY force him to choose?! He told me on his way out of the manor that he even asked her to try and work out a relationship with both of them should Athela agree!"

Nitidi rolled her eyes but nodded in agreement. "We already told her this almost verbatim before she took such rash action. Neither of us is pleased, either, Tupper."

"Well, then, let me try to talk some sense into her, if you two couldn't!"

Again, Nitidi shared a look with her mother. "Unfortunately, she isn't here."

"What do you **mean**, she isn't here? Where else would she be, since she's not on Panu?" Tupper asked, brows furrowing in worry. "You don't mean . . ."

"In her grief, she impulsively took the first demonic contract that became available to her. She has a new master now. She's in the Drig sector on a middling planet," Saemi replied, irritatedly throwing the last piece of fruit across the room with a loud huff. "Fay is now bound to some crime lord, a cruel nobody with a sick obsession for abuse. I'm not sure if she did it out of self-hate, as a form of self-punishment, or she simply was just stupid enough not to modify the base contract in her grief. And I'd had such high hopes for that daughter, too."

The other leaders, gathered from Dawn, Chicago, Brightsville, the kingdom of Tereen, and very recently even Deepnest—they'd have to wait. For now they'd been instructed to do what they could without him, and he'd meet with them tomorrow after he cleared his head.

He already missed Fay. It was like he'd lost a family member. How things had spiraled out of control like this was beyond him, but honestly there wasn't much he could have done without knowledge of the things happening behind the curtains. And now that he'd been forced to be honest with himself, now that he'd been forced to choose—he was certain in his decision that Athela was one of only two people he cared for more than Fay.

That still didn't make it any better.

He'd hoped to talk them into something less traditional as a way out of this, particularly when he and Fay had talked in his room before she'd abruptly gotten up and left, but he understood why neither of them wanted it. He couldn't blame them for that, either—he hadn't wanted something like that, either, until only very recently—and only because of the consequences if he chose otherwise.

Riven stepped down off the ledge, dropping onto a flat expanse of mountainside. To his right, the ruined gas station they'd teleported to out of Negrada was in even worse shape than it'd been in months ago. The view was also a lot different, due to the landscape being terraformed into an Unholy version of its old self. Various kinds of wild undead, as well as other creatures of the night, stalked in the shadows—but due to his aura, even they were very aware of just how dangerous it'd be to approach him. So he'd been left alone, absolutely unhindered.

Continuing to walk forward and wiping away the moisture from his eyes, he stopped behind the woman he'd come to love. She was curled up with her head resting on her knees and silently crying—her pitch-black skin only barely reflecting any of the starlight that sometimes penetrated the fog of these haunted woods.

"Out of all places, you chose to come here?" Riven said softly, startling her when he sat down next to her.

She looked up at him, shocked, and blinked her red eyes rapidly while wiping them and sniffling. "Riven, I'd like to be alone for a while. Please."

"Why's that?"

She shot him a glare that could kill, not even bothering to answer.

He stared back with a soft expression, trying to keep down his burning emotions before reaching out and putting a hand on one of her knees. "Are you okay?"

"OF COURSE I'M NOT OKAY!" Athela screamed, tears bursting out again before she slapped him hard across the face, shuddering and getting to her feet in a huff. She opened her mouth to scream at him again but abruptly calmed herself and took in a deep breath while closing her eyes—retracting the claws that she'd instinctively extended before straightening. "I . . . accept . . . your decision. I just need time to think about it before I decide what I want to do. Please, respect me enough for that and give me some space. Please, Riven."

Riven touched the bruised spots on his face where blood trickled down one cheek before his vampiric regeneration quickly sealed the cut. He looked up at her, sighing and standing up before putting both hands on her shoulders while her lips trembled and snot began to leak out of one nostril.

He wiped her face with his sleeve, and she didn't bother stopping him. "Your version of ugly crying is something else. Athela, Fay left—she cut the contract and disappeared. I didn't tell you to leave the room because I'd chosen her."

His voice cracked upon his admission, and Athela's eyes widened yet again as she took in a shuddering breath. "Athela . . . I just needed some space to let her know that I chose you."

Hurt was obvious in his expression, and he bit his lip to try and keep from crying again. "Honestly, I'm angry with both of you for forcing me to do this. I'm not going to lie, Athela, I liked her. A lot. Telling her was one of the hardest things I've ever done. But if there's anyone on this planet other than my sister who I care for even more than her, it's you. I'm not willing to lose you, Athela, and if you want to try this out . . . If you really want to date and maybe one day marry me, then after everything we've been through together—I owe it to you to try."

Athela's body remained stiff in a state of shock. "You chose me over her?"

He nodded once, trying to maintain a quivering smile but failing. When she noticed with a frown of her own, he gave an apologetic shrug. "Sorry. It's just . . . it was hard. Not that it was even a choice. I love you, Athela. I'll just miss her. I hope you can understand and give me a bit to come to terms with it."

She slowly nodded, biting her lip with mixed emotions and continuing to stare at him, unblinking. Then, suddenly, she threw her arms around him and started wailing with pent-up tears exploding from her face while she shook and hiccup-sobbed.

"Riven, I . . . I love you so, so much . . . I won't forget this for as long as I live. I promise you, you didn't make the wrong choice . . . I'll show you, I promise!"

Riven held her close, kissing her forehead and rubbing her back to calm her down while a feeling of warmth overcame him. In this moment, seeing his partner in crime like this, it made his soul settle down despite all the emotional trauma they'd all recently undergone. "I love you, too, Athela. I love you, too."

The next morning, Riven, with Athela buried under one arm with her head lying on his rising chest, woke up to a knock at the door. It was brighter out today, and sunlight managed to shine through an open window.

Dr. Brass had been right all those months ago. Athela had always worn an exoskeleton over the top of her body, a very thin and formfitting one—but Riven could certainly tell the difference now that she was naked and pressed up against him. Watching her shed the thing like a tight suit had been a very interesting sight to behold—before she'd aggressively pounced on him in an emotional lovemaking he'd never forget.

She twitched in her sleep, groaning and pulling him in tighter before mumbling something inaudible. A silly smile was plastered on her face, and she gave off a soft giggle before drifting back off into dreams.

The knock repeated itself, and Riven responded with a call for whoever it was to come in—after he'd drawn up the covers to make sure Athela's backside wasn't exposed.

The door opened with a click, and Genua walked in with two other elf maids and her daughter in tow. They each carried a variety of platters with refreshments for breakfast, along with a goblet of blood. They were all silent and left quickly, with the exception of Genua, who curtsied and kept her eyes lowered.

"Allie said we needed to wake you. I hope you're not angry with us for obeying orders, but here's your breakfast. She says you need to eat and come downstairs, because the other leaders are waiting and it's nearly noon."

Riven chuckled at her words, but nodded—only stopping her when his vampiric senses picked up on the strange but familiar smell coming off the woman. "Wait. Genua, why do I sense vampirism on your person?"

Genua stalled, then her eyebrows raised. "Oh. That is your sister's doing. While you were gone for those many months, I told her that I'd accept your offer to become a thrall. I'm not one yet, but I'm mostly finished with the transition. I've been drinking the blood of your sister, and sometimes Gurth'Rok, in order to complete the transition. I believe it was their plan to let you do the completion at the end, though, in order to bind me to you. I was told your other thrall, that old man Luke, does not supply enough blood and that I would likely be needed. Does that satisfy you?"

Riven thought about it, rubbing Athela's bare back as she groaned again beside him and adjusted her position. "Yeah. It does."

Genua nodded with a bland smile. "I must say, the transition is going well. I feel . . . happier. I'm told it'll only get better when it completes."

"Because you get to see your daughter now?"

"Yes. But also I believe the vampiric effects of becoming a thrall are shifting my mental state. It was needed; I was in a severe depression after my family's betrayal—and after you killed Ethel and my husband. Now, though, I can honestly say it stings a lot less. If I am to be in this position, I'd rather do it as happily as I can—at the very least for the sake of Len. Is that all, Master?"

Riven's gaze drifted to the ceiling. The way she phrased it made him feel . . . evil. Villainous. The previous raw emotions he'd had toward Genua and her family were fading away now that many months had passed, and he didn't really know how to feel about their attempt to murder him anymore. Not after what she'd just said.

"I'm glad you're feeling better about it," Riven finally said. "I'm glad you and Len are back together."

Genua nodded and curtsied again. "Very well. If you are ever in need of my blood, or my body again, please feel free to let me know. The last time we had intercourse was quite enjoyable, likely due to the drugs and my mind changing—but nevertheless, I'd like to repeat it sometime. Perhaps Athela would like it, too. I believe I find her more attractive than I do you, actually. As for the cage . . ."

Genua looked over to the cage that Tupper had been keeping her in, positioned in the corner of the room. "Tupper told me to stay out of this room last night, and if it is okay with you, I'd like to continue rooming with my daughter across the hall."

Riven blinked. His heart clenched when he remembered the first night he and Fay had engaged in promiscuous activities, and he had to forcibly push those thoughts away while nodding. "Yes, that's fine. The cage was a bit overboard anyways. You can stay across the hall with your daughter—and if Len ever needs anything, let me know. Just be sure she continues attending those reeducation classes."

Genua gave him a warm smile, brushing her locks of blonde hair behind her pointed ears. "Thank you, Master, I will do so. I'll be leaving now unless you need anything else."

"Nope. That's all. Tell the others I'll be down there within the hour."

"I shall do so. Have a good breakfast, Riven."

The eastern wing of the manor was filled with people. Elf servants and slaves rushed around in maid uniforms under the direction of Tupper—who looked rather downtrodden after the news Riven had given him yesterday. There were various guards posted along the halls and all around the compound outside from the Thane Necropolis—a mix of different species but mostly undead, humans from Dawn, rat-kin from Deepnest, and even some of Gaia's dryads.

Inside the eastern wing, the indoor pool wasn't in use—but the kitchen and dining areas up on the elevated platform beyond the pool were quite busy, with people seated around a very large circular redwood table that'd replaced the previous rectangular ones.

Kathrine, the vampiric princess, sat next to her counterpart Allie. Beside them in turn were Mara, Lahn, Vin and Nin, Shovi, and the rest of Lahn's family, who all looked rather pale. King Arthur Brix, his spymaster, Kassius, and Lord Nikola Lucio were all in deep discussion about something or another. Dr. Brass and Gurth'Rok were there, having become prominent figureheads in the running of the necropolis during Allie's absence. General Bruner sat beside them along with the new mayor of Chicago, who Riven still didn't know. Snagger and Mesha, the rat-kin, were there, along with Rashtalia, the broodmother of Brood Tarrow in Deepnest, representing the rat-kin queen. Gaia and a couple of her greater dryads were also present, and beside them were two nervous blonde elves in very fancy but scant clothes that showed off their bodies with blue paint decorating their faces and arms. No doubt these were the king and queen of Tereen, the elvish country that'd just surrendered, who had come to negotiate on behalf of their people.

There were two chairs still vacant, no doubt for Athela and Riven, with Azmoth standing beside the open spots to gesture them in. "You two are late."

The room went silent when Azmoth's proclamation was heard, and all eyes turned to Riven—who stared at the group before being gently tugged along by Athela. She held his hand, leading him forward, and sat down beside him with a gushing smile toward Allie when Riven's sister gave her a wink.

"Now that my lazy brother has finally decided to make an appearance . . ." Allie said loudly, getting a laugh from the table—some of them nervous and others genuine, "I believe it's finally time to get to the heart of the issues we couldn't discuss last night. First and foremost, let's bring up the topic of integrating Dawn and Tereen as vassal states into the necropolis. Do you have any objections to this, Riven?"

Riven blinked, then he shot a look over to King Arthur Brix. "I'd been expecting Tereen to fold, but why Dawn? You want to become our vassal?"

The rest of the room became silent as the king stroked his short, well-cut beard, and he let out an audible sigh before putting his clasped hands on the table. "It became very apparent to me when Rippenvire invaded that we are not up to competing with the aggressors from beyond. Our own fleet is decimated after the attack; over half of our forces are dead. It will take decades to regain what we lost, to repair our city, and to get our fighting forces back in shape to what they once were. Without the intervention of the necropolis, I know without a single doubt that it would have been an absolute slaughter. Not only do I want our country to become a vassal to yours because of the military protection it would provide, but also out of thanks for what you did for my people. This world is changing, fast, and we wish to be under the umbrella of a greater power for these trying times."

Riven considered the man's words, slowly nodding. "Then it is agreed."

Allie beamed victoriously, then stood to gesture to the elves sitting on Riven's right. "That was fast; I like it. Moving on, this is King Glassleaf of Tereen and his wife, Queen Glassleaf of Tereen. They said they would only negotiate when you were present, and I believe they have a proposal to make concerning the terms of their surrender."

Riven's red eyes shifted over, a simple stare as King Glassleaf pushed a nervous, shaking hand through his long blonde hair. His wife grasped his hand firmly before he stood up, a green and blue robe of minimal proportions, similar to many elvish garments, showing off a lot of his body. His green eyes settled on Riven, then traveled back to Allie, before he cleared his throat.

"I am King Glassleaf, leader of Tereen, and I have come to negotiate on behalf of my people. I would like to repeat the same words I spoke yesterday, that if either I or my queen fail to return from negotiations, our country will continue to fight under the orders of our generals until the last man—and that we have come in good faith that we will be treated fairly. Our offer is that we become the vassal of your Thane Necropolis in exchange for the end of this war and the return of our people that you have enslaved. What particulars you wish in return for this end are on the table, are negotiable, and I am hoping we can come to an agreement before my wife and I leave this meeting."

CHAPTER 33

Riven tapped his fingers against the wood, acknowledging the elvish king with a nod before gesturing for the man to sit. "Please relax—you look rather stiff."

The older man did as Riven asked, and the two men stared at each other in silence until King Glassleaf lowered his eyes to the table.

"Let me ask you a question," Riven started, picking up a piece of cheese that Allie unceremoniously slid across the table—eliciting a loud squeak from the friction. Chewing and swallowing, Riven lifted a finger. "Tell me, what exactly makes you think that we are afraid of your people continuing to fight?"

There was a long, drawn-out silence after that, and the elvish king merely blinked Riven's way while becoming paler by the second.

Thus Riven continued. "You make it seem like, should I not allow you and your wife to leave here, your people fighting until the last man would be something of a problem for us. Let me be very up front by saying that I could, by myself, go and crush the remnants of your country without much fuss. We all know this; don't pretend otherwise. The fact that I have not already done so is twofold. One, conflict itself breeds warriors that we'll need in the trials to come. I couldn't force you to surrender but while you didn't, some of my own soldiers were gaining levels at the expense of lives. Two, I don't slaughter people mindlessly—despite what the world seems to think of me after I tore apart Daskus. That was . . . a special case."

Riven glanced over at Athela and touched her hand, and he could have sworn that she blushed while averting her eyes—getting him to grin. Though concerning the color of her pitch-black skin . . . it was hard to tell. "I am not saying this to intimidate you, Mr. Glassleaf. I am merely making it very clear that this war is over whether you like it or not, and meeting you and your wife is merely a formality to make the transition go more smoothly. Allie and I had considered just killing both of you when you arrived, but doing so would likely make the populace of your old kingdom inherently rebellious and would leave us with the choices of either mass enslavement, like we've already done, or a slaughter to use their bodies to create more undead. The latter is what Allie wants to do, I can tell you now."

"It would be a lot easier." Allie nodded in affirmation, getting a choking sound out of the elvish queen, but Riven held up a hand to stop them from replying.

"I've already told her I'm not going to allow that. Allie may run things here in the Thane Necropolis, but there are things I put my foot down for, and as I said earlier, I will not just wantonly slaughter your people without good reason. This would mean, however, that your people would need to be introduced to reeducation classes—specifically the children, who will be separated from the adults and set up in camps for a good amount of time, and there would be an almost absolute reduction in any military capabilities your people could have while being a vassal of our state. This would mean laying down all arms and handing them over to us as we appoint city guards from the necropolis. Instead, your people will be pushed into things like farming and agriculture, construction to rebuild your country—which is now OUR country—and other various crafting trades, at least for the time being, and people will be able to apply for exceptions. I agree with your proposal to release elvish prisoners, and your people would be allowed to pursue fulfilling lives. However, anyone that has already proven themselves an enemy to our cause will be sentenced to continued slavery as long as their crime is not punishable by death. We will establish the equivalent of a martial law in your country for the first three months in order to make sure you aren't trying to attempt anything sneaky, and depending on how that goes, we will discuss potentially withdrawing our troops. We will need all the slaves you took from Dawn's borders to be given back to them as well. Lastly, you will be my direct subordinates should anything of significant concern arise. You will report to myself or Mara, not Allie, as I know there is a lot of bad blood concerning the slaughters she orchestrated on your people and I want this to go as smoothly as possible. I have very little wiggle room to negotiate on these topics, but if there are any disagreements, let me know now so that we can start moving forward."

The elf queen hesitated, then cleared her throat to speak. "My only concern is the children being separated from their parents. This is concerning, on many levels, and I'm not sure our people would abide by this. It would result in mass panic."

Riven shifted his gaze to Mara in the background. "How is it coming along in the reeducation camps we have now? Are you having any problems?"

Mara shook her head. "No, sire. But that situation was far different than this one. The elves we have already taken were taken by force; integrating the remaining cities and village communities that Tereen commands would be far harder unless we actually put them all in chains."

"Do you feel confident you'd be able to handle it your own way, then?"

Mara nodded. "As long as I have the backing I need."

"Then do it." Riven turned to the two leaders of Tereen with a blank expression. "Anything else?"

Queen and King Glassleaf hesitated yet again, muttered to one another briefly, then King Glassleaf shook his head. "Other than the specifics of each of those topics you mentioned . . . it seems fair. When can we expect the return of our people?"

"One month at most. We'll need to fill the spots that they were keeping as slaves on our farms or in our mines. Those who have committed crimes will be branded along the tops of their hands to show their status as kept slaves of the crown."

King Glassleaf nodded again, resting back in his chair with an expression of mixed anxiety and relief. "Very well. I would also like to propose that perhaps we could seal this pact by blood—perhaps this would strengthen our relationship over time."

Riven raised an eyebrow. "By blood?"

"Yes," King Glassleaf said with another anxious nod. "I have a daughter, Princess Shay Glassleaf, who is about your age and would make a fine wife or concubine—"

Riven held up a hand to cut him off. "I refuse. Allie, please move on."

Disgruntled, the elvish king sat back in his chair as his wife gave his hand a comforting squeeze, and Allie chuckled while pushing the next topic forward. "Next we have to decide what to do with the vampiric prisoners of war."

Riven frowned. "We have prisoners of war?"

This time, it was King Arthur Brix who spoke up—and he stood to bow Riven's way before straightening his posture and putting his hands behind his back. "Hello again, Riven. I believe I can answer this in more detail than anyone else. Most of the prisoners of war were taken during Rippenvire's invasion of Mandon. They started surrendering near the end of the battle. We have a little over seven thousand of them."

General Bruner raised a hand and grunted his acknowledgment. "Along with another two thousand or so prisoners under our command."

Riven met Allie's gaze. "Can you explain to me why they're still alive?"

Allie returned a mischievous grin. "How'd you know it was my doing?"

He only gave her a flat look back.

She snorted, crossing her arms and leaning back in her chair. "They'd make good foot soldiers if they were absorbed into our forces. Think about it. Why not?"

"Why not?" Riven repeated, shaking his head and letting out an exasperated sigh. "Because there are thousands of them and they all require blood to feed on, because they still haven't left the planet as a faction yet, and neither because their base nor their beacon were ever found. Keeping them around is asking for a prison break after they showed they can portal in like that."

Allie held up both hands to either side with a shrug. "That's why I wanted your opinion on the matter. Many of them are offering allegiance to us after figuring out who we are."

There was a long pause.

Riven glanced back over to King Arthur Brix, who wore a grim expression and remained standing but said nothing. "How many of your citizens died that day? How many of your troops?"

He looked to General Bruner next. "How many of our own died that day?"

"An estimated sixty-four hundred of our own troops died taking back Mandon, my king," General Bruner replied flatly.

King Arthur Brix kept his gaze fixated on Riven, but he slowly shook his head as his jaw clenched. "I don't even know the number yet. We haven't had the opportunity to count, but the number could be hundreds of thousands."

Riven nodded, motioning for him to sit. The king did so, and Riven looked over Allie's way. "Screen them for anyone really useful. Execute the rest."

"My prince . . ." Kathrine Vonsilla Crushada the Ninth, eldest daughter to the duke and duchess of House of Crushada, 107th in line for the vampiric throne and outer sect princess of the Blood Moon Requiem, stood up. She smoothed out her black dress with red flowers and curtsied respectfully. "Perhaps it would be wise to keep our brethren alive as a sign of good faith to our neighbors. Rippenvire is an underling state, subordinate to one of our friendly competitors concerning vampiric power in the multiverse. Not butchering their promising young ones would be . . . appreciated."

Riven glanced her way with a frown, then pulled up the world quest concerning the invading forces just to confirm his thoughts.

[World Quest 3 Update, Invaders From Beyond: Other factions of the multiverse have been watching your small planet greedily, wanting its resources for themselves. Be it mass slavery, genocide, forced societal integration, or being farmed as literal food, your planet's people are in danger. Invasion tokens have been distributed, and the invasion portals have finally been opened.

Invading forces have until the end of the five integration years to either conquer Panu entirely or alternatively survive that long in order to acquire reinforcements from the homeland. Any invading force left at the end of five years will have free access through system portals until a victor is decided. To rid this planet of an invading force, you must destroy their beacon—which will be highlighted by a marker in the sky above its location with the symbol of their empire. Invading Forces:
- **The Empire of Dying Suns**
- **Pagaroth**
- **The Kingdom of Shatterstone**
- **The Black Sky Azag Hive Cluster**
- **Rippenvire**

Prepare yourselves, natives of Panu. The enemy is coming.]

He nodded. "All right. Then have them withdraw from the planet, and I will do so. Destroying their beacon should evict them, yes?"

Kathrine hesitated, then shook her head. "Not necessarily . . . The invasion tokens are a one-way ticket. The only way to get back home would be to either win the quest early or wait until the five years pass after keeping their beacon intact. Otherwise they stay on the planet, even if the beacon is destroyed."

"So you're saying we should keep them alive for five years to appease these . . . pseudo-allies of yours?"

"Of *ours*," Kathrine corrected with a frown. "And they aren't necessarily allies . . . they're more like acquaintances, but they're still our kin."

"Well, letting them keep the beacon intact is out of the question; there will be no portals between this world and their own. And how much blood does an army of approximately nine thousand vampires need regularly to survive?"

Kathrine grimaced, but her gaze turned on the elvish queen and king. "We could use their people as cattle."

"You did not answer my question. And even if we did, is it sustainable for that many vampires at one time?" Riven cocked an eyebrow and leaned forward in his chair. "I drink from either Luke or Genua at a bare minimum of once every three days—and they often alternate when they begin to get sick from lack of blood. That would mean we'd need to bleed about nine thousand people once every three days, but we'd need even more than that to make sure they weren't being drained. Perhaps fourteen thousand elves, and they'd possibly be out of commission concerning any work in agriculture or labor-intensive positions. Am I right?"

"You are probably correct, yes."

Riven's lips formed a thin line. "And this is hinging on the idea that they killed thousands of my own people, and won't rebel against us, and will accept our proposal to destroy their beacon."

Kathrine hesitantly nodded. "Yes, but . . . I am not exaggerating about the ramifications it would send across our social circles in the wider multiverse. For a high prince of the Blood Moon Requiem such as yourself to show mercy on them would be . . . a needed change, in my opinion. I know it is a hard pill to swallow, but even someone like me, as a duchess of my noble house and as an outer sect princess of the requiem, would not have such a lasting impact should it be my decision—versus a decision coming from you."

Riven glared her down. "Allie, how much money in Elysium coins did we make by killing all those vampires over the course of the battle? And will it be enough to sustain an entire population at current capacity with food for at least three years until our agriculture settles into a rhythm?"

He looked left to his sister. "If we have enough, then put the vampires in concentration camps. We will then sift through them and systematically execute all those who we deem as threats. We will incorporate those we can find useful and who swear new allegiance. If we don't have enough money to do that using the Elysium altar to sustain us, then kill every last one of them and display their corpses on pikes along the roadways. Which will it be?"

Allie smiled as she exchanged a glance with Kathrine. "We have more than enough. I will begin putting them into concentration camps and killing those who won't comply."

The king of Dawn frowned deeply at this news but gave an affirmative nod that he'd accept the decision when meeting Riven's eyes. Kathrine looked thoroughly relieved and even a little bit happy, and Allie seemed excited.

Riven closed his eyes. "What next?"

"Trade routes and diplomacy concerning new alliances, republics, and king-doms on this side of the portal and on the other as well," Allie replied when flipping over another paper on her stack to take a look.

"Not interested. Figure it out yourself; I have faith in you. Next?"

Allie turned another page. "The war with the dwarves in the underdark is hitting a climax. Deepnest calls for aid, and vampire diplomats from another native underdark sect have come forth to deliver a message concerning news on the vampiric elder god world quest."

At this, Snagger stood up with a wave—getting frowns from Kathrine and some of the others in the room at the perceived lack of respect. "Snagger sees-feels Riven has grown-stood strong since last seen-met! Am happy to see-observe your growth-gains!"

Riven smiled lightly, having forgotten how his underground friends talked. "Ah yes. Good to see you, too, man. Let's definitely catch up later over drinks, but for now—what's the deal with this war you're requesting aid for?"

Snagger's large rat face, brown fur and all, turned to look at his cousin Mesha—a smaller white rat-kin woman, and then to their broodmother, Rashtalia. Broodmothers were essentially the equivalents of nobility under the rat-kin queen, and she was just as Riven remembered her from their brief visit to the underdark.

Rashtalia was slightly taller than Riven, standing near Snagger's height of seven feet, and wore the same platinum necklace that hung down over her chest that he'd seen her wear before. She was thinner than him, with brown fur, and was dressed in a formfitting white robe. Her long bare tail, the clawed hands and feet, and her mouselike ears and face were a stark contrast to any women Riven had ever known—but he could still tell she was feminine for a rat person.

She bowed low, her twitching nose almost touching the table before she straightened as Snagger took a seat. "Rashtalia is honored-relieved to be stand-sitting in presence of great bat-kin such as you-yourself! Alliance-friends with Thane Necropolis has made-created much wealth-loot for Deepnest, and your armies-troops have kept-made our trade routes safe-sound. But now that we-us push dwarves back-dead into their hole-tunnels, they grow-rage fiercer-strong. Defensive holds-castles in the underdark stop-prevent us from moving-getting farther. Us-we ask for Riven-Allie friend-kin to help lead swarm-armies to battle, to crush-kill enemies and take their gold-stone for ourselves! Queen is willing-hoping to pay-trade for help, and will attempt-try to make it worth to you-us mutually!"

Despite only having gone to Deepnest once himself, Riven was very aware of how the conflict between their allies in Deepnest and the dwarves had started: The dwarves had essentially tried to commit a genocide against the rat-kin for more resource-rich land to expand into, pushing them back and even attempting to slay Riven on his initial trip into the underdark. Even now, Deepnest provided the Thane Necropolis—and primarily the engineers in Chicago—with an absolute abundance of minerals those on the path of the Machine pillar could utilize to create different weapons and machines of war, like mechs, tanks, jets, and helicopters. This alliance of theirs had quite literally become an absolute gold mine, along with other minerals, and he had no reason to say no to their request for help.

"I'll personally attend the war effort myself," Riven eventually said after mulling it over, getting an overly excited squeak from the broodmother, who nearly slammed her head in another low bow upon his words. "It'll be another week or two, but I'll be there. Let your queen know I'm coming, and I'll likely bring some of our more weathered and experienced troops, too."

Rashtalia eagerly nodded before sitting down. "This one is very happy-merry to hear it and will see-tell queen of Deepnest this happy-good news! You are great-good ally-friends, oh great bat-kin!"

Riven smirked, then waved at Allie to get on with the tedious task of being leaders. "Next. Didn't you say something about the vampiric elder god world quest?"

Another squeak from Rashtalia caught his attention, and she stood one more time. "Oh yes! They wait-seek you in Deepnest, wanting to meet-come to their aid-help and address such things-omens there!"

"So the diplomats aren't here, then?"

Allie and Rashtalia shook their heads simultaneously.

"Very well. On to the next, and I'll talk to them when I go to the underdark."

The meeting delved into a variety of topics after that. Questions on how to set up the governing structure now that the Thane Necropolis was head of this small alliance were at the forefront. Talk about paving roadways and culling various wildlife in the area to help caravans was another issue. Just like how King Glassleaf of Tereen tried to pawn his princess daughter off on Riven, so did King Arthur Brix of Dawn—but Riven quickly made it very clear that he wasn't interested in either offer. As it was, he had Athela, and that was enough. If she wanted to play around with other women, then she'd let him know; until then it was a no-fly zone and that conversation hadn't come to pass yet as it previously had with Fay.

There were talks about regulating access to the cube, which he intended to access himself this week after going over the details one more time.

[Puzzle-Box Cube Labyrinth: This stone cube is a permanent fixture on the world of Panu, granted to Daskus, the city of canyons, by Elysium as a prize to the populace after the king of Daskus completed a difficult system quest with perfect marks. After Daskus was destroyed, it was stolen and taken to the opposite side of Panu. Rules: The trials are formed by outwitting monsters, mazes, and puzzles with a real possibility of death. Only ten may enter an instance event at once; instance events that are not full may be entered by outsiders at any time as long as they are within the same tier of trial. Any number of instance events between different groups may be ongoing at any time. You do not require sustenance while inside the cube, you

may only complete the Puzzle-Box Cube Labyrinth event up to three times with scaling difficulty and scaling prizes via attempt tiers one, two, and three, and you may leave the Puzzle-Box Cube Labyrinth instance events at any time—but only through the single entrance and single exit points inside. Leaving the instance event will forfeit all remaining attempts at completing this system event or collecting its prizes. To create your own instance event or join another's, just stand underneath the cube and focus on it while thinking "Activate."]

Riven declined to monitor it beyond making sure people weren't being *forced* into attempting the trials for other people's benefit. Who was he to stop people from pursuing power in a world like this?

Taxation was brought up.

So was an official written script of laws to be published for everyone to read across the lands the Thane Necropolis now controlled—including Dawn's borders, Tereen's borders, Brightsville's surrounding lands, and those on the other side of the world across the Riven's Eye Wormhole, where Chicago, Rockford, and Milwaukee were located. Most of this was set up for Dr. Brass to handle, as he'd taken a very keen liking to administrative duties.

Though he and Riven didn't talk much anymore.

More and more, on and on for over twelve entire hours the talks dragged on until Riven called it and said they'd continue this meeting the next morning. Thankfully, Athela had taken to spoiling him with deep-tissue back rubs and back scratches, and food had been delivered multiple times over with a couple of breaks, so it hadn't all been bad.

Standing up at the end of the day when the meeting was dismissed and the sun had long since set, Riven let out a groan and turned into a kiss from Athela—putting one hand on her left cheek and smiling down at her before a mischievous grin crossed her face.

He raised an eyebrow in suspicion. "What's that look for?"

She only grinned wider and pushed her body up against his, groping him and causing his eyes to go wide as she whispered in his ear, "Can we go have some fun now? I'm horny!"

"AHEM!" Azmoth interrupted, pushing them apart and turning them both around to look Allie's way. "Lady Allie want talk. Both go. Sleaze time later."

Athela snarled at the bigger demon and started muttering under her breath, but Riven began to laugh and tugged Athela over by the base of her neck to kiss her again before heading forward. "Come on, Athela, I think I know what this conversation is about. And it's been a long time coming, if you ask me."

Up in her supersize bedroom, where Allie had once housed her numerous male concubines, she closed the door behind the other occupants and locked it with a click. Turning heel to face the room, she smiled at Lahn and Shovi before turning her gaze to Riven and Athela. "Thanks for coming. I wanted you to be here in case I got out of control . . ."

She didn't even bother looking over at Lahn's father, siblings, and bully, who were all very pale and sitting at a table to her right. Lord Nikola Lucio wore a typical frilled shirt and vest, well made with fine threads and gold trimmings. His son and daughter also wore Victorian-style outfits of their noble rank. Lahn's brother stared at the floor. Lahn's sister, Linela, had not stopped gaping at Riven ever since recognizing him as the man she'd hit on in the store a while back.

Back when Fay and Riven had still been together.

The thought obviously troubled Riven, and Allie could tell, but she ignored it. This was her time for vengeance and justice, and she was going to draw it out long and hard until she was satisfied that things were officially dealt with.

That made her turn to the last person in the room . . .

Gleetus Nefrand, the bully who'd shattered Lahn's good limbs in an act of spite. He'd somehow survived the vampiric purging, much to Allie's satisfaction, because if anyone was going to brutally murder this motherfucker . . .

It was going to be her.

A wicked smile with protruding fangs illuminated her beautiful features as she stepped forward to where Gleetus remained bound to his chair—the only one who was tied up. She leaned over, smile widening and red eyes flashing to meet his gaze as he pissed himself, lips trembling. "Oh, I've been waiting for this day for a long, long while. I believe it was interrupted last time, but now we get to finish the job. Don't we? The question of the evening is this . . . will anyone be joining you? That, my friend, has yet to be revealed—and I have some curiosities that need to be settled here in front of Lahn and his lovely family in order to make those decisions final. If you're helpful, you might not experience as much pain before you pass."

CHAPTER 34

Gleetus broke and admitted to everything immediately after his left kneecap shattered. Everything from regularly picking on Lahn for fun to sabotaging his efforts to make it to class on time to eventually beating him nearly to death at the request of Linela—though he had admitted to going a bit beyond what Lahn's siblings had originally asked. Shovi was absolutely horrified and sat speechless throughout the interrogation, giving her other two children rigid and infuriated glares, while Lahn just looked sad.

Gleetus's begging and screams of horrified pain only grew louder and louder as his insides were ripped out and plastered against the wall, much to the terror of Lahn's family—and even Lahn himself to an extent. Allie was an absolute maniac when she got mad, and she didn't hold back at all while butchering the young man who'd dared hurt her friend. Though Riven could tell that both Lahn and Lady Shovi Lucio were far less bothered by the sight than were Lahn's two siblings.

Lord Nikola Lucio was rather stoic about the whole thing and just continued to watch while occasionally adjusting his frilled shirt and vest like he had an impulsive need to scratch an itch.

"Are you quite done?" Riven asked after a while when Allie's slim, bloodied figure stood panting over the ruined remnants of what had once been a young man.

She held up the parasitic worm, squirming, in her right hand, and tossed it into a small cage she'd prepared before clicking the lock shut and turning around. Funny that they'd gone to all that effort to shove the worm into Gleetus only to rip him apart not long afterward.

Pushing fingers through her matted hair and sighing in satisfaction, she turned to the pale occupants of the room. Parius and Linela sat rigidly still with sweat beading on their faces and nostrils flaring as she turned her gaze to them. "Not quite."

"Allie," Lahn protested, finally getting up and grimacing at the bloody sight on the floor—putting himself in between the vampiric queen and his siblings. He gave her a stern look, then shook his head slowly. "Please. Let it go."

He could barely hold himself up. He was struggling, still weak on his left side, but he managed.

Allie's red eyes flared, and she was about to protest when she caught Riven's raised eyebrow. Shoulders slumping and glancing back to Lahn, she let out a long exhale and nodded. Wiping blood off her shirt and stepping forward to give him a peck on the cheek, she glared over his shoulder at the siblings—and then to Lahn's father. "We'll talk later, bitches."

Getting Lahn's spare wheelchair now that everything was out in the open, she wordlessly helped him into it and angrily kicked the door open before wheeling him out—with Lady Shovi Lucio following.

The three of them left, leaving only Riven, Athela, Parius, Linela, and Nikola sitting awkwardly in Allie's room, a bloodied, messy pile of flesh scattered on the floor between them.

"I'd say you guys all got off pretty well!" Athela chimed in happily with a clap of her hands. "Be excited—you three get to live after all! Riven and I were taking bets. Riven lost."

Riven rolled his eyes but let himself be yanked out of the chair with a tug of Athela's hand. "You're all dismissed. I wouldn't be here when she gets back—Allie gets rather violent when she's in a bad mood nowadays."

Parius and Linela immediately got to their feet, avoiding the gaze of their father, and power walked out of the room shoulder to shoulder. Lord Nikola Lucio shook his head and slowly stood before shoving his hands into his pockets, taking a backward glance at the remnants of Gleetus, and gagging once before exiting behind his children.

"Do you think there's still going to be a royal ball?" Riven asked absent-mindedly while watching them leave and take the spiral staircase down to the second floor.

Athela's warm body pressed up against his, hands groping his chest with a contented hum. "Don't know, but if not, we need to have our own! Maybe that'd be a good idea considering all those other factions want to meet with us. It'd be a good opportunity to undertake politics, and it'd give me a reason to wear that dress I bought so long ago!"

"Bought?" Riven repeated with a raised eyebrow and a sly smile. "Are you talking about the one we found in Brightsville when we first arrived? We looted it out of a broken-down clothes shop."

Athela's lips pursed and she poked him in the forehead. "Same thing! Now, as I was saying earlier, I've been very deprived. Come, take me back to bed—I've been stuck daydreaming for so long and now that I finally have you, I'm taking full advantage of it!"

A twinge of sadness overcame him when thoughts of Fay came unbidden, but he brushed them aside with a massive amount of willpower.

And thinking about recent events concerning the night prior, he couldn't help but smile slyly. "You gonna do that thing with your tongue again?"

Athela's long black tongue flicked out and licked the side of his face before she pulled him down the hallway. Then she winked. "Absolutely. I loved seeing you squirm."

Daylight streamed through cracks in the otherwise dusky cloudscape of the haunted woods surrounding Brightsville, and leaves cracked underfoot as Riven and Athela walked under the branches hand in hand. It wasn't too far away from the city's edge, because Kathrine couldn't leave the three-mile radius surrounding his guild hall, but it was far enough that they had privacy. Kathrine kept pace beside them, clutching something akin to a tablet, cycling through videos that she displayed as holograms ahead of their path while they walked.

One such hologram showed a large, sleek tower crumbling and falling over—crashing to the ground as vampires fled and slaves cheered. The slaves were the humanoid Sarak, who had pale eyes, purple skin, white hair, and two smooth antennae that looked rather soft and fleshy as opposed to those of insects.

"Slave rebellions happen from time to time, but this one is no doubt orchestrated by your competitors," Kathrine said, flipping through the images to settle on one of a burning manor. "It is true that there are only fifty million vampires on Luteski, and there are six billion enslaved Sarak, but even a tenth of the vampiric cohort there could overpower these weak slaves within days. Your fleet, and your legions, are no doubt being held back by those in power there."

Riven raised an eyebrow, glancing over at the vampiric princess as a brisk wind brushed her brunette hair behind her. "Why? What's the point?"

"It makes you look bad. It makes the decisions you made look bad."

"The ones where I granted those slaves more basic freedoms than most would get?"

"Correct. The vampiric nobility don't like it, and they're trying to make you look like a fool. No doubt some of these attacks are orchestrated by the vampires on other sects of vampires in your faction rather than it being entirely done by slaves. The weapons, coincidences, and lack of a coordinated suppression of the insurgence are all indicators of this." Kathrine looked up from her tablet to frown his way. "It is very much impacting trade efforts there. The registered corporations residing on your planet are having to step in, and they're calling for complete area lockdowns and possibly even an embargo on your trading hub if things aren't quelled soon."

Riven snorted with irritation. "Well, I'm here and not there, and I know very little about vampiric politics. Tell me, Kathrine, how would I go about fixing this? You're far more experienced, and I trust your judgment."

"As a prince: Openly going against you is going against the crown unless they can prove absolute negligence or incompetence. The latter is what they're trying to frame you for. They can only take actions in the shadows or under pretenses—they cannot oppose your will directly unless they hold a similar rank," Kathrine replied promptly, dismissing the holograms with a wave of her hand. "There is good reason to believe the same people who tried to sell your inheritance beforehand are related to the ones now upending the way of life on Luteski. It is your planet, your birthright since your parents went missing, and these branch families of your lineage have for far too long assumed they'd be the ones acquiring ownership of the planet. They are ungrateful for what was provided for them, they did a poor job of running the highly lucrative trading hub in your absence, and they sabotage your efforts to improve the lives of the slaves YOU own. If it were me, I would do two things: make an appearance to speak with the general of House Wraithtide's forces via hologram transmission to address these problems, and publicly execute the troublemakers. Then go back to quelling the uprising however you deem fit."

There was a pause, and Riven stopped in his tracks to think about what she'd just said. "It is odd . . . thinking that I own an entire planet with over six billion slaves there. That I rule over fifty million vampiric citizens there. The numbers are beyond my true comprehension."

Kathrine gave him a sympathetic smile. "Yes, I understand. My parents sometimes throw me to the wolves concerning one or two of the planets my own house rules over, and it's always a staggering experience."

"How would I make an appearance via hologram? And would you accompany me if I did so?"

Kathrine's features immediately brightened, and she gave him a quick nod and blinding white smile. "Of course! Back at the trading commune we have a formation that was just built, and it can be used to talk between worlds! Of course, the use is incredibly expensive at this distance and we won't be able to use it often given the difficulty of operating such a mechanism, but it is possible. If you'd like, I can take you there now?"

Athela got up on her toes to whisper in his ear, "She wants to use you to further her own political agenda, but it isn't such a bad thing."

This was obvious to Riven as well, and he gave a quick nod of acknowledgment when Kathrine was looking the other way. "Yes, that'd be great, Kathrine. I'd like that very much."

Kathrine's excitement only grew, and she quickly changed course to head toward the Elysium altar in the distance—outlined by its green halo of flame surrounding the black spire's tip. "Fabulous! I'll certainly join you, but I must ask— would it be too early or are you comfortable with meeting my parents? Perhaps the high queen? They've been wanting to talk to you for some time but felt that they should hold off until you and I became more acquainted. Now that we've . . ."

Her eyes flitted to Athela, then back to Riven, and she cleared her throat. "Experienced each other's company, perhaps now would qualify?"

"I know the two of you slept together. You don't have to hide it," Athela stated flatly, unamused.

Riven chuckled at the blush overcoming Kathrine and waved a hand to clear the air. "Yes, I am fine with meeting my grandmother. As for your parents, perhaps that can wait. I'm very busy and don't have much time."

Kathrine's demeanor lost some of her enthusiasm, but she was still happy overall. "Very well. I'm sure the queen will be pleased! After that, we can go back to talk to the general overseeing your planet and—"

"No." Riven cut her off with a swiping motion. "We go to talk to the general overseeing Luteski first. I don't want to waste any time as people die and unrest unfurls on a planet I'm apparently inheriting. We will settle that matter immediately, and then I'll meet this grandmother of mine that I keep hearing about."

Kathrine hesitated, but not for long. "As you say, Riven. As you say."

The small castle that acted as a trading commune for the Blood Moon Requiem was thrown into an uproar as soon as Riven arrived. They'd gone so long without having actual contact with the lost prince or princess that Riven almost had to swat off the young nobility who'd remained there in an attempt to try and garner his favor, and the vampiric servants were in a frenzy trying to make things more presentable the moment his foot touched the interior of the entrance hall.

Just like last time, the displays were over-the-top extravagant, but it'd been changed up a bit. Gold plating decorated the paintings and hallways, red-crystal chandeliers decorated the rooms, and heavy plate-mail guards were on full attention with dark armor glistening in the dim light—red eyes straight ahead while he walked by.

"It is so nice to see you've finally arrived back at the commune!" Duke Blemrich, the tall, muscular vampiric nobleman with a black ponytail stated with a grin while quickly trailing his advance down the hall behind Kathrine. "Perhaps we could discuss things in private concerning a business opportunity, or the whereabouts of your sister?"

"You look absolutely handsome today, my lord!" the vampiric Lady Muren said with a low bow when she turned the corner to see him, long orange hair swept to one side and over the shoulder of her seductive, revealing red dress. "What a surprise to see you here! When the guards informed me of your presence, I didn't believe them at first."

Lord Carsion, the blonde nobleman in a purple vest who was walking with a cane, sighed loudly and glared at the others while continuing to trail behind Riven just like Duke Blemrich. "I apologize for the vultures, my prince. Do you wish me to send them away?"

Lady Muren and Duke Blemrich both scowled Lord Carsion's way, but Riven only chuckled and waved it off with his free hand while tugging Athela along in his left.

"I wish you'd ALL be sent away," Kathrine Vonsilla Crushada muttered under her breath. The vampiric princess stopped at a pair of double doors, waiting for the guards to open it for them and step aside.

Through the babbling of the excited nobles peppering Riven with questions and compliments, and after the quiet swing of the double doors let in a gust of cold air, Riven saw through into the next chamber where different-colored crystals were lined up in circular patterns that overlapped with one another in odd diagrams. Runes etched into stones glowed bright purple in the center of each circle, and mages dressed in robes all stood in a line, bowing when Riven and Kathrine entered the room seconds later.

"We received your message, Princess!" one of the mages stated reverently before righting himself again and gesturing to the crystal formation. "We've prepared the room as instructed. Do you need us to set up a silencing array for the babbling trio?"

The old vampire mage pointedly looked past Kathrine to the three nobles, all of whom glared back, and this in turn got a loud chuckle from both Riven and Kathrine in unison.

"Not needed, but thank you, Pladius. You've done more than enough. I'm sure they won't be so stupid as to make noise while our prince deals with internal matters regarding his inheritance—and then the high queen."

At the mention of the high queen, all three young nobles shut up and took a step back—though they stayed inside the room, even if it was at the outer edges, to watch.

Kathrine nodded to Riven and then pointed to one of the circular formations, stepping into an adjacent one herself. "Follow my lead, and keep your feet planted. The experience is a bit jarring at first. You'll see double—one image here in this room and the other on your flagship orbiting Luteski. I already had Pladius contact the military brass of House Wraithtide, and they'll no doubt be waiting for your orders. The connection should take a few minutes to establish as long as we don't have anyone try to jam the signal, so hold still and be patient. The more you move, the longer the connection will take."

CHAPTER 35

A pale, thickly built man stood on the main command deck of an enclosed flagship owned by House Wraithtide of the Blood Moon Requiem. His body was covered in heavy plate armor, decorated with seals and ornaments displaying his rank, with the sigil of his house etched into the center of his breastplate: an orb wreathed in deathly flame. It was smaller than the Blood Moon Requiem's own sigil and was displayed below it, subservient to the empire's own crest. Red eyes stared out at the planet beneath him through a huge glass window, large screens were set on displays to his left and right, and military officers in similar red-black armor gathered information about the surface as well as comings and goings of corporation fleets in the area.

General Viku was a hardened man with a couple small wars under his belt, all of which had ended in victory. Some of them were against other noble houses when conflicts ended in blood feuds, others were border wars concerning core kingdoms that didn't know when to stop pushing their luck. Still others were against pirates or slave uprisings that spiraled out of control.

And in all his years, he'd not been so blatantly held back by the elders.

He stood there, watching neighborhoods and towns burn while citizens were murdered in the streets. He stood there, watching as lawlessness and anarchy erupted in places across the planet of Luteski that were what the elders considered "expendable" to make a point. He stood there, unable to do anything, just so that this fledgling prince would have a light shined down on his incompetence.

It made him sick.

Not only did this reflect poorly on the young prince, who'd given these slaves new rights that'd been unheard-of in the empire before, but it reflected poorly on himself as well. General Viku knew very well that this reflected almost solely on him rather than the elders who were the ones really pulling the strings, but what could he do about it?

Mutiny?

Insubordination?

He shook his head. He'd served long under the banner of House Wraithtide, and he would not throw away his position just to save face or prove a point. He needed this position, for more reasons than one, and despite his pride being stripped from him, he would choose the job over the pride any day.

His daughter depended on it.

The cube in his hand gave off a steady vibration again and then began to blink. It drew his red eyes down to stare at it, and from underneath his helmet, a small smile crept over his lips to display his fangs.

Finally.

"General Viku!" one of the house elders, a man by the name of Baron Orimus Wraithtide, called out as he walked onto the elevated platform of the command deck. His wiry body moved like a practiced snake in burgundy robes, and his eyes glinted mischievously under slicked-back chestnut hair while glaring at the screens on the general's sides. "I see the rebellions are going well. The agents we planted are supplying as necessary, not too much but enough to cause trouble. Are the damages being quarantined to the designated areas?"

General Viku nodded gravely. "Yes. The production facilities and mining operations are all still under our protection, we're letting the slaves sack the Bezin and Norcof districts, where our poorer citizens reside. It'll be enough vampiric blood to get quite a reaction out of the rest of the empire—they'll be calling for a culling." His eyes shifted to the other well-groomed vampire as Baron Orimus Wraithtide nodded in approval. "Do you really think it wise to go against a high-ranking prince like this? Sheline's son, of all people?"

The baron scoffed indifferently, watching cargo ships from other sectors in the galaxy warp in through a spatial gate before changing course to dock at the space station nearby and check in. "Sheline is dead, and her son made it very clear to the rest of us that he can't be trusted to lead the family when he gave those Sarak cattle rights. Can you believe this list of changes to the laws that we have to abide by? Just listen to this!"

General Viku rolled his eyes while turning his head so the baron wouldn't see. He knew very well what the changes were, and to him they weren't all that big of a deal—but to an old-timer like Baron Orimus Wraithtide, it appeared to be the end of the gods damned multiverse.

The old vampire pulled out a list, then put on a pair of reading glasses while loudly clearing his throat and staring at the hastily scribbled lines on parchment down the bridge of his nose. "Ahem! Where is it . . . Ah yes. Just to BEGIN the list, we have protection for the cattle children!"

The baron raised an eyebrow and scoffed again in disbelief, glancing at the general, who continued to stare down at the planet from their perch on the flagship's deck. "Do you realize what that means, Viku? It means no child labor, which cuts down production by an entire 9 percent worldwide. No delicacies at the Rouge Café that I so frequently visit or ANY OTHER high-end establishment on the planet. No training them for unique positions such as concubines or slave warriors. No pets for our own vampiric children. It's absurd! Utterly absurd! And that's just the CHILDREN of these cattle!"

The baron smacked the paper again with his mouth agape, shaking his head violently and huffing loudly. "No gladiator battles between slaves, no torture without reason, oh—here is one of my favorites—NO BUTCHERING CATTLE IN FAVOR OF REGULAR BLOOD DRAINS?! IS THIS MAN SERIOUS?! I nearly got up and left THAT VERY DAY after reading this ridiculous list! We literally BREED Sarak in some specialty lineages to become fatter so we can EAT THEM! WE HAVE TO SPARE THEIR LIVES AND JUST USE THEM AS RENEWABLE BLOOD BALLOONS? THIS IS RIDICULOUS!"

General Viku stared straight ahead, trying to give off apathy, but inside he was struggling very hard not to smirk. He'd never liked Baron Orimus Wraithtide very much, but since the ruling lady of the house left many years ago, never to return, the baron was one of three of the house nobility that was in contention for patriarch or matriarch due to Lady Sheline's absence. It was Viku's great misfortune that he had to listen to this idiot babble, otherwise he would have hanged him from a tree many months ago when Riven and Allie had first appeared.

The baron continued to rant, jabbing a wiry old finger into the paper with each thing he listed off. "We have improved slave housing, which has cost us trillions, compensation built into our tax system for slaves who donate more blood over the course of a year than others, ability to attend NEWLY BUILT CRAFTING SCHOOLS that also cost us a fortune, FREE HEALTH CARE, and a clause that allows slaves to own basic property? HE MIGHT AS WELL MAKE THEM HONORARY CITIZENS! And that doesn't even BEGIN to touch upon the fact that he and his sister are being auctioned off to the highest bidder AS WE SPEAK, with the conclusion of the bids in coming months allowing a FOREIGN vampiric noble house the rights to be WED to them?! We might as well just hand away the keys and pack up all our belongings now! I hear that House Crushada is especially invested in obtaining Riven and has even managed to get their daughter to seduce him on that integrating planet! This is the end for our lineage if we don't do something about it now, Viku! And I'll be damned if it happens while I'm still alive! It may take a couple underhanded schemes and maybe a couple years, but eventually if we're able to prove incompetence we can petition the crown and have him removed. If it were anyone else without the bloodline, I'd just have him assassinated, but the queen would have my head faster than you could say 'Sarak cattle shit' if I even tried. So though I do not want to go up against a prince of our own house, I do not believe I have a choice in order to maintain our way of life. Sometimes, dark deeds must be done for the greater good of the family."

The baron reached out and put a hand on General Viku's shoulder pauldron, patting him twice. "I know I can count on you to do the right thing, Viku. Just remember what we're fighting for, and why we're letting this happen. I expect your full cooperation on this matter, and in future ones. We cannot let outside forces like House Crushada interfere in our internal affairs unless we want to be absorbed by them. I know they've been in contact with you, and I hope you see past their lies. Do you understand?"

General Viku spared the old man a glance, keeping eye contact and clicking his tongue before turning heel and beginning to head down the bridge. The cube in his hand was vibrating again, and he had an appointment to keep.

"General Viku!" Baron Orimus Wraithtide called out, a little more harshly than usual, and he rushed to catch up to the larger man while scowling deeply. "I expect an answer! Let me hear you say it!"

"Say what, exactly?" Viku said with an exasperated sigh, turning to face the smaller, thinner man as officers from along the command bridge curiously shot glances their way. Viku brushed off the hand Baron Orimus Wraithtide put on his shoulder again, and he gave an irritated grunt. "If you're looking for me to turn my back on the head of this house, you have mistaken me for a blood traitor—Baron."

The baron's eyes went wide, and his pale face reddened deeply while he took a step forward. "I would watch your words, General. You are essentially calling me a blood traitor by association, and I do not take such offense lightly."

"Are you threatening me?" General Viku's figure towered over the shorter man as his hand drifted to the broadsword at his hip. The weapon hissed when his skin touched the metal, and a neon red flared along the scabbard with an aura that drenched the room in death.

He stood there glaring down at the baron, and the older man's eye twitched—looking to the general's hand on his weapon. Other soldiers in the room were now dead silent, watching to see whether or not the baron would keep his head on his shoulders. Viku was an A-grade warrior, having taken millennia to cultivate himself to that level. It was nothing to be scoffed at by anyone, an impossible feat by most, so if Viku wanted the baron dead—the baron would no doubt be dead very soon.

"Let me make something very clear to you," General Viku said with a visible sneer between the gap down the middle of his helm. "It was not you who elevated me to this position. Nor was it any of the still-living elders of this house. This house is a shadow of what it once was, thanks to you and people like you. Now that the main bloodline has finally returned, I no longer have to answer to you. My position is due to Riven's mother, a true leader, and I owe her everything that I am. Everything that I have is due to her, and here you come years after she disappears to threaten what is rightfully her children's inheritance? In what world did you think I would agree to such schemes? Ask yourself one more time, Baron Orimus Wraithtide: Is what you are doing wise?"

Riven blinked, seeing two versions of reality just like Kathrine had warned him about. He had his normal body back on Panu in the crystal formation, and then he had this ghostlike hologram that he was now using to stand in a barren metal room.

It was an odd sensation, splitting his senses between the two places, and it gave him a bit of a headache—but it wasn't anything he couldn't manage. When he flexed his ghostly fingers back and forth in front of his face and only barely felt the ground underneath his feet, his attention was brought upward when Kathrine's own ghostly apparition cleared her throat.

"Riven, my prince, this is General Viku—leader of the legions and fleets of House Wraithtide."

She gestured over to a tall man in a heavily decorated black and red plate-mail armor set similar to what the soldiers at the Blood Moon Requiem's trade commune wore, helmet off to reveal a glistening, bowed bald head while he kept a fist over his chest in a salute.

"General Viku, it is a pleasure," Riven stated while straightening, reaching out to shake—but realizing that probably wouldn't work very well and withdrawing it a split second later. "My name is Riven Thane—or Riven Wraithtide, I suppose. I hear you knew my mother and father."

It was both a statement and a question, and the bald middle-aged vampire smiled. "Of course. Lady Sheline Wraithtide and Lord Timvar Wraithtide were always kind to me. They raised me to what I am today, and I owe them my life. Because they are now gone, that debt is passed on to you."

The bald warrior bowed low in respect and held the bow for a solid few seconds before straightening again to look Riven in the eye.

Timvar. It'd been a long, long time since Riven had heard that name uttered. Timvar was his dad, known as just Var back on Earth, and he'd disappeared many years before his mother jumped ship.

Hearing that name caused Riven's chest to tighten.

"I see," Riven said with a quick nod, regretting having brought his parents up. "I'll be counting on you to inform me of what is going on, and why. Kathrine here has been kind enough to help me to the best of her ability, but she does not have the necessary insights or power regarding House Wraithtide to give me much more than theories. Perhaps you could enlighten me as to why I am told a slave uprising is being let loose on my parents' home planet, while our fleet remains in orbit and our legions within their military bases?"

The general's lips twitched upward. "My lord, it would be my absolute pleasure to tell you exactly why in very vivid detail. Unfortunately my hands have been tied this entire time due to house politics, but after I personally supplied House Crushada with the required materials for that array you're using, I am happy to say that I can take orders directly from you."

Riven's eyebrows raised, and he shot Kathrine a look. "You never said it was him that gave you the crystal formation. Based on context clues, I'm assuming this particular long-distance communication is rare?"

Kathrine gave a half-hearted laugh and nodded, side-eyeing the now-scowling general, who glared her way. "Yes, yes, it is quite rare. In fact, it's incredibly expensive to acquire and even more expensive to operate. My house doesn't actually have the materials needed to create one of these formations; it was entirely General Viku's hand that guided this into operation."

"Oh. I'd thought you or the queen set this up."

There was a dramatic pause, and Kathrine sheepishly stepped back to give General Viku the floor.

The bald man snorted. "No, my prince. Outside of the system's own methods, it is very hard to create passage between different universes in the larger multiverse. This was actually acquired using my own personal money, and money taken out of House Wraithtide's coffers. I had to blame it on a profit error when the elders found out so they didn't reroute the funds or confiscate the equipment, as I'm sure by now you know some of your house are rather averse to the idea of your return. At least, Kathrine said she'd pass that along. This flagship, inside this sequestered room with the crystals surrounding you, is one of two pieces of a limited formation that allows us to talk between universes. It will allow you to travel around the ship within a few miles in any direction. Doing that, speaking between entire universes, is a very hard feat indeed. You can't just get on a ship and fly to another universe—after all, the multiverse is filled with numerous universes, and the cost is astronomical and the resources extremely rare. But I do believe it was needed in order for you to retain your hold on your inheritance, otherwise the vultures would take what is rightfully yours. It is a long story, filled with boring details of petty squabbles between cheats. Before anything else, though, perhaps you would want to take your first look at the planet your parents left you? We are in orbit now, and the view is quite beautiful."

Riven's eyes lit up at the suggestion, and a wide grin spread across his ghostly face. "That actually sounds very neat. I'd love to, please—show me the way."

Viku bowed again, then opened the thick metal door to whisper to four guards standing right outside. He motioned for Riven to follow, then started a grand tour of the ship while they made their way to the main deck.

The flagship was absolutely enormous.

Many thousands of vampires called this ship home, with the central docking bay holding many hundreds of small, sleek dogfighting craft that could be launched out large bay doors leading into space. From the first angle Riven got, he nearly fell over because he thought he'd get sucked into space.

It caused Kathrine to laugh and General Viku to grin, because not only was there a force field in between himself and the vast canopy of stars and celestial bodies outside, but he wasn't even really there to begin with.

It'd just startled him to see it like that.

The hangar doors put on full display the absolute might of House Wraithtide's fleet outside. Tens of thousands of ships, some small and some large, hovered in space and peppered the starry sky behind them with a vast nebula in the near backdrop. Some of the ships were absolutely enormous, larger than the biggest skyscrapers back on Earth, while others were as small as the dogfighting craft docked here in the hangers—each big enough to fit one or two pilots inside. They all shared the same basic design with only a couple of variations, most of them being made of dark-gray steel and obsidian—with occasional red metals or paint thrown in for decorative purposes. Most of the ships were very sharp, angulated, and sleek—almost looking like daggers—with a handful of very, very big vessels coming and going from ports like the one he now stood on.

"This vessel is a supercarrier, the pride of the Wraithtide armada," General Viku stated proudly while he followed Riven's hologram to the edge of the bay where the force field stopped them from falling out into the void. "Those other carriers you see out there? They are only half the size of the one you stand in now. The other large vessels guarding the carrier are cruisers and battleships, the bulkier ones are transports and cargo, and the flat circular ones are utility ships outfitted with high-end scanners and barrier fields. The smaller ships are fighters and scout craft. They're all yours."

Riven let out a low whistle, amazed at the sight, and took a long time to comprehend that he really was seeing this. "This is incredible."

His words seemed to please the general, and Viku puffed his chest out with pride while officers and fighter pilots behind him slowly gathered in a perimeter while speaking in hushed and excited tones, pointing or gesturing Riven's way.

"I'm glad you like what you see," Viku said with a large grin. "But you have yet to actually see the planet, the warp gate, the space station, or the corporation trade fleets. None of that is viewable from this location—all that you see before you is the actual Wraithtide armada—but I think you'll be just as impressed with everything else on the other side of the flagship."

CHAPTER 36

General Viku had been right.

Riven's mirage body stood on the bridge, with a large glass half dome in front of him. It gave an expansive view of the planet, the warp gate, numerous fleets of merchant vessels from different parts of the multiverse, and the space station.

That cube-shaped space station was the most eye-catching sight. It was the size of a small moon, about a fiftieth the size of the planet below—which in turn was absolutely enormous. It was layered with dozens of enormous many-mile-wide docking stations, which each had enough room for a small fleet on its own. The entire station looked like a frantic beehive as thousands of vessels swarmed in and out.

Screens on the glass dome identified the different fleets or individual ships, which showed Riven there were at least thirty-two different factions present in front of him—with many private corporations from within the Blood Moon Requiem itself. The makes and models ranged from large energy bubbles with solid cores, to insectoid carapaces and living vessels, to hulking steel creations remnant of what he remembered viewing on *Battlestar Galactica* as a kid.

"Azag Hive Cluster?" Riven asked, pointing to the screen that identified one of the insectoid fleets incoming from the warp gate. "I killed a bunch of those fuckers back on Panu."

"I remember." Viku chuckled with a shake of his head. "Some of your feats are displayed on your equivalent of television here. That was one of them. You're quite powerful for an F-grade mage—a prodigy, even."

"Is the requiem allied to the hive clusters?"

"There are numerous hive clusters, so some of them yes, others no. Politics with that race are always complicated; it's a long story. This particular hive cluster is called the Blue Venom Azag Hive Cluster, while the one invading your integrating planet isn't even in this sector of space and is called the Black Sky Azag Hive Cluster."

The planet below was dark in nature, slightly larger than Earth had been, orbiting a white dwarf star with swirling clouds of black and green in the atmosphere.

The clouds allowed only brief glimpses of the continents below, which was probably a good thing considering vampires ruled the planet now. Even the Sarak seemed more or less acquainted with the dark, given they were natives of this place.

Then lastly, with the backdrop of the nebula present to the left of where he now floated on House Wraithtide's flagship, was the warp gate.

The entire thing was likely created from some kind of magic or was just using some very magic-dense materials along the outer perimeter where it glowed with blue light. It was shaped into a ring, many miles across in diameter, with a swirling orb of condensed energy in the center. The ring activated every ten or fifteen minutes to either bring a merchant fleet here or let one return to wherever it came from. When the warp gate activated, the central ball of energy would expand and then connect to the outer perimeter of the ring before twisting in the center like a whirlpool and blowing a hole in the side of space to create a wormhole.

It was truly fascinating to watch.

After a time, General Viku cleared his throat and looked left to where Riven was still gazing out the side of the carrier. "I had hoped we could do more to help you back on Panu, but unfortunately the system is rather stingy about what we can send. Even this takes an enormous tax for every attempt at communication, and Elysium only barely allows this method. I just wanted to apologize that we haven't done more."

"No need to apologize," Riven said with a smile. He glanced over to Kathrine, and then back to the general—turning his body around with his hands clasped behind his back. "Let's get down to business, shall we? Tell me about these rebellions and what we can do to fix them."

"Rest assured, fixing them will take a matter of days. I am just concerned about recurring problems due to the source," Viku replied with a frown. "This in large part is happening due to certain slaves being given weapons and magical items that can cause a lot of mayhem, mostly being sourced from your own family's vaults. As I am sure you're already aware, this in large part is due to disgruntled family members. Firstly because you're taking what they see as rightfully theirs, which in itself is ridiculous. Secondly because they don't like the changes you've made by giving the Sarak certain luxuries that most vampires would deem over-the-top."

"Do you think my ideas are over-the-top, General?"

Viku shrugged. "It doesn't bother me one way or the other."

"I see." Riven turned back to watch another incoming fleet flash through the portal. "I would have thought the Sarak would appreciate my efforts, rather than trying to kill and destroy civilians shortly afterward."

"It is likely they don't even know it was you who did that. Nor do most of them know the very nobles who wish to keep them down are plotting against you. They have a very limited scope of knowledge because they don't have much access to news networks, information hubs, or the cortex."

"Would opening up those channels of information be a problem? Would I be able to send a message to the entire planet in an address?"

The general hesitated. "Not a problem, but gathering the news networks and transporting the proper communication arrays that are specific to this planet would take some time. Perhaps a week."

Riven nodded. "Then the first step is to do that. I'd also like my entire extended family to be here, please. I'll be addressing them separately."

"All of them?" Viku asked curiously.

"All of them. And make sure you have your strongest soldiers onboard as an escort. In the meantime, I want you to quell the uprising with as little bloodshed as possible."

General Viku's grin widened. "That can and will be arranged, my prince."

"Good. Now let's talk specifics on what I intend to do and what I need to know. Then I'll see you in a week's time when all the necessary items are gathered, and we can figure out just how to go about fixing this whole mess to stop it from ever happening again."

The trip to Luteski was an enlightening one, and it lit a fire under his ass to get a move on all the things he'd been neglecting. To get his life together. Even now there were still talks going on at his manor between Allie and some of the independent factions surrounding the Thane Necropolis on either side of the portal—but he didn't intend to interfere with those talks unless necessary. He simply had too much on his plate to do otherwise, and Allie enjoyed politics more than he did.

Instead, Riven visited a couple places around the Blood Moon Requiem's trading compound with Kathrine. First stop was to meet Instructor Pladius—a well-known scholar and one of Kathrine's teachers. He'd been the same mage who had set up the communication array General Viku had sent them, and he was thrilled to finally be told his services would be needed.

"I hear you tutored Kathrine growing up," Riven said while shaking the older man's hand. "I look forward to taking your lessons, too, and I apologize for any offense I gave by not attending sooner. I've just had a lot going on, and it's been rough trying to fit it all in—but after the trip back to my parents' planet, I realized I have a lot to learn."

The old man bowed enthusiastically with a wide smile, displaying his fangs. "Of course, young prince! I do not take offense at all and am very excited to begin our lessons in earnest! When can I expect you to be here?"

Kathrine looked on from the sidelines with both amusement and eager approval before interrupting her instructor with a quick raise of her hand. "Do not push the issue, Pladius. I know you're excited, but we can hardly expect him to keep a thorough schedule. He'll be here as much as he can be—though he did say he'd try attending his first lesson this week."

That appeared to be more than enough for the old man, who started talking about various topics concerning politics, magical theory, economics, and history that they could talk about when Riven got back.

Next stop were the other nobles who'd come to try and get acquainted with the heirs to the Wraithtide household. Duke Blemrich, the taller man who always had his black hair in a ponytail, was quite surprised and relieved to see Riven intentionally go out of his way to talk, and was just happy to hear Riven would be making an attempt to get to know them better over the course of the coming weeks. Lord Carsion, the shorter blonde man with a sharp nose, was eager to talk trade agreements concerning Luteski—which he explained was a very exclusive arena to trade in, and one his family would pay handsomely for to achieve access. Lady Muren, the rather pretty vampiric lady of the court whose family had sent her here to try and woo him—did very little other than attempt to get Kathrine to leave so they could talk privately.

Of the three nobles, Lady Muren was the one Riven liked the least. But he would not make hasty judgments just yet and told them all he'd be back to talk more in detail soon.

Then came the final stop. Riven was led into a large magically reinforced pagoda on the compound grounds where numerous soldiers were engaged in training exercises. Many of them bowed respectfully and moved out of the way when seeing Riven, but many didn't realize he'd even appeared and continued to clash in brilliant displays of battle that left Riven in awe. Despite his own higher power levels—simply in terms of brute force—each of these soldiers was leagues beyond him in terms of skill, which was quickly apparent.

He continued to observe them for a few minutes, not interrupting the ongoing fights and very much envying the way they moved their bodies to adjust to attacks. Still, Riven was not by any means unable to stand out and drew quite a bit of attention, to the point that even these fights for the most part calmed down with the soldiers looking his way.

It was then that Captain Rusof made himself known.

"Prince Riven Wraithtide, thirty-seventh in line for the vampiric throne, I welcome you to our training hall."

The man who said this pushed through the crowd of gathered soldiers to stand before the prince and princess, bowing low to each of them—then correcting himself and even bowing low to Athela before standing up straight.

This gained him a lot of brownie points in Riven's book, because Athela seemed absolutely pleased that she'd not been ignored like the nobles had been apt to do.

The vampire captain was shirtless, well-built, handsome, and wore his hair in a short mohawk. He was slightly taller than Riven and had a very confident posture. "I must admit, I was unsure of whether or not you'd actually come. I am pleased to see that you have. What can I do for you today?"

Riven gave a slow smile, then with a thought, his armor, Messenger, removed itself. Riven summoned Jackal from his spatial sack and gestured for the captain to follow, heading toward the ring. "Kathrine told me you're pretty good. I wanted to see that for myself. Would you mind sparring with me? I know that I have a level advantage and that you're held back by the cap requirements, but I won't use any offensive magical attacks. What do you say?"

The captain's eyebrows rose, but he followed Riven regardless. "You want to spar in front of everyone here?"

"Is that a problem?" Riven asked curiously, pausing to look back over his shoulder.

"No . . . not necessarily." Captain Rusof shrugged with a grin, summoning a well-decorated spear. "But you're going to get your ass kicked. I don't want to hurt your fragile royal ego too much by doing that in front of a crowd."

Riven sputtered a laugh, now grinning widely as the soldiers around him gasped, shook their heads, or backed away. It was very apparent they hadn't expected this kind of disrespect—or what they considered disrespect—though Riven very much enjoyed the change of tone. "Is that so? I look forward to finding out just how much your words hold true, my friend. Come on, let's see what you've got and just what you have to teach me."

CHAPTER 37

Riven lifted Jackal up, noting the vampiric healers on the side specializing in blood magic waiting hesitantly for the fight to start. The room was dead quiet after the captain's announcement that he was going to trounce the prince, and many of the soldiers exchanged uncomfortable, shifty gazes despite Riven taking it in stride.

"Don't mind them; come at me with everything you've got," Riven said with a serious nod, taking off his shirt to match the captain and getting a whistle of approval from Athela—along with a loud chuckle from Kathrine. "I want you to prove that you have things you can teach me—"

WHAM

Riven's nose crunched and blood sprayed as Captain Rusof retracted the butt of his spear with a smug smirk, running his hand across his mohawk. "First lesson! Never let your guard down!"

Riven righted himself, blinked, and snapped his nose back into place as the captain began to laugh. Grinning and cracking his neck, he wordlessly entered the fray.

Riven was level 130. Despite being a pure-blooded vampire and receiving additional points across the board, he'd put the vast majority of his seven free stat points per level into Intelligence and Willpower, with a little on the side going into Sturdiness.

Captain Rusof . . . had not. He'd put all his points into a purely physical build. And it was very apparent in the way they moved that Captain Rusof was faster than Riven when Riven didn't have his Blessing of the Crow activated. Captain Rusof was also simply much more skilled.

The only thing Riven had going for him in this close-combat exchange was his passive ability. The two men blurred across the room, spear clashing against spear-staff with sparks of Riven's passive ability sending ripples of energy through his attacks and into his enemy. Massive amounts of force tore out of Riven's passive mana strengthening and flooded into his weapon—lighting up his opponent's spear with flashes of Unholy power, acting to counter the large Strength stat discrepancy.

"Shit!" Riven cursed, taking another strike across the flank and stumbling before Rusof kicked him straight in the chest—sending him smashing into the force field enclosing the combat area with a crunch of ribs.

Groaning and getting up to shake it off, Riven spat blood and adjusted the shoulder that'd been pushed out of its socket at impact with a thunk. "This is not going well for me, is it?"

Captain Rusof put his hands on his hips and laughed heartily. The slightly bigger man held both hands to the side in a shrug as soldiers on the perimeter watched intently, called out encouragement, or loudly shouted pointers for Riven to use and counter with. The atmosphere had also become a lot less tense now that the men realized Riven wouldn't be angry if the captain made him look inferior.

Which was exactly what had happened, given Riven wasn't using any mana outside his class passive—which was technically expelling energy in the form of mana, with flashes of Unholy black and green power clashing against Captain Rusof's strikes at each major block or connecting swing. However, Riven didn't actually SPEND any of that mana, so the captain had insisted that he keep the passive even if Riven could switch it off. He'd have agreed to let Riven keep Blessing of the Crow as well, but that particular skill could only be used once a day as a body modification for one hour's time—with the captain arguing that if he attacked while the skill was on cooldown, then Riven would be shit out of luck.

- **Devastator class trait (physical strikes are imbued with Unholy damage equal to 1% of damage being done at full mana capacity).**

"I'm honestly surprised you're doing even this well considering you're mostly a mage! It's a compliment, I assure you!" Captain Rusof blurred forward and swiped Riven's legs out from under him before executing a combo with a knee to the gut and a flip into an axe kick that shook the room.

Riven expelled the air from his lungs but quickly recovered and lashed out, connecting with Captain Rusof's spear and shoving the man back across the floor as he braced for the impact. Even so, the soldier grimaced and flung his right hand around like it was burned after some of the discharged mana from Riven's passive clashed with Rusof's skin.

CLANG
WHAM
BOOM

The two weapons danced and sparked, the two vampires moving far faster than any human could while Riven was constantly put on the defensive.

"WRONG STANCE!" Rusof yelled, smacking Riven on the back of his head with an open palm and twirling away while deflecting a blow. "TOO SLOW!"

Rusof's foot came down on the shaft to pin Jackal and his elbow crashed into Riven's jawline, sending the young prince head over heels while simultaneously disarming him. The captain jumped up and landed near Riven's position while blocking an incoming side kick from Riven on the ground. Rusof countered by yanking that same leg and slinging Riven across the containment zone so fast that the barrier around their dueling area shook and flickered.

"OOOOOOoooooohhhhh . . ." Athela and numerous others simultaneously winced, watching while Riven picked himself up and spat out one of his fangs.

The young prince chuckled good-naturedly, flinging the fang off to the side and holding up his hand—summoning his weapon as the spear-staff flew across the room to land in his outstretched palm. "That one hurt!"

The captain raised his left eyebrow—aura rising in a shimmering red haze around the man that caused the air to twist and turn. "We are vampires, after all. Our bodies can take quite a beating."

Riven's smile widened and his eyes flared. The shifting sleeve tattoo on his right arm sparked Black Lightning momentarily, and he set into a stance. His own aura picked up, and a cold frost began to accumulate around his feet. "Indeed."

With a burst of speed, Riven launched Jackal like a javelin—breaking the sound barrier with a sonic boom as his weapon tore through Captain Rusof's right thigh and smashed through the force field behind. Simultaneously, he tore forward across the sparring arena, accumulating a thick layer of red frost along his arms, forearms, and hands to create claws while grinning maliciously.

The captain had managed to turn left to avoid some of the impact from Riven's weapon, but even at his speed and skill, he'd been unable to miss the majority of it. He grimaced and snarled at the large hole in his thigh and began to fall over while Riven closed in—only to give a mischievous smirk right when the prince was within a few feet of his position.

CRACK

Captain Rusof's spear used Riven's own momentum to impale him through the chest, and with a momentous turn he redirected Riven's body and slung him around like a slingshot—throwing Riven through the barrier and out the arena into the far wall with a crash.

Riven slumped to the floor, and his world turned black.

"Yeah, I got my ass kicked," Riven said, sipping hot tea on a tower balcony couch overlooking the Blood Moon Requiem's compound and the rest of the Elysium altar's trading district while he and the captain chuckled.

They were both being scolded, especially Rusof, by the healers who'd tended their wounds. These same healers continued to rub ointments into areas that still resonated in Riven's body with offensive stamina discharged by Rusof—but neither man seemed to care.

Riven was just happy that he had a suitable sparring partner who knew what the fuck he was doing. "I'm looking forward to sparring again. Hopefully next time we can actually go over what I'm doing wrong and what I can improve rather than just getting an ass whooping."

"That can be arranged! And to be fair, you were at a disadvantage. If you'd used magic, you'd no doubt have won," the captain said with a grin, his smile faltering when he noted the scowl on Kathrine's face. "Eh . . . I said I'm sorry, Princess. I know I went a little overboard."

"That's an understatement," Kathrine said while continuing to glare, holding a cup of her own tea across from them and shaking her head. "If you'd accidentally killed him . . ."

"He's a pureblood!" Captain Rusof exclaimed with a wave of his hand. "He's more than capable of taking a beating like that! And you've got to admit—" The captain turned to look Riven in the eye. "That kind of training is far more useful AND far more entertaining than me just holding your hand along the way while coddling you."

"Agreed," Riven said flatly, putting the tea down and scooting over to make way for Athela when the demoness sat down on the couch next to him. His arm crossed her shoulders and he smiled as she let herself sink in—but a brief pang of grief overcame him as his thoughts turned to Fay.

He shook his head, trying to rid himself of those thoughts. He couldn't dwell on it, but he wondered where she'd gone.

Athela noticed his frown and frowned in turn, sitting up straighter and putting a hand on his. "You okay?"

He nodded quickly, shaking himself out of it with an apologetic smile. "Yes! Yes . . . I'm fine. Sorry."

She frowned deeper, but didn't push the subject and just gripped his hand tighter. "All right. If you want to talk, I'm here for you."

There was a silence after that as the three vampires and one demoness continued to stare out at the mixed races milling around the trade district. It was absolutely booming, especially now that the capital of Dawn had been half ransacked. Crafters, laborers, and various supplies from the Elysium altar were in extreme demand to get the rebuild of Mandon going—and elvish slaves were being rounded up not far outside the trade district to be freed, heading for a mass send-off into the now vassalized kingdom of Tereen.

Riven took another sip of his tea, belched, and stood up, pulling Athela up with him. "All right, it's been fun, but now I have other things to attend to."

"Oh? I'd hoped you'd stay longer," Kathrine said with a frown, but nodded her acknowledgment, standing, too. "Perhaps you and Athela could both visit me in my quarters some time. I think I'd like that very much."

Athela raised an eyebrow, as did Captain Rusof.

"I'll leave that up to Athela," Riven replied with a smile.

His demonic familiar turned to him curiously. "Where are we headed?"

Riven opened his mouth to reply, then closed it and mentally went over his checklist.

He needed to use the Dao treasure related to Blood that he and Athela would share, as it required a bonded partner. The cube from Daskus could wait, but that needed to be done eventually. One week from now he'd need to go back to see his extended family on Luteski. He still needed to acquire a new minion . . .

That last thought made him recoil inwardly. No, it wasn't just one anymore. It was two. Fay had left . . .

He bit the inside of his cheek to stop that train of thought.

The king of Dawn had originally wanted to meet with him in private concerning political matters, but he'd managed to pawn that off on Allie. His sister wanted to go over lessons concerning the Death subpillar before Chalgathi's next trial . . .

And then there was the matter of the dwarves.

He did some mental rearranging of his priorities and nodded slowly. "I believe it's time to get another minion. Then we go see the dwarves."

"Just one?" Athela asked hesitantly, searching his face as it underwent mixed emotions.

"Yes," he eventually said with a nod. "Just one."

"But Fay—"

"I know," Riven said, cutting her off. He met Athela's eyes. "It still hurts. Give me time, okay?"

Athela looked like she wanted to say more, but she nodded slowly and her shoulders slumped. "Okay."

"Thank you. After that, we go to the dwarves—and to see the vampires who have sent diplomats to await me in Deepnest. Let's collect Azmoth from the compound and leave before we're roped into any more political shenanigans."

With that, Riven waved to the vampiric lesser princess and riftwalked away—with Athela quickly following suit.

Kathrine and the captain merely smiled victoriously to one another and went back to sipping their tea while quietly contemplating Riven's recent change of heart. It was nice to finally see him embracing the empire, as all of their lives would no doubt benefit from their success in the future.

It was nightfall, and Riven, along with his two remaining minions, sat in the same exact spot where they'd been spit out of Negrada into this world all those months ago. The broken-down gas station was nearby, and the mountainside was quiet tonight with an abnormally clear sky, considering most of the time these haunted woods were overtaken with dark clouds or mist.

Azmoth continued to meditate on the Infernal Daos, which was a pretty common hobby for the demon at this point, and Riven sipped on some blood he'd bottled for traveling purposes while watching his demonic girlfriend stretch in front of him.

Girlfriend?

Was that what Athela was now?

He glanced her way, a little bit afraid to ask, but smirked to himself and shook his head. He didn't need a title on it, not yet, and was sure he'd get there eventually.

Pulling up his screens and coming to the number of contracts available, he frowned.

[46,402,441 Demonic Contracts Available]

"Jesus."

Riven scratched the back of his head, then gave Athela a sheepish smile. "Mind sorting through these for me?"

He pushed the notification over, and she snorted a laugh, sitting down next to him. Scooching over to where he sat against a dead tree, sighing, and laying her head in his lap while crossing her long athletic legs into a more comfortable position, she nodded. "Sure thing, twerp!"

"Hey! You can't call me a twerp anymore. That's hurtful—I'm your lover now." He scratched his head, thinking about it for a moment. "That's really weird to say—OW!"

"It's not weird. Shut up about it." She jabbed him in the stomach with a glare, then giggled and took the screen away from him to start minimizing the number. "All right, we can sort them by level first, that'll cut out the majority, and . . . We're down to 605,932 demons who are at your max level of 130."

"Can't contract anyone over my level, right?"

"Correct." She nodded, checking off boxes available to her as she scrolled through the list. "Let's see . . . Maybe one of my clan mates is in here. That'd be neat. And . . . no, there isn't. Let's check this tab, and that tab to narrow it down . . . All right, this may take a bit. Give me an hour or two and we'll see what can be done."

Those two hours quickly passed in silence while she went over the options. Athela eventually chose what she considered to be the best five. She unselected the others, at least for now, and displayed them to Riven with a smile. "These are the ones I'd choose, but keep in mind their personalities and how they get along with us are going to be a big deal. If none of these work out, we'll start over with the next best five. That okay?"

"Sounds good to me." Riven smiled, ignoring an undead warg that snarled their way from the tree line, and took the screen from her—shifting it in the air to hover in front of his face as he began to read the descriptions. With Fay gone he had two slots to fill, 454 total Willpower and 198 free Willpower points to use for those two contracts.

But he still held out hope that she'd come back. He was hesitant to fill that last slot just yet, so he'd settle for just one at the moment.

He tried not to frown at the thought of Fay, but failed yet again and had to take in a deep breath as he moved on.

"Athela? Why do these demons have names in front of their species?"

Athela glanced up to him with a smirk, then reached out to hold his hand—interlocking her slender fingers in his. "That's because the demons I chose were all categorized as elite monsters by the system, with the golden flame lettering when identified. Like Negrada's miniboss that we killed. And they're often unique variations of more basic demonic breeds. Have you tried identifying me lately?"

Riven raised an eyebrow, shook his head, then did so. Immediately her name appeared, but to his surprise her letters were outlined in flames just like the satyr warlord's had been back in Negrada's hellscape. The only difference was that the satyr warlord had been listed as ELITE, and the flames were gold. Here though . . . Here, Athela's name was outlined in red flames.

The title of LEGENDARY, and PANU WORLD BOSS, were also plastered onto the end of her title.

[Athela, Level 127 Archdemon: Unique, three forms, Cute Wittle Blood Weaver/Gluttonous Arshakai/Gluttonous Fae Drider. LEGENDARY. PANU WORLD BOSS.]

He raised an eyebrow and failed to speak for a time. "Question. Why does it say 'wittle' in the name? Very lame. Was that your doing somehow?"

Athela snickered and shook her head. "That's what you're going to ask me? Come on! Act impressed! No, I had nothing to do with it. That's Elysium being ridiculous. Don't ask me why. Ask me about the red flames and titles!"

"All right. Why is your name outlined in red flames with the 'legendary' and 'world boss' titles?"

She cackled and flipped over to stare at him with a devious grin. "After the battle in Mandon, the system officially designated me . . . and you . . . as world boss creatures for the invaders to kill."

Riven blinked. "Huh?"

"Identify yourself!"

Riven's puzzled expression turned into a small grin, as he did as she asked.

[Riven Thane, Level 130 Warlock Devastator, Harbinger of Gluttony, Pure-blooded Vampire, Lost Prince of the Blood Moon Requiem. LEGENDARY. PANU WORLD BOSS.]

Just like Athela's name, his own identification information was also outlined in red flames. He was a bit surprised that the system had outwardly labeled him as a harbinger of Gluttony and as a lost prince of the requiem, but that was less surprising than the system considering him a legendary creature and a Panu world boss.

"Why wasn't I notified of this earlier?" Riven asked, glancing over at Azmoth to get a look at his other minion's identification information. Unlike Athela and himself, Azmoth didn't have the titles they did. But his name did now glow in gold flame lettering, and he was labeled ELITE just like the satyr warlord dungeon miniboss had been back in the hellscapes.

That was also new.

[Azmoth, Level 95 Infernal Crusader Initiate, Hellscape Brutalisk. ELITE.]

He looked up again, bewildered. "Athela, why wasn't I notified of this?"

She grinned. "You were notified, I'm sure of it. But with all the drama going on, with the attack on the city, the leveling notifications, the battle notifications, the Harbingers of Gluttony coming to take my shard, the dispute between Fay and me . . . I can see why you didn't notice. You probably just dismissed the notification by accident and never looked. I figured that was the case. I've been waiting for you to say something."

Riven stared, then slowly clicked his tongue. "That's . . . kinda neat, actually. Not sure how to feel about this. What makes us legendary or world boss quality by system standards, exactly?"

"Titles are gained by the feats you accomplish for your level and grade. I may have discussed this once a long time ago with you, but it also incorporates things like your species, too," Athela said simply with a smile. "You can be very strong and not gain such titles, but proving yourself in battle on the scale that you have multiple times now . . . it doesn't surprise me too much. The legendary and elite titles will give whoever kills you a massive XP boost as well as a system reward, similar to how we got all that gold and a prize from Negrada in his dungeon. Legendary titles will give far more, though. As for the Panu world boss title, that's more for the invaders and other creatures who are part of the world quests—ones pitted against the natives. The system sees both of us as major obstacles to world domination and devastation, so it will give any invader or any of the opposition in other world quests a very large boon if they slay one of us."

"But does it do anything for us otherwise?"

"Other than bragging rights when people try to identify us? Nope."

Riven snorted in amusement and shook his head. "Of course not. Whatever, I'm gonna take a look at this list. Should be interesting."

"That I agree with."

Kissing her on the forehead, he turned his attention back to the screen in front of him.

[46,402,441 Demonic Contracts Available. You have manually minimized your list to five. These five demons have been following your progress and are interested in obtaining you as a partner. Click on each for further details concerning the potential minion and their contracts.

- **Chavi, Devil, Unholy/Infernal/Chaos, Level 119. ELITE—A scion of the burning legions and the youngest son of a hellscape warlord, Chavi is a terror to behold. This young devil is wrath incarnate** and has little time to talk in favor of berserking across entire battlefields by himself to slay his enemies by the thousands. Easy to anger, but respects the way of the warrior and those who have struggled to surpass their limits. Despises weaklings and those who have not known hardship. [181 Willpower Requirement]

- Rheufa Chak Tal, Unique: Thousand-Eyes Beholder, Unholy/Shadow, Level 126. ELITE—One of the most calculating and cunning demons of his generation across the multiverse, Rheufa Chak Tal started his rise to power by burning away entire cities in the hellscapes when a certain incubus tricked him into giving up an item of power. Since then, Rheufa Chak Tal has waged wars against entire clans of enemy demons, laying traps and springing ambushes to blindside his enemies with long-range bombardments from numerous angles. Since his recent evolution into a greater demon, his power has seen drastic upgrades and he has become an overwhelming force to deal with as he plunders enemy holds for wealth. He is known as an ambush predator and a loner. [136 Willpower Requirement]

- Fimrindle, Unique: the Iron Scarecrow, Unholy/Blood/Death/Machine, Level 120. ELITE—This truly odd and misunderstood demon created from metal was actually spawned as part of an experiment by black magic users who tried merging a machine, an undead, and a demon. The experiment was a success, but the creators didn't survive the ordeal. After destroying multiple cities, the creature was banished and sequestered into a soul stone laid in a crypt at the bottom of an ocean trench. There he remains, waiting for the right summoner to take him from his wretched prison so that he can once again experience life. He doesn't talk much, and he's a bit creepy even by Elysium's standards, but he certainly knows how to wield a scythe. [159 Willpower Requirement]

- Zrogmanthon, Abyss-Lord, Unholy/Shadow/Depravity, Level 127. ELITE—Zrogmanthon is a very prideful demon who often spends more time gloating about his victories than actually fighting. This is in part because he enjoys boasting and in part because he kills his enemies incredibly fast. His build is focused on tearing reality itself to create critical strikes and gut his opponents before they know what hit them, or at least they wouldn't know what hit them if he didn't tell them about what was going to happen before it happens. Regardless, they still die. As an ethereal creature of doom, this demon is very hard to kill with physical attacks and would be sneaky if he didn't go out of his way to boast so much. [160 Willpower Requirement]

- **Yattazi, Unique: the Devouring Serpent, Unholy/Infernal/Chaos, Level 130. ELITE—Once a tiny snake, this creature devoured the heart of a fallen Unholy god purely by happenstance. Since then, Yattazi has become something of a menace to anything living. She had forgone her draconic evolutions in favor of becoming a great basilisk and from there became something much more when she evolved into a demon. She lives in the lava pools of a volcano, coming out from hibernation to feed and in turn create genocidal waves in surrounding habitats. Yattazi isn't very smart but makes up for it by the sheer devastation she can cause. This creature is lonely, is wanting to find a companion to share in her gluttonous sprees, and is on a quest to find bigger and stronger things to eat. [122 Willpower Requirement]]**

His brows furrowed, Riven glanced down to his status page again, and realized there was a problem concerning any future acquisitions of the fourth demonic minion slot. It wasn't a problem now, but it might be later if Fay never came back. He should have guessed this would be the case because Athela now required 190 Willpower to hold her contract, and if these demons were comparable to her . . .

He only had 454 total Willpower and 198 free Willpower points to use.

Riven would only have enough points to choose one of these creatures to bond with, despite having two open slots.

"Damn." He rubbed his chin in thought. "These descriptions are a lot more intense than they were previously . . . It's like they're telling me their life stories. Very weird, but I like the change."

"That's going to be more and more common the more you grow," Athela stated with a yawn. "Previously, the demons you could pick from were all so low level, including myself back then, that we hadn't had any accomplishments. But as we get older and have more experiences, the system adds those to the descriptions."

He nodded, skimming through the text one by one, deep in thought—when his soul began to shudder. Looking down at his chest, he began to see a dark orb forming in front of his body. He . . . would have been concerned, but Riven could tell just by looking at it that it was actually an extension of his soul aperture taking physical form.

"That's weird," Riven said, nudging Athela, who looked up and began to frown. "Don't worry, it's a piece of me. I can tell it's not dangerous, but . . . do you have any idea what's happening?"

She slowly began to shake her head, and even Azmoth grunted in curiosity while beginning to ready himself just in case.

"That you?" Azmoth asked just for one more confirmation as the dark orb continued to expand.

Riven hesitantly nodded. "Yeah . . . don't attack it. That's a piece of my soul, I think. If you were to damage it, I may—"

His words cut off, and yet another notification appeared as his hand tightened around Athela's—adding on to the ridiculousness he'd already experienced over the past day.

[Harbinger of Gluttony, Sin Class, Secondary Class, has finally finished its construction. Harbinger Soul Clone is now finished. +2 Sturdiness, +9 free points per level will now be distributed with each level-up.]
- **Harbinger of Gluttony (Sin Class Title)—the Harbinger of Gluttony is the most basic sin class specific to the Original Sin of Gluttony and creates a superimposed wraith-like soul clone, a symbiote created from sin inside your body, allowing it to strike out at close distances against any nearby enemy. +2 Sturdiness, +9 free points per level.**

His body flickered with dark light, and it felt like a cold blanket had swept over his skin. Lifting one hand, he saw a dark afterimage of his arm trailing behind his movement before it superimposed itself over his current position. His legs were the same, almost flickering somewhat, before it all settled down and went away.

He didn't feel much different otherwise, and he shot both Athela and Azmoth a look. "Uh . . . Any input as to what this 'soul clone' is, exactly?"

CHAPTER 38

A child of the Scythe, and a botched creation cursed by madmen. That was who and what Fimrindle truly was.

The stick-thin metal scarecrow hung on a cross of his own making. He remained absolutely still, just as he had done for the past many millennia—not moving a single millimeter while contemplating the mysteries of life. In his left hand, an unlit steel lantern hung loosely at his side. In his right hand, he held a simple scythe—showing no markings or any semblance of just how powerful the weapon was. A hinged metal jaw hung slightly open in a creepy smile, exposing an abyssal hole into the back of the scarecrow's throat—and two *X*'s carved into the otherwise featureless face of the scarecrow signified its eyes.

Fimrindle watched in silence, peering through the void and into other nether realms where his potential contractor was speaking to a winged devil much bigger than he was. The soul clone, which Riven still did not know the true nature of, was fascinating beyond anything Fimrindle had seen in quite some time. He only hoped he got the opportunity to examine it in more thorough detail, and now that Riven had begun interviewing candidates for his demonic contract slot—Fimrindle's interest had hit a peak.

Meanwhile, the devil Chavi was boasting of his conquests with wings spread out and aflame. It caused the skies around him to crash with false power.

Fimrindle wondered why the boastful creature was so infatuated with war. What was so great about killing things? Fimrindle had learned the hard way that it wasn't fun and games like he'd been led to believe in the beginning, and it came rather easy. Why did Chavi think it a glorious pursuit? Fimrindle didn't understand. The way the titanic red ape with wings wielded that silly axe around was more for show than anything else, but then again—Fimrindle couldn't necessarily judge the demon. He knew very little about social norms and cues, and this in turn was perhaps the largest reason why he'd been banished to this soul stone. He'd thought he'd been playing a game when he'd murdered all those people. Fimrindle was akin to a small child in that aspect, a soul being ripped apart and formed anew so many times that he had a hard time grasping any of his previous memories over past lives.

The one thing he did remember in vivid detail was the aura of the great spirit that haunted his dreams. The spirit of the Scythe was . . . observant, as was Fimrindle. They watched each other in an endless cycle of silence while the worlds around them passed Fimrindle by.

The iron scarecrow continued to wait patiently. Ever patiently. He did not move, locked away in a cube of energy. He did not rust, he did not rot, he merely waited—having been here an eternity already, waiting for the day that someone would meet the qualifications he desired. For Fimrindle was not driven to act for his freedom unless certain qualifications were met, but he was very patient, and unless he found what he was looking for—why bother leaving this place? It would otherwise only mean a repeat of what'd happened the first few times in the world above that'd so long ago forgotten about his existence outside of legend.

He did not blame his world of origin, though. He just didn't understand. He wished he did, and perhaps Riven would be the one to teach him just what he'd done wrong. Perhaps Riven could be the one to provide Fimrindle insight into the thing he desired most.

But his thoughts were interrupted by the presence of another, and to Fimrindle's mounting curiosity, Zrogmanthon, the abyss-lord, fellow demon of Riven's final five, had somehow entered his soul-stone prison from across the cosmos.

The creature was akin to an enormous black mist, but shifting claws and a grinning mouth full of teeth could be seen like static through a fog when the abyss-lord entered Fimrindle's tiny home. It circled the scarecrow made of metal, letting out a low chuckle while Riven continued to speak to Chavi the devil in another nether realm.

"Ah . . . little scarecrow . . . You aren't in a true nether realm. You remain here instead . . . a fatal mistake when combined with the fact that you are competing with someone as great as me!" Zrogmanthon the abyss-lord hissed, causing the soul stone to shudder and crack as his black eyes greedily gazed upon Fimrindle's stone-still body. "Trapped in a weak prison such as this? How have you not left yet? A demon like me would have broken out of such a place eons ago . . . but you, you're still here. How . . . exciting! To think that I'd be able to travel through ripples in the void to take care of the competition!"

The prideful Zrogmanthon cackled and threateningly ripped a hole in space, exiting from a black hole to squeeze into Fimrindle's home. Enormous black claws, six arms, a body made of shadow, and a shrouded, almost featureless face came forward—smiling at the much smaller Fimrindle and rearing to his full height. "How is it, knowing that someone so lowly as you will be devoured by one as great as me? Have you ever experienced pain before, little scarecrow? Because pain you will have . . . and your dying screams will be the foundation of my growth! I will display your body before my new master and show him that I am the greatest of the five he has chosen to consider!"

Zrogmanthon let the words echo through the cube, his very presence causing the soul stone to break apart rapidly around them—shadow mana radiating across his body and passing over the much smaller, human-size scarecrow beneath him. "Do you have any words for me, abomination?"

Fimrindle had remained motionless this entire time. He remained hung on a cross, scythe in one hand and unlit lantern in the other, staring into nothingness as his mechanical jaw sagged partway open.

Zrogmanthon frowned, tsking in irritation after five or so minutes of hovering over the other demon with his intimidating aura billowing out. Fimrindle seemed to be unaffected by the display entirely despite the soul-stone cage quickly deteriorating. "I see you've been driven into speechlessness by my prowess . . . Understandable. If you cannot escape a place such as this and cannot form your own nether realm despite what you are, you deserve to be shocked into silence."

The abyss-lord raised one clawed hand, and space itself tore open as his hand shimmered in the darkness. "You are by far the weakest of us five, and I am doing you a favor by not allowing you to embarrass yourself. Be grateful, fledgling, for your path will act as fertilizer to my own."

Still the scarecrow didn't move, but a ping of power caused Zrogmanthon's head to abruptly shift right when the image of some ill-defined entity tore through reality beside him.

Zrogmanthon, being an abyss-lord and a creature who could control spatial powers, was shocked. He didn't know what that was, but something immensely powerful had just—

Zrogmanthon turned his head right when he sensed another blip of power near the scarecrow and, to his shock, found the scarecrow was gone. So was the cross he'd been hung on. How had Zrogmanthon, as great as he was, not sensed something like the disappearance of his—

Zrogmanthon died.

The abyss-lord didn't even have time to scream, and his body shimmered and faded away while the soul-stone prison began to reconstruct itself. Fimrindle was back in his spot in the middle of the cube room, hanging motionless on a cross with his scythe in his right hand, his jaw slightly unhinged and his lantern in his left. Though this time, a small light in his lantern blinked repeatedly until it finally winked out—leaving the room in the same state it'd been in only moments ago before Zrogmanthon's interruption.

Going back to contemplating and meditating on the meaning of life while simultaneously observing Riven's proceedings, Fimrindle waited for the fated moment that he would meet this Riven Thane character, for better or for worse.

Yattazi stirred, becoming restless as she felt a new entity enter her nether realm. It'd been a long time since something had been allowed in, and the disturbance was . . . pleasing.

Lonely and hopeful, the gigantic serpent began to worm its way out of the volcano it'd constructed its nether realm around—a very similar one to the real version she was hibernating in every once in a while when out of the nether.

Gills along the serpent's head flared, and molten eyes opened. Rising up toward the heavens, Yattazi broke out of the lava pit to display her majestic figure to the one who would potentially claim her as a friend.

Spines protruded from her back; dark-gray scales even harder than most dragons' covered her large body like armor. Frilled ears flared out to either side of her head, and lava poured down off her body as her head began to lower to get a better look at the summoner.

The man was small, many dozens of times smaller than she was, but she did not mind. She was just happy to have someone to converse with, and she gave an excited hiss while boulders and islands in the lava pool were washed away amid the rising of her glorious figure. The snake put her fangs on full display in an effort to show her potential master just how amazing she was, the teeth crackling with Chaos energy in flickers of deep gray—and a molten inner core flared to life with orange and red hues inside the back of her throat.

"Welcome, vampire, to my lair . . ." Yattazi hissed rather happily, her body trailing out to rise and fall amid roiling waves of magma behind her as she hovered over the tiny figure below. "I have been expecting you, fellow follower of the Unholy path. We have much in common, you and I . . . and I am hoping that you may join me in my quest to feed."

The vampire curiously shifted his head from side to side. His other two minions just stared up at her. "Yattazi, right?" the vampire asked.

"That isss what the great system calls me . . ." Yattazi hissed excitedly. "No need to tell me yours . . . Yattazi already knowsss it, Riven Thane of the Blood Moon Requiem. Yattazi hasss many questions, and many answers, to share with you on your road to power, and I hope it is Yattazi that you choossse for your new minion so that we may one day become friendsss."

Riven stood at the edge of the volcano's basin, looking up at a creature that towered over him, an absolutely majestic yet simultaneously intimidating figure. Dark-gray scales, enormous spines over the top of its head, magma-infused eyes, and a maw that could swallow a small car in a single gulp. In the magma pools behind the creature, its long body splashed around and writhed like a sea serpent for over forty yards—and the flaring, finlike ears coming out either side of its skull only added to that impression.

Despite all this, he could feel only a fraction of the heat that he'd have expected. Nether realms, especially individual ones that weren't shared between demons, were rather tricky in nature and didn't have all the properties that a normal realm would have. Even so, it was quite something.

"Nice to make your acquaintance, Yattazi," Riven said with a smile and a small bow. "I would very much like that. Becoming friends with my contracted demons is far preferable to having servants, as both Athela and Azmoth can attest to."

Azmoth grunted his acknowledgment, and Athela slyly smiled while shifting forms into her Blood Weaver body—then hopping up into his arms to let the vampire cradle her.

Yattazi hissed, a serpentine tongue flicking out between her lips as her mouth closed and her head came forward to more closely evaluate the spider in Riven's arms. "Yattazi knowsssss . . . Yattazi sssssees. It is why I have attempted to contract with you, as I am very impressed with not only your power, but your relationships concerning your chargesssss. However, that is not all I desire, as I also wish to explore the multiverse and find new foodsssss to consume. I am ever hungry."

Riven paused, frowned, and continued to stroke Athela's little spider head as she gave the snake a curious look. "For someone as big as you, how do you keep yourself fed? If you really kill that often, would you not be a far higher level?"

The great serpent seemed to frown. "There are many pathways to growth aside from devouring otherssssss. I have devoured many other creaturesssss, it is true, but many of them were far weaker than I—and I have alsssso grown in size through means of meditation over millennia while I wait for my world to repopulate from the last great feeding. Insight into the Dao is one of many pathways to growth."

"Oh. Got it. Just curious." Riven shrugged. "I likely do have a lot of people for you to eat if you contract with me. Thousands, probably."

Yattazi's molten eyes gleamed brightly, and the frills along her head immediately flared wide. "Really?! What manner of creaturessss are we ssspeaking of?!"

"All kinds."

"Indulge me!"

Riven thought about it a moment. "Well, there are numerous invaders headed our way on the integration of our world. We have to hunt down a bunch of other vampires, there are no doubt human invaders, some Azag insectoids if you know what they are. There are a bunch of cultists I need to kill, too, concerning a certain world quest."

"Anything large?"

"How large we talkin' here? There's a quest for snow giants, and as long as they're not actually made of snow, they might be what you're looking for. They might even be larger than you."

The snake nodded eagerly with a loud hiss that cracked the air, hungrily dripping venom from exposed fangs at the thought. It was obvious this monster was rather gluttonous in its own right; perhaps it'd jell nicely with his sin shards.

Athela held up a leg. "But wait! Are you really always that big? It's going to be a nightmare walking around with you that size! Can't you reduce your power output and—"

Athela's words were cut off after the large serpent blinked, and in a flash the enormous creature's bulk warped. Floods of magma roiled and tore into the sky while the creature's deep-gray scales morphed. The large body began to shrink, condensing more and more while simultaneously removing some of its inborn power that it began storing in a growing black-orange orb swirling amid the bubbling waves of lava.

Seconds later the titanic snake had gone from half the length of a football field and able to swallow a small vehicle to something more manageable.

Athela curiously peeked out over the edge of Riven's arm while she and the others all stared down at the now-tiny creature, and her spider leg scratched at the top of her head in confusion and amusement. "Well, I didn't mean become a slug."

"I am no mere slug! I am Yattazi, devourer of all that movessss!!! My body and energy are merely contained!" the tiny creature called back, hissing in annoyance and slapping the ground impatiently. "Redact your insssult, tiny spider!"

Athela flatly looked down at the other demon. "You a slug."

"It issss not so!!!"

"An uggggggly lil slug. You look like one of those really nasty dumps I took the other day—"

"YOU ARE MERELY JEALOUSSSSS OF MY GLORIOUS FIGURE!!" The spines on the small, pudgy snake protruded out farther in an attempt of intimidation that just . . . didn't work, concerning this form.

Riven began to grin in amusement as Athela teased the once-enormous monster beneath him. Yattazi had transformed into a three-foot version of her previous self.

It still looked damn vicious, though. Riven didn't know where Athela was getting this slug thing from. If he didn't know better, he'd guess she was just antagonizing Yattazi for the sake of antagonizing her. The other demon was certainly becoming rather enraged by Athela's taunting, though.

"I AM MAGNIFICENT!" Yattazi hissed with another smack of its tail.

Athela shook her head in mock disgust. "Slug girl. That's what I'm gonna call you if my glorious master agrees to your contract. Fear not—despite your slimy complexion, he has been known to be a charitable man, so perhaps he'd take pity on you and agree to terms."

Yattazi glared molten daggers Athela's way, then she spit a glob of what Riven could only call gunk at the spider—smacking her in the face. "BEGONE!"

"AAAAAAAAAAAAAAAHHHHHHHHHHHHH!!!!" Athela wailed and writhed in Riven's arms, dramatically wriggling her legs around.

Riven sighed. "Athela, we can barely feel anything physical here. Stop being such a drama queen."

Azmoth agreed with a sage nod. "Yes, yes. Agreed."

The spider in his arms immediately stopped wailing and glared up at him, wiping away the snake glob and flinging it to the nether realm's floor. "Fine! Next time you get smacked in the face with goop, I'm just going to roll my eyes at you, too! HUMPH!"

With that, Athela hopped out of his arms and began to strut over to Azmoth before climbing up his leg and depositing herself on the larger demon's shoulder—giving both men a sideways glare before turning her nose up and clicking her mandibles.

Riven raised an eyebrow. "Why'd you hop perches? You do realize that Azmoth agreed with—"

"QUIET, PLEBEIAN!" Athela pointed a quivering leg his way. "DO NOT DARE INCUR MY WRATH!"

Riven opened his mouth to reply, but snorted and kept his smile hidden from his minion-turned-lover while folding his arms and facing the snake again. He'd not expected to see a shrinking ability, and if he had known Yattazi would have a shrinking ability, he wouldn't have expected something like this. "You don't look like a slug, Yattazi, you just look . . . small. Still intimidating, though."

"THAT'S CHEATING, RIVEN!" Athela squealed from Azmoth's shoulder with a glare. "You're not allowed to tell other girls they're intimidating!"

"She's a vicious demon snake."

"AND I STARTED OFF AS A CUTE LITTLE SPIDER. LOOK HOW I TURNED OUT!"

"Oh, for crying out loud . . ." Riven rolled his eyes—flashbacks of how he and Athela used to be in Negrada coming swiftly to his mind with a fond warmth. He had to fully turn his back on the glaring arachnid—interposing himself between her and the still angrily hissing snake to get Yattazi's attention again. "But let's talk more about you. What do you like to do for fun?"

The snake stopped hissing, blinked, and smiled. "For fun?"

"That's right. Aside from eating things. You want a friend, yeah?" Riven raised an eyebrow.

This truly seemed to stump the demonic creature, and it thought for a good while before eventually answering with another hiss. "All I have ever known is the need to feed and consume, the urge to grow. But . . . if I must choose something else, I would sssay I enjoy cooking."

"Cooking?!" Athela butted in, hopping off Azmoth's shoulder and scurrying over to the slightly larger creature. She crossed her front legs and stared suspiciously. "How would a snake like you even cook?!"

"I don't know what you're talking about. I am very good at cooking and have even acquired a sssssssspecialized crafting category for it. Cooking level is at 86."

"WHAT?!" Athela barked out in shock. "YOU DON'T EVEN HAVE HANDS!"

Riven turned to Azmoth. "Specialized crafting category?"

Azmoth grunted again, four armored arms still folded over his chest. "They level independently of combat level. If stuck with totems, you might acquire one yourself. It take long time, hard work, but rewarding. That all know."

CHAPTER 39

The rest of the time spent with Yattazi was very refreshing—though she did end up reverting back to her normal size after Athela kept pestering her about how her smaller form looked. Despite what and who she was, Yattazi had a very warm personality. She was easy to get along with and eager to please.

When discussing combat power, it appeared that she was heavily focused on close combat and body enhancements. Most of her abilities and insights were focused on making her physical body more powerful both on offense and defense. There were exceptions to this, including a Chaos Cannon martial art that created a blast of raw Chaos energy, a petrifying flash-glare ability that often silenced enemies if they didn't turn to stone, a constricting martial art that utilized her long body, a martial art that used her fangs to inject a potent venom, and a Magma Chamber martial art that was essentially a zoning ability that trapped enemies in place within a designated space that began to fill with magma. She had a variant of the Hell's Armor that Azmoth used, a spell similar to but better than Riven's own Blessing of the Crow, and a handful of different passive buffs that increased resistances against all types of damage.

After parting ways and telling her that at the very least she was under heavy consideration, Riven left and moved on to the iron scarecrow, Fimrindle. Selecting him next, he found himself being pulled out of Yattazi's realm, only to receive a notification.

[Fimrindle has failed to create his own nether realm. Do you wish to use your already acquired demons for use of their nether realms instead?]

He glanced at Athela, then Azmoth. "That's weird. Either of you want to give up your home for a bit?"

"OOOH! OOOH, PICK ME!" Athela exclaimed excitedly, shifting back into her small spider form and waggling her arms in the air. "PLEASE, please, please! I've been wanting to show you my nether realm for a while now!"

"Don't care," Azmoth said simply.

Riven gave an amused chuckle, but nodded to Athela and motioned for her to get on with it—selecting *yes* and then mentally checking into Athela's realm when a strange tug yanked at the borders of his mind.

Abruptly the world around him spun, and Riven felt himself in a . . .

In a temple?

Towering statues of black spiders were on either side, a long hallway to a throne where a woman who looked very similar to Athela, yet older, sat, and pillars of stone held up the ceiling high above them with only trace amounts of barely visible light leaking in through window slits at the very top.

Athela was nowhere to be found—until she suddenly popped into existence and squealed in excitement. Jumping up into Riven's arms and simultaneously morphing into her more humanoid form, she tugged at his hands and motioned toward the throne. "Riven! You HAVE to meet my mom! She's been waiting all this time and I'm SO EXCITED to show you to her!"

In a flash of light, another figure soon joined them. It was a scarecrow, for all intents and purposes, wielding a rather simple scythe in his right hand and an unlit metal lantern in his left. The scarecrow was posted upon a metal cross, and was stick thin, with a metal jaw that lay slack and almost unhinged with sharp teeth smiling his way. The eyes were only *X*'s carved into the otherwise almost featureless metal of the face, and the way it stared at him was . . . rather creepy.

"We'll get to you soon, Fimrindle. Just wait a moment!" Athela piped up, still yanking Riven forward step by step while giddily motioning over to her mother. "MOM, I'M HOME! AND I'VE BROUGHT THE HUNK!"

The old woman on the throne stared with a small smile creeping at the corners of her mouth, but remained seated as Athela pulled Riven her way. She glanced at the scarecrow, frowned, and motioned toward the newly arrived demon. "Honey . . . perhaps you should talk to the scarecrow first? Riven and I can meet afterward. I don't think it is wise to have such a creature enter your nether realm like this only to be made to wait . . . because without me also being here, it would be rather dangerous for you to let him into your safe space. That creature is deserving of respect, and you should show him as much."

Riven's eyes shifted around the rather dark and Unholy temple display, taking in the statues of spiders, driders, and other various creatures of arachnid origin. Numerous sets of red eyes peeked out from the dark corners that even Riven's sight could not penetrate, and shifting figures in the shadows adjusted their positions on the outskirts.

"You've brought a lot of the family!" Athela said enthusiastically, letting go of Riven's arm and running across the room—past Fimrindle—to throw her arms around her mother. "I thought it was only going to be you!"

Riven glanced between this new woman, the figures in the dark, and the demon scarecrow who continued to remain on his cross, unmoving. Apologetically holding up one hand Fimrindle's way, Riven began to walk over to where Athela and her mom were standing side by side—Athela having a wide, giddy grin on her face while bobbing up and down on her toes.

Athela's mother was strangely beautiful in a very sinister way, very close to how Athela looked—only slightly more menacing in her humanoid form. She had three pairs of mandibles coming out of the sides of her throat along a slit that likely opened up into an additional mouth, had smaller red markings across her otherwise pitch-black and patchy white skin, and had four red eyes instead of two. Otherwise, the athletic outline and the six bladelike arachnoid legs sticking out of her back were the same.

Sensing Riven's nervousness, Athela's mother grinned—and she stepped forward with an extended hand. "No need to be wary. After seeing the lengths to which you'd go in order to save my daughter, I am most pleased to make your acquaintance. It meant a lot to me, and the entire clan, that you seem to continually put her above everything else—and we fully support the relationship you two have cultivated together. My name is Ytrikel'Vorindi, although you can just call me Vorindi."

Riven reached out and took her hand, and to his surprise he was actually able to feel it. The tangible nature of this nether realm was somewhat different than others had been, but he wasn't sure why. "It's incredibly nice to meet you, Vorindi. I just was somewhat blindsided! Athela would occasionally talk about you before, and I guess I wanted to make a good impression in case I ever met you."

Athela giggled, and her mother smiled widely.

"No need to worry about that. As I said, you have done more than enough to make a good impression with the clan." Vorindi let go and put her hands behind her back, inspecting Riven and then turning her gaze to Azmoth. "Fascinating. Your path has truly been fascinating. I must ask, Riven, when it is you intend to marry my daughter? I assume her first-time performance was adequate?"

"MOTHER!" Athela barked, clapping a hand over her face and blushing furiously, which turned her skin a different shade of black. "You CANNOT ask such questions! Riven, DON'T YOU DARE answer that question!"

Meanwhile, Riven's own face had turned a bright red, but he promptly nodded with an embarrassed grin. "More than adequate. Just how much did you see?"

"Most of it," Vorindi replied, unperturbed by the loud groan escaping Athela's lips. "It isn't as if we can just look wherever we want to, but I can see Athela's experiences through her bond and I pay an information broker who utilizes scrying abilities to monitor you."

He sheepishly scratched the back of his neck. "I see. I probably need to get antiscrying formations in place around my manor . . . don't I? As for the marriage question . . ."

He trailed off, settling his gaze on Athela, who continued to hide her face behind her hands. But she did peek out at him a moment later to watch. "Telling that kind of information would ruin the surprise, wouldn't it? As long as she wants to, that is. Not any time soon, but perhaps after everything on Panu settles."

He let on a gentle smile, and Athela's body went rigid—eyes wide.

The response was more than enough for Vorindi, who slowly clapped while nodding in approval. "I'm incredibly happy to hear it and look forward to such a surprise. I will refrain from asking more questions on the matter before my child dies of embarrassment, but I approve. Hopefully when things have settled down, as you say, you and I will have more opportunities to become acquainted. I am sorry for interrupting your contractual obligations, but I and the rest of the family now here couldn't help but set eyes on you in a more personal fashion. Regardless, it would likely be wise to go ahead with the contract. I apologize for needing to stroke my own curiosity—if only briefly."

From out of the shadows, a spider leg waved his way—and Riven chuckled, shoving his hands into his pockets. Athela slowly walked over to him and pushed her head into his chest, wrapping her arms around him and avoiding eye contact while he stroked her hair. "Yes, that's likely wise. Otherwise Mother will keep embarrassing me."

She shot Vorindi a glare.

Vorindi smiled innocently in turn, gave Athela's shoulder a kind squeeze, and then gestured toward the scarecrow. "I believe you have a demon to speak to."

He nodded. "That was very brief, but it's been a pleasure. Let's talk sometime soon after the contract is set. Maybe later this week?"

"Stop hitting on my mom," Athela replied with a teasing laugh, head still buried in Riven's chest. She looked up, red eyes wide, lips quivering, and she planted a firm kiss mouth to mouth while getting up on her toes before letting go. "Let's go talk to the scarecrow."

During this entire exchange, Fimrindle hadn't moved even a single millimeter. The large, carved *X*'s for eyes in his metal face did not blink, did not twitch, did not shift. The metal jaw and teeth remained slightly unhinged, and a black void remained at the back of his throat. The lantern and scythe on either side of the creature were utterly still, too, and the rail-thin body of the metal creature was completely undecorated.

It kind of looked like a child's stick drawing taken real form—with a twist of evil to it.

- **Fimrindle, Unique: the Iron Scarecrow, Unholy/Blood/Death/ Machine, Level 120. ELITE—This truly odd and misunderstood demon created from metal was actually spawned as part of an experiment done by black magic users who tried merging a machine, an undead, and a demon. The experiment was a success, but the creators didn't survive the ordeal. After destroying multiple cities, the creature was banished and sequestered into a soul stone laid in a crypt at the bottom of an ocean trench. There he remains, waiting for the right summoner to take him from his wretched prison so that he can once again experience**

life. He doesn't talk much, and he's a bit creepy even by Elysium's standards, but he certainly knows how to wield a scythe. [159 Willpower Requirement]

Riven came to stand beside the creature, taking in the entire rail-thin body. It didn't necessarily look all that impressive just at a first glance, but the description of the demon was promising.

"Tell me, Fimrindle, why choose me as a prospective master?" Riven eventually asked with a frown. "You don't even have your own nether realm, which begs the question as to why that is. Don't most demons choose a summoner because they want to explore the mortal realms without danger to themselves? Yet you're already there. It doesn't make sense to me."

An odd tugging sensation caused Riven to look away for a moment. When Riven's eyes came back to where the scarecrow had been a moment before, he nearly jumped out of his boots and took an involuntary step back—seeing Fimrindle's metal face only an inch away from his own with a wide smile.

"Jesus!" Riven muttered under his breath, heart pounding in his chest while he glared back at the demon. "Don't do that!"

The scarecrow remained stock-still, continuing not to move a single inch while the X's for eyes stared blankly at the spot where Riven had stood seconds beforehand.

Catching his breath and straightening, Riven stared and then sputtered a laugh. "Are you just going to stand there? Or can you not talk?"

Riven blinked, and during that blink the scarecrow shifted its position—inspecting Athela with crossed arms and the scythe-lantern combo settled on its back.

Riven's brows furrowed. How the hell was this creature moving so . . . jerkily? It was like watching a horror film where the ghost or monster made such abrupt movements that it couldn't be tracked.

Eventually Riven blinked again and found Fimrindle looking his way once more. And when the creature finally spoke, the mouth didn't move. Only a raspy, whispering voice was heard—as if someone from far away was yelling through a tunnel. "I am looking for one to teach me . . . one that understands what it is like to be shunned."

Riven waited for the scarecrow to continue, but Fimrindle didn't utter another word. Riven clicked his tongue in thought, shot the others a glance, only getting shrugs, and sighed. "That isn't much of an explanation."

Again, the scarecrow did not reply.

"Mind expanding on that a bit?" Riven asked with a raised eyebrow.

"You are interesting. As is your sister," Fimrindle replied with that whispery voice. The jaw of the creature didn't move, but the words came out anyway. "I do not fear death like so many others. I do not need contracts to live on, nor do I need a nether realm to hide behind like so many other weaklings choose to do.

Should I ever die, my soul will enter nirvana and be reborn. I am already dead, but I somehow remain alive. I am here standing before you, and I am not. I am an abomination in the eyes of the system, a machine by body and a demon by nature. I try to find my path where there is none. I want you to help me find that path, and in return I can offer you help along the one you choose for yourself. That is all."

Riven's eyes narrowed, and he contemplated the words the demon spoke. Dead but still alive probably meant he was also undead. He didn't know anything about this nirvana the creature talked about. Finding a path could mean a large number of things, but in the end it didn't matter too much as long as Fimrindle obeyed commands and got along with everyone else. "I see. While that's a rather cryptic answer, I'll take it for now. What's your fighting style?"

"Assassin. I am a child of the Scythe, the great spirit that brings home the souls of the dead. Every movement I make must have meaning."

Riven blinked. "You being serious? I haven't heard of this Scythe spirit before."

Fimrindle took a while but eventually acknowledged his words.

"By nature, the Scythe is the embodiment of death. It is in many ways an equivalent to the sins, but was a being spawned by the subpillar of Death as a man-ifestation of the end. Speaking of which—I do suggest that you begin to follow your own path more fervently, vampire, should you lose favor with Gluttony due to your lack of proper choice."

Riven's eyes widened, and he crossed his arms. "Well, this got a lot more interesting. What do you mean by my lack of proper choice? What have I done to lose favor with Gluttony?"

The scarecrow paused, then its whispering voice proceeded to echo back at him after a low and ominous chuckle. "You have pleased it thus far. But you hold on to your humanity. I see your soul, Riven Thane, and I find it lacking. I see potential being squandered. I wish to correct you, for both our sakes. Do not confuse violence and gluttonous wants with evil. You may still cultivate sin and the evil inside you without bowing to the notion of evil itself, though this is a harder path than that of embracing the essence of evil. I tell you now that the more you kill, the more Gluttony is appeased. The more you devour, the more you crave power, the more you grow, and the further you will tread. Gluttony's aspect is similar to and almost a combination of Wrath and Greed. You must eat, you must kill, you must grow, in a never-ending cycle of self-indulgence. You must learn to love these aspects of yourself, give in to your wants, for these are the fundamentals of Gluttony. Bathe in the blood of your enemies and drink them dry. When you do this enough, you will one day find your hunger insatiable—but only then will you find the true power your soul now wields. The true power your soul now buries under flawed personal beliefs on the nature of good versus evil."

A shudder ran down Riven's soul aperture, and he felt his soul vibrate and resonate with the demon's words. The five shards of Gluttony surfaced in that moment, acknowledging the scarecrow's words as true with a tidal wave of over-whelming hunger, before fading again into the background once more. He even gained a very fleeting flash of inspiration, which caused him to almost stumble forward—but the images left as soon as they came.

"Are you okay?" Athela asked worriedly, wiping sweat from Riven's brow as he shuddered involuntarily. She glared back at the scarecrow, not sure what was going on, but calmed down when Riven nodded his head.

"It seems you know a lot more about my sin than I do," Riven stated after some time, the maw along his chest plate rumbling in agreement. Jackal came up to his leg in canine form and rubbed against him, and he bent down to stroke the weapon-turned-pet before straightening again to stare long and hard Fimrindle's way. "Tell me more about this . . . Scythe spirit."

The scarecrow remained silent.

Clicking his tongue, Riven continued with another question. "Why should I choose you over the others?"

The scarecrow yet again did not reply.

Riven's eyelids dropped slightly, then he called the demon's bluff and turned around while putting his helmet on. "I guess he doesn't want it as bad as I thought he did. Let's go."

"The devil is a fool."

Riven paused at the scarecrow's words, smiling slightly underneath the metal of Messenger's protective shell. "Go on."

"He is impulsive and violent without forethought to any action. He will get you killed the moment he antagonizes an opponent greater than himself, and it will not be him that dies the true death because of it. The devil Chavi will not care if you die, as he will find another master so he can pursue the glory of battle at little risk to himself."

Riven turned around to stare at the scarecrow, folding his arms and nodding along. "Okay. What about the others?"

"Rheufa Chak Tal is a deceiver. You have not met him yet, but when you do—ask him about what he did to his last master. And if you do choose him, be sure to triple-check his contract. It will no doubt be very long and carefully worded in his favor in ways that you may not see. The snake, Yattazi, may be a monster, but she is also pure in soul. She above all else follows her path with true fervor, and I have nothing negative to say about her aside from the fact that I would beat her in one-on-one combat."

A small chuckle escaped Riven's lips. "Is that so? I would be interested in seeing such a battle. What about the abyss-lord?"

Fimrindle paused. "What abyss-lord?"

Riven raised an eyebrow again and pulled up his list of potential demonic contracts, the list of five that Athela had narrowed it down to, only to see that list had dropped down to four.

CHAPTER 40

The conversation lasted a little longer, but not too long. Fimrindle had an obvious aversion to speaking, and it almost seemed like it pained him to do it. However, Riven did get a lot of valuable information out of the scarecrow concerning his cultivation path revolving around the sin of Gluttony—which was a bit odd considering the demon didn't have a sin shard himself.

The next and last demon he approached was Rheufa Chak Tal, the thousand-eyes beholder, whose realm was far more vast than any of the others' had been.

Standing on the edge of a cliff, Riven looked into the distance where the cliff dropped thousands of feet below. A desolate, burning hellscape roared and erupted with volcanic plumes of magma, and overhead the sky thundered with black clouds crashing into one another in spurts of lightning.

The sight reminded him very much of Negrada, though it lacked the giant flaming eyeball in the sky or any kind of ruins. Otherwise the environment was the same, though, and Riven casually waved to the right where a large beholder demon, very unlike the other two they'd seen thus far, hovered over the cliff.

The previous two beholders had been slightly smaller than him—one in his demonic assortment before he'd chosen Fay as a succubus, and the other one who'd ambushed and helped kill Athela. They'd each had dozens of eyeballs on stalks with a singular central eyeball far larger than the others, and rows of teeth in mouths underneath.

This beholder was far larger, somewhat similar to the size of Athela in her drider form, and its features were slightly different. The largest feature change was that this monster's body was made of shadows very similar to how the abyss-lord had been.

The same central eyeball was present, the pupil catlike and glowing neon green, and it had a large mouth full of sharp teeth just like the others had. It also had numerous flickering stalks of similar but smaller eyeballs just like its weaker beholder counterparts, but extending beyond these and off its back were dozens more of these stalks that split and split and split again until they began to lose substance—black fading into ghostly white before disappearing entirely into the air. They almost looked like snakes, or thick branches of vines that attached the demon to the air about its body, and then those same stalks would reappear only to have eyeballs attached at the end of them in different places all around the area where they now stood.

More and more eyeballs began tearing out of space to glare down on Riven's group, until hundreds and then multiples of hundreds of eyes stared down at him as one.

- **Rheufa Chak Tal, Unique: Thousand-Eyes Beholder, Unholy/ Shadow, Level 126. ELITE—One of the most calculating and cunning demons of his generation across the multiverse, Rheufa Chak Tal started his rise to power by burning away entire cities in the hellscapes when a certain incubus tricked him into giving up an item of power. Since then, Rheufa Chak Tal has waged wars against entire clans of enemy demons—laying traps and springing ambushes to blindside his enemies with long-range bombard- ments from numerous angles. Since his recent evolution into a greater demon, his power has seen drastic upgrades and he has become an overwhelming force to deal with as he plunders enemy holds for wealth. He is known as an ambush predator and a loner. [136 Willpower Requirement]**

"Quite impressive," Riven stated aloud, turning around and around— looking up and down until settling back on the beholder's main body while the stalks moved and shifted in nonexistent winds. "Makes me wonder what else you can do."

"Rheufa Chak Tal, at your service. You may call me Rheufa," a gentlemanly voice replied with an amused hum to his voice. His green eyes landed on Athela, and he began to laugh. "Never did I think to see the day where a summoner of your caliber would consider marrying one of his demons. The prospect is hilarious to me."

Athela hissed threateningly, while the others in the party watched in silence. "It is rude to spy on other people's realms."

"It is in my nature to spy. To collect information. To evaluate my prospects of success when undertaking such a task as this," Rheufa replied with a silky voice—hovering closer and pushing his enormous eyeball up to the other demon. "It would be stupid of me not to do so, but do not think that I am making fun of your situation. I am actually quite impressed that he'd value you so highly; most summoners just look at us as tools—similarly to how most of us look at them. It is a symbiotic relationship—they acquire our power and in turn we are able to level with diminished amounts of danger. Eventually the summoners usually die, and we are left in an ascended state when compared to our prior selves."

The large eyeball shifted around Riven at high speed, examining each party member in full with the vibrant green eye until settling back on him again. It smiled, sharp white teeth glistening under the body made of void-black, shifting shadows. "Now let's play at a question. Why would I, as a rather selfish individual by admission, submit myself to you? A summoner? When I am able to grow easily enough by myself?"

Riven shrugged. "No idea. You tell me—that's what we're here for, right?"

Rheufa sighed, and his eyeballs all rolled simultaneously. "That was somewhat of a rhetorical question."

"Didn't seem like it."

"Just stay quiet for a moment." Rheufa cleared his throat in his gentlemanly voice, far too sophisticated for the demonic body he possessed, and narrowed his sight one more time on the vampire. "What would you say if perhaps I was able to show you a way to acquire not only myself as a contract—but up to ten in total? What would you say if I could guarantee that you become not only stronger and survive the trials of integration, but that I could guarantee you become the first E-grade creature on your planet before even arriving in Chalgathi's next quest? What would you say if this meant your power ranking on Panu's power ladder would shoot you up to the number one spot, that I could guarantee your ability to conquer your world by the end of integration? That all you had to do to achieve this was pick me and accept my terms?"

Riven remembered the words Fimrindle had spoken concerning Rheufa Chak Tal's previous master, and he folded his arms while considering the beholder's words. "That's a lot of promises, and you're giving off used-car-salesman vibes. No matter how good your promises are, I can in turn promise you that I won't be picking you if the contract is shit. But if it is good . . . then yes, I'd be very interested in hearing your proposal. Just how would you follow through on all these promises? I'm quite curious."

The beholder laughed once again, and the green eye in the center of his body lit up. "Your answer is a simple one, but achieving it will not be. You may die trying to acquire it, and the risk is extreme, but should you succeed—I and any other demon you are contracted to will benefit immensely. I am greedy by nature and wish for power, and in you I see the potential to finally enact my plan. Riven Thane, I wish for you to acquire the class of demon lord."

"I'm very grateful for my minions . . . and more is always a good thing," Riven began hesitantly, putting an arm around Athela's shoulders while smiling at Azmoth. "But I'm not entirely sure my way leads down the path of focusing on Willpower. It is growing exponentially harder to keep my contracts as they are, and holding more than a handful of demons will cost me a massive number of stats in the Willpower category. Those are stats I'd rather put toward building up my own body and mind."

"The power you'd gain by gaining our contracts would far outweigh the power you own yourself," Rheufa said with a blink. "Just think of the power you'd gain with ten demons on par with Athela. You would be unstoppable."

Riven stared, then nuzzled Athela with his nose. "Know anything about this?"

Athela was frowning, but she nodded. "I have heard of the class, it is real, but I am not sure how to obtain it. The one downside is you'll have to pull a lot of points into your Willpower, as you said. A LOT of Willpower."

"Yeah, that's a no from me, then. At least for now," Riven replied with a sideways glance at Azmoth. "That okay with you, bud?"

"Do what best for you, not worry about me," Azmoth stated promptly. "I will get strong and catch you in time."

"I never doubted you would."

The large floating eyeball tried to convince Riven a couple of times about the prospects of the class, and Riven was honestly tempted a bit. But he'd been growing at high speed by himself despite what the demon said, and considering Fimrindle's warning—along with this demon having bound itself to the sin of Greed—Riven didn't necessarily trust Rheufa.

"So what happened to your last master?" Riven eventually asked in a pause during their conversation. "Fimrindle told me something happened to him, and to ask you what that was."

Rheufa's large green eye pulsed, almost angrily, and he stared the vampire down. He then grumbled something under his breath and huffed, turning around. "I suppose there's nothing more to be said. If you do not wish to pursue the path of the demon lord, then there is nothing more for us to speak on. I will find another."

Riven blinked and immediately found himself back in Yattazi's realm with Rheufa gone. The transition was a bit jarring because it came without warning, but it wasn't unwelcome. The large coiling snake was still mostly submerged in magma.

Curiously enough, Fimrindle was also there—perched on his iron cross near the magma pool and next to the gigantic serpent who'd resumed her normally sized form.

Furrowing his eyebrows, Riven looked around.

"Have you declined the sssssslippery beholder?" Yattazi asked, huge dark-gray scales shifting with its head swaying side to side in anticipation. "We await your decissssion."

His red eyes shifted to those of the gargantuan beast overhead, and then to the scarecrow. "The beholder will not be joining my team, no. I wasn't all that interested in the devil. As for who I am going to choose between the two of you . . . Honestly, I'm torn."

There was a lapse of silence as Riven pondered his decision.

Fimrindle's head cocked to one side during one of Riven's blinks, and a raspy voice echoed from his dark throat. "Perhaps there is another way . . . Your sister, she is a necromancer, yes?"

Riven slowly nodded, eyebrows raised. "Yes. Why? And how do you know about my sister?"

"I have ways. What level is she?"

Riven shrugged. "Seventy or eighty something. Why?"

"Because minions cannot outlevel their masters," Fimrindle replied with a thick inhale. "I believe it would be best that you take Yattazi as your own and I match with your sister. You see, I can artificially lower my own combat level for months at a time, and truthfully I feel that she is a better fit for me than you are. I do not mean to use you, but my being is both a demon and an undead twisted into one. Perhaps you can talk to her for me, and though I would be weaker until she reaches my true level—I could give her guidance to reach the peak so that she may stand beside you in these turbulent times."

She stood atop the hill with her large undead drake on one side and her new scythe-wielding metallic scarecrow on the other. It was certainly a good addition, and extremely good addition to her forces, with it easily being the most powerful of any servant she had. Why it had asked for her specifically she did not know; the answers he gave her were fickle even when she commanded him to tell her, but she was grateful for the opportunity to acquire him.

Allie watched Riven leave down the mountainside on a huge demonic serpent, heading toward the old hospital entrance that had turned into a gateway into the underdark. The tunnels were patrolled by numerous caravans coming and going from Deepnest where the war with the dwarves still raged, and the entrance to that dark, underground cavern system had been hollowed out to create larger pathways into the deeper parts of the world. Allie still didn't think he'd be able to fit that enormous slithering creature down there with him. The creature was carving entire paths through the haunted forest, simply bulldozing everything in its way as other creatures of the night frantically ran for their lives.

He very well may have to reduce the size or unsummon it altogether until they hit the larger caverns.

Tyranus, the dungeon boss turned undead minion she'd flown here after getting Riven's message, tilted his head to look at the stick-still figure of the scarecrow silently crouching on the ground next to Allie. "This creature is a strange one."

Fimrindle did not reply, nor did he even move.

Allie turned her red eyes to look upon him, smiling slightly, before blinking and seeing her odd minion now had vanished altogether. She could feel him, though, and turning around she saw the thin monster perched on the decimated rooftop of the broken-down gas station. "We're all odd in our own ways. It is unfair to judge one so."

"Apologies, Mistress." Tyranus bowed low, the huge skeletal maw of the flickering monstrosity nearly hitting the ground in submission. "I forget myself. May I ask, what are your plans now that you've sent scouts to weed out the Rippenvire vampires? Do you truly intend to let Riven fight the dwarves on his own?"

Allie nodded, glancing over at a dozen of her elite skeleton minions on the perimeter of the clearing that'd accompanied her here. They were all hooded mages, still somewhat lacking their own will but able to learn forms of her own magic—which made them rather intimidating when compared to most of the populace on Panu. She sighed, then began walking over to the side of the drake to clamber up onto his back. Sitting herself on a saddle specially made for the huge undead creature, she held to the reins and mentally turned him around—pointing toward the northwest. "Yes. Riven is more than able to handle those rock-loving halflings all by himself. They will take the knee, or they will die. As for me, I have my own meetings to attend and a cultivation path to acquire. Mara will finish off talks with Dawn concerning the rebuilding of their city, and the king and queen of Tereen will be escorted home tomorrow. Fimrindle, this is your chance to prove yourself valuable."

She waited for her skeletons to clamber on behind her, then spurred Tyranus to take flight, and his enormous ethereal wings created from death mana and hollowed flesh tore into the air—launching them skyward as Fimrindle disappeared entirely without a word.

"Head northwest, over the mountains, until we see a large river. Then follow that river straight north for two days, and we should reach our destination."

Into the dark clouds gathering in the east and through a light drizzle, the vampiric queen soared toward her destination.

Death pulsed with every step she took, the dying light of the sunset beckoning the night to come forward. The weaker creatures and lesser beings of this world involuntarily cringed and took a step back at her passing, bowing their heads in displays of reverence and whispering to one another as she took up the invitation from the alliance that had sent emissaries only days before.

News of what the Thane Necropolis had become was far-reaching. The feats of her empire, herself, and her brother were plastered across the world's forums. These people, neighbors of her fledgling kingdom, were afraid.

And rightfully so, but for her—it was not enough. Her power was not enough. She needed to catch up to Riven, to stand alongside him. She would not be left in the dust.

The amphitheater was very large, and the hall she now walked down led toward where hundreds more nervous people whispered to one another. The alliance before her had been created from different human factions that'd banded together. Some of them were of Old Earth, but they were in the minority—with most of these people having originated from one of the other two worlds of Zazir and Elhisterii. She wasn't sure which, but they certainly were more acquainted with magic and medieval-style weapons—albeit enchanted ones—than the people hailing from what had once been a city in China.

The dozen hooded skeleton mages all walked silently behind her, their eye sockets glowing with a neon-teal light, and wands out at the ready in case of any ambush attempt while Fimrindle remained out of sight.

That creature truly was stealthy. If she didn't have a connection with him, she wouldn't even have known he was there. He hadn't talked much since their introduction, either, and she was still trying to get a handle on what he was like or what his motivations were.

The stone amphitheater eventually opened up in front of her, with baubles of light held aloft overhead in racks along the walls and stained glass windows painting the room in oranges, greens, blues, and reds.

The room quickly hushed on her arrival, and her crimson eyes searched the stands—identifying three individuals who stood at the bottom and ahead of the others as a greeting party. No doubt they were the leaders of the three-faction alliance that'd invited her to come. One was an Asian man from Earth who wore a pistol at his waist and an exquisite suit. Another was a very pretty young woman with silky black hair that hung down far past her waist in a braided ponytail, wearing a blue robe decorated with golden sigils around a bird in flight. The last was another human man who was completely shaven to the point that he didn't even have eyebrows—though the wrinkles in his face showed he was growing older. He looked very much like a monk, wearing plain brown robes that were frayed at the ends of the sleeves, but he above all looked the most calm.

She stopped only ten yards from them, putting herself into a confident stance and silently staring through the holes in her skull mask while the soul-stitched wand at her side hissed. Six hooded skeletal mages took positions on her left, while six took positions on her right, and people in the hallway behind her continued to whisper and stare from the shadows at the upcoming negotiations.

"This one greets the esteemed queen of the Thane Necropolis. My name is Astrand, great shepherd of my flock—the Golden Bull Sect," the monk said with a small smile, stepping forward and bowing low in a sign of respect—with everyone else in the room doing the same just a moment later. He raised himself and clasped his hands in front of him at chest level, the sleeves of his brown robe nearly causing his hands to disappear entirely. "The ones beside me are Ryu Chen of Beijing, and Authin Verume of the Bluesilk Nest. We have heard of and seen your exploits, Queen Allie Thane, and we wish to extend our most sincere congratulations at your accomplishment of defeating the Rippenvire fleets. To think that one of the invaders sent here by the system was already put to heel and routed so early is a great boon indeed, and our world owes you and yours a great debt for it."

Again he bowed at the waist, and again the entire room followed suit before he straightened up.

Allie sorted through them one by one. She was able to identify most of them, many of them having levels in between fifteen and forty. There were a couple over level 60, though, and even one other S-grade on the power ladder who stood at the very back of the room wielding a claymore, but overall they were quite weak.

Not that it mattered too much. These people were mostly politicians and leaders rather than warriors, and they could have more S-grades waiting just outside. She simply didn't know enough about them.

But she doubted any of them would be stupid enough to make a move. Call it arrogance or confidence, she was certain that she'd be able to escape if push came to shove.

She held up her right hand, and out of it flew a myriad of bones. They began stacking atop one another, building a vortex of magic much like the bone garden atop her tower in Brightsville. Many of the people in the room tensed or reached for weapons and talismans as she summoned the low-tier magic, but when they realized what she was doing, they either sagged their shoulders in relief or gawked in outrage at the blatant insult.

The bones stopped swirling as the last of them came to its intended destination. There, in the middle of their own amphitheater in the center of their heartlands, Allie sat upon a tall throne she'd created from the skeletons of her enemies.

Spines created the armrests. Skulls decorated the back of the support board, which itself was created from numerous ribs. Skeletal hands held up the large chair, and sitting in it caused her to look down upon the three insignificant specks of humans ahead of her just like the rest of the theater looked down on them as a whole.

It was a statement, a statement telling them where she stood in relation to them. But despite this, despite the anger she saw on many of their faces, Allie didn't budge—nor did she see any of them brave enough to say anything about what she'd done. Those scowls turned to slight gasps when she removed her mask to reveal her utterly stunning, pale features—with many of the men even looking on with a lustful envy intermixed into their fear.

"Your emissaries told me you wished to speak, so I came. It was good you called—there aren't many high-density population centers like this one near my empire outside of the Tereen elves we just conquered—even if it is split between three groups controlling the area," Allie said slowly, pulling out a goblet made from the skull of her old archenemy Prophet and filling it with blood from a jug in her spatial sack, taking a sip. "Tell me, what makes you want to speak with me? I wish to hear it in your own words."

Astrand, the hairless older man, nodded sagely while ignoring the fact that he was looking up at her now—as opposed to being on equal footing. "I had hoped, young queen of the Thane Necropolis, that our alliance could exist with your own—peacefully so. We had hoped to establish good relations with a player on the world stage such as yourself, and your brother, so that no unnecessary conflicts or death arise in the future. We had hoped to establish trade and perhaps an exchange of knowledge so that we may all thrive in this new world we find ourselves in. That is why we have summoned you, Your Majesty, and it is my hope that we may someday even become friends in our quest to combat the darkness that plagues this world."

Allie's beautiful smile widened, her fangs on full display without her intentionally trying to do so. She glanced left to where she felt Vin and Nin ready and waiting somewhere outside the building, having gotten there even before she did. "Oh, but my dear friend . . . perhaps I am that darkness."

CHAPTER 41

Trees cast shadows on their cabin. The sounds of the campfire crackling under the night sky grew louder as Julie added a handful of dry twigs. The redheaded young woman gave Hakim a wide smile, sitting down next to him as he roasted marshmallows over an open fire and kissing him on the cheek.

"You look unusually happy tonight," Julie said while wrapping her arms around his waist in the warm forest breeze. She glanced over to her mother, Tanya, and her brother, Tim, who'd managed to regrow his lost limb after they'd spent all their hard earnings from the dungeon experience with Riven on a series of high-quality potions.

Tanya, who was putting another marshmallow on a stick and handing it to her teenage son, smiled back at her daughter, who looked absolutely stunning in her formfitting white healer's robes. "You make us all happy to be around, Julie. Your energy is infectious."

Hakim chuckled and pulled out a flaming ball of what had once been edible, sighing when the others laughed at him before pulling it off and tossing it into the fire pit. His shirtless chest was heavily tattooed now, given the abilities and body enhancements he'd acquired, which only kept Julie's eyes on him longer. "Yes, your mother is right. How lucky I was to have met you!"

Julie flushed in embarrassment, but not before Tim gave a loud snort.

"My sister still snores and farts far too often for my liking."

Julie gasped as her mother and her lover began to laugh loudly. Glaring at her little brother, she crossed her arms and harrumphed. "I do NOT SNORE! And it isn't my fault I'm lactose intolerant!"

"You could stop eating cheese."

"BLASPHEMY! Mom's pizza is too good! I'D RATHER DIE!"

The sound of laughter rose, but the sound of heavy boots trudging through the forest caused the small group to pause. Hakim glanced down the forested hill toward the outskirts of town where tiny lights littered the dark landscape, and coming out of the darkness a familiar figure stepped forward.

It was Caleb, the same man who'd entered the dungeon with them when Riven had shown up. He still carried his semiautomatic rifle, though he'd upgraded some of the runes along the weapon's side to empower its shots, and had the typical camo outfit he liked with a pair of night-vision goggles on top of his head.

He pulled the goggles off when he came around the bend in the forest path and strode forward with a smile, to the cheers and waves of the others. "Hey, guys! Sorry I'm late."

Hakim's large muscles flexed as he gripped his battle-axe and waved it around in mock threat. "Yes, how dare you not be faster! You court death!"

Julie rolled her eyes and handed Caleb a long stick with a marshmallow attached to it, smiling gently when the man took it in turn and sat beside her mother on the other side of the fire pit. "Glad to see you came safely."

"I've got a scout class! I can usually see danger a mile away. Literally." Caleb winked, setting down his rifle and pulling a small sack of goods from a backpack. He tossed over some Twinkies, a couple chocolate bars, some precooked hot dogs with buns, and some paper plates before pulling out the big kicker: the vodka.

"OOOOOooooooh! Caleb!" Tanya said in a teasing, flirty voice while waggling her eyebrows. "You never told me you were bringing alcohol!"

Caleb's face grew bright red when his friends' mother nudged up against him, and both Julie and Hakim began to cackle loudly while Tim rolled his eyes.

Julie grabbed one of the hot dogs from Tim and then shook her head. "Mom, you need to stop doing that or he's going to think you're serious one of these days."

"Who says I'm NOT serious?! I'm totally into handsome younger men!" Tanya retorted with a frown, briefly glancing at Caleb sitting on the log next to her while his face went from red to nearly purple in embarrassment. Her grin only grew wider, but she spared him further stress by giving him a little bit of space and giggling. "So, Caleb, how did you like the new clothes I made you?"

Taking the olive branch immediately, Caleb cleared his throat and shuffled nervously with the food in his lap—arranging it and rearranging it on the paper plate while avoiding death glares from Tim. "They're great! The stat boosts they give me are definitely appreciated. Your skills are getting better."

Tanya beamed and started pouring herself a tiny cup of vodka. "Glad you think so. However, I do believe . . ."

Her voice trailed off and her eyes widened when, under the starry sky and with the backdrop of the small town in the distance, five men silently appeared on the forested edge of their clearing. All were utterly silent, all dressed in black with white masks that hid most of their faces. Tiny metal amulets with the familiar symbol of two crossed daggers hung around each of their necks.

It didn't take long after that for the others to take notice, and Hakim slowly turned to stand while hesitantly reaching for his axe and silently activating some physical buffs. His brows furrowed, and the five masked men turned their attention to him next.

One of them, the central figure, raised a finger and wagged it back and forth. "Do not be so hasty to start such violence, Hakim. We are not here to do you harm; we are merely sent as messengers. How you respond to that message dictates what happens next."

Hakim's nose wrinkled, and he put his body in front of Julie's with the rest of his tiny guild behind him. "I already told Matt that I spent everything I had. Tim's leg took a lot of money to regenerate. I am not hiding anything, and even if I were—it wasn't Matt's to take."

The central figure snorted, brushing Hakim's reply aside with a wave of his hand. "That isn't my concern. What is my concern is that we were paid to bring the lot of you in for a discussion."

"How much did he pay you?"

The figure shrugged indifferently. "The Red Hand paid in items rather than Elysium coins. Not many people have direct access to the altars anyways in this remote section of the world, so items are better suited for our needs unless we wish to travel. But that doesn't matter. What matters is whether you're going to come quietly or you're going to come missing a member or two."

Shadows in the forest began to move, and Hakim's eyes narrowed when more hooded figures on their right and left made themselves visible—if only barely.

Tanya shuffled nervously, and her son, Tim, got to his feet with a gritting scowl.

"This is robbery, a shakedown. Plain and simple," Tim snarled, clutching at a small pistol at his side.

The people on the perimeter drew hidden weapons, a variety of knives, wands, crossbows, and guns.

The central figurehead of the group nodded slowly. "You're probably right. But in this world, where the apocalypse has descended and all around us monsters try to chew away what little we have left, you cannot blame me for attempting to make a living. I am an honest mercenary, and if that occasionally includes escorting particular groups of people to their enemies, then so be it. I will say, though, the Red Hand doesn't seem like they're entirely convinced of your hidden treasures, either—so as a gift to old friends, I tell you now that there's a decent chance you could talk your way out of this when you get there. Matt may be a thug, but he's not stupid. What is not negotiable is the fact that you're coming."

Luke Blissfallen, Level 17 High Elf Thrall (Stormrazor Battle Priest) (Warning: 3% soul decay detected) [10 Willpower Requirement]

Riven stayed in the shadows, a small demonic snake wrapped around his right arm while a spider clung to his left shoulder, and a shadowy jackal with red eyes sat at his feet, dismissing the status page notification. He was impressed with Luke's progression. The old man, an elf turned thrall, was almost completely healed. Riven didn't know how much power he'd retained or if any or all the old man's abilities had finally come back after their link had slowly put Luke's soul back together piece by piece—but he could visibly see the change in the old man's body. Riven was happy that he'd briefly stopped by before going into the underdark, because though he had less savory responsibilities as the most powerful person in the Thane Necropolis, he always enjoyed watching the small, important, and often overlooked things in life play out.

Luke was playing with the children of the large orphanage Riven had set up in central Brightsville, laughing loudly as they climbed over his robes or threw buckets of water at one another. A couple of them were even practicing small forms of magic and miracles, with Luke specifically having taught many of them tiny amounts of wind and water magic from the Storm subpillar—forgoing the lightning-based abilities just yet.

Three stories high and guarded at all times by soldiers, this place was not only a vibrant and thriving school for the children who'd lost their families, but was also an experiment of sorts in real time. Different children were progressing down different roads of cultivation, learning, and even crafting paths.

Crafting paths. He snorted with a shake of his head. He'd been wanting to pursue totem making for quite a while now—it fascinated him, and it'd be a nice stress reliever. But he'd simply not had time with everything going on the way it was.

The thought made him wonder just how Hakim and the others were doing. Hopefully they were all right. It'd been a while, but they did have that artifact to call him if need arose—so he was sure everything was as it should be.

"What thinking?" Azmoth asked in a gruff, demonic voice—leaning his enormous weight on the large magma-infused war hammer in front of him. "Look deep in thought."

Riven glanced left and smiled, his Gluttony-attuned helmet peeling back to reveal his pale features. "Yeah. I was just thinking back to my friends from the tutorial, before I met you. It's been a while. I was just mentally wishing them well."

Azmoth nodded sagely. "Is good to have friends. You need more."

"Oh? Do I?" Riven grinned, slapping the obsidian plates fused into Azmoth's shoulder. "I've got you guys! I've got . . ."

His smile faltered as he remembered Fay. His world quickly turned from an upbeat, warm feeling—to a cold and sad place. It showed on his face, and Athela reached up one of her spider legs to touch his cheek lightly.

"You miss her," Athela said sadly. "I can tell."

Riven abruptly cleared his throat, then looked down to the spider with a nod. "Yeah. I do. But I wouldn't ever give you up. She forced my hand."

"Are you mad at me?"

Riven considered the question, then sighed. "Slightly. But I love you, Athela, and I don't hold it against you. Let's just drop it for now, okay?"

Athela hesitantly nodded her arachnid head, clicked her mandibles twice, and then snuggled into his neck where the red bloodsilk underlayer of his armor met with the ivory plate mail. "Okay."

Yattazi seemed interested in the exchange—molten eyes glancing between the other three as a tongue flicked out underneath dark-gray scales. "Who issss this persssson you talk about? And can we find food sssssoon? I wasss wanting to cook! Dwarf, preferably!"

Azmoth snickered at the last comment but quickly contained himself when he realized laughing right now probably wasn't appropriate. "We eat many dwarves together in underdark. Patience, tiny snake."

"I am MASSIVE, dear brutalisk!"

"Not right now, you ain't!" Athela quipped back with a tiny tongue sticking out. "Right now you're a slug! A teeny, tiny, ugly slug!"

The rather sleek, dangerous-looking snake wrapped around Riven's arm rolled her eyes—getting a chittering laugh from the spider.

"I am going to eat that ssspider, Masssster."

Athela gasped dramatically. "Bring it, bitch!"

Riven sighed with a shake of his head, though he was now smiling again. Yes, he supposed it was good to have friends such as these. Pushing off the wall in the alley he was viewing the three-story orphanage from, he made his presence known while stepping into the light.

Immediately the guards around the perimeter of the orphanage tensed and bowed their heads, clapping hands to their chests in a salute. There were orcs, humans, cyborgs, ghouls, skresh, and even a few goblins in the mix of the guards stationed here for the time being—making it a rather diverse outfit of over fifty people protecting the nearly three thousand kids who lived here. The caretakers, mostly ghoul and human women but also a good number of elves who had chosen to stay behind, all stiffened on the playgrounds in turn when seeing him approach. Some of them even prostrated themselves, while others tried to round the children up to hush them or push them inside.

The only one who did not freak out was Luke. The old man's skin had a leathery appearance to it when he smiled, and his smile only grew wider upon seeing Riven approach. He waved, putting down a little boy he'd been mock wrestling with, and walked forward to meet his master with a hand outstretched.

"Good to see you!" Luke called out, surprising Riven by pulling him into a brief hug and stepping back. "How have you been?! It's been a while since we sparred. Have you come to bring me in for more lessons?"

Riven's eyes softened while taking in the little children who stared up at him from a nearby picnic table and a jungle gym on his left. "No. I think your place is here more than teaching me how to be a pathetic excuse for a warrior."

The elf thrall's eyes widened in surprise, then he began to laugh while putting his hands on his hips. "I suppose you weren't the greatest in up-close combat, but you sure look the part with all that heavy armor you're lugging around. And hello to the rest of you! Azmoth, Athela, Jackal, Messenger, and . . ."

He gave each of them a head nod—even the maw along the armor set that gurgled back at him, before staring at the snake wrapped around Riven's arm. He raised an eyebrow. "New minion?"

"You got it. Her name is Yattazi, and she's usually a lot bigger than this—but I can't go around the city with a massive snake, now can I? She'd rip everything up."

The snake, who'd been curiously examining the children nearby, turned her spined head to the older man and flicked her tongue out to display fangs crackling with Chaos energy. "Hello, fellow servant of the massster! I am Yattazi, devourer of the living and great sssserpant of the volcano! You may kowtow before me one thousand times and ssshower me with giftsss for being allowed to basssk in my presssence!!! For I have gracioussssly chosssen not to eat you!"

Athela chittered in amusement when Luke's face fell.

"I see she's a keeper," Luke replied flatly, ignoring the snake and turning to Athela. "You told her to say that, didn't you?"

Athela took in a deep inhale, aghast. "HOW DID YOU KNOW?!"

"That is exactly something you would say. If Riven ended up getting two demons with your personality, I think this necropolis would be in for a real shit show." He shook his head. "So what is it that brings you here, then, Riven? Anything I can help you with, if not training?"

Riven's smile returned. "I just wanted to check in and see how you were doing. Don't get me wrong, we'll train later, but I have things to do and it's simply been a while. You're looking good—healthy, even. I also saw your soul degradation was only at 3 percent now; you've come a long way. Have your abilities returned?"

The old man grinned mischievously, pulling his hands out of his simple robes and producing a baseball-size orb of water that began to crackle with lightning. "Yes. Though not all of them. My most prominent miracles are still being set into place, but I can feel them. They're almost here."

Riven's smile grew wider. "Awesome. You'll have to teach me more about the difference between miracles and spells later on. I know the basics, but not many people use miracles here."

"That will change very fast if I have any say about it." Luke hiked a thumb over his shoulder to the children in the background. "They're all really fast learners, and I've even captured a couple weak monsters for them to battle in practice rounds! It'll all be controlled, obviously, but cultivating the younger generations is something every great faction starts very early. At least that's how it was on Zazir before the merging of worlds. Now, with the system here and the levels we can gain . . . it may be even more important."

Riven clapped the old man on the shoulder. "Glad to hear it. Do you work with Mara a lot? She is supposed to be overseeing these kinds of things."

"I do," Luke replied with a nod. "That hottie is really something else . . ."

"Mara? The ghoul necromancer?"

"Yes, that's the one."

"You think she's pretty?" Riven replied with a teasing grin.

Luke only blinked. "Well, I'm straight and I'm not blind, so, obviously. She's gorgeous! Just because you surround yourself with beautiful women like Athela, Kathrine, and . . . others doesn't mean the rest of us get so lucky all the time. Contain yourself and save some of the women for the rest of us, damn you!"

Athela let out another dramatic gasp, hopped off Riven's shoulder, and morphed into her humanoid form. She put both hands on the old man's face to pinch his cheeks with affection. "YOU'RE SO NICE! Riven, Wrinkles here just got a lot of brownie points. Treat him well, and that plan you had to eat him—scratch that. We'll just eat Genua instead."

Riven could only face-palm and roll his eyes. "Stop harassing my teacher. Anyways, it was good seeing you, Luke. I've got some rat-kin and dwarves to visit in the underdark, along with some native vampires, too, if what Snagger told me was accurate. Take care, keep safe, and I'll be sure to drag you out for a practice match whenever I get back."

Luke gave him a thumbs-up after swatting away Athela's fingers with a scowl. "This is how you do it, yes?"

Riven chuckled. "Yes, that's the thumbs-up motion. You have it right. Adios, my friend."

"Yes, adios to you, too, Riven. I'll see you later."

CHAPTER 42

The hospital entrance, which had once been a small hole in the basement, was now dug out and fully cleaned. The rotted corpses of swarming nightmare creatures were long gone, and in place of them were stalls occupied by rat-kin and citizens of Brightsville alike where they traded with one another at the mouth into the underdark. Guard patrols from Deepnest and the Thane Necropolis were both present, taking turns escorting people to and from the two cities in caravans. Most of the trips lasted nearly three days due to the goods they traveled with.

Unless they took a spatial sack, of course, but those were rare. Even in those cases, the threat of monsters and dwarvish ambushes were ever present—and one did not just simply walk into the underdark alone because of it.

Unless you were Riven Thane.

Riven casually strolled down the marked tunnels and pathways leading into the depths of the planet, humming to himself with his three demonic servants and Jackal's canine form in tow. The mood was upbeat, in large part due to the hot cinnamon buns and meat-stuffed rolls he'd purchased from one of the vendors before heading down here, as the food was very good.

"I rate it adequate. This is acceptable," Yattazi stated between snarfing down some of the pastries, wrapped around Athela's humanoid form and waiting with open mouth as the other demoness fed her pieces one by one. "I need to start using this . . . sugar substance you speak of. It is quite good."

"Just don't get diabetes," Riven called out rather sagely with a finger upheld.

"What's diabetes?"

"A disease you get from having way too much sugar. Kinda. It'd take a bit to explain."

The twists and turns stretched into enormous underground biodomes, chasms of space that were connected by numerous shafts, and sheltered various creatures that were far different from the norm above ground. Neon-teal grasses, enormous fungi, and molds were all seen in abundance with some mushrooms being taller than he was many times over. Numerous species of large insects, bats, scaled reptiles, rodents with various types of dark vision, and occasionally signs of old battles between rat-kin and dwarves were present along the path leading down. He passed one patrol of rat-kin from Deepnest, who briefly stopped to question him before they realized who he was, and made quick time traveling through the underdark with only a few small exterminations to be had when he took a quick detour for curiosity's sake and stumbled upon a small swarm of huge carnivorous centipedes.

They made good time.

At the end of the day, Riven found himself standing at the entrance to the nesting cavern where a backup of caravans were smushed together and waiting in a slow-going line as rat-kin soldiers were inspecting goods.

"Come-walk faster!" one of the rat-kin soldiers, a four-foot-tall specimen with brown fur wearing chitin armor and a spear, called out while waving a clawed hand. He bade three humans with lanterns attached to their carts to continue down the path toward the city in the background, when he spotted Riven at the end of the line wearing his full plate armor set.

The guard's eyes went wide, and with a high-pitched squeak he quickly prostrated himself. "K-King Riven Thane! Bat-kin warrior-mage of necropolis-friends! I-we make way for you to come-walk!"

The guard quickly got up and immediately started yelling at his fellow guards and the caravans to get out of the way, with many of the disgruntled merchants muttering to themselves until they saw who the rat-kin soldier was making way for. Many people were very familiar with Riven's getup, and his demons Azmoth and Athela were pretty famous, too. They'd been displayed numerous times on both local and world forums across the cortex of Panu, and the most recent battle in Mandon had left a very vivid image of Athela in particular, when she'd taken her archdemon form to wipe out not only the vampiric leadership but also the Harbingers of Gluttony alongside Riven.

The area immediately went silent, before people started exchanging whispers. Many of them quickly bowed or knelt, avoiding eye contact, while others looked up at him with awe and curiosity.

He gave them a polite wave, shrugged, and walked ahead of the line to where a couple dozen soldiers were waiting at the tunnel's mouth leading into the massive cavern containing Deepnest. "Thanks. I was hoping I could be escorted to Rashtalia, broodmother of Brood-Tarrow in Deepnest. She recently visited me in Brightsville and is waiting for me at her compound now for an audience with the queen concerning the war effort."

"You here-come to fight dwarf-killers?" The rat-kin soldier who'd originally addressed him went wide-eyed with delight, and smiles spread across many of the faces of the other rat-kin around him. "I lead-show you to Brood-Tarrow! Come-follow, king-warrior of Thane Necropolis! Much respect-approval for helping us-we in our fight against killer-dwarves!"

And with that, the rat-kin excitedly began running into the larger cavern beyond—with Riven following at a more leisurely pace.

It was just like he'd remembered it, but busier, if that was even possible, given the amount of trade that'd erupted between his own city and this underground dwelling. The nesting cavern was enormous, spanning a couple dozen miles or more—but due to the twists and turns it was hard to tell just where it ended. He certainly hadn't explored all of it the first time he'd been here, either, given the size.

Tens of thousands of bioluminescent vines hung from the cavern's ceiling. Rivers snaked their way into the cavern through an absolute madhouse of activity, with hardly any organization to the mix-and-match of city sprawled out before him. Most of the structures were created from dark-brown wood, hardened clay, or stone. The structures were most often hills, for lack of better words, from the size of a house to many hundreds of times larger than that, each of them having small burrows or tunnels dug into them where rat-kin scurried in and out. Overhead and connecting the mounds were large, dark-brown, interconnecting and scaffolded wooden roadways, while the lower ground levels also had paths that zigzagged between the large mounds or followed the rivers.

It was good to be back. Perhaps this time around he'd have a little bit of time to explore before being burdened with meeting the vampires and the queen of Deepnest. He also wasn't looking forward to slaughtering a bunch of dwarves and hoped they'd back down quietly when they saw him. But at this point, based on reports he'd received, he doubted they'd stop their asinine attacks without a severe ass kicking. They essentially thought the rat-kin were a lesser species, and that kind of mentality was often drilled into people from birth. Regardless, he'd be finding out quite soon. Of that he was sure.

Fay put the plate down on her new master's table, having cooked him a meal and being bidden to sit to eat while they looked over the dark, damp industrial city of smokestacks she now called home. Her stunningly beautiful sky-blue features were scrunched up with a sadness that hadn't left her ever since arriving, and her master—whose name was Ikarius—had taken notice that it'd become worse.

The old man gave her a friendly smile, pushed his fingers back through his graying hair, and picked up his fork to skewer a piece of meat. "This is good, Fay. Thank you for the meal."

She gave him a fond smile. "Of course. I'm glad you like it."

Ikarius . . . was an odd man. He was an F-grade warlock and small-time crime lord, a low-tier one at best, and most of his time was spent trying to carve a better living for himself out of the slums of a vast city in a poorer part of the Nerius Empire. Wrinkles were appearing on his face as time went on, and he'd recently lost his daughter, who had been his sole companion for quite some time after his wife had passed. He wasn't a bad guy, Fay thought, and surprisingly enough he hadn't made a single move to touch her in any kind of sexual way ever since she'd arrived. He'd merely wanted company, and after their interview had passed the initial phase, he'd chosen her when hearing her sob story in the nether realms. He'd even become something of a therapist for her.

"How are you holding up?" Ikarius asked casually, taking a sip of an alcoholic beverage one of his lackeys had delivered earlier that day. "I hope my men aren't making you too uncomfortable with the way they look at you. I can send them off if they are."

Fay glanced hesitantly at one of the younger thugs under Ikarius's employment standing guard a few feet away, and the muscular man stiffened before turning his head to stare at the wall. She frowned. "They're fine. I'm used to it."

"I'm sure you are, but that's still not okay if it makes you uneasy." Ikarius graced her with a kind smile, then put his hands together when he realized she was just staring down at her plate without making an attempt to eat. He let out a sigh and closed his eyes. "Have you thought about what I said?"

Her frown deepened, and her lip began to quiver before she cupped a hand over her mouth. Taking in a deep breath, she let it out slowly. "Yes."

"And?" he asked curiously. "What do you think? Would you like to meet him? My nephew is a very kind man; he'd make you happy."

Fay's black eyes turned upward, and she shook her head no. "Thank you, Master. But I'm not interested in pursuing any kind of relationship outside of my contractual obligations."

He nodded just once. "Very well. Have you talked to your brother recently about how things are going over on . . . What was the planet called again?"

"Panu," she stated simply. "He's tried talking to me, as have my mother and sister, but I think I just need some time. I've exchanged pleasantries with them, but nothing serious. I think it'll be a while before I've truly moved on from this. Riven was . . . He certainly wasn't perfect. But he was kind, and he was mine . . . Or at least I thought he was."

She picked up the fork in front of her, and then slowly pierced some of the food before bringing it to her mouth to chew solemnly. She swallowed, then slumped her shoulders and leaned on her elbows while her fingers dug into her head, trying to hold back tears. Hiccuping once, and wiping away some of the water welling up under her eyes, she sniffed. "Sorry. I don't mean to be like this."

The old man smiled sadly. "You remind me very much of my daughter, you know that?"

She gave a lighthearted laugh despite the accumulation of tears. "Yes, you tell me all the time."

"Well, I mean it." He leaned back in his chair and looked over the balcony at the city streets far below them. "I remember a very similar situation with her. She'd fallen for this boy named Havuski. He chose another woman over my little girl, and she ended up finding someone much better for her before her life came to an abrupt stop in that accident. Despite that, I believe she always regretted that she couldn't be with her first choice. It haunted her until her dying day, even though she loved the man who was better for her in her own way—and it pained me to see her like that."

Ikarius turned his head and tilted it to the side. "You say you loved this man? This Riven?"

Fay nodded but then hesitated with a shrug. "I . . . I think I did. I think I do. I was happiest when I was with him, especially near the end. But it doesn't matter, because he chose her over me when I gave him that ultimatum. He is my person, but I am not his. It is that simple, and I need to accept that fact before I drag myself into a deeper pit of despair. And I . . . ugh. I just wish it'd been someone else. If it'd been anyone else other than Athela, I would have been okay with it. But she just . . . she intimidated me. She was one who already held his heart, and I knew it. Maybe I made the wrong choice in leaving."

Ikarius tapped his fingers on the wooden table thoughtfully. "I think you should talk to your brother. It sounded to me that you two ended on a very sudden, abrupt note, and in my opinion, it'd be wise to have more closure before moving forward. At the very least, you could pass a message to this Riven through Tupper and let him know how you feel. Get your feelings off your chest and have an outlet for the emotional pain you're keeping bottled up inside. It is unhealthy to remain in this mental state, Fay, and you shouldn't allow yourself to wallow in such self-pity."

She didn't look up but absentmindedly played with her food using her fork— ignoring the stare from the hired thug in the background who continued to undress her with his eyes. "I think that might actually be a good idea. It all happened so fast . . . and there are still things I want to say. Thank you for your advice, Ikarius. I'll take some time to think about what I wish to convey, and then I'll let you know what happens afterward."

The old warlock smiled in approval, taking another sip from his cup. "Very good. I look forward to hearing the news."

High Queen Nephridi stood overlooking her great capital on the usual balcony she used in meditation. It was in the highest tower of her sprawling, gothic palace. Her slender hands were clasped behind her back when she heard the faint footfalls of her invited guests.

The rays of sunset cast orange-red hues on the white dress that hugged her skin, and she turned her crimson eyes on the three newcomers while they bowed in submission. One was a young man, the one to be wed to Allie Wraithtide after his parents had won the bidding war for her hand in marriage, and the other two were those same parents. They were all pure-blooded vampires, pale with eyes like her own, all of them wearing red and orange robes with the symbol of a green flame decorating the front of their clothes as a symbol of their house. All had pitch-black hair, and their gazes were excited and expectant when she bade them rise.

She nodded in approval. "Duke and Duchess Barimont, and your youngest son—Lord Justo Barimont. It is a pleasure to meet all of you in person outside of formal affairs. I do believe this is the first time?"

She tilted her head to the side, trying to remember if she'd ever talked to any of them other than during political gatherings.

She hadn't.

"High Queen Nephridi!" Duchess Barimont stated fondly, stepping forward to bow low. "I thank you so much for allowing our child the hand of the princess in marriage! I promise that we will not disappoint you, and our son's union to Princess Allie Wraithtide will bear many offspring with the gift in your name!"

The duke looked absolutely thrilled to be here but let his wife take the lead, having heard rumors that Queen Nephridi got along better with women—which wasn't entirely true, but even the queen had heard them. Meanwhile, the young buck they'd dragged along out of their backwater solar system was jittery with excitement. To land the hand of Allie Wraithtide in marriage meant a massive increase in standing for their family, which had only recently risen to nobility after conquering some neighboring factions in a coalition effort; they'd originally started off as merchants dealing in weapons of war.

They were essentially arms dealers.

High Queen Nephridi put on a smile that didn't touch her lips. "Yes, well, you were the ones who paid for it, after all. To the highest bidder go the spoils. So long as your son does just that, and produces sufficient heirs, I have no qualms."

There was a pause, and when his parents didn't seem to know what to say next, the younger man stepped forward with a bow of his own. His suave locks of black hair were gelled back to the right side of his head, and he looked a little too smug for his own good.

"My queen . . ." Lord Justo Barimont said with a wide grin. "I appreciate your consideration. I truly do! And in the light of wanting to pursue your goals early, perhaps it would be in all of our best interest that we start trying sooner rather than later."

There was yet another pause in the conversation as the queen considered the young man's words.

Nephridi raised an eyebrow and a small smirk. "Oh? You do realize that the integration of their planet still has another four and a half years left. That amount of time is but a blip on the horizon of our life spans, young man. Do not let your hormones get ahead of you."

Seeing the queen's demeanor change for the better, the parents of the young lord both gave nervous laughs of their own.

"I do realize this," Lord Justo Barimont replied eagerly, smoothing out his red and orange robes with a quick motion. "But you see, I am in the F-grade as well. Only level 78. Please correct me if I am wrong, High Queen, as I do not mean to offend. My information may be outdated or just flat out incorrect, but if it is possible, I could potentially travel to Panu on my own. If I were older and stronger, I know this wouldn't be doable—but system restrictions concerning the trade communes would probably allow me passage. I wish to introduce myself to my new fiancée, to let her know in person what has transpired here. It would be a true shame if she were to find out through someone else, and I believe Kathrine—the lesser princess of House Crushada whose family has claimed Riven—would be able to set up a meeting now that we are on better talking terms with the two lost Wraithtide heirs."

High Queen Nephridi rubbed a finger along the edge of her lips in thought, eyes narrowed. "You do realize what Allie Wraithtide's demeanor is like, I hope?"

"Oh yes, I've kept track of the broadcasts that the system allows out! It is a very popular thing to watch among both the commoners and nobility," Lord Justo Barimont replied with a beaming grin, displaying his fangs. "She will make a fine wife!"

Nephridi snorted. "I see. Very well. Just be sure to have guards there when you break the news to her."

The young lord furrowed his brows in concern, glancing to his parents before looking back at the queen. ". . . Your Majesty?"

"You must remember," the queen continued, turning back around to stare out over her great city once more, "that Allie and Riven Wraithtide were not brought up in the Blood Moon Requiem. They do not have the same obligations, experiences, thought processes that we here in our homeland do. She might take the news well—you are a good mating prospect for her—but part of me believes that she may need to be slowly prodded into the mindset of knowing her place here in the empire. She may be a high princess, but just like everyone else of the royal bloodline, she has a duty to fulfill. Even I do. So until you are sure that she has accepted her place, be sure to have the guards with you at all times. She can be rather bloodthirsty and violent . . . positive traits, to be certain, but not when they are directed at you."

"Even if she doesn't wish it, surely she should acknowledge her duty and the right that we paid for," the younger man's father, Duke Barimont, stated with a frown.

High Queen Nephridi nodded without looking back, hand still clasped behind her. "Yes, she should. One way or another, she'll come around—even if, in a worst-case scenario, I have to send a fleet across the cosmos to take that tiny, insignificant planet after the five years are up. I am not saying no to your son, Duke Barimont. He can visit Panu whenever he wants and has my blessing to do so. I am merely saying that he should be careful when off-world, where she might not take kindly to the news—where not even a single E-grade or above from our empire is there to protect the little lord. You may supply your son with protective treasures to subdue her if she chooses to get violent, but I'm sure you're well aware of the incredibly steep taxes to Elysium that come with anything above F-grade during planetary integrations. Some items are even banned."

The young lord's mother, Duchess Barimont, grinned. "Oh yes, we've already looked into that. Our son will be outfitted with the best if you give your approval of his leave to visit our future daughter-in-law, though I hope he doesn't need to use it. We hope above all else that she falls in line and realizes the amazing opportunity she is being presented by joining with our esteemed house. Do not worry, my queen, we will raise her to the expectations you have set for her—and we will create a proper lady of the court out of her just yet."

CHAPTER 43

Approximately one day ago . . .

Kathrine nervously fumbled with the locket around her neck bearing her family's crest. Glancing nervously over to the high prince next to her as the array began to buffer, she caught his gaze and received a wide smile.

"What's wrong?" Riven asked curiously, tilting his head to one side. "You look nervous. Surely the queen isn't that bad."

Kathrine would have paled if she wasn't already so, given her vampiric heritage, and her crimson eyes shifted away. She brought a handful of pristine, silky brown hair out to her side and started stroking it absentmindedly. "Oh, it's . . . it's nothing to be concerned about. Everything is fine."

Riven's eyebrow raised in the lantern light of the array room, ignoring the ritualists as they finished tweaking the last bits for their transition to meet the queen—his great-grandmother. Surely it couldn't be that bad; his meeting with the general of House Wraithtide's forces had gone quite well. Kathrine had also told him the queen was heavily invested in his success. So why was she acting like this all of a sudden?

He shrugged. No doubt he'd find out soon if something was amiss, but he trusted Kathrine. She'd been pretty solid so far, and she had given him little reason to distrust her. "If you say so."

The high prince and lesser princess of the Blood Moon Requiem stood side by side after that, waiting in silence, until they were urged to step into the center of the arrays once more.

The transition was abrupt.

Seeing two versions of reality again just like the last time, when he and Kathrine had visited General Viku of House Wraithtide's military forces, Riven now stood not on a flagship supercarrier with a scene set in outer space, but rather in a small, circular room.

The room was closed off from the outside, with only a single brilliantly red lantern overhead shedding light onto the interior. An abnormally beautiful, scantily clad woman in white lingerie with chestnut-colored hair was meditating, floating cross-legged over a pool of blood that danced and writhed underneath her in intricate patterns drawn in the air using the liquid of the pool underneath. The patterns would shift, reorient themselves, and then disperse to coagulate back into the blood pool below, and when this woman opened up her eyes—the very room shuddered with power.

"Your Excellency! I have brought your grandson as requested!" Kathrine said in a small voice, bowing deep before prostrating herself on the ground in an act of absolute submission.

Red light leaked from the high queen's pupils, and her gaze caused Riven to gasp and fall to one knee when her aura very lightly brushed against his soul. It was as if an ocean of power hid underneath that gaze, and for a brief moment, he could sense something akin to what he could only describe as divinity. A divinity related to the origin of the Unholy foundation and the subpillar of Blood. It was so vast and so powerful that Riven without a doubt knew this woman could blow away his entire world with a quick stroke of her hand, and it made him wonder just how the cosmos had survived ancient monsters like this one roaming around the multiverse.

"You felt it . . . The touch of the blood god. Not many do," the woman said with a pleased hum in her words and a smile on her perfect lips, staring Riven down even while Kathrine gave him a confused look from her prostrate position. "That is . . . promising. Welcome, Prince Riven Wraithtide of my lineage. It is nice to finally meet the son of my favorite granddaughter. My name is Nephridi, high queen of the Blood Moon Requiem, Bringer of the Red Tide. I welcome you home."

Her aura let off, and Riven's wheezing immediately ceased. He took a while to reorient himself after having his very insides blasted with unnatural amounts of insights he could not possibly hope to grasp, a brush against an absolute titan's might, and he stood on wavering legs to get a better look at his great-grandmother.

He took in a shallow breath, evaluating the pale but stunningly pretty older woman in his wraith-like hologram body. "Nephridi. It is finally good to meet you . . . Mom always used to speak of you when I was a kid. Especially after Dad left."

At this, the high queen's demeanor immediately changed. Her intimidating and imposing aura that'd been lingering in the background immediately vanished in its entirety, and a bright smile illuminated her features to show genuine affection. "Did she?! Ah . . . how I miss your mother. Sheline truly was a masterful student, a masterful granddaughter, and the one I loved most out of all my family. As a child, she used to steal pastries from the chefs and bring them to me when I was feeling sad, you know. She and I used to snuggle in bed and read each other stories out of books her tiny hands could barely hold up. I have faith she'll return to us yet, though when that will be or why she's been gone still evades me and troubles me greatly. But enough of that—we have so much to talk about! I only wish you were actually here so that we might eat and drink together!"

He nodded—conflicted between feeling happy to hear of his mother's childhood and sad because of her disappearance. "Yeah. Her absence bothers me, too . . . but if you have faith she'll come back, it gives me hope. I miss her. A lot."

The high queen flicked her wrist, and a formfitting white dress encompassed her body while bare feet touched down onto the floor just beyond the blood pool. The patterns in the air drawn in blood quickly disappeared, and she stepped forward, reaching out to the hologram and barely touching it with two of her fingers to bop him on the nose with a laugh. "I'm curious—tell me what stories she had of me! I'd love to know!"

Surprisingly enough, Riven felt the touch and even flinched back slightly. How she was able to reach through a spatial array like that was . . . interesting, and unexpected.

Though he felt a little off by the exchange, he was genuinely curious about his long-lost great-grandmother. He rubbed his chin thoughtfully while Kathrine remained reverently kneeling beside him in silence. "Is it true that you once dumped an entire cart of rotten fruit on a romantic rival of yours and blamed it on Mom?"

The high queen blinked, then began cackling loudly.

From the reaction, Riven could safely assume that it'd indeed been true.

"And that, my little grandson, is why I don't ever walk backward in swimming pools anymore!" Nephridi grinned and popped a candied fruit into her mouth, humming to herself while sitting on a balcony chair right outside the meditation room.

Riven chuckled, a warm smile on his lips while he gazed out across the horizon curiously. Spires and towers riddled the landscape, portal gates sent people to and from different parts of the city in numerous places, and millions of people could be seen riding airships, crossing walkways between spires, or walking the gilded streets far below. It had the feel of a medieval, magical fantasy city, and would have been perfect if not for the massive number of slaves following the vampires around.

Though he knew that, in some ways, thinking this was hypocritical. Even if what he'd done to the elves, albeit temporarily, was in retribution for what they had initiated, he'd still enslaved them. And the planet he owned as an inheritance had billions of slaves. Freeing them would probably cause massive problems for not only him but the trading hub the place had become. Kathrine had even warned him he'd have riots on his hands and outright warfare between vampire and cattle if he took that route.

Riven turned to his great-grandmother, ignoring Kathrine, who stood rigid and still beside them like a pretty light pole in her own semitranslucent form, and he head-bobbed toward the sprawling city of exquisite gothic architecture. "You have quite the view here. Is it really true that you adjusted the atmosphere so our kind could walk around in the sun?"

Nephridi nodded, humming to herself and popping in another candied fruit. "Yes, I did! Many centuries ago, I perfected the art. Quite something, isn't it? And thank you—this is the view I most often visit here in the palace. I spent a lot of time just watching while in meditation. It helps calm my mind."

The queen cleared her throat, then glanced back at the minor vampiric princess who hadn't spoken a word since arriving. "My dear, have you discussed with Riven the auction your family won?"

Immediately Kathrine tensed, and she bowed her head to slowly shake it no. "I am afraid not, my queen."

"Why's that? Are you ashamed?" Nephridi frowned, then looked to Riven with amusement. "I believe she may be embarrassed."

Riven was still viewing the sights, looking down off the balcony to the palace grounds far below where gardens were attended to by cattle, but he replied anyway despite his mind being on other things. "What's she have to be embarrassed about?"

There was a pause in the conversation while the queen simply waited for Kathrine to speak, and Kathrine failed to do so—fidgeting with her pale fingers and hands while staring wide-eyed at the floor.

Nephridi eventually sighed when Riven turned around curiously, and the older woman stood to join his image at the balcony's stone edge. Leaning against the waist-height barrier, she tsked and let out an exhale. "I suppose it's about time we have this conversation, though you may not like it."

That certainly got Riven's attention, and he stopped gawking at the sights around him to turn squarely on the queen. "What's wrong?"

Nephridi didn't skip a beat. "Do you know why our empire managed to rise to be what many in the multiverse would call one of the peak factions? We are easily in the top thousand when comparing military might, and in a multiverse with hundreds of universes—each having trillions of planets—that's nothing to scoff at. It is hard to tell just what rank we hold beyond that, as in the top tiers of power many secrets are kept from one another—but there are not many who are willing or able to stand against us when our entire might is mobilized."

Riven blinked. "I suppose I don't know how it managed to do that. Enlighten me."

The queen looked up, then smiled sadly. "It's because of our bloodline, Malignant Prophecy, inherited from one of the three great dragons of time. That particular backstory is a long one and not for today, but it can be said that I and the other elders of our empire have cultivated our prophetic gifts to rise nearly to the very top. Our royal bloodline is our most valuable resource, and thus each of our families have a duty to replicate it as much as possible for the good of the empire. That requires a partner who is also a pure-blooded vampire—like you."

She let the words hang there in the air, and Riven digested them before eventually shrugging.

"I suppose this is the part where you tell me I need to make an effort for offspring with the gift, to serve the empire by creating more like us," Riven stated indifferently, much to the surprise of the queen and Kathrine alike. He sighed when he saw their reactions, then turned his attention back to the cityscape sprawling before him. "Athela already told me that was likely to happen."

"Oh. Athela is your demonic servant, correct?" Nephridi asked curiously, relief obvious in her features due to the lack of a hostile reaction. "I was afraid you'd be angry about it."

Riven clicked his tongue in irritation, glancing sideways at his grandmother with a nod. "Yeah, it's a bit irritating, I won't lie. I don't like the idea of being used as a broodmare—or whatever the technical opposite of a broodmare is, as I suppose a broodmare is a female horse. Regardless—I don't like it."

"But you accept it," Nephridi replied after a brief evaluation of his stance. "Don't you?"

"Not necessarily," Riven replied flatly with a shake of his head. "I'll outright refuse if Athela doesn't feel comfortable with it."

Nephridi raised an eyebrow. "You're basing your cooperation on a demonic slave?"

"She's not a slave," Riven snapped in irritation, surprising the queen once again with the venom in his words. "She's my best friend . . . more than that. I love her."

. . .

. . .

. . .

"But you'd be willing to do so without causing trouble if Athela felt comfortable with the idea?" Kathrine eventually interjected, causing both of the others to turn and look at her. She immediately shrank back, bowing her head again when their gazes landed.

Riven snorted, then sighed and closed his eyes. "Perhaps."

"It is a duty we all must bear, Riven," Nephridi stated simply. There was no hostility in her voice, but there was a firmness there that emphasized she'd not back down from the decision. "Kathrine's family is a good one, and she is a suitable match. They've already paid for the opportunity to acquire your hand in marriage, and—"

"Paid?!" Riven interrupted with a laugh. "Marriage?! You're kidding."

Nephridi looked a little put out at being cut off, and her demeanor shifted to irritation. Kathrine looked utterly terrified for a few moments but visibly relaxed when the queen just pinched the bridge of her nose and shook her head.

"I am not kidding. What's wrong with Kathrine, if I may ask?"

"There's nothing wrong with Kathrine. She's very pretty, has been very helpful, and we get along. However, the fact that I was not informed of being auctioned off is a very big red flag in itself, and again, I won't be doing anything unless Athela agrees to this."

"You don't have a choice."

"I do."

"No, you do not."

Riven folded his arms and glared Nephridi's way. "You might be the queen of a cosmic superpower, but unless you want to make an enemy of me forever, you will not force this on me. If you really did love my mother as much as you say you did, you'll back off."

"I cannot do that," Nephridi said with a firm shake of her head. "Even I partake in the effort to create such offspring. Every one of us that is born is a boon to the empire beyond what you can even imagine. Wars have been waged and genocides committed to retrieve just a single one of our number from enemy hands. I will not and cannot back down now. Even if I did, the other elders would rebel and declare me unfit to rule. You will do as you are told, Riven."

His features immediately grew angry, and his fists clenched. He did not immediately reply, but when he did, his words were ice-cold. "Let me be very clear, Grandmother. If push comes to shove, you will be making an enemy out of me forever—and I will simply disappear. Is that what you want?"

"It obviously is not."

"Then you will make damn sure that Athela is okay with this before it is done."

The queen sighed, rubbing her forehead with two fingers. "It sounds like you've already somewhat discussed this with your demonic friend. You won't complain if we make accommodations for your . . . lover?"

Riven lost the tension in his shoulders. "Well, I am a very straight young man in his prime. I honestly would rather have been with 'the one,' but ever since Fay left, I've had time to rethink things . . . Your proposition isn't as bad as I would have once thought. Kathrine and I have already slept together, and I feel like we're compatible. I won't sacrifice Athela's feelings for your gains, but I'm not necessarily opposed to your evil plot, either. If you can find a way to make Athela feel comfortable, and I mean EXTREMELY comfortable with the idea—I wouldn't be against it. It's a dream of many young men—that can't be argued against."

He turned to Kathrine next. "And you'd have to be okay with Athela coming first even if she does agree. Athela and my . . . Athela and Fay, the succubus I had contracted with, were at odds because they couldn't trust each other. They were . . . jealous of one another, is what I gather from talks with my minions. As long as Athela feels secure in our relationship and knows she is loved and won't have me stolen away, that's all that matters. It's your job to make sure that's how it is if you want this to work."

Kathrine visibly relaxed, and then even seemed eager, giving the first real smile since she'd arrived. "Of course. I'll speak to Athela about it when we get back . . ."

Nephridi's happy smile showed her fangs. "Very good! That was far easier than I thought it would be! A weight off my shoulders. Now, we have a couple dozen other young women of the court that'd be more than—"

"Stop." Riven held up an irritated hand to cut his grandmother off again. "Please, for the love of god. Just stop."

Nephridi sighed in mock defeat. "Fine. But we will have this conversation again later!"

Riven grimaced but didn't miss the giggle and the bounce to Nephridi's step when she whirled on a relieved Kathrine to congratulate the minor princess.

"Now we just have to convince his sister! The auction for her hand just ended, and it's a rather good match, I must say!" Nephridi laughed, only to turn and find an absolutely rigid Riven on her left. She frowned. "What is it?"

He adamantly shook his head. "All right, all jokes aside—that's not going to happen. You can have me, but Allie isn't going to be forced into a marriage like that. Zero chance."

"We just had this discussion, Riven."

"And I'm telling you, Nephridi, that so help me god, I will make it my life's goal to get revenge on you and any motherfucker that touches my sister if she doesn't want to enter an arranged marriage."

There was a pause.

"Riven, let me be blunt," Nephridi said with a frown. "My hands are tied here. Though I am the high queen, I am only one of seven elders who run the empire. If I am showing favoritism toward my great-grandchildren, the other elders will evict me from my position—and I am not strong enough to fight them all. Even if it means that at the end of five years I have to send an armada to collect you two from your planet, I will do so. It is nonnegotiable."

"And let me be blunt," Riven snarled back while jabbing a finger at Nephridi in a way that made Kathrine gasp. "You either find a way out of this or Allie and I will disappear off the face of this rock to be lost to you forever. If my mother and father did it, so can we. I am more than sure you are not as infallible as you claim to be, otherwise you'd have long ago found your favorite granddaughter and brought her back. Wars were started for the gift, were they not? You can't just have her running around like that, either—can you?"

The queen and her great-grandson glared at each other in silence until Nephridi's shoulders slumped. "There is perhaps one way to give Allie a small amount of freedom concerning her choice, to back out of the contractual agreement already signed for her hand in marriage, but it will be difficult. And there will be some very major setbacks concerning your political standing in the empire when your integration is over. You'll collect many enemies, some of which are as strong as I am, and your subjects under Wraithtide's banner may suffer for it. And if you fail, things will only be worse for both of you. Far, far worse. You may even both be enslaved, and there wouldn't be anything I could do about it if the other elders stand united against me."

Riven blinked. "Being blunt: I don't care. You're not forcing Allie into a marriage she didn't agree to. Tell me what this is about."

The queen grimaced almost violently, then folded her arms—deep in thought. "Will you at least convince Allie to meet the suitor who won the right to wed her?"

"Just meet him?"

"Yes. Have her give the man a chance. If she doesn't want him, we can proceed with the more aggressive approach. The one that may get you both evicted as royalty, to be used as nothing more than breeding slaves."

Kathrine stiffened again. "Riven, you don't—"

"I don't mean to be rude, but shut the fuck up, Kathrine." Riven glared at the minor princess, then turned back to look at the queen. "I'll let Allie speak for herself. She'll come to talk to you in private and she'll likely agree to meet with this man—but I can almost guarantee you she'll tell him to fuck off."

Nephridi continued to frown, but nodded in turn. "All right, then. If that happens and she doesn't want to take the arranged marriage, this is what you're both going to need to do."

CHAPTER 44

In the old but very large and neatly kept cabin, a poorly knitted banner of a red hand hung overhead, and various people wearing that same symbol on their clothes lined the room on armchairs, sofas, or just stood.

Hakim was in the middle of it, handcuffed and on his knees. He grunted at the impact of a fist on his face, spitting blood and a tooth out while Julie sobbed loudly behind him.

"WE DON'T HAVE THE DAMN TREASURE!" Julie screamed through tears as Hakim was hit again. "WE SPENT IT ALL!"

Caleb lay facedown on the floor, gasping for breath while his lungs filled with blood from a bullet hole. Tim and his mother were pale with tears in their eyes, and Tanya was visibly shaking.

Matt, a brawny man with a thick accent none of them could truly place and a crew cut a little uneven along the edges, just shrugged and hit Hakim again, knocking him to the ground with the last punch. His large frame was adorned with studded, enchanted leather, and he had a revolver on his left hip while a hatchet hung at his side. "Then I guess he dies, along with the rest of you."

"I don't buy it for a second, boss!" one of the ruffians nearby called out while fiddling with a knife—carving chunks out of an apple and chewing loudly while people sat next to him at a table playing poker. "They had way too much money just to spend it all. We saw the records those merchants we robbed kept. This little bunch of nobodies is holding out."

Matt nodded sagely, taking out his weathered hatchet and tossing it in the air to catch it again while muttering to himself. "Yes . . . I agree. You live on my land, and so you pay my taxes. It's that simple. I wonder how many will die before one breaks?"

"You already ransacked our cabin and killed our dog," Tanya said with quivering lips, chest puffed out in an effort to look defiant. "We have nothing left. Your people saw it for themselves when they accompanied the mercenaries you hired."

Matt tilted his head to the side, then to the other, and set a foot on Hakim's hand to push his weight down. He leaned over, getting a grunt of pain from Hakim and flatly glaring back at Tanya and her two children. He then gestured to Caleb, who was beginning to gasp and sputter. "You're really just going to let him die like that? He can't talk for himself, but we've got potions and a healer that can fix him up before he chokes on his own blood. You sure you don't want to redact your statement?"

"WE DON'T HAVE ANYTHING LEFT OTHER THAN THAT STATUE!" Julie screamed again, tugging at the handcuffs she'd been shackled with before being hit in the back of the head by another woman in the Red Hand's signature leather uniform.

Julie hit the floor, spluttering and getting a cry of defeat from Hakim as the large, brave man began to break down at seeing his lover beaten.

Matt took the tiny statue of a knight from his back pocket, examining it with a frown. "It says here the item has already been activated and cannot be used by anyone but Hakim, so that makes it worthless to me. What is this even supposed to do? It doesn't say what the damn thing's name is and says it'll destroy itself if Hakim dies."

"It's gotta be worth something, boss," the same man from earlier called out from the poker table, puffing on a pipe and watching with curiosity as the scene unfolded. "It's definitely magical—maybe have him use it?"

"That could be dangerous," another of the Red Hand members argued with a frown, arms folded. "We don't know what it does, and as you said—it's magical."

"But what if it contains a secret compartment? Maybe it's a spatial object?"

"Not worth the risk."

"If it was dangerous, he'd have already used it against us!"

"Probably, but we don't know that. It was found in his cabin, not on his person."

The two henchmen bickered for quite some time, going back and forth as Matt's eyes drooped farther and farther in irritation. Grunting and walking over to violently backhand Tim for glaring, he lowered his hatchet at Julie's neck and pulled the young woman up by her hair. "Hakim, look at me."

"LET GO OF MY DAUGHTER!" Tanya screamed, only to be savagely kicked by the same person who'd originally hit Julie.

Hakim's face was tear-streaked and wide-eyed. His gaze drifted helplessly from Julie to the man holding his lover, pleading in his features while he shook his head in a silent no.

"Want her to live?" Matt asked curiously, haphazardly tossing Hakim the knight figurine. "What does this item do? Tell me."

There was a brief pause while Hakim considered the man's words, staring at the figurine next to him with building hope now that it was so close. He rapidly shut down that train of thought in order not to give away his true feelings via facial expressions, and concentrated on just surviving this encounter—by lying. Matt was ruthless, cruel, and a basic thug. He was dumb, your equivalent of a high school bully having hit his prime in this small town in the middle of the wildlands, so there was a good chance he'd take the bait.

He would tell Matt what he wanted to hear. "It's . . . it's a temporary and hidden storage device."

"KNEW IT! IT'S A HIDDEN TYPE!" the first henchmen screamed, and some of the men laughed or clapped while the skepticism of others grew even more. "TOLD YA, BOSS. MAKE HIM ACTIVATE IT! If he's lying, just cut off his girlfriend's pretty little head and show him why it's not nice to deceive us!"

Matt considered the underling and smiled. Turning back to Hakim—he hiked a thumb back at the man sitting at the poker table. "Got to agree with Bobby there. If you just lied to us, you just sentenced every one of you to death. If you don't activate it, you all die in that scenario, too. If you activate it and something else other than items popping out of thin air happens, you all die there as well. So go on and show us if you're telling the truth. No pressure."

Hakim locked eyes with the others and shut out more tears when Caleb's final breaths left his mouth—and his friend of many months stopped breathing entirely.

Forever.

Pursing his lips, Hakim got to his knees and tried not to cry. "Put it in my hands. I'll activate it, and you can see for yourself that I'm no liar. A portal will open, and our treasure will be accessible."

Matt's smile widened. "I'm glad you've all decided to come around. Too bad about your friend, but maybe the rest of you will get out of this alive just yet."

Riven's footsteps echoed through the elegant meeting hall, with Athela and Azmoth walking on either side of him. Yattazi was curled around Azmoth's body like a tight hug, and to either side, dozens of rat-kin stood with bowed heads as a sign of respect to his passing.

Surprisingly enough there were even a small number of vampires already there. He stopped in front of the trio, all of them showing red eyes and pale skin as they fidgeted nervously under his gaze—though he could tell that there was a stark difference between them and him. He was a pureblood, so was Kathrine, so was Allie, and even a number of the elite soldiers sent to Panu were, too.

These vampires in front of him, dressed in elegant purple and black silks with hoods over neatly trimmed blonde hair, were all lesser vampires. Their eyes didn't glow at all, and their touch of the Blood subpillar was . . . lacking. At least compared to what he'd seen from vampires of the Blood Moon Requiem.

[Lesser Vampire Assassin, Level 40]
[Lesser Vampire Scout, Level 35]
[Lesser Vampire Warlock, Level 42]

Oh? A warlock? Good choice.

He ignored them for the moment, turning his gaze back to where the queen of Deepnest and her royal guards, all the larger, more muscular variants of rat-kin, were. The guards were heavily armored, covered in thick, spiked brown metal that was far different from the chitin or leathers he'd seen most of the rat-kin warriors put on. They each carried huge maces along their backs, and they looked like walking, tailed tanks given all the layers around their large forms.

They reminded him of Azmoth, but less intimidating.

The inside of the great hall was similar to the one he'd seen when meeting Rashtalia, broodmother of Brood-Tarrow, the brood Snagger and his cousin Mesha belonged to. Vibrantly colored crystals adorned the walls and ceiling, and a throne was set up on a raised level to look down on where Riven was walking. Stands on either side were where the nobility and important figures of Deepnest now stood, various kinds of garments on display in a ragtag bunch of mismatched styles, but that kind of chaos was expected given the way Deepnest was set up.

He briefly stopped again to take his helmet off, waving to the tall brood-mother Rashtalia and his two friends, Snagger and Mesha, before continuing. He made it a point to single them out and continued forward—letting Jackal take its canine form when he was twenty yards away from the throne.

On that very large stone throne was a mouselike figure adorned in finely made blue cloth, a figure that was far fatter than any creature he'd yet seen, aside from the ambushing cyclops he'd killed shortly after trying to take the elves back to Greenstalk all that time ago. The queen was rotund, almost a sphere with rolls, and he was surprised she could even move her black-furred head.

But it did manage to swivel his way when he got up closer.

"Bat-kin Riven-friend! King-ruler of Thane Necropolis!" the queen exclaimed, waving a stumpy nub of a hand out from the rolls of fat overlying most of her arm. "I am excited-pleased that you come-visit us in our time of need-strife!"

Riven tried not to stare at the huge creature's body. There was nothing wrong with some extra weight, but by god this thing was on another level. "Hello, Queen Bez. I've heard about you from Rashtalia, but it's nice to finally make your acquaintance."

"Yes-yesh!!! Do you enjoy-like the grand-great city-nest of this humble one's making?"

"Certainly, Your Majesty. It is truly an interesting place to behold." He gestured to his three minions, introducing them one by one. "This is Athela, the woman I love. This is Azmoth, one of my best of friends. And this is Yattazi, a newly contracted demonic familiar. I hope you can show them the same courtesy you've shown me, and we all look forward to helping your people in the battle to come."

The huge black-furred rat-kin smiled wide. "Is it true-agreed that you-you seek to fight in battle-war yourself? That you will-can fight the dwarf-dwellers in their burrow-holes and bring us-we a victory-win to end this war?"

The nobles of Deepnest were utterly quiet when she uttered the question, and he gave a single nod—getting an uproar of approval with shouts, cheers, and excited rat-kin screams. It was quite unexpected when they started chanting his name, and even more unexpected were the huge barrels of wine and mead that were rolled out of a side tunnel. His eyebrows lifted when corks burst and flowing streams of alcohol started rampaging down the steps to the chants of "Riven-Thane! Bat-kin-friend! Riven-Thane! Bat-kin-friend!"

He hadn't even been in the greeting hall three minutes before insanity broke loose, and servants started flinging pastries, cooked meats, and desserts across the room from hidden alcoves.

The queen sat up with much effort, ignoring the shocked expression on his pale face, and raised a pudgy hand. "WE CELEBRATE THE DEATH-KILLS OF THE SHORT-STRONG BEARDED ONES!!!"

"RRRRAAAAAAAAAAHHHH!!!!" the host of rat-kin screamed their approval, doing weird jigs and dances in the sloshing alcohol while picking up various foods or taking them from the servants who continued to fling food across the room.

"RIVEN-THANE! BAT-KIN-FRIEND! RIVEN-THANE! BAT-KIN-FRIEND!"

"DEATH-KILLS TO THE BEARDED WAR-BATTLE BRINGERS!"

"RRRRAAAAAAAAAAAHHHH!!!!"

Riven's wide crimson eyes stared about him, an incredulous smirk playing at his lips while he used a single finger to wipe a pastry from his chest plate. He tasted the icing, glancing at a dancing rat-kin in orange linens who was obviously already drunk and had probably pregamed this event, and thought it tasted rather good.

Food flew through the air.

His gluttonous chest plate was already licking up food and using tendrils of sin energy to slurp at the alcohol, and looking at Azmoth, who was now wearing a cake on his face, his grin turned into outright laughter.

Athela held up a finger and stared down at the flowing river of alcohol that continued to pour out of numerous barrels near the throne. "Definitely not what I expected, but not unwanted. I dare say these guys throw a better welcoming party than anyone else I've ever met."

"RIVEN-THANE! BAT-KIN-FRIEND! RIVEN-THANE! BAT-KIN-FRIEND!"

"RRRAAAAAAAAAAHHHHHHHH!!!"

Azmoth shared a look with Yattazi after wiping the cake off, shrugged, and started grabbing at the pieces of cooked meat that were being flung across the room. "I like. Get more."

"Agreed!" Yattazi nodded, going HAM on the food nearby with Azmoth while Riven and Athela were left to stand alone.

Looking to his left and seeing Athela standing there, ankle-deep in wine and licking icing off her arm, his eyes softened. She was giggling and laughing, pushing small drunken rat-kin away and then exclaiming to Azmoth that he'd better save some of the orange stuff for her. She quickly got into the spirit of things and joined a wrestling match when the queen threw a particularly large cooked lizard into the crowd. She went in on it more for the sake of the fun rather than actually wanting to eat it, but started squabbling with the locals over what parts she could tear off before her perfect, laughing features turned that bright smile his way.

She saw him staring at her, just staring with kind eyes, and her laughing smile fell slightly. Realization overcame her then, and she let go of the lizard—evading a couple drunkards and dodging a cake Azmoth had flung at her. When she came to stand in front of Riven, her eyes fell to the floor only momentarily—before she firmed her jaw and looked back up at him while wrapping her hands around his waist.

"Why are you looking at me like that?" Athela said, ignoring the splashes of the insanity around them.

He put a hand up to her cheek, gently touching her pitch-black skin inter-mixed with patches of white. "I'm just really glad I met you. Sometimes I take you for granted, you know. Athela . . . we should get away sometime. Spend some time together, just the two of us, maybe take a trip into the mountains before the Chalgathi trials start up again."

She blinked, tears coming to her eyes, and bit her lip before nodding eagerly. "Could we have a picnic?"

He nodded slowly, pulling her in and kissing her softly before letting go seconds later. Their red eyes met again, and with a shred of his aura he swatted away another morsel of flying food amid the chanting of his name. "I would love to go on a picnic with you. Let's make it our first official date. It's been a long time coming, and I'm head over heels just thinking about it."

[Hakim Bluebush has activated a two-time-use system artifact: Heroic Intervention. Two of two charges have been used. Heroic Intervention has selected the five most powerful people Hakim has interacted with since Earth's integration, and you—Riven Thane—are one of them. Hakim Bluebush is currently in need of your help and has placed a live-stream feature in the orb before you that will connect momentar-ily. You will be able to speak to him briefly as he explains his current situation before deciding whether to aid him. You can choose to assist or refuse his request. All or none of the selected participants may go or stay without penalty. If you choose to aid him and risk yourself, you will be teleported to his location until his plight is over. Then you will be teleported back to your current location after a short rest period. Please hold for connection.]

Riven's shoulders immediately sagged, and he pulled Athela into a tight hug after recognizing the notification. "I supposed it's time to tell Queen Bez that we'll be back within the day. It appears we have another job on our hands."

"Your Majesty!" an unfamiliar voice shouted out to him over the hubbub, and Riven turned to see it was one of the three lesser vampires, who was doing his best not to act disgusted by all that was going on about him. The man was obviously trying to look presentable, but that was hard to do with yellow jelly smeared all across the front of his clothes. "Would it be all right if I took but a moment of your time?! I am but a mere—"

Riven held up a hand while Athela bounded across the room to the rat-kin queen, and he shook his head while a flashing bauble of light began to form nearby. "Not now. I know why you're here, but the specifics can come later. It appears I am being summoned, and not to be rude, but this is a call that I cannot miss."

Hakim's heart beat like a drum while his gaze stared daggers at Matt, who was holding the blade of his hatchet against Julie's throat. Blood leaked from a wound atop her head where she'd been struck earlier, and the gang lining the large cabin were in large part focused on the five flashing orbs that began to condense above Hakim in the air.

"So it is true! This is where the treasure lies!" Matt crowed with a wide smile, but he kept his hold on Julie regardless. "I cannot wait to see just what your friend died for!"

The tiny figurine of the artifact—Heroic Intervention—began to fizzle away and turned to dust, while images in the five orbs quickly began to take shape—displaying the faces of men and women he recognized. Each was one of the five people that the system deemed as the most powerful characters Hakim had encountered in Elysium's multiverse thus far—and one in particular above all others who Hakim had hoped would be there.

Hakim's heart lifted with hope growing while shouts of confusion echoed through the cabin as members of the Red Hand adjusted to this new occurrence. His lips parted, and tears began streaming down his face again. "Riven . . . please!"

A portal of multicolored light formed only a half second later, one that was far larger than the similarly constructed bauble, and out stepped a man clad in ivory plate armor with red bloodsilk underlying the cracks and crevices his ivory did not cover. A large gluttonous maw rippled along the center vertically, horned skull pauldrons adorned his shoulders, and an aura of supreme power followed him as he set foot onto the cabin floor. A long black spear-staff with a curved blade and flowing with rivers of living blood lifted up—then the butt of the weapon came down and settled gently against the wood beneath.

BOOM

A shock wave of aura lit the room red. Blood frost rapidly accumulated along the surfaces of the furniture, ceiling, walls, and floor—even freezing some of the clothes people wore as they screamed and backpedaled in shock.

Bright crimson eyes glared daggers through the slits in the full metal plate helm, and out of the portal came three more figures. One was Athela—her long, slender legs dripping wine and arachnid blades spearing out of her back as she sneered malevolently as she caught Julie's predicament. Another was Azmoth, who was carrying an enormous slab of boar meat in each of his four hands—beginning to pulse with flame. Last was a three-foot snake, though given its own aura and the pulsing, crackling Chaos energy around it—it was in no uncertain terms able to kill many, if not everyone, present.

All of them were partially covered in cake and pastry.

Matt stood there, slack-jawed, holding the blade to Julie's throat. In front of him were four identification messages, the same ones that'd appeared in front of many of the others in his gang. Some only showed question marks, but the ones who did manage to identify him displayed very familiar markings if one were to keep up with the world forums. Bright-red flames engulfed the status notifications concerning Riven and Athela, while gold flames encompassed the words comprising those of Azmoth and Yattazi.

[Riven Thane, Level 130 Warlock Devastator, Harbinger of Gluttony, Pure-blooded Vampire, Lost Prince of the Blood Moon Requiem. LEGENDARY. PANU WORLD BOSS.]
[Athela, Level 127 Archdemon: Unique, three forms. Cute Wittle Blood Weaver/Gluttonous Arshakai/Gluttonous Fae Drider. LEGENDARY. PANU WORLD BOSS.]
[Azmoth, Level 95 Infernal Crusader Initiate, Hellscape Brutalisk. ELITE.]
[Yattazi, Level 130 Devouring Serpent, Demonic Basilisk. ELITE.]

"Well, well, well . . . What do we have here?" Riven asked softly, his voice traveling across the room and infused with power that shook the people there to their very bones. The figures in the four other orbs that Hakim's relic had conjured were all gawking, too—all of them except one blonde woman, who'd already briefly met Riven the last time that item had been used.

Riven's gaze turned to Hakim, then Tim, Tanya, Julie, and finally Caleb—dead at their feet. The log cabin they were in was enormous—judging from the size, he assumed it must have been used as a luxury getaway space at one point—but now it was dirty and littered with garbage." Riven tsked in irritation before bringing his glowing crimson eyes back up to Matt. "You done fucked up, my guy. You really, really did."

CHAPTER 45

Matt shifted his gaze from the portal, to Hakim, to Riven, and then to the three demons partially covered in pastry. His grip tightened around the axe he still held against Julie's throat amid the dead silence of the room, and he immediately pulled out his revolver to lower it at Julie's skull with a click. "Hakim!!! Hakim, you backstabbing little bitch! I told you that I'd blow your girlfriend's head off if you betrayed me!"

Hakim didn't reply. He was horrified, and at a complete loss for words facing the potential death of his lover.

"I believe . . ." Athela said with a snarl, red eyes flashing and six long arachnid blades slamming into the ground around her in a rage, "that you're holding an axe to my friend's neck. I wonder just how good your insides will taste when I'm done with you."

She looked like she was about to lunge, but Matt pressed hard against Julie's skin—drawing blood and getting a scream from the young woman as well as from Hakim, Tim, and Tanya.

"I know who the fuck you are! I've seen the forum videos!" Matt growled, half in rage and half in absolute fear. "I don't know how the hell you monsters got here or why you give a shit about these people, but I know damn well you don't have a healer. Why get one when you can regenerate almost any wound, you sick fucking abomination!"

Matt shakily spat in Riven's direction, leaving a glob of the stuff at Riven's feet, while pulling Julie back a step as Athela hissed. He nodded to the three demons next. "And your demon friends can't even be permanently killed! So why have a healer, right? So goddamned cheap, unfair, and overpowered! I'll tell you right now, this girl is going to have her throat slit and her goddamn HEAD is gonna be blown off if you come any closer!"

Riven internally grumbled in irritation, but he actually was worried about Julie's current predicament. He didn't know how or why their group had come into this situation, but this asshole was partially right—he didn't have any healers because he'd never really needed one. He could provide stitching with Athela's webbing like she'd done in the past, though, and he had the Voodoo Doll spell, which he'd rarely utilized—but it could keep bloodstreams of his target flowing even outside a body to maintain oxygen to the brain. The problem was that if sufficient damage was done, Riven would have to continue channeling the spell until an actual healer got to them or he could use a healing potion. Voodoo Doll only maintained the blood flow, but it didn't actually heal a person, and he couldn't use other spells at the same time due to the channeling effect. But if a bullet went through Julie's head? He doubted he'd be able to save her even with Voodoo Doll, even with all the system modifications one could have on their bodies. A slit throat was bad enough but probably manageable, though he'd not want to take that risk—but a bullet in the brain was probably a dead-set deal given his team composition.

[Julie, Level 22 Healer Priestess Initiate]

Yeah, there was no way she'd survive a bullet to the head.

"I suppose we're at an impasse, then," Riven said with a tilt to his head, outwardly unconcerned.

The rest of the room, both Matt's startled ruffians and Hakim's small group, remained wide-eyed and very still—looking from Matt to Riven and then the three demons.

Matt seemed to regain some of his composure at Riven's response, and, realizing he wasn't about to immediately die and had been right on the money, he smiled wickedly. He nodded to one of the men who'd been playing poker earlier. "Hank, get Julie's team rounded up and make sure you have guns pointed at their—"

Riven's hand abruptly lifted, flared with blood magic and then discharged, tearing a hole in Hank's chest the size of a bowling ball and shattering the wall in a spray of debris to the screams of nearby people. He held up a finger and waggled it back and forth. "Tsk, tsk—none of that. The only thing keeping you alive is Julie, but the rest of your people?"

Riven gave an ominous laugh, betting this act on the self-preservation instincts of this man in front of him. He wasn't about to let the others become hostages, too. "Yattazi, Azmoth, Athela—kill the others."

Matt's eyes went wide and he dragged Julie back another step, cursing under his breath as people started screaming and trying to run. Men and women wearing the Red Hand's logo slipped on red ice and piled over one another while lunging for doorways, windows, and even the hole in the wall that Riven had created mere moments ago.

But the demons were upon them.

Or at least two of them were.

Azmoth echoed with a resounding demonic roar and burst into flames, tearing across the cabin and smashing two of the men nearby into paste. He discarded his boar meat and started using his claws, having given Riven his maul earlier that day for safekeeping, ripping off limbs and breathing fire—or clamping down on fleeing enemies with the two eel-like maws coming out of his back. He turned his attention to the people inside, and seeing more people coming up from a basement entrance, he breathed flames into the depths, which resulted in horrified wails, and then continued on.

Yattazi immediately began growing in size from the current three-foot snake she was now, expanding her body at an extreme pace while her muscles, tail, and bones all bulged simultaneously. It was like watching a fire hydrant burst out of a water balloon, and soon her huge tail crashed out the back of the cabin stronghold and took out another wall—causing the building to shudder and partially collapse on more of the enemy group when her head tore through the ceiling. Magma eyes flared, spines on her neck stood up, and as her gaze settled on each of the running morsels, marks began appearing on their bodies so that she might better track them as they scattered. With a hissing lunge, her body turned into a stream of black and gray Chaos energy as she snapped down on one of the fleeing rogues—the woman's scream only coming off as a squeak before her neck was crushed and her body swallowed. The demonic basilisk, half the length of a football field, began to hunt them down like a cat hunting mice.

Athela remained in her position, though, more concerned about Julie than she was with killing the idiots who were running away in droves. There were a lot more of them than Riven had originally thought—what had once been dozens had turned into well over a hundred people. Maybe even two hundred, though in the end they were all insignificant.

They were weak.

Athela's lithe figure slowly circled Matt and his prisoner amid the dying screams of his people, and she took out her ruby-studded black tiara to put it on her head while continuing to walk in absolute silence.

Riven glared at the man while Matt violently yanked Julie toward a wall—putting his back to the wood so Athela couldn't continue to circle him. However, Athela maintained eye contact with Matt, stepping over two freshly charred bodies and then exiting out a cabin door.

"I suppose now the question becomes, how do we proceed from here?" Riven mused, walking forward and sitting at a table that was somehow still intact, and laying Jackal on the wood. The maw along his chest hissed, and black tendrils began pulling in a nearby corpse—devouring it slowly while Matt looked on in horror.

The Red Hand leader only pressed that blade even more tightly against Julie's neck—shivering from the cold while crimson frost collected on his clothes. "You're going to let me go. You're going to give me money to start over, and I'm taking Julie with me so I have an insurance policy on my life."

Riven sighed, tapping his armored finger against the table as a charred leg splattered against the remaining nearby wall. Another part of the roof collapsed as flames licked at the wood, but he smacked the debris away with his aura and set Hakim, Tim, and Tanya in a protective dome of Crimson Ice. "Not going to happen."

"You don't have a choice unless you want her brains splattered on the ground!" Matt hissed with venom in his words.

Julie whimpered, and tears continued to trickle down her cheeks.

"She's as good as dead anyways if she leaves with you," Riven said absentmindedly. "There's zero chance she's going. However, I am willing to make you a deal. I'm willing to pay for her release."

"Not good enough! You'll just kill me when I leave and take the goods back!" Matt protested, ignoring the begging pleas for help and the horrified wails—both outside in the forest and inside the cabin—of his people as they were eaten alive or torn apart. "I'll need more than that or I swear to god I'll pull this trigger!"

Riven gave Athela a very small mental nudge, tugging at the bond between them to let her know he was ready. He then chuckled malevolently. "I see. And how are you going to pull that trigger when the gun simply won't fire?"

Matt's brows furrowed in confusion, and he blinked rapidly before glancing down at the weapon in his hand. His eyes went wide in horror when he realized the revolver was covered in red frost, and when he saw Riven's hand move in his direction, Matt roared in snarling defiance. He pulled the trigger, or attempted to, but the frozen gun wouldn't budge—and he immediately began drawing the axe blade across Julie's neck when two things happened simultaneously.

The first was the lightning-fast hand gesture Riven made, flaring his finger and then quickly grasping at Matt's chest—and immediately Matt went rigid as his heart stopped.

[Voodoo Doll (Blood) (Tier 2): Scan your target to map out their vessels and infuse your mana into their bloodstream. You then gain the ability to replicate their bloodstream regardless of whether they have extensive wounds—enabling you to keep them alive as long as their brain remains intact. You may also use this ability on hostiles to form painful blood clots. Heart attacks caused by this ability do critical strike damage. Dependent on both Intelligence (90%) and Willpower (10%) stats. Medium cooldown. This is a channeling ability and will not work if interrupted by using other spells.]

The second thing that happened at the exact same time Riven made that hand gesture was the wall at Matt's back exploding in six small but different spots. Long black blades, Athela's arachnid limbs, tore through the cabin to take advantage of Riven's stun and tore into Matt's head, heart, and neck.

The move was so fast that the man who was undergoing a heart attack at that very moment didn't have time to react while the blades found their marks, and with a lurch the blades retracted—tearing pieces of his upper body and his head off his body in a spray of wooden chips and bloody flesh.

Julie dropped to the ground as Matt's body was torn apart, beginning to sob, and the Crimson Ice dome covering the rest of them was removed as Hakim frantically rushed over with the rest of the emotional family to hug Julie in a tight group embrace.

Riven smiled at the scene, though he did feel bad about not being there fast enough to help that Caleb guy. He glanced over at Caleb's corpse with a bitter look and shook his head. There was only so much he could do. "Jackal?"

The weapon transformed into its canine image, staring back at him from a shadowy figure on the table and red eyes staring expectantly.

- **Portal Master: This weapon can sync to any stabilized portal you have permission to use from the maker and master. Current locations available for access: Dungeon Negrada, Riven's Eye Wormhole. Takes one week of channeling in the same place to use this ability.**

Riven gestured over to the portal Hakim's treasure had created, then removed his helmet and scratched his chin. "Is it possible for you to stabilize that portal with your Portal Master technique? I was hoping to return here after dealing with the dwarves."

[Guild functions for Panu are nearing completion. Preform a guild of up to twenty people in order to participate; system lock on guild roster has been destroyed. Sole features of guild functions are now as follows in preparation for the worldwide guild introduction event: guild name, guild roster, link to guild hall. Factions options of the Guild and Factions tab will still remain locked until a later date.]

Allie swiped the notification away, uninterested in such things given her current situation, and she gently swirled the blood in her crystal goblet before sipping on it and staring out across the Lucio estate.

Lahn's family home had been left intact for the most part. This was unlike most of the uppermost level of Mandon, capital of Dawn, which had been decimated after the Rippenvire attack. Scouts, both as spies on the ground and planes in the air, were searching rigorously for the remnants of the Rippenvire vampires who'd gone into hiding, and diplomatic envoys to neighboring upstart nations—often spearheaded by none other than herself—made it very clear that any information regarding the invaders needed to be sent to the Thane Necropolis immediately. The prisoners, vampires captured from the battle, were still being interrogated, but most of them wouldn't talk other than to curse their captors.

"How are you liking the tea?" Lady Shovi Lucio asked Mara hesitantly, outwardly nervous in the presence of so many of Allie's friends.

Mara's pretty ghoul features smiled with an unusual warmth—pale eyes burrowing into Lahn's mother. "It is very good, Lady Lucio. Thank you so much for your hospitality."

Lady Shovi Lucio, Allie, Mara, and Linela Lucio were having girl time today at the suggestion of Lahn. All of them sat on the uppermost balcony of Lahn's family mansion while eating pastries and sipping on drinks. Though Allie held only ill will toward Linela and would have preferred to rip her apart and feed on her like she'd done with that Gleetus prick, Allie had given in to Lahn's suggestion when he'd given her that ridiculously adorable puppy dog look. The bastard didn't even do it intentionally; he just looked sad when Allie had initially said no, but she'd quickly given in and agreed after that gods damned look he wore. It was almost like she'd slapped him across the face when she'd said no, but when she changed her tune and agreed—it was all worthwhile to see his face light up.

She chuckled to herself, sipping on the blood in her goblet again and enjoying the awkward silence that was almost entirely centered on the fact that Linela was there. Mara had been giving the young woman death glares, and even her mother had been hesitant to talk to her daughter after learning of the plots against her youngest son.

It was Mara who eventually broke that silence. "My queen . . . We had a message from the Blood Moon Requiem come in, something about an envoy from a high-ranking family wanting to meet you for an important matter. They didn't give details."

Allie only shrugged, still somewhat unwilling to make this meeting any less awkward. She still hadn't looked at Lahn's sister even once, and she could tell that Linela was incredibly uncomfortable by the way she fidgeted in her chair and constantly shifted her blonde hair from one side to the other.

Even from here, on the uppermost balcony of the mansion, Allie could see efforts to rebuild what had been lost. Roads had been smashed apart and the nearby town below the hill that the Lucio estate sat on was in utter ruin. Civilians and military personnel alike worked tirelessly to put their shattered lives back together, and with the entire military having been withdrawn from the front lines against Tereen now that the war with the elves was over, there was a significant force here to help with that rebuilding.

She pulled her hood down over her features when brighter rays of sunlight hit her pale face, and her red eyes squinted in discomfort. "Is my aura putting you off, Lady Lucio? I know my negative Charisma is certainly a thing. I can place the amulet back on if you'd like."

"No! No, of course not, my queen! You are quite all right!"

Allie smirked. Good . . . she knew her aura was certainly bothering that blonde bitch to her right, so she'd intentionally kept that amulet off. Now, with Lady Shovi Lucio's permission, she'd continue to keep it off.

There was another long pause, and Shovi put down her cup of tea to smooth out her green silk dress. "Ahem. Do you still plan on attending the ball with my son?"

Allie's eyebrows immediately raised, and she finally turned to look at Lahn's mother with scrutinizing interest. "The royal ball is still happening?"

Shovi gave a small chuckle and nodded. "Yes, my queen. Though it feels odd calling it the royal ball now that our king has submitted to your will. Perhaps you should start calling yourself an empress rather than just a queen? Since you have two vassal states underneath you—Dawn and Tereen."

"I like the sound of that." Mara smiled with a nod of approval. "I certainly do."

But Allie was still confused. "When is it happening? I had no idea. I guess I just assumed that it'd be called off."

Shovi shook her head, diamond earrings swooshing back and forth. "King Arthur Brix has decided to not only keep the ball, but increase the festivities surrounding it to include many of the upper-class merchants that'll likely be given titles of nobility now that power gaps in the aristocracy have opened up. Political stuff. With so many dead after the battle for Mandon, he believes it will rejuvenate the people he most needs to keep connections with. What better way to do that than throw an extravagant party to have some fun and keep the feel of normalcy in an otherwise abnormal world?"

Shovi gave Allie a warm smile. "And my son is very excited about the prospect of still going with you, if you'd still have him."

"Of COURSE I still want to go with him!" Allie exclaimed, beaming and nearly standing from her seat before containing her excitement. "I've been looking forward to that ball for quite a while! Where is it going to be held?"

"The palace was destroyed, so the academy is our next best option. Last I talked to my husband, he said it will likely be held there. Probably within the next few weeks."

"The academy is intact, too?"

"Some of it. Not all, but much of the grounds are still intact with only a few buildings having been demolished in the fighting. Repairs are underway now and should be complete by the time the ball rolls around. Are you going to come as Allie, princess of the Blood Moon Requiem and queen of the Thane Necropolis? Or are you going to come as Allie of a minor noble house nobody has heard of from out in the country? Not many people know of who you are outside my own family and the king. Even Gleetus . . . his family has no idea what happened—and on threat of treason King Brix has told us not to reveal your secret."

Allie considered those words, suddenly deep in thought. She'd worn her skull mask during the battle, too, and there was no footage that she was aware of on the forums that actually showed her face.

Interesting.

She'd certainly enjoyed the school scene and very much wanted to return to a more relaxing life from time to time, even if needs demanded otherwise on occasion. Smiling, she shrugged and began stirring the liquid in her glass with a pale, slender finger. "I actually may stay my hand and return as a country bumpkin. Today's meeting has been very enlightening, Lady Lucio. I'm quite glad I came to spend time with you."

Shovi absolutely beamed at the compliment, seeing the olive branch for what it was, and her smile almost touched her ears. "I'm incredibly happy to hear it! I've actually been wanting to get your opinion on a couple of dresses for the ball as well—perhaps we could even go shopping together! Would Mara like to come, too?! Ah, I'm rather excited!!!"

CHAPTER 46

The portal stabilized, and a notification appeared signaling that it was slightly different than the prior portals he'd already linked to.

[Heroic Intervention's portal is now accessible through your Portal Master key concerning your spear-staff, Jackal. Due to the nature of this portal's origins, you will need to infuse extra mana to create this portal again and the portal will disappear after a short time of no use, but the origin points have been permanently set.]

So it'd go away and other people couldn't use it if he wasn't around?

That was a shame. Riven had been hoping he could send people to and from Deepnest here, but it appeared his weapon only had so much power concerning the ability to link to such wormholes.

Still, it was better than the alternative of not working at all.

An hour later, Riven stood silently on a hill next to Hakim's cabin, a few miles away from where Riven had initially teleported in. The slaughter had been quick and the dead numbered somewhere between two and three hundred after he'd mopped the floor with the low-life bastards, but despite his quick intervention, he'd still failed to save Caleb, Hakim's guildmate and friend.

He watched silently, holding Athela by the hand and frowning while giving the others space to bury the man who'd helped them survive all these months since the integration tutorial. Yattazi was still hunting down the few stragglers who'd managed to get away, and Azmoth was leaning against a tree with his arms folded—still cindering across his obsidian plate and fleshy, muscular body.

Hakim, Julie, Tim, and Tanya laid the man to rest under a very large pine tree, a species of plant common to these lands, as was very apparent by the sprawling temperate forest around them. They laughed, cried, and hugged each other as they told stories about Caleb in the time that they'd known him since the world had fallen apart, and Riven found himself gazing into a valley where a town a few miles off had lights flickering in the night.

His thoughts were interrupted with a system notification.

[Guild functions for Panu are nearing completion. Preform a guild of up to twenty people in order to participate; system lock on guild roster has been destroyed. Sole features of guild functions are now as follows in preparation for the worldwide guild introduction event: guild name, guild roster, link to guild hall. Factions options of the Guild and Factions tab will still remain locked until a later date.]

"Been a while since the system talked about guilds and factions," Riven mused under his breath, still keeping his distance from the ceremony. "I wonder what this worldwide event is about. The other ones concerning world quests have been very vague—I still have no idea what the Lich King and snow giant quests are about."

"You should read more of the world forums," Athela stated with a teasing smile, tightening her grip around Riven's hand. "You'd understand a lot more about what's going on in your world. Specifically about those two."

"She right." Azmoth nodded sagely, four arms folded and obsidian plates still cindering over exposed, fleshy, skinless muscle. "You on the forums much."

Riven grimaced under the starlight, red eyes once again focusing on the small burial procession. "I have enough to deal with already, but I suppose you're both right. I probably should catch up on world events."

"Want me to give you a rundown on the highlights until you do?" Athela asked curiously, pressing her body up against his.

He chuckled. "That'd be great."

Smiling, Athela let out a content hum and began ticking off fingers one by one. "Essentially there are a couple very big players other than yourself. Most of them are on the rankers list. Remember Judith Marcina? Oh, and you've moved up in the rankings to number four since you checked last."

Athela pulled up the top ten list and pointed to the number one spot, where Judith Marcina was listed. Cherish Lightcrown, the Everlight Witch, had fallen off the list from the rank ten spot and had been replaced by someone else. Otherwise the other top spots had just rearranged slightly.

[Twenty-seven billion current participants have been analyzed. The ranking categories are as follows: Apex rank (top 10), Paragon rank (top 1,000), S rank (top 0.0001%), A rank (top 1%), B rank (top 15%), C rank (top 30%), D rank (top 50%), E rank (bottom 50%)]
[Current Top 10 Native Participants:
  1. **Judith Marcina, Level 169 Human, Apex rank, Angelic Fallcaller**
  2. **Aren Hrall, Level 150 Snow Giant, Apex rank, Frostmage Berserker**
  3. **Retesh Vorath, Level 187 Corpse Lord, Apex rank, Elder Lich**
  4. **Riven Thane, Level 130 Pureblooded Vampire, Apex rank, Warlock Devastator, Harbinger of Gluttony**

5. Nithkik Brutishvase, Level 140 Dark Elf, Apex rank, Depthdweller
6. Thorman Bame, Level 154 Human, Apex rank, Hammer of the Mountain
7. Sinthil Tuk'tuk, Level 166 Lizardian, Apex rank, Wind Storm
8. Chitter Teh-Sneaker, Level 136 Rat Man, Apex rank, Dark-Blade Assassin, Poison Master, Sneaky Sneak Sneaker
9. Brock Longbeard, Level 125 Sundering Dwarf, Apex rank, Battlemaster
10. Netithi Bluskish, Level 121 Naga, Apex rank, Champion of the Kraken

Guild Rankings Currently Not Available. Guild functions are currently being set up. Create a guild of up to one hundred people in preparation for the guild introduction world event.]

Athela pointed to the number one spot on the list, Judith Marcina. "She's probably the best-known of the top rankers, and for good reason, aside from yourself and the dwarf Brock Longbeard. The rest of the top ten don't have nearly as many videos about them available, with Aren Hrall the snow giant in particular being very elusive because he's actually the antagonist for a world quest and a lot of his videos are being temporarily withheld while he gathers power."

Athela pulled up the old world quest notification describing said event.

- **World Quest 5, Realm of the Snow Giants: In the southern reaches of the glacial islands in the Numenor Sea, on the opposite end of the world from where the Lich King lies in wait, an ambitious king of the snow giants has united the warring tribes. He has been blessed by the system with an artifact of immense power, enabling him to clone and create more of his kind with ritual magic, and he is preparing an army for world domination as we speak. He is ruthless, cunning, unfeeling toward the other races that he views as stepping-stones to be slaughtered in the pursuit of power, and a threat that should not be taken lightly. His goal is genocide of all other enlightened races on Panu. Kill the snow giant king, destroy and reforge his artifact to fit your own purposes, and secure his throne on the glacial islands for yourselves. Current Threat Level: High. Catastrophe upon failure of completion when five years has passed: The artifact's power will be tripled, enabling the king of the snow giants to drastically ramp up production of followers. Advanced Details: Not Unlocked.**

"Because Aren Hrall is having his uploaded videos temporarily hidden by the system due to this world quest, it's safe to assume that he is the snow giant king World Quest 5 talks about. No absolute confirmations, but it's a solid guess. Why else would the system hide his uploads?" Athela said with a frown. "Not a good sign that he's ranked second on the power ladder. Anyways, back to Judith Marcina—the human with a class called Angelic Fallcaller. Simply put, she's incredibly powerful. She uses summoned angels to battle for her, similar to how you use demons but in reverse, along with a lot of Holy, Sun, and Moon magics. She's currently a self-crowned empress ruling over the newly created Starfallen Empire, ruling over a dozen or so cities, and her videos show her wiping out entire armies by herself. She's often compared to you as your opposite in that regard and is very aggressive in her pursuits to claim territory. I highly suggest you watch her footage—it's pretty intimidating. There's a reason why she's ranked number one."

"Interesting," Riven said with a nod. "Nothing on Retesh Vorath? The number-three elder lich?"

"Some, but minimal. The only videos I've seen of him are at the back of a horde of undead during a battle with other undead; apparently he's on the front lines concerning World Quest 1. Rumors on the world forums talk about how he's the only reason a certain human city hasn't been overrun by the designated lich king. Other people say he IS the lich king, and other rumors talk about how he's not even involved in the quest. We just don't know—but it doesn't appear the system is hiding his uploads, at least not entirely."

- **World Quest 1, The Lich King's Plague: In the far reaches of the northern Chaos Wastelands, an ancient lich begins to stir. Advanced details are locked.**

Riven glazed over the very brief description of World Quest 1, and his frown grew deeper. "If World Quest 5 and World Quest 1 have two of the top three positions on the power ladder, and this power ladder actually has made natives turn on one another and given these people different sets of world quests to make them the scenario villain . . . that's really bad. I hope those rumors are wrong. And if they are correct, does that mean these people are on the same side—or are they only out for themselves?"

He scratched his head, only turning around when interrupted by Tanya's sore, wavering voice and the crackle of twigs underfoot.

"Riven, I cannot thank you enough for saving my daughter. I was so scared, I didn't think . . . I just . . ." The middle-aged, redheaded woman sniffled and wiped another tear off her face, walking up to Riven and giving him a firm hug. "Julie, and likely the rest of us, would have died without you. Thank you again. There isn't anything that I could ever do or say that could repay your kindness—but if there's any favor I could ever fulfill for you, please don't hesitate to ask."

Riven smiled and hugged her back, letting go after a solid thirty seconds while the trembling woman continued to shake silently. "Hey, don't mention it. You're all my friends; that's what friends do. I'm sorry I wasn't here sooner to save Caleb."

Tanya nodded, not saying a word to prevent herself from crying, and soon the others were walking over from the burial site where Caleb's body had been placed.

Julie gave Riven a quivering, shaky, tear-filled nod of her own while holding Hakim's hand tightly—and Hakim looked almost ashamed. Downtrodden even, avoiding Riven's gaze after his initial muttered thanks.

It was Tim, Tanya's teenage son, who spoke next with a more firm grin than the others could manage. "Man, you just keep saving our asses, huh?"

Tim held out a hand and clasped Riven on the forearm. "Thanks again. At this rate we're going to owe you many life debts over. And you, Athela! You look as stunning as ever!"

"Thank you!" Athela said with a chipper smile.

Riven rolled his eyes with a chuckle and let go of Tim's hand. "Hey, stop hitting on my girlfriend."

That immediately got the attention of all four of them, their eyes wide.

"You and Athela are dating?" Julie asked, brightening up somewhat. "Wow! I'm so happy for you two! I'd thought you might be into that succubus of yours . . . where is she, anyway?"

Riven tried not to let his face fall at the mention of Fay, but it was certainly hard. She'd only left a little over a week ago and the damage was still fresh. A sinking feeling began welling up in his gut, but thankfully Athela covered for him—and she managed to pull him out of his depression quite quickly.

"Yes, Riven and I have been dating for just a week now! We're going on a picnic soon, my first ever!" Athela got up on her tiptoes and kissed Riven on the cheek, both of them sharing a warm smile. "It's going to be so fun!"

"Well, I can't say I saw that coming, but I'm happy for you two," Hakim managed to say half-heartedly, obviously still very bothered about the night's events. His eyes fell again, and he let go of Julie's hand. "Riven, do you mind if we talk in private for a bit?"

Riven rolled one pauldron-adorned shoulder, then nodded. "Sounds good. You lead."

He left Azmoth and Athela to continue chatting with the others, telling them of all the things that'd happened since the last time they'd met in the drake's dungeon. Riven and Hakim walked side by side into the dark, starlit forest with leaves and pine needles crunching underfoot, and once Riven even saw a wolf on the outskirts that quickly darted away when his crimson eyes narrowed on its position with a blip of his aura released.

"Riven, I just wanted to say thanks . . . alone, away from the others. I can't let them see me like this," Hakim eventually said when they came to a stop at the edge of a long slope leading down toward the town. Tears began welling up in the big man's eyes, and he folded his arms and leaned against a tall pine tree while beginning to cry. "I—I don't think I could have s-saved them, Riven. They'd be d-dead, and so would I. That fucking Matt bastard would have k-killed Julie! I'm so ashamed! I'm so weak! If I'd b-been stronger . . ."

He covered his face with one hand, avoiding Riven's gaze and violently shaking with his shoulders jolting every time he tried to suppress a sob.

"You're not weak," Riven said calmly, shaking his head. "Not at all. I'm just a freak. Most people on this planet would have been in the same position you were, up against those numbers. I realize you're upset, but don't take it out on yourself. You're a good man and you did what you could. That's all we can ever ask of ourselves. One day, I'm sure that there'll be a situation where I come across someone stronger. That day, I may lose, I may be robbed, I may be forced to do something I don't want to do, or I may even die. But as long as I do what I can, I can't ever blame myself for the failures I have. You can only move up and move on."

A distant scream and a blaring hiss echoed through the forest, and Riven saw an explosion of Chaos energy where Yattazi had no doubt found another of the rats. He grinned to himself, chuckling at the unknown target's misfortune, and turned to face Hakim head-on while the bigger man just continued staring at the forest floor, covering half his face.

"You gonna be okay?" Riven asked, leaning against a tree opposite Hakim and folding his own arms across his breastplate.

Hakim shuddered, then nodded. He cleared his throat to regain his composure and straightened, taking in a deep breath of the fresh forest air. "Yes. I'm sorry you had to see that. I just . . . I cannot fathom what kind of life I'd have lived if I'd let Julie die in that cabin. That's only assuming I even got away after she was killed . . . which was unlikely in itself."

They both stood in silence after that, staring out across the forest together in the moonlight.

"I wish you didn't have to go back. We could really use you here," Hakim eventually said with a wry smile. "How much longer until Heroic Intervention sends you away?"

Riven raised one eyebrow. "I used an ability concerning my staff to stabilize the portal. I don't have to go back at all if I don't want to."

Hakim seemed surprised. "Is that even possible?"

"It is."

"So . . . you're staying, then? What about the kingdom you run, or your sister?"

"Oh, I can come and go through the portal as needed. The staff created an anchor point for the wormhole and I can open it up whenever I want as long as I put in the mana."

"Is it normal for your staff to create portals like that?"

Riven shook his head. "No, at least not in the way you're thinking. I can't just create most portals, but I can stabilize ones that were already created and recall to them—almost like a save point in a video game."

"That's pretty nifty."

"It is. Which brings me to a question of my own." Riven turned his head back toward the people they'd left behind. "Would you guys like some help power leveling? I could escort y'all around through a couple of the local dungeons if they're still around, maybe work on my crafting while I'm here. I've really been wanting to pursue totem making in my off time—might as well start it up where I left off back in the tutorial with you guys. It'd be a good time."

Hakim stared at him, somewhat surprised and looking mildly confused. "Why would you do that for us?"

Riven shrugged. "Honestly, man, people are scared of me. Like, really scared. I walk around my own city and the people living there scurry out of the way like I'm about to stomp them into oblivion and murder them in the streets. I know some of it has to do with my negative Charisma, and some of it is likely because I destroyed a city—yes, I get it."

Hakim chuckled slightly at that last part. "That'd probably be considered a valid reason to be worried about you. But I understand why you did it. If Julie had been threatened and I had to choose between her and a city full of strangers, I'd have destroyed the city, too, given your choice."

"Exactly!" Riven said with arms widespread. "People don't understand most of the time. They just see me as a monster, as a ticking time bomb. I'm tired of it. I want to start over, go somewhere that people don't know me and do shit that is just for me and my own pursuit of happiness. I want to find time to relax. On top of that, I'm going to need a team, and who better to ask than you guys? It wouldn't take much effort on my part to see it done, and if I can get all of you to a point where you're some help to me, then all the better."

Riven pushed the notification over.

[Guild functions for Panu are nearing completion. Preform a guild of up to twenty people in order to participate; system lock on guild roster has been destroyed. Sole features of guild functions are now as follows in preparation for the worldwide guild introduction event: guild name, guild roster, link to guild hall. Factions options of the Guild and Factions tab will still remain locked until a later date.]

Hakim blinked, then lifted his eyes to meet Riven's again. "You want us to join your guild?"

"Only if you want it. I'd understand if you don't, considering what just happened with another one of your friends. But if this kind of adventuring lifestyle is something you all really want, then let me help out a bit. It'd be nice to come along."

"Would it just be us?"

"No. I'm sure Allie and her necromancer friends would be in the guild, too, and there are a couple others on my mind that I might invite. But whatever this world event is, we can try to get you prepared for it in advance. I'm sure Athela would like that a lot—she regularly wonders about you guys. What do you say?"

Hakim was silent for a time, then nodded slowly. "I think we'd all like that, as long as we're not too much of a burden for you."

Riven smiled, clapping him on the shoulder. "Not a burden at all, my friend. Not a burden at all. Now, I do have somewhere to be and some dwarves to talk to. Try not to get into any scuffles in the meantime, yeah? I may be able to come back through the portal anchor Jackal made, but that doesn't mean I'll be able to intervene like I have been."

Hakim snorted, finally cracking a small but still sad smile. "Yeah. We'll try not to get into any scuffles while you're gone. Are you going to come back soon?"

"I'll try my best. I have a world event to go to, something concerning the apocalypse beasts world quest. But that's still a ways off from now."

"Of course you do. I look forward to having you around. You want a beer before you leave? Do you drink? We have a few stashed away in the cabin for a rainy day." Hakim gestured back over his shoulder with a hiked thumb, then wiped his eyes. "How about it?"

Riven gave him a thumbs-up. "Of course I drink. Yeah, hit me. I can have just one before I leave. Come on, let's go."

Drums beat in the deep, booming out in echoing waves amid tens of thousands of rat-kin chanting his name.

Riven walked along a wooden board down the center of a massive army, an army almost cemented into the surrounding expanse of caverns that'd once held a rat-kin village. Now it was passing through a war zone, past trenches full of rat-kin soldiers in chitin and leather armors wielding spears, pikes, crossbows, and more. It was the front line of a stalemate between his allies and the dwarves who'd slaughtered their people and made this place theirs.

The caverns here were smaller than Deepnest itself. They did span a mile up and down at various points, along with being miles across—which was far more massive than any cavern on Earth would have been—but they still paled in comparison to the rat-kin capital.

Nevertheless he found himself gazing at ruined mounds, craters in the cave walls where homes used to be, and the scattered remnants of mushroom farms.

On the opposite side of that cavern, staring out from trenches of their own and holes or dugouts many hundreds of feet up the cavern wall, were the dwarves. They were outfitted in stone slabs and steel plate armor, armed with various axes, spears, and crossbows of their own. They'd also built a large fortress into the tunnel on their controlled exit, with cannons, magically infused grenade-launcher equivalents, and different types of golems in more prominent view than the soldiers hiding behind nooks in the walls or trenches. They equaled the rat-kin army man for man, and the side that rushed the other—giving up their defensive advantage—was the one that'd likely lose. Situations like these were why the war had slowed into a stalemate.

But Riven was going to use himself as a siege breaker. This could not go on any longer, not when war was coming to Panu on a scale far larger than this relative scuffle between kingdoms in the underdark. Not when he was set to leave for Chalgathi's event and he'd be absent from this area for quite a long time. And if he had anything to say about it, the dwarves would be dealt with over the next few days. Be it a surrender, or something far worse, it was going to get done.

CHAPTER 47

Bridgar Mush was an officer of His Majesty's legions, a veteran of many battles and a dwarf with a truly splendid red beard. Brown eyes above a firm, square jawline stared out underneath a thick stone helmet carved out of the very caves they lived in and molded by forgeries and mages accustomed to the Volcanic subpillar. Most of the dwarves of His Majesty's legions were imbued with that particular subpillar, and thus the army Bridgar now commanded from his stone fortress tower all displayed various weapons, spells, and enchantments primarily from that specialty.

As the man in ivory armor Bridgar knew to be Riven Thane walked across a desolate battlefield between the two opposing armies, alongside the deafening chant of the rat-kin horde just drooling to get their claws into dwarf flesh, Bridgar's frown was a worried one. It was him, without a doubt, identifiable by the two demons on either side of the man and the unique Gluttony-infused items he wore—though the enormous demon basilisk slithering behind them was definitely new.

Their kingdom had assumed that Riven wasn't invested in Deepnest's problems beyond a passing trading partner, that Riven would never actually come down into the underdark himself to fight on the rat-kin people's behalf. It appeared that Bridgar's kingdom had assumed wrong.

[Riven Thane, Level 130 Warlock Devastator, Harbinger of Gluttony, Pure-blooded Vampire, Lost Prince of the Blood Moon Requiem. LEGENDARY. PANU WORLD BOSS.]

"By the beard of Ragnut. Load the cannons and push the rune barriers to full!" Bridgar said shakily, knuckles turning white on the battlements overlooking the cavern ahead of him. "Get ready to drop the ceiling on his head. We're going to wipe this stain clean from the world once and for all."

One of his five nearby underlings, an officer with long, braided black hair hanging from his chin, shifted uneasily. "Bridgar . . . Are you sure you want to do that? We dug those tunnels over the ceiling for a worst-case scenario. Blowing them will lose us this entire area, miles of suitable farmland for the mushrooms and crystals that grow here. We have been fighting for control of this—"

Bridgar backhanded the officer, almost red enough in the face to match his beard. "DO YOU REALIZE WHO THAT IS WALKING TOWARD US?!"

The officer who was smacked stumbled, angrily put his hand on his glaive, then saw the absolute venom in Bridgar's face and thought better of it. Straightening and glaring at Bridgar, the officer pushed past his fellows to nod just once. "Yes. As I was saying, perhaps there are better avenues than to just drop the cavern on his head. Not only will we lose these resources, but it will likely infuriate him. You'd better hope that the resulting collapse would kill him, or else we're all dead. I say we negotiate."

The idea of negotiation got a round of jeering laughter from the other dwarves present.

"He's a vampire! They do NOT negotiate!" Bridgar hissed, spitting on the ground and turning his back on the officers to watch Riven's slow advance across the expanse of underground farmland. "Those bloodsuckers want nothing more than to enslave and feed on all the races they consider inferior. And they consider ALL other races inferior. Do as I say, or—"

The air was split with the roar of cannons.

Bridgar's eyes went wide when a volley of siege weapons erupted from the front lines—targeting the slowly advancing vampire. Explosions of volcanic ash and slabs of magma rocketed toward Riven's position without warning, colliding with the vampire and sending clouds of debris into the air.

Bridgar looked down at his political rival, a lordling from another dwarvish noble house named Ulfensted who'd no doubt tried to steal the glory of killing Riven Thane for himself. Bridgar's head nearly popped off and he almost spat blood. "That little gnome-humping WORM! HE SHOULD HAVE WAITED FOR THE CEILING, DAMN HIM! WE NEEDED TIME TO PREP IT! CANNONS—FIRE ON THE VAMPIRE NOW! SEND THEM ALL! EVEN THE SMALL ARMS! IF HE DOESN'T DIE HERE, WE'RE DONE FOR!"

Not willing to be outdone by his political rival, Bridgar screamed at the rest of the cannons under his command while officers started shouting for the barriers to be reinforced. Cylindrical tubes of rock and molten steel glowed red-hot before spinning up and sending torpedoes of their own, crashing into the cloud of debris where the vampire had been.

Thousands of dwarves immediately lowered their crossbows and began to fire at will after shouted commands from captains overseeing them, and soon volleys of enchanted bolts were being fired like clouds of spines that condensed onto the area the cannon fire had targeted.

Volcanic, earthen spells were launched and crossbows and cannons reloaded before the volleys continued, drowning out the chants of the rat-kin across the cavern complex. Bridgar's eyes narrowed on the spot that the barrage was targeting, and only after an entire minute of constant fire from the dwarvish side did he call for a cease.

The chanting of the rat-kin had stopped.

Smoke, dust, and fire billowed in enormous waves from a crater in the cavern floor.

There was only silence as the two armies stared at the no-man's-land between them.

Bridgar continued to watch, eyes wide and knuckles white. He took in a deep breath of air, then slowly released it as the seconds ticked by. "Is he dead?"

Not one of the officers beside him replied. They all just waited, expectantly, to see the result of their army's barrage.

"There shouldn't be a corpse if he's dead. His body would have been blown apart," Bridgar said under his breath, feeling the saliva sticking to the back of his throat while he nervously shifted his weight from foot to foot. "We have those barriers prepped for incoming attacks, right?"

The officer beside him nodded stoically, staring at the still-flowing plumes of ash, fire, and dust. "They're fully charged and ready to intercept."

Bridgar gave a shuddering nod, feeling his nerves reach a tipping point until suddenly a flash of Infernal light tore away the flaming wreckage of the crater the dwarves had created. His eyes went wide, and he silently cursed Riven's family nine generations back.

There, in the center of the crater, on a piece of cave floor that was largely unscathed, was the warlock. He was surrounded by a dome of fire, while the armored brutalisk demon maintained the defensive ward with help from the basilisk—who was pouring mana into the brutalisk's skill to reinforce it. Athela, known prominently on the world forums as the demon who'd been resurrected from permanent death with one of Gluttony's profane miracles after the sacrifice of an entire city, now stood in her house-size archdemon form.

Beyond them, hundreds of sleek crimson lances were crackling with Black Lightning and being pulled back by Wretched Snares in slingshot mechanisms, and more were being made by the second. Electrified snow began to gather around them as Athela's crystal roses spewed frosted mists, and the basilisk's huge body erupted alongside the brutalisk's—both encompassed with Infernal flames.

The dome fell.

"You engaged me in long-range combat? Really? Before I'd even had a chance to speak with you?" Riven's voice echoed out across the chamber.

Red frost began to rapidly spread out toward the hunkered dwarvish formations along the stone, covering tens and then hundreds of yards in seconds. A flare of his aura produced a swirling whirlwind of crimson snow crackling with Black Lightning, intermixing with Athela's own elementally charged white snowflakes in a flurry of cold that quickly began turning into a far-reaching cyclone.

Through the building storm that raged, thundered, and boomed—shaking the cavern as more and more crackling Blood Lances were created and pulled back in the air overhead and behind the warlock—Bridgar the dwarf watched in horror while taking an involuntary step back.

Riven's voice echoed throughout the chamber one final time, through the haze of whirling snow that was now obscuring him from view, a precursor of violence to come. "I'd hoped that we could settle this like gentlemen. I suppose that was my mistake."

The air ripped apart and the thundering cloud of red and white snow parted as many thousands of piercing Blood Lances imbued with the Path of Red and Black roared forward—causing space itself to rip and tear at the seams.

The semi-invisible barriers flared and shattered almost instantly as a cacophony of explosions tore into dwarvish formations, eliciting screams of horror and pain as body parts, trenches, and battlements were ripped apart like they were made of paper. The volley was followed by the building storm, a storm of chaotic energies and blinding snow that rolled across the dwarven fortress and defensive positions as an impenetrable wave that chilled Bridgar to the bone.

The dwarf dropped back onto his rear, heart beating like a drum, having been spared the initial volley but finding his hand landing on the exploded corpse of a nearby officer.

He screamed through the deafening storm of snow that whipped his beard around, only to cry out again in pain when an arc of elemental lightning tore through an exposed part of his armor into his forearm—splitting it open with a singed wound.

All around him, the roars and screams of his comrades could be heard as the booming approach of the oncoming rat-kin army's battle cries began to rise above the cyclone. All was chaos, and Bridgar only barely had enough clarity to get back to the battlements to begin screaming orders.

Despite his dismay, despite the building dread he felt, he managed to make it to the wall as he tried his best to yell over the howling winds. He tried to yell over the ice that slapped against his skin and cut him in numerous places while jolts of lightning—black and yellow—both randomly hammered into his body and stone armor.

But his voice was lost to the winds, and even to his own ears it began to die in his throat as—through the thick haze of crackling red and white—dozens upon dozens of ice-made arachnids began sweeping over the dwarvish formations to eat his still-recoiling men alive even as they tried to fight back. The huge flaming figure of a basilisk crashed into the fortress wall on his right and below him, sending splintered spears and torn-apart cannons down hundreds of feet while the men stationed there began to scream even louder.

A booming thud and the shake of the wall he now stood on caused Bridgar to trip just as he'd regained his footing, and he raised a hand to block out the whirling storm. But when he uncovered his eyes to try to get a better view of the chaos unleashed on the area around him while debating whether or not he should just run and abandon his men, his gaze fell upon the looming, flaming figure of an obsidian knight torn from the depths of hell.

The towering brutalisk was covered in thick ebony plates, spikes running down his back, and the magma-infused maul in two of his hands flared to life as the fiery demon chuckled. Bridgar abruptly tried to find the axe strapped to his side, but it had been lost somehow in the cyclone, and, going pale, he realized that he was defenseless.

The last thing Bridgar saw was the downward swing of the large stone maul, glowing with lines of magma digging into the outer surface of the weapon, and his life was ended with a loud squelching sound as his body was splattered along the inner defensive layers of the dwarven fortress.

Allie panted, pressed her lips against Lahn's, and violently dominated him on her bed while she pinched his cheeks. She gasped and pulled back to let the man breathe, her red eyes glistening with amusement when he finished.

"That was good! Longer than I expected given your situation," she said, humming to herself in satisfaction and leaving the baffled young man behind when she got up and strode over to the bookshelf. Taking a bottle of blood wine from the top and draining half of it in one go, she gasped again and let out a long burp.

She turned around in the dim light of her room, finding him staring at her longingly with those puppy dog eyes of his. He really was adorable, though a lot of that had to do with his personality. She'd had thralls far more attractive than him in the realm of physical looks, especially due to how Lahn was still regaining muscle mass on his withered left side, but she'd found those fuckboy toys to be lacking in all other aspects. Thralls were something she'd quickly become bored of, and after having found Lahn, she'd executed hers so she didn't have to deal with them any longer.

Why HAD she fallen so quickly for this man?

Pausing to think about it, she really didn't know. Riven had told her that, in his opinion, her infatuation with Lahn had been incredibly abrupt. Too abrupt. Perhaps Riven was right, but her older brother was not one to go about giving dating advice given his absolute failures in that realm. Allie still didn't know what to think about the Fay situation, but at the very least Riven had said he did like and approve of Lahn. So there was that, and Allie wasn't about to fight off feelings like this when she'd been looking for this exact kind of connection for so long. She just . . . felt right, being around Lahn.

"So . . . how was your first time?" Allie asked, a sly smile playing on her lips as her bare, pale legs took her forward in a gliding motion to the edge of the bed. She bent over, booping him on the nose while he propped himself up on his good elbow, and gave him a pecking kiss on the cheek. "Hopefully not too disappointing?"

Lahn just continued to stare, as if dumbstruck, and he eventually blinked while slowly letting his body drop back into the pillows. "I only lasted two minutes."

Allie snorted a laugh. "I expected as much; don't worry about it. You'll get better."

Lahn eyed her up and down while she stood at the edge of the bed, and he reached out a hand to touch her own. He smiled. "I don't know about that. Every time I look at you, I just . . . I get butterflies. I see only perfection, and I ask myself, just how did I get this lucky? How am I supposed to last longer in the face of this?"

Allie squeezed his hand back, sitting and caressing his face with one hand. Then a look of doubt briefly overcame her. "Do you think it was better than it would have been with Marsia?"

Lahn blinked. "Marsia?"

"Marsia Bortrost. The young lady your parents tried to set you up with before you started school."

Lahn blinked again, then began laughing loudly while pulling Allie into a hug on the bed. Their bare bodies rolled onto one another, and the rolling stopped when they settled into a position with their eyes locked. "Allie, she doesn't hold a candle to you. You can't seriously say that YOU'RE jealous. Right?"

Allie grinned. "Of course not!"

There was a pause, and Lahn's face grew bright with smug satisfaction. "You WERE jealous! Oh my gosh! WOW! Allie Thane, queen of the Thane Necropolis and princess of the Blood Moon Requiem, is JEALOUS of MARSIA BORTROST! This is great! I'm definitely telling Mother."

Allie's eyes narrowed and she abruptly jabbed him in the side, getting him to squeal. "You'd better not, you little turd, or I'll suck your body dry and leave it for the roaches."

Lahn's eyebrow raised teasingly. "I may like that."

"Shut up."

They both laughed, and eventually Allie stopped the cuddlefest by getting up and stretching with a yawn. Donning a robe and heading for the door, she turned to look over her shoulder just once. "I've got to go change and see Kathrine now. The Blood Moon Requiem apparently has an important guest that I need to talk to, and she's been hounding me about it for a while. I'll be back in a few hours, but you should get some sleep. Your body needs all the recovery it can get."

Lahn sighed in disappointment. "Could we try again when you get back? I want to make up for my failures here."

Allie rolled her eyes and snorted again, but her smile was wide and displayed her fangs. "Of course. I look forward to it. And we can watch a movie afterward!"

"What's a movie?"

"Oh, I forgot you're not from Earth. I'll explain when I get back!"

With that she blew him a kiss and left the room, shutting the door behind her with a click before her footsteps faded away. After that, only the faint rustle of leaves of the garden tree outside Allie's window was there to keep Lahn company.

CHAPTER 48

Lord Justo Barimont was a handsome man, even for a vampire, and he let that fact be known as he swaggered around the compound giving orders to the various soldiers or maids while two personal thralls from the heartlands waved large white fans to cool him off. His eyes were bright crimson, as all purebloods' were, and his platinum-trimmed robes had the symbol of a green flame embroidered on the chest to symbolize the house he hailed from.

"This place truly is a drag, isn't it, Puncie?" Lord Barimont muttered under his breath to one of the two thrall women nearby, sipping wine from a crystal goblet while gazing over all the cattle that were just so flippantly let loose to run about this dreadful marketplace. He glanced at Kathrine where she sat rigid and stiff in her chair across from him on the balcony, as beautiful as ever, and frowned at her. "Have you not taught these lost royals about proper etiquette concerning slaves? These cattle should be locked up at all times when not accompanied by one of our kin. It is disgraceful, I must say. Truly disgusting. Like having cockroaches in your home, only this isn't one or two—but it is a swarm of cockroaches. Diseased, ugly, smelly cockroaches."

He gestured with a grimace at the roiling crowds of bartering orcs, humans, undead, and more below him, his nose tilted up in a look of absolute disdain. "You have been failing your duties, obviously, Princess. I'll have to speak to my fiancée about changing things. Immediately."

Kathrine's face flushed red with anger, and it was all she could do to not reach across the small glass table between them to strike the man. Instead, she took in a deep breath when her instructor, Pladius, put a hand on her shoulder to calm her down. Settling herself, she replied, "Truly, I wonder what your wife-to-be will think of it when you start telling her what to do, as you say you will."

Lord Barimont snorted a laugh, then grabbed one of the thralls fanning him and yanked her down to face level. Waiting for the young woman to expose her neck and brushing away a hanging diamond earring, the young lord sank his fangs into her neck and began to suck. After having had his fill—and after a few grimaces and winces from the woman—he pushed her off and shoved her back. "You speak as if Allie has a choice in the matter. Let me assure you, Kathrine, she does not. I even came prepared."

Kathrine snorted right back, glancing at the personal guards he'd brought with him. They were soldiers bearing the green flame of House Barimont on their plate armor in a similar fashion that the elites of the Blood Moon Requiem did with the blood-moon emblem, only the elites here were sworn to the imperial throne, while Barimont's men were personally contracted. Then she looked to the three warding rings on his fingers and the large amulet on his chest.

"If you speak of your soldiers and your little trinkets that you managed to pay ungodly amounts of tax to bring to this F-grade world, that's quite amusing," Kathrine said with a raised eyebrow, crossing her legs and puffing on her pipe. "If you're already worried about an attack from your fiancée even before meeting her, it does not bode well for your future interactions. You'll need to do more than just survive if you wish to win her heart."

"I do not need to win her heart," Lord Barimont snapped back with a glare. "I bought her hand in marriage. She is mine."

"She is a high princess," Kathrine retorted. "Unlike me, a lesser member of the nobility, you cannot just talk to her however you wish. The queen will have your head. Allie is her favorite granddaughter's daughter."

"The queen is not the only one with power in our empire, need I remind you. There are seven elders and seven great houses—the queen is just one of them," Lord Barimont replied with a wave of his hand, looking up to the sky when gathering thunderclouds clapped with lightning over the mountains a few miles off. "I have the backing of one of the other elders."

Kathrine raised her eyebrows in surprise. "Truly? I find that a newly raised house like yours having such support is unlikely at best. Even if that were the case, what's your plan? You're just going to tell her of your wedding and leave? What is your purpose here?"

The young lord slowly turned his head to look at her, evaluating her for some time. "What else would I be here for? The high queen and council want children. I intend to give them one. We will consummate our marriage today."

Kathrine's fists tightened in anger. "You cannot give her some time to digest the news before just throwing yourself on her?"

"No. Unlike you, Princess, I have a house to maintain," Lord Barimont said with a shake of his head and a grin. "I am not of noble birth, but I am a pureblood. My family made our fortunes off the dealings of war, not taxation. If I wish to remain in the highest realms of the political field, I must make sure that my blood is intertwined with the royals', so my parents have deemed it necessary that I start now. Soon I will be the father of a new princess, one linked directly to the throne just like you—but with a higher place in the pecking order. That, in turn, will make me even better than you. I will be of higher rank."

Kathrine blinked, then immediately began to laugh—in turn causing Barimont to frown. "Lord Barimont! You are quite delusional, aren't you?"

Kathrine brought a dainty hand to her mouth and giggled to antagonize the man across from her. "I will be married to Allie's brother, who is the technical heir of House Wraithtide. Not only that, but I am already a princess, and my standing will only go higher after the betrothal is made public. In what possible way would you be better than me?"

Lord Barimont, for all his blustering, had completely forgotten about Riven. His face turned a shade of purple-red, and his grip cracked the wood on the chair he sat in. "We will see whether or not your young prince even survives this integration, Princess. We will certainly see."

The mood immediately grew cold.

"Careful how you say that, lordling," the princess stated with a venomous hiss to her words. "Should that be interpreted as a threat, I will have you and your entire house beheaded before the day is over in the name of the queen. Do I make myself clear?"

Captain Rusof, head of the military and the man who trained the elites here at the commune, immediately put his hand on his blade. His black-and-red armor shimmered with a flash of distant lightning, and his red eyes bored holes into the lordling and his personal house escort on the other side of the balcony. He'd been standing idly by until then, but upon the announcement that Kathrine saw this offhanded comment as a possible threat, he and the three soldiers beside him made it abundantly clear just where they stood on the matter of decapitating people who'd stepped out of line.

The guards Lord Barimont had brought also shifted to their own weapons, gazes narrowed as Barimont tried to keep his composure—though there was certainly a mixed bag of emotions underneath that forced stoic gaze he evaluated Kathrine with. "It appears you have read my words incorrectly, Princess. I would never dream of intentionally harming a prince of the main bloodline in any way, ever. Please call off your dogs."

There was a pause, and Kathrine held up her hand—causing Captain Rusof and the three other elites to stand down. The tension in Lord Barimont's face eased, as did the postures of the guards and thralls who accompanied him.

The silence lasted for another five minutes, no words spoken between anyone there while both Princess Kathrine and Lord Justo Barimont continued to watch out over the commune grounds.

"When can I expect her? I am growing bored of this dreadful place," Lord Barimont eventually said, smoothing back his already-perfect dark hair. "Please send word to Princess Allie Wraithtide once more. I do not like to be kept waiting, and these system rules regarding how far I can travel outside a commune are downright infuriating."

"I have already sent the message three times," Kathrine growled under her breath. "I believe she's with someone at the moment and cannot be bothered, according to the workers at her manor."

"With someone?" Barimont said, eyebrows furrowing.

Kathrine's expression became smug. "Yes. With that crippled cattle boy she likes. I believe she planned on taking his virginity today. But don't tell anyone—it's supposed to be a talk just between us girls."

Lord Justo Barimont's jaw went rigid, and a second later the wooden arm on his chair shattered underneath his clenching grip. "Disgusting. I will have words with her about this. My future wife will not be allowed to sleep with cattle, cripples, or anyone, for that matter, except me. And I will show her what a real man is like after I deal with that insolent boy who dared to lay his hands on her. Puncie, get the collar."

Kathrine took another puff of her pipe, confused when the thrall woman handed over a thin leather collar inscribed with runes. She could immediately tell that these runes were the real deal, a powerful set of threaded suppression bindings. "And what exactly is that?"

Barimont slammed it onto the glass table between them. "You'll see for yourself when Allie Wraithtide arrives in person. After all, it was made for her by Elder Thune himself."

Allie stopped her approach in the shadow of a two-story pub on the outskirts of the trade district near the Elysium altar. High above, the halo of green flames encircled a dark spire, at the base of which were thousands of people buying and selling things directly with the system store. They'd place their hands on the spire's base, select what they wanted to take or sell, and exchange Elysium coins—more often than not leaving with goods to carry away. As she got into position, Allie spotted the two trading communes: a fortress of the Blood Moon Requiem—which was closed off to the public—and Negrada's commune, housed in a huge red tent where they would actively trade with anyone who walked in. Outside the altar's perimeter were the buildings she now found herself hiding between, where dozens of restaurants, trading halls, auction houses, and crafting workshops were bounding with business.

"Mistress . . ." The hiss of her newest minion, Fimrindle, called to her from the shadows. "I bring news."

Allie stared stoically toward the Blood Moon Requiem's compound. "Does Riven's story check out?"

She blinked, and the iron scarecrow was suddenly right beside her with a motion that she hadn't even seen—its carved X eyes staring at her. Despite being her minion now, Fimrindle was certainly off-putting due to how and when he moved so abruptly.

"It does. Your designated fiancé is waiting for you inside, and from the queen's perspective this is just a formality—but it appears your future husband is more eager to begin than expected," Fimrindle said with a voice that sounded like wind being blown through a pipe. "They do not know you know. However, there are more findings that are not within Riven's account of his talk with the high queen."

Allie's eyebrows furrowed, and she turned to look at the creature next to her. "How so?"

"It appears the queen warned this young lord about the potential for a volatile reaction on your end. There are also more players on the board—an elder of the clan, likely from the council of elders the queen spoke of. His name is Elder Thune, and Lord Justo Barimont speaks of him as a backer for reasons that I cannot understand due to a lack of background information. They created an item of some kind for you, a collar. I can sense sedation and suppression magic coming off it."

Allie's features immediately grew malicious, and a spark of teal death energy erupted involuntarily from the ground under her feet. "Why would she warn him? Is she playing both sides? Do you know what my supposed fiancé intends to do with the collar?"

"The assumption I have is that he was going to use it to keep you sedated should you become angry. He needs to give you a child. I'm sure you can draw the connections."

Her jaw became unhinged. Her soul flared as the souls of the dead called for blood. A barrel nearby exploded when her eye twitched, and she began to see red. "Is Riven back yet?"

Fimrindle only barely moved his head back and forth. "No. He is still on the expedition with Deepnest to conquer the dwarves and will be gone for at least a few days, by Mara's estimations."

. . .

. . .

. . .

"And what if I do not go meet this man? Did you get a sense of what would happen?"

Fimrindle tilted his head slightly, shifting left when a pair of squabbling merchants passed by the alleyway. "If you do not comply within a reasonable time, and if the conversations I overheard are accurate, it is likely you will be taken into the heartlands against your will at the end of this integration to be trained properly in accordance with behaviors suiting a princess of the requiem. Then they would enslave the locals of this world and take them to sell on the galactic slave markets as labor and cattle. The world would be torched when they leave. This is also assuming that Riven would attempt to help you, disregarding the laws of the requiem, and thus making him unable to claim sanctuary for this planet should he go against the will of the council."

"And what of Lahn if I cooperate?"

"I do not know. My assumption is that he will likely be killed should you resist, but there's a possibility he'll be killed either way."

. . .

. . .

. . .

"I see. I suppose it is time to meet this fiancé of mine, then."

"Do you wish to wait for Riven in case he does not want to negotiate?"

Allie shook her head. "No. This is something I need to do on my own."

Allie wore her usual outfit while approaching the large front gate of the requiem's trading commune fortress: her formfitting soul-woven bone armor, along with the skull mask, and her wand hooked to her belt. Her heart pounded nervously in her chest, and the doors started to creak open.

She didn't have to knock, as they'd already been expecting her, and mere moments later she found herself face-to-face with the man she could assume was her betrothed only a couple yards off. He was disgustingly handsome, well muscled, with a strong jawline and an obviously fake smile on his face. He had bright-red eyes and swooped-back dark hair and wore an emblem of green flames on platinum-trimmed robes. Standing beside him was Kathrine, who had taken on an unfamiliar look of discomfort, wearing her usual black dress that emphasized her curves, and behind the two nobles were armored vampire guards and thralls or vampire servants standing in rows.

Kathrine stepped forward with a slight nod. "Princess Allie Wraithtide, I am glad to see you again. We have much to discuss. Please, follow me."

CHAPTER 49

The dining hall had been redecorated according to the description Riven had given Allie prior to this, though she couldn't be certain because it was her first time here, after all. She'd never had reason to visit the compound before now, but the looming threat of planetary annihilation by an intergalactic vampire empire that her mother had been part of—should she spurn the rules of the queen and council—was nothing to take lightly. Despite not knowing much about the greater multiverse, she was relatively certain the Blood Moon Requiem could follow through on that promise after Riven had described the visit to their inherited planet and the fleets surrounding it. If her mother's house alone had such a force, what kind of force did the main army of the Blood Moon Requiem have?

The room contained only a singular rectangular table, carved from a strange deep-gray wood that'd been polished to a shine. Dozens of dishes formed through works of art were on display, with numerous bottles of fine wines. Two very attractive thrall men and two equally attractive thrall women on a table of their own were decorated in sauces and flowers for live feeding out to the side of the main dining table. Ruby chandeliers cast warm auras, and hundreds of candles all around the room gave off a gentle glow. Black banners with the red crescent moon, outlined with gold, hung overhead, and servants were standing next to the kitchen door and around the room to heed the call of the nobles at a moment's notice.

Aside from those servants of both vampire and thrall origin were the soldiers standing on the perimeter of the room—either those who'd first arrived with the commune, or the ones sporting green flames on their breastplates who'd come with the young lord. The people sitting at the elongated table numbered only four, however.

Lord Justo Barimont sat at one end with his head held high and a cocky smirk on his face as he blatantly eyed Allie while slowly stroking the green flame emblem on his chest. Allie sat at the other end, having placed her skull mask beside her plate—glaring defiantly back at him. Kathrine sat in between the two, uncomfortably crossing her pale legs and clearing her throat while servants poured her a drink, and finally there was Lady Muren, another vampire noble who had her hair up in a vibrant orange ponytail and wore a formfitting red robe.

The small orchestra of string instruments on a raised platform started as the final desserts were placed on the table, and the scent of perfume wafted through the air.

"Do you like it?" Lord Justo Barimont asked with a fanged smile, nodding his head to the small orchestra of violins and cellos nearby. "I'd heard they were the best in your city, and that this was what many high-class citizens of your homeworld listened to. I hope I was not misinformed."

Allie raised an eyebrow, slouched in her chair, and spared the human musicians dressed in fine attire a momentary glance. "Yes, it's quite nice."

She turned her head to Lady Muren with a frown. "Weren't there supposed to be more of you? Riven told me there were two other lords expected to attend, Duke Blemrich and Lord Carsion. Are they not attending the luncheon today?"

Lady Muren spared Lord Barimont a quick glance, then smiled Allie's way. "They decided to leave the planet after Lord Barimont . . ."

"After I secured your hand in marriage, my dear," Lord Barimont said with a wide, greedy smile. "I'm sure you're already at least partially aware of these things, but my family wanted me to meet you after the fact so we could become more intimately acquainted with one another."

Allie snorted in derision, then took a fork and—in a very unladylike manner—tore off a piece of finely cooked meat and began chewing while continuing to glare across the table. "Humorous."

"What is?" Lord Barimont asked pleasantly, folding his fingers together.

"That you seem so entitled to me." Allie then turned back to Lady Muren. "And why haven't you left? Didn't Kathrine already take Riven from you?"

The orange-haired vampire's eye twitched, but she kept a pleasant smile. "Princess Kathrine Vonsilla Crushada has indeed secured Riven's hand in marriage, but unlike us, who can only incubate one pregnancy at a time, males obviously have the opportunity to sire many children at once. Malignant Prophecy is a highly valued gift that the queen wants more of. I know marriage is now out of the question, but I was hoping I could perhaps become a concubine. A shame, really—my family outbid Kathrine's but it was deemed by the elder council that her relationship with Riven had already taken fruition after she whored herself off a while ago."

Kathrine adamantly rolled her eyes, huffed, and started digging into her own food with rather exaggerated stabs. "That's rather a funny thing to say, coming from someone with aspirations to become a concubine. He hasn't even met you more than twice."

Allie continued chewing on a roll and wiped her hands on a napkin after swallowing. "Mmm. So I can assume, Kathrine, that the person you wanted me to meet so much is this pleasant gentleman ogling me at the other end of this fine dining table? Let's just cut to the chase, shall we?"

Kathrine frowned, then gave her an uncomfortable nod. "Yes."

"And he really is my betrothed, according to the queen? THIS guy?" Allie shoved a finger in Barimont's direction, getting a scowl from the overly handsome man as Kathrine nodded once again. "Is it normal for the royalty of the Blood Moon Requiem to be pawned off as breeding partners like this? Without any say about who they get to marry? Or is it just Riven and me?"

"That is a complicated question . . ." Kathrine began while pulling at a lock of brown hair hanging down her shoulder. "The short answer is sometimes. In your case, your parents weren't there to help navigate the political agenda concerning who it would be. So your great-grandmother, the high queen, as your closest kin holding a royal title, was the one who decided an auction should occur after being pressured by the rest of the elder council to choose."

A heavy silence ensued, the sound of Allie's nails digging into the wooden table mixing with the sound of Lady Muren's chewing while Lord Barimont continued to stare with a forced smile. Was the queen really on her side, or was she not? It was hard to tell.

"You should be honored to marry one such as me, Allie Wraithtide," Lord Barimont said, putting his elbows on the table to rest his chiseled, pale chin on his hands. "My house is incredibly wealthy. We have conquered newly settled territories on the outskirts of the empire, owning large shares of two planets and a smaller portion of a third. Millions of slaves, entire cities erected in our names, and a military force that rivals many of the best in the empire. You would not be lacking in resources once you joined my family name."

Allie glared at the man again, eyes narrowed. "And yet here you are, basically trying to buy me as little more than a sex object. And for what? To raise yourself in the political hierarchy? That's what Riven told me."

Lord Barimont's eyebrows rose. "And just what does your brother know about political hierarchies? You and yours have never been to the empire."

"Not in person, but Riven did recently visit to discuss running Luteski. General Viku filled him in on some of the details." Allie leaned back, lying through her teeth. Viku hadn't been the one to tell them about the political landscapes and how to navigate them; it'd been their great-grandmother, the high queen—but Allie still didn't know what High Queen Nephridi's game was. Was her grandmother playing both sides of the field? Or was she truly on Allie's side? If Nephridi really was her ally, it'd be stupid to claim she'd been sent information from her grandmother if other elders of the empire council were at play.

Lord Barimont sighed, then shook his head. "General Viku is known to me. He is a military man. He does not concern himself with politics, but I'd really like to convince you that I am worthy to marry without needing to do things the hard way. Is there no chance I could win your favor? At least let me make the attempt. Reasons for why we bade for your hand in marriage are reasons of our own, and you will be treated fairly as my wife. When you raise our children, I will shower them with the finest of gifts, and our house name will only grow stronger between your inherent gift of prophecy and the might of the Barimont legions."

"I'm not interested."

"It is your duty. I'm afraid you can't decline."

Allie sneered back at the blankly staring man in front of her, then she leaned forward with a hiss. "I'm already courting someone. Someone a lot better than you."

Lord Justo Barimont blinked twice, then pushed back on the table and began to laugh uproariously. His cackles boomed across the large dining hall as Kathrine stared blankly at the table, Lady Muren smirked, and Allie glared. Eventually he calmed himself down, then used a handkerchief to wipe the literal tears streaming out of his eyes from the sheer amusement he obviously felt about her statement. "Are you talking about that crippled cattle whelp? The one with the shriveled limbs?!"

"His name is Lahn!" Allie said, slamming a fist onto the table as she got to her feet with a roar of death mana. The chair and her side of the table exploded into fragments of wood and food, and both Kathrine and Lady Muren yelled out in shock while scrambling away.

Lord Justo Barimont continued chuckling to himself rather loudly as the rest of the room, servants and guards included, came to a standstill. He seemed undisturbed by the building mana roiling around Allie and stood up off his still-intact chair to brush out his robes—clasping his hands behind his back with a smug grin. "Lahn, then. Let me ask you this, Princess Allie Wraithtide: What is it that this Lahn could provide you that I couldn't? And calm down, my dear, there is no reason to get angry. Laughing is a valid reaction when watching someone as esteemed and as beautiful as yourself trying to court a filthy, crippled **PIG** that has less worth than the dirt upon which he stands. When this integration is over, and after I have impregnated you, I will be sure to crush your mutant human pet in the most painful way imaginable while making you watch. Better yet, I even invited him here today so that he could meet the man who would take away his woman. I sent a messenger right as you arrived, so he should be here any time now. Perhaps his death will come a little earlier than expected, and of course—I won't be letting you leave."

He was goading her on; they both knew she knew it.

And she would have his head for it.

The flowing river of death mana surrounding Allie surged, and her mind clouded over with rage. She'd never been talked to like this before, especially not after having acquired the power of the system and her heritage—and she would not suffer this fool to speak as he pleased.

She took in a long breath, calmed herself, and closed her eyes as the river of mana slowly converged and disappeared back into her body. Then she let out a long exhale, shoulders slumping. Riven had told the high queen that he'd try to convince Allie to at least meet the man to talk to him, in order to appease this elder council, but Nephridi had known things likely wouldn't go well.

"At least I've kept my promise," Allie muttered under her breath, slowly opening her red eyes to witness Lord Justo Barimont's smug grin growing wider.

He slowly began to clap now that Allie's surging aura had dwindled, but he was the only one in the room making any noise. "Very good, my bride-to-be. Very, very good. Perhaps I'll spare his life after all, since you appear to be submitting—after I humiliate him, of course. I am glad you've come to your senses and have stopped that silly little tantrum of yours. Now that you've destroyed most of the room in your flippant, childish display of power—perhaps we can enjoy ourselves in private while we await your pet's arrival. The high council demands that we give them a child with the gift sometime within the next century, so there's no time to waste."

Allie's smile widened. "Yes, of course, my dearest betrothed. Let us not waste any more time."

Her bone wand whipped forward, and the room erupted as an Unholy obelisk crashed through the ceiling with a tidal wave of energy and a shower of debris. Teal runes along the black creation flickered to life and rapidly drew power from the surroundings, feeding mana into her body when the obelisk shattered with an influx of power. A vacuum formed around her within half a second before the wand exploded with a shock wave of death as the sound barrier broke.

CRASH

Lord Justo Barimont's eyes widened only for a split second before the ceiling was torn asunder by the obelisk and he was sent rocketing out of the dining hall. Servants and warriors around her screamed or scrambled to safety, but frankly Allie was surprised she hadn't just decimated the entire fortress with that attack. Instead, she'd only blown the smug bastard through three different rooms—landing him in a crater of rubble along one of the far walls of the armory.

Allie clicked her tongue, annoyed that the Blood Moon Requiem had invested so much money into building the compound—and acknowledging that although they'd still only used F-grade materials for this particular world, the enchantments engraved into each block of the fortress made them far sturdier than normal material.

She bent over and picked up her bone mask, placing it back on her face and turning to Kathrine, who was paler than usual with her back up against the far wall. "I believe I'm done here. Tell Grandmother that they'll need to find a replacement for the prick I just killed."

WHAM

Allie's body shuddered, and she screamed as Infernal chains tore out of the ground, latching onto her wrists and ankles and neck to pull her into a kneeling position. The laughter of Lord Barimont echoed through the compound, and his figure emerged from the wreckage beyond the dining hall with his rings all rusted and his amulet cracked.

He looked down at his protective jewelry with a bewildered expression, then hummed in amusement as more of the Infernal bindings continued to clamp down onto Allie's writhing body. "By the blood god! I knew you had a temper, but this is just uncalled-for! And to think you have so much power at only level 84! These amulets should have held up far better in the F-grade. I'm impressed."

Allie struggled and screamed, her death mana suppressed by the Infernal chains that seemed to eat away her own energy stores while simultaneously keeping her tied to the ground. Her soul-woven armor and wand both began to wail, and then, to her surprise—the items began to shudder as they started eating away the fiery chains born of hellscape magic at a rapid pace.

Even Lord Barimont looked surprised, and he raised a hand to reinforce his spells with a strained look as sweat started beading on his face. "I will say that your genetics spell great things for our children, even outside the realm of prophecy. It makes me wonder what your Death affinity is. Surely 90 percent or better."

"Lord Barimont!" Kathrine shrieked over the flames that'd started spreading onto the carpet and tapestries above, where remnants of the ceiling still shadowed most of the dining room. "Unhand the high princess right now! You may be her fiancé, but harming her like this is treason!"

The vampiric soldiers wearing the sigil of the blood moon all tensed at Kathrine's words, and in return their counterparts bearing the sigil of the green flame—the sigil of House Barimont—all tensed as well. Hands gripped swords or halberds tightly, and they started eyeing each other with appraising looks as Captain Rusof held up a hand to stay the violence.

"I was obviously attacked first; I am merely restraining my beloved fiancée in turn to make sure she does not harm me or anyone else," Lord Justo Barimont replied slyly, coming over and tucking a finger under Allie's skull mask before ripping it off to expose her sneer. He bent down next to her, smile gleaming dangerously in the Infernal light. "I believe I'll take her back to my room now. Servants, you are all dismissed."

The remaining servants who'd stayed behind, wide-eyed and watching events unfurl, all quickly left as Barimont picked Allie up off the ground by the roots of her hair—then he produced a collar. "This is for you, my dear, to calm you down. Don't worry, there's no reason to fret. The rest of the night will be far more enjoyable for the both of us."

Captain Rusof took a step forward, chin lowered and red eyes flashing. "Lord Barimont, I thought you were merely jesting when you said you were going to use a suppression collar. Those are prohibited by—"

"High Elder Thune made this collar specifically for her. Do not preach to me about what can and cannot be done here, **Captain**!" Lord Barimont sneered to his right, pointing a finger at the military man. "I am well within my rights, especially after being attacked! Princess Allie Wraithtide has committed what is akin to treason herself after attacking me and thereby defying the orders of the council. She has no choice but to obey!"

The two men glared at one another amid Allie's screams, but eventually Captain Rusof gave a curt nod and retreated.

Barimont snorted in derision, then turned his attention back to Allie. Leaning forward and smiling victoriously, he forced a kiss onto Allie's lips while she still flailed and her limbs were being burned along various points of restraint. Lord Barimont savored the feel of her soft body against his, and he hummed in satisfaction at the act.

Allie's eyes went wide in sheer rage, but whatever items he'd brought with him were just too powerful to overcome. She could feel much of his energy being leeched out of that cracked amulet he wore, a reservoir of power that tripled her own reserves even if the man himself didn't pose a threat without it. Her body flailed, her mind roared, and then—something blurred in her peripheral vision as Barimont's men screamed out at him in warning.

BOOM

The remaining amulet around Lord Barimont's chest exploded as a protective barrier erupted from the innermost jewel, sending Allie and Barimont blasting out in different directions right when Fimrindle's scythe sank into the vampire lord's upper back. The attack would have been a killing blow directly to the heart, but the amulet was destroyed now—and Allie could feel the reservoir of power on Barimont's chest dwindle before completely fading away as she picked herself up from a smoldering pile of rubble in the wall near Kathrine.

She spat blood as she stood up, cracking her neck and holding out her hand to summon her mask, which flashed to her. Putting it on and sizing up the vampiric soldiers who'd drawn swords and conjured Unholy fireballs in front of their lord, who was cursing loudly across the room in a pile of his own rubble, she pointed her wand one more time.

She visibly shook with anger, wiping off the saliva he'd left on her lips. "Now that your toys are broken, let's see how strong you really are."

The iron scarecrow cocked his head to one side. "On your order, Master."

Allie screamed, and the room around her exploded as her formerly suppressed death mana howled in a storm above her head with flaming skulls materializing out of the air above her to come hurling down onto her enemies. Fimrindle's odd body blipped in between positions in unbelievably elegant sweeps and scythe attacks—dancing in between elite vampire soldiers and her flaming skulls while killing three of House Barimont's men within seconds before he vanished and reappeared once again.

Lord Barimont's soldiers rushed the metal scarecrow, and a few of them tried to lunge directly for Allie—a few of them activating movement abilities only to be set upon by dozens of cloaked skeleton assassins that seemingly phased out of thin air to clash with the vampires head-on. Her bone creations flashed forward, each of them the best of her minions as they twirled enchanted short swords and daggers. They ripped into vampiric flesh with precision strikes or were crushed and demolished in ivory explosions as their bodies were ripped open by vampiric blades, but none of them felt a thread of fear as their necromancer mistress urged them onward.

"ALLIE WRAITHTIDE!" Lord Barimont roared over the din of battle that'd erupted between Allie's minions and his own soldiers. "THIS IS TREASON! YOU WILL BE WED TO ME WHETHER OR YOU LIKE IT OR NOT, AND THE MORE YOU RESIST, THE MORE THINGS WILL END BADLY FOR YOU!"

Allie grinned underneath her mask. "You should be more concerned about yourself."

She held up a hand to the sky, and from the hole in the ceiling and up in the clouds far above them, cracks in space began to tear themselves into reality. Screams erupted from the beyond, and a gigantic neon-teal eye wreathed in deathly flames glared downward upon the vampiric compound like the eye of the death god itself.

Stone shattered, and those she viewed as enemies all began to scream as its judgment radiated down hatred and crashed into their bodies like a tidal wave of pain. Lord Barimont was one of them, screaming in agony as his bones cracked and shattered—the sheer weight of the eye's presence causing him to slam into the floor and create a crater there before his broken fingers managed to pry out yet another item from a pocket on his right side.

He crushed a pill of some sort, and a blinding flash of radiant white light blew open the doors to the room and raced toward the heavens—quickly blasting apart the Eye of the Scythe spell Allie had conjured with a flare of golden-white energies.

The backlash was not insignificant, and Allie stumbled, blood dripping from her nose while she caught herself on a wall. Princess Kathrine, Lady Muren, Captain Rusof, and the other elite warriors of the Blood Moon Requiem all stood by silently and helplessly—not willing to impose themselves on this fight lest they be caught up in a power struggle involving people far above their pay grade. Be it the High Queen Nephridi and Elder Thune, or Princess Allie Wraithtide and House Barimont—the bystanders didn't seem willing to put themselves in a line of fire regarding this dispute.

"KNOW YOUR PLACE!" Lord Barimont shrieked, blasting Fimrindle when the demon-undead hybrid managed to bypass two guards to take a swipe at the lord himself.

The iron scarecrow was sent skidding head over heels across the ground, only to recover with inhuman agility and blur back to engage. He was quickly intercepted by House Barimont elites, though, who doubled down on their efforts to kill the creature and keep their charge safe in a whirlwind of clashing, sparking metal.

Lord Barimont then charged with collar in hand, flames erupting along one arm as he torpedoed through the air with a boost of power from flames at his feet. He crashed into Allie's position as the bystanders backpedaled toward safety, only to be repelled by Allie's bone armor and a whiplash of death-mana strings that cut deep into his chest and spiked the vampire into the ceiling.

Allie blurred left, dodging a thrown fireball from one of Barimont's men and retaliating with another roar of death mana from her wand before her free hand rose into the air. While Lord Barimont crashed into the ground and stood up, snapping his neck and then an arm back into the correct position—she closed her eyes and began to focus on the scattered bones and corpses around her.

The air hummed as she activated Speaker of the Dead and A Path of Bones, combining the spirit-summoning spell with the ability to bend and sculpt bones to her cause. The afterlife responded with a howl of shrieking voices that filled the sky, and the remnants of the ceiling shattered as a roar of ghosts rushed at Lord Barimont in an attempt to possess him like a tidal wave.

Lord Barimont screamed in horror, and the room flared with an explosion of Infernal energy that rocked the very building they stood in—killing numerous guards, skeletons, and thrall servants in the attempt to ward off possession. He huffed, his flaming body reducing to cinders only to go wide-eyed when he saw an avalanche of bone erupting from Allie's spatial sack on her hip.

She grinned mischievously, waggling a finger at him as the ocean of ivory soared high—ghosts still circling him like birds of prey would a rabbit. "I don't marry maggots."

She shoved her hand forward, and the ocean of ivory descended like a maelstrom of violence—crashing into Lord Barimont and cutting into him in hundreds of places while simultaneously trying to flatten him into a pancake. The ivory ocean began to compress, compress, and compress even more as it turned into a sphere with the vampire lord inside.

He roared in pain and cursed her, spurts of flame trickling out of the dense ball of ivory hovering in the ruins of the dining hall. Ghosts began to shriek and dive into the mess of magic, using Allie's own death mana to keep them safe from the Infernal fires as their spirit bodies dug into Lord Barimont's own—turning his pained cursing into a frantic and horrified wail.

Allie's fanged sneer grew wider, her crimson eyes burning with malice while her hand continued to tighten on the strings that connected her will to the swirling orb of compacting ivory. "DIE!"

"AAAAAAAHHHHHH!!!" His screams were growing fainter, and the struggles were growing less obvious as fewer and fewer flames escaped the holes in her bone prison, but a neon-red blast of light from one of the soldiers tore across the room and shattered the hold Allie had on the young lord. The bones disintegrated, and the ghosts trying to tear into the man's soul were evaporated instantly.

"NOOOO!!" Allie screamed in rage and summoned more flaming skulls, launching them at the vampiric soldier and turning him into paste before she was slammed back into the wall with a sickening crunch.

The flaming chains from earlier tore out of the wall and from one of Barimont's hands, binding her to the stone and wrapping around her neck, legs, and arms to hold her still. Lord Barimont picked himself up—a bloodied, haggard mess with one eye missing as he glared hatefully toward her. Standing in a pile of ash, he slowly began to regenerate as his vampiric body healed the wounds inflicted upon him.

"You raggedy BITCH!" Lord Barimont howled, only to turn at the sound of a door being flung open—and his hate-filled sneer turned into a look of absolute glee.

There, in the entrance to the hall, was Lahn. He was in his wheelchair, frantically looking around and taking in the sight with growing emotion. He saw Allie's figure bound and burning as she screamed against the wall—her mana battling the suppressive effect of the chains that were extending out of Lord Barimont's hands.

He saw her minions battling the vampiric knights in fierce combat with Fimrindle at the head of them all. He saw the one-eyed mage smiling sinisterly his way, and Lahn drew out the gift Allie had given him all those weeks ago.

A brilliant white light illuminated the darkness of the vampiric compound, and Prophet's artifact tome blazed with Holy energy that radiated across Lahn's skin while his shriveled hand frantically tried to flip the pages. Tears welled up in his eyes, and he glared daggers at the man who was hurting Allie while he screamed at the top of his lungs, "I'M HERE TO HELP, ALLIE!"

Allie's body twitched, and her death mana roared in an explosion that sent ripples up the chains binding her—causing Lord Barimont to stumble, giving her a moment of respite. She turned her head, a look of absolute horror in her eyes when she saw who it was.

She screamed, her voice shrill. "LAHN! LAHN, GODDAMN YOU, RUN! FUCKING RUN!"

Then Lord Barimont lunged.

CHAPTER 50

Allie was in trouble. She was being attacked and her life was in danger.

And his reaction was instinctual. Without any thought of his own safety, he would persevere for the woman who'd taken his heart with the kindness she'd shown him over these past few months—a kindness he'd only ever known from his mother prior to meeting her.

Lahn's shriveled fingers on his left hand, still devoid of any real musculature despite the slow going recovery process, flipped through the pages of the shimmering white book that oozed Holy power on his lap.

He watched the vampire lord before him, the asshole who'd attacked Allie, lunge toward him at a speed Lahn couldn't quite comprehend. He knew his death was likely impending, and tears were already trickling down his face as he pushed through the mental blockade of fear to do what must be done.

But he was too slow, and though he knew what he was looking for, the vampire lord was just too fast.

"Hello, PIG!" the one-eyed vampire hissed venomously, still holding Allie to the wall as the battle between her undead and the vampire soldiers bearing the sigil of the green flame raged behind him. The vampire's shadow loomed over Lahn in his wheelchair, and he backhanded Lahn's face so hard that spit and teeth flew out of his mouth.

Lahn spun around, flung from the chair but barely managing to keep hold of the Holy book. He landed in a crumpled heap, grunting a scream as his weaker arm snapped and his jaw unhinged.

The vampire lord began to laugh despite his wounds, which were slowly beginning to regenerate—though more slowly than they had earlier. He turned and sneered Allie's way. "This?! THIS creature, of all the people you could choose, is the one you prefer as your mate? OVER ME?! How ludicrous!"

Lahn's fingers, despite the pain radiating across his broken body, continued to dig at the glowing pages of the book with frantic abandon. In truth there was no way he could defeat this monster; there was no way to save Allie the way he was.

That's why he needed to change, and though the sacrifice it would take to get there was steep—the words of power written into the pages of this text were as clear as day to him.

There was a path to save her. A path that even the previous owner of this book hadn't taken due to the cost.

The vampire lord shook his head, sending a bolt of flames tearing through two of the skeletal assassins that charged him—only to glance uncaringly at one of his soldiers who died at the hand of Fimrindle. Pausing just a moment to make sure the iron scarecrow was preoccupied while more soldiers tried to hold him down with blurring movement abilities and exchanging lightning-quick attacks, the irregularly handsome man began walking toward Lahn with a malevolent grin. An ebony dagger of intricate, jagged, evil design appeared in one of his hands, and he loomed over Lahn like the spirit of death when he raised it up high for a killing strike. "I will purge this world of you for tainting our royal bloodline with your filth, you disgusting pig!"

"YOU WILL NOT TOUCH HIM!!!!" A flash of teal and black roared to life and Allie's scream echoed throughout the compound, causing the earth to quake among a sea of ghosts that tore from the air around her—launching themselves at the flaming chains binding her to the walls in a mad rage.

The dagger descended toward the vulnerable human man, Allie not having freed herself in time despite her herculean effort to interrupt the attack, but the blade was stopped short by none other than Kathrine.

Kathrine Vonsilla Crushada the Ninth, eldest daughter to the duke and duchess of House of Crushada, 107th in line for the vampiric throne, had stopped his attack with a thin rapier. The silver blade's tip was held just inches over Lahn's face, flaring with ribbons of blood that lifted off the weapon like calm waves before the storm as it sparked against the black dagger that'd almost taken Lahn's life.

Lord Justo Barimont was stunned, glaring at Kathrine in uncomprehending rage as the vampire royal held his blade at bay. "What are you DOING, Princess?!"

His eyes grew wide and he nearly tripped over his own legs when Kathrine's arm shot out, collar in hand, to try and put it around his neck. The runic enchantments Elder Thune had placed on it were more than recognizable to his eyes—he must have dropped it without realizing—but Kathrine's advantage of surprise passed as quickly as it'd come. He would not just sit there and let her put that damned, profane object around his neck if he could help it—and violently slapping it away and out of her hand was more than enough to keep himself out of harm's way. "You just expect me to sit there and let you nullify me like that? Did you really think that would work? You'd need to knock me out completely for that kind of plan."

The words hissed out of him like a snake, and he bloomed with fire—exploding backward to barely avoid a death ball by mere centimeters with Allie's wand pointed his way after she'd finally broken free of his chains.

He literally shook in rage, eyes open wide and becoming bloodshot while glaring at the two princesses—Allie coming to stand beside Kathrine, who was obviously rather shaken despite her quick intervention to save Lahn's life. "You do know what this means, don't you? The interference you have just committed is akin to a blood feud."

The man's words were deep, malevolent, and his red eyes narrowed while staring directly at Kathrine's nervous figure twenty yards away.

Kathrine nodded hesitantly, keeping his gaze and still pointing her rapier toward him in a stance that was meant more to ward him off rather than threaten him. "Yes. I know what this means."

Barimont's sinister smile spread. "Your house is not a match for mine without the crown protecting you, even if yours is of a higher status. I hope what you just did was worth it."

Kathrine shuddered but stood her ground as Allie helped Lahn sit up against the near wall. "You forget yourself. I will have House Wraithtide's forces to aid my family. Your house, though known for its conquests, will not be able to stand up to the might of our combined forces if a blood feud is put forth."

Allie stood up from where she'd been helping Lahn, then walked over and put a shaking hand on Kathrine's shoulder before giving the other woman a firm squeeze and a nod.

Barimont spat, then flung the dagger off to the side and summoned a long whip with flaming blades protruding from it. "We will see. But truthfully, it won't even matter if I'm able to capture both of you. Your house will not dare to attack mine if I have you as a hostage."

"To what end?" Kathrine quipped back, anger in her words now as an aura of red spread around her—flaring to life with a whirlwind of blood. "Even if you did manage it, you'd still have to deal with Riven after this is over! What are you even thinking?! He'll just kill you when he gets back! Nobody you can bring is over level 90—you'll be slaughtered for this!"

Lord Barimont rolled his eyes, then smirked victoriously when the sparking clashes of the battle nearby were joined by the sound of marching feet. From the interior catacombs of the fortress came two dozen more vampires in two columns, each bearing the sigil of a blazing red phoenix. They were dressed very similarly to the other soldiers originally stationed here with Kathrine, wearing black-and-red plate armor and using either halberds or long swords, but at the front of their ranks was a man with a very distinct look to him.

His hair was a shiny silver, his features were thin but toned under an exquisitely made satin battle robe. His jaw was locked and clenched, and he looked around the ripped-apart room before his eyes landed on Lord Barimont. "Where is he?"

"Not here," Lord Barimont said with a sideways glance at Allie and Kathrine. "This battle is just for us now present."

Kathrine, in the meantime, was blinking rapidly, and she held the flickering sword in her right hand while her left came to rub her temple in disbelief. "Jalel?

Jalel, is that you? What are you doing here? You're too high level to even be here! How did you get through the portal?"

Jalel remained stone-faced, while Barimont began to laugh.

"I would have been too high level if High Queen Nephridi hadn't punished my scheme to claim the shard, and now *shards*, plural, of Gluttony for myself," Jalel said flatly, his men spreading out in the room to halfway encircle the two princesses. He came to stand next to Lord Barimont, not even looking at the other vampire lord even once. "I was given the choice of death or being allowed to eat demotion pills to reduce my level hundreds of times over. Now that my cultivation and level gains have been completely demolished, I am barely level 87. The amount of money that spiteful queen spends just to make a point is truly absurd. The level cap for invaders is 80, but the cap here for trading communes is 90. I am here on behalf of Elder Thune to make sure that Riven behaves himself when he gets back. Even though Riven is currently higher level than I am after such a steep loss of power—I am more than capable of subduing him even in my currently reduced state, due to my skills and knowledge of countless battles over centuries of life. It will be me, Kathrine, who keeps your fiancé in check. I have been given permission to put you down if need be, because unlike the two lost royals here—you're expendable."

Allie snarled. "ENOUGH TALK!"

CRACK

Her hand whipped forward and rapidly smashed tendrils of death into Lord Barimont, propelling the distracted man through two walls and causing him to scream as the mana ate away at his flesh and regeneration. It was an absolutely thunderous strike, and Jalel's eyes widened before he sprinted forward to intercept the channeling power.

BOOM

Kathrine's rapier sliced down, sending a solid wave of rippling red blood mana tearing through the air—making impact with Jalel's summoned barriers that sprang to life immediately before they hit.

Power boomed in an echo resounding for miles.

The fortress compound shook.

Kathrine screamed in horrified pain as a dagger sank deep into the back of her left lung, and she fell to the ground wide-eyed when looking over her shoulder only to see her romantic rival—Lady Muren. Lady Muren's orange hair whipped about in the wind, a venomous smile on her rosy lips, and she twisted the blade while pouring Unholy poisons into Kathrine's body.

"Riven's name is mine to claim!" Lady Muren hissed, only to have Allie's foot crash into her face—sending the other vampire careening into a far wall.

Jalel's men leaped into action, flashing forward as two dozen blades sought to kill Kathrine or maim Allie—but the sound of more unsheathing weapons rang through the air when even more vampires joined the fray.

"Let's see if you really add up to all that bluster!" Captain Rusof's long sword flashed forward, decapitating one of Jalel's men before he met Jalel himself in battle with a flaring smile on his lips—soon vanishing in movements so fast that normal mortals wouldn't be able to follow the blows. Metal struck metal and screams echoed through the compound as vampire fought vampire. Captain Rusof's men immediately followed his lead—having made their choice to take a side in the political feud when the man they respected most had set his example.

The battle was on.

Lahn's jaw and arm were broken, and he'd probably snapped a few ribs. His face was beginning to swell and the fingers of his hand trembled while flipping through the pages. Why couldn't he find that damn page?

Why now, of all times, was he having an issue finding the single page that could help him here?

A fire-laden, bladed whip lashed out and struck at Allie as she blasted it away, sending Lord Barimont's attack to the side before retaliating with numerous skulls blazing with neon-teal mana. She dodged and vanished out of sight while more of the dead began to rise, fighting alongside her as new corpses that screamed and roared toward her enemies with wild abandon. Blades clashed and magics flew, and all Lahn could do was helplessly turn page after page, trying to find the passage he'd read all those weeks ago when he'd first been given the item as a gift.

His eyes sped down the walls of text, complex runes rearranging themselves to create words of gold across glistening white pages. He winced as he saw Allie's body skip across the ground, only for her to rebound, spit blood, and send waves of death mana spiraling in a tornado of screeching skulls, ghosts, and black-teal flames into a trio of enemy vampires. The battlefield was quickly being widened as more walls and ceilings fell, and combatants pressed one another into the surrounding fortress.

Why was he so useless?!

Why could he not do this one thing to help her?!

He tried not to cry, praying silently to the gods that she would win—that she and her allies would prevail and that they'd not even need him. But even now, he could see that they were losing.

Kathrine was being pushed back, severely injured by Lady Muren's initial attack; lines of poison were spreading through her veins, while the two vampire women flashed back and forth with blood magics in elegant attack patterns. Captain Rusof was exchanging blow for blow with Jalel, but it was apparent that Jalel was slightly more skilled than he—scoring hits when Captain Rusof left openings time and time again. Fimrindle was in a stalemate with five elite vampiric knights from House Barimont that'd locked him down, and the skeletons were mostly gone by now—though they'd certainly taken a number of the vampires with them.

That left Allie and Lord Barimont, who were locked in a back-and-forth duel of flame and death. Allie's strikes were more powerful and packed more punch, but

Lord Barimont was obviously well trained and the skill gap was obvious by the way he manipulated his magics to push aside and divert Allie's own while opening up opportunities for counters.

Then, after two entire minutes of flipping pages and feeling absolutely useless, having been completely forgotten by the rest of the combatants in the room, his eyes finally rested on the passage he'd been looking for.

Lahn's shriveled, trembling fingers touched the page and slowly trailed the golden words that began to sing to him in his mind's eye. His soul resonated with the book he held in his hands, and, taking the plunge, he began to initiate the price while reading out from the tome in frenzied whispers that hurt like hell due to his dislocated jaw. Simultaneously, his good hand started undergoing the motions required of this act in bizarre and intricate patterns in front of him.

"A shield of light in the darkest night, standing before a shade of woe that never has seen the dawn, I mark my soul as a vessel of the heavens and beseech you—oh heavenly warriors—to aid me in my time of need so that you may smite the evil before me! Banish the blight from these tainted lands, and hold my heart in your hands, so that I may find the path to heaven and tread lightly upon its sands! Glory to the pantheons of light!"

He held up his hands, emitting a small spark of golden energy from his outstretched palm, but nothing happened.

He waited through the chaos of battle, hoping beyond hope that they would hear him. Hoping that he'd undertaken the ritual correctly. Hoping that his voice would be heard.

Lahn's eyes lit up in excitement and relief when he felt something tug at the edge of his consciousness, the feeling of angelic beings on the other side of the veil, but they quickly left just as fast as they'd come. Hope turned into worry, and worry turned into despair when he heard a faint feminine whisper that echoed directly into his brain:

"Your soul is pure, young one, but we do not help the children of the dark. Your wish is selfish and misguided. The taint of the blood god is upon the one you seek to protect. She is a creature of evil, in both deed and origin. We will not intervene."

Lahn's face paled, and despair turned to rage as he screamed and tried to rip the page of the book out so that he might crumple it in his hands and tear it apart. He slammed the book against the ground, not caring about the pain radiating up from his broken arm as he began to cry violently in frustration and anger. "YOU'RE SUPPOSED TO HELP! THIS IS NOT HOW THINGS ARE SUPPOSED TO GO!"

Allie's scream brought Lahn about, and he stared wide-eyed when he saw the flaming whip tear off one of her legs. The vampire lord who was fighting her merely laughed and mocked her, telling her that if need be he'd take all her limbs before locking her away.

The idea of this unknown man putting his hands on Allie again made Lahn's stomach churn and his mind roil like a hot metal poker. He looked at the book again, then slammed a small, wiry fist into it. "HELP ME, DAMN YOU!"

The angelic creatures were receding. Their energies, once drawn to him by the book, were quickly fading away. All except for one, however, who made its presence known to him with a faint touch of mana.

Golden energy gently crept out of the pages of the book, tethering itself to Lahn's wet face while tears dripped down his puffy cheeks.

An exchange of feelings and thoughts flashed through Lahn's mind, and slowly he began to calm. He nodded, acknowledging what the being on the other end of the mana tether was telling him. "Yes. I know what will happen to me if I choose to do this, and I am willing to pay that price. Please, help her. If you do not, I fear that terrible things will happen to her—and that I may die as well."

Another pulse and exchange of thoughts flashed between them, and then Lahn shuddered involuntarily. He took in a deep breath, steadied himself, and lifted up the book into the sky. Smiling with quivering lips, he nodded one last time as the book began to disintegrate—using its energies in lieu of his own life force to extend the duration of what they were about to do. "Thank you, Denaskus. I will never forget this."

The angelic being on the other side of the veil sent him a warm pulse of acknowledgment, and then the transformation began to take place.

Lahn's skin began to burn with a blinding white light, and his clothes lit aflame—burning away as golden, feathered wings ripped out of his back. A halo formed over his head, and his eyes completely burned away—only golden flames being present where his eyeballs used to be. His shriveled arm completely withered and fell off, but his shriveled left leg became just as strong and sturdy as his other side was. A spear of light formed in his one remaining hand, and sculpted musculature began to build along his abdomen, chest, arm, and legs—making him look like he'd been carved out of marble in the image of a Greek god.

The resonating boom of the Holy foundational pillar and the Judgment sub-pillar roared around him, tearing apart two of the enemy vampires that'd been close enough to the transformation to take an immediate hit. Lahn's body flexed, and he felt the angelic spirit possessing him take control as it turned his head to stare down at Lord Barimont's gaping gaze from where Lahn floated majestically in the air dozens of meters above the hole in the compound's torn roof.

The resulting voice was a deep and resounding boom.

"I, Denaskus, arbiter of the Celestial Prax, have been summoned onto this pitiful world to smite the unworthy into damnation." Lahn's body shifted his spear of white light, golden wings, eyes, and halo flaring with the fires of judgment as the radiant aura around him intensified. The ground shook with power, and the entire battle stopped temporarily while all combatants stared upward at the new display of prowess.

Lahn's body shifted his spear of solidified Holy light, pointing it directly at Lord Barimont. Lahn's eyes were gone, but the flaming eyes of Denaskus—the angel possessing his body—narrowed into slits. "Prepare yourself, vampire, for I will be the last thing you ever see."

CHAPTER 51

Allie was missing a leg that for some reason wouldn't regrow, Kathrine was severely poisoned and beginning to decline, Jalel was overpowering Captain Rusof, and Fimrindle was finally breaking out of the stalemate—slicing off limbs and heads before pushing Allie's way with incredibly fast and jerky movements. A protective dome now encased the Blood Moon Requiem's trading hub—preventing anyone from going in or out, and the battle within and around the compound had become an absolute madhouse of vampire-on-vampire battles.

Very obviously, there was a rift in the power dynamics between factions of the empire.

Turning his head, Lahn focused on the enemies before him and felt his soul roar to life with power channeled by the heavens themselves. His body burned hot with magic, and a potent sense of justice to be carried out lingered on the borders of his mind.

Possessed by the angelic being Denaskus, he hovered overhead for only a few moments before launching himself back down toward Lord Barimont with a speed that far surpassed anything he'd deemed imaginable. The sky burned with white light, enveloping him in his dive as angelic wrath encompassed his winged form. His combat level was only level 2, but here with this possession he'd surpassed even Allie's might—rising to the challenge to save the girl he'd fallen for.

As he dived downward with a scream of vengeance on his lips, golden, feathered wings flared out to either side with a spear of Holy light pointed at Lord Barimont's heart—and Lahn felt himself begin to break. His body couldn't hold such a powerful being inside him for long; he'd simply die before even a few minutes ran out. He'd already sacrificed one arm and his eyes just to initiate the transformation, and thus he was in a race against time to kill the vampire before his body gave out.

Allie watched wide-eyed as Lahn's body crashed into Lord Barimont's protective barrier of flames at immense speed, sending a shock wave of white-gold light out in all directions that tore through stone and sent warriors sprawling or caused them to stumble. The floor shattered, and a crater dozens of feet deep erupted in the middle of the dining hall. Magically reinforced stone walls cracked and Lord Barimont screamed as the spear of light pinned him to the floor, pulling out enchanted items one after the other as each of them shattered under the immense Holy aura of the angelic creature now standing over him like a judge of fate.

She saw Jalel disengage Captain Rusof with a kick to Rusof's chest and rush to help Lord Barimont a second later, and Allie saw red. Activating her spell A Path of Bones, the scattered remnants of her supplies and the dead bodies around her tore ahead in a swarm of ivory—blasting Jalel back.

Or at least that's what she'd originally intended, but Jalel activated some sort of movement ability and almost teleported forward—spiking his long sword into Lahn's back—

CRASH

Lahn's one-armed angelic figure spun and blocked the sword strike with his remaining right hand, slamming one of his golden wings down onto the vampire prince with a shattering crack of thunderous power.

But it wasn't enough.

Jalel blocked Lahn's golden wing just like his own blade had been blocked by Lahn's hand, and the narrowed golden eyes glared back at bright crimson as Lahn's halo began to flare with brighter light.

"Insolence," the deep voice of the angel possessing Lahn's body said, only to soar upward and out of reach when two of Lord Barimont's elite soldiers rushed him with the intent of impaling him.

Having released Lord Barimont from where Lahn had impaled the vampire, the angelic being crashed back down onto the reinforcements—cutting through limbs and burning them alive with Holy flame as Jalel was pressed from behind by the captain once more.

"Master, you are cursed." Fimrindle suddenly appeared before Allie, his thin metal body covered in gore and blood. His scythe hummed and his lantern vibrated with souls of the dead he'd ripped from the men he'd recently killed, using the souls as fuel to boost himself in battle—but he set the lantern down to lightly touch at the open wound where Allie's right thigh had been completely cut through.

A metal finger picked up the writhing black mass along Allie's flesh that continued to dig into her body, fighting her regeneration as she winced. The scarecrow looked up again and blurred—a spray of blood behind her telling her that he'd killed another of the soldiers before he knelt beside her once more with his scythe planted onto the stone floor. "This curse will take a long time to get rid of, and it is draining both your regeneration and your mana. In a short time you will be useless in this fight. Do you wish to flee?"

"Fuck that!" Allie spat, summoning her bones to create a makeshift ivory leg for herself. The bone dug into her flesh, impaling her vampiric body in numerous places to anchor itself—but it worked. Testing out the poorly made limb and grimacing at the thin tendrils of death mana that ran along the surface of the newly formed leg, she glared up at Lord Barimont, who'd taken to the sky with green flame forming balls of fire all around him.

She pointed to where he was battling Lahn overhead. "Help kill Lord Barimont. You're in a better state than I am. I'll move to help Kathrine."

Fimrindle nodded and then vanished once again as thunderous booms echoed in the sky between the protective dome surrounding the compound and the ground far below.

Allie cast a worried look skyward one more time, then firmed her resolve amid the clash of steel and spells around her—propelling herself forward and rushing headlong toward Kathrine's position in what had once been the kitchen not far off. She could already tell that the poison was wreaking havoc on the princess's body, with oozing green wounds dripping acid and numerous slashes refusing to heal and battling her vampiric regeneration, while Lady Muren's bright-orange hair flared about her and blood magics clashed along sleek silver blades.

Allie would not let Kathrine die here, not after what she'd done for Lahn, and so she reentered the fray with the intent to tear off Lady Muren's head.

Riven walked next to Azmoth's hulking form through underground city streets littered with dead dwarves. A city of square and rectangular architecture burned around him, and a storm of red and black swirled overhead—crackling with thunderous applause at the destruction he'd wreaked upon his enemies. Blood mana from all the dead, infused with the power of his path.

A combination of the aspects of Blood and Shadow.

The cavern above echoed his ominous approach, and rat-kin swarms pursued his advance at the vanguard—overtaking remnant holdouts while nearing the main gate of the dwarvish palace. He'd absolutely steamrolled the defenses here; he'd killed tens of thousands of them by himself and obliterated the outer walls, and yet he still didn't even know the name of the civilization he was conquering.

Nor did he care.

Despite having killed so many, Riven hadn't grown many levels. It made him realize that the XP he was getting for each kill was diminishing with these weaker enemies the further he grew himself, and that he'd have to find stronger enemies to handle if he wanted to progress fast. He couldn't just farm a bunch of weak dwarves and expect to get growth spurts for it.

His vampiric senses picked up heartbeats in numerous houses he passed by, his red eyes sifting through the dark crevices—bearing witness to cowering civilians. The young, the old, the women—all huddled together and barricading themselves whatever ways they could.

He ignored them. He didn't want to hurt them—he honestly didn't even want to fucking be here at all and had even given the rat-kin explicit orders as impromptu leader of this military operation to not hurt anyone who didn't put up a fight. However, he knew there would be casualties regardless, and though it bothered him, it certainly didn't bother him like it would have when he'd first arrived on Panu.

Sacrifices needed to be made for the greater good, and he'd given them two chances to speak to him with only a barrage of cannon fire for a response. These dwarves had started this war in an attempt to commit genocide against the rat-kin he now called friends, having killed hundreds of thousands of rat-kin in the process—so the dwarves had this coming.

"It almost feels too easy . . ." Riven muttered to Azmoth, casually holding up one hand and creating a network of Wretched Snares in front of him. The Unholy, needlelike nets layered on top of one another by the dozens in a split second when thunderous booms echoed from the palace in the center of the city.

Dozens of magma-infused cannonballs roared toward him after the explosions bloomed on the palace wall, and they slammed into Riven's nets a moment later—only to fizzle out and drop as smoking chunks of metal one by one.

He turned but continued walking, watching Athela's house-size figure battling three earthen elementals twice her weight a couple blocks away with ease as she wove about them—spearing them with her icy limbs. Her swarms of ice-made arachnids toppled guard towers, and the screams of dwarvish sentinels being over-run echoed out through the city before the tower fell with a resounding crash.

"Azmoth does not like this. Feels like we are bullying. Azmoth wishes for a true fight," Azmoth replied a moment later, walking in stride on Riven's right—magma-infused maul hoisted up over one shoulder. On the other side of his body, he carried the shield Riven had gotten for him so long ago from Negrada's trading compound at a staggering price of 140,000 Elysium coins—but had failed to use up until now. Up until today, the shield had refused to bind to Azmoth and was unwieldy—but now the shield had seemed to undertake a change of heart.

[Immortal's Grasp (Tier-1 Awakened Shield) (Heavy Armor): 640 average defense, 83 average damage on strike. +209 Sturdiness, +42 Strength.
- **Grasping Fingers: A hand can launch out of the shield to grasp enemies, pulling them toward the shield or you toward an enemy.]**

It was a very large and round shield, big enough for Azmoth to hide behind with over half of his body. It was made of a darker shade of gray steel, was many inches thick, and looked like it could have been the door to some kind of bank vault—only to be ripped off and used as a barrier instead. Bolts and screws had been drilled into the external perimeter, and the sigil of a black hand was displayed on the front.

But that hand wasn't painted. The fingers of the hand twitched and even pushed out against the iron on the front of the shield—causing the metal to creak and groan as it bent, only to be re-formed moments later. Riven had already seen the shield in action twice while using Grasping Fingers—launching the black metallic hand out of the shield to grasp and yank back enemies or crush them outright. It was certainly an odd piece, but Riven was happy Azmoth was finally getting some use out of the shield after having it for so long.

Riven nodded while he considered Azmoth's words, forming a storm ball in his free hand to stare at it while he walked. Cannon fire continued to crash into his nets while they moved, but nothing the dwarves could throw at him managed to break through. "Yes . . . I agree. This kinda sucks. But we've gotta do it, otherwise the senseless deaths and this stupid-ass war the dwarves started will never end. We'll kill the king and put someone else in charge as a subordinate to me. Hopefully that'll be the end to this nonsense."

Concentrating on the storm ball and passing by burning houses, he frowned underneath his helm and concentrated on the shape. These upgraded storm balls from what had once been Bloody Razors were certainly more powerful, there was no doubt about it. The storm balls also had homing abilities on par with his Bloody Razors, but they lacked something the Bloody Razors had.

That was piercing power.

These storm balls would launch and either eradicate his enemy, which was what usually happened, or they'd blow up and fizzle out. This latter option had happened a couple times now against higher-leveled enemies who'd managed to deflect the attacks with various abilities, and based on the amount of power he put into them, he could tell that if the shape had been different, more concentrated, sharper even, they'd have pierced through before exploding.

He remembered back in Negrada when he'd first been able to infuse his Bloody Razors with excess mana, causing them to explode. He'd been overjoyed at the idea that he could cause them to erupt, which was a big step up from the original sharp shards of mana he'd first been able to control. However, he was now having the opposite problem—these storm balls were simply too unstable and blew up too quickly. He needed them to pierce first, allowing them to bypass barriers more effectively by condensing the mana in these projectiles onto a single razor's edge of contact.

He wanted the shape of his old razors back.

Grimacing at the attempt and getting a headache, he began to mold the storm ball hovering over his hand into a razor just like his old ones used to be. The chaotic, lacerating buzz of energy over his palm swirled with Shadow and Blood magic—rippling and sparking in an attempt to resist his will.

But in the end the magic obeyed.

It condensed into a spinning, multipronged circular razor similar to the ones he used to have. Only this time, instead of being solely blood magic, this was a solid crimson intermixed with black shadow mana—sparking with Black Lightning and having a much more solid, compact texture to it.

He smiled, having no doubt this version of his storm ball would be far superior to either previous versions of the spell he'd had. It had slightly less explosive potential because of it, but that was fine in his eyes. Being able to rip through defensive formations more easily was well worth it in his opinion, despite a decrease in area-of-effect damage.

> **[Storm Ball has been modified. You may now either summon Storm Razors or Storm Balls based on which you prefer. These are two sides to the same coin and feed off the same spell. Storm Razors gain a 20% piercing bonus when compared to Storm Balls, and Storm Balls gain a 35% wider explosion radius when detonating when compared to Storm Razors. Your status page has been updated.]**

He cocked an eyebrow. Two versions of the same spell, eh? And his thought process on the matter had been spot-on. Scratching at his chin, he supposed he could see uses for both versions of the spell depending on the scenario—but he was also rather amused that it took so little effort to create such a modification.

Then again, how long had it been since he'd truly broken through? He needed to focus more on the study of magic and take lessons from the tutors back at the Blood Moon Requiem's compound. He had a lot of questions regarding magic that he was certain could be answered by that Instructor Pladius guy, and frankly, Riven loved magic. Despite being up close and personal a lot of the time given his hybrid Warlock Devastator class that infused all physical attacks with a percentage of Unholy damage passively based on his mana pool, he was still a mage at heart. And if he seriously put his mind to it, just what could he accomplish? So far he'd only undergone brief epiphanies due to battles or small attempts at experimentation over the course of his integrated life, so just what could he achieve if he really gave it his all?

The thought excited him. Maybe when he went back to spend time with Hakim's group and dabbled in totem making again, he'd truly give the exploration of magic a real try. A smile tugged at his lips, and he almost forgot he was in the middle of a siege when Azmoth's large body tore through the street and smashed into a dwarven mage who'd tried to ambush the group.

The dwarf's four-foot-tall body smashed into paste underneath the huge maul, and another dwarvish man—an assassin—lunged five feet toward Riven with daggers in hand before a black metal hand whipped out of Azmoth's shield.

The assassin screamed, then was yanked back and pulled into the grip of the shield—latched onto the heavy metal front plate before Azmoth picked the shield up and smashed it down onto the ground. The dwarf died immediately, and Azmoth wiped the man's guts off before burning the remnant blood and walking casually back over to where Riven stood.

"You look like a real demonic paladin with your getup. The black armored plates you naturally wear, the shield and the maul," Riven mused, tapping Azmoth's left shoulder with Jackal's blunt end. "I like the look. It inspires me."

Azmoth merely snorted in amusement, and the two continued their walk to the palace gates.

That's when a single, extremely loud war horn—deep and foreboding—blew out from the boxy stone palace ahead of them. Riven stopped in his tracks and dismissed the dozens of nets ahead of him, revealing in more detail the large palace gates that were slowly creaking open.

The horn echoed again, and then again, and a thunderous voice roared out from the inner palace grounds as a short but heavily armored man wielding a jeweled stone claymore twice the man's size walked out. "RIVEN THANE! I, KING OF BRYA, CHALLENGE YOU TO A ONE-ON-ONE DUEL! WINNER TAKES ALL!"

The deep voice echoed unnaturally through the city, causing many to slow their fighting in anticipation of what was happening.

Riven lifted an eyebrow. Brya, was it? Well, now he knew.

Riven patiently waited for the approaching man, alone and armed only with his claymore and the thick sheets of stone armor encasing his body. Eventually the king stopped a hundred yards away, though Riven was still able to make him out rather easily due to his vampiric senses.

The dwarvish king had a crown of emeralds laid into his stone helmet, and a long black beard hung braided across his chest. The thickly built warrior slammed his sword into the ground, and with one hand he pointed Riven's way. "CALL OFF YOUR ARMY AND LEAVE MY PEOPLE BE! WE WILL SETTLE THIS LIKE MEN, JUST YOU AND ME! OR ARE YOU A COWARD?!"

Riven blinked. He looked around at the partially burning city about them and knew full well that the city would fall. This was a desperate man's last attempt to salvage the situation, or at least he'd die trying. Or, even more probably, the king was sacrificing himself to save the lives of his people. Riven glanced up to the walls, where fearful dwarvish warriors stood ill at ease, glanced to the surrounding buildings where civilians still hid from the rumbling of rat-kin feet or the battles his demons were involved in.

If it spared these people, even if there was a chance at him losing, Riven would take it. He might be jaded after all the things he'd gone through, but he still wasn't a heartless murderer.

Not entirely, anyway.

Raising a hand and using his aura to project his voice, the storm of black and red radiated with the words he spoke. "This is Riven Thane. All units from Deepnest, and the guilds or mercenary groups participating in this battle from the Thane Necropolis, stand down immediately and withdraw. Anyone seen disobeying this order will be gutted. Anyone seen killing civilians unprovoked will be gutted. The king has challenged me to a duel, and I will take his word that the winner takes the victory here. But let it be known to the people of this city that, should your king die and you not comply and lay down your arms to accept your conqueror—I will be forced to continue this senseless killing."

Riven's red eyes stared unblinkingly at the dwarf down the road from where he stood. Just with the power he'd infused into his voice using the thundering storm of power overhead, he was sure the king knew what was about to happen.

There was simply no way this man could win against him, and either the king was delusional about his chances or he was making this final stand as a symbolic gesture, one that would stop Riven from killing any more dwarves other than himself.

[Dwarvish King, Level 90 Earthen Swordmaster]

Riven looked to Azmoth standing at his side, the hulking demon having grown far more levels than Riven had since the battles through the underdark had commenced. "You'll be the one dueling for me. He's slightly less leveled than you, but it'd be a good fight, and you'll get more experience for it."

Azmoth grunted his acknowledgment and started walking forward. Two hands held the large stone maul, one hand held the thick shield, another clawed hand was free for grappling—and the two eel-like, armored maws coming out of his back rippled with Infernal flames as fire built inside. The huge demon's spiked tail swayed back and forth, and the dwarvish king nodded to Riven in what he could only assume was respect.

"Give me an honorable death, as a warrior king. Spare my people, I beg of you," the king said in a lower tone so that it didn't echo across the city, and he held up the large stone claymore to point it at Azmoth. "LET US BEGIN, THEN!"

The ground underneath the dwarf's feet surged up at an angle, launching him like a catapult toward Azmoth's larger form. Orange and brown light illuminated the dark, and the dwarven king screamed a battle cry with determination in his eyes.

Azmoth didn't break his stride, activating Hell's Armor and flaring to life with Infernal energy. Simultaneously activating The Burning Crusade, his physical attacks and weapons got additional fire damage boosts. Flames rippled across his entire body, shield, and weapon in an instant, and he brought the round metal shield up to take the charge head-on.

The resulting crash caused the ground underneath Azmoth's feet to shatter, but the shield threw the dwarvish king into a nearby house—crashing through the far wall.

Azmoth turned, leaned down, and activated Propulsion. Flames roared even higher behind him as they launched him like a rocket into the place where the king had landed, and using Crushing Meteor Strike, his titanic swing blurred with a resonating thunderclap of power that was followed up by another martial art—Shock Wave.

The buildings around them and the street Riven stood on were vaporized, turning into clouds of dust that were quickly burned away with swaths of flame radiating out of Azmoth's body. When the dust did clear, Riven saw the large demon holding up the smoldering, broken corpse of the dwarvish king high in the air for those on the palace walls to see. The houses for blocks around them were starting to burn, and Riven's Crimson Ice quickly went to work putting out those flames as civilians started to scream in horror.

"Good job, bud." Riven grinned at Azmoth, then walked over to give the demon a pat on the shoulder while three other well-dressed dwarves nervously stood at the entrance to the palace—waiting for his arrival. No more cannons fired, and soon the dwarves along the walls were throwing their weapons and even their siege machines off the edge in a sign of absolute surrender.

Riven's voice boomed over the city one more time for all to hear, and the resulting roar of cheers and screams of excitement from the rat-kin army behind him could be heard as a deafening cacophony. "We have won."

Drums started beating in the deep, the sound of a victory march, and he approached the palace at a steady stroll while his demons quickly joined him. He had a lot to do to iron things out, and he . . .

Riven shuddered, and the world froze about him. Everything just stopped, and colors faded into gray.

[Malignant Prophecy has activated. Desired Action: Medium-Tier Manipulation. Current Willpower stat: 460. Sufficient Willpower to perform desired action. Performing this act will put your Malignant Prophecy on cooldown for significant amounts of time. Desired Action: Save Kathrine Vonsilla Crushada's life. Malignant Prophecy's only available option will be demonstrated to you upon acceptance. However, you are currently at four total Malignancy Points. When you achieve five Malignancy Points, your first tribulation for repeatedly dabbling in taboo arts will begin shortly after the prophecy has been fulfilled. Elysium's wrath will be unchained. Do you wish to proceed to save Kathrine's life while incurring the wrath of the system?]

. . .

. . .

. . .

[Your manipulation of fate has gained you one Malignancy Point. Current total Malignancy Points: 5. Should you succeed in following the outline of the prophecy, your first tribulation will commence and your soul will be judged. Malignant Prophecy has entered an extended cooldown stage and cannot be activated for the next two years, should you survive your tribulation. Good luck.]

CHAPTER 52

Allie's world was a stark gray. Blood dripped from her eyes, ears, nose, and mouth as she locked gazes with Jalel only a few feet away. He was the only other one moving in this out-of-body experience, but even he could only move his eyes—so he was limited in the same way she was.

[Malignant Prophecy has activated. Desired Action: High-Tier Manipulation. Current Willpower stat: 800. Desired action: Processing . . . . Processing . . . Processing . . . Insufficient Willpower to perform desired action due to interfering and opposing Malignant Prophecy nearby. Entanglement of bilateral Malignant Prophecy users and their opposing wills has canceled out both thread-weaving attempts to secure fate.]

The entanglement broke for the third time, and for the third time she and Jalel both began to scream in agony—each dropping to the ground and writhing around as time after time their opposing Malignant Prophecies clashed violently.

"KILL HER!" Jalel screeched at his subordinates, picking himself up and kicking the barely moving body of Captain Rusof—who was choking on his own blood and failing to regenerate. "KILL HER NOW!"

"But sire, she is—" one of his soldiers protested warily with a glance over his pauldron.

Jalel cut him off with a sneer of rage. "OUR WILLS ARE BECOMING ENTANGLED. WE WILL BOTH DIE IF SHE ISN'T DEALT WITH! Do you want ONE user to die or TWO?! IT IS ME OR HER—CUT OFF HER HEAD!"

Wait, did she hear that right?

Was he lying?

Allie blinked away bloody tears and shakily got to her feet, still having one of her legs molded from bone due to the curse burying into her amputated thigh. If the Blood Moon Requiem knew an entanglement like this could happen, why would they send Jalel here? If HE had known this, why had he come? If there was even a chance at one of them perishing and their gift really was all that valuable, what was the thought process behind it?

Was she being set up by Elder Thune? Or was it Jalel acting on his own accord? Or was someone else at play here? If what Jalel had said was true, and especially if Jalel had come for Riven in particular, were she and her brother being specifically targeted?

Did the queen know?

None of this made sense. Not after so much effort had been put into securing Riven and Allie for the empire, so there was certainly a larger political game going on here that she didn't have a full picture of just yet.

Nevertheless, Jalel's soldiers seemed to agree and braced themselves before rushing her yet again—this time with bloodlust in their eyes.

"You will NOT TOUCH HER! She is MINE!" Lord Justo Barimont screamed in rage, flinging fireballs at Jalel and turning his back to do so—opening himself up for a staggering strike of Lahn's spear as the angelic figure blurred forward.

The spear of light pierced Barimont's chest and sent him rocketing into the protective barrier surrounding the compound with a sonic boom—only for the light of Lahn's angelic possession to flicker. Lahn was quickly losing power, that much was obvious to Allie, but she grimaced and faced Jalel's oncoming soldiers just before another racing surge of pain electrified her spine.

[Malignant Prophecy has activated. Desired Action: High-Tier Manipulation. Current Willpower stat: 800. Desired action: Processing . . . . Processing . . . Processing . . . Insufficient Willpower to perform desired action due to interfering and opposing Malignant Prophecy nearby. Entanglement of bilateral Malignant Prophecy users and their opposing wills has canceled out both thread-weaving attempts to secure fate.]

She screamed, dropping to the floor in unison with Jalel yet again.

Fimrindle was already intercepting two more of Jalel's soldiers, and they'd even begun to fight one another after Jalel had been attacked by Barimont. It was now a three-way battle, with Jalel's forces, Barimont's men, and Allie alongside the originally stationed garrison all duking it out. Then there were still Princess Kathrine and Lady Muren, who'd disappeared to fight elsewhere.

It was a fucking madhouse, with even more soldiers from House Barimont having poured into the compound through the portal as reinforcements for the young lord. Funnily enough, within minutes four more groups were also entering rapidly into Panu via the portal:

Princess Kathrine Vonsilla Crushada's parents had sent through their own soldiers, bearing the sigil of a rose. Then soldiers from House Wraithtide, probably sent over by General Viku, bore the sigil of a neon-teal orb wreathed in deathly fire. More soldiers from Jalel's own house bearing the sigil of the phoenix poured through as well, with the final group of soldiers bearing a sigil of a wolf. This last house primarily focused their attention on House Crushada soldiers and were calling out for Lady Muren while rushing into the periphery, where the princess battled the other lady of the court.

Obviously sent through other entry points in the empire or somehow using system shenanigans that Allie didn't understand, dozens upon dozens of vampiric soldiers in the inner sanctum of the keep were erupting into an already blazing battle between House Barimont, the house Jalel hailed from, House Muren, House Wraithtide, the original garrison from the imperial throne, and House Crushada, with bodies and blood piling up left and right as they came. Soldiers from Wraithtide and Crushada were teaming up against House Barimont after leaping into Panu from the portal's spinning orb; House Muren remained neutral to others aside from House Crushada, which they actively engaged; and now the battle was spilling out into all areas of the keep with many of the Wraithtide soldiers rushing toward Allie's position after fighting through masses of enemies.

The cacophony of blades, battle cries, screams, and erupting magics from an ever-growing number of hundreds of level-70 to -90 elites of the Blood Moon Requiem killing one another was almost deafening.

The training pagoda was aflame, and smoke billowed up around the two combatants—far removed from the main course of fighting in the adjacent building.

Kathrine gurgled incomprehensibly due to the sizzling hole in her throat, dropping to her knees while acid boiled out of numerous wounds covering her body. She managed to send another wave of blood magic at the vile bitch who'd poisoned her, but Lady Muren merely laughed—blurring left and avoiding the attack but also staggering due to how tired she was.

"Is that all you've got, you pompous, arrogant brat?!" Lady Muren wheezed while holding two wicked daggers, a long, seething gash along her stomach with part of her intestines hanging out to mar her dress. She stood upon a hanging platform farther up in the training pagoda, the place all but abandoned due to the more intense fighting going on in the main building of the compound. Seven soldiers' bodies lay around them.

"Come on, Kathrine, show me what you've got!"

Kathrine vomited in the firelight of roaring flames, hitting the floor with both knees and getting a cackling laugh from the woman ahead of her as Lady Muren's red eyes flared brightly.

"I guess not, then! I do believe you're at your end, wench. This has been fun, but I think we'd better end it now—don't you?!" Lady Muren pulled up both blades in front of her ripped dress, blinking away the smoke and ash that partially obscured her vision. One dagger rippled with flames, and the other with blood magic—and with a screech she launched herself toward the royal.

A thunderous crash sent both women stumbling when an angelic figure smashed the overly handsome Lord Barimont into the barrier nearby, smearing his guts all along the translucent wall as onlookers from Brightsville all watched the fighting with both awe and horror. Most of the outside soldiers had no idea what was going on, but due to the noise and explosions coming from the compound, a perimeter had already been set up by the Thane Necropolis military for the protection of the civilians should the barrier come down.

"As I said, vampire . . ." the angelic figure of Lahn, or Denaskus, said in a booming voice with burning golden eyes. He leaned back from the vampire lord in disgust, as if the thing he was pinning to the barrier was some kind of grotesque bug. "I, Denaskus, will be the last thing you ever see."

"I'LL BE SEEING YOU IN HELL!" Lord Barimont roared back, exploding into flame and detonating the spot he and Lahn had landed in.

Stone erupted about them and Lahn staggered, his golden wings flickering in and out as the last remnants of his power began to fade.

But it was not enough, and Lord Barimont's exhausted crimson eyes went wide in horror as the angelic figure remained in the flames that crackled and burned at the ground beneath them.

Denaskus grew a wide, malevolent smile. Raising his hand and summoning a bolt of pure white lightning like the god of thunder himself, he arched his back and positioned himself to throw—but then abruptly disappeared when Lahn's body couldn't handle it any longer.

There was a pause, both vampire women and the man pinned to the wall watching as Lahn became nothing more than a mortal human once more. His eyes were burned out, gone completely, his left arm nothing more than a stump. His flesh was completely charred, and the brilliance he'd once radiated now sent damaging sparks of lightning all up and down his body—causing him to shudder and jolt before he dropped to the ground in a smoldering mess.

Lahn hit the ground, and he didn't get back up.

"HAAAAAAA!!!" Lord Barimont screamed in excited victory, only pausing to cough up blood and yank the spear of light out of his body—dropping it to the ground next to Lahn's unmoving frame. The vampire lord retched, then doubled over and began laughing like a madman. "THE PIG HAS DIED! THE PIGGY HAS DIED!"

Devolving into a fit of giggling, the badly injured vampire lord rolled on the ground in a state of hysteria—finding massive amounts of amusement in Lahn's demise.

Kathrine, too, soon doubled over, her eyes sagging and her body unable to support her any longer when her left cheek hit the burning pagoda floor with a wet thunk. Shakily beginning to draw herself out of the flaming building, she felt an abrupt pain in her stomach when Lady Muren's foot crashed into it.

Kathrine doubled over and flipped twice before landing on the stone outside, Lady Muren following gleefully close behind while twirling her curved daggers in either hand. In the background, the area near the Riven's Eye Wormhole lit up with magic that abruptly turned the dark clouds above a bright red.

"Lights out for you next, bitch!" Lady Muren crowed gleefully, oblivious to the change above her and jumping up in the air and aiming to land on Kathrine's prone form when a thunderclap of sound rocked the compound.

The barrier around the compound shattered.

A black spear-staff covered in flowing blood crashed into Lady Muren's body halfway through her leap, obliterating her torso entirely and splattering her remains on the pavement. With a wound like that, there would be no regeneration. There would be only death.

The ground quaked, the civilians previously watching the scene ran screaming, and an aura far more powerful than any other on this part of the planet descended upon the compound with overwhelming force.

The sky above cracked, and the sinister visage of a great maw opened up to reveal an abyss among the clouds. A storm of crimson and shadow roiled overhead as the temperature abruptly dropped, and red frost began accumulating all across the landscape.

CRASH

Like a meteor from the heavens, Riven descended upon the compound and shattered the earth. A booming echo reverberated from his impact, sending debris high into the sky as the maw across his breastplate hungrily shrieked and wailed. He straightened, slowly raising his head to where the sound of battle echoed in the nearby fortress before turning a curious glance on Kathrine.

He teleported to her, and she stared back up at him wide-eyed while choking on the green acid burrowing into her flesh.

Riven didn't know what to make of this. Infighting? Here? At the Blood Moon Requiem's compound?

He abruptly got to one knee and yanked out half a dozen high-grade health potions he'd bought from the Elysium altar for occasions such as these. Usually he relied on his own healing and didn't often need a healer, but it was always better to be safe rather than sorry—and he was thankful that he hadn't forgone the option despite spending a fortune on potions that were far superior to what locals could make at the moment.

"You are in seriously bad shape," Riven said, dumping the contents of three red vials all over Kathrine's upper body before pouring two more down her throat. "Jesus . . . That poison is nasty stuff. You gonna be okay? Do I need to pull out more? What's happening inside?"

Kathrine gasped for air and immediately stifled a sob, taking in huge gasps and breaths while wiping tears away. "Your-your sister! And L-Lahn!"

Riven cocked his armored head to one side, brows immediately furrowing. "Tell me."

Kathrine took in another desperate gasp, ripped the last health potion from Riven's hands, and poured it onto other wounds on her body that were still fighting the acid. Sinking down with momentary relief, her eyes darted to Lord Barimont, who was just staring at the two of them with a blank expression. "You need to go! He did this—he tried to take Allie away, and he killed Lahn! And now Jalel is inside trying to kill Allie because—"

"TO KILL ALLIE?! INSIDE?! WHO THE FUCK—" Riven didn't even finish his sentence before he whirled around—his eyes briefly landing on Lahn's prone form. He briefly paused, sparing Lord Barimont only a passing glance before disappearing through a rift in space—leaving Kathrine to stare daggers at Lord Barimont in silence.

Lord Barimont's red eyes slowly narrowed, and his fangs began to show when he picked himself up and headed Kathrine's way. He cracked his neck on the way over, pulling out his flaming whip while Kathrine staggered painfully to her feet.

The two vampires only had a moment to stare at one another, though, before Athela's blinding form ripped Barimont's head off and buried it into the ground below with a single, violent tearing motion.

Lord Barimont's body fell, never to get up again.

Allie's whimpering scream was only emphasized by the sword being shoved through her armor and into her heart.

Jalel's eyes were bloodshot even beyond their normal crimson appearance. He breathed heavily and was putting all his weight down onto the weapon to finish her off as his men desperately fought off reinforcements from House Crushada, the original garrison, and House Wraithtide.

He hissed scornfully, specks of saliva slapping her in the face while he suppressed her magic with his own. "If one of us has to go, it isn't going to be me!"

She struggled, feeling her beating heart rapidly pounding as the steaming metal dug deeper and deeper into it. She began to spasm, kicking and lashing out violently but unable to do much more than sob. She was simply out of juice, having used most of her mana battling Lord Barimont, and didn't have any more to give. Fimrindle was banished, too, having been killed by Jalel himself, as was Captain Rusof, who had also died at Jalel's hand.

"Sorry to see you go, cousin, but just do us both a favor and stop resisting!" Jalel said between his teeth—pushing as hard as he could but having a hard time of it due to the quality of Allie's soul-woven armor. "All that screaming and crying isn't going to save you—so just—LET—GO!!!!"

BOOM

Jalel's body shattered when a portal tore open in space and released an exploding Blood Nova directly into his face—the mana engulfing Allie protectively at the same time while tearing apart the room around her. The vampiric prince was flung through a reinforced wall and then again through the next when a myriad of Blood Lances crackling with Black Lightning crashed into him like a storm—the frost around the room quickly building and freezing the battling vampires.

Out of the portal stepped Riven, coated in radiating Blood, Shadow, and sin energy. His bright-crimson eyes seemed to have expanded beyond their normal range. Jackal hissed in his right hand, and his left arm flared with oozing, writhing red mana—dozens of spinning storm razors snapping to life.

Due to his sheer level discrepancy and his natural affinities, even when compared to the level 90 elites of the Blood Moon Requiem's younger warrior class, his mere presence sent some staggering to their knees. Some froze over when he fully emerged, others passed out, and still others seemed to have a hard time breathing while his aura radiated malice onto the entire compound with absolute authority.

Only a third of the vampiric elite were able to completely ignore his presence with auras of their own, yet they were like candles in the abyss—only protecting themselves and unable to do much for their comrades no matter what house they hailed from.

Riven did a quick check on Allie, seeing that though she was sobbing, she was still alive and her wound was regenerating as normal. He looked back up just a moment later to see Jalel blur ahead—far faster than a normal level 90 could do, even considering he was a pureblood. The act surprised Riven immensely and he barely had time to react, but he did so nevertheless with a quick activation of Blessing of the Crow.

Jackal whipped up and smashed Jalel's long sword away, leaving the man open to a swinging kick that shattered the vampire's right arm and sent him spinning into a stone pillar—knocking the support beam over with a groan and crash.

Riven held up a hand and pointed toward the other man, who was getting up from the rubble with bloodlust in his eyes. A roar of wind howled around them and dozens, then hundreds of spinning storm razors with sharpened blades of black and red swirled in a cloud behind Riven's position. "Die."

Hundreds of projectiles torpedoed forward—causing the air to shriek upon their passing and leaving trails of blood ribbons behind them.

Jalel's eyes narrowed and he activated one, three, seven, twenty protective treasures from his spatial sack—each of them shattering as more and more of the barrage smashed down onto his position.

As Jalel used up his treasures, Riven charged up Jackal with torrents of Black Lightning. His spear-staff howled with glee, and he pointed the curved blade in Jalel's direction just when the barrage ended.

A snapping sound accompanied the rupture of Shadow-infused lightning, and the mass of energy larger than Riven's torso shattered space and crashed into Jalel's body.

The other prince, however, activated an ability of his own, flickering in and out of existence to dodge most of the attack but cursing loudly when his right arm and shoulder were ripped off entirely.

Jalel lunged forward, disappeared, and reappeared next to Riven with a snarl of rage. He lifted a glowing red hand and reached for Riven's neck, only to be yanked back down by tendrils from Gluttony's maw across Riven's chest as the visage in the sky howled hungrily.

"I remember you . . . and not just because of what Kathrine has told me concerning your punishment from the queen," Riven muttered, staring down at the silver-haired man with ice-cold hate. "You were as annoying back then as you are now. Let me finish what I started in Negrada."

Usually Riven avoided punching things because he simply didn't need to. However, in the few instances he DID need to, Messenger had a unique feature that could be utilized.

> Ripping Claws: Punching someone with the spikes of your gauntlets will cause massive hemorrhaging damage over time.

CRACK

Riven's gauntlet smashed down into Jalel's pale face, its jagged edges protruding from the knuckles as blades tore flesh from Jalel's skull.

Jalel screamed in agony and hate, attempting to teleport away again but unable to do so when Riven's aura clamped down onto him. Jalel's struggles became more frantic while blood poured out of his face, hemorrhaging onto the ground underneath them when Riven raised his fist up once more for a second strike. "THAT SHARD OF GLUTTONY WAS MINE!"

Riven didn't even respond.

CRACK

This time his knuckles took bone, his fist blurring forward and shearing off Jalel's lower jaw entirely amid yet another scream.

CRASH

Jalel was flung through another wall, and Riven stepped forward to follow— smashing through two more vampiric guards bearing the sigil of the phoenix on their breastplates like they were nothing before continuing forward into the next room.

"Insect," Riven said with venom, kicking Jalel when he tried to get up and then stomping down onto the other prince's neck.

Only Riven was surprised when Jalel melted away and a silver mace smashed into the back of Riven's armored head.

The effect of a silver-infused weapon was felt despite no skin contact, with just the mere presence of the weapon having a more severe effect than Riven would have liked to acknowledge. He stumbled forward, holding the back of his head, a headache starting to blare, only for another strike to snap up into his jaw.

"You may have the levels on me now, but you do not have the experience." Jalel spat blood, his jaw having regenerated rather quickly even for a vampire. He huffed and pulled out yet another talisman, snapping it and healing his wounds fully while simultaneously banishing the red frost on his body before audibly cracking his neck when Riven turned to stare at him. "I am a warrior hundreds of years old, and I will not be defeated by a nobody like—"

Jalel abruptly screamed, as did Allie in the next room, and he sank to his knees while clutching at his head when the entanglement of Malignant Prophecies flared yet again.

"Warrior?" Riven repeated, cocking his aching head to the side while blood began to flare up around him—engulfing him entirely as the earth began to tremble. "No, Jalel. You are a fool. A proud and arrogant fool."

With that he teleported behind Jalel right when the other prince recovered and used Jackal to uppercut right between Jalel's legs. He felt something crunch under the blow, heard Jalel scream, and then sent the other prince high into the air hundreds of feet up with the impact that left a huge gash in his lower abdomen and groin.

Riven followed, teleporting yet again behind Jalel's airborne position and using a network of Wretched Snares to entangle him before whipping Jalel's ensnared body around and flinging it at the ground with immense force.

His hands blurred into clawing motions to charge lance after lance before impact, summoning a swarm of storm balls and razors beside them.

Jalel crashed with an explosive thud, and red ice rose up from the ground to secure him tightly along with more and more layers of Wretched Snares that sprang up around him. High above him the storm of black and red abruptly changed, and the massive swath of mana overhead that hadn't created projectiles was pulled into Jackal like a swirling river of red and black.

The heavens descended.

Black and red crashed down upon Jalel with a thunder, sending pieces of the Elysium altar's base platform sky-high amid the blurring bombardment that shook the earth. Jalel created a dome of blood to protect himself but was unable to defend against most of it—only barely managing to slip out with another teleport, only to be met with Riven's own portal ripping open next to him.

Jalel turned, horrified and bewildered that Riven's mana control was so good. "HOW?!"

Riven's weapon snapped forward, and the jaws of a canine created from blood flashed ahead. The air split apart and the blade tore through Jalel's weapon that he'd raised to block like it was nothing, splitting Jalel's body in half entirely and crunching down on the two remnant halves with the bloody jaws of the ability. When the crimson jaws snapped shut, a reverberating cloud of deep-purple sin energy sparked along its teeth.

- **Jackal's Lunge: Point this weapon in any direction and activate this innate and unique martial art, charging the blade with blood mana to create the visage of a jackal's maw and blasting forward. When your blade strikes an enemy, the red jackal will close down on them to deal additional blood and sin damage.**

Jalel's splintered body flashed a bright crimson a second later and re-formed, gasping for air and turning to run. He staggered, though, remnant sin energy remaining along unclosed wounds before Riven's body burst into flame and crashed into him from behind.

Soldiers bearing the sigil of the phoenix were seen dashing Riven's way, but they were quickly intercepted by others bearing House Wraithtide's orb of flames. Riven blinked once, then tore Jalel's men apart with a crash of red ice that blew holes in their bodies via spikes in the ground.

"You're really starting to annoy me," Riven said softly in Jalel's ear upon turning, grasping the other prince behind the neck while Jalel screamed as hellfire licked at Riven's fingers. He picked Jalel up, then smashed him back down into the ground. He did this over and over again, keeping a firm grip on the other man and repeatedly beating him to death against the metal floor of the Elysium altar's outer body.

A swift strike with a hidden dagger snapped the blade off on Riven's throat, but the bloodsilk of Messenger held firm—much to the surprise of both men.

Riven blinked, momentarily stopping his beating, and began to laugh—while Jalel's swollen, bloody, and regenerating face fell into a horrified panic.

"HOW?!" Jalel screamed again, trying to fish out another item from his spatial sack only to be stopped with a violent clamp of the wrist.

Riven sneered, snapping the man's hand off. "Some warrior you are, eh? How's that experience coming in for you now?! A classic case of overconfidence!"

He stopped Jalel's screaming by slamming his armored fist into Jalel's open mouth, shattering the man's fangs and gripping his spine. Yanking once, twice, and then three times, he decapitated Jalel with brute force and then opened Gluttony's mouth along his chest.

The head of the vampire opened its eyes wide, and in similar fashion to how he'd ended the fight with the Azag Hive Cluster in Chicago, he shoved Jalel's head into Gluttony's maw.

The mouth snapped shut, crunching onto Jalel's skull before pulling the remnants into the abyss in Riven's chest with black tendrils that licked up the remnant flesh.

[Malignant Prophecy has been fulfilled by saving Kathrine's life, and your battle is now over. You have acquired one Malignancy Point. You have a total of five Malignancy Points. Elysium's wrath now descends in the form of a tribulation.]

The sky above him depicting Gluttony's maw fractured, creating golden cracks along space itself. Brilliant multicolored light shattered space around the cracks moments later, and Riven grimaced when he saw a storm erupt from the beyond overhead.

His shoulders slumped. "Shit."

CRACKLE-SNAP-BOOM

A roaring ocean of power crashed down onto Riven's position, engulfing his body in searing energies that caused him to scream. His vision immediately began to blur, but he pushed through the pain and managed to summon the visage of Gluttony once again.

The great maw tore through the ground underneath his feet upon his request, roaring to life to challenge the system itself—to protect the bearer of its shards as the abyss rose to the challenge.

His mind snapped.

His body tore apart.

All that was left was darkness.

[Your mana channels have been destroyed. Your pillars have been shattered. You have been temporarily afflicted with the debuff Soul Crippling. You have temporarily lost access to all your abilities. Your soul crippling temporarily negates the effect of up to 1,809 stat points from Strength, Agility, and Intelligence at random for any given moment, severely weakening you for random amounts of time at random moments throughout any given day. You have condensed your Malignancy Points into a Malignant Fertilizer, and your Malignant Sapling grows. You have condensed enough sin energy to finish Mark of the Sinner. Mark of the Sinner's buffs cannot be accessed due to Soul Crippling. Congratulations! You have survived Elysium's tribulation.]

Half a day had passed, and the sun was setting on the horizon.

Lahn was barely breathing, but he was still alive. He'd played dead after Denaskus had exited his body to preserve what little life he had left, but the remnants he'd left behind were in absolute ruins.

Burns marred his entire body, his eyes and left arm were gone, and his lungs were a seared and painful mess. His soul was in ruins, and the channels written into his pillars were all garbled or just outright gone, similar to Riven's own situation. He could barely function, let alone stand, and it was likely that Lahn would never be able to cultivate or grow his mana channels ever again.

But to help Allie, it'd been worth it.

"You're a damned idiot!" Allie said softly, wiping tears from her face and cradling his charred head in her lap while various healers from the Thane Necropolis did their best to stabilize the young man. "A damned idiot."

Salves were being poured all over Lahn, spells and miracles were being cast, and Riven sat exhausted in a wheelchair beside them with a blank expression on his face. Yattazi was curled up behind him, and Azmoth sat on the large snake, protectively looking over his master, who was now rather helpless.

Riven stared down at the sleeve tattoo on his right arm. The ever-moving tattoo still contained some of the black markings it once had, but other sigils now glowed a deep purple—and the entire thing gave off smoky wisps that trailed off his skin with whispers of power, which he could not access due to his recent soul crippling.

"You okay, Riven?" Allie asked, looking up at her brother from where she sat cross-legged on the ground. She knew he wasn't okay, but not asking would make her feel even more guilty. Her amputated leg was now back to normal flesh after using a bone mold in its place, but her soul-woven armor was heavily damaged and she wasn't sure if it was repairable or not.

Riven nodded her way, even smiling slightly when Athela walked over to sit in his lap—wrapping her hands around Riven's neck and leaning into him while soldiers of Houses Wraithtide and Crushada cleaned up the mess the battle had left behind. "I'll be fine. Though I don't know how things are going to progress from here."

There was a pause while the two siblings locked eyes.

"You might have to be the one that takes Messenger into Chalgathi's trial if I don't recover in time," Riven said eventually, averting his gaze from his sister with a frown.

The burned wreckage of the Blood Moon Requiem's compound smoldered and smoked, only a part of it still intact and undamaged after hundreds of warriors had died there in the political struggle between noble houses. Kathrine had left to go home after Riven had turned his ire upon House Muren, House Barimont, and Jalel's House Firebird. But those noble houses were all still very intact and absolutely irate about what had transpired here, with only their youngest and lowest-leveled soldiers being able to even visit Panu. Kathrine had told him that the political upheaval was so big that the rest of the elder council had to get involved to settle things down after the entire empire had watched events transpire. Elder Thune and the high queen, surprisingly enough, remained absent from the public scene.

Apparently, the Blood Moon Requiem was on the brink of civil war. It was unknown if it would happen or not. What was certain, however, was that if the empire didn't split apart into fragmented pieces, there'd be a reckoning in the form of a blood feud. It was the way vampires in the empire dealt with these kinds of things, according to Kathrine, when entire houses would sometimes be wiped out in miniature wars to settle disputes and keep the greater whole of the empire from fracturing.

Allie thought over recent events, then reached out and grasped Riven's hand—squeezing tightly and keeping eye contact. "Thank you."

Riven chuckled. "No need to thank me. I love you."

"What happened is my fault."

"Nah, I used the prophecy to save Kathrine. If anything, it's my fault for choosing to do it."

"But she wouldn't have been in danger if not for me."

"Stop blaming yourself, Allie. We're fine; that's all that matters." Riven gave Athela a quick peck on the forehead, and his smile grew wider. "It isn't permanent. Plus, this gives me an excuse to really go at it with totem making again in the meantime. You know Hakim and the others I talked to you about? I told them I'd be spending more time with them and would power level them—and that I'd get back around to craft again. It's been a long time coming."

Allie averted her gaze, ashamed of what had happened and sighing when she saw Lahn stir in her lap. "How are you going to power level them like you are now?"

Riven looked her way a second later and raised an eyebrow. He gestured to his minions. "Athela and Azmoth, of course. They can do it. Yattazi, however, will probably leave for another master soon; we spoke about it already, and she doesn't want to stay with a crippled warlock who can't level himself for an undisclosed time—thus inhibiting her own growth. I get it, and I'm not mad."

The huge basilisk behind him gave a low hiss of acknowledgment. "Thank you for underssssstanding, Riven . . . I hope you are not upsssset with me. You have been a good friend while I have been here, but I hope to ssssssuccccceeeed in my ascension to higher power ssssssooner rather than never."

"Don't worry about it. We hardly knew each other anyways, and your help has been appreciated, for what it's worth." Riven smiled somewhat sadly over his shoulder.

"I never leave. I stay," Azmoth said with a wave of his clawed hands. "I annoy you till end of time."

Athela giggled, then nodded in agreement and ruffled Riven's hair, shooting the basilisk an annoyed glare. "Yeah. I agree. Who'd take care of you like this if not for us?! Even if it were permanent, I wouldn't leave you. We've been with you since the beginning, and we're here to stay. We don't know how long this will be, but I'm sure it can't be too long."

A heavy silence permeated the area while Riven contemplated their words, but eventually another smile tugged at his lips.

Riven gave a salty laugh, then closed his eyes and let his head drop. Yawning and leaning into the demoness on his lap, he let the smile on his lips remain. "Thanks. It means a lot to me. But for now, how about we talk about this later—eh? I'm rather tired after what happened, and I'd really like to enjoy a nap."

CHAPTER 53

Athela slowly pulled the door to Riven's manor room behind her, leaving only a crack open, smiling at his rising and falling bare chest while he recovered. Then her eyes fell to the pair of feathered boots that Riven still kept at the side of his bed, and her smile faltered. The past few days had been . . . difficult, with the serious damage to his soul very apparent. He could barely summon mana at all. Frankly, she'd been surprised that he didn't have permanent damage, because that kind of event would have outright destroyed most cultivation efforts forever, but she was thankful the worst hadn't happened and that in time he'd be fine.

"You'll stay here to watch over him?" She turned to Azmoth, and the large demon gave her a curt nod. "Good, thank you. I have business to attend to in the nether realms."

She turned to go but was stopped by a large clawed hand that landed on her shoulder.

"Say hi for me" was all he said, and Athela stiffened slightly.

She nodded, removing his hand and turning back to look up at him with pursed lips. "What do you think I should do? When Tupper came to get me, I . . ."

Azmoth slumped his shoulders, looking away and out a window in the hall where faded sunlight pierced through the fog of the haunted landscape outside. "I not know. But I like her. Fay always kind to me, even if dirty succubus."

Athela's frown deepened, and she clutched the sides of her body in a self-hug, looking down to the floor in shame. "I think . . . I may have overdone things. Back in Dawn's capital at the battle of Rippenvire, when I ate her. It was really mean. I was just so angry. I . . . I felt betrayed and like she was trying to steal him away. Perhaps we should have talked more first."

"Yes." Azmoth nodded in agreement. "You should have."

"What do you think she wants to talk about with me?"

"Not know."

"Will Riven abandon me if she comes back?"

Azmoth reared his head back and had to stifle a laugh, putting two hands on his hips with two more behind his head in a stretch. "No. Riven love you."

"But I can tell he misses her. He talks about her in his sleep."

"Yes, but he chose you. You not know what he was like when you died. Was very, very bad."

Athela gave a half-hearted smile, shifting her long black hair off to one side behind her ear. "Yes, I know. I suppose he did choose me—but I'm not sure it was for the right reasons."

There was a silence after that, and eventually Athela muttered a goodbye— waving at Azmoth while she disappeared down the steps and exiting two stories down on the bottom floor. There, she met Tupper. The blue-skinned, white-haired incubus, dressed in a tuxedo, was waiting patiently for her, and he bowed his head upon her approach.

She nodded to him in acknowledgment and took in a deep breath, fingers clenched. "Hello again, Tupper."

"Mistress Athela," Tupper replied with a hesitant smile. "Thank you again for agreeing to meet with my sister. You didn't have to do so."

"I know. But there are things that've been on my mind, things that I'd like to get off my chest probably just as much as she does. It wasn't all that long ago that we were friends."

Tupper opened his mouth to reply, but hesitated—then shut it again. Without a word he opened up a blue-rimmed portal leading into a private nether realm, then gestured for her to walk inside.

The nether realm she'd created was only a temporary one, displaying a simple octagonal room with low-hanging yellow lanterns overhead that gave off a warm glow and two fluffy couches facing one another across a small table.

Fay fidgeted nervously, taking in deep breaths over and over again with long exhales to calm herself down. She'd been sure to make herself look presentable and wore a modest white dress, plain and simple but still formfitting. Her black eyes stared vacantly at the table in front of her as she crossed her long blue legs, and a ball was forming in the pit of her stomach as she went over all the possible scenarios that could go oh so terribly wrong. She just wanted to . . . to change how things had ended. She wanted to have a clear conscience after what had transpired.

"Hello, Fay."

Fay startled, looking up to see a slender, athletic woman she'd come to know rather well over the past year. She abruptly stood up, still clutching her sides invol-untarily and giving a forced, nervous smile. "Hello, Athela. How've you been?"

There was an awkward pause while Athela considered this, and she gave a noncommittal shrug while looking away. "Could be worse, could be better."

Well, at least Athela hadn't snapped at her. That was promising.

"Have a seat?" Fay asked when the portal to Panu shut behind the other woman.

Athela nodded, then stepped forward and sat herself on the couch on the opposite side of the table. She straightened her posture, put her hands on her bare knees, and then made eye contact when Fay sat across from her. "What about you? How have you been doing? I hear you have a new master."

The words stung, though it was unintentional and there was no malice hidden there.

Fay grimaced, but thought about the old man and some of the tension left her shoulders. "I've not been good. Not at all, but the person I've contracted with is helping me out. He's something of a therapist."

"Going for the older guys now?" Athela gave a half-hearted, teasing smile.

Fay couldn't help but frown and shook her head. "No, I . . . we haven't done anything of the sort. He's just a friend."

"Ah. That's rather unusual, considering the type of people that usually contract with your race."

"Yes, I agree. It is." Fay paused, gathering her courage and clasping her hands in front of her while avoiding eye contact. "Riven was like that, too, at first."

The silence reigned heavily on the two women after that, each mulling over their own thoughts.

"I was told he recently got injured, pretty severely," Fay started again, glancing up for confirmation.

Athela nodded with a grimace. "Yes. We're not sure how long it will last, but he should recover. It isn't the end of things, but it is enough that his newest contracted familiar left. She was a basilisk of some kind; she didn't want to wait. Shortsighted, if you ask me, but at least we weeded out the bad apple, if you catch my drift. Riven is a great master to have and I wouldn't choose anyone else over him even if he could never cultivate or level again."

"I suppose that's a point we both agree on." Fay's gaze fell, and tears began to well up underneath her eyes. "I wanted to talk about what happened between us. What I did. I . . . I was hoping that you'd accept my sincere apology. I was immature and selfish, and I sacrificed our friendship over what happened. I've thought a lot about it, and I was willing to let him be with any other woman except you there at the end. That was . . . That must have been rough for you to hear. And you and I both know that I knew how you felt. I'm sorry, Athela. I really am."

There was a pause.

"And you're telling me this . . . why?" Athela asked uncomfortably.

Fay gave a quivering smile, wiping away some of the tears dripping down her cheeks. "I just feel bad. And I miss all of you. I miss Riven, sure, but I miss you and Azmoth as well. I know it likely isn't repairable, and I'm not asking to come back. I just don't want to go the rest of my life knowing how badly I fucked things up, and without trying to reconcile with the people I wronged. Namely, you. It is why I asked to meet only with you and not with Riven. I owe you that much."

Athela silently gazed ahead, staring while Fay continued to talk.

"I was also hoping that you'd pass along a message," Fay said with a self-loathing laugh. "To Riven. Tell him that Tupper has a letter; you can look it over first if you wish—but tell him that you were right. That I tried to manipulate him while you were gone because I was so head over heels, and I was jealous of you. I wanted him for myself. The time I spent with all of you was the happiest I've been, even though it was rather short—and I ruined it."

Athela clicked her tongue. "Yes . . . He told me about the date the two of you went on."

Fay outwardly cringed at its mention. "I . . . see . . . What did he say?"

"He told me what you two did and described to me how it made him feel," Athela replied sadly. "He said he wants to find that with me. He invited me to go on a picnic and a nature walk with him sometime as our own first date. I'm excited to go."

"You're implying he doesn't already feel that way about you?" Fay asked warily.

Athela shrugged. "Honestly, I'm unsure."

"He chose you over me, Athela. I'm sure he feels that way about you."

"He did, but even in the beginning he admitted that he hadn't seen me as a romantic interest. He treats me like one now, certainly, but I get the feeling he's doing that out of . . . obligation."

"Don't be ridiculous," Fay protested, frowning.

Athela laughed. "I'm not being ridiculous! I know he loves me—I don't doubt that at all. But the way I love him is perhaps different from the way he loves me. I view him as a romantic partner and have ever since my transition into this body. Meanwhile, he views me as a best friend—as family. It is different, you know. When he sleeps, I'm not the one he talks about."

Athela's eyes lifted to meet Fay's. "He talks about you. He still keeps your boots at the side of the bed."

The succubus just stared. Then Fay's eyes and face scrunched up, and she immediately began to sob. First it was mild, but then she began to cry more violently, holding her head in her hands as her shoulders shook.

Athela bit her lip, her voice cracking. "Fay . . . Why didn't you just talk to me?"

Fay didn't reply, only continuing to sob fiercely.

"I wish we could have stayed friends, you know," Athela eventually said in a low whisper. "I don't like seeing you like this, and I want to apologize, too. I'm sorry for eating you back in Mandon."

Fay managed to calm herself down, sniffling loudly, and then laughed at the mention of it. "I deserved it. Didn't I?"

"Probably, but that doesn't mean I don't feel bad about it."

The two women shared a smile, and Fay even managed a curt laugh between sobs.

Standing up and walking over to the other side of the small room of this nether realm, Athela motioned for Fay to scoot over and sat down next to her. Wrapping her arms around the succubus and letting tears fall down her own cheeks, Athela shuddered.

"I really am sorry," Fay muttered under her breath, surprised at the embrace but leaning into it. "Really, really sorry. I was a shitty friend. I have a lot of growing up to do."

Athela snorted, wiping off her cheeks. "Yeah, I know. In some ways, so do I."

The two women sat in silence after that, only their chests rising and falling in the otherwise still room.

Fay moved to hug Athela back, pulling her in close one final time before pushing the demoness away. "I think this is goodbye, for good. I should leave and finally move on . . . It was nice seeing you again, Athela. I mean that. I won't bother or pester you anymore, I just wanted to end things on good terms. Thank you for coming, from the bottom of my heart. I'm sure you and Riven will have lovely children one day!"

Fay began to stand up with a gentle, shaky smile directed Athela's way, but was yanked back down to the couch with a surprised grunt.

Athela glared at the other woman menacingly. A strange mix of emotions crossed her black and white face, but eventually she put a hand up to Fay's cheek and gently touched her wet skin. Private nether realms had quite a lack of actual feeling, but shared ones were more tangible as it drew on more than one demon to use—so the intimate touch startled Fay even more.

"Is your summoner able and willing to let you go, should you want to leave?" Athela asked curiously—searching Fay's face for clues.

Fay, despite being startled, hesitantly nodded and sniffled again. "Yes . . . Why?"

"Riven gave you the option of staying right before you left, under a condition. Do you remember what that condition was?"

Fay momentarily blanked, her heart beating at a much faster pace while she took in the implications of what Athela was getting at. "Riven asked me if there was any way the three of us could work this out. That he'd rather not lose either of us, and he'd rather try to go forward with both of us rather than just choose one."

"And does that idea still not appeal to you at all?" Athela asked softly, fingers twining around Fay's on the couch. "I would like to be friends again. I liked how we once were."

Fay's composure quickly dissolved again, and soon her face was scrunched up and tears were running down her cheeks for the third time during that meeting. She nodded violently, voice wavering. "I w-would like that v-very much."

Athela smiled, put a finger to Fay's lips, then leaned in close and nuzzled the succubus's cheek with her nose. "Then there's only one way I see this working out. We should work on our own relationship first. I think . . . I think it would make Riven very, very happy."

Grazing Fay's left breast with a hand, Athela tugged on the fabric covering Fay's cleavage and pulled it down. She slowly reared back a moment to soak in the look of surprise on Fay's face, then went back in and gently locked lips with the succubus—before pushing her to the couch as Fay began to undress.

Captain Vros Kinal, champion of this expedition to Panu, planetary leader of the Empire of Dying Suns, was vexed. He looked the group from Rippenvire over with a bemused expression, glancing over at his subordinates while conquered natives labored in the wheat fields below his perch on the tower. "You want to team up? Did I hear that right?"

The representative from Rippenvire nodded. The man was a tall vampire, pale-skinned and red-eyed just like all the rest—but lacking the distinct glow of the purebloods. He wore gadgets and steampunk pistols on either side, with a top hat that shielded his face from the sun and a satin vest. "Yes. You are correct, human."

"And just why would I agree to something like that?" Captain Vros Kinal asked with a raised eyebrow, motioning for the vampire to come stand with him at the ledge of his tower overlooking the landscape. "The Empire of the Dying Suns is doing just fine without you. Unlike you, we chose not to go head-to-head with an Apex ranker immediately upon arrival and have been flourishing for it. Our men grow in level quickly, our profits are soaring, and we already hold many towns and cities while recruiting the best of the natives we capture to our own cause by holding out shiny trinkets and the promise of power to them. What reason have I to ally with bloodsuckers like you?"

The vampire beside him grimaced but didn't take obvious offense at the human's jab. "We have developed a means to kill the one known as Riven Thane, but we need the manpower to back us up after our forces were demolished at the battle of Mandon."

Captain Kinal blinked, leaning on the railing and resting his armored shoulders while the stiff horsehair down the center of his helmet shook in the breeze. "That's very interesting, but I doubt we'll be fighting Riven Thane anytime soon. If anything, I want to avoid that monster at all costs until we get to the point that we can receive reinforcements from the homeland."

"You won't survive long enough for that to happen."

"Brazen words coming from a group of failed nobodies like you. Rippenvire might be respected in your part of the multiverse, but here on this planet, you're nothing but a bunch of washed-up dogs tucking your tails between your legs after a severe beating." Captain Kinal gave the stoic vampire a knowing look. "But I will admit I'm curious. Theoretically, if what you say is true, I would be open to potentially working with your kind. Just what is in it for all of you, though? What would you get out of helping us? Surely you can't expect to actually succeed in conquering this planet now that over 90 percent of your forces have been crushed. You're all still in hiding, and I doubt you'll come out unless forced to do so."

"What do we get?" the steampunk vampire repeated with a blank expression, meeting the other man's gaze and folding his arms in front of him. "What we get is our regained honor before returning home after murdering the man who took this victory from us. Do not worry about why—all you need to worry about is the how. Perhaps you and your men could follow me to a remote island out to sea; it is there that our secret lies. I'm sure that, one day when that bastard comes knocking down your door, you'll be thankful that you agreed to this."

Riven sat in a wheelchair in the garden of his manor, next to Jose's tombstone with Azmoth nearby. The sound of crickets under a large tree infused with death mana after the terraforming was rather peaceful, and the neon-teal leaves glowed pale light down onto his position as he contemplated life. His body felt weak, but he could already tell there were signs of repair in his soul aperture. His pillars were beginning to re-form, albeit slowly, as were the mana channels he'd cultivated over the course of integrated time.

"Yattazi was so hasty to leave," Riven muttered, looking up at Azmoth with his hands clasped in front of him. "It surprised me. Kinda hurt my feelings, honestly."

Azmoth grunted in irritation. "No loyal. No need for snake to be here. Not bad, but not one of us. It okay."

Riven let on a warm smile. "Yeah. I suppose I still have you and Athela. Do you . . . Do you think Fay's doing all right?"

Azmoth turned his spiked, armored head—obsidian daggers for teeth smiling back at him. "Yes."

Riven sighed. He did that a lot nowadays, the sighing. No matter how hard he struggled, he just couldn't seem to escape this bombardment of bullshit that chased after him almost endlessly. Just sitting here in the garden and taking in breaths of fresh air with his eyes closed made him realize that he'd been constantly on the move without giving himself a moment to really pause and consider what it was he wanted to do outside the obligatory NEED to do things.

This was the cost of power, he supposed.

"I still can't believe what happened at the trading compound. Kathrine was very shaken," Riven stated while looking skyward. "I hope she's all right. I hope Lahn's all right—he was in even rougher shape than she was. Kid has a good head on his shoulders, though. It'll be a while, but at the very least, his body will heal. His soul, on the other hand . . . I'm not so sure about it. Maybe, maybe not."

"This multiverse very big," Azmoth retorted with folded arms, leaning against the manor's outer wall. "Lots of treasures. Lots of powers. He get fixed, I sure."

Riven snorted a laugh, glancing down at the shifting, flickering sleeve tattoo covering his right arm. "Yes, I suppose it is a big place."

The sound of footsteps and a beating heart caused him to turn, and from around the corner he saw Genua in a maid's outfit—her long blonde hair swaying back and forth as the pretty older woman headed his way. Her eyes were starting to turn a pale red, which was unusual for thralls but not unheard-of—and she hadn't even made her transition yet.

Though he was sure that was likely to come soon. Her attitude toward him and pretty much any other vampire had also drastically changed to one of both servitude and reverence—an opposite reaction to many mortals concerning vampiric negative Charisma. This change was a common side effect of the transformation as well. When he finally did turn her into a complete thrall, those feelings would only solidify. What was even more interesting to him was that he simply didn't care that she'd essentially had her mind warped. Not only had she chosen this—although she'd been coerced into doing so—but in his opinion the punishment of everlasting servitude was fitting after she and her family had tried to assassinate him for no good reason.

"Here you are, Master," Genua said with a low bow, handing him a stack of tomes with a huff. "These are the manuals you requested. All that we could acquire concerning totem making and runecrafting. There wasn't much that we could find, even in the altar's system store, but there's enough to get a head start."

Riven nodded, happy that he had at least something to go off. "And the supplies?"

Genua unhooked a spatial sack of her own, handing it over to Riven with a smile. "Of course. These are some of the supplies listed in those books. Again, not much, but we got what we could. It should last you for at least a short time while you endure your recovery."

"I see. How's your daughter doing?"

"Len is fine. The schools Mara set up are very good, and she's slowly stopped talking about her father and sister."

"What about you? Are you still thinking about them often?"

"Of course," Genua admitted, though without much emotion. "It does make me sad. I did love them, especially Ethel. Farrod was . . . not the greatest husband, but he was still mine. However, I'm doing much better now thanks to Gurth'Rok and Dr. Brass. They regularly infuse me with vampiric venom in preparation for when you claim me as a thrall. It has helped my mood tremendously. I find myself enjoying life once again."

"Oh? How are those two doing, by the way? I haven't talked to them for some time now."

"Very good. They have taken up managerial positions under Mara and help run the city. General Bruner from Chicago is also in Mara's inner circle, and I get to see the four of them quite often since I work at your estate. They're far busier than you'd imagine."

Riven snorted. "Well, I'm glad SOMEONE enjoys that kind of work. It certainly isn't me."

He pulled up his status page and scrolled over to the quests menu. From there, he selected the most recent Chalgathi update.

[Chalgathi, The Apocalypse Beasts World Quest, Panu:
Congratulations on being the third person to collect all five Chalgathi artifacts. Now that all artifacts have coalesced into one item set, you are to be given eventual access to the subevent Altars of Dread and Hope.

The Altars of Dread and Hope are exclusive areas designated by the Elysium administrator, where only the chosen of the apocalypse beasts may enter after having acquired their given artifacts. This applies to all apocalypse beasts, not only Chalgathi. Here at the Altars of Dread and Hope you will be divided into two groups: cultists and noncultists. As previously described, the outcomes of this world quest differ greatly depending on which of the chosen acquire the

prizes for these quests. Thus, cultists will be pitted against noncultists when reaching these altars. Noncultists across all three apocalypse beast categories will arrive at the Altar of Hope, and cultists across all three apocalypse beast categories will arrive at the Altar of Dread. You will be highly incentivized to work together with your given team upon arrival, and severe punishments will be handed down to those who intentionally harm any others within your own category while involving yourself in this subevent of the quest line, with more details to arrive upon event initiation.

The Altars of Dread and Hope will first open with an event initiation two months, nineteen days, and eleven hours from now. Upon opening, the next phase of World Quest 2, The Apocalypse Beasts, will begin. You can expect to enter an alternate pocket realm at that time along with various people, places, artifacts, and events drawn in from around the multiverse. You can expect to be gone for a minimum of one year's time. Participants who do not collect all the necessary apocalypse beast artifacts upon event initiation will still be able to join the Altars of Dread and Hope subevent upon completion of the item sets.]

He reread the "two months, nineteen days, and eleven hours" part.

Would that be enough time for him to heal?

And damn, being gone for an entire year or more . . . that was rough.

Had it really only been a month and a half since he'd collected Messenger? So much had happened in that short amount of time . . . It was almost unfathomable. His thoughts trailed back to that day, the day Athela had died—the day he'd saved Fay from the cultists. He was simultaneously sad, angry, and happy all at once when thinking about it. Sad because Fay had left, angry that the cultists had dared harm people he cared about, and happy that Athela had returned to him.

Perhaps it was selfish to think he was angry that things didn't turn out better, given the ridiculous circumstances he was in.

Taking a look at his own spatial bag, he pulled out two objects. The first was a system-proclaimed treasure map related to a Dao treasure of sin that he'd acquired from finishing the quest to save Fay. The other was a Dao treasure related to Blood that Athela had acquired herself after the Harbingers of Gluttony had been defeated in Mandon.

Unlike most treasure maps, this one was a three-dimensional hologram projecting from a small metal cylinder, with the top of the cylinder creating a very intricate diagram of a part of Panu from a zoomed-out view.

The hologram displayed a tropical island with a volcano at its center. It had a very distinct boot-shaped protrusion that formed a cove on one side, with trees and other features on the island so tiny that they were smaller than a pinhead but still somewhat discernible. The map spanned many meters across in any direction from the cylinder, and he was even able to get up and walk through it—identifying a glowing dot underneath the volcano through a large sprawling set of ancient ruins that were built into the ground underneath the island. There, where a ruined city lay long forgotten by the looks of how decimated the architecture was, were flowing rivers of magma that eventually led to an odd-looking temple.

It was here, at this temple, that the icon continued to flash.

It had no description otherwise, no details, only the outline of the island, the ruins, and the path down the magma rivers leading to the temple where the Dao treasure of sin was located. The very large problem now, though, was that he had zero clue where this island was. It could literally be anywhere, and he had no doubt that the combination of three merging planets would only make it all the harder to find.

But people in Chicago were already working on finding the treasure's location by using drones. The mapping of Panu was underway, and many of these drones were already far out to sea to the south of Dawn. It might be a long time from now, but he'd find the island he was looking for eventually.

The Dao treasure of Blood he already had, but using it required a bonded partner. Probably made specifically for Athela by the system itself, it fit in the palm of Riven's hand—only being the size of a tennis ball, rounded with a point like a tear, and it glowed a bright red similar to the color of Riven's eyes.

[Tear of the Blood God (Legendary F-Grade Dao Treasure): Must have a bonded, contractual partner to use. Reveals insights into the Dao of the Blood subpillar and drastically increases the resilience and size of both partners' Blood subpillars after use regardless of what your insights gain for you.]

It was perfect. Not only because the Blood subpillar was his specialty pillar, one that he had a 100 percent affinity for, not even because he had the accomplishment title of Bloodthirsty, which increased his damage output for any blood abilities he used. No, it was perfect because this treasure in particular would be able to reinforce both his and Athela's pillars—and perhaps it could even heal his Blood subpillar entirely.

He'd be finding out sooner rather than later, that was for sure. He felt rather exposed the way he was right now, and was pretty certain that even the weaker members of the Thane Necropolis military could likely put him down in his current state. He needed to recover fast, and this treasure perhaps held the key.

"Do you intend to use it before you leave to meet with Hakim?" Genua asked curiously, cocking her head to the side. "Or not until you get there?"

"Probably before. Might as well use it here where I'm safe, rather than waiting until I'm in relatively unknown territory to expose myself if anything goes wrong. But Athela has to get back first. After that I plan to work a bit on totem making, power level Hakim and the others, then maybe go after this other Dao treasure before Chalgathi's quest happens if I'm recovered before then," Riven replied, putting the items both down on the stack of tomes next to his wheelchair and grunting with pained exertion upon turning the chair around. "Oh, boy . . . This chair is a real pain to use. I don't know how Lahn manages to . . ."

Riven's voice trailed off, and he nearly choked when his eyes locked on two figures standing at the corner of the building behind Genua.

Genua turned upon seeing his look of shock, then her eyebrows rose—and she quickly dismissed herself with a polite bow.

Athela stood beside Fay, holding hands with the other woman while smiling fondly down at Riven's seated form. The succubus, on the other hand, looked incredibly nervous, avoiding eye contact and only managing to spare Riven brief glances while biting her lip.

Eventually, as the silence wore on and Azmoth turned to look as well, Athela nudged the horned succubus in the ribs and then gently shoved her forward. "Go on. I know you've been looking forward to this."

Fay looked over her shoulder, legs shaking slightly, and her head hesitantly turned to look Riven's way while her hands fidgeted with the long silky white hair trailing down her front. She caught Riven's watery gaze while he stared her down, and she gulped with a light wheeze. "Hi . . . Riven. It's . . . it's nice to see you again."

Riven's hands balled into fists, and his red eyes hit the floor, ashamed and unable to meet Fay's own while his body began to tremble.

"Are you unhappy to see me?" Fay asked worriedly, stepping back and almost tripping over her own feet. "I—I can leave, if you want. I just thought that maybe . . ."

Riven held up a hand, shaking his head. He turned to stare at Athela, who gave him a warm, smiling nod, and then he turned his attention back to the succubus while slowly beginning to wheel himself over to where she stood. Looking up at her and coming to a stop a foot away from the young woman, he barely got out a whisper while trying to contain his emotions. "Are you here to stay?"

Fay bit her lip, trying hard to fight the urge to cry and failing. "Do you want me to?"

"Of course I do. I never wanted you to leave."

Fay choked, and she nodded adamantly—kneeling down and wrapping her arms around his waist while shuddering. "Okay. Then I'll stay."

Azmoth watched the silent crying duo embrace one another before lumbering over to where Athela stood watching over them—arms crossed in satisfaction. He turned to match her posture, looking back and forth between her and the succubus who was shaking in Riven's arms. "I surprised."

"Are you now?" Athela asked curiously, raising an eyebrow up at the currently larger demon before punching him in the shoulder lightly. "I'm full of surprises."

He nodded in agreement. "Yes, yes. I proud of you. Did you forgive?"

Athela let out a long sigh, and her shoulders relaxed while leaning into the armored titan beside her. "Yes. I did forgive her."

"And she forgive you?"

"Yes."

Azmoth smiled. "Good. Maybe it go back to way it was, or better. I hope better. You made Riven happy, too. The way he looking at you says lots."

Athela blinked, then followed Azmoth's nod to where Riven was still sitting in his wheelchair, hands holding Fay's kneeling figure while she quietly sobbed into his lap. Happy tears trickled down his cheeks, and he was giving Athela the most genuine look of appreciation she'd ever seen.

Her heart nearly stopped, and a faint blush started overcoming her. Then she straightened and huffed, pointing his way. "I hope you appreciate the things I do for you, mister! You don't even WANT to know what I had to go through to get her here! Humph!"

With that, Athela twirled around—black hair swishing out behind her, and she made her way into the manor to get some food. "Come on, Azmoth! Let's get breakfast. I'm starving, and a spider princess needs to keep up on her diet!"

Azmoth chuckled, gave Riven a wave, and then followed his friend inside.

Unbeknownst to Riven, in that very moment, as his heart thundered approval with every beat while holding Fay close, his soul aperture was undergoing more changes than just a self-repair.

Tendrils of sin energy were spreading from the Mark of the Sinner on his right arm, silently spreading like a cancer into the demolished pillars and scattered fragments littering his soul. They pulled and pushed, yanking the pillars back together piece by piece—infusing each of them with Gluttony's presence while the great maw watched in avid fascination. It was a unique situation that the main body of Gluttony had not encountered before—having a harbinger finish his or her sinner's mark immediately upon a soul shattering.

It provided a very unique opportunity to weasel himself inside, to circumvent laws that would otherwise hold him back.

[Estimated time until soul repairs and symbiosis are complete: sixteen days.]

"Riven . . ." The great maw hissed at its notification in the eternal black of its abyss—tendrils from the deep places of creation spiraling upward and outward, waiting for his soul to re-form. "Oh, Riven . . . How I cannot wait to see how you turn out. You and I . . . we're going to be very close friends . . . very . . . close . . . friends . . ."

ABOUT THE AUTHOR

Ranyhin1 is the pen name of Trent Boehm, author of Elysium's Multiverse, an apocalypse LitRPG he originally released on Royal Road. A lifelong lover of fantasy, Boehm is also a science nerd, Dallas Cowboys fan, and wannabe gym rat. He hopes one day to pursue writing full-time.

Podium

DISCOVER MORE

STORIES UNBOUND

PodiumEntertainment.com